# We Fished All Night

AMS PRESS
NEW YORK

**By the author of:**

**KNOCK ON ANY DOOR**

# WE FISHED ALL NIGHT

BY

Willard Motley

APPLETON-CENTURY-CROFTS, INC.

New York

1951

Library of Congress Cataloging in Publication Data

Motley, Willard, 1912-1965.
We fished all night.

I. Title.
[PZ3.M8573We4] [PS3563.o888] 813'.5'4 73-18875
ISBN 0-404-11370-2



Reprinted by arrangement with Hawthorn Books, Inc.

From the edition of 1951, New York
First AMS edition published in 1974
Manufactured in the United States of America

AMS PRESS INC.
NEW YORK, N.Y. 10003

**This book is for all the soldiers who fought for all the countries that failed them in the hope that they will never again have to fight for all the countries that will again fail them.**

*I gratefully thank*

**THE ROSENWALD FUND**

*and*

**THE NEWBERRY LIBRARY FUND**

*for fellowships that greatly aided*
*in the writing of this book*
*conceived in the lean years of*
*1945 and 1946.*

*The new world was being born, as a baby born, in blood and pain and afterbirth. The world was something raw and naked and bloody.*

*Down the black asphalt the parade of returned soldiers comes. The soldiers come nine abreast in tight formation. Come in the steady, measured one hundred and twenty to the minute march step. Come with the sun striking and ricocheting from their pointed, polished bayonets.*

*The soldiers come in even rank, in rigid march, their carbines slung from their shoulders, their hands free, swinging in measured cadence. The soldiers come, thirteen thousand pairs of boots in hooves of hammer blows against the asphalt. The soldiers come in steady clump, in combat jacket, and staring straight ahead. Come in funeral effect.*

*Mist has lifted. Sun breaks through the gray clouds. And the soldiers come their long way back. Their long way back from death and dying and killing. Back, their long way, the weary soldiers from the weary lands.*

*"The boys are back!" a woman shouts.*

*The boys are back. But not the same. They have seen things, been places. Done things of a night and of a day. And now the killers come home.*

*A paper snow descends from skyscrapers. In the sky airplanes drone salute. And the disabled veterans are here to see. Are propped up on their litters and in their wheel chairs. Are in the reviewing stand.*

*There are shrill whistles from the crowd, and waves of clapping, and hoarse cheering.*

*The soldiers march home. Their shadows march along in even rank with them. And shadows of cries lost and bodies given. And shadows of shadows.*

*There are voices in the crowd:*

*"Thank God, they're home! Let's hope they never have to go again," cries an old colored woman, clapping in revival-meeting fashion.*

*"Let's walk on the street too," says a little boy to his father.*

*"That's just for soldiers, honey," says the father.*

*Across the black pavement in funeral procession the soldiers pass.*

*From a third floor window a woman shouts "Welcome home!"*

*"This ain't home," one of the soldiers says.*

*The flag goes by and men start taking off their hats.*
*"See the flag, honey?" the man says to his little boy.*
*"I want one," the boy says.*
*"I'll buy you one, honey."*
*A woman shouts, "Welcome home!"*
*And a soldier answers, "Same to you, lady."*
*The soldiers march through masses of sunlight and shadow. Their boots make muffled thunder on the asphalt. The canyoned street pours its blizzard of confetti down on the nine-abreast combat helmets.*
*There are two middle-aged men and a grandmother in the crowd. They have brought a chair for granny to stand upon. She calls out "There it is! The good old American flag! The only flag in the world!" The men with her know all about guns: "That's an old gun—they're going to melt it down. . . . Now there's a new gun!" Every once in a while granny injects something about the flag.*
*At the curb stands a one-legged soldier on crutches. Near him a gold-star mother weeps with her face in her hands. The man is holding his little boy up in his arms and tilting his head back. "See the airplane, honey?"*
The soldiers march home. . . .

## We Fished All Night

***Lord, we fished all night and caught nothing.***

# Book One

## WATCHMAN, WHAT OF THE NIGHT?

### I

On the fringe of the Loop, in alabaster white, it dominates the western sky. Out front, in the middle of the street, a policeman sits on horseback. At the base of the building a Negro polishes the huge bronze plaque anchored there as a cornerstone:

THE HAINES COMPANY

A NATION WITHIN A NATION

Every day . . . about a million alarm clocks, thousands of factory whistles and some church bells awaken the people from rest. Street cars, Els, buses and suburban trains are alerted. For a hundred and twenty minutes of each morning the people are rushed to the center of the city. In the earth the subway wails. Overhead, on its rope of steel, the El spears to the city's center. Swaying streetcars cut their burdened paths across the cobblestones. Automobiles nudge one another and trucks broad-shoulder their way through narrow streets.

Traffic roars: Moving the people in steady streams. In a rhythm. Like the tide flows. Like the heart beats.

Traffic lights with peaked roofs are like hooded maestros, orchestra leaders, RED-AMBER-GREEN, beating out the orchestral rhythm to its crescendo:

Stop, GO!

The people move to work. At a given signal they will all move back again.

Before industry takes over, the neighborhoods become slums. Across the broken area of the slums streetcars and El trains move. The eaves of the houses droop down like the fedoras of bums. Pigeons are making love on them. The rusty cornices of the slum buildings are ready to fall on the heads of the people walking below.

Much of traffic moves in long arrows toward:

THE HAINES COMPANY

A NATION WITHIN A NATION

Against the skyscraper towers of this city, Chicago, it rises forty-eight stories high. It rises forty-eight stories high among the nations of skyscrapers and is said to be the most beautiful, powerful and wonderful of all. It rises in twin buildings, one on either side of the river.

One seems to mirror the other. One seems reality; the other the dream.

From his chauffeur-driven car, attended by his secretary, comes aristocratic Emerson Bradley. His old and wrinkled face has the look of one accustomed to command. You can see, too, in his face, all the drinks he has drunk, all the steaks he has eaten, all the women he has slept with.

The people, from streetcar and El and shuffling close together like a herd of cattle, come up the broad marble steps, in through the wall of glass doors and into the pink marble lobby on their way to elevators, delivering backs for lifting, fingers for file cabinets and typewriters.

The huge stanchions of the building thrust up and out mightily. The concrete, the marble, was built to last forever. Rub your hand across it. It is cold as ice. The people are just the pulp to be used by the building. They trudge toward elevators.

Another group of workers meets them coming from the building, from the bowels of the building far below the bargain basement. From the night shift the workers come in overalls, grease from head to foot, their bodies slack, boneless-looking, held up by the stiff overalls like scarecrows suddenly propped on the city street. They couldn't leave the dirt behind. They had to take it home with them. No place to wash up. No place to change clothes.

Up from their jobs of making nuts and bolts, screws, in the bowels of the building. Nuts and bolts shipped by train. By boat. Shipped to Europe. This is America! To Africa. This is America! To Asia. This is America! The year 1937.

Some employees said:

If you want to know anything about Emerson Bradley go out to the car line at midnight or early in the morning and get on the car with them. Did you ever ride in a cattle car? They're boiling with hot grease and human sweat. Their feet and their face are the same color. They remind you of someone who has fallen into the river.

But other workers said:

Emerson Bradley is a duplication of the deity. Look at him sitting up there. If we all forsake him he will die of hunger. Who will pick his cotton? Who will manufacture his goods for him? Don't we owe something to the boss?

And Emerson Bradley knew that if he made a move the people would go home and sit in idleness. The goods would stop going across the counters. The machines would halt. The trucks would lie idle. Even the river, the artery of supply, would stop.

Sun touched the bronze plaque to brilliant color at the foot of the building and rose higher. The people come increasingly to the building. Chet Kosinski, a seventeen-year-old, pimple-faced boy, goes to his job as a messenger boy. His sister Helen to her day-long duty of inspecting garments. Papa Levin, stooped beyond his years and with a finger missing from one hand, goes to the basement. O'Keefe to his elevator and his odd jobs. Sue Carroll goes many stories up in the building to her typewriter, dreaming of her little-theater production. Dave, a Negro, runs across Jim Norris by accident in the corridor and they talk of high school days and football and do you ever see Milo? Through the long, low, concrete hallway the people swarm, Edna among them. Edna, whose husband is dead, thinks of her two young daughters whom she is supporting singlehanded. From behind a large glass-partitioned section five hundred typewriters beat out their staccato. Mr. Wilmington, a department head, walks majestically toward the elevator in his business-gray suit. Along the edge of the river a Milwaukee Road freight train snakes its way, like a slow-moving caterpillar, bringing goods to the greedy mouth of the Haines Company. Max backs his truck up to one of the unloading platforms.

The Chicago River moves sluggishly between the twin buildings of the Haines Company, its murky waters stained by industry.

# II

*the way of an eagle in the air*

Don Lockwood stood in front of the mirror. "Tonight," he said, "tonight, Don Lockwood, you will give the greatest performance of your career." His foot was up on a stool in front of the full-length mirror and he twisted it from side to side, looking at his leg encased in the black tights. He looked admiringly at his leg. He was proud of his calves, large and muscular, on so slight a frame. Tightening his calf and leaning down he squeezed his fingers into his leg, hairy and healthy under the tights. He chuckled and leaned back at his full height with his arms folded across his chest. "To be—or not to be: that is the question," he quoted softly. "Whether 'tis nobler in the mind to suffer the slings and arrows of outrageous fortune—or to take arms—" He lifted one arm away from his body in a theatrical gesture, pausing, posing, looking at himself.

He had pulled a spotlight over close to the mirror. Dressed completely in black he stood in bold highlight in the dark and dingy dressing room. The reflection of the mirror gave back the leg, its calf balled under the skintight cloth and the knobby knee. The mirror gave back, too, his lean, thin, twenty-one-year-old face with its lean nose, its green deep-set eyes and the little mustache.

". . . and by opposing . . ." he said, forming the words with his mouth and watching his gestures in the mirror, ". . . end them." His voice dropped still lower to a hollow key. "To die—" He slapped and clasped his right shoulder with his left hand and lowered his head; but glanced up through his eyebrows to see what effect this gesture gave. He liked it and smiled at himself. He pulled at the tights, pulling them up more snugly over his legs, and saw the bulge that suggested sex and was pleased with this too. He ran a carefully guided hand over his blond hair and, tilting his head, laughed in pleasure. He flourished his sword.

Someone knocked sharply on the door. A woman's voice said, "Hurry up, Don! almost time."

"Ready, Sue!"

He turned each profile to the mirror. And his full face. Then, carefully adjusting his shoulders and pulling in his stomach, he opened the door and started up the stairs out of the basement dressing room toward the wings.

The little group outside the Uptown Players' Theater on North LaSalle Street moved into the building. The little clump of admiring parents, relatives, personal friends and well-wishers crowded into the front rows and filled the theater to one-third of its capacity. On the seats they waited, whispering, fidgeting, going out into the lobby to smoke.

Behind the curtain Sue called, "Clear!" Juanita fluttered her admiring eyes away from Don and returned to the audience. Earl, the sound-effects man, got up from the castle step where he had been reclining. Carrying his long, cork-tipped cigarette in the hand that wore a ring on its little finger, he walked off the stage.

"Places!" Sue called.

Don cleared his throat, melodiously.

The theater lights dimmed. There was trouble getting the curtain up, an awkward silence as the audience waited in embarrassment and then several titters as the curtain groaned on its ropes and came open. Don, on cue, stepped out under the spotlight and flourished his hand.

" 'Tis not this my inky coat alone, good mother, nor customary coats of solemn black," he said, improving on Shakespeare. The Queen, made up beyond her twenty-seven awkward years, moved near. In the wings Sue slipped on her harlequin glasses and followed the script. Earl, whispering to an assistant in his irritated and effeminate voice, put the thunder and storm recording on the portable victrola.

The first act was ended. Some of the nervous strain had gone. Carmen, the Queen, had stopped trembling. Don went out in the alley to smoke and look at the cold, frosty sky and feel the part of the melancholy Dane. He stared at the far Tribune Tower and the Wrigley Building. And thought of Hamlet and Barrymore and himself. He tossed his cigarette away, watching its red coal descend in an arch to the valley. Now what are my first lines? He cleared his throat and spat and went back toward the wings. Oh yes.

The final curtain closed to hand clapping. It opened to show the cast, holding hands and bowing. In the center of the group and moving forward to the footlights, Don Lockwood bowed gracefully, smiling, turning his profile to left and to right as the spotlight played on him.

Relatives of the cast and friends from the audience already hurrying backstage crowded around Don, congratulating him. He smiled and turned his profile left and then right, thanking them. This seemed to be a bigger moment for the actors than the play itself. The girls in the cast were running around giggling. Don stood in his makeup and costume taking congratulations, taking them as if acting Hamlet was nothing. Smiling casually, tossing his head back to exhale, he moved past them. "I have to talk to the director—she's so grateful," he said, chuckling. A cameraman had been hired to take stills of the cast and he began setting up his equipment in the aisle. The Queen's mother had a bouquet of flowers for her. Juanita, carrying a book of Saroyan's plays and a paper-covered copy of the *Rubaiyat,* came to tell Don how wonderful he was and let him know that she would be waiting for him in the lobby.

The actors' parents took turns walking out on the stage. In a way they were sharing in the honor. Earl, running back and forth to greet friends, rushed up to Don for a moment to say, "Oh, Donald! You were wonderful!" The cameraman was setting up his tripod and putting bulbs into his camera. Proud parents were still congratulating their children. Sue kept clapping her hands together and calling, "Everybody get ready for the pictures now!" No one paid much attention.

When at last Don got to his dressing room he closed the door, and leaning back against it, posing now for himself alone, he laughed. Laughed in pleasure. Outside he could hear the continuous murmur of voices and the delighted squeals of girls. He had wowed them! He laughed again and moved to the looking glass.

In the dressing room he stripped and before the mirror began creaming the makeup from his face. He was only half finished when someone knocked at the door.

"Who is it?"

"Susan."

"Okay, Sue," he said casually. He had nothing on but a jock strap. He unbolted the door and let her in. "You were wonderful, darling!" she said. She was a plump, youngish-looking woman in her early thirties, had short-cropped blond hair, and had once been in a play on Broadway.

"I wanted to see you a minute, Don." Her plump hand shoved the bolt across. She put her arms around him and raised her lips to his. Their mouths clung together. She brought her hand up into his hair from the nape of his neck, mussing it and forcing his mouth closer. He stepped back, holding her firmly from him with his hands on her shoulders. "Hey, control yourself!" he said, laughing. He turned and moved back toward the mirror. His large and hairy legs carried him across the room.

Sue unbolted the room. "You'll join us later?"

"Later," he said. He was already stripping to put on his shorts.

In the toilet under the stage Don dampened his hair until it was almost wringing wet, combed it, and with his fingers set a wave in the front of his otherwise completely straight hair. Pushing his hair forward with the palm of his hand and then squeezing the front part of it tightly between the fingers of both hands, he set the wave in place over his forehead. Five times he executed the operation before he got it to his liking. His hair was so long that on either side of his head it came back from his temples, up over his ears and to the nape of his neck. From the back it looked like the stiff folded wings of a bird. The wave in front was all right now. He looked at it and gave it a final smoothing with a gentle palm. Then he adjusted the knot of his tie, his collar clasp, his tie clasp. Finally he laced a white silk scarf about his neck and made it blossom out of the front of his overcoat. Above the scarf his Adam's apple was a sharp point.

Juanita was waiting in the lobby. The caretaker also waited there, impatient to lock the building. "Oh, Don, you were wonderful!" Juanita said again. He smiled his appreciation and took her arm.

Outside the building he stopped to look at his picture in the glass display case advertising the play. It was a flattering photograph done in a low and dramatic key, one that he liked so well that he had it framed above his dresser at home. Juanita read the poster aloud, pleased to be with him tonight. "The Little Company presents Don Lockwood in *Hamlet* with Carmen Lowry and Leo Adams—it's a lovely picture of you, Don!"

"Oh, I don't think so," he said, not meaning it. He read his name again and then moved on down the street with her.

They joined the rest at B/G's restaurant on Dearborn and Division, where they had gone to celebrate; there was little else they could afford.

It had been rough going. For two months they had rehearsed every night just to put the play on for one evening. To meet costs each of them had to sell twenty-five tickets or buy them themselves.

They were discussing Stanislavsky with almost self-conscious earnestness and the table was already filled with empty coffee cups and cigarettes crushed out in the muddy saucers when Don and Juanita came over.

"A wall feels, doesn't it?" Don said, winking kiddingly at Sue. "Sure, it has emotions. Become a wall. That's Stanislavsky, isn't it?" He pulled out a chair and sat down.

Two tables ahead of them a young artist from the neighborhood nodded his head in a pointing gesture. "A perpendicular pronoun just walked in—Don Lockwood."

"I just came from the play," the fellow with him said. "I know one of the girls in the cast. That ham thinks he's the *greatest*. Hot guy himself. From the little insignificant theater group." He laughed in amusement. "I was there to a couple of the rehearsals and nobody holds his stomach in like that. His stomach was in all the time. He must have had a sore stomach after the play."

Carmen, thumbing through a copy of *My Life In Art,* read authoritative quotes from Stanislavsky. *"Now* does that prove what I said?" she asked, ready for an argument. Juanita put her copies of Saroyan and the *Rubaiyat* on the table. "Are we going to have coffee?" she asked Don. He shrugged. "I'm broke," he said; and laughed to cover up his embarrassment.

Juanita searched in her pocketbook while Sue looked at her with a secret and amused smile. "Do you want some pie too, Don?" Juanita asked.

"Well rawther!" he said, stroking the end of his mustache with his forefinger. He looked at Leo in a superior way and back again at Juanita, in an effort to carry it off well.

Juanita brought the coffee and pie. She pulled her chair close to Don's and looked at him admiringly when he talked. Don sat with his hand on the back of her chair, casually, and smoked a cigarette. Sue looked across at them several times quickly, then away. She began to talk animatedly about Broadway to Earl and Carmen. Juanita had slipped her hand into Don's. Sue saw this too. She said, in a pause in the conversation, "Do you like the *Rubaiyat*, Juanita?"

"Oh yes!" Juanita said. "I think it's beautiful! You like it, don't you, Don?" Juanita asked, turning to him.

Don cleared his throat. He looked at both of them as if awaiting a cue. No cue came. Sue was smiling at him in friendliness. "Well I—I read it years ago. Yes—it's all right."

"Miss Carroll—" Juanita began, and when she had caught Sue's eye, she continued. "I'd like to act. Don told me to ask you. I thought maybe he would but he told me to. I'll study hard and—well, could I have a chance?"

Sue ran her fingers into her hair and inclined her neck toward her hand. "Well, dear, the thing is we have too many women now. We need more men—and with so many men going away to the war—" She let her words trail into nothing and smiled at Juanita regretfully. Behind the smile was the fear that Don found this girl attractive.

Leo had picked up a newspaper left on the table by someone. "Look at this headline!" he said. They all looked.

U. S. SINKS 7 JAP SHIPS.

For a moment Don felt his heart pounding. He hoped that he wouldn't have to go. He hoped it would be over soon. His number might come up at any time. He swallowed. He laughed. "We'll beat their pants off," he said.

They talked about the war for a while but it didn't hold their attention. Their talk drifted back to the theater. Don went to the toilet. Over the trough someone had penciled: ROOSEVELT FOR THE DURATION OF ROOSEVELT. He chuckled and hurried out to tell the others. "Don was wonderful, wasn't he?" Juanita was saying. When he sat down next to her she turned to him and said, "You could go right onto Broadway."

Don wrinkled his eyebrows modestly. "Oh, I'm not ready for Broadway yet," he said, believing her.

Don laughed a great deal and talked loudly and was the center of attraction. At twelve o'clock he left to take Juanita to the subway.

"I don't like him," Leo said, following Don out of the door with his eyes. "He's always dramatic. Even when he sleeps he'd be dramatic." Sue looked at him but said nothing. "He's theatrical all the time. He's dressed for the part and he never takes off his costume," Leo said.

"You're just jealous," Carmen said.

Leo laughed. "Where does Don live?" he asked everyone.

"No one knows," Carmen said. "He's very mysterious."

"He's really a very fine person," Sue said. And thought, remembering all she knew about him, remembering him on the stage: What courage, self-confidence and ego he has. It's too bad he never had any chances. He's intelligent. He's quick. He could have been— Her mind delved deeper. They shouldn't have done *Hamlet*. They weren't ready for it. But Don had kept after her. Don had wanted to play Hamlet. He had done—yes—a pretty bad job. As I knew he would. Can love make such a slave of you? . . .

Sue clapped her hands together. "Okay, kids, let's clear out," she said. "Remember, improvisations tomorrow at eight. And be there on time."

"I didn't know it was so late!" Leo said. "I've got to get to the Chain Gang in the morning," he said, using the nickname people had for the Haines Company.

They struggled into their coats and, still discussing theater, straggled out to the sidewalk. Sue caught a southbound car and went home immediately.

When Don put Juanita on the subway he crossed the street at Division and caught the 51st and Indiana streetcar and rode to Wabash near 12th street. He climbed the stairs of one of the several decrepit limestone-fronted two-story buildings on the east side of the street. From under the hall rug outside the upstairs door he got the key. He waited on the bed in the dark. At length he heard the key in the lock and then the door opened.

"Don," Sue whispered, entering her one-room apartment.

"At your service, madam," he said in a British accent.

She had a bottle of wine. She found it in the dark, and glasses. The raised shade at the uncurtained window gave the room its only light. It showed the bookcases, the edge of the phonograph, the stark lines of a surrealistic painting. Sue put some Tschaikovsky on the turntable. Then she came over to the bed, twisted her shoes off and leaned over to kiss him. "Hello, Mother," he said teasingly. She chuckled half-sadly and slapped his face playfully.

They sat for a while on the bed drinking the wine, setting the glasses on the floor while they embraced. He pressed his lips hard against hers, forcing her mouth open. He felt his need growing. "Let's monkey around," he said.

They stood up. Laughing they undressed together, and quickly, because the room was cold. He rolled close to her even before the sheets had taken warmth from their bodies. He wrapped his arms around her. "Mother, give me the sun," he said.

They lay in the bed together, their eyes accustomed to the dark. It was very cold in the old house and they had piled all the blankets and their coats on the bed. Don lay on his back in a pleasurable exhaustion. His eyes stared at the moon patterns on the ceiling. With him Sue was like a girl. Not the director, the Miss Carroll they all knew. There was pleasure in this for him, the secret, hidden meeting of their bodies. Their knowledge, when together, of these nights. And there was attraction for her in him. Her age. A woman in love with him. Not just a girl. A woman. In the dark her body was not stoutish to him and her clasp was warm and tight, her love something he had experienced with no girl. His eyes rolled toward the window, his ears listened to the night sounds and he felt an elation. He was the kid whose mother was on relief a few years ago. The kid with ragged socks tucked in under his heels and toes inside his shoes. The kid in the relief Mackinaw. "Oh, you're on relief too, huh?" Tony had said in the schoolyard, proud of his Mackinaw and the kinship it gave them. But he was ashamed. A lot of Mackinaws showed up on the playground that day. . . . He was the kid with vinegar in his hair for the lice. And here he was in bed with a woman, not a girl, a woman. She had even been married and divorced . . . what Sue's husband hadn't achieved he had achieved—it proved something to him. He stroked Sue's body with his hand. Suddenly he felt her stiffen. "That little bitch!" she said.

"What little bitch?"

"Juanita."

"Oh!" He laughed the oh. And rubbed his chin against her shoulder.

In the bed she stirred and her hand in his hair dropped away. He put his fingers to her cheek to stroke it. Then he felt the tears. She turned her face away to hide them from his touch. But he turned it back, roughly, with the palm of his hand. "Now what's wrong?" he asked gently.

"Oh, Don, I love you so much, so much."

He drew her toward him. The blankets were over them, her arms tightly about him. In the room's cold darkness, with snow on the slab of the window sill outside, the phonograph had been playing the last Tschaikovsky record over and over. But neither of them cared or heard. And Don felt free. . . .

When it was over, Don dressed and went down on the street toward home. From a tavern the words of a song assailed him:

*We're gonna have to slap*
*The dirty little Jap*
*And Uncle Sam's the guy who*
*can do it.*

Don grabbed a Clark Street car for home. He got off at Grand Avenue and walked west half a block. It was a slum block. It was like a diseased finger attached to the dirty palm of the Skid Row of North Clark Street. A diseased finger pointing to the Negro slum area and the factory buildings. He climbed the sagging, weather-beaten steps between the black cast-iron rails and came to the crusted black door from which the paint was peeling in blistered ovals, leaving the rotten wood exposed in large pockmarks. Under the rusty bell was tacked a dirty, yellowed card upon which the name KOSINSKI had been printed in pencil. He climbed the inner steps between the plaster-broken green walls that grinned darkly, sardonically at him, to the upper hallway and pushed the door open with his foot.

"Chet! Is that you, Chet?"

"Yes, Ma," he said tonelessly.

Her bare feet carried her to the center of the room where, in the oval of kerosene lamplight, she stood clad only in a dirty pink slip. She raised her fist and shook it at him. "You didn't want me there. You're ashamed of your mother. Don Lockwood, indeed! Blood of a dog!" She spit it at him. "Ain't Kosinski good enough for you? You're ashamed of your people."

Don lifted the corner of his mouth in a sneer and threw the playbill on the floor. "I'm no goddamn Polack! How do I know who my father is anyway?"

"You dirty-dirty bastard you!" his mother shouted. She brought her fist up against her forehead, and swaying there in the lamplight with her eyes roving across the ceiling, gently tapped her fist against her forehead. "God witness my suffering with so horrible a son."

"And why don't you stay off the bottle?" Don said.

*"Panna Marya,"* his mother moaned, still beating her forehead. *"Matka Bosha."*

A form stirred in the rocking chair behind the stove. An old man slowly emerged from it, helping himself with a cane. Slowly, feebly, he took the first steps forward to the scraping of the cane against the bare and dirty floor, his weak eyes blinking, even in the dim light. *"Kto tam?"* he asked. "Don?"

"Why does God bring such a disgrace as a son like this down upon my head?" his mother said to the walls and the ceiling.

"Hello, Grandpa," Don said.

The old man hobbled forward. He was very old, his gray hair matted and growing around his ears and over the back of his collar. Though dressed in rags he wore a tie neatly knotted.

He hobbled between mother and son, one hand on the rough brown handle of the cane, the other against the small of his back. He turned to the woman and his phlegmy, quivering voice spoke to her. "Now you leave this boy alone." His old and wrinkled neck turned toward Don and his white, bloodless lips smiled. *"Inteligencja!"* he said, tapping his withered knuckles against Don's forehead. Then he winced from the pain in his back and tried to feel it out.

"Always," Mrs. Kosinski said to no one, "they take sides against me. Always my family is at me about something."

*"Jeśli mię Bóg uchowa—"* the old man said.

Mrs. Kosinski put her hands on her hips and laughed a short, bitter laugh. "If God spare you, old man! If God spare you! Oh, God will spare you. You will be here to bury us all. And Chet, nothing good will happen to that lazy bum. Me, I work for you and him, but does God see me?"

*"Jeśli mię Bóg uchowa,* I will see him famous," the old man said.

"Famous! Him famous!" She snorted and twisted her hips away.

*"Inteligencja!"* Grandpa Kosinski muttered after her.

Don lit a cigarette.

"Mark my words," the old man said. "He will be a great actor some day. Then you will be sorry for the way you talk now."

Don puffed on his cigarette and knew that what his grandfather said was true.

They stood in the front room of the two-room apartment. Two windows almost the height of the room looked out on Grand Avenue. There were no curtains. None were needed. The panes were so grimed by the weather, so pockmarked with grit, so seldom washed, that it was difficult to see out of them. The room was large. Once, many years ago, the wallpaper had been painted over, and once again. It was neither dark-green, nor brown, nor purple, nor maroon, but a muddy combination of all these colors. The bare plaster ceiling was cracked in many places and in one large, jagged spot over the bed there was no plaster, only the bare laths, grinning at the floor. The floor was bare, dirty, warped. In a corner one of the little kids had messed but no one had seen it. There was a sink piled with dirty, cracked dishes, an old-fashioned round table cluttered also with dirty dishes and a few pots containing dried food in their bottoms, a coal stove for both heating and cooking purposes. The only other furnishings were a few rickety chairs, a broken-down davenport against one wall, a bed against another wall and Grandpa's cot against a third wall. Nine people lived and slept in this one room. Grandpa, Mrs. Kosinski and seven children. Ma slept on the davenport. The bed was never made. It was dirty. They slept in shifts. Grandpa sat in his rocking chair and slept by the stove late into the night, waiting for Don to come home. Sometimes the little kids would sleep in his bed until they had to get up to go to school. Then Grandpa would go to bed. But more often they slept on a mattress on the floor behind the stove. Only Don had his own room and his own bed.

Tonight the little kids were behind the stove. Tonight, for some mysterious reason, Don's older sister was not at her 26-table on West Madison Street but slept in the bed. She lay on her back and snored slightly in the semidark. With her slept two of her younger sisters. Kazio, the thirteen-year-old boy, slept on Grandpa's cot with his clothes on.

"He will be famous."

Don inhaled happily, dreamily on his cigarette knowing that Grandpa was right and that he would be a great actor.

"You are tired," Grandpa told Don. "You had to act tonight. Go to your room. Your grandpa will make you some cocoa." The old man turned back to his daughter. "Why should he want a name like Kosinski!—*Kosinski!*" He spat on the floor. "Kosinski on the name place of a theater!"

Mrs. Kosinski turned from the old man and smacked her palms against her buttocks at him. She walked to the davenport and sat down angrily, looking in the ash tray on the floor for a cigarette butt. Don picked the playbill up off the floor and went to his room. He returned immediately and lit the second kerosene lamp, that stood on the table. "So they turned the electricity off," he said.

"Why don't you get a job and help pay the bills?" his mother said.

He smiled at her condescendingly, but didn't answer.

He carried the lamp into his room. "Lazy Polack pig!" his mother called after him.

The lamp lit Don's room insufficiently. There was a pipestem bed and a battered dresser. Against the wall on a coat hanger under a cloth was his only other suit, a salt-and-pepper tweed still in good condition, that he had bought for twelve dollars in a hock shop. On top of the dresser was a small pile of plays and books on technique. Some he had stolen from the library, standing close to the shelf when no one was near him and working them down under his belt, covering them with his sweater, then his coat. Some had been given to him by Sue. Over the dresser was a large framed picture of John Barrymore, a small picture of Rudolph Valentino, torn from a book—and his own photograph. On the opposite wall near a large mirror was a flattering caricature of him in costume that Sue had drawn. Tacked up near it was a small portrait of Edwin Booth as Hamlet—also torn from a book.

Don put the playbill in his dresser drawer. From the drawer he took a hand mirror, and pulling the lamp closer, looked into his own eyes. He had deep-set eyes. He had very large eyes and they were very green. His forehead was broad with the blond hair flaring away from it. His mouth was long, the top lip thin, the lower one pouted out a little, petulant. The lips were reddish and there was a cleft in his chin. Sometimes he thought his chin looked weak . . . no, it's sensitive . . . the cleft in his chin saved it from looking weak. Yes, he had a sensitive face with his deep-set eyes staring out. And unaware of it he had a gesture attractive to people. When he smiled he showed his teeth and his eyes narrowed, one of them coming down in a long squint that was like a wink; it was quite an attractive smile. He wasn't handsome. But good-looking, yes. And, strangely, in an English way. He had poise and there was a certain cut to his features, making them sharp if not classic. And there was something he had been aware of for a long time, since he was only seventeen in fact. There was something in his face that made it attractive to women. Something half-menacing in his deep-set green eyes. Something about the thin mustache and his lips beneath it. That had been a master stroke, growing the mustache. He tilted his head, looking in the mirror at himself. "Don Lockwood," he said aloud, thinking of how it would look in lights on Broadway. Trying now to remember where he had found the name was difficult. In a book? Or had he heard it somewhere? Anyway it was a damn good stage name!

The door was fumbled open and Grandpa Kosinski hobbled in carrying a dish on which was the cup of rich brown cocoa and some little stale wafers he had pulled out of his secret cardboard carton under his cot where he kept his meager but precious luxuries and keepsakes. He set the dish on the bed and lowered himself onto the mattress. "Come, boy, drink," he said. "It will help your throat. It will coat it."

Don sat alongside the old man and made a pretense at drinking the cocoa. "Don't pay no attention to your old lady," Grandpa said. "She's going through that difficult time for a woman—you understand what I mean—"

From his trouser pocket with a palsied hand Grandpa Kosinski drew the five wrinkled dollar bills. He smoothed them out against his knee and laid them on the bed. "My old-age money came today—" his voice became a sly whisper, "now don't tell your ma or she'll be trying to squeeze every last penny of it out of me." He shifted the chew of tobacco to the other end of his mouth where it balled out and took some of the wrinkles from his cheek. His wrinkled hand gestured at George Washington on the top dollar bill. "That's for you, boy." He patted Don's shoulder. "You may need some cigarettes. Buy yourself some fancy socks. Maybe a nice tie. You have to look good in your work." Don's eyes concentrated on the money. He was ashamed and drew them away. But they went back. He didn't want to take the money right away. "Thanks, Grandpa," Don said, patting the old man's shoulder in return and laughing.

In the cold light of the frosty morning, Ma Kosinski arose. She shook the stove, coaxed it with kindling and newspaper, put the last of the coal into its yawning mouth in which the slow flames licked like tongues in an almost empty bowl. Behind the stove the old man had gone to sleep with the chewing tobacco showing in a knot in one cheek. Ma Kosinski looked at her father wryly. He stirred in his sleep and muttered, "Cold! *Mnie zimno; ja marzne.*" His daughter shrugged and pulled the frayed shawl up closer about his shoulders. She put the coffeepot on the stove. Then she went to Grandpa's bed and pulled the covers off the children sleeping there. "Get up! *Wstawaj pan!*" she said in both languages. *"Wacek! Kazio! Weronika!"* When they didn't stir she slapped them awake across the thighs with her hard calloused palm. *"Wacek! Kazio! Weronika!* School!"

When they were up and already in their clothes that had served too, for covering, when they were only still rubbing the sleep from their eyes she told them, "Go to the alleys. Bring wood." Then she awakened her father. "Go to your bed," she told him.

She awakened Eva. Eva, fifteen and darkly colored like an Italian or a Syrian, stood shivering in the cold but watching her mother's face for its command. "You will cook the breakfast and get the kids off to school. Oatmeal. Bread." Eva nodded without answering but her black eyes flamed for a moment in rebellion. "You will get to the factory on time today." Again Eva nodded without answering. Listlessly she moved to the sink and filled a pot with water.

Mrs. Kosinski drank her coffee and pulled on her cheap cloth coat, ready now to go to her factory. She glanced at the bed at her oldest daughter to see if she were asleep and then opened Helcia's purse, took out her gloves, pulled them on. Eva regarded her from the sink with unwavering black eyes. Mrs. Kosinski moved quickly to the sink. She slapped Eva, hard, across the arm. "You see too much. You talk too much."

Mrs. Kosinski went into Don's bedroom. For a moment she stood with the door closed, looking at him. This, her son from her husband. Only he and the girl, Helcia. The others. She shrugged.

Moving to the bed she looked down at her son. *"Wstawaj pan!"* She shook him.

*"Ja wstane,"* Don mumbled.

But he didn't get up. His breathing came heavier.

His mother stood looking down at him. She was tall, statuesque, with a thin, bony neck in which the cords stood out, and blond hair wavier than it was curly, naturally so. Way off some time she had been halfway good-looking. But it was all gone now. Her nose was thin and sharp, like Don's, and her fingers long, thin. Her cheekbones, each like a sore and swollen knuckle, were in no need of rouge.

Impulsively she stooped down and stroked the hair off Don's forehead, continued to stroke it a moment longer. When she stood again erect a few tears rolled down her cheeks. She wiped them away on the back of Helcia's glove. She tightened her thin lips. She left the room.

In the kitchen she and Eva glanced at each other in a sullen, misunderstood way and Eva's black eyes did not waver, did not fall. As she went down the hallway steps the kids were coming up and the wind took the door back and forth behind them. Their faces were red and their fingers stiff with the cold. They dragged two old boards covered on one side with grimed and frosted snow. Their mother looked first at the boards and then at them. "Now you be to school on time," she said, "or the Mother Superior will be after me. I have enough to do."

Don slept until noon. When he awakened he lay comfortably in the bed, not wanting to get up for a long time.

Grandpa stuck his head in the door. Grandpa said softly, "Are you awake, boy?"

"Uh-huh."

"I'll fix you a bite to eat," the old man said.

Don lay back on the bed and remembered the night. Fully awake now, he sat up in his underwear top, the cold air of the room goose-pimpling his thin, white arms. He breathed deeply, in the exercise necessary to his art for correct breathing. "Make the tones pear-shaped—breathe from the diaphragm," he said, laughing, remembering the John Barrymore movie. He inhaled as the book, as Sue, had instructed.

In the kitchen he could hear Grandpa's cane feeling the floor in the pecking sound of a bird, then the eggs frying in the hot grease. In practice Don breathed again and breathed ag—something bit him on the leg. He pulled his leg from under the covers and between thumb and thumb captured the bedbug, squeezed it until it popped and the blood ran on his fingernails. He wiped the dead bug against the bare floor and examined his leg. He found three red bumps where bedbugs had been. And in winter too. But his leg was cold now and he stuck it back under the covers. He wondered how many bedbugs lived in the tenement house of the mattress and springs.

Grandpa Kosinski brought his breakfast to him in bed: eggs, stale bread, a cup of coffee without enough canned milk. When he had finished eating, Don jumped out of bed in his shorts, got quickly into an old pair of pants and went into the other room by the stove.

Helcia was already up and preparing to go out. She had washed the dishes and cleaned up as best she could and had applied her makeup.

"Don," she said in greeting.

"Helen," he said.

She was a large girl, almost plump with full lips, red-painted, large eyes, plucked eyebrows and artificial gardenias at each temple. Her large nose was sprinkled generously with freckles over which powder had been drawn. Her bushy brown hair stood out in a full crop about her head and gave her an even plumper appearance.

Grandpa leaned forward in his rocker. He tried to speak to both of them in Polish, to make them both speak Polish with him. Helen laughed. "I never did go for that stuff," she said to Don, laughing, "even in school." She had a voice like Ma's but with a sexy undertone.

"Me neither," Don said, avoiding Grandpa's eyes.

"All I know," Helen said, "all I know is—*Smiało!* Be of good cheer!"

"You and me both," Don said.

*"Smiało,"* Grandpa said. "And you, Don," Grandpa continued, emphasizing by clicking his cane hard against the floor, "you are—how do they say?—destined—yes, destined—to be a great actor." His daughter was at work and he, he was head of the family with the children, head of the family as it had always been in the old country, as it should be here, now, and forever, the oldest male. His palsied voice reached out to surround them and engulf them and take them home to his heart. "Always remember the old country. Always remember Poland. Always remember home. That way luck lies." He twisted in his chair, leaning forward with his withered hands clutching the arms of the chair. "And you, Helcia, don't grieve, for you are sick from grief," he said, again imagining that there must be some secret sorrow in Helen. "You will get a nervous illness. When you are so you are neither healthy nor sick, and no doctor can help against a nervous illness. Work as much as you can, then you will have no time for grief."

"I do not grieve, Grandpa," Helen said, coming past him and for a fleeting second in the passing taking his chin between her forefinger and thumb. "I always say," she said, "nobody's going to hold against you what you can get for free."

"That's for sure," Don said.

Kozie, thirteen years old, was asleep on the mattress behind the stove, truant from school, and no one cared. In the rumpled bed now the youngest children slept, having crawled there from behind the stove. Helen got into her coat to go. Grandpa had wandered over to the window and was looking out the half-blinded, frosty pane. "Everything is frozen out of doors," he said.

Helen in coat and hat, searching in her pockets for her gloves, approached him. "It freezes very hard," he said.

Don rubbed his arms near the stove and put in another piece of wood.

"Icicles are hanging from the roofs," Grandpa said.

"Here," Helen said, taking his cheeks between her hands and kissing his old forehead. She left for work.

"The river is frozen over," Grandpa said in the same melancholy tone.

"How do you know, Grandpa?" Don said from the stove. "You can't see the river from here."

"I know," Grandpa said, sucking his thumb. "I hold my finger thus. And I can tell from the chill that comes into it."

Grandpa moved to his bed and then turned toward Don, happy now in being alone with him. In his hand Grandpa held a necktie. Childishly extending the tie, childishly speaking, Grandpa said, "My necktie, Don!" He smiled. It was a very broad smile. One tooth stood out like a great skyscraper in a void in the otherwise nude mouth.

"Sit down, old man," Don said as every day, in his half-rude, half-joking tone. Carefully he knotted the tie as every day and his grandfather smiled and the lone tooth gleamed yellow-white.

"You look like a young beau," Don said, finishing, and twisting his head to see his handiwork from an angle. Then Grandpa Kosinski went to look in the mirror at himself. He wore a blue work shirt beneath the tie, its collar frayed and dirty. His trousers were much too big, trousers that you could have fit him in half again, and were held up by suspenders. Old fireman's suspenders that had been good long ago but were now frayed, their elasticity gone.

He chuckled at himself in the mirror. He walked around with the pants wobbling back and forth. Walked around with the cane and in the high shoes to his rocker and settled himself in it.

The coalman came, saying Mrs. Kosinski had stopped by on the way to work, and set the bushel basket on the floor. Already Grandpa was nodding.

Don went into his room. They were all asleep. The kids. Kozie. Grandpa. Don went and sat on the edge of his bed and felt the cold touch his forehead and his fingers. He put his fingers over his eyes and sat there. When he was alone he felt inferior. He recognized his awful limitations. When he was around people he could laugh and kid—but alone. Sure, he could put on the charm. He was healthy, half-handsome, likable, and willing to be sincere, he guessed, if sincerity was necessary. But he didn't know anything. Not really. And he realized, now, what a fool he had been to quit school when he was only in fifth grade. Sure, he tried to improve himself, but hell—

He got up and put the suit he had worn last night under the cloth with the other one, keeping it neat for those times when he was with his friends and had to look good, impress them, not let them ever know anything about where he lived, who he was, who his people were.

He sat again on the edge of the bed. Sure, secretly once a week he went at night to a grammar school far on the South Side where no one would know him and there at the children's desks with middle-aged and old people, with Poles and Italians and Lithuanians from the steel mill, his knees scraping the underside of the desk, he sat learning grammar and, once again, the fundamentals of arithmetic. He couldn't spell at all. He had a good ear for words and knew it. Yeah. From the conversations of well-educated people he picked up big words and enjoyed using them. Maybe he forgot and mispronounced many of them or used them wrong. People probably laughed at him behind his back. He lowered his head. Yeah, they probably did.

He got up and opened the door a little more to let more of the heat into the room . . . the only jobs he had been able to get were as a messenger boy at the Haines Company and as a dishwasher and counterman at Thompson's. He had quit these jobs, afraid that he'd run into some of his friends. The work was beneath him anyway. Oh yeah?

Now he didn't work. And he wouldn't as long as his mother didn't kick him out of the house. Why should he? He bit his lip. He lit a cigarette. Why should he work? Wasn't he devoting his time and thought to the theater?

Don rose from the bed and got the red pasteboard-covered fifth grade speller from the bottom drawer of the dresser where it was hidden under his shirts. He propped it up on the pillow and, using a book for a table, copied words from it onto sheets of paper. He made a column of words. He copied each of them a hundred times. Then, thinking about them, he spelled them to himself. Then he wrote ten sentences using them. Every day he took at least half a dozen new words.

When he had finished, he went into the other room to warm himself. Grandpa was awake and sitting on the side of the bed. Don looked for some food. There was none. "Christ, I'm hungry!" he said. "We are getting thin because the winter is big," Grandpa said. He was silent a moment. Then *"Siądz pan koło mnie,"* the old man said, patting the bed. Don did as he was bid and sat alongside him. *"Mów pan ze mna po polsku,"* the old man said. Don disliked the unclean smell of old age. He tried to move away a little without letting his grandfather notice. He tried not to breathe as deeply as he had been. "I understand better than I speak," he said, in answer to Grandpa. As a child he had been ashamed and cried when his mother made him speak Polish. In the Polish Catholic School off Division Street they made him talk it; they had made him learn it well. He could even spell in Polish. He still disliked talking in Polish.

The old man rambled on in Polish and Don didn't listen until the words: ". . . write a letter for me."

Don got the tablet of paper and sat waiting, thinking: Letters! letters! always letters to Bronislawa, this sister of his, this old-maid sister.

Grandpa said, "Write this for me. Write—And now I write to you and say 'Praise be Jesus Christus' and I hope you will answer 'in centuries of centuries.' I, your brother, send you bows and ask you not in your old age to forget your brother. . . ." The letter went on and on, "it freezes here and all the world is sad. Even the river is frozen over. . . . And now I write you of your health. . . . I have no health, particularly my arms are bad. . . . I have tears in my eyes always when I remember you. Let us kiss each other, at least by letter, at least through this paper, let us give hands to each other."

At last Grandpa said as always, "My address North America, 121 West Grand Avenue, Chicago." There were tears in his eyes as he finished.

Grandpa went to the window and looked out to hide his tears from Don. "To see that dear land once again," he said.

At length he came back from the window, his oversized pants wobbling comically and looking in the seat as if a heavy load weighed them down. "My box, Don, get my box. There is something I want to show you."

Don knelt on the floor and from under the cot pulled the dirty and worn cardboard carton in which Grandpa kept all that was precious to him. Through the small brown wrinkled paper bags tied with string, many windings of string, through the loose letters all bearing Polish stamps, through the little matchboxes and tobacco cans, tied too with string and containing valuables, past open boxes holding a few mildewed crackers, past a few jars containing yet a little more jam, rotting, through all his little pile of treasures Grandpa searched until at last from the very bottom of the box he pulled what he had been looking for. He set the little packet on his knees and his eyes misted. It was a small treasure, no bigger than a package of cigarettes. It was wrapped in yellowed newspaper. It was tied and again tied with frayed and blackened string. And now as Grandpa's withered fingers took the string away the brittle yellow newspaper crumbled to flakings of dust and sprinkled agedly down his trousers. Inside the newspaper, opening and crackling and falling away like a dried leaf, was a handkerchief. It too had been tied and again tied, first in one direction and then in the other.

At length Grandpa had the handkerchief untied and with gentle, caressing fingers unfolded it. Inside was a dried brownish-black substance, powdered until it seemed that nothing else could be so dry. Don looked at it in puzzlement and then up into the old man's eyes.

"Polish earth," Grandpa said. He fingered it lovingly, but carefully so that no grain of it would be lost on the floor. "It will be buried under my head when I die. Then I will not be lonely," he said. "The first night in the grave is the loneliest but—" again he fingered the dirt, "this is home." He held the handkerchief in his palms, over which the thin skin held the bones together, and held the treasure out so that Don could touch the Polish dirt. "There will be enough left for you," Grandpa said. He yet fondled the little heap. He smiled. "I had forgotten," he said, "in my excitement about coming to America." He smiled. "And just before I entered the ship I stooped down and scraped up a little of the earth. The earth of Poland."

Don arose and, moved by feelings he didn't know the name of, walked toward his room. "That was in 1887," the old man said to his back.

Quietly Don closed the door. For a moment he sat on the edge of the bed. Then he arose and walked to the mirror. He looked at himself dramatically in the mirror, trying to feel better. He ran his fingers through his hair, smoothing it back. Damn, but it was straight! He pulled some of it down over his forehead and along the sharp line of his nose, and holding it there, fingering it, examined it curiously. Like string. Thin blondish hair. There was enough of it but it was real thin. It was long. He needed a haircut. He'd always had long hair with little points sticking around by his ears and neck because it was so long. Even as a kid, because Ma didn't have the money for a haircut. Sometimes Ma would clip it with the scissors. She always cut the little kids' hair. But it wasn't artistic to have long hair when he was a kid. As a kid, outside on the street, he always managed to look fairly clean and fairly well dressed. They were poor clothes but they were clean clothes.

Don looked at his face, trying to be theatrical, trying to be dramatic, but failing. That white, pasty skin. Sharp nose. Too sharp. And, of course, his lean, thin face. Here was the kind of guy he was.

He went to the bed and lay across it, face down, with his head in his arms. Here was the kind of guy he was. He was the kind of a guy who was a fake. And he knew it. But there was nothing he could do about it. And he wanted horribly to be liked. Maybe it was because he had always felt, since he was nothing but a kid, that Ma didn't care about him. He even knew that he loved her and wanted her to be different. He went out of his way to make people like him. Strangers. Anybody. Everybody. He always hid his real feelings. Like with Grandpa. Grandpa bored hell out of him. But he laughed with Grandpa, and patted his shoulder and kidded him even when he was most bored.

Don, face down on the bed, twisted one ankle roughly against the other. He went deep into himself. He went where he lived. So much of him was pose and he knew it. Sensed that this acting wasn't real. Just a chance to show off. That he was playing a part. That he wanted to be something. That he was trying to be, was pretending to be something. That he wasn't anything. That he didn't fit with this crowd and didn't even like them. Not even Sue, really. That was why he laughed and treated everything like a joke. What would Carmen call it—compren—comprensation?

He rolled over on his back and covered his eyes with the crook of his arm. Here's the kind of a guy he was. A guy from a worse than slum background—thinking of Ma and her men. Here's the kind of guy—just an ordinary Pole—Polack! Name of CHET KOSINSKI. Just an ordinary guy like you meet on the street every day. He should be a stable, simple little guy never amounting to anything much. He should marry a rather dumb Polish girl, work in a factory, get drunk on week ends, bring kids like himself into the world and prepare them to work in factories too but try to beat them into staying in school so that they could go a little further and be a little better than he was.

He thought again of Chet Kosinski. . . .

The boy, Chet Kosinski, sat on the back porch crying. Nobody loved him. His mother didn't. Nobody did. He rubbed his grubby knuckles into his eyes and sucked up the water of his nose. He put one thin-soled tennis shoe on top of the other and leaned his forehead against the porch rail. Some day when he amounted to something everybody would like him. But it wouldn't matter then. It was the right-now that counted.

Maybe you can't sit down and think about your whole life and have it come back to you in chronological order. Anyway he was trying to as he turned and twisted on the bed. It came out to him like this:

"Ma," he said and shook her. She was drunk. No, that wasn't the first thing he remembered. . .

Then—the shock of remembrance. He began to tremble. . .

It was Christmas. He was a little boy. There was just he and Helcia and Eva, a baby sucking at Ma's sagging, dry breast. They were the poorest people in the neighborhood. Ma scrubbed floors in a downtown office building. They weren't even going to have a turkey. Ma came home Christmas Eve. She must have been crying on the streetcar coming home with the happy holiday crowd. Her eyes were red and baggy. She had two pounds of hamburger and some Irish potatoes. Christmas Day she baked the hamburger and boiled the potatoes. Somewhere she had found a turkey feather and stuck it in the hamburger roast before she brought it to the table. "See, children," she had said, "we have turkey too. Just like everybody else we have turkey." She had laughed with the tears running down her cheeks. And laughed with her elbows on the table and her hands up to her face. It was cold in the house. The hamburger was good. Grandpa had patted Ma's shoulder and said, "Now, now, my little girl." There was ice all over the windows. He and Helcia licked their plates. Eva sucked at Ma's breast while Ma went on crying.

That night, somehow, Ma had gotten drunk. There was a man in the house with her. Don remembered that he had awakened in the night, thinking someone was hurting Ma, and had cried himself back to sleep. In the morning Ma had awakened him and held him fiercely to her with her blond hair hanging down her back because she hadn't bobbed it then. Ma held him fiercely, until it hurt and, still crying, she had said, "I never did that before." She said it over and over. Then she laughed. Real loud. Then she cried again. Then she said, "There are ways! There are ways!" She said it many times. Then she said, smoothing his hair, "My children won't go hungry again." She said this many times too.

Don lay staring at the ceiling for a long time, then lay a long time with his eyes closed and his lip caught between his teeth. Bit by bit the memory faded away into the recesses of his being. Again he thought of Chet Kosinski. . . .

He was eighteen and he still had a few pimples and he got a job as a messenger boy at the Haines Company for twenty dollars a week. . . .

There's a beginning to all things. There are the accidents of life. This was the accident of their meeting.

He went to Yeros' restaurant across the street from the Haines Company in his messenger uniform. It was crowded. Way over against the wall was a table for two. It was the only empty space in the whole restaurant. A woman sat there and he held his tray, not knowing whether to sit down or not. He stood there awkward. The woman looked up and smiled. "Want to sit down?" she asked.

"Yes, ma'am."

She moved her tray over and made room for him. He sat down.

And the accident of the next day. He set his tray down and pulled out a chair. Then he saw her and two other people at the table.

"Oh, hello," she said.

"Hello." He was embarrassed. He tried to eat fast so that he could leave.

"How do you like working at the Haines Company?" the woman asked when, with his head down, he had almost finished his spaghetti and meat balls. He glanced up. "Oh, it's all right." He dropped his eyes. She lifted her coffee cup for the last of the coffee, squeezed out her cigarette and stood up. "Good-by."

"Good-by," Chet said.

And two days later it was she who came over and sat at a table with him.

"Hello," she said.

He nodded embarrassedly and his large green eyes fell away from her face. She looked at him in his embarrassment and smiled in sympathetic amusement.

They finished eating at the same time and were ready for their coffee. Chet pulled out his pack of cigarettes. Awkwardly, shyly, he shoved them toward her. "Want a smoke?"

"Thanks," she said. "What's your name?" she asked.

His face burned with color. "Ah—ah—Don," he said. And looked down.

The woman ran her fingers through her short-cropped curly blond hair, up over one ear, reflectively. "My name's Sue," she said, "Sue Carroll. I work at Haines, too. But I have a little theater group on the side."

"What—what's that?" Don asked.

She explained.

"Did you ever think you'd like to act?" she asked.

His blond face flushed up color. He lifted his arms in awkward surprise. "Who—me?"

Sue smiled at him. "Look," she said, "my group is an amateur group. It's awfully hard to get men. Why don't you come up and watch one of our rehearsals some night?"

"Well," looking down, "maybe I will."

She wrote the address on a slip of paper and handed it to him.

"Thanks," he said and pulled his legs from under the table and picked up his messenger cap. "Thanks a lot." He flushed again and worked his way between tables toward the door thinking that Miss Carroll and everybody else was watching him.

He could tell she was surprised when he showed up. He hung at the back of the room, gawky and self-conscious. She welcomed him in friendliness and the rest of the people were nice to him. He showed interest and began coming the three nights a week. She worked with him as a beginner. He was smart and learned quickly. Soon she was devoting a good deal of time to him.

One evening when there was no rehearsal she invited him up to her room for some private training.

"Gee, this is swell!" he said, looking around her room at its artistic arrangement and furnishings, his eyes taking in the modern paintings on the walls, the low bookcase crowded with books, a couple of pieces of sculpture on top, the large phonograph albums, the candles stuck in wine bottles, the low thick-topped cocktail table, miniature iron skillets used as ash trays, a set of tin masks on one wall.

He grinned at Sue boyishly in his enthusiasm. "I wish I had a place like this!"

"Come," she said, "sit down. I'll play some music."

She put symphonic records on the turntable and he sat with his eyes turned down, not really listening, not liking nor understanding the music.

"Would you like a glass of wine?" Sue asked.

"Uh-huh."

She brought him a glass of Chianti and put some popular records on the phonograph. He sat sipping the wine, his mouth wincing on it a little, and patted his foot to the rhythm of the music. When the records had played down to the last one Sue said, "Well, we better get to work."

And it became a pattern. Twice a week he came to her room for private training. And one evening, after they had been working together for two months, he asked her, in gratitude for what she was doing for him, to go out to the show with him. He was dressed in his only suit. He smelled of chewing gum and hair oil and men's cologne. He took her to the show and was as self-conscious as he would have been if he had been out with his big sister. But he sensed that Sue felt motherly toward him. Recognized the good in him, the alertness of his mind. Wanted to bring it all out. Up to the surface, for him to recognize and use to advantage. She was a good teacher. It began to bubble inside of him and come toward the surface. He learned to use his voice, to project it. To read lines well. To use his body not awkwardly, and to gesture artistically with his hands.

In the next play they gave she cast him in the juvenile lead.

She devoted all of her spare time to coaching him in her room. Gratefully, humbly he worked. With humility he thanked her, his green eyes looking at her and almost showing tears. She looked away. "Oh now, cut it out!" She poured him some wine. And she was right. He was wonderful in the part.

After the play Sue gave the whole cast a party in her room. They stayed late and drank beer and wine and ate many sandwiches, and the phonograph played all the time and when they left the room was dense with cigarette smoke.

Sue stood in the hallway watching them all leave together. They turned on the stairway, waving, shouting good-bys.

On the sidewalk Don said to the rest of the cast, in quick impulse, "Wait for me—I'll be right back."

He went up the steps again and knocked. The door came open and Sue stood in the doorway. He smiled at her and moved back into the room. In that movement he was awkward and shy. He said, "I told them to wait for me a minute. I—" he gestured self-consciously, "I—just wanted to come back for a minute and—and thank you for—" he stammered, "for all you've done for me." He moved toward her with his hand stretched out. "Thanks." And when he stood alongside of her he put his arm around her. Then, in the next moment he didn't know what he was doing. He didn't want to spoil it. She would probably tell him to get out and never speak to her again. And yet he couldn't help it. He was carried away by his affection for her. And he couldn't stop. He put one arm and then the other around her.

He was surprised when she clung to him and lifted her mouth to his.

And then they were both breathing hard in emotion.

"Come back," Sue asked, "please come back."

With his arms around her and his cheek against hers he nodded his head.

He came back to her room when he had left the rest of the cast. He was scared and excited and embarrassed and averted his eyes.

"Sit down, Don," she said and drew her eyes away from him, and the embarrassment was in the two of them. She came quietly and sat next to him. "I didn't think this would ever happen," she said. Self-consciously she got up and poured two glasses of wine and came back. There was silence between them and neither seemed to know what to say. Sue drank her wine quickly, for courage it seemed. Then she said quickly, in a sort of a confession, "That time at the restaurant when I asked you to try out for the group—that was when I was first attracted by you. Something about you—your slimness—" she went on even more quickly, but softly, tenderly, "the boyish awkwardness and uncertainty about you, speaking to a stranger. Your large green eyes in your slim face. And—" she gestured, "I was thinking about how you would look with theatrical makeup." She smiled and looked up at him. Don's deep-set green eyes regarded her with grave youthfulness and slowly lowered themselves. "The first time you came over here," she said, chuckling a little and gesturing at the room, "I said to you—I remember exactly—

'You're so much like a little boy that I want to reach my hand out to you and help you.' I felt foolish right after I said it and on your face was the pleased yet painful look of the boy growing into a man. . . . I," she chuckled at herself, "I—I thought of how I was going to say all of this to you when you came back." She stopped self-consciously. "More wine, Don?" He nodded without answering.

She got the wine and came back and sat next to him, put her hand on top of his for a moment, then withdrew it. "You know," she said, "I was proud of you and the way you were learning. And then I was guilty." Again she chuckled at herself. "I knew I was attracted to you one day at the Haines Company when I was opening a letter. And I told myself that it wasn't right. That you were too young—that I was thirty—"

Don put his hand on top of hers.

She looked down at his hand. "I used to watch your long, sensitive fingers when you gestured with your hands."

The ash trays were filled with twisted-out cigarettes and the empty glasses from the party. "I didn't think this would ever happen," she said. Don's arm slowly encircled her waist. "I used to buy records I thought you'd like to hear—"If I Had You," "I'll Get By," "If I Didn't Care"—They embarrassed me. But they said what I'd never say. You were just a young ki—you were too young."

Don's lips moved over her mouth. Their mouths worked together.

He got a better part in the next play. He went to Sue's room at least twice a week. Sue poured wine for him. He grinned at her. "You know," he said, "that first time I came over and you gave me wine—that was the first time I ever had anything to drink."

In her room at least two times a week they'd drink wine to chase the embarrassment, to relax. And after a bit he'd touch her body and say, "Hello." And after a bit he'd say, "Let's monkey around."

A thin mustache came to his upper lip. He learned to flirt. He liked to flirt. Sue would become hurt or angry at him. There was a certain pleasure in hurting her every once in a while. He'd go into places—exclusive bars, night club bars where he felt it was good to be seen. He'd have two beers. Only two beers. That was all he could afford. If a girl happened to leave the bar and then come back he'd think, The broad walked back in because I was here. He found out he was attractive to girls. And he got as many as he could. He was really living. And he was an actor now. He walked around with his chest poked out and his stomach pulled in. His stomach was pulled in so far that his pants were beginning to slip a little. He was an actor! The way he placed his feet on the floor was a pose. The way he held a cigarette. The way he held his shoulders. His head. Someone was looking at him. Everybody should look at him.

He rolled again on his stomach, his thin blondish hair stalklike about his head. And he knew himself to be neither very good nor very wicked. Only clever. He couldn't act. Why kid himself? . . . And he began hiding. . . . No, no, that wasn't true. He began dreaming . . . He was a good actor: he would be a great one. Grandpa was right. He would be a great actor. All he had was acting.

When he arose from the bed he had again hidden all these things from himself that he had just told himself, lying there. But all during the day, at unexpected intervals, he thought of the Christmas hamburger roast with the turkey feather stuck in it. He could even see the hamburger and how it was shaped, the platter it was on, the color of the turkey feather.

That evening he went to Sue's apartment with her. He was quiet, even when they pulled the covers over them. "What's the matter, Don?" Sue asked. "What was the matter this evening?"

He told her that he had lied to her when he said that he was an orphan and had come to Chicago from Oregon when his parents died when he was sixteen.

He told her about the turkey feather. Told her everything he could remember about himself. The things he had been ashamed to tell her before now. He told her all about his family. Told her about his shame of being from poor people, inferior people, he said, and from the slums. He should cry. He tried to cry. But he couldn't.

Sue held him in her arms as a mother would, and stroked him. "There, there, Don," she said. "It's all right, Don. I understand."

*the ants are a people not strong*

Aaron Levin held the world close to him and held it away from him. He set the pencil against the paper and added another word. Carefully and in precise Palmer Method, with the final stroke in a perfect half-arch, he wrote the word, dotting it with a little *o*. Like all young people he was writing poetry. He was sixteen.

Aaron bit his pencil and laid it aside. He searched through his thesaurus for a big and pretty word. Sitting hunched over the desk, his warm, dark eyes searched the column of words for the right word. His desk was a kitchen table drawn up to the window. It was neatly arranged. The pencils were all sharpened and evenly lined along one side of the desk, and on the other side clean white sheets of paper lay under a volume of Shakespeare's sonnets. At the upper corner of the desk between two green-painted and shellacked house bricks used as book ends were his dictionary and volumes of Keats, Shelley, Longfellow. Directly in the middle of the desk but toward the window with sunlight slanting off it was an old-fashioned inkwell stuck with a quill pen. The quill had come out of a turkey and Aaron had attached a pen point to it with a rubber band. On the floor under the desk were his schoolbooks: English III, Latin, American History.

Aaron had found his word now. It would be either *halcyon* or *euphrosyne.* He liked the sound of halcyon but euphrosyne looked better. He explored the dictionary to find out what euphrosyne meant. It was from Greek mythology and was the name of one of the Graces. He didn't know which one and, not having a book of mythology, didn't know how to find out. Halcyon, halcyon: he said it quietly. It sounded good. He liked the music of it. How would it look on paper? He leaned over to write it down and his long, straight hair fell over his forehead in a black gash. A sparrow had come to sit on the slab of limestone sill outside the window and was pecking busily. Aaron watched the sparrow. Once, in cold, bitter anger his father had told him he looked like his mother.

Aaron leaned on his elbow, biting his lip. He laced the black gash of hair off his forehead and behind his ear. He stood up. He was a large boy for his age, almost six feet tall and already somewhat beefy, with a round open face and wistful dark eyes. He walked to the window and stood staring out. The afternoon sun struck obliquely against the dirty pane and gave him back a dim reflection of his face. With a forefinger he outlined its roundness, the rather full lips and the sharp, straight nose. Then he leaned his forehead against the cool, dirty pane and closed his eyes.

"Hello!" someone yelled. "Hello!" And he opened his eyes. Across the narrow courtway, leaning out an open window and over another crumbly limestone sill, he saw young Rebecca waving at him. Their eyes met and her voice came again through the glass to him. "Hello, Aaron! Mama says I can bring you a piece of cake. She just made it."

"Aw, go 'way!" Aaron said, and turning his back, walked from the window.

His eyes took in the dingy room, clean but unattended by a woman's orderliness. His desk, the only nice spot in the room. The ugly library table, the cot he slept upon, the sagging overstuffed sofa, the spindle-legged radio with the china dogs and elephants set on a faded doily. His eyes slipped unhappily over all the furniture, the ugly pictures on the wall: "Lone Wolf on a Hill" that his father liked, a photograph in an oval frame of his father posed with his little sister and himself when they were kids. Walking back to his desk Aaron kicked at the frayed rug. He hated the cheap ornaments and pictures, the tall mahogany-painted doors, the high ceiling and the foot-tall baseboards. Not as an artist lives.

Aaron picked up his volume of Shelley, and standing tall and bushy-headed at the desk, fingered it, turning the thick linen pages, running his palm over the heavy coarse-grained binding. Maybe it was good about his mother. Everybody who had been an artist had suffered. He had to suffer too. And it didn't matter how much he suffered so long as in the end he wrote, really wrote things that were good. Again he took up his pencil and the melancholy was pleasant. A few more lines came. He inscribed them carefully on the smooth white paper.

After a bit he heard the back door bang, and his sister came rushing into the front room and threw her Freshman English textbook across the room at the sofa where it hit one of the cushions and skidded under the radio.

"Where have you been?" Aaron said, looking at her angrily because the whole line of poetry that was being molded in his mind had been destroyed.

"Oh, I was playing volleyball," she said casually.

"Go away and let me alone," Aaron said.

"All right, sour puss."

"You wash the dishes," Aaron said. "You fix the dinner tonight. I didn't go to the store. The list and the money Papa left are in the kitchen." Why hadn't his father told her? Just because she was a girl was she better than him? He, he corrected himself.

"Can I use your bike to go to the store?" his sister asked.

"No, you can't—oh, all right!"

Now she was home. Now he wouldn't be able to write.

He wrote anyway for an hour more and added another two lines and a half to the poem. He copied what he had already written, copied it several times, trying to improve on the handwriting. Then he knew that it was getting late and he wanted to be out of the house before his father got there.

He went into the kitchen to see what time it was. His sister had cut up all the vegetables and started the stew. She had made herself a hamburger and was fitting it between thick slices of pumpernickel. "Have a bite," she said, walking over to him. He looked at the walnut-brown pumpernickel with the thick slice of onion like a section of white marble peeping out between the crusted bread and wondered how to describe it. Then he fitted his teeth around the sandwich and took a bite. "Thanks."

Aaron went back to his desk. He put his writing materials and his thesaurus into a brown paper carrying case. Then he felt in his jacket pocket for the round shape, the cool touch of the tin.

"Muriel, I'm going out," he told his sister.

"All right, sour puss!" Muriel said, still teasing him.

Aaron walked down the street. He was alone and lonely. He would go to the park. He would be able to write there. He would have the proper atmosphere. Through the West Side tenement-house neighborhood he walked in the warm summer sunlight, trying not to notice the decaying brick and weather-ragged boards of the houses or the skinny kids that played on the sagging steps. A young aspiring writer, alone, he walked. Chicago, the city beautiful, he said, repeating billboards erected by the city fathers. He didn't know whether he hated the city or loved it. Someday! he said, whispering it, and pounding a fist into an open palm.

He went into the underpass toward park and beach. On the concrete walls of the underpass the kids from the West Side on their way to the beach had left their scrawlings: J. C. BILL LOVES RUTH. SLICK LOVES ELEANOR. In lipstick the girls had written their names or made a heart with two sets of initials inside.

Aaron looked at the scrawlings in disgust. He waited in the long tunnel until he heard no echoes of footsteps. Then quickly slipping a pencil from his pocket he printed against the concrete: THE YEARS LIKE GREAT BLACK OXEN TREAD THE WORLD. TIME, THE HERDSMAN, GOADS THEM ON. I AM CRUSHED BENEATH THEIR PASSING FEET. Quickly he finished and hurried to the upper lawn on the other side of the street.

In the park he found a place for himself far away from anyone and beneath a tree. He lowered his largish body to the grass and placed his writing material close to him. Looking around self-consciously he drew the pipe and the tin of tobacco from his jacket pocket. He lit it, coughing a little. He liked the fragrant rum and maple smell of the tobacco and the purple-bluish cloud of smoke that clung low over the green lawn.

When he had finished the pipeful he propped his back against a tree trunk and made a desk of his knees on which to hold his composition notebook. He would be able to write here with trees, sky, nature all around him.

But nothing came.

He sat a long time with the pencil poised, ready, trying to coax the words up out of him and onto the paper. Nothing came. On his stomach and then on his back he tried to think of things to write. And he was unhappy, feeling that he'd never be able to write if here, with nature all around him, he couldn't think of a phrase to set on paper. He thought of single words and tried to find new words with which to rhyme them. But soon he wasn't even thinking of writing. He was thinking about leading his class. About the 98.2 average he had. Funny that he should lead his class and that it didn't make him proud or happy.

At length he gathered up his writing material, headed back toward the neighborhood and walked around the night streets, trying to feel what the streets told him. And felt a failure because nothing came that he could write down.

He wouldn't go home until they were in bed. He stopped in a delicatessen store and bought a quart of milk and two apples. He squatted on somebody's doorstep, still half a mile from home, and uncorked the milk. The apples were rich mahogany under the street lamp and at first cool, and skidded in the fisted palms of his hands before taking warmth. On the doorstep he drank the milk and ate the apples. And that was good. That was the way an impoverished writer would eat his supper in Paris. On a strange step. And wander in the night. And find inspiration in the night.

Then, having eaten, he dusted the large seat on his pants and continued down the tenement neighborhood streets feeling his insides squeeze when, in house after house, he saw the squares of lighted windows with people somewhere behind them. People living out their lives. Like ants, people not strong. Poor people. People with stories, with poetry. He was not surprised but rather pleased to find that his eyes were moist with tears. It told him that he did have what a writer needed. But it was something he could never tell to anyone—either that or about the lighted windows. He felt locked in himself. Always he felt this way. It wasn't good to feel this way. Maybe, some day, in words.

They were in bed. He let himself in quietly and lit the old-fashioned iron grill floor lamp, pulling it over to his desk. He glanced fearfully at the door to his father's bedroom which, as every night, was ajar. Quickly he got the spread from his cot and shielded the light of the lamp so that it shone only on the top of his desk. Then he took off his shoes so that his footsteps would not give him away.

At the desk he seated himself unnaturally stiff, toyed with his pencils, arranged his paper for writing and waited for the words. *Belatedly* was a good word. He wrote it down. He heard his father move on the bed and cringed against the sound. Again his father stirred. "Aaron, turn out that light!"

He turned the light out and waited in the dark for half an hour with his forehead against the desk top. When he heard the low rumble of snoring he again switched on the lamp and more carefully secured its light against detection. He would try something loose and unrhymed. Then he had an idea. He began writing.

In half an hour he had finished it. Silently he read it:

> Energy, strain, and perhaps insanity
> Destruction and creation of ninety-nine
> And an infinite number of ciphers
> Of brain cells.
> Thought, thought, thought.
>
> But how calmly my books lie
> In their six-dollar bookcase.

It didn't seem much like a poem. *But how calmly my books lie in their six-dollar bookcase.* That, he supposed, wasn't bad.

Then he started in terror. His father was standing in his doorway. His father was short and lean, gaunt-faced and unesthetic there in the dark doorway in his underwear. "All day I work hard." Aaron sat stiffly, feeling revulsion at the Jewish dialect of his father's voice. "All day I am providing for you. And what do you do? You keep the light open all night." His father moved into the more discernible light and stood near the desk. "You know I am not sleeping with the light open. And the bills! Mr. Edison, he is rich enough."

Aaron lowered his head and laced his black hair behind his ear. What is he complaining about? I don't ask him for anything. I have my paper route and I buy my own stamps and writing paper, my own lunch.

"And what are you doing?" his father said, gesturing with his open palms, thin and leathery in the dim light.

His father was a strangely silent man and Aaron dreaded his words. When he spoke, what he said carried weight and was law in the house. Aaron, with his head lowered, looked at his father's bare feet with hair heavy at the ankles and his toenails needing trimming, and waited silently for the rest of the words.

"You are doing this—" his father said, scattering the papers on the table with an angry hand. "You are *writing.*" He spoke the last word contemptuously. "And what are you writing? You are writing nonsense!"

With the back of his hand his father smacked the bottle of ink and the quill feather off the table. It fell on the floor underneath the table. Aaron saw the ink ooze black into the rug. Hit me but don't destroy my writing, he said to himself, not looking up at his father. His father waved and then crumpled the sheets of paper impatiently in his fist. Aaron was afraid he would cry. "A hulk of a boy like you writing poetry," his father said. He didn't want to cry. It would be something else his father would accuse him about for not being a man.

Mr. Levin walked into the bedroom. Aaron sat where he had left him. When his father returned he was smoking a cigarette between lean, bony fingers. "Aaron," he said, and his voice was cooled of anger now, "you must listen to me." His voice was patient and pleading.

"Yes, Papa," Aaron said.

"All the time you waste your time writing. And what kind of writing is it?" Again he picked up the sheets of poetry and looked at them scornfully. "A man doesn't wrote poetry." His voice became reasoning. "You must use business acumen, son. You are a Jew. You must remember that." Aaron tried to keep his mind cold and stiff to the word *Jew*. He didn't like the sound of it. People were all the same. The artist had no race or country. The artist is a man of all men. "In Russia—" his father said, and paused. He sat on the edge of the sofa and looked across the room at his son, pleading with him now. "You must make yourself a business or a professional career. You are a good boy. You are a smart boy. You must have security." His father worried his bare knee with the leathery palm of his hand. "In this country you have a chance. You must have the things I didn't have—a good education and security." Then his father said no more. His face became lean and taut and his eyes dull. He finished his cigarette and went into the bedroom. And he closed the door.

Aaron lifted the inkwell from the floor and put it back on the desk. With his handkerchief he blotted what ink he could from the quill feather and put it back into the bottle. He smoothed out the crumpled sheets of writing paper. Then he pulled off his clothes and lay face down on his cot. When they were kids and without a mother, when the neighbor woman had cooked their meals and, on Fridays, cleaned the house he would, from his bed, see his father sitting in the rocking chair in the front room with Muriel on his lap, rocking back and forth with his arms around her and her head on his shoulder, rocking and softly humming to her.

At four-thirty in the morning Aaron softly bumped his bicycle down the steps from the second floor and rode to the newspaper depot. The doors were already open and the grammar school boys who delivered the papers were rolling and stacking their newspapers into their wire bicycle baskets. Aaron counted out his hundred and fifty-eight papers and began rolling them. The young kids cursed and lit up cigarettes and talked about behind the school with the girls. Aaron tried not to hear the curse words. One of the boys in his every-morning joke said, "Hey, A-ron! When are you going to shave?" Another boy said, "Hey, A-ron! When you graduate high school are you still gonna deliver papers?" Then still another kid said to all of them, "The fat boy supports his old man. His old man drinks." All of them laughed.

Aaron said nothing. He wheeled his bicycle, heavy with the morning edition, out onto the sidewalk and under the lightening sky.

It was Saturday and after delivering his papers he could sleep until noon.

He had just dressed and washed when his father came home from work. Mr. Levin paused as he crossed the threshold, touched his fingers to his lips and with his fingers ceremonially touched the mezuzah by the door: the little metal case containing a strip of parchment made of the skin of a clean animal and inscribed with biblical words. "Hello, Aaron," his father said, looking at him with a consoling eye.

"Hello, Papa."

His father washed and fixed lunch. "You eat with me, Aaron?" Aaron shook his head. Mr. Levin drew a chair to the table and set out the half grapefruit, a herring, two hard-crusted and glossed bagels, cheese, a glass of coffee and a shot glass of whisky. First he swallowed down the whisky and then, rolling up the sleeves of his work shirt, lifted the spoon toward the grapefruit. Aaron came through the house with his hat.

"Where are you going?"

"To collect on my news route."

In the hallway he got his writing materials from under the newspapers in the bicycle basket where he had hidden them.

He rode the subway to the Washington Street stop and went to the library, climbing the wide white marble staircase with its green and gold mosaic patterns. His eyes read along the walls near the ceiling—*BYRON, SCOTT, TENNYSON, DICKENS, POPE, WORDSWORTH*—and he thrilled inside as he did each time he came to the library and saw their names set eternally in the green and gold mosaic.

He liked the library. His imagination always seemed to work there. He liked the quietness: it was so quiet that if someone coughed it seemed as if the walls turned around and looked at you; if the phone rang it shook the building.

He went to the reading room and filled out a call card for volumes of T. S. Eliot and Ezra Pound. Saul had talked about them and he didn't even know who they were. He had been ashamed, he a poet and not even having heard their names before. He couldn't tell Saul that. "You like *The Hollow Men,* don't you?" Saul had asked him. "Oh yes," he had answered, turning his eyes away. "I think it is—is very well done, and—and with feeling." Saul had said, "Well, a lot of the critics call it his best work." He had grown afraid, thinking Saul might want to start a discussion of the poem and would find out that he was lying. Saul was really intellectual. He envied Saul. And Saul was his own age. But he had had a good background and all those things all his life.

Aaron took the volumes of poetry from the call desk to a table. He read them slowly. He couldn't understand much of it but it excited him and it must be good poetry because it was so hard to understand. He decided to take the two volumes home. And what else did he want? Miss Reynolds in English had mentioned Plato's *Republic* and she had talked about Nietzsche's *Thus Spake Zarathustra,* saying, however, that it took an adult mind to read Nietzsche, even mentioning a recent murder by a high school boy and how he had been quoted by the papers as being a devout reader of Nietzsche. In Saul's father's library Aaron remembered seeing the name Nietzsche on a large volume. He'd take it home too. After he had read it he would mention something about it casually to Saul.

Leaving the desk with the books he held them in his arm so that people passing him here in the library and on the street could read the titles. They would know that he wasn't just a kid. They'd know he was a serious reader. They would admire him.

He walked down Michigan Boulevard, arranging his books so that Plato's *Republic* could be plainly seen by the people who passed him.

He went up the broad steps between the two lions and into the Art Institute, glancing curiously, shyly, at the nudes.

He spent the rest of the afternoon at the Institute wandering through the galleries. Saul had been talking more and more about Gauguin, Picasso, Van Gogh and Dali. He stood a long time in front of their works. Then he looked at the works of the contemporary abstract and surrealist artists. It confused him, the lines and the colors, but he felt that he should understand it, if he had any real artistic feeling, or he should try to understand it in order to fully develop his sensitivity. Secretly he liked the Italian classics best.

Before going home he walked through the park. In the distance he saw a bush in full red bloom. He walked over to it, thinking, I want a louder look. That was good! He laughed aloud and wrote it down in his notebook.

At seventeen he was completely absorbed in the things of youth. He was thinking of graduation, less than a year off, and his future. There was no job he wanted. He'd like to go to college and to perfect his English for writing. He'd have to work his way through, of course, but that was a challenge. Saul and Len were going to college too, but their parents had the money to send them. Saul would be a doctor like his father and Len was unhappy because his mother had browbeaten him into promising to become a lawyer.

Pedaling his bicycle, Aaron flipped the paper overhand and heard it bang against the front door.

He had started thinking about girls now. All the fellows at North Tech were dating several times a week. He had gone out with Len twice on double dates but hadn't had much to say. Girls seemed to like him but they told him he was the big brother type. Len said you had to get smart with the girls. He compressed his lips in a scowl. The big brother type! Missing the second-floor porch with the rolled newspaper he had to prop his bike against a lamppost, retrieve the newspaper, and try over.

Twenty more papers and he'd be through. He pedaled down the sidewalk, bumping off the curbstone at the corner. He wondered dimly about the war. But it was far away, far removed from a schoolboy and a student's world. At school a teacher criticized Roosevelt's policy. That was all the war meant.

That afternoon while writing at his kitchen table desk Aaron heard someone knock on the door. It was Rebecca Friedman. He noticed that she was growing up and even getting breasts. But she still looked like a kid. She had two large bundles, and dropping them over the sill said gruffly, to keep the embarrassment out of her voice, "Those are some clothes—some things—my mother sent for your sister." And quickly, "You want to go to the school baseball game with me tomorrow?"

He found himself blushing.

"Aw, go away," he said. He looked funny, standing there blushing, this six-foot boy, before this girl.

She stood in the doorway without moving but holding one side of her face away from him. She toed the doorsill with her shoe. "I got a three-pound box of candy," she said. "From—Joe," she added.

"That was nice," Aaron said.

"Will I see you tonight?"

"No." He closed the door.

With the door closed he started thinking about being home alone and Rebecca there and sending Muriel out somewhere. No, he told himself. But, strangely stirred, he got into his jacket and went down to the school store. Eight or ten of the fellows were there, inside with their feet up on the benches, and standing around outside in sweaters adorned with big block N's, or in shirts with the tails worn outside the pants. The fellows, as usual, were telling about their world-shaking experiences. The women they had had. No one was safe with them! They told it braggingly, and cast sneaking looks at each other to make sure that the others were believing them. Each was afraid he'd appear weak before the others. They piled it on. Saul and Len seemed to have had the most experiences.

Aaron pretended to himself that he was shocked by what they said but he listened even if he added nothing.

Of all the people he knew he liked Saul best and, in the senior year, they began seeing more and more of each other. It was to Saul's home that Aaron went to listen to the many albums of symphonic music his parents had in two huge cabinets and it was Saul who explained the music to him, the history of it, and gave him a real appreciation of it. Saul talked too of politics—Communism, Anarchism. Together they discussed North Tech, and analyzing the school and the school system, Aaron grew cynical about education.

The kids were clannish, he and Saul decided. The Jewish kids were one group and the Poles and other gentiles another. The jitterbugs were those kids who went in for social things. They loved the excitement of ditching classes and insulting teachers. They smoked because they thought it was smart. They didn't like school but didn't know why. They just didn't want to learn. The teachers were biased and all the textbooks, bought through a syndicate, were outdated.

Saul and Aaron, talking excitedly, told each other how most of the teachers were reactionary and how all of them gave their own opinions on politics and religion. "They give the kids phony stuff and the kids laugh at them," Saul said, "but once in a while a teacher loses her temper and says how lousy the schools are. Just last week old lady Walton let loose—" He laughed in recollection.

Aaron and Saul laughed about Mrs. Spencer, who had said, "Now you people who are religious, don't go home and tell your parents I'm teaching you evolution. You can take it for what you think it's worth."

"Mr. Shaw even refused to discuss evolution," Aaron grunted.

"Have you ever noticed how Miss Dawson likes to hurt England?" Saul asked. "And she advocates war against Russia after this war."

Aaron laughed, "Hey," he said, remembering, "Miss Isaacs said I should help you. She said you were anti-Semitic."

Saul laughed. "She told me I shouldn't talk very much—a Jew should keep in the background."

It was Saul who took Aaron to the Near North Side to stand in Bughouse Square listening in the dark to the soapbox orators talking religion, politics, philosophy under the lampposts. It was Saul who took him to the Thompson chain restaurant on Chicago Avenue. "They're all Bohemians down there. You'll get a kick out of them," Saul told him. Aaron became immediately interested. Bohemians meant to him artists, writers; meant serious, starving people who were creating in the field of art.

They pushed through the plate-glass door of Thompson's. Aaron's eyes took in the table tops covered with cups of coffee and squeezed-out cigarette butts and around which sat the odd assortment of young and middle-aged people who wanted to be artists, writers and poets. They talked loudly over their coffee cups. They talked about art, about psychology. But mostly about sex, normal and abnormal.

Aaron followed Saul with his head turning from one table to the next in this new and exciting world. Saul seemed to know everyone and spoke or waved. But he led Aaron to the back table.

"Hi!" Saul said when he got there. The middle-aged man, the young man and the youth looked up. "Oh, hello, Saul!"

"The Three Musketeers," Saul said to Aaron; and to the men at the table: "I want you to meet my friend—Aaron Levin. Aaron, Morry." Aaron shook hands with the tall, slim youth who was about his age but had a little mustache. "Sean O'Keefe," Saul said, indicating the middle-aged man. O'Keefe smiled embarrassedly. "Now, now," he said, "John—not Sean." He folded his paper and stood up with his hand out to Aaron. "Glad to meet you." "Milo," Saul said, nodding toward the young man in his middle twenties. "Milo lives on Halsted Street. He's writing a novel. How are you, Mi?" Saul said. Milo grinned at Saul and shook hands with Aaron. Saul drew chairs up to the table for Aaron and himself.

Morry and O'Keefe began discussing capitalism. "I insist," O'Keefe said, "that the system of capitalism has murdered many, many people—and, the proofs? There are many—" He smiled wryly. "Murder is a very primitive crime."

"War is a very primitive crime, too," Milo said.

Saul leaned over toward Aaron and whispered, "Milo's a conscientious objector."

"The terrible thing is," O'Keefe said, "that we have not substituted anything for force—not referring to one nation or another." He smiled. "But look. There are so many ways of killing a man. You can plan a little war of your own and millions get killed." He stroked his cheek. "One man kills in passion. But another man has a warehouse of food. And all around him are a bunch of kids. And they die, one after another, like flies. All of hunger, all of malnutrition, one by one. Both of these men are murderers." He paused. "Just think," he said, squeezing the bridge of his nose with his fingers and then looking across the table, "what human beings could become if they were fully developed. Life should be like a river flowing deeper and fuller with every stream contributing. But no! Why, we're more interested in developing flowers than we are human beings. The Lady Smith Rose! We bring some orchids from the jungles of Brazil at the cost of thousands of dollars and develop them and guard them and sell them for hundreds of dollars. We're more interested in botanical life than we are in human life!"

Milo looked across the table at O'Keefe: my God! Running an elevator and sweeping up floors at the Haines mail-order company! Aaron looked at him with his deep brown eyes and felt an immediate fascination for him. Why couldn't his father be a smart man like this? He wanted to talk to O'Keefe. But in his shyness he didn't know what to say.

Inside himself, looking at Milo and then at O'Keefe, he felt tears of gratitude water the dry and sore spot. Here was identity. Here were creative and intellectual people.

Aaron began spending much of his time at the table at Thompson's. The people there were interesting to him, exciting and different. They were someone to talk to, share intimate conversations with on art. Milo he admired most of all because he was writing and spoke of hundreds of pages of manuscript. Morry had self-assurance and was likable. O'Keefe was the most intelligent man he had ever known. O'Keefe carried an index file in his head. Ask him about anything you wanted and he could talk about it. If you asked him some historical questions he came up with the date. Over there he also met Dave, a Negro who worked in a lab out at the University of Chicago and Max, a husky Mexican in sailor uniform, who was on leave.

And then he met Steve. Steve was in his thirties. He had come to their table one night. Nobody introduced them. Morry smiled a little. O'Keefe said hello and went on reading his paper; and it wasn't like O'Keefe to be impolite. Milo talked with Steve.

Steve had a wonderful manner. When he tapped ashes from his cigarette, lifted his head and dropped his eyes around from one person to another in that sophisticated, urbane way of his you thought he was from the Gold Coast. He spoke lightly, cleverly, and then all of a sudden grew very quiet. He sat a long time, toying with his cigarette, moving the live coal on the edge of the table. He dropped the cigarette on the floor and stepped on it. His eyes moved slowly, sadly to Milo's face. "If I had one wish," he said, quietness, a poetry of rhythm coming to his voice, "I'd wish for a castle and I'd seal up the doors with concrete and put all the people inside that I like so that nothing else could ever hurt or touch them." He looked down at his hands, thin, sensitive hands; weak, nervous hands. He looked up into Milo's eyes, pleading for understanding. "I would like to have lived three hundred years ago. I like to hunt. I like to fish. I like to sit around and talk. I could have gone off into the forest and been happy. I don't want to be anybody's slave and I don't want to be anybody's boss." He looked with sad, broken eyes, weak, red-rimmed eyes, into the past. His voice touched the table, touched their ears. "It's been so long since I've looked at an apple tree in blossom, or picked a bunch of violets, or got my feet into a brook, or walked through a meadow to smell it, or climbed a hill to feel the wind . . ." Aaron looked at Steve and lowered his eyes into which moist emotion was creeping at Steve's words.

Steve smiled. "Well," he said, "there's one thing you can say about us—we're awfully sad."

"Who is he?" Aaron asked, when Steve had gone.

"That's Steve," Milo said.

"What does he do?" Aaron asked.

"Sometimes he writes poetry," Milo said.

Writes poetry! Aaron's mind leaped with the words.

"Most of the time," Morry said, "he plays the horses, drinks and runs after women."

O'Keefe stayed behind his newspaper.

After that Aaron came more often to Thompson's than ever before, looking for Steve, always disappointed when he wasn't there.

It was several weeks before he saw him again. "You write poetry," Aaron said excitedly when he did find Steve at the table and O'Keefe behind his newspaper. Steve laughed sophisticatedly, nodded in pretended modesty.

"I—I try to write it a little," Aaron said. "Could I—would you let me see some of your poetry sometime?"

Steve laughed. "Sure." He looked at Aaron and a little flicker went across his eyes, a cynical darkness flushed his face for a moment. "Poetry is . . . " he said. "Don't try to write for the masses. The hell with the masses. Poetry is an individual thing. Express yourself in new forms and the hell with everybody. Read the moderns. Try to improve on them. They've only scratched the surface of the new form which is the individual." He flicked ashes from his cigarette urbanely. "The modern artists have the key to that individuality," he said.

Aaron took a new interest in modern poetry after that and read everything he could find. He went many times to the Institute to look at abstract, cubistic and surrealistic art. To write he had to feel.

Aaron also hung around the school store now, after classes, filled with a vague need. With Len, Len in his blue sweater with the large gold N on the front, Len swaggering around the streets near school whispering wisecracks out of the corner of his mouth at the girls who giggled and liked it while pretending not to.

"There's a good lay," Len told Aaron, nodding at one of the passing girls.

"Have you been out with Alice too?" Aaron asked, excited.
"Yeah."
"What's she like?"
"Oh, she's all right."
"Co-operative?" Aaron asked, trying to assume Len's attitude of worldliness.
"To a point."
"That's interesting," Aaron said. Terribly he needed identity.
A full-bosomed girl passed them, the wind blowing her skirt up sharply from around her legs. Len nodded and grinned wisely. "Eating stuff," he said.
Aaron shuddered, in his sensitivity, hearing Len's words. But he thought about it later. And the next night in Thompson's, Steve showed him some poetry he had written. Aaron read: *We have a bed and we have all this night. Look! I am naked without apology. Turn yourself . . . turn yourself, give yourself to my lips, press down your hips. Why waste the bed, emasculate the night. Come . . . come . . . and come again . . . we could be gods if you would. Why starve yourself, the food is good.*
He thought about Steve's poetry. His own poetry began to take on a sexual tinge.

The football season came. The school had little hope of a good team. Aaron, one of the biggest fellows in North Tech, was soon noticed by the captain of the team. The captain asked him to come out. Aaron's friends heard about it and coaxed him to try out. Hating sports but wanting to be accepted by his classmates, he promised.
Aaron's feet were so large that they had a hard time finding a pair of shoes to fit him. He pulled the smelly jersey over his large, soft-muscled shoulders and went out to the field where he was pitted, in the initial practice, against a small, wiry veteran guard. The coach gave preliminary instructions while the rest of the players, in two lines, waited their turn.
"Charge!" the coach snapped.
Aaron picked himself up off the ground.
"How much do you weigh, Levin?"
"A hundred and eighty-eight pounds."
"You, Gapinski?"
"One-forty."
"Okay, Levin," the coach said, "get in there, boy, and take him back—*back!* Okay!" He blew his whistle and shouted, "Move! *Move!*"
Aaron picked himself off the ground, bruised.
Twenty times the coach had him and Gapinski face each other,

and snapped sarcastic remarks at Aaron when the veteran guard each time charged him back five yards and knocked him off his feet.

The other members of the squad stood around, pleased with the respite, and grinned. "You ought to be able to stay off your can with them gunboats, Levin!" they shouted, and, "You ain't going to let that little guy make a fool of you, are you, Levin?"

Aaron stayed the practice out. Toward dusk he limped around and around the oval of track with the rest of the squad for five miles. He limped on a Charley horse. His legs and arms were sore and bruised. There was a lump under his eye. In the showers the rest of the squad grinned at him in superior amusement.

Aaron handed in his uniform. "I guess you weren't cut out for football," the coach said.

Aaron turned more toward his writing.

Coming in from collecting on his newspaper route Aaron saw his father sitting at the kitchen table eating his Saturday dinner. The little whisky glass was empty. The bagels looked like highly polished wooden knobs on their saucer.

"Hello, Papa."

"Come eat," his father said.

Aaron looked at his father's hand stirring the spoon in the glass of tea and saw the nub where one finger had been lost in a factory machine. He shuddered. It always made him shudder to see it. He went to the stove and dished up some of the stew. He knew his father had cooked it when he saw the big hunks of vegetables and meat and wondered where Muriel was.

Aaron sat across the table from his father. Papa Levin's small, thin body was stooped in its chair, leaning toward the food. Aaron, big on the chair at the other end of the table, towered above his father. Sunlight fell on Papa Levin's lean face in need of a shave and his sharp, pinched neck above the blue work shirt. Uncomfortable as always in the presence of his father, Aaron ate in silence. Occasionally his father looked at him and smiled as if he wanted to start a conversation. Aaron avoided his eyes. In doing so he looked at his father's lean and leathery hands. And remembered, as a child: the index finger of his father's right hand, leathery then too, moving slowly across the backward printed letters of the Hebrew alphabet, teaching him. He had repeated them slowly after his father and the finger with the dirty fingernail moved on to the next. Then selections from the Torah. In succession, as he grew, the Bible, Mishnah and Talmud. Aaron tossed his head, whipping the black hair out of his eyes. He laced it behind his ear. His father cleared his throat and Aaron knew this was preparatory to saying something.

Mr. Levin stood up and walked to his work jacket which hung

against the wall on a nail. From the pocket he drew out a booklet and carried it to the table. "Aaron, you are a smart boy," he said. "Almost a high school graduate now." He smiled kindly and proudly. "Yes, a smart boy." He nodded his head several times. His hands trembled a little on the cover of the booklet as he held it out to Aaron. Aaron was surprised to see his father's hands shake. He always thought of his father as a cold and emotionless man. "Here is something I want you to read," his father said. Aaron took the booklet and was more surprised to see what it was: Communist Manifesto.

He looked up at his father with his mouth open slightly and his eyes blinked wide. His father a Communist! He couldn't believe it! He had thought of his father only as ignorant. Had disliked him for his ignorance. Never had he seen him read anything but the Jewish *Forward* and religious books.

"But, Papa—" was all Aaron could say.

Papa Levin went and sat opposite his son at the table. He looked across the table and into his son's face. "Truth is heavy, therefore few care to carry it," he said.

"You mix the Talmud with communism," Aaron said.

His father shrugged.

"What about your religion? Your God?" Aaron asked.

The old man squared back his thin shoulders. His eyes, flanking the thin, pinched nose, looked into his son's face. "My God I can worship in the open field," he said, "or if need be, in the secrecy of my room."

"You would like Sean O'Keefe," Aaron said, chuckling.

His father's lean hand across the table silenced him. Again Aaron was surprised to see his father tremble. The old man said, "My God is my own here." He placed his trembling hand against his heart. "But in a country where to defame a man's race or his color is a crime and you go to jail for that crime, that country I am for."

"But this is America, Papa," Aaron said. "Here there is freedom."

The old man laughed contemptuously. "The place honors not the man, 'Tis the man who gives honor to the place," he said, again quoting from the Talmud.

"What about freedom?" Aaron said. He was arguing with his father. And in his mind:

The artist was an individual. He needed most the individuality of his soul. How else could he express himself?

Papa Levin rose and moved close to Aaron. He held out his palms, callouses heaped there. He smiled. "You call that freedom, do you?" He stuffed an angry hand into his pocket. "You go look at Emerson Bradley's hands. Go look at the hands of all like him. Go see if they eat stew. Go see if their children, big boys, have to deliver newspapers at four in the morning." His eyes grew dull. He rubbed his bristle of beard. He turned and walked into the next room, slamming the door after him.

Aaron sat staring at the door incredulously. It was more than he had ever heard his father say at one time before and—his father a Communist! He put on his coat, looked at the closed door and slipped out of the house. He went to the park. Across the lawn he saw, under sunlight, the lagoon shimmering and a single boat tossing on it. "Blessed be he who has such things in his world," he said, half-aloud, and was surprised that he, a nonbeliever, remembered that from his religious background: when one sees beautiful persons, cattle, or trees, or even a beautiful non-Jew, he must say this—and he had said it. He was amazed.

Chilly in the false warmth and sunlight of the fall afternoon, Aaron rose and wandered through the park, unconscious of where his feet took him. . . . Passover, that was the holiday he remembered most. There was no mother. But his father observed the holiday with them. They were awfully poor then. He ran down to the store to buy the box of matzoth. It was fun looking all over the house for leaven bread. Papa with the necessary wax candle led the search. He and Muriel followed him in excited expectancy in this game of search. "Oh, Papa! Papa! Here's a piece of bread!"

And Muriel, sticking her tongue out at him, "I found a piece too, smarty!"

"Children, we must not quarrel on this night," Papa said. The flickering candle flame made large shadows loom up into Papa's eyes and his cheekbones stood like those on a skull. The candle moved to another part of the room, and Papa. They found another piece of bread. Later, at the heder, Aaron learned that it was lawful to place pieces of bread in the corners of the rooms so that the search would not be in vain.

Papa carried the bread out onto the back porch and crumbled it in his palms. He gave it to the wind. Then they had to scrub the kitchen cupboard.

The feast was what he remembered most of all. It was always the only *good* meal they had for a whole year. Papa invited the old Jewish junkman up from his basement room for the meal because one must be hospitable to the poor who have no family board for the Passover feast. Papa and the junkman, both so lean, looked like ghosts in the light of the kerosene lamp.

It was the law that the table must be adorned with the most beautiful dishes possible. They had only their everyday dishes, cracked, the cups without handles. They had to recline at the table instead of sitting up straight and Papa told him and Muriel, "Recline on the left side."

"But, Papa," Muriel said, "why do we have to recline at all?"

Papa held his arms open and motioned to her with all his fingers to come. He took her on his lap, and smoothing her hair, smiled at her kindly. "Because, my little girl, it means the Jews have been delivered from Egypt. It means only the Pharaoh reclined before, while the Jews were slaves. It means the Jews now will have political and social and intellectual and personal ease. Big words, my little girl," he had said, stroking her hair, "but some day you will understand." Aaron had watched with a pang of jealousy. No one ever stroked his hair.

Papa lifted Muriel down off his lap. He spanked her once, playfully, with his open palm. "Now—go recline." He smiled again.

On the table was the feast. On the cracked plates. Three matzoth wrapped in a cloth. A cup of salt water. An egg. Roast lamb. Bitter herbs and vegetables. A mixture of apples, almonds and nuts. At each place at the table was a glass for wine. For him and Muriel little whisky shot glasses for their wine. Glasses that would be less than half filled.

The wine glasses had the bottle turned down into them. And now Papa said, "Blessed art Thou, O Lord, who createst the fruit of the vine." Papa went on and on to the end of the prayer and they all said "Amen." Then Papa touched the matzoth and said, "Behold, this unleavened bread is to remind us of the bread of affliction which our forefathers ate in Egypt."

The second glasses of wine were filled. The ceremony went on. And each of them received from Papa a piece of matzoth and bitter herbs dipped in *charoseth*—which was a funny name for the mixture of apples, almonds and nuts.

Then Papa saying to them, "Chew hard on the bitter herbs, children, and remember the bitter days when all Israel stood as a bondman before Pharaoh."

Then came the part that frightened him. In through the door would come Elijah. Elijah about whom they had heard so many stories. Papa smiling gently and saying, "In Russia as a boy they told me that thunder was the noise of Elijah's chariot wheels among the clouds of heaven." And smiling, nodded his head.

Now in a little while Elijah would stand in the room. His chariot would draw up to the door. He would march in. Aaron had begun to tremble. He trembled now a little, remembering. The door was opened and the wind tugged at their clothes, at the table covering. The kerosene wick flame stood crooked in its glass and smutted one side of the globe. The glasses of wine were filled for the third time. And the extra glass for the welcome guest, the prophet Elijah. Aaron again trembled with the memory. Maybe it was only his imagination. Of course it was. But—in through the door—he had seen him come. He had seen Elijah enter. That was silly. But he could swear it. At least he thought he could. One of those tricks of the imagination. The imagination of a child.

The part of the ceremony they waited for, he and Muriel, with the filling of the fourth glass—

"A lamb! A lamb! which my father bought for two farthings," they had sung. And continued:

*"There came a cat and ate the lamb*
*There came a dog and bit the cat*
*There came a stick and struck the dog*
*There came a fire—"*

Aaron looked up. He was surprised to see that he stood outside Thompson's restaurant. He went in.

O'Keefe was saying, "Yes, yes, there will be a strike, all right. Emerson Bradley will find that he cannot run the Haines Company with white-collar workers alone. The whole danged place will be closed down."

Aaron sat and listened without really listening.

Steve came in and Aaron was glad to see him. "Read the *avant garde* writers," Steve told him. "Read Nietzsche." Aaron hung on to every word Steve said. And Steve, looking at him in hidden amusement, realized the influence he had over him. "Read Freud," he said; and with a malignance Aaron didn't recognize, "But above all read Nietzsche and Schopenhauer."

Aaron did as he was told. He began reading from *Thus Spake Zarathustra* which, until then, he had only carried under his arm on the bus and subway. He became a serious student of philosophy on his own, feeling that the more he knew about the deeper things in life the more profound his writing would become. He found himself more and more interested in modern poetry and art, in anything new and experimental.

Papa came into the house. He looked at Aaron, "Have you read yet, from the book I gave you?"

"A little," Aaron said.

"Teach thy tongue to say, 'I do not know,' " his father said, quoting from the Talmud. "And read with an open mind." He turned toward the door. " 'Man is born,' " he said from the Talmud, " 'with his hands clenched; he dies with his hands wide open. Entering life he desires to grasp everything; leaving the world all that he possessed has slipped away.' "

"I'll tell that to Emerson Bradley," Aaron said.

His father walked into the other room and put his lunch pail on the table.

The young, smooth, crisp, cheerful voice said over the radio at the break in the music: "How about it, fellow? Are you between seventeen and twenty-five? Are you in good health? You're a cinch for the Army Air Force. You get $21 a month plus a dollar for food and—in the army they spell food capital F-O-O-D! . . . If you want that girl of yours eating out of your hand come on down and join up! How about it? Come on down to the old Post Office and say, 'I'm here for my silver wings!' "

Aaron clicked the radio off. For a long time he sat with his elbows on the desk and his hands in his hair. Then he again picked up the pencil.

He sat writing until it got dark. Then, in old clothes and gym shoes, he let himself out the door and, under the stars, began to trot against the hard concrete sidewalk when Rebecca, coming from somewhere out of the dark, fell in step with him. "Why are you running?" she asked. In slacks she matched his stride, her face turned up to his questioningly. He was going to chase her away. Then he saw the oval of brown-splotched birthmark on one cheek at the corner of her mouth. He let her trot along. Once or twice he glanced at her. Her long brown hair was in braided pigtails. There were little red ribbon bows at the ends of them, like the wrapping off a candy box. That was nice. He'd write a poem about it.

Their feet made soft-treaded sounds, lifting and striking the sidewalk. He felt like a fool. He slowed to a walk. She slowed too, tossing her head and throwing the pigtails back across her shoulders. There was a drugstore on the corner.

"Want a soda?" Aaron asked.

"I don't care."

They had sodas on the tall stools and went back out onto the night sidewalk. "Now go home," he told her.

Rebecca went.

Aaron washed up and went down to Thompson's. He dressed with great care. For three months he had been saving for his new clothes to wear down there. He put on the loud red, yellow and green flowered sport shirt and the long-lapeled, canary-colored sport coat with its accentuated hand-stitching. Under his arm he carried *Modern Trends In Art.*

They were all at their accustomed table and greeted him cordially; all but Milo who sat quietly as if in deep thought.

"Jesus Christ!" Morry said, giving a friendly chuckle to his voice. "You're all dolled up tonight."

Aaron smiled his pleasure and, placing the book where they all could see the title, sat down between Mildred and Kitty, two girls who often dropped by the table.

"Aaron," Kitty said, indicating the young man across the table, "this is Don Lockwood. He's an actor." To Lockwood she said, "Aaron writes poetry."

Don wore dark glasses which he took off for a moment to acknowledge the introduction and then replaced on the sharp bridge of his nose.

"How do you do. Pleased, I'm sure," Lockwood said. "Cawn't say that I've seen you around before." He ran a lean forefinger along one side of his thin, blondish mustache.

Kitty giggled in pleasure and said, loudly, to everyone at the table, "Don't mind Don's English accent. He's been in three English plays in a row."

"How'd you do in your last play?" Mildred asked Don.

"Are you kidding?" Don said, smiling tight-lipped.

Aaron liked Don's looks; he was the first actor he had ever met. He began an immediate conversation with him. Milo was jotting something down in his notebook and O'Keefe had retreated behind the newspaper. Now O'Keefe was talking angrily, leaning toward Morry and pointing out one of the war dispatches that was anti-Russian.

Don stood up to go, again taking off his dark glasses and glancing at the table with his green eyes. "Sorry. I have to run. Rehearsal, you know." He made a slight bow, and slipping on his glasses, left with the girls.

Aaron turned toward Milo. "Gee, Milo, how are you? How is your writing going?" His hand had slipped into his pocket to draw out a poem he had written. He badly wanted Milo's approval of this new trend he was following.

Milo was watching Don out the door with his lips tightly pressed. He now looked across the table at Aaron. "Why do you come down here dressed like that?" he asked bluntly. "Are you trying to make people notice you?" Even as he said it he was sorry and ashamed of himself; but also glad he had said what he felt. He liked Aaron. He saw the changes coming and knew Steve's influence and the influence of the whole Near North Side Bohemian crowd.

O'Keefe put his head behind the newspaper. Morry went to the counter for coffee.

"Do you want to be like the rest of these people around here?" Milo said. "Christ, you don't have to dress like a clown to write."

Morry brought the coffee and, avoiding everyone's eyes, set the cups on the table. Aaron's fingers shoved the poem back into the well of his pocket. He lowered his head.

At that moment Steve, in his disheveled clothes, pulled a chair up to the table and flopped down. He pushed his swollen, thirty-five-year-old face, looking fifty, out over the table. His eyes, hanging in deep bags and filled with fear and cynicism, looked from face to face. He pulled his notice to appear for an army physical examination from his pocket and waved it loosely over the table. His mouth tightened to one side of his face in a bitter sneer. "It's nothing but big business on a highly glorified scale at *fifty dollars a month.*" His eyes took on a deeper fear. "It's like death only you'll never come back from death and you may come back from war—anyway—" the bitter smile again creased his mouth, "my neck wasn't built for a noose or a uniform." He started to tear the notice in half, then thought better of it.

Aaron pushed his chair back from the table. "I've got to make a telephone call," he said. He didn't look up.

"We don't fit into the little puzzle they've rigged up," Steve said, laughing.

No one said anything to Steve. He stood up, and shoving the notice into his trouser pocket where it stuck out at an angle, moved away from the table.

"You hurt Aaron's feelings," Morry told Milo. There was disapproval in his voice.

"Yes, I know it. I like him." He gave no other explanation.

In an hour Aaron returned. He had changed his shirt and his coat. "I'll get coffee," Aaron said. No one made any mention of the fact that he had gone the long distance home on the streetcar, changed clothes, and returned. Aaron brought the coffee from the counter and set the cups before them. He sat down next to Milo and smiled at him. O'Keefe became very talkative and joked about his job at the Haines Company and began a long discussion of the war. Finally Aaron turned to Milo with the poem in his hand. "Would you—do you mind looking at this and telling me what you think of it?"

Milo took the poem and read:

Flower, open to me, tulip
Whisper my love
From bulb to bulb
Liquid yellowness
Bucketful my love

Flower, open to me, thy dew
Butterfly my love
Leaf-spear
My lush-lust
Wax my upright antenna

Nest, open to me:
My eggs of love
Dropping, shell white
Tanures,
I am thy seed.

Milo lay the poem on the table. "Well—I—I think it has a nice feeling," he told Aaron.

"It's just experimental yet," Aaron said apologetically. "I have a long way to go. I'm tired of rhymed poetry and the obvious."

O'Keefe had picked the poem up and read it, frowning.

"What does *tanures* mean?" Milo asked Aaron.

In his embarrassment Aaron laughed softly and self-consciously. "Oh, it doesn't really mean anything. I—well, I thought it sounded good—gave—gave a feeling."

O'Keefe handed the poem back without comment.

"Did you like it, Sean?" Aaron asked.

"I don't understand this modern stuff," O'Keefe said and would add no more.

Morry reached across for the poem. He read it and was about to laugh out loud when he saw Milo and O'Keefe frowning at him.

Len and Saul dropped into Thompson's looking for Aaron, and dragged him off with them. Looking for youthful excitement they went over to the North Clark Street Skid Row and into a low-down tavern. They had to coax Aaron inside, each taking an arm and razzing him across the sill. Walking to the crowded and noisy bar Aaron stared fearfully at the hard faces of the middle-aged and elderly women. Once he had stood outside and then gone into all the taverns along North Clark and along West Madison, first down one side of the street and then the other, looking for a face among the many faces.

The bartender didn't question their ages. Saul and Len ordered beer but he asked for a glass of wine: poets drank wine. "Don't drink out of a glass in here, you fool!" Len said. He drank, anyway, sipping the wine: wine was the drink of Paris.

"It's late," Saul said. "My mother is going to raise hell."

"Mine too, but what do I care?" Len asked. "A lawyer!" he snorted. "So I have to be a lawyer to please my mother!"

"My mother is dead," Aaron said. He knew it was a lie but he had to say it. He had told Len and Saul the lie before. But he had to hear it out loud again.

# IV

*the locusts have no king yet go they forth all of them by bands.*

Jim Norris held the people in his hand. Jim Norris held the people in his hand and didn't even know it. In his blue jeans and white sweat shirt with its oval of neck he stood on the rough board platform in front of the union headquarters on North Canal Street. His large, hair-curled arms were upraised, his angry voice rang with indignation and his words flowed down to the people, and over them, and into them. "This—this colossus that spans the river—" He pointed his long, tanned and muscular arm at the white-walled building of the Haines Company across Canal Street. "—and Emerson Bradley—"

"BOO!" the crowd of workers shouted in angry chorus.

"—Bradley, this cyclops who can see but one way—sitting in his penthouse office—"

From his perch above the crowd, the thighs of his legs showing above the tightly packed heads, he looked like an athlete. Slightly over six feet tall, his shoulders were square and broad, his hips slim in the blue faded tight-fitting trousers. At his back in the gloomy day and almost like the backdrop of a stage set were Bernie's Tavern on the corner of Canal and Lake Streets where Milwaukee Avenue starts, a restaurant and Local 33 housed in an aged two-story building from which the weather had eaten the darkened paint. Below him the crowd was packed in until it overflowed the sidewalk in a huge, uneven arc and took up part of the street. Jim stood on the platform with his hands upraised. His voice strode out to the crowd. The river flowed toward him from the lake and bent into its north and south branches a short distance from where he stood, the south branch flowing immediately under the Lake Street bridge toward Madison Street, the Daily News Building, the Northwestern depot and on southward to lose itself in the country, the north branch wandering in many twists and turns northward under bridges like a huge eel caught in a net. At this branching of the river stood the Haines Company, one building on either shore.

On the south shore of the river directly in front of Norris was the administration building and the retail department store; across the river on its other bank stood the mail order building directly in front of the Merchandise Mart. The buildings were twins of the exact size, shape and height and rose against the sky in shining alabaster.

November bruised the sky. November chilled the air. Up the river north and above the bridges lacing the river stood the Wrigley Building and the Tribune Tower pointing silent fingers at the threat of a snowstorm. The El rumbled continuously over Lake Street.

Jim faced the crowd. Over the heads of the crowd he shook his fist at the Haines buildings. "The people," he said, "are shaking a calloused fist at the Haines Company. The workers are pounding a fist against the castle door—*demanding!*—union recognition—*demanding!*—decent wages—*demanding!*—a closed shop—and Emerson Bradley—in his penthouse office *must* listen to our cry—*will* listen—"

The crowd moved in closer. The women smiled up into Norris' face or bit their lips or pushed the hair off their foreheads with their hands, their eyes intent on him as they listened. The men stood nodding in agreement, tightening their fists, working their hands in their pockets, and somewhere in the crowd a high school girl making wartime money by working after classes said aloud, to no one, "Ain't he cute!" And Don Lockwood, waiting for Sue, was hemmed in by the crowd, stood listening with curiosity and some agreement.

Jim looked into the upturned faces. Slowly he looked, forcefully. He tossed his head a little in his anger and the curly blond hair verging on copper flowed back off his forehead. His mouth bared itself to white teeth. "Is man's right to life a right to work and live decently or—is it at someone's whim and pleasure? Are we just dirt out here on the sidewalk?"

The final day shift was now leaving the building. They swarmed out, covered all the sidewalk and part of the street. They streamed out of the Canal Street exits and out of the retail department store exits on Lake Street. They flowed from the upper entrances and onto the Lake Street El station that had direct access to the building. The early-evening mob moved as one huge octopuslike creature from work toward home, a miscellaneous crowd of clerks, typists, secretaries, accountants, order fillers, supervisors, executives and maintenance men. . . . A policeman tries to keep traffic moving smoothly. People rush across the street against the light and snarl traffic. A truck driver jams on his brakes, puts his head out the window and curses a pedestrian. Union organizers pass out mimeographed handbills to all who will take them. Some stuff them into their pockets. Some, knowing what they are, refuse. Some, seeing what they are, crumple them in their fists or let them drift out of their hands to the street. Streetcars blot up the crowds at corners. El trains take them from platforms. More crowds gather where the others have stood. And still they flow out of the Haines Company. Almost ten thousand employees. . . . Everybody is in a hurry to get home. There's something about the way a man walks away from his job. Something of this in all of them, leaving from the forty-eight floors of the twin buildings of the Haines Company. Tired. Headaches. Backaches. Burning eyes. Weary. But released. Free for a while. All in a hurry to get home. Tired. Hurrying to suppers, wives, husbands, families, newspaper, radio and show. Or perhaps to just a room somewhere. Maybe they won't enjoy their suppers. Maybe they will fight with their wives. Maybe they will have to go to the show whether they want to or not. But hurrying to get there . . . and all they had to do was to lift their feet and they'd be on the streetcar automatically. The crowd would see to that.

On every car they're hanging off the edges . . . a little office girl, very much painted and powdered and with an artificial flower in her hair and large earrings, stands shivering in the cold. She has an Irish face. She's snobbish. She doesn't talk to the common help. The mob on the street. And she has to wrestle with these big burly colored women, and with everybody, the Italians and everybody, to get on the car. Her feet are killing her . . . little nurse McGrath with a tired face. Waiting in a doorway for the mob to melt away a little.

The mob moves toward transportation and home. Some stop to listen to Jim Norris or the other speaker in front of the building on the opposite side of the river. Many move away. "Aw, one of them union organizers." "Another goddamn Red." "One of those crackpot organizers." The majority of the white-collar workers move on toward home with stiff faces and straight-ahead eyes as if they haven't seen the organizers. . . .

Jim Norris stood on his platform, the next speaker already standing below, ready to take over. Jim, tall and statuesque and standing out against the blackened buildings at his back, again tossed his curly blond hair off his forehead with a vicious snap. His long and flat and strong mouth hurled the words of his anger against Bradley at the crowd, or became reasoning in its tones, confident, militant. His voice lowered. He ran the palm of his hand over his forehead and smoothed his hair. "Man," he said, "has traveled a long, weary road. All the sweat and blood that has been spilled at machines and in factories has not been spilled in vain. . . ." A little secretary, shivering in the cold and dampness, looked up admiringly into his face hearing nothing of what he said. This was the man who had fixed her typewriter. Her eyes slipped along his shoulders, down to his hips, along his loins in their blue jeans and then back up to the planes of his face. To her he looked like the billboard ads of the male in Jantzen swimming trunks.

Jim's voice lowered. He said, "You can't stop the people in their forward march. The people, like ants, live by co-operating. They—the Emerson Bradleys—can't divide man against man forever."

He climbed down from the rough stand, jumping down the last two steps to the sidewalk. The next speaker climbed up.

Jim pushed through the crowd. Some of the men slapped him across the back. A woman stood with her little girl, looking at him. Jim put his hand on the child's curly head and smiled at her. He then moved through the crowd toward the restaurant. It took him a long time to get there. Everybody wanted to congratulate him.

Jim pushed into the restaurant for a cup of coffee. He rubbed his hands together, warming them and grinning. The place was crowded. At the counter the union officials pushed over, making room for him. He moved toward the cleared space. As he walked several men slapped him on the back. "Good going, Norris! Good going!"

Jim grinned. He had a disarming smile. His candid blue eyes, dark-lashed, gave their direct look in a friendly, straightforward way as if he had never met an enemy.

"Was it all right?" Jim asked Kovac, the union president.

"Was it all right?" Kovac said gruffly. He hugged Jim over to him. "It was great stuff! Didn't know you could talk," he said in the same gruff voice.

"Hello, Mr. Baker," Jim said to the man on the other side of him. Mr. Baker nodded his head in approval. "You did very well, young man! Very well, indeed!" Mr. Baker spoke in cultivated and precise English. He was a man in his sixties, neatly dressed, with pared fingernails and a stickpin in his tie. Jim glanced at him in respect and then reached for his cup of coffee. He had admired the man since he first met him. He had heard the story. Jim drank some of his coffee and glanced again at Mr. Baker respectfully. He had been a department head at the Haines Company, one of those men Emerson Bradley considered dispensables, and they had wanted him to get out. He had a month's vacation coming. They gave it to him cheerfully and he went to California to visit his wife's people and when he came back his desk was no longer in his office. It was out in the middle of the floor with the other workers and among all the girls in the department. Before this, his office had been shut off by partitions and only the girls had been out there on the floor. Well, there was his desk right out on the floor. And he had to sit there in humiliation among those girls who had previously taken orders from him. Worst of all there was very little work on his desk for him to do. There was a brand-new man in his office, a young fellow from college, younger than the number of years Baker had spent at the Haines Company. It was a wonderful way of squeezing a man out. Mr. Baker had stuck it out for just two weeks. Then he couldn't stand the humiliation any longer. They say that one day just about noon he stood up by his desk and said, "Well, I know where I can go." He had jammed his fist into his hand. He had jammed his hat on his head. He had walked over to union headquarters. He had put his hat down on the desk and asked, "Is there any work I can do over here?"

Jim again glanced at Mr. Baker in secret admiration. Mr. Baker smiled at him and said, "They tell me it was your first speech."

"Yes, sir." He grinned. "My wife helped me with it."

"My wife has always helped me and encouraged me in everything I've done," Mr. Baker said.

One of the other organizers was asking Jim how it felt. Again he grinned. He couldn't tell anybody how he felt inside. He'd just have to tell himself, thinking about it along the way home. Still another organizer had joined their group, smacking his hands together to warm them. "Just came from across the river," he said. "Joe Abrahams is giving the company hell over there." He rubbed his arms, warming them. "Big crowd, too. Cold as hell out."

Jim put his long legs down off the stool and on the floor. "Hey, Yeros!" he called out to the proprietor, setting the coffee cup down and wrestling his big finger out of the handle where it had stuck. "You got my coat?"

"Sure thing, Jimmy-boy!" the proprietor yelled back. Bundling the coat into his arms he tossed it over the counter to Jim. "I guess you fixed their typewriters today, Jimmy-boy!" he said.

"Come on next door and have a drink," a couple of the men said to Jim in invitation.

"No," Jim said, disentangling himself from their big, encouraging hands. "No, I've got to get home." Turning up his collar he waited on the corner and boarded a Lincoln-Peterson streetcar.

Gee, it was good, speaking for the union. For months, for too long, he had been an undercover man repairing typewriters and adding machines on the floors of the Haines Company and organizing as many of the workers as he could, slowly, safely. Maintenance Department. Yes, it was good to come out in the open! He continued to grin. A woman glanced at him and he looked up at her, feeling good, with the grin still on his face. She smiled back at him.

He averted his eyes. He glanced out the window. Repairing typewriters with the girls giggling when he came in, and putting their heads together and calling him over to change a ribbon or fix a typewriter that had nothing wrong with it. He looked at his shadowy reflection in the windowpane of the moving streetcar. It rode along outside the glass with him. Yes, he was good-looking. It could be an affliction being good-looking. Louise. The girls giggling. Especially the high school girls who flirted with him openly and even made passes at him once in a while. The older women, women in their twenties and thirties, were quite different in their approach. Something about the way their eyes opened a little wider, looking at him, or their lips parted a trifle, or their voices becoming soft and warm, very cordial. Each time a woman showed interest in him it embarrassed him. Even angered him. And sometimes he'd tell himself, okay, be charming. Smile, damn it! And joke with them. Or look back into their eyes. If it gets people into the union—women in, and they're hard nuts to crack—play along, boy, play along. Sometimes he'd kid with the teen-aged high school girls. "Want to buy me a cup of coffee?" one of them would ask, or another, "I get off in half an hour. I'm gonna be over at the restaurant when I get off. I always go there for a cup of coffee before I go home."

"Oh now," he'd say, "I'm an old married man."

"Oh, you are *not!*"

Several of the others, giggling, would say, "You're only nineteen or twenty . . . No, he's about twenty-two . . . Hey, kid, don't you wish you had curly hair like him!"

"I'm married and I have a son," he'd say.

"Oh, you have *not!*"

"Yes, I have. He's almost as old as you are."

This would bring squeals of laughter. None of them would even believe he was married then. These were the kids, once you got them interested in the union, who would be all out for it. Like rooting for your side at a football game.

Again he glanced at his reflection in the streetcar window. Goddamn it! He *did* look his twenty-seven years! He made a gloom-ugly face at his reflection and saw it grimace back. He grinned. It was good to be out in the open, on the side of the people. Damn it, it was good!

He thought of Edna and had a warm feeling. It was people like Edna he was for. A woman, her husband dead. Two kids to raise and put through school. High school, too, she wanted for them. . . . Her forty-year-old face, always cheerful and a little defiant. Her cheap clothes, mended. Her desperate attempt to keep them neat. Her pride. Wanting to look as good as anyone else who worked there. Her tired hands and her weary body, her tired legs, keeping up her rate day after day, every day, all year. And the years moving one into the other. Working even on Saturdays for the little extra money she would get. Money needed to keep the house, give the kids a little bit more. Nine hundred units of work a day. That was a hundred—a hundred and twelve pieces of mail to handle an hour. My God! He stroked his tanned face with his hand. Edna, one of millions. She had worked at Monkey-Ward's and Spiegel's and now at the Haines Company. It was the only work she knew.

Jim, in memory, was no longer on the streetcar. He had picked up his tool kit and was walking to the elevator in the Haines Building.

"Hi, O'Keefe!" he said to the elevator operator.

"Hello, Jim," O'Keefe said, smiling. "And how goes your work?"

They had gone up in the elevator. They were alone. O'Keefe seemed to be running the elevator very slowly today. "Tell me, Jim," he said, "when you played high school football that was a lot of co-operation, wasn't it? I mean, all the players had to play together to win."

Jim smiled. He nodded yes.

"That's why I like the sport," O'Keefe said, "even though we never had it in the old country and I don't know all the terms. And how's your little boy?" he asked quickly.

"Oh, fine."

They went up two more floors in silence. Suddenly O'Keefe stopped the elevator. "Let's sneak a little smoke," he said. He offered Jim a cigarette. Jim set his tool kit on the floor. He lit up. "This elevator is always slow," O'Keefe said. "I don't have many people to take up this time of day. I replace Bob for two hours every day." He lit his cigarette. "You know," he said, "some day we're going to have a union in this place. Now, I don't know—I want your opinion—"

The elevator buzzer rang. "Dang it!" O'Keefe said. But he puffed on his cigarette and didn't take the elevator down to the floor that flickered in the red button. "It's your opinion I want about unions," he said. "Whether you think they're a good thing. I mean—don't you think working people should stick together?"

The buzzer rang again. "What floor did you say?" O'Keefe asked.

"Seven," Jim said.

They went up the two flights to seven in silence. Again the buzzer sounded from the third floor, in an irritated persistence. O'Keefe peeled the door back so Jim could get off. Jim slapped him across the back and laughed. "I think I'd vote for a union," he said. He wished he could tell O'Keefe that he was a union organizer. Not yet. He'd sign him up later though.

Outside the elevator he fished in his pocket and drew out the assignment slip. *Department 35,* he read, *conveyer belt.* He picked up his tool kit and walked along the tomblike low-ceilinged room that took up the entire floor. Packages were piled to the ceiling. Packages made the only aisles across the whole of the floor. Painted cardboard signs, both lettered and numeraled, gave routed directions to merchandise and to departments. In the dim light with boxed and loose merchandise piled to the ceiling as if holding it up he walked, searching for Department 35. Behind him O'Keefe's elevator peeled open its door to let off some passengers.

Jim found Department 35. There were about ten women working at a long bench, sorting sales slips, checking them, inspecting merchandise and wrapping packages. One of the women said, "How long is it to our rest period?"

"Oh, two hours yet, dearie," another woman said.

"Well, I'm going to take time out for a smoke," the woman said. "Emerson Bradley won't sleep tonight if you do," a younger woman said in a joking way.

"Well, he can croak for all I care. I'm going to smoke."

This was the first time Jim had seen Edna. "If Bradley only knew!" one of the women said, in a manner that meant she was glad whenever they could put something over on Emerson Bradley.

The next day Jim had happened to carry his tray of food to one of the tables for two people that were set against the wall in the restaurant across the street from the Haines Company. It was a popular restaurant with the truckers and shipping clerks, popular too with poorer women, and cheaper than the company cafeteria. There was a woman at the table. "Do you mind?" Jim asked. She looked up. It was Edna. "Help yourself," she said, clearing more space for him. Jim sat down. "I've seen you," he said. "You work in—in Department 35—on the conveyer."

"The conveyer belt is beyond where I am," she said. "I work at a long bench—" and laughing, "they call it my desk."

She had finished eating and reached for her cigarettes. Jim noticed the many gray hairs that she had attempted to comb under but hadn't tried to dye. Jim lit a match for her. "Thanks." She nodded at him. "The other day a couple of efficiency experts came through," she said. "Two of them. One with a pencil and pad. But they don't allow for stoppage. What you can do in one minute they expect you to do for eight hours. And the thing is everybody works faster than they would normally." Her coffee was cold. "Wait, I'll get us a couple more cups," Jim said.

He brought them back and they drank, smoked another cigarette together.

After that he had lunch with her whenever they were in the restaurant together and could sit at the same table. The young girls who knew him tried to get him to sit at their tables and were jealous. They asked if that was his mother. Seriously meaning it. Or giggling when they asked.

He told Louise about Edna. They invited Edna over to dinner. They both asked about her job and her work. Jim went down to the corner and got a half-gallon bottle of beer. They sat in the front room drinking beer and talking. The conversation turned back to the Haines Company. "Some day we'll have a union over there," Jim said. Louise looked at him and, womanlike, seemed to be trying to tell him to go ahead, Edna was with them. Jim rolled his empty glass between the palms of his big hands. "How do the women in your department feel about a union?" he asked.

"Well, now," Edna said, stroking her hair back, "they're all for the union in their heart but kind of afraid of their job. I don't know," she shook her head in disgust, "they have a slavery sense of justice to Haines—some of those workers. Ah—a loyalty. Some of those old workers, you'd be surprised, the *loyalty* they have for that company—and why, I don't know." She shook her head. "And if you aren't company-minded, you better let them think that you are if you want to stay there."

Jim smiled and set the empty beer glass on the table. "I want to tell you something, Edna. If you don't agree I hope we'll still be friends. Well—here it is—I'm working for the union. We're signing people up. If you're for the union—"

Edna had signed up....

Jim was suddenly and excitedly back on the streetcar. He jumped to his feet. He had ridden past his stop! He pushed through the homeward-bound evening crowd toward the door.

He walked back to North Avenue and down North to Wieland. His house was midway in the block on Wieland at 1447, a two-story frame building in need of paint. There was a stoop and one step up to the front porch beyond the fence. He lived on the second floor and a plank walk led to the middle of the house on one side, a flight of steep wooden steps led to the second-floor entrance with a little uncovered porch at the top of the steps.

He ran up the steps two at a time, whistling, and banged the door open, smelling the clean, string-beany, inky smell of the four rooms. "Hi, Skinny!" he shouted and went through the house to the baby's room, looking for his wife.

Louise was bent over the mimeograph machine, cranking the handle and twirling the sheets out of the machine. "Hi, dear!" she said, glancing over her shoulder and smiling, then continuing with her work. At the far end of the room the baby slept in its crib. The papers kept sliding from the machine in a precise rhythm.

Jim wound his way past the scattered boxes and baby formula set on the seat of a chair, the kitchen table that held the mimeograph machine, and kissed her on the neck.

"Oh, darling!" she said, startled out of her concentration.

He kissed her on the neck again. "What was it like?" she asked.

"Like?" He grinned. "Your speech was wonderful!"

She stuck out her tongue at him. "You know very well I didn't do much on it," she said. And her arm kept twirling, cranking the sheets from the machine.

He picked up one of the sheets flashing off the machine and read:

BRADLEY VERSUS THE UNION

"When?" she asked, looking up at him, and pushed her long hair back off her cheek with her unoccupied hand.

"Tomorrow, I think," he said, and, "Good job!" looking at her work.

He put the sheet back on the pile of handbills. "D'jew eat?" he asked.

"Waiting for you, dear. Busy." She kept cranking the machine.

He began wrestling with her.

"Oh, don't, Jim!"

"Ain't it awful, being married to a working stiff?" he asked, getting her head in the crook of his arm. He ran his knuckles along her ribs.

"Oh, please! Please, Jim!"

"Wish you were back typing old man Bromwell's letters?" he asked.

"Not on your life!" she said.

"Sure?"

"Even this is better." She laughed, pulling his hair. "Now, stop! Please, please . . . !"

The baby began to cry. Jim let Louise go. He took the baby up in his arms. "Damn you," he said to the baby, "interrupting a family quarrel." And to Louise, "Let's eat."

They went into the kitchen, Jim experimentally feeling the baby's diaper. "Anything's better than being a private secretary—to an old man," Louise said; and then more seriously, "Oh, Jim, it's wonderful, being part of it all—I love you, you great ugly brute!"

"The women at work don't think I'm ugly," he said, jokingly and unthinkingly. A slight and anxious frown passed over Louise's face. He saw it. Shouldn't have said that. "I'm going to wash," he said.

He went into the bedroom and washed. Drying himself he paused with the towel at either side of his face and looked into the mirror. He frowned at himself, seeing the good-looking, regularly featured face. Straight nose. Curly blond hair. Tan skin. And those damn reddish cheeks high on the tanness of his face. Silly girls flirting with him. The strained look on Louise's face when they were walking together down the street and some girl or woman looked at him—in that way. Damn it, didn't Louise know? Of course she knew he wasn't interested in other women. Just her. Was it a feeling of insecurity? Well whatever it was it was damn silly. He hated to see that strained look in her face, and her eyes coming up to his for support. Pleading eyes. Eyes saying, I love you. Always afraid that some woman would get him involved. And in high school. All the girls making a big play for him. Being on the football and basketball teams made them even more interested in him. Sure he had laid one or two of them when the need was on him. But girls, as such, having a lot of women running after him, had never interested him. In high school it had been more fun to sit around talking and kidding with the fellows. To break training occasionally and drink beer with Milo and Dave. In summer the three of them went out with a football and practiced for the fall. He and Milo going camping up in northern Wisconsin. He and Dave sitting on Dave's front porch nights in the old neighborhood, talking. He looked again into the mirror at himself. Damn his good looks! The person was the thing, inside. Louise and to work for the union, for the people, was the only thing that was important. In his life, anyway. Louise ought to know that by this time.

He went into the kitchen. Louise had dished up the string beans and brought the tomato salad from the icebox, drowned in mayonnaise as he liked it. The slight irritation was gone and she was smiling. "Hi!" she said.

They ate.

Louise was a rather plain girl, two years older than her husband and very thin, with almost no breasts. She had large and expressive dark brown eyes, heavily lashed, and hair in which there wasn't much curl. A face, thin-featured and already beginning to gather tiny wrinkles at the corners of her eyes; but a sensitive and intelligent face. Her standard joke, dressing, looking in the mirror at herself with the powder puff posed while he struggled with his tie at the bureau, was, "Darling, why is it handsome men always marry ugly women and the other way around?"

"Now, Skinny, you know you're very pretty. You know that."

"But I'm not, darling. Look, I'm looking right in the mirror. I hope all of our children look like you, darling."

. . . Theirs had been an ideal romance and marriage. It would always be. He had walked into the downtown office with his repair kit. A middle-aged, distinguished man had preceded him.

"Miss Martin," the man said, "if Jenkins calls I'm not in." He went into the inner office.

Jim stood in the doorway. "There's a typewriter to be repaired here?"

"Yes—this one," Louise said, indicating the machine on her desk.

His broad back was bent over it and he was squinting into it when the telephone rang.

"Sorry, sir, Mr. Bromwell isn't in."

Jim looked up. He made a tishing, clucking sound with his tongue and shook his head at her in a reprimand.

Louise looked back at him and frowned.

"Any message, Mr. Jenkins?" she asked into the mouthpiece.

"Shame on you," Jim said.

"No, Mr. Jenkins."

Louise put her hand over the mouthpiece. "Will you *please* be quiet!" she said to Jim. "No, I don't know when he will be in," she said into the phone.

"You know he's in," Jim said, his eyes sparkling with mischief.

She frowned at Jim again. And into the phone: "No. No. He left a short while ago."

"Aren't you ashamed of lying like that?" Jim said.

"No. No, Mr. Jenkins, I don't know."

Mr. Jenkins was giving her an argument on the other end of the wire. When she could break in, Louise said, her voice pleasant, even friendly, "Okay, pal, you're right. He is in . . . well, that's what he told me to tell you. I'm sorry. I only work here. I'm sorry—"

"Good girl!" Jim applauded, grinning at her.

"No, I don't know why he won't talk to you. I'm sorry. Try tomorrow. Yes, good-by."

She turned from the phone. She looked at Jim. The frown was beginning to crease her forehead. Then she smiled and laughed a little. He grinned back at her and darted his blond head back toward his work.

"Hey—" he said five or ten minutes later, "why doesn't your boss buy a new typewriter for you? This thing—" He lifted his arms in despair and went back to work.

Ten minutes later: "Hey, you, hold this, will you?" he asked, handing her a tool while he tilted the typewriter up and unscrewed something underneath it.

A week later he was called back to work on the machine again. "You were right," Louise said.

He went to work. Somewhere a whistle blew the lunch hour. Jim took a thermos jug and sandwiches out of his tool kit, sat on the floor with his back against the wall and started unwrapping a sandwich. Louise had twisted her hat on. "Have a sandwich?" he asked, holding one out in his large square-fingered hand. She looked at him; then smiled, chuckled. "All right. You don't expect me to sit on the floor, do you?"

With his forehead and mouth puckered he poured the thermos top full of coffee and handed it to her.

A month later he was back to fix the typewriter again.

"You know," he said kidding her, "I didn't fix this machine last time. Do you know why?" He laughed. Then, "Has Mr. Jenkins seen the boss yet?"

Louise laughed.

"When are you going out with me?" Jim asked suddenly and then, flushing boyishly, pushed the blond hair off his forehead with the palm of his hand.

"I don't like good-looking men," Louise said.

He had copied the telephone number down. A week later he called.

"This is Mr. Jenkins. Is the boss in?" he asked.

"Hello, typewriter man," she said.

There was an awkward pause. Then he said, "Will you go out to the show with me?"

There was another long pause. "Yes," she said.

"Say," he said, "I don't even know your name!"

"Louise. Louise Martin. I don't know yours either."

"Jim Norris."

He took her to the show. Then every week he was taking her out to the show and for food afterwards. They began seeing more and more of each other. There were nights and there were week ends. He had an ancient Chevie and he picked her up in it and took her home. He taught her how to drive and then, to show his confidence in her driving, sat in the back seat. He'd squirm down on his spine and put his feet up on the seat in front. From his pocket he'd pull his harmonica and play while she drove down the boulevard. They went to the beach, swimming, lolling in the sand. He was blond, healthy, good-looking and had played end on his high school football team and was handsome and bronze and perfectly built and stood wide-legged, broad-shouldered, deep-chested and tall in his trunks with the lake as his backdrop. She was deep-brown-eyed and slim, graceful in her movements, intelligent and serious; more serious-minded than any girl he had ever known. There is more than the beauty of a face in a person. And she had this beauty of personality. This beauty of sincerity, honesty, intelligence. The beauty of the deep-thinking eye, the purposefully tilted head, the honest lips in conversation, the honest hand in the gesture of underlining her statements. And she was a college graduate. More than he could have hoped for himself in a girl. They saw each other every day. Day passed into day and it was a lovely summer.

He said, let's go to the ball game, and she went gladly to see the Cubs play though she knew nothing of the game. To be with him. To sit alongside of him. To glance secretly at his blond profile even when the bat hit the ball and the players were streaking for first and third. In a T-shirt and blue denims rolled up at the cuffs Jim drove her to Wrigley Field, to many hot-dog stands, out to the midget auto races at Soldier's Field, and to Riverview where they rode the high rides and he pitched baseballs at wooden milk bottles. And they came to know each other well, very well. Nothing was too insignificant, no detail, nor was anything too important, too significant, not to be shared with the other.

"I never asked you, Jim," she said when they had known each other only a little while; "are you from Chicago?"

"Not originally. Originally from the South." He smiled a little. He held the fingers of the grass and turned his face away remembering. "On one side of the tracks in the South where I lived there were shacks with poor whites in them. On the other side of the tracks were shacks with Negroes in them. Each group hated the other. I came North when I was nine. On my first day in school up North there was a tragedy." He sat up smiling, clucking his tongue, shaking his head over the tragedy. "I had to sit next to a colored girl." He looked at Louise. "I had been taught that I was better. Since then—" he smiled slowly, his white teeth showing in the darkness, "I've often worked with Negroes. I'm glad and proud to work with them. The pimples still come out when I think about it." He rubbed his hand over his forearm as if feeling the pimples of emotion rising there. He leaned back on the grass. "Now one of my best friends is a colored fellow—Dave. You'll have to meet Dave." He laughed. *"One of my best friends.* That's funny, isn't it? You know—the old thing people say—" She put her hand on his wrist and smiled while her eyes filled with tears.

He wanted to talk. To unburden himself of all of it. He told her about going back to the South with his high school football team for a game and Dave not being able to go with the team. His own guilt about it. He told her that he thought the big hope of the country, of bringing all men to an awareness and finally an equality, was the unions. He told her that that was what he wanted to do with his life, become a part of the union movement.

Louise nodded, and he was more to her than just this very handsome young man who attracted her.

"I'm all for you, pal," she said casually. Then more seriously, "That's how I feel about things too." Then, her eyes lighting with humor, "Proud of me?"

"Yes," he said, nodding. It was a warm and serious and sincere yes.

And, looking at her, he remembered his path. Chicago when he first came to the city. The slums. Knowing, remembering the lives of the people there. Then, when his family could move to a better neighborhood, he had met Dave and Milo in high school. And, through them, moving further away from any yet-standing slum structures of pride and prejudice he had left.

Fall came and they had been seeing each other almost six months. Early fall. When the most pleasant days of the year are over Chicago. They were in love with each other but had never said so.

They had kissed and held each other close. It had not been more than this.

Spring came again. On the first really warm day they got into the old Chevie. Jim wore his blue denims and a jacket. They stopped along the way and bought several quart bottles of beer to take along with them, after Louise had said, "Let's go out to the Midway and just sit."

They parked the old Chevie. Jim uncorked the beer and they sat out at the Midway with the University buildings across the lawn from them. The trees wore the youthful green of spring. They sat under the trees, under the starry sky, sipping on the cool necks of the beer bottles and looking, occasionally, at each other in the half-dark.

"How you doing?" Louise asked.

Jim nodded his head seriously.

"I like it here," Louise said.

He answered her, then tapped the palm of his hand down against the grass in a shy gesture, laughing. He said, "You're kind of nice"; then looked down at his wrist.

And conversation drifted away. . . .

Slowly they drank, slowly the bottles lowered their liquid. Jim rolled over and lay on his back. The cuffs of his blue denims were twisted up. He edged his hand into his pocket and pulled out the harmonica. He gave his lips to it and the sad-sweet music lifted up toward the young green of the trees.

"Do you know the 'Marseillaise?' " Louise asked.

His lips fitted the harmonica to the notes of the "Marseillaise." They marched up and out toward the stars.

And at length the harmonica was laid aside. Jim twisted over on one hip and lifted the beer bottle to his lips. She watched a truant trickling of beer run down his chin and onto his neck. Then he lay on his stomach, not talking, staring through the trees.

For an hour there was no conversation. Just the beer bottles sitting in the grass. Just the lifting of the bottles to their lips. Just the two of them together. The crickets in the grass. The university buildings anchoring the city like a great mountain. Just their own silent thoughts. Louise sometimes smilingly wondering what her boss would think if he could see her.

They both lay on their stomachs with the last bottle of beer between them. They both, leisurely, took turns drinking from it. It was the kiss between them.

And, finally, with midnight far past, Louise sat up. "Look, pal, I've got to get home. Job tomorrow, you know." She put her hand on his shoulder to arise. Her insides pinched a little, looking down at him. He spread his hands on the lawn. "Some day," he said, "I'm going to ask you to marry me." She sat down again. The pinching feeling was greater. She put her hand, the back of her hand, up against his forehead. He had large, strong hands. He put them on her shoulders. "Will you?" he asked.

She nodded and leaned her head against him. "I'm almost crying," she said.

She sat up straight and pushed him away, looking into his eyes. "I'm not a virgin."

"I don't expect what I can't give," Jim said.

Driving home, he reached for her hand. She gave it to him. But she sat far away from him and looked at him all along the way.

"What's the matter?"

She shook her head. "Nothing."

She was afraid. He was too handsome for her. Too many women would be interested in him. He would be tempted too many times. She wouldn't be able to take it.

Three weeks later they were married in the city hall. Dave and Milo were there.

"Hey, Skinny!" he called her on their wedding day, affectionately.

She put her arms around him. "I didn't let you think about how skinny I was or about my thin nose," she said. "I've got you now." She pulled his hair lovingly. "Now try to get out of it!"

Her pregnancy. The long, long pull through the nine months. The hospital. Coming home with the baby. Both of them looking down at it. The wonder and awe of their two bodies in this little body. . . .

Theirs was the ideal marriage. It would always be.

# Book Two

## EVENING

## I

Grandpa, standing by the window and looking out, said, "It thaws a little today." He moved to his rocker. Saturday afternoon. Everybody home. The day would not be so long. He stroked his tie. But the shorter they were the sooner the dirt under his head. And this he feared.

"Ewa!" Ma called.

The dark girl's eyes met and held her mother's. "Eva, Ma. Eva! Eva!"

Her mother laughed. "Go, take the kids and wash them. See that they sit on the toilet."

Eva took the little children out into the toilet in the hall.

From the stove the old man murmured, *"Mnie zimno; ja marzne."*

Ma Kosinski turned her long, corded neck toward the old man. "Cold! Cold! Always you are cold. Why don't you die, old man?" She said it monotonously.

"For Christ's sake!" Don said. "Why don't you leave him alone?"

"Blood of a dog," Ma Kosinski said at him.

Helen, awakened by the loud talking, stared out of the bed at them with puffed eyes and then again sank wearily to the dirty sheets.

Ma Kosinski wrung her hands and implored God. "My children do nothing for me. After I have bred them out of my own body. My children do nothing but talk back to me and disobey me. What is this dirt I have on me?" Again she wrung her hands.

Don tossed the book down. He went to the stove. At the window Alina sat with her back to the room, looking out. And now she pressed her little nose against the cold pane.

Don looked in the pot. The thick grain porridge bubbled slowly. He dropped the lid. *"Kasza* again!" he said disgustedly. He put on his coat and, as always when he had the money, went down to the hot-dog stand, preferring hamburgers to the Polish food his mother cooked.

"He thinks he's *szlachta,"* Ma said.

Grandpa laughed. "Polish nobility! Don!" Grandpa kept chuckling.

Don returned and sat on the bed with his book. Helen's hips lumped up in the blankets behind him. Today Grandpa was filled with the Poles and wanted to tell Don about it. "The villages they are beautiful. The roofs are thatched and moss grows from them. In Polish villages people go barefooted and the feet are strong."

"Uh-huh," Don said.

"The houses have low doors and small windows. The houses are clean. Even in America the Poles are clean. The Poles are a clean race. My wife—your mother—" he turned to his daughter accusingly, "there never was a cleaner woman." He looked around the dirty room. *"Humph!"* and went on: "Never a better wife. Never a cleaner house. The copper pots hung by the stove and were as bright as the sun. The bedsheets were white—the—the—" His voice began to tremble and his arms and legs, his eyes to fill with tears. "I spit on all this—" he said, looking around the room. He spat tobacco juice on the floor. Some of it dribbled down his chin and onto his tie.

Alina sat at the window staring out. The buildings across the street, how many windows did they have? The windows winked at her. The new snow on the stone sills was like the lace on the altar at church.

"Die, old man, die," Ma Kosinski said under her breath. Without meanness. In complaint.

"Always in the cities of Poland and the villages there are beautiful, wealthy Catholic churches," Grandpa said, trying to shape them before everyone's eyes with his hands.

"There is always a wealthy Catholic church in Polish neighborhoods. Even here," Don said, "and the poorer the neighborhoods—aw, nuts!" he finished for himself.

"A good Pole is always a good Catholic," Grandpa said.

Wacek was wetting a stream against the wall in the corner and Eva went to grab him and drag him to the toilet.

Grandpa was full of Poland: "The young girls wear their hair in pigtails—" the old man would doze, and wake, and continue his story from where he left off, "the women wear bright kerchiefs tied under their chins."

"Yes, Grandpa . . . uh-huh," Don said and went on studying the new play.

"Ewa!" Ma called commandingly. Eva came but made no word. Her mother examined her critically. "You are getting big now. Your breasts are coming fast. You will soon be sixteen. So you like it in the factory, no? In Poland—" She turned her column of neck and sneered at the sleeping old man. "In Poland they marry when they are fourteen. Go with some man who can help support us." The dark girl's eyes flashed defiantly at her mother.

Grandpa awakened. His weak old eyes groped for Don, and his trembly voice. "Don in—in—" he scratched his head and ran his tongue out of the end of his mouth, trying to remember, "—in 1887 —no, in 1889 . . . "

"Uh-huh," Don said.

"You silly girls wait for love and marriage," Ma went on, "and many opportunities go by."

Grandpa's head jolting down suddenly toward his chest awakened him. He grinned and the one tooth glistened in front of the wad of tobacco. "In the old country we sing the *Kolenda,* a Christmas song, and the good priest comes to examine the people on religious matters and gets gifts from them."

"Ewa!" Ma called irritably. "Why don't you say something?"

"Eva, Ma. Eva! Eva!" Eva said.

Ma slapped her hard across the arm.

"Eva!" the girl said without flinching, and her eyes looked with deep hostility into her mother's.

"Bitch!" her mother said, and slapped her again.

"Well, some of them could of had American names," Don said. "Some of them have American fathers."

Mrs. Kosinski turned on her son. "I never did the sin to God of throwing away the seed he gave me. If I had you wouldn't be here to face your mother down like this. Never did I give them but good Polish names. And now all of you want to take the names of this country. Eva! Eva! Eva! Not Chet! Don." She frolicked across the dirty bare floor with her hand on her hip. "Don, Don, Don Lockwood." She made a little song of it. "Helen, not Helcia." She looked toward the front window. "Alina! Come here!"

The little girl at the window turned quickly into the room. "Yes, Mama!" Fear and intensity were in her face. She came forward to her mother. She was a beautiful child, this little girl of eleven or twelve. Physically thwarted though. She was so anemic and small. She didn't have any breasts and her legs were like stilts. But still a very beautiful face. Shy and withdrawn. With large, sad eyes and beautiful blond hair.

"Don't you like your name?" her mother demanded. "Do you want to change it?"

"It's a *beautiful* name, Mama!" Her voice was as she was, shy, thin, with undertones of soft sadness. "Oh, Mama, it's *beautiful.*" Her eyes filled with tears of pleasure and she tried to hug her mother.

Ma Kosinski's quick, instinctive hands clutched Alina's shoulders affectionately. Ma Kosinski hugged her for a moment, then thrust her away, and the child went again to sit at the window with her little nose pressed to it.

Her mother turned back to Don and to Eva. Angrily she said, "The Relief wanted to sterilize me. *Matka Bosha!* Sterilize me to keep their bills down! Saying I shouldn't have children because I have no husband. Saying I shouldn't do the good Lord's work. Stopping the hand of God! None of you would be here if I had let them do that to me."

Don was angry. And with his anger was shame, shame for his mother. Eva regarded her mother with calm, unblinking eyes. In the bed Helcia lifted herself to one weary elbow. "Jesus Christ, it's Saturday, Ma! I worked till five in the morning." She dropped back to the bed and rolled her face to the wall. In his rocker Grandpa awakened. "And at *Wielkanoc* we carried the food to the priest to be blessed," he said.

"Get out!" Ma yelled at Don. "Get out! Go with your fine friends who don't know you are a Pole. If they knew—" she smiled wisely, "would they be so quick to have you around with all your put-on and big ways?"

"Aw, for Christ sake!" Don yelled. "Leave me alone, will you?"

"Get out!" Ma yelled. "Get out!" He laughed at her. "You think you will live off me. This won't be," his mother said.

But it was. She argued with him every week about going to work but every day kept him on.

That night a visitor came to call. Don knew he was Polish and from the old country. When he came in, a big-boned ugly man with lumped-up cheekbones, he kissed Ma's hand. Maybe just over on the last boat, Don thought, laughing to himself. Then remembering: as a boy he had been forced to kiss the hands of all the men who came to visit his mother. "Aw, nuts!" he would say, flushing. But Ma: "Greet Mr. Cugowski." Again he'd say, "Aw, nuts!" But it did no good. For many years, as an older boy, he had had to kiss Grandpa on the shoulder as was the custom.

Now Ma thrust his little brothers forward and made them kiss the strange man's hand, as was the custom. Then she chased the kids to bed, telling them that if they didn't shut their eyes and go right to sleep the horrible *Wil* would terrify them and they would not be able to sleep all night, that "The *Wil* stands always where you look."

Eva put on her coat, and defying her mother, looking straight at her, walked to the door. "Where are you going, Ewa?" Eva's black eyes didn't move from her mother's. "Did you hear me?" The corners of Eva's lips smiled and she let herself out the door.

Helen had already gone to her 26-table on West Madison Street. Grandpa was in his rocker behind the stove. Alina lay in bed, already asleep.

Don went to his room, put on his coat and left the house without telling Ma or her guest good-by.

The stranger, the man called Walenty, had brought a bottle in his hip pocket. He and Ma sat on the side of the davenport where she slept, whispering, drinking, smoking. Ma got up and turned the lamp down even lower, as low as it would go. Ma watched the wad of tobacco in Grandpa's jaw and saw that now it moved not at all. On the sofa their forms melted closer together.

"Your father?" the man said.

"He will not hear. He is deaf. He is old."

Weronicka, the baby girl, awakened behind the stove. She began to cry.

Ma held the man fiercely away until the sobbing stopped and the child had gone back to sleep.

In the morning Grandpa was angry. To his daughter he said, "You sit up all night holding that man's hand. You think I was asleep. But I watch. And such an ugly man."

His daughter smiled.

"Yeah," Don said, "what do you see in him, Ma?"

Ma shrugged. "When candles are out, all cats are gray," she said in Polish.

And Grandpa, still grumbling: "You had better be careful or some man will give you a baby. At your age, too. What sin!" He shook his head from side to side.

"From holding hands, a baby?" Ma laughed at him. "A Polish woman never mentions that she is going to have a baby," she said. She minced away from him.

Don laughed. It was partly in amusement, partly in disgust.

*Wielkanoc* came. And at Eastertime Ma sent Eva and Kazio to the church with a package of all the kinds of food they would eat during the year. The old Polish priest blessed it, his consecration purifying all the food of the same kind that the family would eat until the following Easter. Kazio and Eva brought the bundle of food back home.

Grandpa was at the window. "The dear sun is shining," Grandpa said. "The little buds are on the trees."

Taking the blessed food from Eva, Ma said to her, *"Matka Bosha,* how your breasts grow! They are almost ripe." And cleverly, "You do not like the factory. Why do you not hire out as a servant with some wealthy people? In the factory the foremen will take you but they will not pay."

Eva flushed. "You make me sick!" she said.

In sudden fury, Ma slapped the color brighter in her cheek. Eva smiled at her with narrowed eyes.

At the window Grandpa said, "The little clouds go over."

"You are like a tiger," Ma said to Eva. "A man will have his fill of you in short order unless you change."

Grandpa walked back to his rocker. His head, in sleep, jolted down toward his chest as if it would leave his body, slowly rose, and jarred downward again. Don came in from being out all night. He carried a copy of the *Dziennik Chicagoski.* Grandpa was always asking him to get the Polish paper and giving him the money for it. He always forgot. Today he was pleased that he had remembered. "Where have you been?" Ma asked. Don smiled tight-lipped but did not answer. He put the newspaper on Grandpa's lap where he would see it when he awakened. "What is the matter with our family," Ma said angrily, "that they keep things secret from one another like thieves?" Don went into his room.

Aline rushed into the house, breathless. In her hand she carried a little brown paper bag. "Grandpa! Grandpa!" she called and ran to him. From the bag she pulled out one of the little wafers representing the body of Christ that she had bought at the little religious goods store on Milwaukee Avenue.

Grandpa awakened. He broke off a piece and ate it, saying, "The best of everything" and "All good wishes." He and the little girl smiled at each other and Grandpa made his head dance from side to side in a playful gesture. He tried to pull the little girl onto his lap but she dashed away and to her mother. "Mama!" she said, holding out a wafer.

Ma took one and broke it, passing a piece to Eva. Grandpa caned his way to the window, his loose pants wobbling from side to side. He looked out. He said, "The weather has changed. There is a thick fog."

Alina rushed into Don's room, offering a wafer. He took it but instead of eating it put it on his dresser. Alina looked up at him with a lowered head, because he didn't eat it.

At the window Grandpa, looking out, was saying, "The sky mingles with the earth."

The seasons moved quickly to the old man. He stood by the window saying, "The rain is falling in drops." Saying, "The dear sun shines brightly and the trees are putting forth their leaves." Then the days came when the Grandfather went down to the steps of the sidewalk to sun himself and watch the Grand Avenue streetcars go by. And this was every day for the old man for a while, this and Don tying his tie every morning.

Summer began to draw toward its exhausting end in Chicago with long hot days and no breeze off the lake, with people sleeping at the beaches and in the parks all night and on newspapers on the sidewalks in the poor neighborhoods.

At the window Grandpa was saying, "The mornings and evenings are rather cold already." Looking wistfully at Don he moved back to his rocker. He settled himself there.

From his rocker Grandpa said, "Soon it will be my Name Day. Soon we will celebrate my Name Day." His old eyes went over to Don's head, bowed over the book. His old eyes filled with tears. "I hope I will be here with you, Don, for another Name Day."

"Sure you will, Grandpa," Don said without looking up.

*"Mów pan ze mna po polsku,"* Grandpa said.

"I understand better than I speak. You speak it to me," Don mumbled into the pages of the book.

The old man began speaking Polish. Today he was filled with himself. "In the old country," he said, "propaganda was carried on by agents of the steamship companies about America. And the bosses from jobs over here, needing workers. We would all have much here. The foreign agents said so too. . . ."

And Grandpa went on. "I came to America in 1887, Don, a young man of twenty-two. And now age creeps on." His withered hand rubbed his knee. "I came here with nine dollars in my pocket—are you listening, Don?"

"Huh? Oh—uh-huh."

Grandpa's recital went on. Don turned the page of his book. Grandpa had fallen asleep.

# II

They gave no plays during the summer. It was the "dead season" in the city. They practiced technique, held readings, did improvisations, pantomimes, studied plays. And during the summer Leo was called into the army. He went, saying that if he could help get the bloody mess over with, good; if winning the war would guarantee more for everyone, if the words they were preaching were honest words, then this war was good and if only the Jews would, after two thousand years of suffering, be better off, why he was for it and wanted to do his share. That he just hoped nobody was kidding. "Communist!" Carmen whispered to Earl, so that Leo wouldn't hear.

They had a letter from him in camp, and then a second one. Then the news came that he had been killed in camp, in an accident, of which there had been many but about which few people ever heard.

Don was with Sue when they heard the news. She cried. Don was surprised. Sue said, "He was good—*good*. He loved something. He believed in something. To die in an accident when you are training to fight for something you believe in—" She put her handkerchief up to her eyes to stop the tears. Don felt that she was romanticizing Leo. He couldn't feel anything about it. He and Leo hadn't liked each other particularly. Sure, he was sorry he got killed. But the only thing about it that frightened him was that his number might be called any day. He had come through most of the summer. He'd hate to get killed in camp—or at all.

He lived with more energy that summer, trying to live up as much of his life as he could just in case he got killed. He was with Sue in her room as much as possible and made one of the new girls in the group and was bringing Juanita more and more around to the point where she would lay.

He went to the taverns with Sue. She stuffed the money for the drinks into his pocket before they left her room. They went out to the Negro neighborhoods where Sue said she learned so much about the "liquid action of the body" watching Negroes. Don sat in the Negro taverns feeling a momentary compassion for them as Sue talked about their economic and social sufferings. He listened to their songs and enjoyed them. He went to other taverns with Sue and heard the juke box songs of the times:

*Praise the Lord and pass the ammunition*
*Praise the Lord and pass the ammunition . . .*

*Ven der Fuehrer says*
*"Ve iss de Master Race"*
*Ve Heil! Heil! Right in der Fuehrer's face . . .*

And with the singer Don put in the farting sounds.

He walked down Maxwell Street or far west on 12th Street with Sue where she went to buy pumpernickel bread and Jewish sausage that they would later eat in her room. And when she talked about the Jews, their long struggle against prejudice and propaganda and hate, he felt a fleeting sympathy for the Jew, too. Through Sue's sympathetic aid and explanations Don became, in his mind, a liberal.

In his room Don sat on the floor with his back propped against the bed and with the kerosene lamp on the seat of the chair. He sat with *Wuthering Heights* open in his hands. Sue had told him in her dark room that it would be their next production and he wanted to begin memorizing the part; it was always damn hard for him to memorize the lines and get the cues straight.

The group rented a hall on North State Street. The evening of the initial reading of the play came. Sue let her eyes drop away from Jessica. And Earl. She wondered why the little theater attracted so many strange people. Well, she supposed, every field off the beaten path attracted its fringe of eccentrics. The theater. Art. Radical movements.

Knowing her business, extremely serious about her work, honest, doing the thing she wanted most to do despite financial setbacks, despite the fact that she beat her brains out daily on a job she hated, despite the vagaries of the people with whom she had to work and the knowledge that any one of them might disappear the day before a production, she felt a moment of despair and futility. She glanced at Don. He had his head back in a theatrical way and was exhaling as if trying to shoot the smoke against the ceiling.

She glanced momentarily at Don and felt a tinge of distaste. Then sympathy. There was a real and decent personality under all those layers of pose and egotism. Disappointing in imagination and sensitivity. Voice neither good nor bad. Body sufficiently trained. His self-assertion. Refused so much direction from her, or seemed to accept it until he was on the stage and then there was nothing you could do about it if he invented his own stage business. His lack of both knowledge and intellectual interest was the most disappointing thing about him. And his pretense of knowing so much. But she had helped him. Had built something there. She knew these things about him. But she also knew her secret desires. Oh how you love the things you love, she thought. And smiled. And turned her eyes away. Then quickly she picked up the conversation Jessica had started, knowing that to propel herself into a discussion of the theater was, as always, a cure for her blues.

And her mind dropped away from depressing thoughts. Her face and eyes and movement became animated, girlish. Her body lost its look of fleshy tiredness. She drew her chair in closer and made a unit of the group by speaking as she now spoke, and her voice went out, bringing them in, warming them, giving them all the feel of the theater, its art, thrilling and inspiring them. "Olivier—and—and—Maurice Evans," Sue said, "people like that are mimics with a tremendous amount of conscience." She pulled off her harlequin glasses and stroked her scalp under the short-clipped blond curls with the stem of the glasses. She gestured with her other hand. "They're guys—" and she pronounced the word *guys* with a warmth and a feeling that showed love for actors, acting, "guys who studied the backgrounds of the times in which the persons they depicted have lived. They understand it. It's not just a matter of study. It's a matter of human understanding. Of social consciousness. Of political understanding." Sue leaned forward. She said, "Good actors, I think most good actors with rare exceptions are guys with very acute political consciousness. Throughout the arts, of course, you find that—but—but the better actors are all guys who really have something to say and want to say it. Something in social concept. So!—they aren't just reading lines—they *really* make those lines mean something." She tapped her folded glasses into the palm of her hand. "And an actor should be able to be uninhibited too. And—and—and—" her glasses tapping into her palm searched for the words, "to—to—really roar his way around in a part and do what the part takes."

Don smiled, knowing that she spoke of him now. Knowing these as his abilities.

Sue now walked across the room nervously, while their eyes followed her, lit a cigarette, took a puff, crushed it out, came and sat down again. "A guy like Barrymore. John Barrymore hardly ever got into his part. Completely he was always Barrymore. Sure. And yet he wasn't—he wasn't—standing off and looking at the thing as an artist, as a craftsman."

Don warmed. He and Barrymore. It was an identity he had long established.

Sue said, "He was just having a great time. He was a *great* natural talent. Like Caruso—" She stood up, unconscious of her movement in her enthusiasm at bringing the meaning of art to them. "My God! You hear him straining on some of those high notes sometimes and you wonder what the hell! Who ever told this guy he was a singer? And yet you listen to him for a while and you know why he was a singer. He was a singer because he was born that way. The guy could sing. Well, Barrymore just acted. So Barrymore would come on the stage with a different attitude and a different mood and play the part differently every night but not because he was living a part. Just because he was playing John Barrymore. Well, I guess, in a sense, that's playing a part too."

Sue paused. She glanced up at the clock. "Well, I've got to stop running off at the mouth. We've got some work to do." Then as an afterthought she said, "It would be interesting to sometime investigate just how far the social and political atmosphere of a city, the flavor of a city, affects its art. Here in Chicago, for instance—" She smiled at her own wordiness. She stopped. She smiled. "I guess I'm talking too much."

"Oh no!"

She smiled again. Because they were sincere. Because she had cured the blues. Because despite everything this was her life and her love. Because most of these poor kids here, false as some of them were, had a feeling for the thing. Respected acting as being something great. Worked all day. Grubbed at their jobs. Came here at night, even without supper, some of them. Came because there was a drive to their lives, a desire after art and beauty. Came because they wanted so desperately to be more than clerks, typists, order fillers.

The hard, hard work of production began. And as with every little theater group there is always somebody who is the big cheese. Don was the big cheese. He gave free advice to the other actors. He began trying to develop a master gesture for Heathcliff. He wondered how Barrymore would do Heathcliff. All the little bees worked hard and didn't get anything. Some of them were not even in the play. But they worked like hell and Sue was God. They worked and worked, thinking that sometimes maybe they would get a bit part; but they were all so objective about it. The play was the thing. If there wasn't a part for them they didn't care. Actually many of them would be there for years before they got a lead. And Sue was using them. Using them without even completely realizing it. Using them the same way she used her own abilities and talents in the almost hopeless calling of the little theater. But they, Sue and the rest of them, had a feeling for the thing. They respected acting and the theater.

A month of rehearsals went by. Two months, and then it was the night of the play.

Don sat before the dressing room mirror with his hair curled and blackened. He looked in at himself and shook his head, touseling the curls. "Tonight," he said, "tonight, Don Lockwood, you give the greatest performance of your career. . . ." Don stepped from the darkness of the wings to the full light of the stage . . . Don gave his heartbroken cry at the end of the play. "They say the dead do haunt their murderers. Haunt me, then! Be with me always—take any form—drive me mad—but don't leave me alone—not alone—" Don got many curtain calls and bowed, bowed left and right, his curled and blackened hair falling over his forehead.

He knew that he had given the best performance of his career. Sue was especially happy about it. She was always happy after a performance, cooking him his favorite dishes on an electric plate, having a bottle of wine for him before they monkeyed around. His best performance! Sue even got items in Kup's column and Dale Harrison's column about him. He began thinking about Broadway. It was almost an obsession with him. He knew he was ready for the big time. He knew he was good enough. Better than most of the leads in second companies that came to Chicago. He'd go to the theater and, sitting in the cheap balcony seats, silently analyze and criticize their acting ability, their technique, their voices. He knew that all he needed was for some producer or director to see him in one of Sue Carroll's productions. He'd be in!

# III

At eighteen the rounded innocence of his face gave Aaron the look of a sixteen-year-old. His eyes held a wistful expression and his full lips were slightly pouted. He began to worry about his weight and every morning after the newspapers were delivered and every night before he went to bed, even if he had written until late, he ran a mile. Graduation was only a month off. He worried about being a virgin.

More and more often he went to Thompson's to see Steve and Milo. He had grown shy about showing his poetry, afraid that people would not understand what he was trying to do, but now that he felt that in this last poem he had come closer to individuality and a style of his own, now that he felt the words looked good on the page and said something tersely, sharply, he wanted Milo to see it. He sought him out.

Milo handed the poem back, his face tightening slightly.

"What—what do you think of it?"

"But you don't know anything about sex," Milo said. "Write what you know about. Write some short stories."

"You don't like it?" He was hurt. He tried not to show it.

"No, I don't like it. I think it's posed and artificial," Milo said, bluntly honest.

Aaron ran his fingers into his long hair and leaned on his elbow, talking to Milo with his eyes fastened to the table top. "You're probably right. I don't know if this poetry is any good. I'm young. I don't know if it's what I want to do. Maybe I should write prose. I'm young. I meet a girl. She goes roller skating, she necks, she likes the movies, she simply adores the movies. I say, 'Levin, you hang around with too many erotic people. You go with her. Get down to her level.' I take her out. Then I go home and say, "You're a prostitute. You've given up art.' Then I say, 'You're living in a bourgeois capitalistic society. You've got to conform, Levin!' " Aaron lifted his large arm and hand over the table in a humble gesture to Milo. "All I know is that I want to write. Why can't art be just a hole in the wall?" He waved his hand at the hole in the wall. "That's art—that represents something. But no. Anyone who is interested in literature is like being a member of a royal family that stretches back to when the first man sat down to write."

Aaron looked at Milo with his childish and wistful eyes, leaning his hunched and beefy shoulders forward toward him as he spoke. "You're right," he said. "I want to be close to the people. I want to say things to them and for them. I guess that stuff is posing. I guess I was posing because of my background—something I can't tell you. I guess I was trying to hide my background or get over it. I want to be a poet. Not a precious one. Not one who smirks and twists his face and says 'Oh, I am! I feel!'—Not a delicate phantasy butterflying, but a sweating, salty, tear-mixed try at life."

"You should write that down," Milo said in quiet good-nature.

Aaron smiled sadly. "I guess even the way I talk is posing." He shrugged. "I don't know." He grinned fleetingly and then his eyes became serious again. He looked down at his large hands, turned palm up under his eyes. "But my fingers are cramped."

"If you don't write that down," Milo said practically, "I will."

Steve came to the table and flopped down. He tore the racing stubs in quarters methodically. Milo brought coffee to the table. Steve had Aaron by the sleeve of his coat, staring at him and saying, "You don't know what fear is. Wait until you're in the army. Wait until you go into battle. Wait until—" He looked up at Milo and smiled, slowly releasing Aaron's wrist. As Milo sat down he said to him, "I'm going to lay off the Four Freedoms. I think they're a little premature." And sneering bitterly, "I played Santa Claus last year and he didn't come in. Now look—" he lifted the fingers of one hand and with the index finger of his other hand said, counting them off, "they talk about the Four Freedoms. Freedom from want, freedom from fear, freedom of religious worship and freedom of speech." He looked at them and said very seriously, "Do you know the only place where they have the Four Freedoms? In jail and in insane asylums." His eyes went to the entrance of the restaurant. "What's that coming in the door," he asked, "the neuter gender?"

In the weeks that followed, Aaron began to mature. Some of the fatness went from the seat of his pants and from around his stomach. He took his diploma. He got a job as an order filler at the Haines Company.

He had given up the writing of poetry and into notebooks was scribbling his impressions: *Clouds and sky, trees, flowers, green hills, streams in a valley, a herd of wild horses—the city—the city, buttered in warm, flowing colors. A woman smiles. An old man smiles. A little boy, eating a chocolate bar, laughs. The zoo. Laughter, laughter. A ball game . . . a double-header. Score cards, Coca-cola, and "Get your fresh roasted peanuts here. Peanuts!" The farmer, a red-wrinkled forehead—crow's-feet—large, hairy hands—standing close to a shy, canary-delicate wife—grins. The artist. The clowns, baseball players, farmers, artists.*

And one night he awakened in that period just before dawn when there is a gray hush over everything and silence is about to be displaced by the noises of the morning. He lay a moment, very still, and then squeezed the palms of his hands together. He had it! It would be a lot of work, it would take several years, and study, and many notebooks of observation, and hardships—but he would get it all outside himself. It would be a novel. It would be humble and simple. It would be about the city, about Jews and gentiles. It would attempt to bring understanding and tolerance to its pages. It would be neither pro nor con but would show all the fallacies and prejudices of both groups. Some people would call it anti-Semitic; and some an attack on gentiles. That didn't matter. It would be the truth, and that alone. Milo was right. He knew his path now, and knew it to be good.

He began, that day, outlining the idea of his novel.

On Sunday, Saul came by for him. It was a beautiful, warm Indian summer day. "I saw Rebecca," Saul said, "and promised her I'd go to the park with her. Want to come along?"

"Sure," Aaron said.

They called by for Rebecca and then walked to Lincoln Park. Rebecca had changed. She wasn't a nosy kid any more. She was grown up. Well, almost. Her hair was combed loose and her skirt was long; he couldn't see the bony knees he remembered. She spoke quietly and walked with dignity. He was surprised to see lipstick on her mouth.

It was a long way to the park and under trees they stretched themselves. Rebecca's skirt slipped up over her legs a little and, when he looked, her knees weren't bony any more and her silk stockings made her legs shapely and attractive.

When they were rested they sat up. Rebecca smiled at Aaron and, with slim fingers, stroked her hair back into place, pulling grass from it. She had green eyes and healthy chestnut hair. "Gee, I'm still tired!" she said. She leaned back on the grass, shut her eyes and stretched. Her cheek with the blemish of birthmark was turned away. She was wearing a wine-red sweater and, stretching, it tightened out over her breasts.

Aaron looked down at her and so did Saul. Then they looked up and their eyes met. They looked down again. Her skin was very white, and delicate, like a child's. Her hair was long and loose. The two boys looked at her. They again met each other's eyes. They wanted to get the day over fast, so that they could tell each other how much they liked her.

Aaron was in love. At his desk, writing, he tried to catch glimpses of her at the window across the courtway. He asked her to the show and they took long walks. They had nothing personal to say to each other. She encouraged him to talk about himself and his writing. He said, "When a fellow tells a girl that he's a writer, in a way he's saying 'I'm different.'" Aaron gestured with a big open palm. "I'm not different. I don't want to be different."

Rebecca put her hand in his. They walked along silently. His hand trembled and became moist. Trying to keep her from noticing, he carefully withdrew his hand. He stuck it in his pocket and wiped it dry.

They saw more and more of each other. In a strangely childish and yet adult way she knew how he felt about her. And with a certainty, a finality that needed no words, the way a child gives its love she gave her love to him.

In the park, with sun breaking through the trees, she, in a simple way, told him, without words, that she loved him. He was sitting near her, talking about what he wanted to say in his book. She smoothed out her skirt and patted her lap with her hands. He put his head in her lap. She put the palm of her hand, quietly, on his forehead and left it there. "Now tell me," she said. He talked: and was glad that she was only sixteen. He would never try, because she was only sixteen. While he talked, with her hand on his forehead, she stared straight ahead and across the park with her green eyes.

Fall began to turn to winter. At Thompson's restaurant O'Keefe talked of little but the war and the possibility of a strike at the Haines Company. Milo was trying to finish his novel and expected any day to be sent to camp or to jail for being a conscientious objector. Aaron sat often talking to them. They began inducting eighteen-year-olds and the war came closer. I want to live, I don't want to die. When I'm dead the world is dead. He hid his fear from everyone. He purposely avoided war talk and discussed writing.

"Milo," he said, "in my writing I want to take the people by the hand. 'Look'—I want to tell them—'I'm living on the top story and I want to show you my room. I want to show you how nice it is up here.' " He reached out and put his big fingers over the wrist of Milo's coat. "Milo, you've got to help these people—all of them. Not only for themselves but as a testing ground for greater things. You've got to look at them not only as a writer but also as a scientist. Every night you look through the microscope. You don't see what you want. But you make your observations and your notes. You set everything down. Every night you polish up your microscope and look. Then one night you see what you want and you set it down."

Steve had come to the table and sat listening, sneering with his ugly mouth, looking at them out of his baggy eyes. There was an embarrassed silence as Aaron finished speaking his intimate thoughts.

Milo wrote something into his notebook. Steve watched the notebook slide into his breast pocket. "For Christ sake, Milo," Steve said, "what's the use of trying to write? What's the use of doing anything? The world's going to pieces, man! Your writing stinks, wipe your ass with it—that's their point of view." He waved his hand, taking in the whole world. The muscle between his lip and nostril jerked. His yellowed teeth showed a moment, and a sneering, sardonic smile curled his lips in a flash, then fell away, like the lens of a camera opening and closing. He leaned across the table and grasped the wrist of Milo's coat. "There's nothing that counts but you—as an individual—as a personality. The laws are made for the jerks. There are none that you couldn't make better for yourself. They're made to be broken by strong people." He smiled again. The lines of his face still weakly held the remnants of good looks. "People who have discovered what is inside of them—poets, writers, artists—belong on an island. You don't need them. They need you. There's nothing you can contribute now. You've got to hypnotize yourself while all this is going on." He crunched out his cigarette in the saucer of his coffee cup. His hand trembled slightly. "My number's coming up," he said. "My draft board will be getting around to me any day—every morning I'm afraid to look in the mailbox . . . just two years and I'd be past draft age . . . just two years standing between me and life. . . ." He shook his head. "Nothing good ever happens to me. I haven't had one goddamn good thing happen to me in my life."

At the table in front of them a voice said loudly, "We'll kill all the goddamn Nazis!"

"Yeah, that's the human thing to do," Steve said to Aaron, Milo and O'Keefe in contemptuous bitterness. He stood up, smiling weakly and nervously. "I think I need a drink." He walked out without saying more.

"Goddamn it!" O'Keefe said, lowering his newspaper. "He could sit for five mortal hours and never let up on that stuff!" O'Keefe pulled off his glasses angrily, and shoved them back on. Despairingly he turned to Milo. "Why do you come down here? They're all beaten and broken people down here. It will only hurt you. You will get like them. Go see some of your friends. Don't sit down here night after night.

"Why do I come down here?" Milo said slowly. He smiled sadly. "I'll tell you," he said. "Max and Eric and Bruno and Frank are my reasons." He smiled again. "They're my friends and they're all in it or going." He motioned helplessly with his hand. "I'm a conscientious objector." He shrugged. "I can't go to see them or their wives or their parents. What they may think of me—"

Steve wandered back in. "Changed my mind," he said. "I'm afraid to drink—if I get started. Give me a cigarette, Milo." He laughed. "Afraid to drink," he said again. He laughed again.

At the table behind them a voice said, "The fellow who lived next door to me was killed. He was away a year and never had a leave. He was at Bataan and then they shipped him to Guadalcanal. He was killed up there."

Aaron heard, and said flatly, "My draft board will be calling me up soon."

"Why don't you become a conscientious objector?" Milo asked Aaron, and going on, "Quite frankly, I don't think you can take war. Some people can't."

"I can't be a C. O.," Aaron said. "It's what people would say about me—my friends—the neighbors—and my father."

Milo shrugged.

"I'm not as brave as you are," Aaron said.

"I'm not brave," Milo said.

Steve leaned forward, smiling, speaking in a cynical and bitter voice, "You should be a psychological case, and if you aren't you should strive to be because that's the only way you're going to be able to live in this goddamn world that a bunch of sonofabitches have created to make robots of us."

"What did you say?" Milo said impolitely. "Let's have it again."

Steve smiled with a tight mouth that set his mustache to bristling. "The man who said that has gone around the corner." But he leaned forward and looking at Aaron, said craftily, "You'll see the psychiatrist when you go for your physical examination. Don't be too belligerent. Don't rant and rave against the capitalistic system. They're not afraid of violence. They can bring violence into order. It's nonviolence they're afraid of."

Aaron stared at Steve in the fascination he always felt when Steve talked about anything. He felt his legs tremble under the table in fear, in the old nervousness. He said he had to go. He walked home. On a city street he saw a baby-faced sailor in his teens sucking a popsicle.

Aaron was supposed to see Rebecca but he walked past her door. He walked past his own house too. He walked to the car line and stood looking into the darkened store window. Inside, throwing a sickly white glare of their own, was the display of row on row of artificial arms and legs.

# IV

The city was still dark. On either bank of the river the twin Haines buildings stood like giant sentinels, like the posts of a gate allowing the river to pass through. On Canal Street the light was on in union headquarters.

They were having a meeting in Kovac's office. Kovac, the president of the local, sat on the edge of his desk in his Mackinaw, rubbing his big-palmed hands together and laughing. "We'll break their back in a week," he said. "Bradley will have to recognize the union. Got a cigarette, Baker?"

Mr. Baker sat behind the desk. He was neatly dressed and looked as if he were at an executive board meeting rather than sitting in a ragtag union office at five in the morning preparing the final strategy of a strike. He looked up from the sheet of paper on which he was writing the assignments for the principal organizers. "Of course, Stan." He passed his package and his lighter.

Jim sat with his hands clasped behind his head and leaned back against the wall. The union lawyer sat in an armchair and looked as if he were asleep. Rosenfeld and Olson were speculating on how many Negroes would stay out of the plant. Vazanni said to Kovac, "Goddamn it, it's the ideal time for striking—just before the Christmas rush! We'll tie up their stores all over the country." Kovac nodded grimly and continued to rub the palms of his hands together. Mr. Baker looked up from his work. "They're ready in Detroit and Minneapolis and Albany." Kovac nodded. "If we're successful here they'll walk out whenever we give the word."

Jim stood up and stretched his long legs. "I'm going to get to my station."

"Man, it's hours yet!" Vazanni said.

"Can't sit still," Jim said, smiling. He picked up an armload of the mimeographed sheets that were the official union newspaper and walked toward the entrance.

Voices came up from a narrow stairway that led down into the basement. Jim lowered his head to keep from bumping it and went down into the basement.

The floor was of dirt. There was a pot-bellied stove, glowing a cherry-red, with a pile of ashes at one side of it. Benches and long tables were set up across the floor. Women in slacks and blue denims and woolen dresses with buttoned sweaters busied themselves pouring water into large containers and opening cans of coffee. They stoked the fire. They stacked paper cups on a table that would serve as a counter and filled miscellaneous jars with sugar, stacked little wooden spoons near the paper cups. They laughed and talked in the early-morning gossip of women. Three of them had already begun to make sandwiches.

Near the stove several men were painting the last of the signs to be carried by the pickets. Most of the signs had the word *Haines* painted on them in black preceded by a red letter C, making the sign read *Chaines*.

Jim sat down in the hum of women's voices, the cheerful, encouraging conversation, and stirred his coffee with the little wooden spoon. He gulped his coffee and started up out of the basement to the street.

A few pecking snow flurries came from the bleared gray sky. They hit the sidewalk. Hard, like a bird against a tree. As if they were testing the day, its coldness.

Snow began a monotonous and lazy swirling to the sidewalk where the wind kicked it back and forth. And now the Negro porter came out of the Haines Company and, with polish and rag, began shining the plaque, bringing its embossed bronze letters—THE HAINES COMPANY—to a golden luster. And now the watchmen began unlocking the doors of the building. And now, in front of the Haines Company, the strikers began to walk with their posters. The snow flurries beat down on them from the gray sky. They walked slowly, back and forth, in front of the plant on either side of the river. Slowly, carrying their banners, in a complete chain around the buildings on either side of the river. And now the employees began to arrive from streetcar, El and subway. And O'Keefe began handing out his leaflets. Jim and the others began handing leaflets to the workers.

The employees arrived. The strikers' ranks swelled. Employees who were union members fell into line, or went over to union headquarters, or took the car back home. Soon there were several hundred moving up and down in front of the doors of the Haines Company. Their posters bobbed up and down as they walked. They began to sing, lifting their voices to the cold November sky. The police arrived as from nowhere; many of them, almost outnumbering the strikers. Police under the command of the Industrial Squad. They took their positions a few feet apart, all around the buildings and inside the ring of strikers who marched and sang, brandishing their placards, calling out the name of Emerson Bradley in jeering and angry tones, shaking their signs in the faces of all who came toward the buildings.

Other employees arrived. The department heads, supervisors and little clerks, the typists. They smiled, stiff-faced and self-consciously, at the strikers; or frowned, looked straight ahead and hurried a little, anxious to get inside and away from the jeers, the insults, the physical threat. They entered the buildings escorted by the police.

Jim, marching with his *Chaines* sign, spotted Edna. "Hello, Edna!" he yelled.

"I came out! I guess you thought I wasn't coming!" Edna shouted, falling into step with him.

The truckers and the railroad workers arrived at Haines but refused to deliver goods through the picket line. Shoppers came to the retail store. Most of them went in. Emerson Bradley's long black Cadillac drove to the side gate of the administration building. It was greeted with boos. The private police hired by the Haines Company swung open a steel door and the chauffeur drove the car into the yard. The gate was closed and locked to the deep-throated boos of the pickets. More snow began to fall. O'Keefe, buttoning his sweater under his coat, took his turn among the weaving line of marchers. Some of the truckers who had refused to drive across the picket line had joined the strikers. Some of the other unions in the city had sent members to march and bolster the Haines strikers. Newspaper photographers had arrived, taken some shots, and now loafed over warming cups of coffee or shots of whisky, waiting for the possibility of a struggle between police and strikers and the front-page photos they would be able to take.

Another shopper started toward the building. O'Keefe sidled up to her. "You don't want to go in there, lady. The stuff in there is no good." He wrinkled up his nose. "I know because I used to work in that awful place. You can do much better at Sears and Roebuck."

The woman smiled at him and kept right on walking, right in through the Haines front door.

The strikers soldiered back and forth, their placards bobbing above their heads in a sea of protest. There was one girl in the picket line who was short and Irish. She wore a brown cloth coat and let it swing open against the chilling winds. She walked around cussing and singing. "Scab! Scab! You lousy scab! You lousy bastard scab!" she'd yell when anyone went in. She'd see some Irish girl: "Ya Irish sonofabitch! What ya going in there for!" O'Keefe, though modest and shy and reverent about women, kept encouraging her. He was laughing because she was doing so much cursing. When she cursed someone out he'd echo, "Yeah! Atta girl, Irish!" as if he could use that kind of language. He was for her because she was a fighter. She even looked at him hostilely. When she wasn't in the picket line she was walking around tough, frowning. The police laughed at her in enjoyment because she cursed so much. The photographers were watching her too, hoping she'd start some trouble.

The strikers made a circle in front of the door. A painted typist came along. Instead of walking along the building to the door as the other scabs had been doing she walked along the curb to the strikers and cut through the circle. Irish grabbed her by the coat sleeve, grabbing for her hair with the other hand, and swung her around. "What do ya think you're doing, ya lousy bitch!" They were right in front of the main door. Irish socked her. The girl looked stunned and shocked and began to cry. The strikers had closed up the line and the action so the police couldn't see. Voices yelled. "Come on, Irish, give it to her—goddamn it!" A flash bulb went off. The strikers closed the line tighter as the cops started toward the action.

The cops had to push their way through. Three or four policemen were in the inner circle now. They grabbed Irish by each arm and lifted her up. She was squealing and kicking, and beginning to cry herself now, from temper. Her hair was thrown up in a mess and her coat was flapping in the wind. Another flash bulb went off. No one was marching now. They stood watching and yelling to the cops to leave her alone. Irish kicked one of the cops in the leg. He grunted loudly. The crowd roared approval. The next issue of the newspapers would report: GIRL ATTACKS POLICEMAN.

From union headquarters Mr. Baker came running across the street and tore his way through the crowd. As he was moving through the crowd the strikers told him what had happened.

"Turn that girl loose!" Baker said. "You have no right handling her like that."

The cop gave him a who-the-hell-are-you look and shoved him away. The tears were streaming down Irish's face. She was yelling and cursing and snarling at the police; cursing mostly now because she was crying. One of the cops was twisting her wrist one way and her elbow the other to make her shut up. Mr. Baker was facing the police again. "I'm a union official. You have no right to hold that girl and I'd advise you to turn her loose. That woman had no right to break up the picket line."

The girl Irish had tangled with was still crying and stood behind the glass door with two policemen. A couple of late cameramen had rushed out of the tavern across the street and, holding their cameras above their heads with one hand, holding their hats on with the other, were trying to squeeze through the mob. Traffic was snarled. People were getting out of their automobiles to come and see what was going on. On streetcars people craned their faces close to the windows. Every cop had his hand on his billy. The strikers had their fists doubled and were cursing. They can't get away with this, was the attitude of cop toward striker and striker toward cop. And they were egging each other on. Were almost anxious for a clash.

In the circle around Irish a cop shoved Mr. Baker in the face, pushing him back against the wall of strikers. His hat flew off. A striker caught it and held it for him. Roaring, yelling shouts of anger rose up and swelled and remained in a storm of protest above the heads of the mob. Jim, who had remained in the background, respecting Mr. Baker's ability to handle the situation, now dove into the closed circle. He faced the cop. Jim said, very quietly, very distinctly, "If you touch that man again, I'm going to punch your teeth down your throat." He smiled when he said it, with a tight, hard grin. The cop acted as if he didn't hear Jim and turning, pointing at someone else, told them to shut up. Jim continued to smile in the cop's face. He stood next to Mr. Baker protectively.

A squad car pulled up to the curb and a captain got out. He called several of the patrolmen over and had them form an aisle to the circle. He walked majestically down the aisle in his neat uniform with its gold braid. He stopped and looked at the strikers derisively and as if they were insane. The strikers were whole rows of faces. Cords standing out in their necks. Teeth showing. Fists clenched. Yelling.

One of the strikers shouted, "MacArthur has come back!" People started laughing and it quieted down some of the shouting.

The captain talked a moment to one of the policemen, finding out what had happened and that Mr. Baker and Jim were union officials.

"We're going to lock this girl up," he said to Jim. He turned to the two policemen holding the girl. "All right, bring her through here." To another policeman he said, "Come on down to the station to make out a report on what happened. All right—" he said to Jim and Mr. Baker, "which one of you—?"

Jim looked at Mr. Baker as if he'd like to go. "No, Jim, you stay here and get the circle going again." An aisle was made to the squad car. One of the strikers handed Mr. Baker his hat as he walked down the aisle. Irish, proud and with her fists on her hips and her coat still flapping, with the tears still on her cheeks, walked trying to tear her arms loose from the hold the police had on her.

Jim began organizing the circle again. Traffic began slowly moving at the direction of the police.

Morning moved its cold minutes forward in slow monotony. The strikers marched slowly back and forth. It wasn't yet ten o'clock. . . .

Men and women on later shifts arrive. "Hey!" several of the strikers call out, derisively pointing to their noses. "You've got a brown spot on your nose!" Derisive laughter as the scabs hurry in. "Yeah, you know where your nose has been!" one or two of the strikers call out to the backs disappearing through the huge glass doors. And the voice of the strikers, swelling:

*Solidarity forever!*
*Solidarity for-eeeeever!*
*Solidarity for-eeeeeever!*
*For the union makes us strong!*

The shoppers continue to arrive and stand indecisively before the strikers. Some, snapping their heads angrily, push through the strikers. The pickets walk along beside them urging them and pleading with them not to cross the picket line. They are obdurate and the police prod the strikers away with their night sticks. The more timid shoppers stand indecisive and the police urge them to go through the picket line: "We'll take you through." The police escort them into the store.

Jim, his blond curly hair catching and reflecting the dull sunlight, came out of the union headquarters carrying a scarecrow with a broken neck dangling from a rope and a battered straw head hanging loosely on its chest. To the back and front of the scarecrow was pinned a sign bearing the one word: BRADLEY. The mob of strikers shouted in laughter and pleasure. The mob yelled: Bradley! *Boo!* The strikers moved Jim up to the head of the line along with the old man carrying the large American flag. The strikers fell in procession behind him. And the voices of the strikers, everybody singing, rose in enthusiasm and confidence and gay spirits:

*We will hang Emerson Bradley to a sooour apple tree!*
*We will hang Emerson Bradley to a sooour apple tree!*
*We will hang Emerson Bradley to a sooour apple tree!*
*'Cause the union makes us FREE!*

# V

The man they were reviling in the street sat at his desk. Emerson Bradley, seventy-five years old, was a small, short man, inclined toward obesity, baldheaded, with an aggressive jaw and a stubby, bristled gray mustache. Everything about him was pinkish. His old face was an ashy pink and through the pink-polished scalp of his bald, bulbous head muddy-blue ropes of veins showed. His nose was large and loose on his frowning face with fleshy lines coming down either side of it to a thick mouth under which his aggressive, thrust-out chin was wrinkled like a prune. His eyes, behind rimless glasses, were humorless. The eyelids were the loose flesh of a turkey's neck and much the same color and, half-drooped, gave his face the appearance of perpetual peevishness. Pinkest of all on that pink-shaded face were his puffed jowls. His hands were pink and white hands, small and stubby, like a baby's. He had the look of one accustomed to command.

His office, atop the forty-eight floors of the administration building on the west shore of the river, was huge, three stories high, quietly decorated with huge windows on all sides giving him a complete and panoramic view of the city below. On the south wall was the room's only decoration, an original Rembrandt etching. At either side of the picture was a door. One door led to his private elevator with his private policeman standing outside on perpetual duty when Emerson Bradley was in his office. The other door led to his suite of rooms: shower, bath, kitchen, conference room, dining room, bedroom, small bar. A full-time servant worked and lived there.

Emerson Bradley pulled a box of crackers from his drawer. He broke a few of them up in his little pink and white hands. He walked to the wall of windows above the river and opened one of them on its smooth steel arm. "Hello, Mr. and Mrs. Brown," he called, waving and chuckling. Pigeons crossed and circled above the window. Emerson Bradley opened his hand and tossed some of the crackers out to the pigeons. The birds winged and dove, catching the crackers between their beaks in mid-air. He tossed more of the crackers. The pigeons swooped and caught. More circled near the window. Emerson Bradley chuckled. It was almost a mean chuckle—phlegmy, half-sneering. He talked to the birds, scolding them as if they were naughty children, telling them to wait—to be patient. He tossed a few more cracker bits. "Now, now, FDR, don't be so greedy! Wait, Eleanor! Your husband first. Well!—Old Morgenthau himself—morning, sir!" Again he chuckled his sarcastic chuckle. He had named all the pigeons that came each morning. He could tell them apart: "Howdy, John L.—God, your eyebrows are shaggy this morning!" For a moment he looked down to the city street and saw the pickets, like toy people from this height, weaving around his building across the river and around his building below, marching slowly with their placards. On his property! Distantly, like a sound heard in an echo, Emerson Bradley heard the words climbing up the sides of the walls . . . *"Emerson Bradley to a soooour apple treee . . ."* For a moment he frowned. Then he chuckled without humor. He closed the window and walked back to his desk. It shouldn't disturb him—*didn't!*—those people down there on the street. He would follow his usual daily routine. This isn't a catastrophe or disaster at all. Only a little ripple on the smooth surface of water. It will pass away.

He leaned his chin on the pyramid of his fingers. He smiled. His jaw tightened and jumped at each end in his smile. There had never been a union in *his* company and there never would be! He could, as always, defy the world.

He glanced at his watch. He looked across the room at his Rembrandt. No. Never. He was a fighter and the whole goddamn country knew it! He smiled again, thinking of the puny little strikers on the pavement below. He pulled the phone over and ordered full-page ads in all the city newspapers, telling his advertising manager exactly what he wanted the ads to say.

A little restless, but not upset, he went to the bathroom and swallowed one of his pills. Then he walked back to the window. He looked at the squat one-story building below: BRAUN BOTTLES. He smiled superciliously. Julius Braun. Too idealistic. Too liberal. He'd never get anywhere in a business way, in a power way. Nosy, Emerson Bradley knew everybody's business.

He looked north from his penthouse office and could see the sinuous form of the river circling Goose Island and moving on toward North Avenue. He chuckled a little, looking at the equally white walls of the Montgomery-Ward buildings. Chuckled contemptuously but tolerantly. No, he wasn't like Sewell Avery. He wouldn't fight the Administration openly. The mailed fist in the silk glove. Get them down with a gloved hand. And he'd win! He smacked his fist into the palm of his hand in the same way Jim Norris would have done it. Damn, he liked a fight! Since he was a kid. He smiled at the kid. Bullied as a boy because he was small. Well! Yes, that summed it up. Well! the kid was proud of the man.

He looked at Chicago. In the river's southward bend, the Loop. He glanced north at the Wrigley building and the Tribune Tower along Michigan Boulevard. Brought his eyes back to the roof of the Merchandise Mart across the river, squat and flat. He looked at Chicago. Looked at it as if it were a pie that he was slicing into pieces for himself. Just a pie to be cut open. The contents meant nothing to him.

He looked down at the white mass of the Haines Company rising above the banks of the river. He smiled. His business. He had built it up from nothing. Made a nine-hundred-million-dollar business of it. He glanced again along the sidewalks and saw the strikers. Pigmy men. Baker. So Baker had become secretary of the union. He moved back to his desk, chuckling.

He glanced at his watch. Nothing against Baker. Damn fool, that's all. His first act was to clean house when he got in. And the ax fell on some of the biggest heads in the company. Vice-presidents and executives and department heads went out by the dozens, thrown out without hesitation. It also fell on the little fellows. He had gotten rid of about thirty per cent of the working staff. And they stayed out with the exception of a few who—Emerson Bradley shrugged his shoulders—were harmless and got in again by worming their way back through vice-presidents and others. He wasn't running a kindergarten. This was a business he was going to make into a going concern. There was one fellow though. Isaacs. He angered thinking of Isaacs. When Isaacs came back from his vacation his desk was there but there were no papers on it. There was no business for him to transact. But he sat right there at his desk and took out a book and started reading and waited for a telephone call. When the mail girl went through she left no papers on his desk. He was ignored completely. But he sat there and sat there for three months without doing a stroke of work. Damn gall! I suppose in the meanwhile he was fishing around for a job downtown. Jews. That's Jews for you. Always managing to get the best out of every situation.

He glanced again at his watch. One minute yet. He picked up the microphone and toyed with it until it was time. Then, as every morning at ten-thirty, Emerson Bradley's voice spoke into all the buildings and on all the floors, basement to roof. Emerson Bradley's voice reached out like a benevolent father, through all the house: "Good morning, everyone. We are now in the middle of our Christmas rush business. We must all work a little harder, give a little more to our work. And I must give notice that all those people who went out on strike are no longer members of the Haines family." . . . He cleared his throat a little. . . . "And—due to the rush of business the company has decided to give a pair of nylons to every woman and a carton of cigarettes to every man who brings in a new employee. If these new employees stay on the job for two weeks a—ah—bonus will be paid to those who brought them into the Haines family."

When the microphone was switched off Emerson Bradley was smiling. Good idea! The nylons and cigarettes. Hard articles to get hold of now. Again Emerson Bradley gazed at his Rembrandt. What beautiful line and chiaroscuro! His thoughts wandered back to when he had taken the company over. . . . Haines had gone broke during the depression. They held a general stockholders meeting and decided to go to the San Francisco bank for a loan. The bank had said, "Certainly—but we have certain conditions. . . ." Emerson Bradley grinned with his pink face. Remembrance was good. Deserved a drink. He poured himself a very little Scotch from his silver decanter and added a lot of soda. He sipped slowly.

Emerson Bradley turned back to memory, slowly stroking one hand with the other. "We have certain conditions. And one of these conditions is that we must have a representative on the board of directors." They found their man. They found him.

He was their strong man. He had put the Haines Company back in the black. Their strong man. He didn't fool around with little things. He was, of course, an enemy of labor. That had been recommended by the bank too. He moved in, a representative of the Walker National Bank. Moved in, took possession of an ordinary executive office.

He had certain conditions too. He must get two hundred thousand dollars a year. He must be allowed to buy stock at a certain price, no matter to what height it might go. The price was eleven dollars. That was bottom.

Emerson Bradley sipped his Scotch, looked at his Rembrandt, looked out at Chicago; and back at his Rembrandt. He had put the stockholders into a cheerful mood: "If we can boost the stock of Haines to thirty from eleven, almost three times as much, then I'm entitled to buy as much stock as I want—up to a certain amount." He couldn't buy fifty-one per cent. But there were unlimited quantities of stock on the market because the small stockholders didn't want any. It was a drag on the market. The stockholders grumbled. Emerson Bradley smiled at their remembered grumbling. But they yielded finally. He bought forty thousand shares of it. It started to climb on the market as soon as people found out he was buying it. The stock went up and up. It went to seventy-seven dollars. The difference alone made him a millionaire. Not that that mattered. He was wealthy before that. He was born wealthy. His father, all the Bradleys, were very successful men who had explored the lead-mining possibilities in Western Missouri. He grew up in great business.

Emerson Bradley in happy reverie strode around the office . . . the first year there was a very substantial dividend. It put the company on its feet. And one of the old-timers—old Jim Smithers—suggested that, to make everybody feel good, all the employees should get a Christmas bonus. . . . Emerson Bradley looked at his reflection in the window. He didn't fool with little things. He had said, slurring it, "NO! They're lucky to have jobs."

Emerson Bradley looked out again at his city . . . one of the stockholders' meetings. One of the *large* stockholders had challenged him about the size of his salary. Challenged him! He had snatched off his glasses and smashed them down on the table so hard that he had broken them and said, *"You people are purchasing prosperity at a small price!" Damn,* but he liked a good fight!

. . . His strategy had been excellent. He had given up the vice-presidency when he took the company over because, for one thing, there was a lot of unpleasantness and he now evaded it. Bosworth, the president of the company, now had to stand the gaff when there were complaints of any kind. He became merely the treasurer. He didn't even control a worthwhile amount of stock any more for there were enormous amounts of stock on the market. But his friends did. The conservative members, the pro-Bradley group. At several of the meetings the minority stockholders had come to Chicago from all over the country. They had tried their best to beat him down and force a more liberal policy. But he had always marshaled in his legions and he always beat them when it came to a vote.

He laughed. He sipped his Scotch.

But what kind of a man is Emerson Bradley behind his stern pink-wrinkled face, under his blue-vein-roped bald head, beneath his quiet gray business suit?

He was always a spoiled boy. As a child he had screamed for what he wanted and had never relinquished this technique. He still blew up like a child when he got angry. He had a quirk in his head that soldiers are terrific. During the first World War many big executives had been called to Washington to help out and were given commissions in the army. He came out as a major, about which he privately complained ("after all I did for the country!") but which he had forever after used as a title: Major Emerson Bradley. He was jokingly spoken of throughout the city as the Major of Lake Street.

He was really in a fog. He lived in his own little world. When he went to the ball game he automatically ordered six seats in width and depth so that he wouldn't have to sit by anyone. He'd stay for an inning or two and leave. He'd go to the opera and stay one minute. To the theater and stay one act. Then he'd get nervous.

He wanted everything big. Out at Lakeview he had a huge farm estate enclosed behind a ten-foot-high stone fence topped by spikes. There was but one gate as entrance to the estate in the two-foot-thick wall. You almost expected to see a moat and drawbridge before the lone entrance gate.

Occasionally he gave parties out at the farm for his employees. His estate was like a little duchy or kingdom in Europe. He was the lord and all the little people were peasants. He invited them out to his farm as though to treat them—but they were put out to pasture. They were never invited into the house. He indicated that they should play softball—artists, executives, department heads. They played ball. There was croquet for the women—secretaries, models, typists. But that was the way this outwardly dignified organization could be turned upside down by some quirk in the mind of Emerson Bradley.

As a young man he had squandered as much money as his indulgent father had thrown his way—and this was considerable. He had indulged himself in rich foods, liquor and women. There had been one woman after another. He was not interested in them as women but as an extension of his ego and lust. Then, when it came time for a young man of his wealth and social position to marry, he went about it cold-bloodedly, sifting the field of eligibles, and went to New England for the woman to bear his illustrious name.

She looked twenty years older than Emerson Bradley but, in reality, was ten years younger than he.

She never complained, and after—early in the marriage—she bore him a son, life went on day after day.

She gave him no more children for reasons of her own.

She had the house and the child. He had the business and his woman after woman outside the house. If she ever knew about any of these women, nothing in her face or actions indicated it.

The boy grew. The father dominated him completely. The boy, James, thin and nervous, was not especially bright. Nor did he have any desire to go into his father's business. But from the age of sixteen, though Emerson Bradley's father had handed him a vice-presidency when he finished college, Emerson Bradley's son had to work his way up from the bottom, learning the business on his vacations from prep school and college.

And the boy became more nervous and was more cruelly dominated by his father.

Emerson Bradley lived his business life by routine. He drove himself out of pride. Each morning he got to the office at eight—before anyone else arrived—and worked hard until noon. Then he went to the club for a couple of martinis and a spot of lunch. Afterwards he played golf for a couple of hours or swam in the club pool before returning to work. He called his wife at a certain time every day to let her know whether or not he'd be home for dinner.

If he was going to be home she saw to it that a fire was built in the library. That he had his paper and cocktail there in front of the fireplace before dinner. She arranged that James be in the library to talk to his father for a while.

Day in and day out she delivered this routine. Then, in quiet despair, she committed suicide.

Emerson Bradley never understood it. He hired detectives to find out if she had been seeing anyone. But there had been no love affair. There had been nothing extraordinary about her life. Nothing. The evening before she had killed herself she had had his fire in the fireplace, his newspaper and his martinis for him as usual.

Emerson Bradley never understood it. That she had had no life. That she had been dead for a long time.

He could still manufacture some artificial tears when he thought of her.

The war came. The First World War. To get out from under his father's domination, James enlisted in the army. As a private.

Emerson Bradley blew up. Emerson Bradley bellowed: "If he wanted to go into the army! Ask me! . . . Commission! . . . Officer!"

When the war was over, James returned. Shell-shocked. He brought a German wife home with him. Again Emerson Bradley blew up. But there was little he could do about it: the woman was pregnant. He dominated and browbeat her too.

James lay around the house. His lungs had been impaired. He had three children and lingered, a half-invalid, for seven or eight years before he died. Emerson Bradley made a war hero out of him. The latest story was that he had died in action. He could shed a tear over him, too.

There was the German wife. The three children. "Give the children to me. Give me these two little girls and this little boy. I can do much for them," he told the German wife. "You will want to marry again. If you don't give them to me I won't do anything for you."

He dominated his grandchildren as he had his wife and his son. His three grandchildren, Hazel, Barbara and Ogden.

When they were still young, Emerson Bradley married again. This time he picked a woman almost as wealthy as himself, who had married young, divorced young and had remained unmarried. Childless, she took care of the grandchildren and fell into much of the same routine as his first wife had.

He was very formal with his wife and they were very polite to each other but no one ever saw her very much. They rarely went out together. He liked to think that his wife managed the home—that branch of the business—just as his various employees managed the other branches of it.

If Mrs. Bradley didn't love him she was too gracious to admit it even to herself. There was something resigned about her, though.

She had her clubs, her social functions, the Bradley grandchildren. She was a much respected and loved woman.

Meanwhile Emerson Bradley continued with his series of clandestine love affairs.

He brought his women into the firm. He put them on the payroll. He wouldn't spend his own money on them.

One was at the head of the catalogue department. One was brought in as a model, though her best days were over. One was put in charge of display.

And there was Loretta Lawson, his star on the Haines Family Hour. This was at the time that Emerson Bradley discovered radio and saw in it another advertising medium for his mail-order house.

Loretta Lawson could see the end of her career as an actress. She and her husband, Gregory Martin, didn't like each other but lived together and connived together. She was still rather good-looking, especially under evening light with her makeup expertly applied, and was twenty-five or thirty years younger than Emerson Bradley.

When Emerson Bradley took an interest in her, she and her husband began to scheme. She started to work on the Major of Lake Street. He was the most wonderful man she had ever known, a *great* man. She gave him an awful play. She gave him the works. And ended as the star of his weekly radio plays. She had her own dressing room. Her maid. Her gowns free. And she had most of the important Hollywood male stars appear opposite her. And, in order to know where her husband was, Emerson Bradley made him announcer for the weekly show. When he and Loretta slipped out the back entrance door of the studio to his waiting limousine Gregory Martin was on the air. Would be on the air for an hour.

But nothing was ever enough for Emerson Bradley. No one woman fed his ego well enough. And now, an old man with heart trouble, he had page girls come to his office and entertain him in an unusual way.

The Haines Company was completely dominated by his passions and his prejudices. He had a private phone to each of his executives—and they jumped. There was no waiting. He was unforgiving to anyone who made a mistake. He had a secret system of listening in to any of the top executives' offices at any time that he wanted. *He* ran the mail-order house empire. Life, in the business world, was all dollars and cents to him. Nobody talked except to answer him. He never talked very long to anybody. He never let himself be in a position to be interviewed. He directed everything. He stayed up all night, if necessary, deciding what questions he would allow to be asked and what his answers would be. He was the absolute boss and dictator of the Haines Company. He ran the train. He got it there on schedule.

He had manipulated half the judges in town. The police were practically in his pay. During strikes he paid each policeman assigned to his plant fifteen dollars a week plus their meals every day and their cigarettes. He paid the sergeant and the sergeant paid the men. They were paid to be on his side.

His promotion manager, a man who had been a great bootlicker for twenty years and had been known to cry when one of his ilk died, knew how to put it factually when speaking of the company: "Half the people love the Haines Company and half of them hate it but they all buy here."

Emerson Bradley went his individualistic way. He dominated everybody and everything.

If:

He wanted an apple pie cooked a certain way in the middle of the night by his chef in Chicago, squad cars with sirens whizzing rushed it at breakneck speed to his Lakeview farm.

The police would be told to go to the back door and butler or maid would say, "Thank you."

Or:

One of Emerson Bradley's flunkies would come into the Haines building saying, "Gee, I had a hard day! I've been out greasing the cops from here to Lakeview: 'Watch for this car'—I'd give them the license number—'Never stop him. If he kills a chicken or a child we'll fix it later. Just don't stop him.' "

He was an old man now. Nobody loved him but his little granddaughter Barbara. Hazel had moved out half a year ago to Chicago's North Side, was studying at the University of Chicago and taking lessons at night at the Art Institute. The envelope containing checks he sent her the first of every month were returned unopened. The boy Ogden, whom he himself had named, was completely spoiled and wild. He drove his car too fast, got into too much trouble with both the police and the newspaper columnists, ran around with too many girls, started too many brawls in night clubs and seemed to be trying to spend every cent of the money his grandfather gave him. And the more he spent the more Emerson Bradley gave him. To keep him in tow. To break him. To control him.

No, nobody loved him but his granddaughter Barbara. In effect he had said to her: If you leave me no telling what will happen to me—and I'm a great man. He put all the responsibility on her. It was his domination over her.

Barbara said to a girl friend in response to an invitation, "I can't. I didn't arrange it with my grandfather." She looked away and continued, "With a man like my grandfather there's only one way to do things and that's his way, and if I stick with him it'll take the pressure off the other kids."

This was Emerson Bradley.

# VI

The pickets wound their slow-moving human chain around the Haines buildings. The morning hours wore away in a thin gray coldness. The afternoon came, colder, and snow fell intermittently. The pickets stuck to it, all day long. O'Keefe, now marching along with Jim, said—seeing scabs come down and file into the employment office—"I'd like to scrape that stuff off the bottom of the Chicago River and pat it in gently, all over them."

The pickets stuck it out. There were almost as many women as men. They went to the restaurant for coffee and to warm up. Or to the tavern for a stein of beer. Then they returned to their posts, relieved other pickets of their poled placards and dropped into the long and weary line once again. There were old men in the line, men who had been at the Haines Company for years and were almost at the pension age. But union men. Marching. Jeopardizing their jobs in the picket line. There were boys and girls who had cut classes at the University of Chicago and come down to lend their support. There were the young fellows and girls who worked at the Haines Company and who had come out. They were the noisiest and most enthusiastic. They marched and shouted and sang and didn't wear out. All day long. And got a big kick out of the strike. High school boys and girls who were working part-time.

Word came down from the top of the Haines Building that the major was going to make a speech. Emerson Bradley, thinking of using it also on his five-minute radio speech during the Haines Family Hour Sunday evening program, said into the microphone that piped his voice throughout the Haines Company, "Unions are trying to destroy a fundamental principle upon which our government is based. Only an established thing can be torn down. Unions are not a traditional, established thing. There is no fight to fight."

Late afternoon came. Evening came. The line dwindled. Emerson Bradley took his private elevator to the ground floor where his chauffeur met him. They drove out of the side gate. "Hugo," Emerson Bradley said, "drive through the park for a while."

Emerson Bradley relaxed against the cushions of his limousine. He placed his little hand against his forehead for a moment. Carefully he put his hand to his mouth and took out his false teeth. He set them on the seat alongside of him. They grinned there. He relaxed a little more against the car cushions. His face had shrunken, especially around the cheeks and mouth and nose. His chin didn't have that thrust-out sternness. It was only a wrinkled prune. The Emerson Bradley face was a shrunken old-man face. He sighed and tried to relax even more. He was just a lonely old man and realized it. A lonely old man being driven home by his chauffeur.

Emerson Bradley had his dinner.

He went to bed. When he laid his head on the pillow he liked to think that everything was perfect—even the floor of his garage was swept. And it was a good world.

Night and the strikers were the only sentinels on the street outside the Haines buildings. At eleven o'clock Jim turned in his placard. He limped, tired but happy, to the streetcar and rode to his North Avenue stop. Poor Louise, missing it all. Dead-tired from running the mimeograph machine and typing up one of the new protest sheets. She was probably asleep.

She wasn't asleep. She sat on a stool in the kitchen with her legs drawn up on the top round and was reading an old copy of *In Fact*. Behind her, on the stove, the kettle of water boiled, the coffee was warmed and waiting, his supper was on the lowest of flames. "Hi!" she said and jumped down off the stool. "Hello, Skinny." He was dog-tired. He kissed her on the cheek. She immediately poured him some coffee and began dishing up his food. "I think I can make it tomorrow," she said. "I think Mrs. Bush will come up and watch the baby for an hour."

When he had eaten and sat in the easy chair with his head resting back against it and his eyes closed she brought the pail and the kettle of boiling water. Making the water the right temperature by dipping an experimental finger into it, she knelt down in front of him and unlaced his shoes. Without moving his head from the back of the chair he looked down at her tenderly. She pulled off his shoes and his socks and, lifting one foot, put it in the pail of water. The long, yellow hairs of his leg floated on the water. With her hand Louise tested the water again and played in it. Jim reached down and took some of her brown hair between his fingers. Suddenly he laughed. He lifted her up from the floor and jumped out of the chair. "We're going to beat them! Beat the bastards!" he shouted, laughing heartily. And grabbing her, he started to dance with her. His big foot was jammed in the pail and as he swung his wife up into his arms in the first step of the dance he upset the pail. Nevertheless they danced around and around the room in happy abandon, he in his bare feet, and clasping her close. Then, out of breath, he stopped. He laughed again. Then he and Louise knelt down on the floor and, with their heads close together, wiped up the water.

# VII

The strike at the Haines Company shared the front pages of the newspapers with the war news. Into Thompson's in the chilly November night Sean O'Keefe limped, tired and happy, his jaw jutting out a little, his face stubby with beard. He bought his cup of coffee, hung his coat against the wall and sat at a table in his blue knit, button sweater. Shortly Aaron arrived and slipped into the chair opposite O'Keefe. "Hello, Sean."

"Oh, hello, Aaron!" O'Keefe said in an unusually pleasant voice.

"I see by the papers that the strike came off."

O'Keefe nodded emphatically. "I've been on the picket line all day," he said cheerfully, "and," he added, grinning, "my feet hurt."

"You have!" Aaron asked in surprise.

O'Keefe nodded with his coffee cup at his lips and drank more of the warming liquid. Then he set the cup down. "There were a lot of young kids in the picket line—kids who work there—kids from out at the University of Chicago—God, but they had a lot of fun! They stuck it out all day long too." He looked into Aaron's eyes.

Aaron averted his eyes. It seemed too vulgar. Walking in a picket line. Sure he was for it. But he couldn't take part. He'd be embarrassed. When he had arrived at work and seen the strikers he had taken the next streetcar home. He wouldn't be able to tell his father this. Or how he would feel if he walked in the strike. His father would be mad at him. His father had been out there in front of the plant all day long. He knew that.

Aaron ran his fingers through his long black hair. There was a little man in his head who had *the opposite viewpoint to everything.* It must be his father.

"We'll give them a fight this time, boy!" O'Keefe said. He pounded his fist on the table. "As long as the pay goes to white-collar workers, men with dignity, there's no harm in it," he said. He slurred the word *dignity.* "They'd rather spend it that way than pay it in taxes to the government. But if the little fellows who are scrubbing the floors or pushing the parcels around ask for a nickel more, that's almost treason—why, that's a shooting crime!"

Milo and Morry had come in. Milo stuck his finger playfully into O'Keefe's back. "Who's shooting who?" he asked. O'Keefe grinned. He stirred his spoon in his empty cup, almost boyishly, and continued to grin as Milo and Morry drew up chairs.

"How's it going?" Milo asked.

O'Keefe nodded his head grimly.

"Tomorrow's Saturday," Milo said, "I don't work. I'll march."

"Me too," Morry said.

Aaron was ashamed of himself. But he said nothing.

"Many people go in?" Morry asked.

"A few scabs," O'Keefe said.

"You say scabs as if you don't like them," Morry said, chuckling.

"I love them—" O'Keefe said, "because they are my brothers. Otherwise I'd like to attend their funerals."

O'Keefe began to chuckle. "Let me tell you about Chuck Miller!" he said. "Jeez, he walks like a young farmer! He's the oldest man in my department. He's in his sixties. He looks like an ex-baseball pitcher. God! He's got arms and hands! I could imagine him stabbing out his hand to stop a grounder getting away from him—and thick neck—" O'Keefe felt his own neck, illustrating, "and straight! He walks straight as—he walks like a young farmer. That's what Chuck's like. Well, he's spent fifty years almost at Haines. He was there since he was eighteen. Almost fifty years." O'Keefe nodded his head. "And he was laid off during the depression and he got back only by begging one of the executives that he knew personally because in that place you get to know a lot of people. It's amazing how many people you get to know if you're the knowing type. And you can take advantage of who you know. Chuck, he had a good job as a minor executive and had to come back as a freight operator. Chuck is never going to retire unless they force him out. He has no money. I know he has no money. What he had he lost during the depression. When he was idle he worked on the WPA. His wife was sick. His wife is dead. He's alone in the world. His children have all gone away from him. He doesn't want to get in anybody's way. Just come to his job, keep it, talk to the boys, smoke his pipe, come to work every day. He wants to be left alone until he's ready to die—which may be about twenty-five years from now judging by his physical condition." O'Keefe smiled widely, looking at Morry and Milo. "Well, by gum!" he said. "I see Chuck walking in the picket line today!" O'Keefe smiled broader. "I know men who went out who've been forty years there. Due for a pension. They've been in there all their life. You'd think they'd say, 'Why should I sacrifice my future?' " O'Keefe smiled grimly, shook his head slowly.

They sat half an hour talking. Dave arrived and sat next to Milo, saying that he hadn't seen him in a long time. Don came over from another table. He took one of O'Keefe's pamphlets and said several times that he was all for the strikers. He was introduced to Dave and was very friendly to him. When Dave left, Don asked, "Who is that colored fellow, anyway?"

"A very good friend of mine," Milo said. "We work out at the university together."

Don said to all of them, "You always sit up and take notice when a colored guy doesn't talk with a Negro accent, don't you?" And, after that, whenever Dave was in the restaurant Don came over and talked to him.

Aaron, who had had little to say all evening, stood up and left. On the street outside he felt depressed and decided to walk home.

In the night street, in the cold, walking home, his thoughts wandered far and returned to him . . . the next three grades had been taught by Mr. Bloom. He was also fat but bigger than Schwartz. He wore glasses without rims and looked shrewd. . . . Aaron shivered from the cold and lifted his coat around his ears. . . . He used to walk up and down the aisles with a ruler. He used it too. The bastard! I was deathly afraid of him until one Saturday when I went to the show. . . . Aaron chuckled to himself, remembering that it was against their religion to have money or work on the Sabbath. . . . He used to sort of sneak in. He made sure that no one was around who knew him and would tell his father or any of his Jewish friends or teachers. He'd buy a ticket. At the right moment he'd dart into the show with his heart beating fast. This Saturday he was about to buy his ticket and race in when he saw Bloom coming down the street. He stuffed the ticket into his pocket and looked at the ads in front of the show. Bloom didn't see him. Bloom just bought a ticket, jangling the unholy money in his hand, and went into the show. I don't know what I thought. Yes, I got the feeling that I had something on him and I was never afraid of him again. That was the day I lost my religion. . . . Aaron went up the steps and into his house.

Papa was still up. He waved the evening newspaper and said, "Today I didn't work. Tomorrow I don't work. Tomorrow I walk in the strike. Tomorrow I walk for my fellow workers." He wanted to know, again, if Aaron had read the book he had given him.

"A little," Aaron said.

He undressed, climbed into his cot and pulled the covers over his head. Yes, the little man in his head who had the *opposite viewpoint to everything* was his father.

# VIII

All night long the few pickets moved in front of the Haines Company. Daylight came. The strike moved into its second day. Irish was back in line. The strikers increased as the day increased.

The full-page ads, advertising for help and condemning the union, brought a crowd of people looking for work. Most of them were young men and women anxious to make money for the Christmas holidays.

The second day of the strike brought a furor. Emerson Bradley's granddaughter came down from her economics class at the University of Chicago, took a placard and marched with the strikers. She was soon recognized and the news photographers and reporters gathered around her. Flash bulbs burst. The strikers improvised a song and began singing it in jeering tones to the walls of the Haines Company:

*"Hazel Bradley doesn't belong to the Bradley family ANY MORE!"*

It was only one line but they sang it over and over, marching and cheering with renewed vigor. And finding out who she was and where she was in the crowd they cheered her and lifted her to their shoulders. The reporters shot questions at her:

"What do you think of the strike, Miss Bradley?"

"Why, I'm for it, of course, that's why I'm out here."

"What does your grandfather think about you joining the pickets?"

"He doesn't know. I guess he won't speak to me for a while." Her lips came out petulantly. "I don't care." She laughed. "Every Christmas I buy his Christmas present in the bargain basement of his store."

The reporters ate it up.

"Now, Miss Bradley, why—why are you for the strikers?"

"Because—" her eyes became serious and sullen, "I think working people have a right to decent wages and Grandpa isn't giving them decent wages. Because—I think workers are entitled to have a union and bargain—and—" She laughed again, almost in the way her grandfather would, the same fighter he was. "Grandpa is going to give me hell!" she said. She righted her placard and tried to struggle away from the reporters and the admiring union members. More flash bulbs went off.

She was not a publicity seeker. She marched all day long with the strikers, had coffee and sandwiches in the union basement and went back in line.

The front pages of the newspapers all carried her picture. They featured her remarks.

Kovac and Mr. Baker were arrested that day. Kovac and the gentlemanly Mr. Baker, for disorderly conduct.

On the third day of the strike Judge Raven handed down an injunction regulating the picket line to three people.

The next day the Haines Company mail-order plants in Philadelphia, Albany, Minneapolis and Detroit went on strike.

The strike lasted three weeks. The whole Haines plant was snarled. Christmas orders piled high and were undelivered. The Haines Company lost thousands of dollars every day. The three pickets moved in front of the buildings day and night. The strike went into its fourth week. Then newspaper headlines said in big, black type: BRADLEY RECOGNIZES THE UNION!

# IX

Len enlisted in the army. Saul said he was a fool. But Saul too enlisted and dropped into Thompson's on his first leave. He had changed. He bragged about army life and cocked his cap to one side of his head. He talked about the women and good times he was going to have. Looking at him Aaron remembered how Saul the sensitive had introduced him to an understanding of symphonic music, how Saul had taught him so many of the things of a full and intellectual life. Aaron looked at him and knowing him well knew that what he really meant by enlisting, by talking in bravado about army life, was simply—I want to have something to talk over with the boys. I don't want to be alone and listen when the war is over. Aaron lowered his eyes from his friend's clean, hard, bragging face. He wished this damn chaotic moment was over.

Aaron began to think of himself. He put his hand down under the table to try to stop the trembling of his leg. Him. Soon they'd call him to go to the war. Him.

On the streets, in the neighborhood, people asked him why he wasn't in the army, when he was going. The old men asked it in an angry insulting way. Old Mrs. Kaplan pushed her gray head out the door of her notions store and beckoned him with her bony finger.

"You must enlist, Aaron," she whispered, looking up and down the street. "For you I have been looking to tell you this. It is a war to save the Jews, they are saying. The Jews are buying their way out, they are letting other people fight their war for them. This they are saying." She tapped her long, hard finger against his chest. "About you, you must not let them say this, no."

"Thanks," Aaron said, tipping his hat and getting away from her as soon as possible.

The eighteen-year-old draft was only a few weeks old. His father came into the room when he had his head down on the desk. "Aaron," he said, and Aaron sat up. He looked at his father, short, lean, with his balding head and wearing his blue work shirt—and thought, No one knows another person's life, the desires, the hopes, the blunted ends. "Aaron," Mr. Levin said, "I have been waiting for you to speak. You are now a high school graduate. This war—Aaron—now that you are a man—now that our country is taking men your age—"

He was surprised at how gently his father spoke. He had never noticed that before. Then he tightened his lips and shoved his hair off his forehead, knowing what his father was going to say.

His father sat on the cot and his knobby knees tightened against the cheap cloth of his trousers. "It is your war, too, son. Our people—in Europe."

*Our people* . . . Aaron put his forehead down against the cool top of the desk, unable to be the man his father wanted him to be. His lips trembled. "If it means—" he said, "if it means that the Jews are accepted by all people as just people, part of all humanity, if it means the Jews will stop being clannish and will become assimilated—"

"Silence, Aaron!"

"—I'm willing to fight—and die—"

He could hear movement in the room: "And my other child, this sensitive plant, male, eighteen," Aaron thought for his father. He lifted his head from the desk top. His father was standing by the cot stripping his work shirt off his body. He was stripped, now, to the waist. Aaron saw with a shock of surprise the weak and puny chest, the thin arms. His father moved nearer to him and into the circle of light. "I want to show you something, son." He turned his back to Aaron.

Aaron saw the aged marks a knout had left. He saw them but did not know his father's life, desires, hopes and disappointments. He looked and saw where the whip had cut the flesh, years ago. Cut it jaggedly and brought blood and left its markings forever. He looked and saw the livid lines etched there forever in his father's dark-skinned back. Lines that looked like the rivers on a map in the fifth grade, but slick and white. Ghastly white. Smooth as marble, the long, irregular rivers of the unforgotten pain. Jagged scars that crawled across the dark-skinned back in a broken spider web and looked like the cracks in an aged plaster ceiling. "In a pogrom in Russia," his father said. "When I was a child," his father said. And his father moved away, out of the circle of light, put on his blue work shirt, stuffed the tail into his trousers. "Do you wonder," he said, "why I hate the Russians—no, not the Russians, not the new government, not the Soviets. But those in power everywhere who do harm to a man because of race. Yes, even here. Even here."

After that neither said anything. In silence his father smoked a cigarette. When it was out and the red coal had been crushed black in the bottom of the ash tray like old and seared angers, his father came and stood alongside of him. His father put his hand on Aaron's shoulder. Aaron would have liked to pull his shoulder away but he did not want to hurt his father. In a voice gentle as a woman's his father said, "Will you go and fight, son? Please, for me, will you go and fight?" His father raised his hand from Aaron's shoulder and laid it against his own forehead. "I am too old."

Aaron went into the quiet room of his mind and thought it over before answering. When he returned, he said, "I'll enlist, Papa."

All night he lay on his hard cot, not sleeping, thinking, and the dawn bruised the skyscraper and factory sky. He arose and pulled on his clothes. Milo was wrong. It was his war too—if he believed in people—not just the Jews—but all people—

# X

The days turned colder and colder. Grandpa stood by the window, saying, "It is cold out of doors," and, looking toward Poland, talked of how the war must have seen bombs falling on his native village, how, perhaps, the house in which he had been born had been destroyed by the bombs. Don looked at the old man and felt fear. The thing he avoided thinking about was the army. Yet the thought of it lay at the surface of his mind, forever, and in little ways stepped out front onto the theater of his conscience. A soldier passing on the street. The recruiting office billboards. The headlines in the newspapers. Only a little while ago: PASS 18 YEAR DRAFT. NO YEAR TRAINING. If they were taking the eighteen-year-olds, what chance did he have? He had only been lucky, ducking it this long. Lucky. "Soon it will be zero," Grandpa said, waddling back from the window. Lucky. Maybe he was a physical coward. But he told himself no, that he wanted to pursue his career now while he was getting more and more recognition.

Then the war caught up with him. The envelope was stuck in the rusted mailbox hanging half off the wall with the name Kosinski penciled above it.

He was scared to death. He carried the envelope up into the house and sat with it on his knees.

"*Jaka pogoda?* How is the weather?" Grandpa said.

Don didn't even answer. He sat, feeling his legs and his arms tremble.

Grandpa came over to him. "My tie," he said, chuckling. Don tied it mechanically.

"What is the matter?" Grandpa asked him.

"I got my papers for the army today," Don said.

He didn't even notice that Grandpa sat next to him with his withered hand on his knee.

He stayed up all night, the night before his physical, smoking cigarettes and drinking coffee, hoping that this would run his constitution down enough to disqualify him for the army. If he was nervous, real nervous, maybe they wouldn't take him. He was a trained actor. Maybe he could act his way out of it. He was an actor. That's what he resented. This interfered with his life. His ambitions.

In the morning, his eyes red-rimmed from lack of sleep, he went down to Van Buren Street for his physical.

Up all night and the cigarettes didn't do any good. He was classified 1A.

"I was classified 1A," he said at home. Grandpa was home alone and had been waiting for him. Grandpa caned his way over. "When do you go?"

Don didn't answer. He saw himself lying dead somewhere, blown to bits. The old man sat alongside him and put a withered hand on Don's shoulder.

*"Dzis?"*

"No, Grandpa," Don said, "not today."

*"Jutro rano?"*

"No, not tomorrow."

*"Pojutrze?"*

"No, Grandpa. *Za dwa tygodnie.* We get two weeks to put our business straight."

"In the evening?" Grandpa asked. "In the night?"

"In the morning, Grandpa."

"Then we have a fortnight."

Don showed up at rehearsal. He stood in the doorway before entering. "O blood, Iago! Blooooooood!" he shouted from the door dramatically. Then he strolled in smiling. "I enlisted today," he said loudly and to the whole room; and carried the lie off well.

"Oh no, Don!" Sue said.

The cast stared at him in awe and respect.

"I'm going over to win the war," he said.

Nora kept eying him and he felt he could make her before he left. His mother surprised him by babying him now and even brought his breakfast to him in bed on Sunday when she didn't work. And coffee every morning before she went to work.

There were still a few days left and Don lived them to the hilt. He even began to wish he could knock Sue up, or some other babe, so that he'd leave his name in case he got killed. Then he thought what his name was and laughed. Well, leave the name *Lockwood*.

Sue held him very tight on her bed in her dark room the last night. Sue cried in the dark too. And that made him feel good. He stroked her and told her he loved her, that he would write often. He stayed with her all night.

At home Ma didn't even get sore and ask where he had been all night. Eva came in and kissed him quickly, with her arms tight around his neck, before she went to the factory. His younger brothers and sisters were all there to tell him good-by, even Kozie, who was always on the street. Helen hadn't come home last night from her 26-table but she had left a note and a five-dollar bill propped up on his dresser for him. Grandpa hobbled around on his cane looking at him from all sides and saying what a fine-looking soldier he'd make, that this was his big scene, that—and Grandpa pointed the cane—he'd shoot a dozen Germans down out of the sky, that he would help make Poland's sky Poland's sky again. And when he got the chance Grandpa Kosinski pulled the secret carton from under his cot, unwrapped the many, many coils of mended string from around the little newspaper-wrapped package. From the package, first looking to see that no one else saw, Grandpa Kosinski pulled two five-dollar bills. These he gave to Don, saying, "You might want a drink to carry you through some battle." Winking and saying, "You might sometimes need a woman. I am not too old to remember these things, and how youth lays on youth for sadness and pleasure and the fears that come—" He poked the head of his cane into Don's stomach and cackled, his mouth opening wide to show the one tooth.

Alina came quickly, shyly, to Don when, unnoticed, she had the chance. Into his hand she pressed, without words, a little medal. On it was the *Panna Marya.*

And now it was time to go. The impersonal depot waited. And the many other soldiers, like himself, sitting there going to—no one knew what. Don rose swiftly, smiled quickly. He went to Grandpa. He kissed him on the shoulder as, for many years, he had not kissed him. He turned to his mother, still smiling.

A cold gray winter sky was over the city and the tightly drawn streetcar wires and the towers of the Loop. Mrs. Kosinski looked at her son with a pale, drawn face. "Chet! My son! My son!" She hugged and kissed him. Pushing the hair off her forehead, she said, "My little boy! My little boy, a soldier!" Crying she put her arms around him. He returned the embrace and patted her shoulder. He kissed her pale lips and stroked her hair and remembered the turkey feather in the hamburger roast a long, long time ago. Then he pushed her gently away. "All right, Ma." And he laughed.

He ran down the decaying steps between the rusty black rails. The shadows were just beginning to retreat from the sidewalk. The hard-packed dirty snow was under his feet. The kids and Grandpa were at one window. Ma was leaning out the other one. Lifting his hand he waved to her and to Grandpa.

And he laughed. Weakly.

# XI

Aaron went to tell Rebecca goodby. "I think I'm going to leave tomorrow." Her face paled and he could see the birthmark stand out ragged and brown-red on her cheek. He had often found himself staring at her birthmark. It detracted from his artistic ideal of beauty and perfection.

"Sit down, Aaron," she said. Her voice trembled. At length her mother left the room. They had little to say to each other. He could see her heart beating very hard under her dress. "I'll write to you," she said.

"Will you write often?"

"I was going to say I'd write every day. I don't know if I'll have enough to say that often." Her hand was up to the side of her face and she was trying, unnoticed, to pull her hair over her cheek so that the birthmark wouldn't show. "Let's take a walk," she said.

It was cold out. Their feet and their hands soon got numb. They warmed themselves at the fire in a tin drum by a newsstand. "I wish you weren't going," Rebecca said. He took her arm and could feel it tremble. He walked with her and stood with her under a lamp-post. "Will you wait for me?" he said. He saw the tears on her lashes. And almost automatically she brought her mittened hand up to her cheek and over the birthmark.

"Let's go home," she said.

In the hallway he stood facing her with his head down. She reached with her arms and put her hands on each side of his face and then her arms around him. It was the first time he had kissed her.

When he got down to the sidewalk he wiped his eyes.

The following day Aaron Levin went for his physical. Going out of the house he touched his fingers to his lips and touched the mezuzah. It was silly to do that, he thought. But he did it for his father, he told himself.

He would go to the war. He would go with the knowledge and hope that if he, all of them, could strike—not at human beings but at all the evil in the world—that it was a good fight.

He felt a kind of joy at the imagined sight of prejudice everywhere being bayonetted, himself standing with the hard face of zeal, spearing evil everywhere.

He had never felt such ecstasy before. He would write when this was over. After the bayonet, the pen. . . .

Into the white-fronted building on Van Buren he walked, and to the proper floor. He swallowed hard and was conscious that his legs and arms were trembling.

The lobby entrance was almost like an amusement center. There were pinball machines along one whole wall. Rows of enemy soldiers to be bowled over with little pinballs, Nazi airplanes to be shot down, submarines to sink. Groups of boys waiting their physicals idled at the toy pinball machines, aiming and shooting in their preliminary military practice. The most popular game was the one with Hitler, Mussolini and Tojo as targets. The soldiers stood in a long line waiting to play the game. They shoved. They yelled in applause when anyone shot Hitler, Mussolini or Tojo.

In the room where the physicals were given Aaron was marshaled into place in the line of nondescript boys who that day had received their GREETINGS from the President. Boys. Half-grown. Used to wearing polo shirts and blue jeans, autographed blazers. They had wiped windshields, taken care of parking lots, delivered groceries.

They drove crazy, junky cars without mufflers. They were proud of their muscles. They bragged about girls. They swam and boasted and hung on street corners.

Aaron's knees began to tremble and he hoped no one would notice. He was made to stand up against the X-ray machine so that his lungs could be examined. He was told to strip to his shorts, and his clothes were put in a basket on a rack. With the rest of the nude and nondescript line he was herded, slow-step, forward. The stethoscope was held to his heart and his back. He was given a bottle in which to urinate and his arm was stuck with a needle. Their sex organs were examined. In front of him a young kid was having trouble. "Come on, skin it back!" the doctor ordered. The kid still had trouble. "If you don't hurry up and do it I'll do it myself," the doctor yelled. Aaron waited. And on to the next line. His eyes and his ears were examined and he was told, with his shorts down, to bend down. He was sent to the psychiatrist.

The psychiatrist laid aside his glasses and his pencil and smiled. "Well, there isn't much to talk about to a big, healthy fellow like you, is there?" he said to Aaron. Aaron felt the trickle of perspiration oozing from his armpit, dropping on the smooth mahogany desk; and clamped his arm tight.

The psychiatrist sent him on down the plaster-roomed channel, down the maze to exit. He offered his paper to the sergeant at the designated desk. The sergeant with a worn and much-used rubber stamp stamped ACCEPTED across the papers. Stripped of individuality he now offered the back of his hand, as instructed, and on it in Mercurochrome was painted a large A.

He no longer had anything to say about it.

They returned the money he had spent for carfare to get down to the induction center. Then lunch at one of the long tables set up for the purpose, with his arms and knees trembling.

And down the chute.

# XII

New Year's Eve came, a sad, wrinkled New Year's Eve, noisy though, with people trying to squeeze the most happiness they could from life, and forget about the war, and get as drunk as they could, and for a while forget about those over there, their sons, brothers, husbands, sweethearts, friends and their fear for them. Whistles shrilled and guns cracked only in play and celebration.

Jim stood on a chair, refitting the curtain rod that had fallen to the floor. The first whistles sounded. He got down, went to the pantry, and bringing two glasses and a bottle, poured wine for his wife and himself. They clicked glasses. They smiled slowly, quietly at each other. The guns of celebration sounded. Jim looked across the table at his wife. She was getting quite fat with the new child.

"Louise—" he said. He cleared his throat. He filled the glasses again, leaning forward, his wavy copper hair taking high light from the naked kitchen bulb. He bit his lip for a moment and gestured with his arms. "Louise—" he said, "there's a larger thing outside—" He nodded toward the window and the night. It was the only way he could explain it. Louise put her arms, outstretched, on the top of the table and knitted her fingers. Jim said, "I—I'd like to go help."

Louise nodded. "I've known it for a long time," she said.

"Would it be asking too much? If it is—just say so."

She shook her head.

"It's—it's not fair to you—one child—another coming," Jim said.

"We're all in this together," Louise said.

"I wouldn't be with you—when—"

Louise stuck her bottom lip over the top one in a wry grimace and smiled. "A lot of people are parted." Smile. Smile! she told herself.

"The allotment wouldn't be much," he said.

"I'll manage, darling."

"Sorry you still aren't typing old man Bromwell's letters?" he asked, trying to joke. But his voice cracked.

Louise came around behind his chair and hugged him tightly. "I'm not glad you're going," she said, "but I'm proud of you." Her tears streaked his neck.

Jim sat at home for the last few minutes before having to leave for camp. He played with the baby, watching it toddle on its sixteen-month-old legs to him and grasp the pillars of his trousers for support. Louise looked at him. She looked at the worn and friendly rooms that were all their married life together. His favorite chair. The dishes they had been given for their wedding gift, and not a piece broken. Her eyes came back to Jim. She sat looking at him. He laughed and swung the baby up over his head. Then he put the baby in its playpen behind the table holding the mimeograph machine. Then he came and sat looking at his wife. He glanced at his watch. He looked at his wife, fearfully. She folded her hands and looked back at him. They were folded around her rounded-out stomach.

He stood up. He put his hands on her shoulders gently. She rose to his embrace. They clung in each other's arms for a long time.

He sat down and lit a cigarette. Smiling, she reached across for his cigarette, took a puff, handed it back to him. Jim finished the cigarette. He crunched it out.

"Take care of yourself, Louise," he said. He stood up. "Well, so long," he said. He grabbed his duffel bag and went out. She followed him out onto the porch and looked down over the steep banister. Jim patted their dog, who came to meet him from around the side of the house. "So long, Feezer." The dog tried to follow him. "No! No! Go back!" he said gruffly. Very gruffly. He locked the front gate and looked up at her. He waved to her. She waved back.

He didn't look again toward the house but disappeared down the sidewalk.

Louise lowered her hand. She didn't blink. She went back into the house and sat on the edge of the bed and said, "He's gone."

She sat there a long time. She began to tremble a little. She got up and walked into the other room. On the shelf near his favorite chair she saw his three cheap pipes and the bowl of tobacco only half empty. She picked up one of the pipes and kissed it. Then she laid it aside. "You're not going to cry," she said aloud. Her fingers toyed with his harmonica on top of the dresser.

She walked into the bedroom. On a chair she saw his shirt and twisted on the floor by the bed where he had squirmed out of them and left them were a pair of his socks. For something to do she got a box and packed his clothes away. Then she unpacked them and put them in the dresser drawer. Oh, come back, come back, darling!

Again she sat on the side of the bed. She sat there a long time. The telephone rang and she answered it. She knew he was smiling at the other end of the line. "I'm sorry," he said. Then she knew he wasn't smiling but that his tan face was serious and taut. "The thought of going away and not seeing you indefinitely—maybe never—and the baby coming—hit me between the eyes all at once."

"Oh, darling—it's all right," she said. She heard a train coming into the depot. "Is that your train, dear?" In the pause she could see him, boyish and a little awkward, sticking his handsome blond head out of the telephone booth, looking to see. She could see the first big wave of blond hair before it got curly. She put her lip between her teeth.

"That's it," his voice said from a long way off, "take care of yourself, Louise."

"Take care of yourself, Jim."

Click!

She stood a full minute holding the empty, dead receiver against her ear. She lowered it and looked at it. "Come back to me, Jim," she whispered.

# XIII

. . . And their lives moved off into night. Don. Aaron. Jim. The millions of others.

# Book Three

## DAWN

# I

*the way of a serpent upon a rock*

Don swung slowly from the back step of the Grand Avenue car after it had come to a full halt. He walked along the dirty, newspaper-strewn sidewalk toward home under the grayed-over sky. He stood outside his house at 121 West Grand, looking up between the corroded black banisters. Over the door the crudely crayoned sign said on its square of white cardboard:

WELCOME
HOME
DON

His throat filled up. They had even printed DON instead of Chet. Moving closer now, and with his hand on the banister, he looked up at the sign. It was dirty from hanging there for so long a time. The bunting around the door was frayed. There had been delays and more delays before he had been discharged.

Hanging onto the banister he limped slowly up the steps. He took his key, carried all the way to war and back, out of his billfold and fitted it into the lock. The sky was grayed over a chill winter day as when he left. Painfully he climbed the stairs to the upper door and pushed it open. The same smells. The same dirty apartment. . . .

His mother, looking to the door as it swung open, stopped combing her hair with the comb drawn halfway through it. She stood up. "Oh, my son! My son!" She drew out a chair. "Sit down." She began to cry.

He looked at her. "I don't have to sit down," he said; and to himself: Already it starts like the guy at the Rehabilitation station said.

He sat down.

He looked at his fingers and laced them together. "Don't cry, Ma." He didn't know what else to say.

She went on crying.

"Where's Grandpa?" he asked, looking around, and for something to say.

"It is all over with him," Ma said, crying harder and blowing her nose on the hem of her skirt. "We didn't want to tell you—bother you with our troubles—you with your troubles." It made her cry all the harder.

Grandpa dead. He felt himself go dull inside. It hurt worse than the loss of his leg.

"He lay ailing a long time," Ma said. "He asked me to write to the old country for *zmijecznik*. But—" She shrugged. "When the bones are dry and want to lay down? What good then is magic remedies?"

Julka, the baby, came from behind the stove, step by step, her grave eyes on Don, her tongue reaching for her nose that dripped. She stood with her little arms around Ma's legs, her eyes still gravely watching this strange man.

"And when it was bad," Ma said, "when it was bad he said, 'Give me some water to rinse my mouth.' The next day he said, 'Clip my whiskers a little.' "

The child climbed into Ma's lap.

"Then the next day he said, '*Jeczcze nie pozno . . . jeczcze nie pozno.*' "

She began to cry again.

It is not yet late, Don thought, translating into English. The baby was trying to wrap its arms around Ma's neck.

"The next day he lost consciousness," Ma said. She slapped the baby across the behind in reprimand and went on without interruption. "How fortunate it was that the priest, with our Lord Jesus, came in time."

Don's eyes moved away from his mother and across the room.

"We put him away nice," Ma said.

"Who tied Grandpa's tie?" Don asked. He didn't expect or want an answer. He lit a cigarette and awkwardly pulled his false leg from its sprawled position to a more natural pose, using his hand to adjust it.

"A priest came," Ma said, "and led the burial procession—not without speech—and thanked the dead before the grave."

"And how much did that cost?" Don asked cynically.

"We had mourning banners on the house. And the wind waved them for three days," Ma said, stretching her skinny hand toward the door.

I got my drama from her, Don thought, looking at her, the tense face, the outstretched hand.

Ma said, "Grandpa said you were to have all his things. We were not to touch them. And I didn't. Only the Polish earth." She put her hand up to her face and the tears ran down beyond it. "I put it under Grandpa's head as he would have me do. And a little I saved for myself, as my good mother in heaven would have me do."

Wayne. Don twisted his fingers together. Wayne, buried in foreign soil.

"Where's the kids?" Don asked for something to say.

"They're out," his mother said. "They will be glad to see you." This made her cry worse.

"How's Eva?" he asked, trying to bring a hard or at least casual tone to his voice. "Where's Eva? Still working at the factory?"

"She got in some trouble with a sailor. They got her at the Catholic Welfare." Ma held his eyes for a moment, then looked away. "They will adopt it out."

Don remembered Eva's dark eyes and her defiant smile like his own. He shrugged his shoulders.

"I try to be a good mother," Ma said. Again the tears ran down past her shielding hand.

"Where is Alina, Ma?"

"Alina is at the church. She is always at the church. She fancies she wants to be a nun."

Ma pulled Julka's arms loose, set her on the floor and sent her scampering away crying with a hard palm across the behind. "Poor Grandpa," Ma said, shaking with silent sobs. "He would have loved seeing you in your uniform." Her eyes rested on the lapel of his uniform. "What is that medal? Is that your Purple Heart?"

Don's hand came up quickly, proudly, to the Purple Heart. And he smiled.

"Poor Grandpa, he would have liked to see it," Ma said. *"Umart jak swiety."*

Don, laughing, said, "Grandpa a saint! So he died a saint."

He laughed again and getting up, limped into his room. When he walked his leg was like a joint that bent both ways. It was both stiff and flexible.

He sat heavily on the side of the bed. Grandpa dead. Poor Grandpa. He put his forehead against the cold iron upright of the bed. Poor Grandpa. He rubbed his forehead against the iron post. He ran his fingers through his long hair. He wished now that he had been kinder to the old man, had listened to him when, lonely, the old man talked to him, leaning forward in the rocker and searching him out with his dim eyes. He rubbed the palm of his hand across the bed.

Then he was unreasonably angry at all of them. Their stupidities, their superstitions. Magical remedies! Priests! Sacred Polish earth! Their vulgarity and ignorance. So Eva was going to have a baby! And for a sailor! The good old Armed Forces of the U.S.A.! She didn't get the rich man Ma wished for her.

He put his head back against the bedpost and laughed. And stopped laughing. So another Pole was going unnamed and without family out into the world. Another bastard Pole. Maybe the kid would get a better break than he did. Maybe rich people would adopt it. Or movie stars. He'd have a nephew or niece and never see the kid. Or maybe he'd see it often as an actor on the screen and never know. Alina a nun! That was funny as hell. And sad. The priest-ridden Poles. That was what was wrong with his people. His people! And he thought in Grandpa's words: I spit on all this.

His leg itched where the knife and saw had been. He scratched it with his hard nails. Scratched hard. It felt good and he arched his back a little, like a dog being scratched. Scratched, and it felt good. He hoped he wouldn't make the stump bleed like last time.

He thought of Ma, of her face. And he couldn't, or wouldn't, believe that he was from her body. Maybe, like Eva's bastard, he had only been adopted.

At length he sat upright and looked about his room. Saw Grandpa's cardboard box sticking from under the end of the dresser. Saw it with a shock of sadness.

He arose with his false leg unsteady under him and went to the dresser. He pulled the box out and dragged it to the bed. Sitting down, he opened it.

The little newspaper-wrapped packages tied with the many bindings of strings. The letters with Polish stamps on them. The jars and glasses with a little scum of rotting jelly yet in them. A cracker box with a few broken and mildewed crackers. This was Grandpa. All that was left of him. . . .

He opened the packages but there was nothing he wanted. He found three aged dollar bills in a tobacco can and put them in his billfold. He found a few pennies, a rusty nickel and several old dimes in the bottom of the box. He put them in his pocket and as he did so found the *Panna Marya* medal Alina had given him. Alina a nun! And from this whorehouse! He opened Grandpa's letters and began reading them. . . .

1898, the date said in faded ink on the yellowed sheet of paper . . . *Dear Brother: You write me not to marry until Michalek comes here with his fiddle. But so it could easily happen that I should remain an old girl. But never mind, if at least one of you were with me. As it is I live in a prison. I have nobody even to speak with. Our parents are old and go to sleep early, and I often think that my head will burst, I must weep so, and I long for you, for I am alone like an orphan. If I did not pity our parents I should go at once to you for with this needle I can earn a little, and money is needed everywhere. But is it possible to leave our parents to the mercy of fortune, while they have raised us? Well, I will bear it as I can and pray to God that he will bring here at least one of you, for I long terribly. Goodbye, and don't be angry with me for writing this, for I have nobody to whom to complain. Bronislawa.* So this was Bronislawa, to whom he had written so many letters. This was Grandpa's sister. His sister, the young woman, not the old, old maid to whom he had written for Grandpa.

1888 . . . *I am beginning this letter with Praised be Jesus Christus and I hope you will answer in centuries of centuries, Amen. May the Lord God grant you not to be spoiled in America. May you always be good, first toward God and towards God's mother, then towards us, your parents, and toward all men, as you have been up to the present. Amen. Now I thank you heartily for the shoes you sent me. They are so comfortable that I can walk as far as I need without feeling that I have anything on my feet. I always remember you with tears. We are very glad that you are in good health and that you speak to us. People envy us that you write so often and that on every holiday you send something, either money or a photograph—that you don't forget your parents. And now I beg you, if you intend getting married don't look at her dresses, but esteem only whether she loves our Lord Jesus. Then she will respect you also. We send you consecrated wafers. Although there are also wafers there, yet you are entered in the registers of this parish, so we send you them from here. Now I send you other words. Work and economize as much as you can. I long very much for you because I never see you. I kiss your photograph on the wall. Your Mother.*

Don took the dry half of a wafer from the envelope. He sat for a while looking at it. Thought how old it was, thought of Grandpa the young man and these old parents of his. Without knowing why, Don bit off a tiny bit of the wafer and swallowed it.

1912 . . . *May this letter warm your frozen blood. You send only bows. And now, we beg you, send us as soon as possible any money which you can, for we need it very much. . . . You wrote, dear son, that probably we shall not see one another any more. We were very grieved, and particularly I was. May we at least merit to be in heaven together. I have had so much trouble with you, I bred you, and now in my old age, when I can work no more, you left me, all of you, all but Bronislawa. I am now weaker and weaker. I often fall sick, so I should like to die in peace, when the last hour comes. And now, my dear child, remember me at least, your mother, who bred you. God alone knows how many tears I have shed that, for all my sufferings and troubles about you when you were small children, I have now nobody, save Bronislawa, to comfort me. Nobody to speak merrily with. If I could I would fly to you, were it not for that water I would go at once into the world after you. But surely now I shan't have any opportunity to see you in this world, for I feel by my bones that everything is more or less diseases. So I beg you once more speak to us, at least through paper. May I not have this disappointment at least. Your Mother.*

*. . . Our parents are both dead and I am old. . . .*

Don read. Read and halted with the faded, crumpling pages in his hand. So these were his great-grandparents. The cause of his being. Being a Pole in a slum of America. A Pole, looked down on by Americans of older stock here in this new country that was old in its ways of pride and prejudice. Read—and was suddenly proud of the Poles. Their humanity. Their history. These were his people. People like other people everywhere across the whole length and breadth of the world. Little nobodies of people who lived, suffered, died.

In the other room Ma was making pressed cakes of cabbage. "Don, come eat. My poor, dear boy, come eat," she called.

Don dressed to go out. "Wear an arm band," Ma said, "or someone will think you didn't mind the death of your grandfather." Don let her sew it on his arm; he liked it because it looked dramatic.

For two weeks he had stayed home carrying the heavy weight around on one leg, learning to walk, feeling Grandpa near to him in the apartment, feeling that he was old by fifty years beyond his age. Old in his one bad leg. Stayed home practicing to walk until the false leg became as a matchstick and he could walk without pain or awkwardness. With some agility on the government-issue leg.

Then Don went down to the Loop office where Sue and the Little Theater Group would be. On the door he saw the newly painted sign. THE SUE CARROLL PLAYERS. He pushed the door open, ready to make his grand entrance.

He stood on his false leg in the doorway with his hand on the knob. "Hi!" he called casually.

They were doing improvisations. They stopped. They crowded about him. "Oh Don, Don!" Sue said, taking his hand. Her eyes were moist. They all crowded closer about him.

"Nay, press not so upon me—stand far off!" Don said, striking the pose of a Mark Antony and swinging his arms outward as if actually pushing the mob aside. He laughed.

Everybody started to talk to him at once. They talked again about trivialities and avoided, as best they could, looking at his legs. Earl was there and in an army uniform. Earl with his little hands and soft voice. Don, looking at the uniform, was surprised that they had taken Earl into the army. Finally Carmen, unable not to mention it and shaking her head from side to side with her mop of hair flying across her face, said, "We're all so sorry about your leg!" She was almost on the verge of tears.

Everyone gave her a dirty look. Don laughed. "Oh, I'm not sensitive about it. Really, it's better than the other one." He tapped it with his knuckles and grinned. The leg gave forth a hollow sound. He stood on his good leg and waved the other in front of him like a man on a tightrope. He laughed. He came further into the room, chuckling. He sat down. "You were doing improvisations, huh?" He chuckled. "I can do an improvisation of a soldier awakening in the hospital and finding that his leg has been cut off." He laughed. "I can do an improvisation of an old man sitting in the sun thinking about his youth and stretching his old back to the warmness of the sun." He laughed again. "Got a cigarette, Sue?" She lit one and handed it to him but couldn't look at him. He chuckled. "But seriously, Sue," he said, "I'm still an actor. How about taking me back? I could do character parts—old men's parts. How about it?"

"Why sure, Don." She still carefully avoided looking at him.

He chuckled. "I'll wow them. With makeup. A beard. Maybe a cane." He grinned. "I'll wow them!" He became enthusiastic and he and the others began suggesting plays that would suit him.

Afterwards he was alone with Sue. "I'll buy you a beer," she said.

On the street, looking across to the other side, Sue asked, "Don, do you really want to come back to the group?"

Don twisted his hat to another angle. He glanced sideways at her, trying to explain. "Through—" he waved his hand, "all the mess—that was all I thought of."

Sue nodded. "All right, Don."

With a crash a streetcar ground to a stop behind a truck. Don felt the hair on his neck bristle and his arms began to tremble. In that field. The whine of explosives—

"Where do you want to go, Don?"

"West Madison Street."

They went to the Long Bar, to the Cobra Club, and finally to Kaplin's where they sat in a booth pushed up near the 26-table.

"This is swell, huh?" Don asked.

Don drank a lot. He laughed a lot. "This is like home," he said, without reason, looking around the tavern. He grinned and for a moment took her chin between his thumb and forefinger. "Let's have another drink," he said, tightening his fingers on her chin.

"Don't drink too much, Don," she said.

They drank again and again, at Don's insistence.

"Don't you think we've had enough?" Sue kept asking.

"I like it down here," Don said. He laughed. "Notice all the one-legged men on crutches and the one-armed guys?" He winked. "Vets of the last war." He winked again. "Maybe I'll end up down here in ten, twenty years. Great joke, huh?" He laughed. "But dramatic."

Sue wiggled a finger at the waitress. The waitress came over, a woman of fifty with a blotched face, caved-in chest and hair hanging about her thin neck. "Yes?" Sue pointed at their glasses. The woman swept them up in her dirty hands and went for more.

Don stood up, a little drunk, on his false leg. "Got a quarter, Sue?"

She put it on the table. He winked at her. "Going to play twenty-six."

He half staggered to the 26-table. "Got a sister who's a twenty-six girl down here somewhere," he said over his shoulder to Sue. That hurt her; she felt like crying. She watched him in his uniform, stagger to the 26-table.

Leaning there he laughed and talked with the girl for a while, then rolled the dice out of the black cup. He didn't win.

"Look!" he said suddenly. He threw his GI leg up on the top of the 26-table and stood on his good leg. "Look!" He pounded the false leg hard with his knuckles. The 26-girl stared at the leg, at him, tried to smile, thought better of it and only looked at him.

Don dropped his false leg down to the hard wood floor with a bang. He walked over to the bar. He fished around in his pocket. "Gimme a beer," he said to the bartender.

Sue came and stood beside him at the bar. "Want to go back to our table, Don?"

"Aw, leave me alone!" Don said. He said it angrily.

She went back to the table.

Don looked down into his beer—with the whine of ammunition, the thud and boom of explosives—he stared across the bar—in that field there—swilled his beer. One minute a healthy young fellow. They taught him to run miles with a pack on his back, go without food, live in a foxhole, live with lice and dirt, in cold, snow, rain. Kill with his bare hands. They had taught him that. He had been proud of himself, his endurance, his healthy alive legs under him with their bulging calves. The next moment—a cripple. Pain. Shame. Deformed the rest of his life, deformed. He laughed and banged the empty bottle, called for another. Always there would be pain. The kind that shame and deformity bring, a feeling of difference. The worst kind of pain. Subtle in so many ways. But always sneaking up on you. Gnawing at you. Was it true that it would ache with the changes of the weather? Pain. It had been his closest acquaintance. His enemy and his comrade in arms. For months. Months? It seemed a lifetime. A young lifetime. Everything focused only on the dead leg, the rotting stump under the khaki blanket. Draining away the pus. Taking away the soaked and crusted bandages. Red and green running to a pale yellow. The war, then, was only with pain, the condition of his leg. Minute after minute, hour after hour, day after day. Did it stink? Would it kill him? Gangrene? Doc, tell me the truth, goddamn it, tell me the truth: I can take it.

Fear, pain. Pain, fear. He'd never be normal again. He grinned tight-lipped in the back-bar mirror. Love? But sex. Unstrap your leg in the whorehouse and leave it standing in the corner. Sue? He lifted a shoulder and dropped it. Bleeding stumps. Dying men. Oh God, please leave me as big a stump as possible. That's all I ask, God. Please, God. Can I wriggle it? Knew a guy, broke his finger. Died of gangrene. In three weeks. There isn't gangrene in it, is there, Doc? You can tell me the truth. "Beer, bartender! Bring me another!" The arms and legs piled like cordwood. That's what we did, Uncle Sam. For you. For you, you bastard sitting at the end of the bar feeling that babe up. For you, you bastard who made a million on the war keeping it going. For you, you bastard right here in Chicago all through it running a black market, not wanting to see it end too soon. Burned the legs and arms for heat like low-grade mine run, to keep the other half-dead men warm. Ever hear a man scream in pain? The tears of soldiers are horrible. Wonder what they did with my leg? Burned it, of course, you fool. Don't think they buried it, do you? With full military honors, do you, you fool? Salvo of cannons. It kept the other dead and half-dead men leaning toward warmth, hope. Good enough! Good enough! He'd always hate the smell of roast bubbling its gravy over in the oven and burning. Look, fellow, you aren't a basket case, he told himself. Just a little scratch. He smirked. He got up and walked back to the table where Sue was.

"Hi!" He sat down, heavily. He drank what beer was left in her glass. "Sue, do you know something?" He grinned. "I'm mildly shell-shocked. Everybody who's been to the front is mildly shell-shocked. That's what the guy at the rehabilitation center said. I'm mildly shell-shocked." He chuckled. "Sure, I'm mildly shell-shocked." He staggered to the toilet. It was full so he staggered out the back door and into the alley and used a telephone post. Coming back in he saw a drunken woman leaning against the wall looking as if she were going to vomit. "Lady, were you ever shell-shocked?" he asked. She looked at him and grinned, staggered toward the ladies' room, kept grinning at him over her shoulder. Don looked over tables at Sue to get her reaction. She smiled at him weakly. When he sat down in the chair across from her, she said, "I'm sorry that the first time I saw you was in front of the gang. I wanted to kiss you so badly."

Don said, "Over there I thought about you a lot."

"That's all right, Don, you don't have to lie to me," Sue said. A little sad smile went with the words.

Don drank the rest of the beer in her bottle. "Let's get the hell out of here," he said.

"All right. Anything you want, Don."

On the sidewalk outside Don said, "Did you see me throw my leg up on the 26-table?"

"That was worthy of Douglas Fairbanks," Sue said, laughing, trying to bring humor to her laughter: and recognized the pathos of the moment. Recognized his pain. Pain that had nothing to do with his leg. Recognized, too, her feeling for him.

"I guess I'm an invalid, huh?" he said.

"Oh nonsense," she said, squeezing his arm. And to herself: Be casual. Be hard-boiled, at least to his face.

They went to her room. The drinks had left him in a bad condition. In the hall he talked too loud; laughed too loud. She kept hushing him, afraid that some of the other roomers in the house would hear, and at last got him up to her room. In the darkness of the room before she turned the light on, and after, she kissed him quickly.

Sue made coffee and insisted that he drink it. He wanted more liquor but she told him that she had none. She sat with him on the bed, holding the cup of coffee and occasionally bringing it to his mouth where, grumbling, he took small sips. She set the cup on the floor and with her fingers fondled the little mustache.

Don said, "Do you want to monkey around? I mean—now that—"

"Oh, Don, Don!" She leaned toward him and kissed him gently on the cheek.

"The sight of me—this—are you sure—?" He questioned helplessly. He awkwardly got to his feet.

She tried to hug him. He walked away from her.

"Undressed—" he said.

They talked about it without saying anything. He sat on the side of the bed. She with her arms around him. "Jesus Christ!" he said. "One moment I was—" he laughed, "in perfect physical condition. An actor—" He laughed. "And the next minute—" He laughed. "This cripple that you see before you now." He swept his hand down the length of his body, dramatically. He laughed again. "What do you think of that little scene from the director's point of view?" Laughing he got up and walked the length of the room, looked down through the window and into the well of the black alley.

Sue sat on the bed, staring at his back. "Come here," she said quietly. He came to her. She took his hand and pulled him down alongside her and took his head in her arms. Don's first tears came. He pulled away and stood up, walking to the end of the room. She watched his awkward stride.

"Sue, I'm not different," he said drunkenly. "I'm not different." He shook his head no. "I'm the same guy." He grinned at her from across the room. "I'm still the same ham." Tears ran down his cheeks.

Sue seemed to dissolve. She sat on the floor at the side of the bed. Don came alongside and took her hand. He sat down next to her. It was painful for him to sit on the floor. She was crying. "I'm crying," Don said, "you're crying. Let everybody cry!" Sue put her arm around him and her forehead against his forehead. They sat there. They fell asleep. They slept there a long time. Sue with her arm around him. Sue fighting sleep. Finally sleeping with her arm around him. The woman in her thirties and the boy who had lost a leg.

When they awoke they went to bed. After a while Sue's head was resting in Don's armpit and she was playing with the few hairs on his chest. Don lay smoking a cigarette and blowing languid smoke rings at the ceiling. Suddenly Sue snapped her fingers. "I've got it! Just the play for you!" She sat on the side of the bed. "Get up, Don!" She lit the light. Kneeling, she searched in the bookcase and drew out a copy of *On Borrowed Time*. "Oh, you'll love it!" she said. She made coffee.

He was still a little drunk and she took his face between the palms of her hands and massaged it. She made him drink more coffee.

He went to the bathroom and washed his face in cold water. They sat on the floor side by side with their backs against the bed. Excitedly they read the play. Don laughed and hugged himself and lay back on the floor, thumbing through the book for the passages he liked, finding them, shouting them in glee to the ceiling. "Old Gramps Northrop!" Don shouted, slapping his thigh sharply with the palm of his hand and throwing his head back. "Yeooooow! I'll wow 'em, Sue! I'll wow 'em!"

It was almost daylight when they went back to bed.

In the afternoon Don awoke, not in a hospital, in bed with this woman, this woman he knew so intimately. The shade was up. She was awake, with her face and her eyes turned toward him. "Nothing has changed, Don," she said to the first blinking open of his eyes. He smiled.

"Why do you smile?"

He didn't tell her that he was thinking of the many times, in this bed, he had awakened with the shades up because she had wanted to look at him. On bare feet he had always got out of bed and pulled the shades to the sills. In the dark he couldn't see her face. Nor the longing to look at him. All of him. But she had always come up with a laugh. "You're so modest, Don." Under the sheets she would kick him with her foot. He looked down at the foot of the bed. There had always been four bulges under the blanket at the foot of the bed. Their feet. Now there were only three.

He did not look in the corner where his leg stood.

Don sat at the dressing table amid the confusion of lacquer pots, grease paints, powder, brushes, powder puffs, cold cream, orange sticks and hare's feet. He leaned close to the mirror, squinting at his face with its thin coating of cold cream. Pulling the ground color marked "sallow old man" over to him, he rubbed the stick lightly over his face and neck.

He chuckled as he worked, and with spirit gum stuck the artificial white hair over his eyebrows. He hollowed his eyes and gave them a watery look by drawing a soft red line above and below them. Chuckling, he added wrinkles above and below his mouth, a depression on either side of his chin, shadings at his temples and on his neck.

Finally he took some crimped hair and, shaping it, attached it to the sides of his face in wispy lamb-chop sideburns. He chuckled. He leaned way forward toward the mirror, looking at his aged face. In Gramps Northrop's voice he said, "Don't make no difference. That's what you say. Etiquette. Matter of fact my hands feel kind of dirty, too, but I guess I'll wait until they're a little dirtier . . . I got you up that tree and you're gonna stay there until I tell you to come down!" And in his natural voice, looking proudly at himself, "Tonight, Don Lockwood, *tonight* you will give the greatest performance of your career!"

# II

*lost, and by the wind grieved*

The bus hissed on its slow brakes and cushioned springs and came under the evenly spaced street lamps. He awakened. "Chicago!" someone said. And someone else, looking out the black window, "We're in Chicago!" Others began to awaken and stir, to reach for luggage and stretch their tired legs and arms. One or two people switched on their lights. Others still tossed in restless sleep, their coats over them or balled up into pillows behind their heads.

Awake, he rolled his face toward the window. For a moment he didn't know if the streaks of water were against his cheeks or against the windows. Chicago, he thought dully. He looked out the black prison of window. They were in the fifty hundred block west on 12th Street. The bus rolled monotonously on, monotonously. He looked out: shoeshop, A & P, restaurant, theater, drugstore, dime store, tavern, hardware store, hot-dog stand, filling station, grocery, barbershop, laundry, fruits and vegetables, butcher shop, plumber, jewelry store, cleaner and dyer, greeting card shop, automobile dealer, theater, tavern, bank—CHICAGO!

He got off the bus in his olive drabs. It hadn't rained. The Marshall-Field clock showed 4:20 A. M.

He didn't go right home. He wandered around the streets of the Loop, along Michigan Boulevard to the Water Tower. He peered into the Thompson Restaurant from across the street, afraid someone—who knew him—would see him. He wandered aimlessly, down the Rush Street night club district. He wandered to the West Side.

It was all here. Just as it had been when he left. It had always been here.

Nearing his house a funny little rhyme came into his head: *If you can write by candlelight, there's hope for you, and more like you.* He shook his head. No. He would never write again.

He climbed the stairs to the door. He knocked. On the other side, after a long while, he heard his father's voice say, "Who?"

"Aaron."

There was a fumbling with the lock. The door came slowly open. He stood in the door with dawn at his back. His father stood looking out at him. His father was in his long woolen underwear. Thin in the legs and arms and body of the underwear. Thin and old in the face. His father groped out to him with a shaking hand. Aaron lowered his head. His black hair fell, long and straight, over his eyes. He looked down at his father's bare feet, the nails needing trimming and the long black hairs edging out to the end of each toe.

Aaron laced his hair behind his ear and let his eyes come up slowly to his father's. His father drew him in across the door sill.

Aaron sat on a chair in the kitchen and lowered his head. He sat down dully. His father sat opposite him, in his long underwear, looking at him.

"I'm sorry, Papa," Aaron said without looking up.

When he heard his father sniff very quietly, he looked up. He had never seen his father cry before. It was strange to see his father cry. He stared again at Papa's thin toes with the long, curled black hairs. He remembered the stripes on his father's back from the pogrom in Russia. He remembered his father showing them to him. He could see Papa's hand come up and the back of it wipe his cheek. The hand with one finger a stub.

He watched his father cry. He watched unmoved.

And now his sister had awakened and come from her bedroom. She was almost grown now, almost a woman. She had slipped on a gown and her hair was drawn into a knot at the back of her head. Her eyes were sleepy.

"Muriel," he said, and nothing more.

She came to him. She knelt alongside of him, at his feet, and tried to encircle him with her arms. "Oh, Aaron, I'm so glad to see you." But she cried too. What did *they* have to cry about? He stiffened his body and withdrew from her encircling arms as much as he could. He frowned.

And now Papa's eyes were dry and piteous on him. And now Papa was smiling and putting his hand on his shoulder. Aaron let it rest there. "How do you feel, my son? How are you?"

Aaron put his forefinger against his upper lip and rolled his eyes away. "I'm all right."

"Come, we will fix you something to eat. Come, Muriel, we will fix your brother something to eat."

Muriel fried the eggs. Papa set the plates out.

When, smiling, they called him to the table he ate obediently, stuffing the food down.

When he was finished he went to the bathroom. He knew this would happen. He vomited the food. He tried to vomit it quietly so they would not hear. There were so many secrets now.

They didn't go back to bed. Papa went to work. Muriel went to the office where she worked.

He was glad when they were gone. He knew the one thing he wanted more than anything else in the world. He built a fire in the garbage burner. Quickly shed his army uniform. He put it in the fire. He poked it to quicker flame. He chuckled at the smell of charred cloth. He laughed at the sight of flames in the olive drab like vengeful daggers. Never, never, never. He watched the fire eat the uniform. One prison was gone. Never, never, never.

Now that the anger is over, now that the deed is done, now we can speak, under the sun. That he thought. And stabbed the uniform viciously with the poker. Now we can speak . . . no . . .

And suddenly his head ached. He hoped he wouldn't vomit again. He wandered into the next room. He didn't even look at his desk. He went to his cot and threw his large, almost fat, awkward form across it. He drew his body up into a knot with his arms between his legs and his head curled in. . . .

He couldn't sleep. He got up. His hands were sweating profusely. He hated that. He dried them on his handkerchief, almost scrubbing them.

What happened to the morning and the afternoon he did not know. He had wanted to get out of the house before they came home. And there was Muriel standing in the door, shouting in cheerfully that she had stopped by and told Rebecca that he was home, and that she was coming over to see him.

"I don't want to see her," he told his sister. "Not yet—I mean. . . . "

"All right, Aaron."

"She doesn't know—about—?" he asked, watching his sister suspiciously.

She shook her head no and began to cry.

"Aw, for Christ sake—shut up!"

In a very few minutes there was the sound of running footsteps and a sharp, happy knocking at the door. Muriel looked at Aaron. He shook his head no. He closed the door of the second room and sat behind it.

The outer door had opened and he could hear Rebecca saying quickly, happily, "Oh, Muriel, where is he?" And a pause—and Muriel saying, "He wasn't here when I got home."

"Oh." That was Rebecca. Her voice dwindled in disappointment. "Tell him—tell him to come over when he gets home."

Behind his door Aaron sat grim, silent, moody. His tension relaxed only when he had heard the outer door close.

He got out of the house. He didn't even look at Muriel when he left.

Night crouched over the city. Crouched and hung there in a ghostly blue-blackness. Aaron walked under the night sky. He wanted to see Steve. He wanted to talk to Steve. The wind put his hair on end. He brushed it smooth with his hand. He didn't want to see Milo or O'Keefe. He wouldn't know what to say to them.

He walked into Thompson's. O'Keefe was alone there at a table. When O'Keefe saw him he looked at him in surprise and pleasure, a slow smile coming to his face. "Aaron! Well, well!" He grasped Aaron's hand and pulled him down into the chair across the table. "It's good to see you!" He made no mention of the fact that Aaron wasn't in his uniform. Aaron slumped in the chair across the table and looked at him with pleading eyes. O'Keefe seemed not to notice.

"Where's Milo?" Aaron asked, not knowing what else to say.

O'Keefe ran the palm of his hand along the edge of the table and glanced down at it. "Milo's in a C. O. camp."

Aaron looked at O'Keefe. So, Milo had gone through with it. "Is Steve in the army?"

O'Keefe smiled with slow, tight lips. "They didn't want him. They were never going to take him, all that time he ran around here with that—oh awful—doleful face—looking for sympathy because he was going into the army and be killed."

"How's Dave?"

O'Keefe looked across the table at Aaron. "In jail," he said. "He was a conscientious objector too, you know."

"Yes, I know," Aaron said. That didn't surprise him either. Nor could he feel sorrow. Just a gloomy tension inside. Then, quietly, "Sean—"

O'Keefe glanced up at him. Aaron looked into Sean O'Keefe's face. "I'm not in the army any more."

O'Keefe rubbed his chin and waited. Aaron didn't speak again immediately. O'Keefe smiled in his shy, polite way. "No?"

"No," Aaron said. "I'm out for keeps. I just got out of the veterans' hospital. I lost my mind." His voice was very calm, slightly humorous.

Someone came up to the table and put a hand on Aaron's shoulder. "Hello, keed!"

Aaron glanced over his shoulder and felt relief. "Hello, Steve. I cracked up," Aaron said in the same quiet, half-humorous voice. He felt relieved talking about it, not so depressed now. He smiled a little, at Sean and at Steve. But his eyes were pleading, wistful eyes, filled with an enormous sorrow. His voice was a voice that could break into weeping at any moment. Steve was smiling a little. Sean O'Keefe averted his eyes from Aaron's tense face and rubbed the soles of his shoes against the floor in embarrassment. Aaron said, in that quiet, quiet, monotonously half-humorous voice, "The army said we're sorry, first from a selfish viewpoint, then from a Christian viewpoint. We'll keep you for a little while and then we'll turn you loose." He shook his head in a large and impotent protest. "A wounded man is better off—a man who comes back wounded to some family warmth has something. A man whose mind is shot—just turn him loose—" Again he shook his head back and forth. And was silent.

He saw his hands on the table in front of him. He saw them trembling agitatedly. He withdrew them and put them in his lap so that the others couldn't see. Coarse tremor of both hands, they called it. The psychiatrists called it.

O'Keefe went for coffee and brought it back. "Here, Aaron," he said cheerfully, setting the cup in front of him. Steve had been saying something with his lips drawn down in a cynical smile. O'Keefe drew his chair back to the table noisily. He rubbed the palms of his hands together and lowered his nose to the steaming cup. "*Ummmmmm!* Smells good!" he said, smiling across the table at Aaron. Steve laughed. Aaron averted his eyes. O'Keefe said, "Look, Aaron, some of us were meant maybe to be soldiers. Some—" He shrugged. "You're better off here at home. You can go on with your life as before."

Aaron was staring at a war headline in bold black type across the front of the newspaper that a man at the next table was reading. "They're killing so many," Aaron said, shaking his head slowly back and forth in protest.

Steve leaned his face over the table at them. Dissipation was cut into every line of it. He said, "I can only see men as zeros. I have seen them that way for years. I think of us as people who dwell in caves and live in trees. We're all killers."

"Well, there's the tiger and the ant," O'Keefe said. He slurred it at Steve. His eyes narrowed at him. "And after all, maybe the ant is a better citizen than the tiger." He picked Aaron up with his eyes now. He leaned forward and said, in great earnestness and for Aaron, "A man shouldn't cut himself off from the world. A man shouldn't shut himself up in a cave. He shouldn't be allowed to. The race needs every man."

"Aw—" Steve said, motioning a deriding hand at O'Keefe, "we're all killers. Only the hallelujahs and the theorists and the economic messiahs say anything else."

O'Keefe stood up. He tightened his lips. He stared at Steve and nodded his head in anger as if making up his mind finally and irrevocably about him. He gathered up his newspaper, stuffed it in his pocket and walked out of the restaurant.

"You hurt Sean when you said that," Aaron told Steve.

"I'll say anything in front of O'Keefe," Steve said, "because the man defeats me."

Aaron looked at Steve with his wistful eyes. "In camp," he said gesturing awkwardly, "I said sunlight must be someplace. Wait for the sunlight." He shook his head.

"You're not crazy," Steve said. "It's them, the goddamn bastards." He began giving Aaron his tools that he used against the world. "All of them out there. Each guy trying to get the better of the other guy. Everybody out for himself. It's a stinking world, keed." He smiled a little. "People are pigs." He sneered at all of the pigs.

Then he was silent for a long time, bitter and brooding. Aaron felt himself relax and become calm. He felt better, better than he had felt since before he had enlisted.

Steve said, "Yeah, you're not like them, so you're crazy. You don't like war. You don't like to kill. You're crazy. You're an artist. You're crazy. You want to build. You don't want to tear down. You're crazy." And suddenly Steve was silent.

Aaron leaned forward on his elbows with his head between his hands and stared at the table in abstraction. . .

. . . he had to go home. He must go home. He had to hurry home. . . .

He got up from the table. He walked rapidly through the door. He started hurrying for home. He became excited. He started to run. He slowed to a walk. But he still felt like running.

He looked up at the sky. It is Sunday, three-thirty in the afternoon, black rolling clouds overhead and rain. The area around the barracks is filled with large yellow-gray puddles of rain water. Most of the men are resting in their bunks, their faces blank and calm, their eyes following the grain in the wood along the ceiling. I know what most of them are thinking about: home. They move steadily on waves of thought through the thick curtains of rain, beyond the hills, along large strips of wasteland, above the green tips of tall trees, along the snakelike shoreline of streams at the edge of forests. Faster and faster. Past telephone poles along the highways and muddy roads. Faster and faster. Above farmhouses and silos and church steeples and barns. Faster and faster. Crashing down through the tall, sharp, wet grass in the valley. Faster and faster . . . then home . . . home at last . . . up the stairs, and you knock on the door! Ma opens the door. You rush in and grab her around the waist and dance like a pair of kids through every room in the apartment. The rain has stopped. The slowly setting sun breaks through the clouds and wraps its rays around your heads and dances with you. You are both breathing heavily and you fall on the sofa in the corner and laugh and laugh. You kick off your shoes, throw your legs up on her soft lap and close your eyes. "Gee, it's swell to be home." There is no rain, only warm rays from a slowly setting sun. "Gee, it's swell to be home." You know you're home. You can feel home. You can taste home. "Gee—"

"Gee—it's swell to be home," she says, laughing and twisting the short hairs along your hairline. "Gee it's swell to be home." The music stops. The dream ends. It is still raining. The ceiling is an ugly thing to keep looking at. . . .

He wondered where his mother was. He rubbed one eye with his knuckle. He walked alone in the lonely city and up the lonely steps to home.

At home he looked at his belongings for the first time. His desk. His papers. Dust-gray. He would never write again. He touched his desk, his papers, with alien fingers. He picked up the inkwell still stuck with the turkey feather quill. He looked at it and thought, Put them in fear, O Lord, that the nations may know themselves to be but men. . . .

The desk drawer sliding open. Inside, covered with the dust-gray, the one record, "Clair de Lune." His record . . . his? Belonging to that other Aaron Levin now long dead. He took the record in his hands. He sat on the side of his cot. He began to hum the tune with the record hugged to his chest, and, swaying back and forth . . . he began to cry. Men cry as much as women. They don't tell. . . .

He should go to bed. In the hospital (the kind word they used for the asylum) he would have been in bed long ago.

He lay a long time. Always, always so hard to go to sleep. Feeling of tension. Depression. Fear. What was he afraid of? He hoped he wouldn't have to get up to vomit. He should have stayed on the street walking all night long . . . then maybe . . . sleep. . .

. . . he began tumbling downward into the chaotic night.

When he awakened it was because the bed was damp beneath him. He jumped and his heart beat fast. Then he knew where he was. No guards. No soldiers. No hydrotherapy. No electric shock. Again he felt the dampness beneath him. Slowly, cautiously, he got out of the bed. Carefully he pulled the covers back. He stared at the bed. Then put his hand over his eyes. He had wet the bed. He hadn't done that since he was eleven.

He hid the sheet. He couldn't let Papa or Muriel find out about this.

He pulled on his socks. He put on his right shoe first, without lacing it, then the left. He laced the left shoe. Finally his fingers reached down to lace the right shoe. Then he stopped his action. He hadn't performed this Jewish custom since he was a little boy and went to the heder. Not since he had lost his religion . . . yes, once since, once in the hospital. He had thought he was back in the heder. And then a soldier uniform had shattered that picture. Any morning at home he could look through the door and see Papa putting his shoes on that way.

He took off his shoes, tearing at them to get them off in a hurry. He would put them on without any ritual.

They were off now and he'd reach down and just put on whichever one he happened to touch first. He reached down. And he knew where he was . . .

. . . that fleeting moment of recognition—where you are—before you reach down to put on your shoes—where you are, what you are—for the rest of your life.

This, then, was his postwar certainty. This, forever and ever, always and always. It was the worst kind of prison. He had seen men tied down in flesh and blood, ready to die. Men imprisoned to whole large families they had to support, having to go to a hateful job every day of their lives all their lives long. There were men and women imprisoned with fatal, incurable diseases, dying by inches and knowing it. Men serving life sentences. Men going to gallows. But nothing as horrible as this.

His eyes were like a child's eyes rolling in his head. He looked at everything in fright. In a pleading stare. He had been pronounced unbalanced. Insane. He knew nothing could be done for him. He knew he was in prison to insanity for life.

He turned his head to the side and scratched his chin against his shoulder. He felt like crying. He cried so much. They say, the fine doctors say, that crying takes away the tension, keeps people sane.

Again he scratched his chin against his shoulder and stared at the floor. I'm psycho! I'm psycho. I'm Psycho 1944!

He wandered into the next room. Some music from the radio slithered its tune into his ears.

*God bless America*
*Land that I love*
*Stand beside her and guide her . . .*

His gun. His country. These things have been told me above all things that be. Do it in a stomach beyond protest. Do it in a day beyond reproach.

*From the mountains to the prairies*
*To the oceans white with foam*
*God bless America—My home sweet home* **

He drifted back to the room, to consciousness, to contact with reality.

"Goddamn it!" he yelled at Muriel. "Turn that radio off."

Kate Smith was saying, "That soldier boy of yours is waiting for a letter right now. Remember, if you don't write, you're wrong." And click! Muriel had turned Kate Smith's voice off. He lay again on his cot.

Papa Levin awakened and as every morning, as it had been taught him, thought of God and his own soul and whispered, "My God, the soul that thou gavest me is pure. Thou hast created it, thou hast formed it, thou has breathed it into me. . . . "

Papa Levin arose. He went into the kitchen. He glanced sadly toward the door to the other room and the large form of his son twisted in sleep on the cot. My son! My son! He fixed and ate his breakfast. He put on his hat and his denim work jacket and went toward the door. He lifted the little door of the mezuzah and saw the word *Shaddai.* He touched it devoutly with his finger tip and then kissed his finger. He went down the steps toward the early morning streetcar.

First his wife and now his son. He sadly rubbed the back of his hand across his chin. When his wife—he had mourned her as if she were dead. In the Jewish custom. For seven days he had not gone to work. He had put off his shoes. He had reversed the bed. He had remained indoors. He had not cut the hair of his head or his face for the prescribed time. All the water in the house had been poured into the street. And he had rent his clothing at the neck to the extent of a hand-breadth.

Papa Levin sat on a side seat on the streetcar, drawing his shoulders and legs in tightly against his body in his agony. His thin head lowered and his chin rested on his slight chest. His boy. He had tried to do right. He could not get him redeemed because he was not from a Jewish mother. But on the legal day, as in Bible times, on the eighth day after the boy's birth, he had taken him to be circumcised. A godfather had been there. And a chair in readiness for Elijah. Everything was as it should be. He had tried to be a good father. He had tried so hard to do the right thing. Always he had tried to be one of the first ten men saying their prayers at the synagogue. Why was this affliction on him? Why must his boy suffer?

Papa Levin worked overtime and came home when it was dark. Opening the door he saw a figure shrink into the shadows against the wall. He took the girl gently by the arm. "Child, why are you here?"

"I—I thought that maybe Aaron would come out and I could—I could see him," Rebecca said with her head down.

Papa Levin looked closely at her. Muriel had told him that each night Rebecca waited in the hall to see Aaron. Not since Aaron had been home had she seen him. Papa Levin patted her gently on the shoulder. "I will see if he is home," he told her.

Papa Levin tiptoed quietly up the steps and to the door. With a soft hand he cracked the door open a few inches. In the front room

Aaron sat alone, moving the fingers of one hand on his knee with his other hand.

Papa Levin tiptoed to the steps. With all his fingers he motioned Rebecca up the steps. He nodded his head and pointed toward the door. He went down the steps quietly, aiding his descent by holding to the banister.

Aaron went into the toilet. He leaned over the bowl. They were dry heaves that left him gasping and his eyes running. But only dry heaves. He was getting better.

When he went back into the front room Rebecca was sitting on the edge of his cot. Her hands were clasped together in her lap. She was afraid to look up.

"Rebecca," he said, and "how did you get here?"

She looked up slowly, frightenedly. "The door—it was open."

She had no more to say but only sat there with her head down. He sat in a chair looking at her. She was pretty. He saw that. Wearily he realized that she was pretty. Thick, thick chestnut hair. Curly. Her skin was so white. Creamy. Unmoved he noted each detail of her face and figure. Pretty. She didn't use any makeup. Didn't need it. Only the birthmark was bad. Red-brown. On an otherwise perfectly featured and formed face. She looked up quickly, and down. He saw her eyes in their rapid flight to his face and away. Green eyes. Heavily lashed. Full breasts. A good figure. He catalogued abstractly, removed from any personal feeling. How old was she now? Seventeen. Almost, anyway.

He ran his hand wearily over his eyes and forehead. "I was sick," he said.

It was as if she had waited for his words. She sprang from the cot and ran to him. She put her arms around him.

"Don't," he said. She lowered her arms; and her eyes.

"I was sick," he said again, monotonously.

"It doesn't matter," she said.

"It should matter."

"It doesn't matter." She put the palm of her hand up across her birthmark as was a habit with her. "It doesn't matter," and very simply, "I love you."

"Do you," he said dully. How can she understand the life I am now? She can't follow me where I'm going. She's too normal. Too sane. She should marry some nice bookkeeper. Two rooms and the bathroom down the hall.

Standing alongside him, she had put her hand into his hair. She smoothed it off his forehead, stroking it back into place. He let her. Her stroking hand felt good. He thought of his mother. Funny that he should think of his mother. He wondered if she had ever stroked his hair. "I've got to go out," he said.

Swiftly Rebecca slipped down on his lap. She took his head between her hands. She kissed him swiftly on the lips. Many times. He let her. Too sane. She put her cheek against his. Too sane. "I've got to go out," he said again and stood up slowly. "I'll see you," he said. He smiled at her. It was a superior smile.

"When, Aaron? When?"

"Soon," he said. Too sane.

He went out. He walked. Walked. Walked. From out a tavern door he heard a juke box blare:

*Well, huba huba huba*
*Hello, Jack!*
*Well, huba huba huba*
*I just got back.*
*Well, huba huba huba*
*Let's shoot some breeze*
*What's the sit-u-a-tion*
*With the Nipponese? . . .*

Aaron stood for a moment on the sidewalk in front of the tavern door. He clamped his hands over his ears and moved on down the sidewalk. Behind him the music said:

*. . . Well a friend of mine*
*In a B-29*
*Dropped another load*
*For luck.*
*As he flew away*
*He was heard to say . . .*

Aaron wandered aimlessly, helplessly, through the night streets. I'm psycho! I'm psycho! I'm Psycho 1944!

# III

*the spider taketh hold with her hands and*
*is in kings' palaces*

He set his duffel bag on the sidewalk and stood at the gate in his khaki uniform, looking over the fence at the little two-story frame house. The dog, barking wildly, came bursting down the steep flight of steps on its short legs, and with his tail wagging furiously, ran along the sidewalk to the fence as fast as he could. He jumped against the fence with his front legs and began yapping happily. Jim put his hand wearily inside the gate and let the dog lick it. Then he saw his wife.

She had come out on the little second-floor porch. Her face paled and she put her hand up against her neck. In the other arm she carried the baby he had never seen.

Jim's eyes watched Louise coming down the steep stairs to meet him. The dog barked and ran around excitedly, racing halfway up the steps toward Louise and then back down them toward Jim. The dog barked and tried to leap the fence. It was then, in the tall trampled-down grass, that Jim saw his other child playing with a large wooden soldier. The boy had grown. He must be three—three and a half years old. How old was he anyway?

Jim was still looking in at the boy when his wife got to the fence.

"You didn't let me know you were coming, Jim," she said. Her face was strained and excited.

"No," he said. "I guess I wanted to surprise you."

Louise opened the gate.

He picked up his duffel bag and set it on the sidewalk inside the fence. He put his arms around her and kissed her. The dog jumped against his legs and ran around him in a circle, snapping playfully at his trouser cuffs.

Louise was crying.

"This is your other son," Louise said. She offered the baby to Jim. He took the child, looking at it strangely. So—this was the one he had never seen. The one Louise had given birth to, alone, in pain and suffering, when he was overseas.

Louise wiped her cheeks on her apron. She was smiling now, and her eyes moved across his face, up and down the form of him, back to his face. She took him by the hand and led him down the sidewalk toward the steps. "Jimmy!" she called. "Jimmy!" The little boy rose from the ground and came forward gravely, carrying the wooden soldier in one hand. "He looks like you," Louise said, laughing with her voice close to tears. "Remember, I said I wanted all my children to look like you. This is your daddy, Jimmy," she said, squatting on her heels and pushing the child's hair out of his eyes. "I told you your daddy was a soldier and that he would be home one day." She looked up into Jim's face, and laughing, said, "Every soldier that he saw he'd ask me 'Is that my daddy?' "

"Hi there, fellow!" Jim said to his son.

"Are you my daddy?" the child asked.

"You bet I am!" He handed the baby back to his wife. From the boy's hand he took the wooden soldier and threw it over the fence and into the street. Then he lifted the boy up into his arms and carried him up the steps behind Louise and the baby.

"Home," Louise said.

"Home," Jim said. He sat down wearily on a chair in the kitchen. He had waited for this moment. He had lived for it. Across the room, seated on a stool, little Jimmy sat silently watching his daddy. Louise put the baby in its crib. "Jim!" she called from the bedroom. He got up and went to her. "Look!" she said. She had opened the drawer and she showed him his civilian clothes. She held his trousers in her hand and put her arms around him.

When they had kissed again he took the trousers. His hands shook a little. "I'll put them on," he said. He took off his army cap.

"Oh Jim!" Louise said, looking at his hair. It had been cut so short that it stood up on his head in a half-inch turf.

He rubbed his head and grinned. "It'll grow back." Louise threw her arms around him and searched again for his mouth. He stiffened a little and held her off. "I'm tired," he said. Louise looked at him and lowered her eyes. She remembered what she had read in books on the rehabilitation of GIs. She smiled at him. "I'm sure you are."

He was glad to get into his civilian clothes again. He was surprised that the trousers still fit.

When he had changed into the trousers and stood barefooted in them and nothing else, Louise came into the room. Her eyes were bright, bright with tears and laughter. She came to him and ran her hands over his shoulders, his arms and down to his hands. She held his hands and stood looking into his eyes. "Not a scratch!" she said, looking at him. "Oh, Jim, we're lucky!"

He looked back at her. Not a scratch? He wondered.

Louise took the baby from its crib. She handed it to Jim and then left them together in the bedroom. She went into the kitchen but a moment later tiptoed back to the door to see how Jim and the baby were getting along.

Jim had put the baby back into the crib and was staring out the window. His shoulders were slumped, his hands listless on the window sill.

Louise turned back into the kitchen. From the shelf she got one of his pipes and took it to him, carrying it in both hands. "Here, Jim."

"Huh? He turned back from the window with moody eyes. "Oh! Thanks."

He lit his pipe. Then he took her hand and drew her down alongside him on the bed. They sat there, he holding her hand and smoking. He had thought about it for months, being back with Louise. Sure, he was glad to be back. He was glad to see her. But he wondered why he didn't feel anything. All he really felt was being all dried up inside. Forget it! Don't go moody. Don't spoil things. He let his body fall back against the bed and made the springs squeak under him. "God, Louise, it feels good to be back home! Have a bed to sleep in."

She lay alongside of him for a while with her arm around him. Then she sat up. "I'm going to cook dinner."

After they had eaten, Jim said suddenly, "Let's go out and celebrate!"

"But the baby—" Louise said.

He was irritated. She could see it in his face. And she too wanted to go out and be with him in a homecoming celebration.

"Maybe Mrs. Bush—" she said. She ran down the steps and next door to ask Mrs. Bush if she would watch the children. Then she ran back upstairs, laughing breathlessly, and began to dress.

They walked down Wieland Street. Jim held Louise's arm. Halfway down the block he tightened his fingers on her arm and brought her to a halt there alongside him. She looked up at him in surprise. Jim was looking at the honor roll attached to the flagpole in the little cleared space of a vacant lot in tribute to the city block's soldiers. The names were dim and weather-beaten. Some had gold stars in front of them. The place was unattended. Weeds grew where flowers had once grown. The whitewash had peeled away from the decorative stones.

When he had finished looking, Jim moved on down the sidewalk with his wife. He was very silent. They turned down North Avenue. They went to the Vine Gardens.

"Let's have champagne," he said.

He sat staring at his hand. Then he grinned at her and made a face. She took his hand and, sitting beside him at the bar, swung it back and forth. All around them, couples were laughing and dancing and talking. Funny. He should be happy. He only felt tense and immeasurably sad. Funny, goddamn funny.

. . . He had wanted to see his wife but was in no hurry to get home. He had taken the bus to Chicago. When they had arrived at Chicago he had bought a ticket to Omaha and had ridden the bus in the night, not three miles from home, out of Chicago. . . . Then he had gone to the West Coast.

He ordered another drink. And another. Louise didn't force him to talk. She didn't try to make conversation. She didn't stare at him. He felt a throb of love and drank again. He looked at her and was surprised to see that she had aged. There were lines around her eyes. Not distinct. But there. All the time, overseas, he had thought of her as the most wonderful woman in the world. Beautiful, too. Louise glanced quickly at him, smiled, and then looked away. He noticed her thin neck. She wouldn't be a good-looking elderly woman. Let's see, how old is she? I'm thirty-one. She's thirty-three.

"Let's have another," he said. He ordered another round. . . .

On the bus. His head against the seat of the bus. Looking out. Farmers contributed more than any city dweller to the welfare of the country. More than industrialists. Looking out the bus window at passing scenery . . . there was a vulture sitting on each of those chimneys there. But if you told the farmers about it they wouldn't even get their guns. There was a banker sucking blood out of the soil over there. . . . And a broker picking apples in the orchard over there. . . . And the bus carrying him his restless way across the country.

He tapped the bar with his glass for another round. . . . In Portland he had walked along Burnside and Third Avenue, gone into the taverns of the city's Skid Row and watched the card players at their round tables beyond the bar. He had talked to the Negroes, Chinese, Japanese, the lumberjacks and dock workers, the labor union men. He had slept in a flophouse there. He had gotten off the bus in strange towns and wandered around, slept in strange hotel rooms. The bus had dipped down into California.

Jim ordered another drink. Louise had never seen him drink so much before. He drank silently, speaking to her only once in a while. He didn't get drunk though. Just drank. She was not having a good time, nor was he. But both of them tried to pass it off as a swell evening. At last Louise touched his arm. "The children," she said.

A high, piping Italian voice sounded along the bar. The middle-aged Italian man carried a large basket of artificial flowers and trinkets bulging and pushing their way to the top and over the sides. Gaudy flowers. Pins made of sea shells. Little Hawaiian dolls made out of pipe cleaners, and frozen in dance poses. "Pretty flowers, mister, for the pretty lady," the man said to every couple along the bar. And now he stood beside Louise and Jim.

"Pretty flowers, mister, for the pretty lady."

"She hates flowers," Jim said laughing.

Louise pinched Jim's arm in protest.

"Looka pretty!" the vendor said, holding one against Louise's hair for Jim to see.

"No, we don't want any, Bud," Jim said in slight irritation.

"No," Louise said, smiling at the man and shaking her head. She looked beyond the man at Jim carefully.

"Looka, lady, maybe you lika dis?" the Italian voice said. "I maka myself." He held up a pin made from a sea shell. "Painta myself." He was very excited about his art work.

"I don't think we want anything," Louise said.

The bartender started down along the bar to tell the vendor to leave the customers alone.

"Looka, maybe you lika dis." He held up one of the dancing Hawaiian dolls and, wiggling it between his fingers, made it dance on the air.

Scowling, Jim looked up from his glass. Then he saw the doll. "Say, that's kind of cute!"

"You lika? How many you want, one, two, three?"

"Isn't that cute?" Jim said to Louise. "Do you want one?"

"Oh, I don't think so, Jim."

The bartender began wiping the bar in front of Jim. "Is he bothering you?" he asked Jim.

"Oh, no!" Jim said; and to Louise, "Don't you want one? You want one, don't you, hon?"

The vendor looked at Louise and tried to coax her with his eyes and did his own little dance with waving hands and patting foot.

Looking at Jim and smiling, Louise shook her head. Then she saw the disappointment in Jim's eyes. "Yes, I think I *would* like one, Jim," she said.

Jim paid for it and Louise put it in her purse. Again she touched Jim on the arm. "The children—"

They went to bed. He tried to make love to her brusquely and without tenderness. His hands were rough on her. His love-making was almost like a rape. Louise was shocked at his violence. And in the end he had been impotent.

She lay away from him, puzzled, worried, rubbing the wrinkles from her forehead with the palm of her hand. Mustn't worry.

"I'm sorry, honey," he said. His voice sounded like that of a boy.

Time. The adjustment period. She had read about all of this adjustment period. But it worried her anyway. She smoothed her forehead with her hand.

"Did you hear that?" Jim asked in the bed next to her.

"What, dear?"

"That noise."

"Relax, honey," she said, putting her hand on top of his.

Jim threw back the covers. He got out of bed and turned on the light. "I thought I heard a noise," he said. He tried the windows. He tried the door. Then he came back to bed.

The days passed into a week. Jim was restless. He took frequent walks or sat home holding his clasped hands between his knees. His walks sometimes lasted two or three hours. Sometimes he walked only to the corner before returning home. His thoughts were a mingling of a nameless fear and horror and guilt, a confusion of action, a dulled memory of deafening sounds. In the tensed quietness of his own home, with sunlight on the floor and the baby gurgling in its crib, he could actually hear—in the dullest rumblings—the sounds of battle. Sometimes in the night he would awaken with a start and lie trembling, staring at the ceiling. During the days his mind began to run over the names of his buddies, those dead and alive. A longing to see them . . . death, always death: coming to them or given by them. Death. Constant companion.

He was irritated when the baby cried or little Jimmy demanded too much of Louise's time. Irritated and angry at himself for his irritation, for he knew he had no cause.

At night he got up and investigated the slightest sound. Sometimes he arose five or six times, peering out the window into the dark, trying the door, before he could go to sleep to be pursued across his sleeping by the menace that was sound and movement and terror and hopelessness.

At night in bed he was often impotent these first few weeks. And sometimes it was only like emptying his bladder. He was angry at Louise about this. Angry at her because, somehow, she could not give him comfort and assurance and confidence, though she tried. Her solicitude at night angered him, and her saddened glances during the day.

Then one day he opened a cardboard carton where some of his things had been packed away. He began sorting things, discarding some, piling a few old pipes on the dresser. Then, when the box was almost empty and he was reaching down into it, he saw his harmonica.

He drew his hand away, shuddering. He stared at the harmonica a long time. Then he went and sat on the window sill with his hands over his face. He sat there for ten minutes with his face in his hands and the noontime sun gilding his back and the blond hair on top of his slumped head.

At last he stood up, heavily, moved through the rooms and, without telling Louise where he was going, went out onto the street and to the tavern. He didn't get back until after ten that night.

Louise was sitting in the front room looking worried. "Just don't say anything," he said. "Please don't say anything." He staggered toward the bedroom. His shoulder hit the door and he went inside. He sat on the side of the bed and unlaced his shoes. Louise watched him undress, pull the covers over his head and turn his face toward the wall.

Then one day, a week later, he asked where the garage keys were and went down, opened the doors, looked in at his old Chevie. He lifted the hood. He pumped up the tires and lowered the car off the jacks it had been stored on. A few minutes later the tinny sound of the motor could be heard and his head was thrust under the hood tuning it up.

Then one day he said suddenly, in his first mention of it, "How's the union doing?"

Louise sighed in relief—at last he had mentioned it. "Oh, darling, we ran off so many pamphlets! I—why I cranked that machine all day long! But things are going swell. Of course Emerson Bradley"—she pushed hair off her forehead—"is still trying to kill the union but we're here to stay." She came behind him and put her arms around his shoulders. "Mr. Baker and Kovac came here several times to bring the carbons and helped me run the pamphlets off."

Jim blinked. So Kovac had been there.

He didn't know why he thought that. He tightened his hands and loosened them.

"They were very nice," Louise said, "and they always asked about you—oh, I wrote you all that."

"Not that Kovac had been here," Jim said looking at her carefully.

"You must have forgotten," she said, kissing him on top of the head. She wrinkled her nose from the tickling in his short-bushed blond hair. "I'm going down to the grocery."

She went instead to the drugstore and telephoned union headquarters. She talked to Mr. Baker.

The next day a car drove up in front of the house. A man got out. Little Jimmy was playing in the tall grass and came forward when the man opened the gate. The boy had a toy gun in his hand. "Are you a robber?" he asked the man.

"No," the man said, chuckling, "I'm a policeman." He went up the stairs and knocked. Jim opened the door.

"Mr. Baker!" Jim grinned and, holding out his hand, pulled him across the doorsill. "Come in! Louise, guess who's here! Mr. Baker!"

When she came into the front room Jim and Mr. Baker had their chairs drawn close together and were discussing the union.

An hour later Jim walked to the door with Mr. Baker and stood watching him walk to the gate toward his car. Little Jimmy came from the grass with the toy pistol in his hand. "Are you a robber?"

Mr. Baker smiled and patted the boy on his head. Little Jimmy put the toy gun through the picket fence and began to shoot the tires out from under his car.

Jim saw the boy. He ran down the steps angrily and along the sidewalk. He stopped and looked down at his boy as Mr. Baker's car drove away. "Come on now, son. Put that gun down." He smacked the child across the behind, half playfully, half in command, with the big palm of his hand.

# Book Four

## EVENING

### I

In the cities there had been young men wearing uniforms. Each day now more civilian clothes appeared on the streets. It was the time of peace.

And the city moves its million faces over sidewalk and streetcar track and its great heart pounds on in its three million pulsation and the city does its work, day by day, of being a going concern, a big, impersonal place of mortar and brick and asphalt and steel. The crowd moves, shoulder to shoulder, hip to hip. The eyes brush, unseeing or cold or impersonal.

In the city, in that crowd of people on the Near North Side, Don walked. In that crowd Aaron walked aimlessly.

Suddenly from out of the crowd of people a voice called to Aaron. Aaron halted and looked around. It was Max. Max was in his sailor uniform. "Oh." Aaron dropped his eyes. "Hello, Max."

"Hi, Aaron! How are you?" His hand grasped Aaron's and his other hand patted his shoulder while his face grinned in all its tan Mexican friendliness.

"I'm okay," Aaron said. With Max was another sailor swinging a white duffel bag from one arm.

"You're looking good," Max said to Aaron.

"Yeah."

"S'good to get out of service, huh?" Max said. "You feeling good?"

"Yeah. I'm feeling all right."

"S'good to be back, huh?" Again the warm Mexican grin.

Aaron nodded.

"Well, pal," Max said, grinning even more broadly. "I'll see you, huh?"

"Yeah, I'll see you."

Aaron hurried away.

Leaving Aaron, Max and his friend climbed a flight of steps and knocked.

The Negro looked out of his brown face at the southern boy. The southern boy was long, lean, slightly humpbacked in his navy jacket, the ropes of his white duffel bag winding around his wrist and fitting into the folded palm of his hand in a handle. The Negro smiled in a friendly manner, but with a slight reserve. He wondered if the sailor was embarrassed. Or felt prejudice. Or would try to be polite. He wondered if Max had told him that he was a Negro and glanced quickly at Max.

The Mexican boy pushed in between them in his sailor's uniform and threw an arm around the shoulders of each. His light tan face shone in many highlights as it tightened with his grin and his black, black eyes hid in little slits. "Dave," he said to the Negro, "this is Ollie." "Ollie," he said to the southern boy, "this is Dave." And Max grinned again, looked proudly from one to the other.

The duffel bag, suspended a few inches from the floor, came from its little swaying back and forth and settled to the rug. Ollie stuck out his hand. He took and squeezed Dave's hand. "I wanted to meet you, Dave," he said. It was a southern voice, soft, the words flowing one into the other in a quiet rhythm. "Max told me all about you. He told me about you and Milo. He told me about all his friends but he always came back to you. And I told him 'I'm coming to Chicago after the war before I go home. I want to meet your folks, Max, and I want to meet that guy Dave.' "

"Max wrote to me about you too," Dave said politely.

"Not that I give a damn about either of you," Max said, moving them toward the front room with a warmly clenched hand on the shoulder muscle of each of them.

"You fellows had a lot of fun," Dave said.

Into the front room Dave brought the half-gallon bottle of beer and glasses. They sat, the three, facing each other. They sat, sipping the beer, looking from one to the other. One bottle. Two bottles. Three. These were hellos and good-bys. These were the best of words and the saddest of words. And the words had a flow of their own. The words flowed one into the other, loosely, from one subject to another.

The beer brought them closer. The beer loosened their secret thoughts and feelings. Made boys of them speaking their minds as boys of ten speak to their fathers, their mothers, their best friends in moments of confidence before they are men. Yet they were men by every known test. By every inherited right of war and death and hell and three years' continual fear. And it was fear and loneliness and horror that still gripped them.

They sat, speaking one to the other:

"Pete? . . . Pete? . . . Oh yeah . . . did he go across? . . . did I know him? Yeah, yeah, I knew him. Where did he live? Nobody knows where he lived."

And glasses refilled with beer.

"He knows everything about me," Max said, indicating Ollie with a jabbing thumb. "And I know everything about him. We don't hold nothing back. That's how close we are."

"You know, Dave," Ollie said, "we gave each other our letters before we opened them. Maybe his would be from his broad and mine would be from my wife."

Max refilled the three glasses. He lit three cigarettes in his mouth at one time and passed one to Dave, one to Ollie, kept one for himself. He looked, grinning in friendliness, at Ollie and Dave. "They say the war is over. Is it true?"

Smoke curled up toward the ceiling from the three cigarettes. The head of Dave, the head of Ollie, turned toward Max. Ollie spoke slowly, spreading his hand toward Max with the cigarette sending its trail upward between the clenched fingers. "Two things you got to realize—two things—you're out of the navy—and you're on your own." He laid his hand with the navy dogtag looped around its wrist on the blue knee of Max's bell-bottoms. "Don't screw up any more, Max. I got to leave you now. I got to leave you tomorrow after I meet your folks."

Max laughed. He put out his big hand and mussed Ollie's crew cut. "This big jerk," he said to Dave, "he's got a wife and three kids." He wrestled his arm around Ollie's neck until it was a vise across his Adam's apple, and squeezed hard.

When the beer stopped slopping out of the glasses and the table came down again on all its legs, having been almost overturned, Ollie turned to Dave. "That's right," he said. He pulled out his billfold and without words handed Dave a picture of his wife and children, mildewed, worn thin and dirty from the inside of the billfold across a whole war's time. Dave looked, and handed it back. "Dave," Ollie said to the Negro, "I haven't got much education. I'm not smart like you. I never went to high school. I never voted in my life. Now I'm going back home and I'm going to vote. I've seen things and I know you should vote." He sipped his beer slowly, looking over the rim of the glass at the far wall at nothing. He set the glass down. "I want my kids to get an education."

"Hey, pal!" Max shouted in gruff humor. "Pass the beer!"

"Keep quiet," Ollie said, lifting his fist and grinning. "I want to talk to Dave."

"We're home," Max said. "It's time to drink." He scowl-grinned in a menacing way. "Pass the bottle!"

"You've had enough. You're drunk now," Ollie said.

"*Ay chinga!*" Max said; and to Dave, "Hey, Dave—you know how I met that bastard? He walks in on his first day in our outfit and walks over to me—" Max pounded his hand into his chest. "Me! And you know what he asks me? He asks me if I want to have a drink. And now he's telling me I've had enough. And me the only Mexican in the outfit. An insult to my people!"

Grinning, Ollie shoved the bottle down along the table to Max. He turned again to Dave. It was a southern face, red-flecked, freckled, wrinkle lines around the eyes from the sun and wind; it smiled at Dave, the little blue eyes crinkling and the thin wrinkles stretching out across his temples toward the blond, half-curled hair. "You tell that damn fur-ner—" He pronounced it jokingly, the way they had on shipboard. The smile fell away from his face and his hand touched Dave's wrist. "You tell him to let Mercedes alone and marry Alma and settle down and be somebody."

"When the planes came over we wished we had some of this," Max said, drinking.

"The war's over, Max," Ollie said.

"Yeah. We can all go home. We can forget about it," Max said cynically.

"I got to leave him tomorrow, Dave. You see that this bastard doesn't start getting drunk all the time and screwing up like he was before he went away."

"I'll try," Dave said.

"I'm not good at talking," Ollie said. "I haven't got a good education like you and I can't explain—" Again he touched Dave's arm. "You and Max, you guys, come to Lexington and see me and my wife. We're poor. But we've got a extra room you can sleep in."

"Yes, we will," Dave said, knowing how impossible it was—he a Negro; Lexington, Kentucky; Ollie's house—but glad that Ollie, for the pleasant moment, had forgotten how impossible it was.

"The bottle," Max said, waving impatiently the fingers of his hand. "No," he said to Dave who offered the beer bottle. And Ollie, knowing, pulled a whisky flask from his pocket. "See, Dave?" Ollie said, as Max drank. "See what I mean?"

Max handed the flask back to Ollie. Ollie handed it to Dave. Dave took a drink. Then Ollie took a drink, corked the bottle and put it back into his pocket. "That's all, Max," he said.

Max grinned sheepishly, his eyes running off into slits.

"I don't know what I'm going back to—what kind of job I can get," Ollie said. "I used to shingle roofs."

"Look, Ollie," Max said. And he hitched his chair up close to Ollie's. He balled his hand into a fist in the collar of Ollie's jacket and shook him gently but urgently. "I want you to go back to your wife. I want you to go back to your kids and I want you to make them read! read! read! books! books! books—Hit them in the mouth with them! Kick them in the ass with them! But don't let them read trash. Don't let them read dime novels. Let them read books! books! books! Let them read Shakespeare. And give them another book. Give them *Crime and Punishment* so that they can see what a man's mind can do." Max had been talking with his face close to Ollie's and his fist in the cloth of Ollie's jacket. Now he let loose. Now he said, "Don't let them be damn fools like us!" Almost roughly he lifted his glass to his mouth. But he drank slowly, enjoyably.

"You know what I want to do?" Ollie said. "I want to cry. I just want to cry."

"Oh, you want to cry," Max said, razzing him.

"I want to cry," Ollie said. "I'm leaving you. I may never see you again. I have a feeling I will never see you again. We can have a big cry. Yeah! Sure! We can have a big cry." He said it roughly, yet wishing they could.

"I wish I could join you," Max said, "but I can't."

"More beer, guys?" Dave asked.

"You know when a plane comes down—when lots of planes come down—" Max said.

"Don't bring that up! Don't bring that up!" Ollie said in short, clipped, angry words.

"See?—See how you are?" Max said, raising his hands and arms in a puzzled and irritated gesture. "One minute you want to cry. The next minute you want to fight." Max grinned. "Pass your glass, bastard!" he said.

"They came in against us and we fought them off," Ollie said. "We won," he said.

Dave filled a glass and, eyes lowered, looking down into the amber fluid, he drank. Even when he set the glass down he did not look up.

Ollie stood in the room in his blue sailor's suit. Talking to no one but himself, he said, "Did you ever get the behind knocked out of you by an explosion? That happened to me. They did that to me. That happened to me." He took a few exploratory steps forward across the room and a few back. "It still hurts." He felt the base of his spine. "There's a sore spot there." He came back and sat down. "Look, Dave," he said, stretching the palms of his hand out for Dave to see. "My hands are calloused from using guns." He looked into Dave's eyes with a blue, unblinking stare. "It was *my* duty to put *my* fingers on the trigger." He turned again toward Max. "Max, damn you," he said, "I've cried over you. That's not because I like you. I think you're full of shit."

"They say the war is over. Is it true?" Max said, grinning.

"Yeah . . . them tears coming in my eyes," Ollie said. "I want to cry."

"I can't cry any more. My tears are gone," Max said.

"I got a bunch of tears in my eyes, Dave, about this guy. I'm a cry-baby," Ollie said.

"There was a time when I could cry," Max said. "I cried. Yes, I cried. Every goddamn man—woman—child cries. I can't cry any more. Now when it is necessary to cry I just think about it. That's all I can do."

# II

Leaving Max and Ollie, Aaron walked on.

Outwardly he had a calmness. He could wear a mask now. No one knew what went on inside him. No one would believe what went on inside him. He was improving. He knew it. He wouldn't have to go back to an asylum. Not if he took it easy. He would always be a little crazy. Genius is controlled insanity. Where had he read that? But he wouldn't have to go back to an asylum. No. Not that.

He looked up at the sky. The sky, heavy with clouds, was like a torn sheet of paper: *an open letter to all my friends:* . . . don't lose me, Steve, Sean, Milo . . . please write soon . . . don't lose me . . .

He looked up at the sky. The sky and the earth and the sea had been an enemy.

He walked into Thompson's. They were there at their tables, the people he knew.

He smiled at them and nodded and walked to O'Keefe's table.

Into the restaurant came Don Lockwood in his soldier's uniform and wearing his Purple Heart. A dowdy middle-aged woman at one of the front tables whispered loudly to her woman companion. "There's a war hero now!" Her eyes followed him the length of the restaurant.

Don laughed greetings to the people he knew and shouted "Hi! Hi!" He lifted his hand in salute to friends at a far table and mugged a grin as he approached them. He walked dramatically on his GI leg, about which everyone in the restaurant had heard. He made a dramatic scene of sitting down.

Someone at Don's table looked to the next table, and seeing Aaron, said hello to him.

Don swung around on his chair, making it seem more difficult to do than it was, and winced a smile. "Well! Hello there—ah—ah—Aaron!"

Aaron nodded. "Hello, Don."

Don rose from his chair laboriously and leaned way over the other table to shake hands. "So you're out of the service too. Where did they hit you?"

Aaron looked at Don for a moment and slowly withdrew his hand. "No, they missed." And to himself: I got hit right in the heart but they didn't give me a medal for it.

"Where were you?" Don asked.

"Europe," Aaron said.

"I was in Africa—lost it there," Don said. He tapped his false leg with his finger, hard. It gave its hollow sound. Then he sat down slowly, pressing the palm of his hand on the table and frowning at his own clumsiness.

Aaron slumped back in his chair. Thinking: there is a guy with a fettered body and here I am with a fettered mind. He can hobble away from himself. He picked a cigarette butt out of the ash tray and began peeling it open. The tobacco made a small pile on the table. With a burnt match he began shaping the tobacco into different designs.

In his mind Aaron had gotten up from the table and walked away. He was in another place at another time.

. . . at that moment, if it had been possible, he would have wept and laughed to see such sport. I would weep loudly and laugh loudly. I would recite Shakespeare and lines written on the bathroom wall aloud, because that's life, isn't it? From the sublime to the ridiculous. It is Sunday afternoon. The sun is combing her long, blond hair in the garden, while I sit on the porch in a comfortable leather-covered armchair behind bars.

. . . I'd been working in the genito-urinary ward in the hospital in Long View, California. A few nights ago I suffered from a spell of despondency. I took poison. I was rushed to the main building in the hospital and given emergency medical treatment. I had a notebook on me. They stole it. It wasn't much. A few poems. A famous quotation or two. Some notes I took in a small, cheap café in Los Angeles. It wasn't much, but they robbed my pockets, threw me into a dark room in D-16, the Psychopathic Hospital, and watched me twist and turn in bed all night, with saucer-large suspicious eyes. They whispered to one another all night. "Did you read his notebook? All sorts of crazy half-prose, half-poetry scribblings in it." I wanted to die just then and leave them weeping in the long, dark corridor of conscience, unable to sleep or eat or laugh for the rest of their lives. I wanted to die, but it was Aaron and not they who wept that horrible night.

. . . the next morning, a friendly psychiatrist questioning me, a major who didn't understand me. He may think he does, but I know differently. . . . I don't trust any of them, because I know they are soldiers rather than psychiatrists. I'll listen to what they have to say, co-operate with them and attempt to adjust myself to this new life.

. . . I have said this. But I am not worried for I have said nothing that will give the enemy any comfort. I have not revealed the movements of troops or war materials. I am not a seditionist or saboteur. I buy war bonds. I have absolutely no ties with foreign agents or powers. I am innocent . . .

. . . I am listening to the New York Philharmonic play Brahms' Second. Most of the other patients are in another room watching a full-length film from Hollywood with Ann Sheridan. I am listening to Brahms and the sun combs her long, blond hair . . .

Aaron got up from the table and without saying anything to anybody walked out.

It was night. It was always night. That's how he felt. He wandered, a stranger in the familiar city, down Clark Street to the river and stood on the bridge. The river was a wide black treadmill under his feet, stabbed with the reflecting lights of the night. Before his gravely searching eyes the Chicago skyline rose in impressive blocks of steel and stone with high-climbing ladders of lighted windows reaching to the rain-threatening sky. Wrigley Building, Tribune Tower, 333 Building —he began cataloguing them. They were like a high wall he could never scale. They hedged him in, like an animal caught in some cruel trap. And now they seemed to be floating down the river toward him in a solid front, closer and closer, a wall moving to crush him. He put his hands on the iron rail of the bridge to steady himself. It was cold to his touch. He put his forehead down against its coldness.

. . . people are just people. That belongs to you. You wrote it, I believe. You've repeated that phrase over and over in the conversations we've had. People are just people. It used to hold some weight. But today, at this moment, I don't understand it at all . . . people are just —what are they, Milo? Pigs? That's Steve. I'm really not interested. I wish the pigs would forget about me, leave me alone, go away.

A poet in a psychopathic ward. I've ruined my head. I can never return to normalcy. The doctors are optimistic. All doctors are optimistic. That is what doctors are paid for—to be understanding, polite and optimistic . . .

Against his head the cold black rail of the bridge. Behind him the rumble of traffic.

. . . every today tomorrow dies, every today tomorrow dies . . . It became a song in his head.

Aaron lifted his head from the rail. He shook his head as if to clear it. He moved slowly on his big feet down Clark Street, north into the tangled overhead maze of neon advertising beer and taverns and all-girl strip shows.

From across the street a figure came out of the shadows of the high rampart of the bridge, crossed the streetcar tracks and followed him.

Aaron shuffled on, the red and yellow neon light falling on his hunched shoulders for a moment and then slipping back to the dirty sidewalk. He began to carefully avoid stepping on the cracks. His neck hung loosely and his chin almost touched his shirt front. I'm going to get stinkin' drunk tonight. I'm going to make a goddamn fool of myself. I'm going to make love to every girl I get my hands on. I'm not coming home until tomorrow morning—about eight o'clock.

Someone laid a hand on Aaron's arm. He jumped violently, his neck craning up stiffly out of its drooped position.

"I was following you," Rebecca said.

"Startle reaction, they call it," Aaron said.

"Can I walk along with you?" Rebecca asked.

"I don't care." He worked his hands angrily in his pockets.

Rebecca moved to the side of him where her birthmark wouldn't show if he looked at her. She took his arm. "I like to be with you," she said. She tried to put her cheek against his shoulder. "Don't do that," he said. He pushed his bottom lip out sullenly.

"I like to be with you," she said again.

"That's good," he said. There was no emotion of any kind in his voice.

They walked along the night street. Drunkards staggered past them. A few stars sprinkled the obscuring sky. A little wind whispered in their hair. Rebecca kept her face turned toward Aaron and her eyes looked at him, wistfully, pleadingly. "It's nice tonight," she said. "It seems like rain but I don't think it'll rain." Her wistful eyes watched him.

Aaron halted on his big feet. "Why do you hang around me?" he asked.

Rebecca made her voice chuckle. "I like you—do you mind?" She was afraid he would say yes. Her fingers on his arm encouraged him to continue walking. He moved ahead on reluctant feet.

They walked to Chicago Avenue and on north. Walked in silence, Rebecca tightening her fingers into his arm for the feel of him but pressing them secretly, gently, so that he wouldn't notice and get mad.

Suddenly Aaron stopped. He faced her. "Look, I just want to be alone. Why don't you stop bothering me? Why don't you go home?

Why don't you leave me alone?" He turned abruptly and walked away from her.

There, that's that! He kicked the sidewalk with the toes of his shoes. He walked on past several store fronts. Then he turned back.

She was standing under the lamppost where he had left her. She was crying. "I'm sorry," he said.

"It's all right, Aaron."

"Let's go," he said. "You can take my arm if you want."

Her fingers closed and pressed on his arm.

He didn't talk to her, but she was glad to be with him and held his unresponsive arm.

Then, at a corner, Aaron saw Don coming toward them and averted his eyes but it was too late to avoid him. Don climbed up the curbing on his GI leg and grinned at Aaron.

"Hello."

Why do I have to meet people? Why can't they leave me alone?

Don glanced at Rebecca quickly with his deep-set eyes and then back at Aaron.

"Rebecca, this is Don."

She turned her head away from Don a little to conceal the birthmark and, tilting her chin, looked up into his face with her large green eyes. She smiled and said hello. Don arched his eyebrows and smiled a little in the way that he knew was attractive. "I'm pleased to meet you, Rebecca." His eyes took quick inventory: a good-looking Jewish girl. He guessed she was Jewish or else she wouldn't be with Aaron. She didn't look Jewish. Straight nose, milk-white skin, chestnut hair. What the hell did it matter if she was Jewish? "Drop by sometimes with Aaron and see us rehearse," he told her. Quickly his eyes looked down as she blushed and said thanks, she'd like to. Legs okay. What did he mean by thinking she didn't look like a Jew? What does a Jew look like? That was what Sue had said. Right too. In the dark he didn't see her birthmark.

"Say!" Don said. "I haven't got anything to do right now. Have you people? Let's go to Bughouse Square for a while!"

"What's Bughouse Square?" Rebecca asked.

"Oh, the soapboxers," Don said. "You know—free speech."

"Oh! I'd like to go!" Rebecca said, pressing Aaron's arm.

"All right," Aaron said, frowning.

They turned and went into the square. Rebecca walked so that her good profile was turned toward them. Secretly, yet with a panic, she tried to pull her long curly hair, bushed at the bottom, over her birthmark.

The park was dark. The soapboxers used the half-block-long street in front of the sedate and aged stones of the Newberry Library. One street lamp gave the only light. There were several speakers tonight with their little knots of listeners crowded around, looking up into their faces. On the first box stood a man with a lined, fifty-year-old face above a wiry body in a frayed salt and pepper suit. He had naïve, childish blue eyes and wore a battered and sweaty straw hat. He had just finished speaking and was trying to sell Marxist literature. Aaron, Don and Rebecca walked past him.

Encircled by the next crowd was a huskily built man with a swollen neck in which the cords stood out tautly. One of his arms was stretched out over the heads of the crowd in the attitude of a bully. Faces looked up at him. He pointed at the little man in the battered straw hat. "On that next box—" he bawled, "on that next box—is a man named Reeves. He is a—Communist!" He slurred these words and went on, pointing his accusing finger. "They tell me—they tell me—that Reeves was shot in the heel in the Spanish Civil war." There was general laughter. The speaker waited for the laughter to subside. Then he continued. "Now, I ask you—I ask you—how could he be shot in the heel if he wasn't running away? *Ohhhh!* He's very brave when he's braying from a box here in Bughouse Square—and he wants to see a bloody revolution here to overthrow our *great—democratic—government* and install *Bloody* Joe Stalin as dictator of America—he and the Jews who are trying to gain control of this country—"

Aaron pulled in his shoulders and shivered. There it was again. Rebecca dropped her eyes and was ashamed to look at Don. Don, embarrassed, put his hand on Aaron's arm. "That's one war we haven't won yet, the racial war," he said sympathetically. It made him feel good saying it. Aaron would know how he felt. Sue would be proud if she could hear him.

Aaron pulled his shoulder away and walked fast to hurry them away from the accusing voice. He thought of his father. And his father's back.

As they moved away they could hear an old woman's voice in the crowd say, "Jews—yah—that's the only thing I agreed with Hitler on." She was old. Her hair hung raggedly about her shrunken face and a few crooked teeth still fitted into her jaw.

Don, Aaron and Rebecca walked in silence to the other end of the street. In the dark there, standing on the stone embankment, were several young men who spoke with the voices of women. Among them Don saw Earl from the theater group. Don looked away quickly and pretended not to see him. But Earl's eyes, sad and somewhat haunted, had looked into his for a moment.

At the other end of the park a large crowd had now gathered. "Let's walk back down there," Don said, "and see what's going on."

The speaker was surrounded by a tightly packed circle. He stood on the box from which the little blue-eyed man in the battered straw hat had spoken. He was a Negro, tall, lean, very black. His eyes were sad and patient. His voice was slow and doleful. "On July 4th," he said, "King Lynch—took the lives of four of our people—two women and two men. The lynched men were in the armed forces of our country." He spread his large black hands under the street lamp. "What are we going to do about Libertyville, Georgia?"

A soldier lifted his face toward the speaker and said in a loud, jeering voice, "Overseas we put the niggers behind barbed-wire and that's where they belong."

The Negro seemed not to hear. "In the quartermaster corps—" he said.

A rather elderly man in army uniform broke in, saying, "What did you niggers do over there? All you did was drive trucks." A man, hidden in the crowd, asked anyone who knew, "What did they kill the niggers in Georgia for?" The man next to him said, "You don't need an excuse to kill a Negro in this country." He was a lean man, sharp-featured. He looked like the political cartoons of Uncle Sam without the beard. Some of the listeners nodded, glad that he had said what he did. He was their spokesman, saying what they didn't have the nerve to say.

The Negro speaker looked down into the crowd. "They were killed," he said, "because they were Negroes." He smacked his black fist into the pale palm of his hand and his patient eyes snapped anger. "American prejudice must be done away with—"

"Get down!" a man hidden in the crowd shouted. "Let a white man up there!"

Don stepped away from Aaron and Rebecca and moved closer into the crowd.

"In China and Russia—" the Negro said.

"I don't care what's happening in China and Russia!" a voice in the crowd shouted back. "When is my son going to get out of the army? That's what's important!"

The Negro smiled sadly. "Well, brother, you'd better be concerned," he said.

Don began to edge through the crowd toward the speaker. It was hard on his handicapped leg. He used his shoulders to help him knife his way through. A man's sneering voice said, "How can a white man get up there and speak after this?" And now Don stood alongside the soapbox. He wished he was wearing his uniform. He turned and confronted the crowd. "I want to say something," he said loudly. His lips were thin and angry as he spoke and his eyebrows were squeezed together in a frown. "Here in this park tonight," he said, facing the crowd, his eyes moving from face to face angrily as he spoke, "I've heard a lot of anti-Jewish and anti-Negro talk."

"Let's go—" Aaron told Rebecca. His head was down in embarrassment and he tried to find something to look at on the ground.

"Please—" Rebecca said, touching his arm. "I want to hear what he says."

Don faced his audience. His voice was sincere and he projected it in the manner he had learned from the stage. "I'm a veteran. I enlisted," he said. "And I did my part." His forefinger snapped angrily against his leg. It gave a hollow sound. "I lost my leg." Again he snapped an angry forefinger against his false leg and it gave its metallic thud. "And I want all of you to know that we soldiers who fought this one are going to see to it that we don't have in this country what they had in Europe. I saw plenty of action. I saw Negro troops unloading ships under shellfire. I saw them die for this country, and I saw Jews die for this country." Unconsciously Don lifted his arm in a dramatic and stagy gesture and unconsciously turned his profile left and right. "That's what America is—" he said, "all of us, not just—" his lips tightened on the words and he snapped them out, "the pure white race." Along Clark Street an ambulance's siren wailed in a long, shuddering vibration. Don looked toward Clark Street and the wail of the siren. His good leg trembled under him and he breathed in sharp pain through his open mouth. His eyes moistened. To the crowd he said, "Wayne—a friend of mine—" He gestured out into the night and the trees that shrouded the little park in darkness. "He died over there—" Again his arm jerked at the concealing night. "He believed in America. He believed in making America a better place."

The wail of the ambulance siren was a low, screeching, seeking thing, a mile away on Clark Street. Don set his teeth. He jerked his head back and sent the hair leaping off his forehead. "That's all," he said and began moving out of the crowd. The Negro and the people gathered around the box watched him go. There was sudden applause. It grew louder. Several people patted Don's shoulder as he edged through the crowd.

On the fringe of the crowd stood a handsome middle-aged man whose well-dressed look suggested that he might have, out of curiosity, wandered down into the park from the Gold Coast. His friendly eyes in his handsome red-flushed, blue-veined face were cold, flat, without depth. They were calculating eyes and seemed not to belong to his otherwise kindly face. He put one hand on Don's shoulder and held out his other hand. Don saw the tie clasp, the three-pronged silk breast-pocket handkerchief and the gold cuff links. "That was a fine little talk you gave them, son," the man said, shaking Don's hand. "They need that, son." His voice made itself chuckle a little.

"Thanks," Don said, pleased. His eyes looked over the man's shoulder for Rebecca. The man had pulled a card from his pocket. He handed it to Don. There was a large square-cut diamond ring on his finger. "Look me up some time," the man said. "I'd like to talk to you some time. Like your ideas." He patted Don's shoulder again.

But now Don caught Rebecca's eyes. She was staring at him in admiration. He smiled at her and held her eyes. To the man he said, "Thanks. I'll do that." He slipped the card into his billfold without looking at it and moved to where Aaron and Rebecca waited. Rebecca smiled at Don. "That was wonderful—what you said."

"Oh," Don said, scoffing modestly at himself, "they needed it."

They had now come to the sidewalk. "We go this way," Aaron said.

Don held out his hand. Aaron took it, loosely. "I'll see you, Aaron, old boy," Don said. There was the slightest trace of an English accent in the casual and friendly tones of his voice.

"Yeah," Aaron said dully.

Don looked at Rebecca. "Hope I'll see you again." He smiled his best smile. Lifting his arm to them he moved south down Clark Street.

# III

Smiling to himself Don walked along Clark Street. He guessed he had made an impression on her. Yes, he was sure of it. The way her eyes had looked up at him. Aaron was a lucky guy to have a nice-looking girl like that tagging after him. Tears in her eyes when she congratulated him on his speech. . . . That was a *good* speech he had made. He was proud and pleased with himself. He'd tell Sue about it. She'd be proud of him too. Let's see, what were some of the words? He dampened his lips with his tongue to recite them half-aloud to himself. "I'm a veteran. I gave my leg for my country," he said, gesturing with the words. "That's what America is—" he said and again the ambulance siren sounded across his conscience: Wayne.

. . . he had had to take guard duty that night. At midnight he came out of the guard tent, sleepy and stretching. Then the night, warm, with a coolness fanning the warmness, awakened him. There was a moon, bright over the barracks. He swaggered along, swinging his gun, thinking how he would do it if he were acting the scene.

Down the long length of wire fence he saw the fellow he was to relieve. The fellow stood with his back against the fence and his head touching the wire diamonds of the fence. His eyes were calmly, almost serenely surveying the night. His short-cropped blond hair stood straight up on his head and was only an inch tall, made copper by the moonlight. Some of it was sticking through the wire diamonds of the fence. His gun stood beside him, and he held it by the barrel in the balled palm of his hand. Slowly, gently he rubbed the back of his head against the fence and looked deeper into the night, took a deep breath which filled his lungs and squared his chest. Slowly, pleasurably, he exhaled. Then he heard Don and came to an alert position.

"Halt! Who's there?" His gun snapped up into both hands, the bayonet catching moonlight.

"Your relief—Kosinski." Every time he had to say his Polish name he hated to.

"Advance, Private Kosinski."

Don advanced until he was a pace away.

"Halt!"

He halted. Then the guard recognized him. "Okay, buddy," Wayne said.

"How's it going?" Don asked.

"Oh, pretty good." Wayne set his gun against the fence.

"Officer of the guard been around?"

Wayne shook his head no. He dug into his pocket for his cigarettes. "Smoke?"

"Thanks," Don said.

"Jesus, I'm glad you're here. It's going to feel good to hit the sack."

"Yeah. I hated getting up."

They stood in the peace and quiet of the night, smoking. They looked in curiously at the row after row of jeeps and trucks drawn up in tight formation behind the close-knit wire fence. There were hundreds of them, each sculpturing its stark shadow on the ground in hard, geometrical precision in the moonlight.

"Lot of equipment," Don said.

"Yeah." Wayne took another long inhalation and the spark of his cigarette came to ruddy life in the night. Don stepped out his cigarette. "Wonder how many doctors they'll need in this war?" Wayne said. Don shrugged. Wayne said, "Well—I'll see you." He started to move off.

Two days later they had to dig foxholes. Wayne walked over and began digging near Don.

"Hi!"

"Hi there!"

It was hot and soon their shirts were sticking to their backs. Sweat rolled down their foreheads and gathered in their eyelashes, was salty-tasting on their lips. It felt good to Don trickling down the calves of his legs inside his pants, tickling a little. Suddenly Wayne turned toward him, holding his pick outstretched. "Hey!" he yelled, thrusting the pick at Don. "Catch!" He threw it. Don caught it. Wayne immediately put his hand above Don's around the handle and Don his above Wayne's as if they were choosing up sides in a sand-lot baseball game.

Wayne laughed in his infectious way. Don started laughing too. They stood there laughing with their shoulders shaking and the sweat rolling from their faces. All around them the other soldiers worked at their digging. Wayne grinned at Don. "Say," he asked, "what did you say your name was?"

Don stopped laughing. "Kosinski," he said. He looked down at the ground. "I'm just a Polack." He laughed, trying to be casual.

Wayne frowned slightly.

They want back to their digging. After a while Wayne looked over. He grinned. "Hey—you shouldn't say *polack*. Even if you are Polish." With his pick he tossed a little dirt at Don. Then he grinned again and went back to digging. "Neat little grave, huh?" he asked, patting the foxhole with his pick.

Don looked at him with admiration. "You remind me of a woman I know," Don said.

Wayne laughed; then they both laughed.

"No, I mean you talk like her," Don said.

"She your girl?"

"Sort of. She runs a dramatic school."

"Sounds interesting. I did a little dramatics in high school."

They went into town to a U.S.O. dance and to the show. Coming home, walking through the darkened and deadened camp, Wayne lifted his head and looked out across the field. Don glanced at him. Wonder what he's thinking? Maybe of home. I wonder what his home is like? Don thought of his own family. He pulled out his pack and they each took a cigarette in the dark. Lit up. They walked on in silence. If he knew about my family I wonder if he would still like me. Don tossed his cigarette away. Wayne had accepted him and he couldn't understand it. But he was grateful for it. He glanced at Wayne in gratitude. Wayne grinned. He nudged Don with his elbow and began trotting. Don fell in step with him. The trot became a race. Unconsciously they were in competition with each other. Don put on a burst of speed. Wayne thrust his broad-shouldered body through the air and brought Don down with a flying tackle. Don skinned his knee. They sat down side by side in the road and Don, with his trouser leg up, pulled away the bruised skin. Wayne lay back breathing hard and looked at the sky with his hands behind his head "Nice night," he said. "Say!" he said, sitting up. "Let's go into town to church tomorrow. What church do you go to?"

Don was ashamed to tell him that he didn't believe in God. "Catholic," he said.

"Well, we'll go to the Catholic church, then," Wayne said.

"What are you?" Don asked.

"Congregational," Wayne said.

"Let's go there, then."

Wayne smiled slyly and looked out of the corners of his eyes at Don. "Don't you believe the propaganda that one church is better than the other?" he asked.

"I'd like to go to the Congregational church," Don said.

"Okay. But it's my treat. I'll take care of the collection box."

They stood up laughing. Don pounded Wayne on the shoulder with his fist. "Sue would like you!"

It was strange how a friendship could grow out of such small things. Wayne coming over to dig next to him when they had to make foxholes. The resemblance between Wayne and Sue. Wayne's sensitivity for him about the name Kosinski. That was like Sue too. They had talked about it since the day Wayne had asked him not to say *polack*. He tried to remember it because it was important to him. Wayne had said something like the less we think about race, color, nationality, the accident of being born in a certain country and the more we think of the good of all humanity, the quicker we'll make a—yes, that was the way Wayne had said it—world worth living in for everybody. And something about: We may not be thanked by the present or even by our children. But our wise grandchildren may thank us or some people five hundred years from now.

He had stared at Wayne in deep admiration. Had wanted to touch him and say "I like you," or "that makes sense" or "goddamn it, I agree with you!" Instead, chuckling a laugh, he had said, "Hey, where'd all that come from?"

Wayne had laughed too and said, "Let's go get a beer."

One hot night they had sneaked off to the swimming pool. They hopped over the fence, first making sure that no one saw them. They pulled off their pants and gave their bodies to the water, slipping noiselessly into the water from the edge of the pool.

At first they swam quietly. The water was cooling. Don did the breast stroke, snapping his legs like a frog and feeling the water surge around them and ripple away as he propelled himself forward. They began to wrestle in the water, first with their heads out and then going under the surface, pulling each other under. They rested on the edge of the pool, lying full-length on the concrete that first made them shiver but then became warm under them. The water dripped off their bodies and formed little pools near them. They lay silent. First peering at the sky. Then with their eyes closed. And the army, at this moment, wasn't so bad. Don opened his eyes and turned his head toward Wayne.

"Why did you enlist, Wayne?"

Wayne was silent a moment. He grinned. "Speech coming up," he said. "I enlisted because I believe in America." He spoke slowly; his voice was earnest; it was embarrassed too. "And democracy and the

Bill of Rights and because—well, I acted—no, not heroically—but like a good American." He chuckled a little. "Leave me alone, will you!"

They had talked about many things. It was strange how close you got to a fellow in the army. Don looked up at the sky, scratching his head against the concrete. Then he turned his eyes back toward Wayne. "I wish I could talk about things like you do. I've practiced diction in the little theater but it doesn't make sense when I open my mouth."

Wayne laughed. He sat up too and let his feet hang in the water. He looked down into the water, remembering. "I guess I talk that way because of my mother and father and a college professor—two—one was a history teacher and the other was an anthropologist."

"College!" Don's admiration grew. "You went to college?" And he never told me this before!

"Two years."

"What did you take up?"

Wayne swished his feet back and forth in the water, his heels gently kicking the pool. "Oh—just general subjects—first I wanted to be a football coach—then a teacher. Maybe an anthropologist. Anthropology interests me. Or maybe some sort of social work when I get out of the army and finish school." He grinned a quick grin. "But it looks like the war will never end." Then with quick and sudden movement he pushed Don into the water and followed him.

They swam some more, then once again sat on the edge of the pool. Don tramped down on bare, squishing feet to their pants and brought the cigarettes back with him. They smoked, their fingers getting the cigarettes wet and making them hard to draw on.

"What did you do in civilian life?" Wayne asked Don.

Don glanced sideways at Wayne. "I worked in a bank." Then quickly, "What college did you go to?"

"I didn't go to college right away—I bummed around the country for a couple of years after I graduated from high school, working my way and looking at the country." He chuckled. "Mom and Dad didn't want me to at first." His face grew serious. "What I saw in the South and—" his hand gestured impotently, "and in the slums of big cities—I guess I feel guilty because I never knew what it was to be poor—"

Don looked at Wayne in envy and some resentment too: I never knew anything else. He saw himself in the relief shoes. Saw himself sneaking home down alleys with the packages marked NOT FOR SALE that he had to bring home from the relief station and was ashamed to have anybody see him carrying.

Don said, without looking at Wayne, "I lied to you about working in a bank. I didn't do much work in civilian life. All that's going to be changed when I get back."

"Let's go swimming again," Wayne said. "Last one in—" He popped into the water. They swam for a while and then again loafed in sprawled positions at the edge of the pool.

"What sports were you in?" Don asked.

"Football. Basketball. Some track. A little baseball."

Don whistled. "You must have been good!"

Wayne laughed.

"How many letters did you get?"

"Oh, a couple. It was tougher in college." He shook his head. "I was lucky to make the football squad."

They smoked again. Don sat, hugging his knees, and looked at Wayne secretly. Wayne liked him for himself. Nobody ever had before. He didn't have to act big shot in front of him. He could just be himself.

"You've got a good build," Wayne said. "Were you an athlete?"

Don shook his head. He rubbed his cigarette out. "What's your mother like?" he asked, guardedly, thinking of his own mother.

Wayne lay back and looked up at the sky. "She's the most wonderful mother in the world." He smiled. "That sounds corny, doesn't it?" He sat up. "She's swell! That's all I can say about her." He shrugged. "Well, what can you ever say about your mother?"

"Nothing," Don said.

They sat in silence for a while.

"Tell me about your home," Don said.

Wayne sat, smiling gently, looking into the distance beyond the wire fence of the swimming pool and over the roofs of the barracks. "We live in Omaha," grinning, "that's not as big as your Chicago. But we have slums too." He lit a cigarette, shook the match out and for a moment watched its acrid purple smoke rise in a slow, dying trail. He looked up over it at Don. "My folks are sort of well-to-do. Upper class, I guess you'd call it, for Omaha."

"You must have had a car," Don said in admiration and envy.

"Yeah, since high school."

"What kind—a big one, I bet."

"An old Ford."

They walked down to their clothes and began to pull them on. "After the war you've got to come home with me and stay there a while," Wayne told Don.

"I'd like to."

"Before you go home," Wayne said. "You'd like my folks." Wayne grew enthusiastic. On the way back to the barracks they planned the visit.

And Don told Wayne about Grandpa. It was the only thing he could tell him about his family. He told him about tying Grandpa's tie every morning. About the letters to Poland. Grandpa became a symbol to them. Wayne enjoyed him as much now as Don did;

and Don loved Grandpa more now, found more value in him. Grandpa sent Don a package of Polish pastries which Don shared with Wayne. They sent Grandpa some ties from town. Ma wrote for Grandpa: *The ties I received, dear Grandson, and they are like none I ever had before. But your grandfather wishes you were here to tie them for me. Hurry home, dear grandson, you and your friend from your war to see me.*

They went to town.

"I've got hot rocks," Don said.

Wayne laughed at him.

"Let's get layed," Don said.

Wayne walked in silence for the length of the block. Then he said, "This is silly, I suppose—but there's a girl waiting for me and I think I'll hold out as long as I can."

Don tapped him on the shoulder understandingly. "Let's have a couple of brews."

"You go get a woman and I'll wait for you in a tavern."

"No," Don said, "let's get some brew together."

"Sublimation, huh?" Wayne said when the beer was in front of them and their heels were hooked up on the bar stools.

"What's your girl like?" Don asked.

"Very pretty." Wayne turned his glass on the bar. "We've got sort of an agreement." He lifted the glass abstractedly and made another wet circle with it. "I wouldn't marry her before I left—not knowing—" He shrugged and smiled a little sadly and swallowed some of his beer, wiping his mouth with the back of his hand. "You'd like her. I'm going to introduce you to her." He grinned boyishly and slapped his legs with large, healthy, athletic hands. "Some guys—going into the army—get married just like that." He snapped his fingers. "Want to leave their name behind just in case. Not me. It isn't fair to a girl. Maybe a kid coming and— " He shrugged. Then grinned. "How about another beer?"

"Sure thing, pal!"

They drank six or seven beers. Don said, "I've still got hot rocks."

Wayne said, "Tell you what—I'll wait for you."

Wayne sat on the bottom front step of the old building that looked dead in the night with all its shades pulled to the sill and no appearance of life inside. Don, when he came out, wore a little mustache of sweat and his forehead was damp. "Have a good time?" Wayne asked.

"Oh boy!" Don said. He whistle-sighed his satisfaction.

They went back to camp, walking all the way so that it would take a long time to get back.

Their friendship grew. They were together as much of the time as they could be. Wayne's mother mentioned Don in her letters to Wayne. She said to tell Don that she was remembering him in her prayers too. She sent packages containing homemade cakes, candy bars and books. To Don, Wayne was everything he would have liked to have been and had everything he envied and admired. He was good-looking, sincere, educated, well-to-do. He had a respectable family, money, a car, the girls chasing him. He still couldn't understand why Wayne liked him but was grateful and felt inferior in their relationship and tried always to measure up to Wayne's ideals. He identified with Wayne. He took Wayne's standards as his own, as he had taken Sue's standards.

. . . Wayne, Don thought, wandering the streets aimlessly. He was tired and limped noticeably on his false leg now. He turned into the first tavern he came to.

He had been drinking too much in the last few weeks. Sue didn't understand it. Nobody did. Too much, but he needed it badly. It helped him. It numbed the gnawing despair and loneliness that were at the center of him—when he thought of his life—the rest of it—when he thought of Wayne, of the war, of his family and background, of himself. Too much drinking. But the lonely, torturing cravings and despondency. The dependent needs. Liquor eased them, relaxed them into the far corners of his mind. And alone he had a different attitude about his leg. Not the laughing, casual pretenses he assumed in front of people. Nobody knew the despair that faced him every day when he awoke and every night when he unstrapped his leg and pulled the covers over him and tried to sleep.

He sat smoking and drinking, drinking and smoking, one after the other. Just to forget. But it was impossible to forget. Sue: he thought.

# IV

Sue was getting ready to go out. She had already slipped into her coat when Don knocked. He didn't speak but stepped past her and into the room.

"I'm awfully sorry, Don, but I was just going out. I have an appointment." She looked at him and knew that he had been drinking.

"Well, go ahead," Don said roughly.

Sue closed the door and looked at him. "You can stay here until I come back."

"I know that."

Sue shrugged in irritation. "You've been drinking again, haven't you?"

He smirked at her. "Yeah, I've been drinking again."

Sue turned and started for the door. She didn't quite get there but turned back into the room, facing him. He laughed. "Well, why don't you go?" He continued to smirk at her.

Sue looked at him as if she wanted to say something. She bit her lip and held it between her teeth for a moment and continued to look at him. She knew herself. Knew that she was too soft-hearted and sympathetic.

"Well, Miss Carroll," Don said, "you don't like it because I've been drinking. You want to give me a lecture. Go ahead—but make it short." He leaned back against the dresser in a bored way.

She knew her love for him. She knew that she wasn't pretty and that there was no security for her love. But she wanted him to straighten out for his own sake, even if there would be nothing in it for her. Why should he talk to me like this? Be hard on him. She flicked her gloves against the palm of her hand. She flicked them again, and harder, until she was slapping them. At length, never letting him free from the contemptuous hardness of her eyes, she spoke. "All right, I'll make it short."

He watched her with amusement and anger and, when she began to talk, resentment. "You're the guy," Sue said, "who posed as the great liberal when he went into the army. The guy who talked about helping people." A little mocking smile flickered at the ends of her lips. "Help people? Now you're sorry for yourself. You're bitter." Tell him what you really think, she told herself. Don't hold back. Be offhand.

Don stuffed his hands roughly into his pockets, and turning, frowned into the mirror. Their eyes met in the mirror. Sue's eyes moistened. She took a step toward him. "You don't have to be bitter. Don't be bitter." She put her hand on his shoulder. "You're the same person. You can do something worth while." Standing alongside him, she looked at him appealingly.

Don whirled around, his false leg plopping on the floor noisily. "Sure I'm bitter! Sure I'm thinking of myself! I lost a leg, didn't I?" He shouted it. "Why shouldn't I think of myself? I'm one of the guys who's going to be standing on West Madison Street twenty years from now saying 'Buddy can you spare a dime for coffee and for a war vet?' Sure, why shouldn't I think only of myself? Sure, I'm bitter! Why not!" Then suddenly he halted.

The room was quiet after the violence of his voice and words.

His face seemed to drain of all color and become taut. For a moment despair stood in his eyes. Then they became expressionless. He moved to the bed and sank down on it. He lay back and put the crook of his arm over his eyes: Wayne.

Sue took off her coat. She put her hat on the dresser. Walking to the bed she leaned over him, and putting the palm of her hand on his forehead, smoothed his hair back. "I won't go out. I'll stay here with you." She spoke as if to a child whom she would comfort.

"Leave me alone, Sue." He said it not bitterly but despairingly, pleadingly. "Please leave me alone."

Quietly Sue left the room.

Don lay behind the crook of his arm. They were on the ship. They were being taken to the war. They were the implements, the tools. Scooped up off the land, poured into the mold, processed, hardened, lifted off the drill press, lifted off the forge, stamped from the jaws of the punch press. Shipped now, into the jowls of the night. Like cattle, or any other thing, when space is important. In the hold, in the great guts of the throbbing ship, they slept. Hundreds of beds in the huge bunkroom. Iron poles for supports and the bed a piece of canvas slung between them and only six inches off the floor. Two feet above the first bunk another, and two feet above it another, and another in layers of four and five. Each soldier sleeping practically on top of the other in the packed bowels of the ship that smelled of the sickening odors of heat and sweat and oil and vomit and urine.

And as the ship plows on through the sea, day and night, night and day, day and night in the relentless voyage to war and to death, the men feel a quiet fear inside them and try not to show it in their eyes. They wisecrack. They play cards. Read. Shoot craps. But it lies deep. The thoughts are of home, of a familiar room, a house, a city block or a country mile. Home. Never did the word mean more. And loved ones. A corny phrase. But never more real. And home is something each feels he will never see again as the ship takes them closer and closer and closer to the mauling night of war.

And the ship plows on in convoy with many others over the treacherous sea that has death in its stomach. The ship heads for its appointment. The men for they know not what.

But the days were not all unpleasant. The men lay on blankets on the deck, reading, writing letters, playing chess or cards. There were big, reckless crap games. For money meant little where life meant little. Where the stars and the horizon moved to the appointed hour.

He leaned over the rail with Wayne, looking at the water. In the distance he could see the great gray hulk of another ship of the convoy. "Well—I guess we'll get in on the big push—the big thrill."

Wayne held his forefinger between the leaves of a book to mark his place. "What are you going to do when the war is over?" His serious brown eyes, warm and surprising brown because of the blond hair, looked into Don's.

Don laughed. He turned and leaned his back against the rail. "Well—" he said, "I know the fine art now. I've learned three methods—shooting, bayoneting and hand grenades. I think I'll start a mob after the war. We'll put the gangs of the twenties to shame with all the wonderful training we're getting."

*"C'est la guerre,"* Wayne said, smiling with his lips while his serious eyes watched Don.

Then, "Let's go lie on the deck."

He and Wayne lay silent on their backs, gazing at the blue, changeless sky. Five minutes, ten . . . then softly Wayne quoted, "And we are here as on a darkling plain. Where ignorant armies clash by night." He was silent again, but his lips moved without sound . . . and at length, aloud, "And what are we but infants crying in the night? Infants crying for the light and with no language but a cry."

. . . and the boat slipped on quietly, serenely, to the land of war, to the menace of the far shore, to the large dark threat.

Twelve days they were at sea, the convoy needling its cautious, alerted way across the ocean; taking its zigzag pattern across the water toward the embattled land. The men began to speculate, and made wild guesses as to their destination. The sea gave no answer. The officers gave no word. The ships plowed the water. Then, one evening after supper, they were called together and told that they were not far off the coast of North Africa. And each man's heart beat a little faster now that the imminent became the actual.

In the dark the landing barges were prepared. And the hearts all beat a little faster. The dark land loomed up dimly in the slate-dark evening, was peopled perhaps with the snouts of a million guns. Was peopled with their fears and their lives and deaths. The land gave no answer, nor the stretches of desert sand, the ridges and rock outcroppings, nor the trees calmly waving.

They waited for the night. And the early morning. Then the landing barges were ready. This was it. When you go into the army your fear of death is greater and greater—then it diminishes—then it all comes back on the eve of battle. This was it. Don began to tremble. He bit his lip to stop its trembling. Wayne glanced at him and, grinning, winked at him. It was like tightening his belt for him. He winked and grinned back. And moved, unconsciously, a little closer to Wayne. "Soon," Wayne said. Don was still trembling a little. His only defense was a laugh. It was a nervous laugh. He said, "Tonight we give the greatest performance of our lives."

The assault barges cast off from the transports, started their engines. The motors droned together in many awakening voices. Helmeted, wearing leggings, packs on their backs, water canteens strapped to them, Don and Wayne stood together in one of the launches. Wayne grasped Don's arm for a moment and his fingers tightened into Don's muscle. His grasp said "Hello," or "Friend," or "Well—"

The launches headed for the dark shore line. Panic seized Don. Run! Nowhere to run. The sea hissed and bubbled behind them. Ahead of them the dark, secret, menacing shore line. There were palm trees on the beach.

Close, close to shore now.

The soldiers hopped from the landing barges and ran through the water toward the beach. They hit the beach. They went down on their bellies. Digging in in a piece of naked sand.

The silence became a thing of noise. The enemy had been lured to shore. The enemy had been found out on shore. Coastal batteries set up a barrage. Steel birds strafed the shore line. Red tracer bullets etched their pattern.

Some of the men around Don didn't get up when they charged to their second position.

A full day of fighting. Two days.

They were still alive.

The infantry continued the pursuit on the third day. The captain said, "Down the road about half a mile there's a bridge." He cleaned one fingernail with another, watching his work as he did so. "Just beyond the bridge there's a nest in a building there." The captain didn't allow himself a sigh. He only went on cleaning the nails of his left hand with the index finger of his right and didn't look up at the soldiers, had never been able to, asking this request that might bring death with it, but spoke gruffly, watching the dirt being pared from under his nails. "We need a couple men to clear that bridge. There's no artillery with us and we need that bridge by nine o'clock. I want—" and now he was looking at his cleaned nails, "a couple of men to sneak across the bridge and to the back of that building and mop up that nest with grenades."

There weren't any heroes in the split second after he had spoken and still went on looking at his nails while each man mentally grasped himself and held what was dearest to him, not knowing whether or not in the volunteering the bullet would have his name on it, would be the one you don't hear.

"I'll take it, captain."

Wayne had stepped up out of line and spoken

Then the captain looked up from his nails at him. "It's a rough deal."

"I'll handle it, captain."

Don looked at the back of Wayne's head. And Don stepped up next to him.

"Me too, captain." Under his breath he said to Wayne, "You goddamn fool!" Wayne grinned and winked at him.

"You better grab a smoke before you leave," the captain said.

They started off. There was an inhuman quietness to the night. The night was ghostlike and they two ghost figures against the night and its silent darkness. They moved off into the unknown.

The moon was not much and threw but dim shadows. There seemed to be nothing else in the world in this darkness but themselves. And they matched their voices, their steps, with the quietness. "I'm plenty sore at you," Don grumbled. "Whadda you want to be, a hero?"

Wayne chuckled and threw an arm around Don's shoulders.

They walked in silence.

They came to the marker the captain had mentioned and knew the bridge was now less than a block away.

"No use rushing it," Don said. "We can be heroes five minutes later." He sat down on the ground and, lying full-length so that he could get his hand in his trouser pocket, pulled out a candy bar. He broke it in half. There in the night he and Don sat side by side eating the candy bar. When they were finished they still sat there. Silent. Neither speaking.

At last Don said, "What is your father like? You've never talked about him." And Don wondered what his own father had been like.

Wayne smiled. Don could see the smile in the darkness. "He has a little beard." Wayne smiled again. "He's a doctor." Then, when the silence had gone on a long time and they had both been thinking their own thoughts, Wayne said, "Dad's a fine guy." He was silent a moment and then went on. "He donates a day a week to the settlement house in Omaha." Wayne's voice chuckled. "Lucky there was money in the family or we'd have been awfully poor." When he spoke again he said, "Even in this little time over here I've seen a lot of suffering. You know, when I get back I think I'll be a doctor and work down there in the slums. I think Mother and Dad would like that." He sat up straight and stretched. Then he punched Don on the leg with his fist. "Let's go be heroes."

. . . "Wayne," Don said aloud from behind the crook of his arm. On Sue's bed he twisted, pulled his lip in between his teeth and bit hard.

It was taking that point. I remember. It was coming down the road. I remember this broken bridge. I was climbing up on the bridge. The hypodermic needle entering his arm. The nurse's cool palm. No, it was beyond the bridge. Him and Wayne. First they had sat a long time in silence. They both wished they could smoke. He couldn't tell what Wayne was thinking. Wayne's face was calm, handsome in the darkness. It was the clean, strong face of an athlete. His eyes were calm too. Then the smile. The punch on the leg. "Let's go be heroes." Don stood up. He was scared and he told himself, for courage, tonight I give the greatest performance of my life. He was trembling.

They had crossed the bridge, waiting for a cloud to completely obscure the moon, crossed it on their bellies. It seemed to take an hour, inching cautiously across the bridge. And circled away, on their bellies, in a half arch across the ground toward the back of the building which, formidable against the night, looked like a fortress against which they would pit their puny strength.

"Cover me with your rifle," Wayne whispered and snaked slowly along the ground toward the building, the grenade ready in his hand. Don tensed and trembled. Then his deeper fear, his watchfulness, calmed him. He was steady, alert, ready. Crawling along the ground there he had gotten outside himself. Something was bigger than he was. He had never felt fuller, bigger, freer. He crawled along behind Wayne with his rifle pointing up above Wayne's head at the upper window of the building.

Their bodies were too loud, crawling along the ground. Their figures made too distinct an outline snaking slowly along. It was as if a million eyes watched them. A million guns pointed.

Momentary moonlight revealed a uniformed figure in the window raising a gun and taking accurate aim. Don squeezed the trigger of his rifle.

Trite as it was, all hell broke loose. That was the only way he could remember it—all hell. The figure slumped forward over the sill as if kneeling there looking down into the yard for something. Wayne leaped to his feet and hurled the grenade. It fell short. All of the windows of the building seemed to send a separate fusillade of bullets at them. Wayne grasped his stomach. Wayne fell over backwards. Don dropped his gun. He forgot his purpose. He knew but one thing. His friend was hit. He stood up and ran toward Wayne. He didn't quite get there. The bullets stopped him. He tried to crawl to Wayne. More bullets splattered around him like hard rain falling. He couldn't get close enough to Wayne to touch him. To say "Wayne," or "I'm here," or "friend." From his own flesh-tied-down pain he rolled his head sideways on its limp neck toward Wayne. Wayne was staring at him. Wayne's lips tried, tried hard to smile.

But his eyes held some pleading, begging request. Maybe: "I don't want to die" or "don't let them get you," or "please—please go see my mother and father," or, perhaps only "it hurts so much, please hold my hand while I die."

And Wayne's eyes went on staring at him that way until, slowly, they closed.

And Wayne was a soldier, dead, with his empty hands clutching the empty sky.

Don closed his own eyes, waiting to die.

Hell was still going on. The artillery had come up after Wayne had tried to get it the hard way. Commanders make mistakes. Commanders change their minds. Commanders don't worry about one or two guys.

The Americans took the bridge. And went on.

The soldiers advanced swiftly, crouching, running forward to the newly won position with their guns blasting. They were tripping over him in the dark. He cursed at them. "Goddamn you! Keep off me!" Many khakied legs ran across the field. He was left lying there near the dead Wayne. The battle sounded farther away. He wondered if they had left him there to die? His pain was almost unbearable. His leg. As if the bullets had sawed it half across, and down. From above his knee to his ankle, it was a burning torch of pain. He fastened his teeth into his wrist as hard as he could, trying to nerve himself against the pain, and tasted the salty blood on his lips. His eyes moved to the grotesquely humped figure of Wayne, thin and small in death, anchored to the ground as a stone is anchored. He clamped his eyes closed. But the tears of hurt and pain and loss squeezed through and fell in their small pool to the ground while the blood of his leg soaked into the ground from its large, ragged pool. The earth took both, greedily.

They came for him. They lifted his body and then the loosely dangling leg up onto the litter. I won't look now. They laid him in a barn. A cow kept trying to crap on him. He was crying with exasperation. He didn't want to be crapped on. Hadn't enough happened to him? Then he was gasping with pain. Then he was crying. Just crying. Like a kid cries. Wayne was dead. Hadn't he tried to save Wayne's life? And there wasn't even anybody there to see it. To know that he had tried to save Wayne's life. Wayne was dead. His friend was dead.

They cut the cloth of his trouser leg away. He wished he couldn't look then. The needle entered his arm.

He awakened with a cramp in his leg. It became the severest of pain. He groaned and tried to turn on the bed. There was a woman's soft hand on his forehead trying to smooth away his pain. His leg was gone.

In the days or hours or weeks . . . drifting into consciousness and unconsciousness . . . when the pain was a little less, his first thought was that his dream of the theater was gone. His second thought was of home, of his mother, and making it up to her. That wish, mingled with the morphine, gave him semi-awake, semi-sleeping dreams. He vacillated between dream and reality. Sometimes: the sterile hospital smell with its undertone of rotten flesh and greasy yellow stench of running pus, antiseptic tubes probing under his fever-thick tongue, razor preparing the way for the knife by cleaning off the body hair in the groaning beds around him . . . the sure fingers of the nurse feeling for the pulse, the taking of blood into his sapped body, changing of bandages, thousands of smells, impressions. Sometimes: he and Wayne still on shipboard in the long pleasant days with the open blue sea and sky. Or he and Wayne were home at Wayne's house . . . dancing in a many-mirrored ballroom with a beautiful, daintily perfumed girl, running to catch the streetcar home, the applause of the theater crowd as he strode out for his seventh bow. And Sue with him in her room . . . a bed . . . tottering between the two weirdly intertwined worlds . . . don't have to worry now . . . hospital bed where I can sleep all night without the fear of an enemy awakening and killing. HOSPITAL BED! His heart beat fast against his ribs and his voice choked up into his throat and perspiration stood out on his forehead. *Hospital bed!* What happened? What's the matter with me? The nurse's cooling palm on his fevered forehead.

Then he was getting better. He could sit up in bed now for a little of each day. His mind turned doggedly from thoughts of Wayne. He kept his eyes averted when they changed the bandage on his stump. Each day. And then one day . . . he tried to look over the side of the bed, across the room, anywhere . . . and looked down at it . . . his stump. . . .

The young body does not give easily of itself to death, to weakness. The bandages from his stump were less offensive in odor and sight. He sat up in bed a little longer each day now. To his left was a fellow who had gotten shrapnel through one leg. He couldn't straighten his leg and his knee was swollen. But it wasn't bad. All he needed was rest and some heat treatments. Across the way was a fellow with his testicles shot off. Several beds to his right a soldier went through hellish torture every day when a doctor straightened out his arm. He had been hit in the shoulder and he couldn't lower his forearm all the way. There was hardly any muscle left in his shoulder and back and somehow it had affected the nerves in his arm. But the doctor wasn't coming any more after today. Today the doctor said he had done all he could, that the kid would be a cripple, his arm eventually drawing up to his chest with his fingers drawn up in a clawlike position. Next to him the boy there happens to have an amputation of both arms. He had walked off the battlefield to the dressing station with one arm hanging by only a few tendons and a double trail of blood leading backwards to the memorial of the exact spot on which he had been wounded. We, the dead. Don stared straight out the window at the brilliant blue sky and the timeless sun that gave the dark, baked earth a golden glow.

On Sue's bed Don groaned softly. Behind the crook of his arm his eyes were filled again with the sight of death and his ears with the sound of shells and fire.

He bit into his lip. Wayne was dead. And he wasn't alone, dead and rotting, carried off, what had been left of him, bit by bit, by the worms. Hundreds of thousands of young bodies. Healthy dead young bodies. Disgraced in death. Degraded in death by the weird and fantastic and cruel thing they called civilization.

And behind the twist of his arm Don knew also his own shameful feelings. Knew that deep down inside him he was glad it was Wayne instead of himself. Half a life was better than none. But—twisting slightly on the bed in his self-torture—he had tried to save Wayne's life. He had been willing to give up his life for him. And he knew, also—twisting yet on the bed—that it should have been he instead of Wayne, Wayne who had so much to live for, who had his stake in the future. A good life, decent and helpful.

Don stirred on the bed and again softly groaned. "He was better than me," he groaned. He lifted his arm at last from his closed eyes but put the palms of his hands over his face. He was sobbing into them though no tears came. Wayne had given to the last grain, the last dried drop. Wayne had acted—no, not heroically—but like a good American. I want to be a good American. But what do you do? How do you start?

# V

How do you become a good American? How do you make your country a better place for everybody? How did he carry on for Wayne? What do you do? And how do you start?

The cigarette he had lit and balanced on the edge of the dresser had burned out, scorching the dresser top and leaving a little cylinder of gray, wasted ash, but Don didn't notice it. He put his fingers into his long hair and scratched his scalp despairingly. He lay back for a moment on the pipestem bed and then arose and walked into the other room.

His mother was at the stove stirring, with a long spoon, the gummy food that bubbled there. Her eyes reached for Don's. "My son, are you hungry now? Do you want to eat now?"

He didn't answer her but went to the sink and drew water into a dirty and chipped glass that stood on the wooden drainboard.

Helen, getting ready for her 26-table on West Madison Street, stood before the cracked mirror, circling too much of a bright red rouge into her cheeks. Eva, back from having her baby at the Catholic Welfare, thin and seventeen and wearing a ragged black dress, sat on the window sill watching Helen. She did not seem to mind having left her baby at the Welfare for adoption but watched admiringly as Helen now arched the red, red lipstick over her full lips. She moved quickly to the table, picked up Helen's artificial flower, and again seating herself on the window ledge, held the flower ready to offer it to her sister. Her lips were parted a little, looking at the brazen beauty of her sister's face. Her eyes darted to the back of Don's head. "Don," she said, "take me out with you sometimes, huh? Take me out with you where there's music and I can meet lots of fellows." Her unoccupied hand smoothed her stringy dark hair, and smiling dreamily, she tilted her head a little to the side in a pose that might have been borrowed from the theater billboard heroine.

"Yeah, yeah," Don said, hardly hearing and Ma whirled from her listless stirring of the gummy dinner. "Little bitch!" she said, withdrawing the spoon from the pot and approaching Eva. "Have you not brought enough disgrace on this house with your bastard baby?" She whacked Eva across the cheek with the spoon, leaving a smear of food. "Whore!" She hit her over the head, not too hard but with authority. Helen sighed but said nothing and went on painting her face. Don tightened his lips and scowled.

"I want lots of good clothes and good times," Eva said defiantly. "You take me out with you sometimes, Don." Her voice was edged up toward tears but her eyes looked into her mother's and her smiling mouth mocked her mother.

Mrs. Kosinski's hand holding the spoon drooped to her side. The fire went out of her eyes and a sadness replaced it. She shook her head. "You're too much like me, Eva," she said softly, and going back to the pot, began to stir the food with an angry fury.

"I liked him!" Eva flung the words at her mother in a flood of anger. "He was a nice sailor! He was handsome! He had a swell body! He was some lover!"

"Bitch! Little bitch!" Ma said. There was no fire in her voice.

Don went back into his room and closed the door.

Alina came into the house from the church with her thin little hand clasped over her prayer book. Her blond wavy hair had been combed smooth and was caught in a severe little ribbon at the nape of her neck. Her large eyes looked at all of them and she said breathlessly, "It was wonderful in the church! It was so cool and quiet! The sunlight was nice on the colored-glass windows!"

From her ledge, tightly clasping Helen's artificial flower between her bony fingers, Eva hurled words at her mother. "He was a won-der-ful lover. You said I should. He was won-der-ful!"

"I never gave any of my kids away," Ma Kosinski said. And she crumpled into herself there at the stove, began to sob furiously with her long body bent over and the ladle held motionless in the pot.

Helen came to her mother and put her arms around her. "There, there, now, Ma."

"You said I should!" Eva shouted in challenge.

Mrs. Kosinski's sobs grew louder and more helpless. "Now, stop it, Ma, stop it," Helen said reassuringly. Her large arms moved her mother away from the stove toward a chair. Mrs. Kosinski wiped her nose on the back of a red-worked hand. "I only don't want her burdened with kids—having kids—so young—so young—" Ma Kosinski sobbed.

Alina's prayer book had slipped to the floor. She sat with her hands pressed tightly against her ears and her eyes closed, shutting out everything.

"I know, Ma," Helen said soothingly, "I know."

In his room Don put a book on his lap and a sheet of paper on the book. He started a letter to Wayne's mother. He didn't know what to say and held the pencil tip in his mouth, chewing on it. Then he started the letter. He tried hard to write it but didn't know what he wanted to say, and wasn't sure whether he was writing in sentences or not. They were educated people. They were rich people. He didn't want to make a fool of himself. He balled the letter up in his fist. He tried again, again crumpled the paper. Wayne's folks. He saw their house as Wayne had described it, and the rooms inside. He glanced around his room, heard the angry, picking voices beyond the door, looked up at the picture of John Barrymore on the wall, walked to the dresser and fingered his army disability check that had come that day. His heart began to beat fast in his excitement. Yes!

He had no clear plan yet. It was just to clear out at home. Get out of there. He'd never amount to anything living there. His family dragged him down.

He began, quickly, nervously, to throw his clothes into a battered paper suitcase. From the walls he took his pictures of Barrymore, Valentino, Booth—and the drawing Sue had made of him. He was going to start all over again and he'd become someone Wayne would have been proud of. From the shelf in the small dark closet he took the little packet containing Wayne's belongings. He had never looked at them. Again he glanced into the closet. Grandpa's cardboard box was on the floor, and behind it, leaning against the wall, was Grandpa's gnarled cane. Don gently touched Grandpa's cardboard box with the toe of his shoe. "You're going to be proud of me, old man."

He went into the other room. Helen hadn't gone yet. Eva was automatically setting the table, slamming the dishes down as if she wanted to break them. Ma sat in a chair. Her eyes looked up, pleadingly, into Don's. "Does my boy want to eat now?" Then she saw the suitcase. Her bony hand with the broken-off black nails went up to her withered chest. "Where are you going?" There was panic in her voice.

Don looked across the room at Helen. "You've got a room of your own now," he told Helen.

Ma's eyes came up pleadingly, beggingly, to Don's. Don met them levelly. He smiled a little, in conquest.

There was an agitation at Ma's throat as if something inside wanted to get out and the thin cords in her long neck stood like weed stalks. Her eyes found no relenting of purpose in Don's face. Just the slightest thin-lipped smile, tickling his little mustache. He glanced again at Helen. She nodded at him, an agreeing nod. "We don't mean you no good," she said.

"So!" Ma said. "Not only is the name not good but your people are not good enough for you. So!" She stood up. She laughed shrilly. She put her hands on her hips and her bony elbows, dirty in their creases below the short-cut sleeves, were knotty with the blackened, red, sagging wrinkles smoothed away. "It went to your heels, didn't it?" she said. She laughed at him. "Speak out freely," she said. She spat it at him.

Don set his suitcase on the bare, warped floorboards. "All right. I will speak out freely. I'm sick and tired of you. I'm getting out, see?"

"Go your way," his mother said, "and the devil take you. I tell you without ifs or ands." She smacked her hand across her behind at him.

His only defense was a laugh. There was guilt in his laughter. He lifted his suitcase. It seemed less weighty. To Helen he said, "I've still got some stuff in the closet."

She nodded. But her eyes looked at her mother with compassion.

Don went out. Behind him he heard Eva saying, "I wish I was going with you!"

On the steps going down he was ashamed of himself. In the hospital he had promised himself to make it up to his mother and now he was leaving her.

He took a room at an apartment hotel on North Dearborn Street edging just off the Gold Coast. It was a nice-looking building on the outside. There was an unpleasant odor in the hallways, a mustiness —as if all the rooms were so small that they breathed outward into the hall the body odors of their occupants. There was a self-operated elevator. His room was hardly big enough for him to change his clothes. There was a couch that opened into a bed, a small dresser crowded against the wall, a straight-backed chair, a tiny bathroom. One lone window looked out on a wall of windows. The room was more than he could afford. But he had a good address.

Two evenings later Don stood in line in the ticket office. When his turn came he said into the little cage, "Gimme a ticket to Omaha—round trip."

He climbed on the bus.

# VI

The house, serene and rich-looking under the early afternoon sun in the Happy Hollow district of Omaha, made Don feel inferior and frightened. He stood staring at it in respectful awe. He worked his hands into fists and stretched his fingers wide, nervously, several times, looking at the house. It was a two-story brick building with a red tile roof gleaming in the sunlight and settled gracefully on the wide green lawn behind a single fir tree. Evenly trimmed shrubbery margined the sidewalk and led to the front porch. On the lawn a hose swirled its softly hissing spray and laid gentle drops of water on the grass in a wide circle.

Don smoked a cigarette for courage. After he had finished he stood looking at the house for yet a moment longer. Then he walked stiffly down the red tile path and to the door. He rang the bell quickly so that he couldn't turn back and then stood staring at the copper name plate: DR. R. ALLISON.

A woman answered the door. She was a small woman in her forties and above the collar of her house dress had a friendly face that looked smilingly at him while she waited for him to speak. It was Wayne's mother. He knew that. "I'm Don."

She paled. Her eyes looked into his. They were just like Wayne's eyes. They were warm, liquid brown eyes. For a moment he was looking into Wayne's eyes. She held out her hand. "Hello, Don. Do come in." He felt the slight tremble of her fingers. Then they clasped his hand more warmly as if not to betray themselves and she put her other hand over his and drew him gently forward into the hallway.

They walked into a cool living room with expansive windows that looked out onto the front lawn and caught within their frame the green-needled branches of the fir tree, the lazy spurting spray from the water hose.

"Sit down, won't you?" Mrs. Allison said. "Wayne's father isn't home yet." Her voice was kindly and her brown eyes, like Wayne's, looked more deeply into his. Everything she felt that moment and had been thinking for a long time was in her eyes. Don sat down on the edge of the sofa and placed the little packet of Wayne's belongings on his knees. "You must be warm," Wayne's mother said, and smiling, "I'm going to make you some lemonade. Make yourself at home." She turned away from him because her eyes were swept with sudden disaster and went toward the kitchen.

Don sat uncomfortable. He looked around the room. There was a grand piano. On the piano there was a framed picture of Wayne in his uniform. At the other end of the room there was a fireplace and, over the fireplace, an oil painting. Don glanced around the room with admiration and a growing feeling of inferiority and wondered how Wayne could have liked him. Far into the interior of the cool, comfortable house he could hear the gentle tinkle of ice. He could see the tears, hot, that fell toward the cold ice cubes.

When Mrs. Allison returned she was composed. She sat next to him. Don looked at her gravely as he lifted the glass to his lips and sipped the lemonade. Both of them sat on the very edge of the sofa and turned tensely toward each other and each tried not to think of what was foremost in their minds.

Mrs. Allison said, "Wayne's father isn't home yet. Today is his day at the infant welfare station." She spoke very quickly, then held her lips tightly pressed. "You will stay a few days, won't you?" she asked.

Don nodded without answering and felt fearful, afraid that he wouldn't know how to act in this house and with these people.

Mrs. Allison stood and, smiling, held out her hand to him. "Come, I'll show you the house. Bring your lemonade with you." She took his hand and led him out onto a sun porch. She chuckled a little. "This is my husband's office and laboratory. He's awfully messy.

He and Wayne are so much alike." She said *are* and then put her hand to her throat, but smoothed her neck with her fingers and smiled at Don. The several chairs were piled with books, scientific journals, vials and little cartons of pills. Mrs. Allison said, "Dad doesn't allow Hilda or me to touch anything." Holding his hand she led him through the rest of the lower floor and then up the steps.

"This is Wayne's room." She led him inside. "I knew you would come to see us," Mrs. Allison said. "I wanted you to sleep in Wayne's room." Suddenly, and awkwardly, he put his arm around her shoulders and as suddenly, as clumsily, moved it away.

From the bottom of the steps a man's voice called out, "Mama, I'm home. . . . Mama, where are you?"

"In Wayne's room."

Doctor Allison stood framed in the doorway. With his head lowered a little Don looked up at him, seeing, first of all, the little Vandyke beard Wayne had described. It was sharp and turning gray.

"Dad," Mrs. Allison said, "this is Don."

The doctor moved out of the doorway and into the room. He held out his hand. He grasped Don's hand tightly. He said nothing. He looked deeply into Don with his sharp, penetrating eyes. Seemed to be measuring him and loving him for having been his son's friend; seemed to be finding Wayne inside of him somewhere, in the conversations they had had, the experiences they had shared together. Then he nodded and smiled and released Don's hand.

"It's warm, Dad," Mrs. Allison said. "Too warm for that coat and Don isn't a stranger here." She unbuttoned his coat and began working his arms out of the sleeves. Over her head, his sharp little beard at an angle, Doctor Allison winked at Don and said, "She's always like this. Always treating me like a baby."

"He gets more colds than his patients," Mrs. Allison said.

"That makes me a good doctor," he said, again winking at Don. With his coat off he stood in his vest, a large, old-fashioned gold watch chain seeming to hold it together better than the buttons.

There was silence, strained and confused and crashing around their thoughts of the dead body in the strange soil. Mrs. Allison's hands became a trifle shaky and then almost panicky. They seemed to search for something to do or touch. She smiled at Don. "Perhaps you would like to see Wayne's album."

She got it from the top drawer of her son's dresser. She smoothed the bed next to her, motioning Don to sit alongside. He did. Doctor Allison sat sidesaddle on the footboard of the bed. Mrs. Allison turned the pages of the album. The pictures of Wayne came up. Grammar school graduation picture. High school football captain, his face lean and young, the mouth stern but the eyes smiling. Action picture, turning the end and stiff-arming a tackler. Wayne with a baseball bat. Wayne in swimming trunks, in a basketball suit with the school name lettered across the shirt. Wayne in graduation gown, looking a little absurd with the mortar cap tassel down over one eye. Senior class president. Snapshots of Wayne in different cities and towns on his trip across the country. Pictures he had snapped of share croppers, shanties along rivers, Mexican road gangs. A large photograph of a girl on which was written: *With all my love—Sally.* Snapshots of other girls.

Mrs. Allison told Don about each of the pictures. They were something she wanted him to see to bring Wayne alive again, but something unbearable too. Dr. Allison said nothing but puffed slowly on his pipe. Sometimes he glanced at Don's face, bent over the album. His wife's eyes were hot and dry and staying away from tears.

The pictures turned up for a few moments and then the black leaves of the album were turned to other photographs. Doctor Allison occasionally slipped his watch from his vest pocket and looked at it in a nervous habit he had, as if there were a patient he must call on. And Mrs. Allison sometimes pressed the trembling of her lips to a tight line. And sometimes Don drew his shoulders in stiffly and wished he hadn't come.

The last picture was turned up. The album was closed.

Mrs. Allison said, taking her husband's hand and turning it over, "Your hands are dirty. Go wash your hands." She stood up. "I must go see about something to eat. Hilda is all alone in the kitchen."

She left the room. Doctor Allison stood up. He cleared his throat. He seemed to want to say something, then thought better of it and merely tapped Don on the arm in the same way Wayne had often tapped him, said, "Make yourself at home, boy," and left the room.

Alone in the room Don stood looking at the floor. Slowly his eyes came to the bed. He walked to it and picked up the tennis racket. "Hello Wayne," he said. He took a swing with it, as if at a ball and then gently laid it back on the bed. He looked around the room. There were two pennants above the bed bearing the names in the school colors of Wayne's high school and college. On the dresser in a narrow-necked bottle was a miniature model of a pirate schooner. He moved about the room, looking at it, Wayne's room. He ran his fingers listlessly over the covers of Wayne's books in their bookcase. There was a lot of poetry: Shelley, Keats, Whitman, Sandburg. There were books on history, and novels. He sat on the edge of the bed looking at the room and then staring out the window. Wayne, his mind said, Wayne.

Dinner was served. They sat down at the table and the maid came in. "Hilda, this is Don, Wayne's friend in the army," Doctor Allison said, standing and making the introduction.

Hilda was a plain-looking, heavy-boned Swedish woman only a few years older than Wayne's mother. She shook hands with Don, pressing his hand as hard as a man would have. "I raised that boy," she said. "I helped raise that boy."

She sat at her place at the table. Don was surprised. If he had a servant she wouldn't sit at the table with them.

The dinner was a quiet affair. The soup spoons clicked the plates gently and everyone thought his own thoughts. The conversation was general. There was little of it.

The roast came and the vegetables.

"Tomorrow is Sunday," Mrs. Allison told Don. "Are you going to your own church or would you like to go to our church?"

Don laid his spoon aside and looked at Doctor Allison. Wayne's mother said, "Oh, he never goes. Sundays he looks through his microscope." Her voice was both scolding and affectionate.

"I'd like to go to your church," Don said. "I went to the Congregational church with Wayne and—I liked it." He glanced down at his plate.

Hilda, across the table from Don, suddenly burst into loud and violent tears. "They took my boy away," she sobbed. Scraping her chair noisily from the table she got up, and with her hands covering her face, almost staggered out of the room, looking sadly humorous on her fat, short legs.

They ate the meat and the vegetables in silence. Mrs. Allison got the dessert herself. It took a long time for her to bring it in. She set the cake and ice cream before them.

Don looked down into the heaped-up ice cream, wondering if he could swallow even a mouthful of it, and the angel food cake with its brittle white frosting and too soft insides. He saw Wayne standing against the wire fence serenely surveying the night. "How many doctors will they need in this war?" Wayne had said. It was almost the first thing he had said to him. He felt Wayne tackling him from behind that night and felt again the bruise of the skin on his then alive leg. He remembered Wayne stretched full-length with his hands behind his head and his eyes staring at the sky.

"What are you thinking?"

"Thinking of home," Wayne had said.

This was home. He was an alien here. Trying to carry a message across the awful void that would always be until these two people here were, themselves, part of that void. And the name lost. No others to carry on the ideals of these two and their dead son. Only he. He clenched his hands. He would. For Wayne. He wouldn't fail them.

He searched for words, shuffling them in his mind, wanting to blurt this out, say this in kindness, or this in gratitude, or anything they wanted to hear. He searched for words. He said at length, drawing the unused spoon across the linen tablecloth, "Wayne was the best friend I ever had." His voice choked up and he didn't know how to say what he wanted next to say. He had no more words. He stopped. He couldn't look at them but played in the unwanted ice cream with the lamenting spoon. There would be no children. No grandchildren. This was the end of a name and a family. Wayne alone to carry on, and Wayne dead. There would be no more Allisons.

Wayne's mother's eyes found Don's as he dragged them up from the melting ice cream. "It's up to you boys who came back," she said, "to see that the boys who—" the word was hard to bring out, "died—didn't die in vain. That—that—" her hand made a helpless little circle above the tablecloth— "that it's a better world for everybody." She wiped the corner of her eye with a lace handkerchief, smiled at Don over its edge. She reached out across the table and patted his hand, smiling at him.

At night, in the quiet night of the house, they wanted to know about their son. Mrs. Allison suggested that they sit on the front porch. Her smile was too bright, her eyes too sad. She said that she would make lemonade and bring it to them. Oh God, for a bottle of beer, a shot! Don tightened his jaw and went to the front porch with Dr. Allison.

The father sat silent next to Don on the porch. His rocking chair made its creaking noise. Crickets were in the night grass.

The mother came and set the lemonade before them and took a chair. There was only the outline of their bodies in the dark, and the chair squeaking a little and the smell of the doctor's pipe.

There was a long silence. The lemonade remained untouched in the glasses. They wanted to know about their son. The mother asked. Don told them everything he could remember, every detail of their friendship. He knew Wayne's mother was weeping in the dark. Sparks came from the father's pipe and occasionally he drew his watch, that he could not see in the dark, from his pocket and glanced down at it. And the night moved about them, toward lateness and deeper darkness.

"Ask him, Dad," the mother said.

The father sucked on his pipe a moment longer. He set it on the table. It made a clicking sound. His voice, when he spoke, was very soft, very low. "How—how was it with Wayne—when—?"

Quickly Don put his hand across his chest as if to conceal from them Wayne's blood where it had spattered on his uniform.

Don trembled. He saw the scene again. Under the ragged edges of the night they lay together. Wayne's hands were pressed to his stomach as if he had a cramp. But was he only trying to hold his entrails inside? Wayne's eyes were looking into his. They were dying, pleading eyes, holding an unfathomable desire and request. Wayne's lips were trying vainly to smile but they only trembled and there was a gurgling in his throat and a bubbling of frothy blood from his gaped-open mouth. The wind walked over the night as over a grave.

Don shivered. He stared in fright at Wayne's parents. They couldn't see him. He could see only the outline of their bodies. He lied to them. He said, "He didn't know at all. It was easy."

The father turned to his wife. "See, Mama, it is good."

Don knew that the mother was crying harder now. Her body on the chair was bent double. But there was no sound.

They sat in the night.

She had turned Wayne's bed down for him. And late that night they were still in the front room, sitting together on the couch with but one dim lamp burning. He brought the little packet of Wayne's belongings to them. On the bus, one hundred miles from Omaha, he had for the first time looked inside: one of Wayne's dog tags; his watch with the engraving on the back—*To our son, with love. May time see you through;* his wallet, pictures in the wallet of his parents and Sally, three faded dollar bills in the wallet; his keys, the keys to his home and his car. Don had laid his head back against the seat. He had closed his eyes. The next thing he knew was that the bus driver was saying loudly, cheerfully, "Omaha!"

Don approached the parents. He held the package out to them. "These are Wayne's." The father took them. The mother looked at him and her eyes were filled with the same unfathomable request that had been in Wayne's. He wanted to leave them with some words that would allay their grief. He said, "Wayne said he had the most wonderful mother in the world." He saw his own mother, his mother's house; he saw Wayne and Wayne's mother. He lowered his eyes. He said, "Wayne said that when he came back he was going to become a doctor like—" He nodded at Wayne's father. He left the room and climbed the stairs.

The next day he went to church with Wayne's mother. He was very gentle with her. He helped her up and down curbs. She introduced him to the minister, to her friends and Wayne's friends. At lunch Dr. Allison did an unusual thing and came from bending over his microscope to eat with them. Hilda piled more and more wheatcakes on Don's plate because her boy Wayne had liked them. And yet she looked at him with an unconscious wish secret in her eyes that it had been he instead of Wayne.

When they were finished eating, Don said he'd like to go see Wayne's girl, Sally. The father and mother exchanged quick glances. The mother said, "She's married now. She lives in Drake Court."

Sally was as pretty as Wayne had said. She was soft and beautiful and had a wonderful figure and was worth waiting for as Wayne had said when he couldn't go to the whorehouses with him. She looked a little frightened when he told her who he was and a young man in an officer's uniform with captain's bars on the collar came to the door to see who was there. She introduced him to Don as her husband and said she was glad that an old friend of Wayne's had called on her, that she had known Wayne in school. They invited him in. They mixed a drink for him. He asked her how long she had been married. She told him. He figured it out and it was a month before Wayne had been killed. He left as soon as he could.

Don wanted to leave the next day but Wayne's parents insisted that he stay longer. He explained that he had no clothes with him. Wayne's mother got one of Wayne's suits and made him put it on. Looking at him in it and turning him around she said that with just a little tailoring it would fit him perfectly. She brought some of Wayne's shirts and socks to him.

Don stayed five days. He had never been more content in his life. They wanted him to stay longer but he told them he had to get back to Chicago. Reluctantly they agreed to let him go. Wayne's mother and Hilda, still with the secret look at the back of her eyes, fixed him a final meal.

Don walked around the Happy Hollow district the morning before he left, imagining that Wayne was walking beside him. He found Wayne's grammar school and his high school and imagined he had lived next door to Wayne all his life, had gone through school with him and that there had never been any war but that Wayne had a sister and he was engaged to her.

When he got back to the house and looked into Wayne's room he saw Mrs. Allison busily engaged inside. She was taking Wayne's pennants from the wall and packing them, with his other belongings, into a large cardboard carton. She was putting away the last mementos of this boy who had been so brutally torn from her, with so much pain, in childbirth and again torn away from her in man-made death.

When he was ready to leave, Hilda shook hands and wiped her eyes on her apron. Wayne's parents walked him to the door. Outside, on the porch, was a large wardrobe suitcase. "You were Wayne's best friend," Mrs. Allison explained. "These are his clothes. If you can use them—or know someone who can—" Again her smile was too bright and her eyes too sad.

They moved out onto the porch. Don shook hands with the doctor. The doctor looked deep into Don, and smiling, tapped him on the arm in Wayne's gesture.

Don stood on the top step for a moment. He glanced back at them. "It should have been me instead of him." He meant it.

Wayne's mother came forward. She put her arms around him, and holding him tightly, kissed him. Then she released him.

He knew she was crying. He didn't want to see her tears. He picked up the suitcase and limped down the steps. He didn't look back when he got to the sidewalk.

# VII

Don climbed the steps to Sue's place awkwardly, swinging the large suitcase up to the step above each time and then dragging his false leg to that step while his hand on the railing gave him additional support.

He knocked. Sue opened the door. "Haven't seen you lately," she said coolly. Bitterly she thought, He doesn't know how I've thought about him, how I've missed him, worried. He doesn't know because he'd never feel these things about me. You fool, she told herself, why can't you accept what you have! She was torn between gratitude for what love he gave her and anger at the indignity of having to be grateful.

Then she saw the suitcase. Her voice became alarmed. "Where are you going?"

"Been out of town."

"Oh." There was relief in the single word.

Don lugged the suitcase over the sill and closed the door. "Went to see Wayne's folks."

"That was nice of you."

"They're nice people."

"I missed you." She said it casually. But her heart wasn't casual. If it only could be. Not care too much. "Want a glass of wine? I'll take you to supper."

"I'll take *you* to supper," Don said. Sue looked at him in surprise but said nothing. Bringing glasses she filled them with wine. "I have to wash up a bit," she said, "and then we can go out to eat."

"Wait," Don said. He motioned her to come sit beside him on the bed. She did. "You could kiss me," she complained. He kissed her. "There—now keep quiet." He pushed her away playfully. Then his eyes became serious. "I want to talk to you." He laughed. "This will kill you—I want to get a job." Sue looked at him but said nothing.

"No. I really do." He ran his hand along the bedspread and looked at it. "I'm through being a bum." Sue put her hand on top of his. "I don't know where I can get a job," he said, nodding toward his false leg, "but I'm going to try."

"Don," Sue said, "maybe you could get on at the Haines Company. I'll tell you what—I'll ask around the place tomorrow and then let you know." She took his hand between both of hers. "After all you're a vet and—" she nodded in turn toward his false leg, "well, they should be willing to do something for you." She placed his hand against her cheek.

While she tidied up, Don lay back across the bed thinking about the good people he had known: about Wayne's parents and Wayne and Sue.

"Hey you! I'm ready!" Sue said.

"Please sit down," Don said, holding his hand out to her in a helpless, pleading gesture. When she sat down he lay back on the bed and put his arm over his eyes. He told her about Wayne, all about him, and about his parents, all about the trip to Omaha. For a long time after he had told her he lay there. She didn't say anything but her heart responded. A kinder Don. With a kinder Don she had less to fear. If she could only say how she loved him and not have to be afraid of driving him away by that loving. But she couldn't chance it, couldn't show it. She didn't show it now.

He wanted to tell her what he thought on the bus—how he was against war. Finally he sat up. "There's something else I want to tell you. I don't know how to say it. I—" he laughed his nervous laugh, "want to live a useful life. I've been a phony long enough. I've—well—I've seen people suffering when I was across—" He ran the palm of his hand across his eyes as if to erase the sight. Sue stood watching him. He looked at her, asking her with his eyes to understand him. "I think I even understand my mother now." Again he laughed his nervous laugh and said, "I—well—" And his eyes implored her to understand. "It means I'll be leaving the theater." He said it and stopped and continued to look at her.

Sue slipped her glasses off and ran one of the stems into her short-cropped curly hair. Surprisingly she understood. "I'm glad to hear you say that, Don." She kissed him and said, "I know, Don. And I'd say I'm proud of you but that would be corny."

She wasn't even going to try to talk him into staying with her acting group and this disappointed him a little.

"I'll be rooting for you," she said. With her hand, and laughing a little, she pulled him up off the bed. "Let's go eat."

He took her to a good restaurant. They ate leisurely and she looked across the table at him proudly, smiled at him or winked at him in her embarrassment when he glanced up and caught the pride in her eyes.

He sat thinking: I've lost my leg. I've lost my best friend. I must tell the world what a lousy deal it was. He made a vow. I'll be a sonofabitch if I'm not going to be as close to Wayne and as much like him as I can be. Wayne, his mind said, Wayne.

He wanted to tell Sue all this. But he couldn't put it into words.

He looked at her. Sue, his mind said. He knew she understood. Sue. He had a warm, good feeling for her and suddenly he felt happy and purposeful and grateful to her for all of her caring.

Sue reached across the table, and held his hand, wanting to say "I love you" to him.

# VIII

Aaron laughed and whistled, walking briskly along the street. He had done it in secrecy and now he could tell them and none of them could do anything about it, talk him out of it.

Half laughing he ran up the steps to the house. His sister and her boy friend were in the front room listening to some jive music, discussing band leaders, Frankie Sinatra and new dance steps. Rebecca's mother was in the kitchen with his father and sat at the table with a cup of coffee in front of her. "To marry a *goy!*" She shook her head in a sharp, underscoring line while her lips tightened out like the blade of a razor. "No, it should never be!" Her cup clicked the table, spilling some of the coffee. "Rather I would see mine Rebecca dead than to see her having anything to do with a goy!"

Papa Levin stood on his tired feet and looked down at Mrs. Friedman with his patient, wrinkled face. He spread his hands away from his body. "But the old times," he said, "the old ways have passed. It is not right that people separate themselves like this."

Aaron, angry because the others were there and he could not make his announcement, locked himself in the bathroom and waited until he could be alone with his father and tell him. Then when Mrs. Friedman had finally left and Muriel and her boy friend had gone out to a neighborhood movie, Aaron confronted his father.

"Papa, I want to talk to you."

Mr. Levin laid aside his paper and, putting his arms up on the table, leaned toward his son. The old man's eyes looked deeply and sadly into his son's and his thick, colorless lips smiled slowly. "Yes?"

Aaron's eyes fell away from his father's face, slipped down the blue work shirt, skidded along the nub of what was left of a finger and stared at the floor. "I got a room. I'm going to move. I think it's better if I live by myself."

The smile dropped away from the old man's mouth, leaving the heavy lines at either side of his nose and the hollows in his cheeks that the smile had, for a moment, tightened away. "Aaron—my son," Mr. Levin said. There was no command, no request, no appealing in his voice, only a weary and painful acceptance as if he had already known. He came from his chair and lifted his hand to the high shoulder of his son. Aaron retreated a step and at the same time shook his head no from side to side.

The old man looked up into the tall boy's face, and wringing his dry, calloused palms that made a rasping sound, said, "This you shouldn't do. You shouldn't hurt me like this."

Aaron smiled. It was a lazy, indifferent smile.

The old man had turned away. He had taken the bottle of whisky from the cupboard and a little glass. He sat at the table and poured the glass full, lifted it to his lips, his eyes again finding his son's and looking at him in a long glance of entreaty. His hand shook, carrying the whisky to his lips, and some of it spilled on their dryness. He gagged a little on the whisky and wiped his mouth with the back of his hand. "You belong here in your home. With your father and your sister. Here, Aaron, where we can look after—" He shook his head. "You are not completely well. If you stay it will be better." He shook his head slowly. "If you will stay all the time you can write and all night you can keep the light open."

Aaron laughed. "I'm going," he said. It was good to hurt someone; he had been so badly hurt himself. He went to his room and started packing. His father came to the door and stood there looking in. Aaron grew angry and hurried, throwing things quickly into the suitcase. Behind him he could hear his father occasionally groan as if in physical pain. He wouldn't do that. He wouldn't dare do that. He couldn't bear that again. Here, in this room, the work shirt coming off, his father turning and showing him his thin, slightly hunched back with the scars the whip had left. "Look, will you leave me alone!" Aaron said without turning around. His father neither spoke nor moved.

Aaron gathered his books and his writing and tossed them into the suitcase too. He buckled the case and his father moved from the doorway as, carrying it, Aaron walked into the kitchen. His father followed him. Aaron dropped the case to the floor and dug into his pocket with a frantically searching hand. He pulled out his door key and placed it on the table.

The old man looked down at the key and, unable to look up at his son, kept staring at it. "Keep your key, Aaron."

Aaron shook his head. His lips were fastened with a tight and rude smile.

"Aaron—" The voice was gentle with a coaxing. "Stay. Do anything you want. Sleep all day." The old man's shoulders shrugged as if now he could accept anything. "Write. Do anything." He shrugged again and went on staring at the key. "If you should get—sick—"

"Then I'll jump off the bridge."

"Please—my son, do not say that to me." The old man moved toward Aaron. Aaron lifted the suitcase. His hand was a tight fist around its handle. He smiled at the pleading in his father's eyes.

"I'm going."

His father's shoulders drooped. His pinched face turned away. "The key, it will always be under the scrub pail."

Aaron walked to the door and opened it. "I'll come to see you," he said. He closed the door and ran down the steps on his big awkward feet.

The room was nice. He was free. There was only one prison that held him. He lay on his back on the bed, staring at the ceiling and chuckling over his new-found freedom. He rolled his head in pleasure and glanced about the room, looking at its warped floor and frayed rug, the old-fashioned faucets, one of which dripped and left a rusty stain down the inside of the bowl. Free! Free!

Here he could avoid life's surgical eye and wear his dark glasses against participation . . . but what if he died and never wrote anything? What have you got to lose? Well, you're a virgin, you know. Oh the hell with people like me who persist in asking ridiculous questions such as, have you been suffering? Has some sort of change come over you? What seems to be the trouble? To hell with people like me . . . the war department regrets to inform you . . . straighten up and fly right for a change . . . Dear corpse, God, draw us all into life again . . . I muff every thought with that damn "poetry." Y-E-SSSSSS! The poem, the poem by all means . . . "dis culture bizness."

He laughed and hugged his legs and rolled on the bed in enjoyment. And suddenly stopped, his face tense . . . straighten up and fly right. He laughed again and again to himself, in encouragement, giving spurs to himself. And he said aloud, "Straighten up and fly right."

For two days he enjoyed life, just sleeping whenever he wanted to, most of every day and all of every night. Then he began wandering the streets, looking curiously at the people, wondering about them, glancing into their faces. And one morning he stood in front of a hockshop and looked in beyond the dingy window at the tawdry array of things once owned and then given to the jaws of business for a little money, a little fun or perhaps only enough to eat and sleep on in the fond belief that some day, somehow, when things were better, the frayed hockshop slips would be called up from billfolds and the money counted proudly out as with slightly embarrassed faces the owners took back their meager possessions identified with better times and sweeter days. His eye was caught and held by a typewriter in the very center of the whole array of lost but remembered possessions, purchases, gifts. He stood looking in with his tongue pressed out tensely against his bottom lips: I am a wax dummy standing in an unlit store window, when I do not write—when I do not think—"poet." I have nothing if I do not write.

He went inside. He counted out, with sweating palms and quickly enthusiastic mind, the twenty-six dollars and took the typewriter into his arms, lugged it the three blocks home, and up the creaking stairs. He set it down on the dresser and all that day, biting his bottom lip, pressed with one finger against the keys and saw the black letters erect themselves against the white paper and leave their impress.

A week, two weeks, shut from everyone he transcribed his meager thoughts to the white paper, telling himself, Be simple, be honest, speak of the war, the people. He arranged the few papers at the end of the week in order, and piling their thinness on the dresser, took a streetcar to the neighborhood that had been home.

Carefully avoiding his father's house he walked with careful tread up the steps and pressed Rebecca's doorbell.

"Will you come with me?"

"Oh yes, Aaron!" And she quickly pulled her arms into the green sleeves of a summer coat and hurried down the steps, alongside him, looking with fondness into his face.

He took her to his room with few words said between them on the way and only her eyes seeking his face, his hair, his eyes, his lips.

He said, "This is where I live—don't tell them."

She said, "It's nice. I like it." She pressed his hand. "I won't tell anybody."

He rubbed his foot against the floor and looked out over her shoulder and through the window to the early night sky hung with its few, dimly shining stars. "I've been doing a little writing. I want to read it to you."

She twisted her gloves from her slim and slightly trembling fingers and sat tensely in the one chair across the room from him. He sat on the bed and, squinting at the official-looking typing on the page of paper, pouted his lips a little. Then glancing at her, hoping she would like it and understand it, he began to read.

Rebecca sat leaning forward as she listened. The words came softly from across the room.

She didn't understand much of it. The words were strange and not like the simple English she understood from novels rented at drugstores and bought from the best-seller lists, but his voice was sweet to her ears and the vision of his face with its black hair leaping out from his forehead as if an artist's palette knife had put it there and his sensual and pouted mouth, his eyes following the words in a brown-blackness, brought tears of love and compassion to her eyes. And she was not listening. She was drinking in, greedily, the look of him, and remembered, for lonely times, the shape of him, the room, the moment and its sad sweetness. She wanted badly to sit at his feet and pictured it out: he reading his poetry with his arm loosely about her shoulders and his hand tenderly stroking her hair. He loved her and when he was finished would sit with his arm around her while the tiny light of the stars would pin-point the dingy window glass.

Blushingly she turned her mind from such thoughts. With love she looked at him. Her body ached to lean against him, to sit on the floor at his feet with her shoulder against his knee.

Aaron suddenly looked up from the lines he had been reading. "Why don't you sit over here?"

He meant that she should sit on the bed beside him. Quickly she moved to him and quickly, in sudden boldness, sat on the floor with her shoulder touching his leg. He read and she didn't hear but only thought, with a mind that would remember every detail, that she was sitting at his feet. And she said to herself that she would suffer anything just as long as she could be near him, forever.

Her tenderness and her feelings made her bolder. She put her head down against his knee. The page, stirring and turning to the next, made the room's only noise. "This—" Aaron said, "is just—" He swept his big hand confusedly. "Well—it's not finished—it's just—just an idea—well, listen—" He pouted his lips. He was embarrassed reading it and yet it was everything he wanted to say to people. It was where Aaron lived. It was Aaron. What he really felt and would perhaps never be able to say. He began to read.

Rebecca listened and put her forehead down against Aaron's trouser knee. "I love you, I love you," her lips said without sound.

She did not lift her head immediately when Aaron had finished. He stroked her hair. She rubbed her cheek against the blue roughness of his knee, the cheek bearing the birthmark, and did not think of it. "I love you," she said.

"I know you do," Aaron said. He smiled sadly, strangely, impersonally. He put his hand on her shoulder and tightened it sympathetically. "You better go home now." She nodded her head and smiled, keeping her eyes and mouth away from tears. She stood up, shaking her hair over her shoulders, smoothing it. "Give me your comb, Aaron."

He gave it to her. She smiled at him. "Will you walk me to the car?"

When he had put her on the car he went back home and lay across the bed, following the nightmare of his career in the army. Never, never, never.

. . . the nightmare, the reality: army life. I can't understand what is going on. I sometimes think I'm lost. I just visited a chaplain. He was squat, bespeckled and ugly. The day I arrived in camp I was interviewed by a personnel psychologist. I applied as a conscientious objector, Milo. He was sympathetic and advised me to see a chaplain. "Chaplains have a great deal of influence," he said. "You see a chaplain. After basic training you'll be placed in a noncombatant unit."

I saw the chaplain. "You'll get used to killing, my son. We all have to do things we don't want to do. That's life. You're young yet. You're inexperienced. You'll have to learn many things. I've done many things I didn't want to do. I once worked in a shoe repair shop. There were bad odors from the shoes. I didn't like the odors. But I did my job. I'm proud of that . . . yes, yes, yes, you'll get used to it, my son."

I saluted and left the chapel.

I continuously make mental notes. I have written about six poems since I've been in the army. The officials may chain my arms and legs but my mind is a quick bird in flight over enormous areas of green plains, free and swift. Nobody understands me. The headaches occur more often now.

I suffered severe pain in my head. I signed the sick call and the first sergeant sent me to the dispensary. A young Jewish doctor from Chicago's North Side examined me. He picked up his pen, black Parker reed, and scrawled "psychoneurosis" across the top of the observation slip. He then sent me over to the mental hygiene clinic. A major, the battalion psychiatrist, put me through a psychiatric examination. "Levin, the army needs every man. I'm sending you back. One month from today I'll see you again. You're fit to go back to duty."

I've looked out of sweat-wet eyes and seen nature. I'd only looked at humans before. I have impressions of evening skies, the camp chapel on top of the hill, sweltering swamps and the snake-filled, silent nights on the field. Stealing a smoke on a night problem. Soldiers cracking their dirty jokes.

I had a headache again today. I reported to the first sergeant and he put me on sick call for the record. I went up to the dispensary by myself.

"What did you do in civilian life?"

"I wrote."

"Oh. You must be neurotic."

They gave me a couple of aspirins.

"Go out and get laid and all your troubles will be over."

His mind began traveling down alleys and into caves. The frantic beating of his heart made the bed and its springs shake.

Gotta get out of here!

He rushed to the door, ran out, down the steps.

On the sidewalk below, collapsing into himself, he clung to the railing and panted through open mouth.

Then, as someone sleepwalking, he felt his way cautiously forward with his big feet and moved on down the sidewalk.

In the somnambulant night he walked. He was sinking into the sidewalk instead of walking on it. Down the endless ways of slum streets leading to slum houses he walked. The sidewalks spread out uncaringly into the deep black depths of the neighborhoods. Night swelled around him like the beating of a heart.

# IX

In her bedroom Rebecca pulled on the new blue and white seersucker two-piece suit and fastened the little silver buttons that ran down the front of the blouse. She fastened them slowly and looked across the room at the far wall. Would she be different? Was it wrong? Abstractedly she adjusted the wide Cavalier sleeves. For a long while she sat tensely on the side of the bed. Then quickly she arose, and walking to the mirror, again combed her hair. She was ready now. She glanced down into her purse. The rouge and lipstick were there.

She went into the drugstore on the corner near his house and carried the soda to the last booth where no one could see her and sat with her back to the front of the store. Pushing the soda aside she opened her purse and took out the lipstick and rouge. She had never used them before and, frowning into the mirror, applied the rouge to her cheeks in amateurish round disks. Then inexpertly she painted her already red lips with the redder lipstick pencil. Below one of the circles of red near the corner of her lips the dull birthmark showed in an irregular blotch.

From her purse she took a package of cigarettes and opened it. Looking over one shoulder and then the other toward the front of the store to see that no one was watching her, she then put a cigarette between her lips. Lit a match. Choked trying to light the cigarette. She again glanced about the drugstore and dropped the cigarette on the floor. Once more she looked into the mirror at herself and seeing, with sad eyes, the oval of birthmark, tried to arrange her hair so that it would show as little as possible.

She walked quickly from the drugstore with her eyes staring straight ahead and hurried self-consciously down the sidewalk, sure that everyone was looking at her painted face.

Aaron didn't answer when she knocked. She tried the handle and the door slid open. Aaron sat in the lumpy overstuffed chair with his head back against it and his eyes closed. The only illumination was a small lamp on an end table alongside the chair and the moonlight that came through the tall window. The rest of the room lay in dark, secret shadows. Aaron's face alone was clearly visible, and his hands folded on his lap. And now, with the door coming open, he lifted his eyelids and looked across the room at her.

Rebecca closed the door. "Hello, Aaron."

He only stared at her. But he didn't tell her to go away and she sat on the edge of the bed with her purse clenched on her knees. Her legs began to tremble. "It's too light in here," she said, and moving swiftly to the window, pulled the shade to the sill. Aaron's eyes followed her in dull watchfulness. She moved quickly back to the bed, again clasping the purse on her quivery knees. She began to breathe hard and was afraid. She had to part her lips a little to get her breath.

Aaron frowned at her. "Why don't you take that paint off your face?" he asked in dull derision.

In that small gesture of hers she brought the fingers of her hand up over her birthmark. She tried to smile. "I thought you liked women of the world." Aaron wondered where she had ever heard that silly phrase, *women of the world.*

Rebecca lowered her eyes from his. She was staring at her purse. Her fingers twisted at the catch and she reached inside the pocketbook and pulled out the cigarettes. "Want a cigarette, Aaron?" He shook his head and some of his black hair fell over one temple, hung limp there. Rebecca put a cigarette between her lips, and the match, making a scratching, hissing sound, added its weak flare to the darkened room. She tried to draw the smoke up into her mouth and gagged on it, coughed raspingly.

Aaron laughed out loud at her. "Here, give it to me." He took the cigarette from her and, sitting again in his chair, smoked it.

Rebecca began to cry. She cried silently, the tears rolling slowly down her cheeks and, like a child, put the back of her hand against her cheek to stop them, rubbed her eyes with her knuckles. Aaron didn't try to console her. It was as if he didn't even know she was crying.

When the tears were dry, when Aaron had lit still another cigarette, Rebecca glanced at him and glanced away. She had to get behind his chair. She couldn't do it here. Her whole body began to tremble. All of a sudden she said in a rush of words, "The faucet is dripping," and moved to the washbasin. He didn't tell her that it dripped all the time. From the faucet she moved the length of the room and stood in complete darkness behind his chair and crowded into the corner. Aaron, lost in his own thoughts, slowly puffed his cigarette and stared out beyond the enclosing wall into space.

In the darkness Rebecca unbuttoned the first button on her blouse, the second. She slipped it off. She pulled her skirt loose and stepped out of it. Took off her brassiere. Her shoes. Rolled her stockings down. Took off all her clothes. Then, with her head down and staring at the floor, she stepped, completely nude, out from behind the chair and stood in the light in front of Aaron. Last night he had said while reading his poetry that sex was the thing everybody needs, was the thing that gave reason to the minds and bodies of everyone. If that was what he needed . . .

She was perfectly made. Her shoulders were soft and rounded, her breasts young, firm, forward standing. Her hips were slim, her legs were lithe with shapely calves and high insteps. About her whole figure there was an unspoiled youthfulness. And she stood in front of him with her head down.

Aaron's unbelieving eyes looked at her. His mouth fell open in surprise. "Aaron," she said. And moved a little closer with her head down and one hand reaching for his hand.

"Rebecca! Put your clothes on!" It was a command.

She came closer, and in her shyness, in her shame, clenched her eyes tight—but slipped onto his lap.

Aaron drew back further into the chair and held her off with his hands. "Rebecca—you can't do this!" She was trembling all over in complete humiliation and tears forced their way out past her tightly clenched eyes. Aaron stood up, lifting her erect with his large moist hands. "Please, Rebecca, put your clothes on." She only shivered the more and became a deader weight against the unyielding palms of his hands. He began to shake her a little as if to awaken her. And suddenly, weeping loudly, she darted from under his hands and disappeared behind the chair.

Aaron sat down heavily. "I'm sorry, Rebecca . . . you shouldn't have done it," he said wearily. Then there was only the sound of her furious weeping and the sound of her frantic body hiding itself again in her clothes. And as suddenly as she had darted behind the chair she now rushed out and ran toward the door, turned, ran to the bed, threw herself across it in a ball with her face in her arms. "Oh, I'm so ashamed . . . I'm so ashamed," she sobbed, over and over.

Aaron sat in his chair with his head down. All he felt was complete discomfort.

"So ashamed . . . so ashamed . . . "

For Aaron the moment, reality, began slowly to dissolve, to drift away to another time, another place . . . where they were bivouacked was the most pleasant place he had ever been in his life. They were near a high ridge where you could see miles of rolling country. It was quite different from the swamps and flat plantations closer to the river. They had been mock fighting on land bare of trees, hot by day, cold and wet by night—low country—but here it was like a different world. He had just built a fire . . . too hot . . . must move . . . He'd always wondered why back at the other site there were no birds. Out here there are robins and wild canaries—beautiful. There are many other wild animals. I caught a lizard, allowed a chameleon to change color on my shirt, and picked up a dead armadillo by the tail. All day the buzzards circle gracefully. I like this country!

This last problem was pretty tough on us all—one day we chased the "reds" twenty miles, fighting all the way. The fire is hot, red and yellow, orange-purple. Rebecca just sent me her picture. I built this fire about fifty yards from the nearest group so I could be alone to look at it. . . .

Aaron sighed in remembrance and was back in his room in Chicago. He lit a cigarette and looked through its long coiling of smoke at Rebecca. Her sobbing was less violent. Aaron pressed the soles of his shoes against the floor as if to stand and go to her, put his arms around her. But he sighed again and leaned back against the chair. He must tell her. He closed his eyes. "Rebecca."

There was a movement on the bed. Rebecca slowly lifted her head from her arms. Her wet green eyes looked at him. "Yes, Aaron." A little catching sob of breath tightened in her throat.

Aaron kept his eyes closed. "What," he asked, "do you know about me? Me and the army?"

"Why—that—that—" Her eyes searched for his but could not find them. "You were released from the army."

He laughed. He opened his eyes, and looking at her, smiling at her, nodding at her, tapped his forehead with his fist.

"No, Aaron!" she said, rushing to him and, kneeling before him, put her arms around him.

"Don't you know—" he said coldly, "that I tried to commit suicide?"

Her hand went up to her mouth as if to hold something inside.

"Don't you know—" he said coldly, "that I'm insane?"

Her tears came again and she tried to put her arms around him, comfort him, tell him it didn't matter. He moved her away and toward the door. He picked up her purse and handed it to her. "Go home. Stay away from me," he said, "I'm nuts."

He opened the door. She stood looking at him in love and disbelief. His hand moved her gently across the sill and he closed the door.

He could hear her crying as she went down the steps. He laughed bitterly. Out of the war he didn't even get that. He was still a virgin.

# X

Rebecca went down into the street and into the night. She was still sobbing and walked with one hand held up to her face so that people wouldn't notice. Don, coming out of his hotel, saw her. "Hey, Rebecca!" He hurried after her clumsily, limping a trifle. He caught up with her. "Hey, Rebecca!" She didn't seem to hear and it was then that he saw she was crying. He caught her by the wrist. "What's the matter?"

They were standing under a lamppost and she looked up into his face with the tears running off her cheeks and making brown dots on the gray sidewalk.

"What's the matter?"

With her eyes closed she shook her head and didn't answer.

"Why are you crying?"

"Because I'm ugly." Her sobs came in small gasps.

"You're not ugly."

"Yes, I am."

He laughed gently and didn't let go her wrist. Smiling, he shook his head no.

"Because of this," Rebecca said, pointing at the birthmark with her free hand. "Look at it. Look how ugly it is." She began to sob again and her green eyes were the color of wet young grass. "Please let me go."

He released her arm. She began to move away. He fell in step with her. "Let me walk with you." She didn't say no but walked with her head down and patted her eyes with her handkerchief.

They walked two blocks. "Feel better?" Don asked sympathetically. She nodded yes. Her breath again caught in her throat and nostrils as a child's does after it has cried long and hard. They walked another block in silence. She looked up. "Oh, I'm going the wrong way."

They turned and walked south along Dearborn. Don lit a cigarette and secretly admired her, her sharp chiseled features, the long-lashed eyes, green behind the brownness of the lashes. "Feel better?" he asked. She nodded. He took her arm. She let him. She had begun to cry again but only a little. "I can't go home looking like this. My eyes must be red," she said; and tried to gain control of herself. They were near Don's hotel. "I live there," he said, pointing. "You can wash your face there and fix up if you want—or we can walk around until you're ready to go home."

"Would it be all right to go there?"

He pressed her arm in friendliness. "Of course it will."

"I don't want anybody to see me like this."

"No one will."

They went into the lobby and took the self-operating elevator. A few of Rebecca's tears dotted the close-cropped green elevator rug.

Don unlocked his room and they went in. From the dresser he took a glass and poured a little wine into it. "Here, drink this. It won't hurt you. Make you feel better."

She took it obediently, her grave green eyes, shining from her tears, looked into his in gratitude. "Thank you." She drank it while he got a towel from the dresser and pointed to where the bathroom was.

While she washed Don searched in the bottom drawer of the dresser.

Rebecca came from the bathroom. She smiled at him shyly. Then her face immediately assumed its sad and disconsolate appearance and her eyes again filled with tears. Her face had been washed of its paint and had a healthy and wholesome beauty. "Hey—come look!" Don said, waggling his fingers.

"What is it?" she asked, looking into the palm of his hands.

"Come over here," he said. "Sit down." He made her sit on the couch that folded out into a bed. He wrapped a bath towel around her shoulders. Then he put his index finger under her chin and tilted her head until the birthmark showed plainly. He sat down next to her. Then, working slowly with his mouth screwed up into a knot and his frowning eyes concentrating and a furrow between his eyebrows, he applied the theatrical makeup expertly to the birthmark. While he worked she sat stiffly and new tears gathered in her eyes. Twice she glanced at him. He was nice. And nice-looking. He was awfully nice to her. A tear fell.

He was finished. He leaned back, squinting his eyes and twisting his head to the side as he studied his work. He was proud of the job he had done. Smiling, he held a finger before her eyes in a command to sit still.

"That was a nice speech you made in the park," Rebecca said.

Don laughed. He moved to the dresser and got the mirror. Her eyes followed him.

Piling books on the seat of the chair he set the mirror on top of them and pulled the floor lamp over so that its light would reflect on her. Then, sitting next to her he put the folded palms of his hands on her shoulders and slowly turned her until she was looking into the mirror. There was no birthmark.

Don laughed. "See, you're not ugly."

Rebecca went on staring at the spot where the birthmark had been. Don gathered up the theatrical makeup, and, opening her purse, dropped it inside. Rebecca's tear-flooded eyes came back to him. "Thank you—Don." He laughed, wrinkling his nose in an engaging way. Getting the wine bottle he filled their glasses and sat next to her. "It won't make me drunk, will it?" she asked.

"Aw, no—and I'll take you home—if you let me."

Her eyes fluttered to his face, and away. "You're awfully nice to me, Don."

Don laughed. Rebecca sipped her wine and looked at him over the rim of the glass. When the glasses were empty Don asked her if she wanted more. She shook her head and leaned back, exhausted, against the couch.

Don poured another glass for himself and sat drinking the wine slowly while he looked at her and smiled with gentle kindness.

"Feel better?" he asked.

She nodded. Her breasts tightened out under the candy-striped seersucker blouse and he saw them. He glanced away. She sighed deeply. Don glanced back. As she sighed her breatsts swelled out full. Don dropped his eyes and looked into his wineglass. But he was aware of her body. Painfully aware of it. He sipped his wine and with half-lowered eyes secretly looked at her body. Told himself no. But his friendliness, his genuine liking of her and sympathy for her, had been shaded over with an urge of sex. No. But his eyes went back to her and he smiled and looked deeply into her eyes and held hers in slight flirtation.

She glanced away. "I better go."

"All right. Can I take you home?"

She nodded and her hair bounced on her shoulders and he saw it and wanted to stroke it. He felt the urge grow larger. Don't spoil things. But he brought the wine bottle over. "Just one more glass, huh?" he asked, nodding encouragement and holding the bottle to pour. His deep-set eyes gazed at her and he wrinkled his forehead in pleading.

"Oh, do you think—?"

"It won't hurt you." He smiled with his lips slightly parted as a little boy would smile and with his eyes teasing, challenging, saying you're afraid.

She held her glass out to him. "If you think it's all right."

"Sure, sure."

"At home I drink a glass of wine sometimes," she said.

"It never hurt you?"

She shook her head no and drew the filled glass from the bottle to her bosom. "Oh, I didn't want it filled!" Don looked at the glass and her rounded breasts where the glass pressed.

"I didn't want it filled!" she said again.

Don made a tishing, teasing sound.

Slowly, seated side by side, they drank the wine. Don took her empty glass and set it on the floor with his empty glass and knew he would try. Even if it spoiled everything. And she was a sweet kid. He'd like to have her for a friend. But he knew that even then, sooner or later, he would try. He felt the urge move keenly and was both ashamed of the desire and more filled with the need.

Rebecca said, "In a minute I've got to go. Honest." She leaned back against the couch, a trifle upset by the evening and the wine. New tears came to her eyes.

Don leaned back too. He put his arm around her. Her eyes were brimming. With his forefinger he snapped one tear from her cheek. He drew her to him and kissed her, gently, tenderly, with just the tip of his mouth softly pressing. "You're pretty," he said. She was. He drew her closer to him. He kissed her again. Her lips quivered under his. She was crying. "Don't, Becky," he said. He tasted her salty tears on his own lips. She laid her head against his shoulder. They sat like this for a while, she with her face pressed into the cloth of his coat, he with his arm around her.

In him, now, was a poorly controlled demand. His fingers touched the softness of her waist and, gently, the firmness of her breast, cupped it. Her eyes opened and stared into his in a fascination and she did not move away. She buried her face against his chest. "The wine makes me dizzy," she said in truth or to cover her real feelings. With his free hand he lifted her chin. "Darling . . . darling . . . darling . . . " he said. He rubbed his nose against her cheek, her neck, and gently bit her neck. His free hand turned the light switch off. She withdrew a little but his hand kept her cupped and he drew her closer to him, clung to her, found her mouth in the dark. "No, like this," he said, kissing her. She was hesitant but he was insistent, rubbing the kiss more firmly into her lips, her mouth. His free hand loosened the first silver button, the second silver button.

# XI

In the union office Jim Norris sat thumbing through the file-cabinet cards. Occasionally he selected a card and put it to the side on the neat little pile of six or seven. These were the nonunion members he would visit tonight. Behind him the file cabinet stood with one of its jaws yawned open and the hundreds of indexed cards smiling in a stiff, white-toothed grin. Here in orderly precision, indexed in alphabetical arrangement, were the names and addresses of every employee at the Haines Company; here too were the lists of the employees who didn't belong to the union. The union organizers visited them by night and talked the matter over.

Since the army, in the short time out, Jim had become a union organizer. Mr. Baker was chiefly responsible for this—and Kovac too. The union had sent him to the summer school session at the University of Wisconsin where he had studied the social sciences, government administration of industrial business and labor history. Jim laid another card on the little pile. He had come back to the same house, the same wife, the work he loved . . . he looked up and stared across the room . . . but the same Jim hadn't come back . . . his home, his wife, even the work he loved so well were strangers to him. Something had dulled in him. He worked now as from habit. He looked abstractedly out the window while his hand, in unconscious action, fondled his chin, pinched the dimple there, pinched it again. . . .

He smiled slowly. Bill Carter was quite a guy! Short, husky, with a screwed-up, scowling face beneath the close-cropped red hair, Carter shouted his curses and swaggered in his uniform half a foot shorter than Jim, flashed his quick grin, drank too much hard liquor. There was an imposed toughness about him as if he were forever testing himself and proving something to himself. . . . The war was over . . . their outfit was breaking up . . . last time he saw Carter. "It's been goddamn good, the whole experience," Carter said. He spat sideways and wiped his mouth with the back of his sleeve. He grinned. "Christ how the German gals flirted with us GI's! But of course we stuck rigidly to the nonfraternization policy—" He threw Jim a sidelong wink. "Like hell. What a laugh." He stuck his hand into Jim's breast pocket, and, taking out the pack of cigarettes, selected one. "I'm engaged to a cute little German gal in Rhineberg—remember when we were back there that three weeks? Pretty little blonde." He used Jim's pack of cigarettes as a baseball, tossing it into the air and catching it as he talked, his eyes climbing the ladder of space after the package and dropping to his cupping hands as the pack came down. All the while he juggled the burning cigarette between his lips, inhaling and sending the smoke out past his squinting eyes. "Show you her picture some day. Should have seen her cry when I left." He grinned. "She's going back to the States with me—she thinks."

Carter leaned back with his arms wide, stretching, and one hand began to playfully but roughly massage Jim's cap into his head. "About women—here's my candid opinion. French women are no goddamn good. They're not very clean and their love-making is too professional. Belgian girls are cleaner and make love about the same way, *sans* professional. Holland—" His eyes squinted along the low line of buildings across the street, remembering. "Dutch girls are very clean, devoutly religious and hard to make. They're husky but amateurish lovers. Rather stupid but capable of heated passion. My dear little Ann Kronfeld . . ." he smiled tenderly . . . "38 Karl Strasse, if you're interested. Have a picture of us eating ice cream together. Awful ice cream. The picture was supposed to have been put in a newspaper somewhere. Don't know if they did. German women, ah—devoutly religious, clean, hot as hell, wonderful lovemakers. Very true and capable of deep love. Very emotional. Hard to make unless their husbands are not around. . . ."

The scene dissolved and Jim was grinning at the empty sidewalk. Two women walked past the window, their skirts billowing in the wind, their hands holding the skirts down. Jim looked at them abstractedly. Once he would have found Carter disgusting—the continual preoccupation with sex, with women. When had he changed?

. . . Carter had, when it was time to go, hit him on the arm with a hard-balled fist and sprinted down the sidewalk. . . . Funny. Funny that he should think of the end pieces of the war. The first and last impression that had stuck. The rest had been noise and confusion and movement. Funny.

Jim pushed away from the desk and walked down the sidewalk two doors away to Bernie's Tavern on the corner of Milwaukee and Canal. He bought a glass of beer and stared down into it, sm  ng. He'd like to see Carter. Wonder what he's doing? Women, of co  rse. He smiled and suddenly, with the glass halfway to his lips, his face became haggard, his eyes dull. He drank quickly and set the glass down. No, the rest hadn't been noise and confusion and movement. His mind shuffled quickly through the memories and half-memories and brought up one he could face, look at. . . .

They moved up toward the front. They were unshaven, dirty, their hands calloused from their rifles. They marched along the roads and highways. All humanity lay strewn about them, lay gasping and bleeding. Weary of foot, one of the group, he moved with them toward the war. They passed roving bands of people straggling along the highway and through the city streets like gangs of beggars. His eyes recorded them. The Displaced Persons were a hungry, ragtag army, the women in babushkas and straight dresses that hung down between their knees and ankles, the men in rags, their faces, under caps, grimed and cut with the lines of war. Children followed along. Many of them were crying. Old men and women, often supported by younger people, feebly picked their way with the struggling mass of the homeless.

The two groups moved past each other. One group was going back to where soldiers had been. The other was moving up to where soldiers would be. Some of the D.P.'s, seeing their liberators, waved and laughed and shouted happily. Some didn't even look up at the Americans. They were going back to destroyed homes and burned land. They took, like pack horses, all of their belongings they could carry on their backs or in wheelbarrows.

The soldiers moved through the city, dragging their feet over endless roads moving toward war. Their faces wore an ugly stamp. Indifference and brutality and bitterness and hate and animal attitude had taken them prisoner even as the war had claimed them hero. It was in their faces, in their laughter, in their ganglike swagger and bluster, moving to rags of night and bones of dark. They laughed, moving toward death and destruction, and cracked their dirty jokes. They were cynic-eyed and sneering-mouthed; they were born of the dark and the night and death. They had been spewed over hill and road and paved city block and they lock-stepped their skeletal way, laughing, under the dome of night. They laughed. They cursed. They spoke of Frogs, going through France. Some of them grabbed handfuls of weeds and threw them at the starving French: "Here—eat this!"

They clambered into boxcars, bellying their way inside, their trim tools of war clutched in their hands. The French were on the field, picking, plowing. The French were in their doorways looking out at their liberators, waving. The French had tears streaming down their cheeks, men and women alike, and on their lips the words, *"Les américains! Les américains!"* In prayer. In thanksgiving.

The soldiers stood in the doorways of the boxcars. And some of them shouted as they rolled along past meadows, fields, towns—"Hello, you whores! Come here, you sonofabitch!" And if a girl was near as the troop trains roared toward death and destruction the soldiers would stand in the boxcar doorways and grab for the flies of their pants and shout: "Come here, you whore!"

Jim leaned his head back against the boxcar wall and closed his eyes, shutting out the scene. Carter crunched his cigarette out against the floor and turning his head sideways to Jim asked, "Did you ever read any Balzac?"

They moved to the front. And death was so common, so apparent everywhere, that when he had time to think he wondered that he was still alive. And felt it was just a matter of time. Time would kill him.

Night. One o'clock when the lampposts started walking down the street and the cornstalks moved in on him in close order drill.

Morning. He was grateful every day to find himself still alive; and surprised.

Just a matter of time. Time would kill him. The bullet with his name on it. There was always a part of him on edge. Always an insecure feeling. He had always to watch what was going on behind him. Not just the fear that someone would stab him in the back. There was some vast, heinous scheme going on behind him.

Always insecurity and a disbelieving hope that he'd somehow get home.

They moved up to death. . . .

Jim ordered another beer and sipped it slowly.

. . . And after being so hardened they didn't, as Carter put it, give a shit any more. They became as animals, boring into the ground for shelter, fearing the mighty man-made phenomena of death-spitting skies, wasp-stinging bullets, rhinoceros-jolting tanks, the sharks of the sea that sank ships. They didn't care any more. They were without heart and of little feeling. Only weary of land and sky and sea and man himself. Let's live today for tomorrow you may—there was an exultation in victory, in moving. You were getting somewhere. The greatest fear and anxiety came in waiting—waiting—

Once you had learned not to give a—his mind hesitated, then plunged forward—say it—*shit* any more, how did you learn the way back to caring about people who you'd learned didn't care whether you did or not? They had all been animals together during the war; but they couldn't have been beast unless that was part of being man. . . .

Jim sipped his beer bitterly. He lit a cigarette. One of the visions that Jim cared not to see slipped, unbid, onto the tavern bar before his eyes.

He and Carter. He could see the field, torn, the very trees bleeding from their shell-torn barks, their leaves withering and drooping. The upturned smoking tank with a headless body sticking out of the hatch. A body like a child's sawdust doll from which the head had been torn. The house there—the door sliding open and the sniper's bullets smacking the dirt near them. On their bellies, he and Carter, not quite out of the range of death. The door sliding open, and for a moment seeing the two figures there. A boy of perhaps twelve and an old woman with gray hair, tall and angular in the slate color of a winter afternoon. The bullets smacked close. Carter's face rolled in the dirt, his chin scraping and having a smudge on it when it was turned to Jim. Carter's eyes looked into his. All the toughness and swagger were gone from them. "Got to do it," he said. The door slid open and the young boy stood, amateurish toy soldier on its sill, with his gun like a little tin gun raised. Carter squeezed the trigger. The boy threw up his hands and jumped across the doorsill like a child leaping from behind a chair to frighten someone. Then he fell face-downward. The woman's scream carried, hysterically, across the quiet field. Carter's face rolled back along the ground and looked at Jim.

The woman had foolishly or insanely, hysterically, thrown the door wide. For a moment she stared out. Her voice was laughter and crying at once. She lifted the gun.

Jim could not leave all the guilt to Carter. And Carter seemed not to care. He only lay there looking at the woman.

Jim lifted his gun and slowly squeezed the trigger. The woman fell across the doorstep, across the little boy in a protective heap. Jim tossed his gun aside and put his face down against the ground. Silence took the battlefield.

This, too, was a part of war. . . .

Jim shook his head. Tried to shake the vision loose, blank it out, blur it over. He glanced down the bar, trying to destroy the memory. Saw a familiar face; a blond fellow. "Say—!" Jim called out, getting off his stool and moving down the bar toward the fellow. "I know you!"

"Yeah, I thought I recognized you too," Don said.

"Know where it was!" Jim said, straddling the stool next to Don's. "At a Christmas party given by Milo." He snapped his fingers in remembrance. "You were doing something from Shakespeare!"

Don grinned, "Yeah, that's right."

Jim kept snapping his fingers, calling up remembrance. "Name's Dan—Don!—Don something!"

Don smiled. "Don Lockwood," he said.

Jim held out his hand. "My name's Jim Norris."

They shook hands.

"Let me buy you a beer," Jim said.

"Okay—if I can pop back."

"Sure thing," Jim said, "I could use a few." For a moment his eyes dulled and the war visions tried to stand in between him and Don. The beer came.

"What are you doing down here? Work at Haines?" Jim asked.

"Trying for a job. On my way up for an interview."

"I'm over at union headquarters—two doors down the street," Jim said. "Drop around and see me sometimes."

"Yeah."

They had a couple of glasses of beer together. Don glanced at Jim in the envious attraction people have for extremely good-looking people. Don wished he was that good-looking. Jim drank the last of his beer and put his foot down against the floor. "Well—I've got to get back." He held out his hand. They shook again. "Good luck—hope you get the job." He started toward the exit and, at the door, turned back. "Don't forget—drop in and see me!" He threw up his hand in a friendly answer to Don's nodded smile and walked, tall and broad-shouldered, from the tavern.

Don drank another glass of beer. He was drinking to get up nerve enough to ask for the job. Nice of Sue to go to all the trouble. Then he was thinking of Rebecca. He'd like to see her again soon. She was darn good-looking; the prettiest girl he had ever made. He was glad she was Jewish. He had never gone with a Jewish girl. He'd be proud walking down the street with her. He hoped everyone would know she was Jewish. But she didn't look Jewish. He had better not drink any more. Didn't want to be a little high when he applied for the job. He'd have to get a stick of gum and, chewing it, walk around for a while until the smell of the beer was off his breath.

# XII

Jim decided to walk the two miles home from work. He walked slowly, whacking himself across the leg with his folded newspaper in rhythm to his long stride. But there was no bounce to his step. His stride slackened. The newspaper hung limp in his hand and his head drooped down.

I've changed. No one knows how I feel inside. Louise doesn't. I'm just going through the motions at the union. From habit. . . . Yes, you're the guy who believed so strongly. What's happened? You know. No. I don't—well part of it but—

He had been a highly moral man. Moral in the deepest sense of the word. He had been constructive, purposeful, positive, idealistic, a man who had checked many of his desires by the visions that had guided him. He was a man with the habit of positive action, but no longer the deep burning conviction. He had been full of love for people. Now he had seen a world gone mad. Live for the present, not the future. Tomorrow there may not be a future. Deeply disturbed by the significance of what he had lived through, Jim searched in his mind for answers.

He barely moved now and his long shadow stretched out away from him. He had been eager, alive, full of love for people, wanting a better life for them. And now their faces were withdrawn. He saw them ugly in the morning light. He felt the evil in them reaching out to him. And wanted not to feel this way, think this way. He was like a man wrestling with himself; with the apathy and soul-sickness the war had cast over him. There was unrest in him and uncertainty about the things he had been so sure of.

What's wrong with me? What has happened? Jim squinted at the gathering darkness . . . the enemy had so many faces. The enemy was big, he was clever. He was forever changing his form. He looked out at you from the places in the night where you least expected him. He masquerades in many places.

Jim walked slowly toward home—things he and Louise had talked about.

The enemy has a loud voice. He speaks in bluster and bombast. He hammers guns into chains and chains back again into guns. He withers small children in slum cellars and closets old men and women in poorhouses.

Jim walked now, slapping his newspaper angrily against his leg, putting face and feature on the enemy. . . .

Who is the enemy? Where does he hide and how do you know his face or his hidden deeds when outwardly the faces of America are sweet smiling faces believing in democracy, in love thy neighbor and do unto others and free enterprise and anybody can be President? How do you lay hand on him and fist to him?

He could be a king or an English, Irish, Jewish, Negro, Greek, German, Italian, Polish butcher, laborer, housewife, white-collar worker, executive, whispering hate of a Greek, Jew, Irishman, Mexican, Negro, Italian, Catholic, Protestant, atheist.

The enemy is not always a rich man. He is sometimes a poor man. He sits in the show next to you and rubs elbows with you in shopping crowds, gives his seat to a mother with child in a crowded streetcar, rises with you to cheer for home run and touchdown. He plays golf on wide green links. Sometimes he picks up the teacher's pointer, sometimes masquerades in the minister's robes, sometimes even looks through the scientist's microscope. He is black, brown, white, yellow, and every color of man. He is clever, but more stupid than clever for he is himself his own prisoner.

The enemy is anything but a child.

Jim stood now at the gate leading to his house. He trembled a bit, in elation. He looked up at the windows behind which would be Louise and the children. He felt his triumph. He felt like the old Jim. And stood there a moment longer, looking up.

Jim laughed aloud. He had found himself. He had come home. He was the old Jim. He bounded up the steps two at a time. He swung the screen door open. "Hey, Skinny!" he called out to his wife, and going through the rooms, found her giving the baby its nursing bottle. He leaned over and kissed her on the neck.

Louise turned, and smiling, put her arms around Jim's neck. "You're kind of nice!" she said.

"You are too, Skinny." He felt, for the first time since his return, that she was the wife he had left and he the Jim who had left her.

She rumpled his blond hair that was growing long again. "Dinner will be ready soon."

After dinner he sat in the front room reading the evening paper. Then he stopped reading and stared across the room. . . . Last night. In the bedroom. Just before going to bed. "Let your hair loose." She turned toward him with a surprised look. Obediently she loosened her hair and came and sat at his feet with her head on his knee. With his fingers he curled her hair as a little girl's hair would be curled. Laughing she tied her handkerchief into a bow over her forehead. He sat staring at her. His hand stroked her shoulder. He continued stroking her shoulder. But something, some feeling, had gone out of him somewhere, somehow. Something of love. His hand continued to stroke her shoulder automatically . . .

When he had first returned he had been impotent. Then, later, his love-making to her had become more and more bestial. His carnal desires for a while had no end. Then he had become bored with the whole thing.

Jim rustled the newspaper open between his big hands . . . began to read—and then laid the paper on his lap. The memories flooded in on him . . .

Dressed in brief authority they marched, hunting their fellow men. Dying, they enriched the soil. Jim shivered and in the memory, perspiration stood out on his forehead in a beaded wreath.

He laid the paper aside. . . . War didn't change people? They didn't carry part of the change back with them into civilian life? At first they, the men he knew and liked in his outfit, were as he was—those he liked—purposeful in getting the killing over, drawn into this thing because of their beliefs, their ideals. Not hating the men. Hating the idea behind the men. And, bit by bit, as the war wore their nerves thin and uncovered the layers of their hidden and unconscious antagonisms and civilized-away hate, he saw them change, day by day, until they had actually become killers. Just as after a while their hands had become calloused from the use of guns, so now the sandpaper of war had rubbed the soft edges off their brains and souls and made of them the hard tools to be used only for purposes of war. With the change their guns had become phallic symbols, takers of life, proof of their manhood and masculinity and heroism. They shined their guns, took the greatest care of them and always had them near at hand. Their guns had become their best friends and their bed companions. And now there was the same elation, the same high point in blasting death into the enemy as giving a child to a woman in peacetime. An exultation in killing, destroying, moving forward, forcing the enemy off the edge of the earth . . . Bill Carter and he on their bellies, firing at the enemy who, besieged from the rear, were trying to make a retreat by cutting across a half-hidden road to comparative safety in the fallen debris of a shattered town. Carter laughing brutally, taking aim, cutting down another retreating shadow of a man, saying, "This is just like a carnival. There goes another—" And ripping a man from his feet to the dusty arms of the earth. Carter grinning. "Like ducks moving along in a line at the shooting gallery."

Jim lifted the newspaper and held it against his face to take the perspiration away. He laid it, damp and creased, across his legs . . .

Two letters from his wife had gotten through to him. He held the letters in his hand. He opened them. He read them. They didn't mean anything any more. It was as if he were reading someone else's letters: "It is a boy, dear. A beautiful boy. I got back from the hospital today. Don't worry, honey." And dully, with the alien letter in his hand, he wondered if the boy would have to fight a war. He was, in that moment, unreasonably mad. Hated his wife because of the boy she had borne him. The order came to move up to the fighting . . .

The weary soldiers were in the weary land. Their lives were weighed by the second. Somehow, miraculously, they were still alive and moved through the insomnious night . . . somewhere in France . . . the Grave Registration Detail had been fighting for twenty-eight days and had now been working, burying the dead, for two days and two nights. They were knocked out and volunteers were asked to help with the work. Jim volunteered. This was war. He'd look at it. He'd remember it. Carter, a little white-faced, volunteered, too, booming his voice roughly and swaggering over toward Jim. "What the crap's the big idea?" he asked Jim angrily. His fist on Jim's shoulder had friendship in it. Evelyn Johnson, the fellow with a girl's name, volunteered too. He was a farm boy. He had slaughtered animals. He volunteered for everything. I love to kill. I'm doing something I couldn't do in the States. He loved to bayonet men to death. On the farm he had climbed over the railing into the pigpen, and when the little eyes lost in their shaggy hoods had turned toward him, he had lifted the sledge hammer and with a mighty blow brought it down against the skull; or backing away for aim sent a bullet into the brain.

Several others volunteered. . . .

One of the truck drivers said, "Now don't be chicken. You fellows won't have to touch the bodies. You use gloves."

They climbed up on the truck and clattered through sunlight to what had been the battlefield a few days earlier. It was now a disinterred cemetery. Enemy and ally lay together across the field, united in the peace of the long night. They rode the earth like boulders, and as fixed in time; they gripped the soil with their rotting bodies in blood-soaked and blood-dried uniforms like the snaggly stumps of long-dead trees.

A stench hung over the whole battlefield. The odor of death was all about them. It came out over the road in a gaseous but invisible smoke and dug its acrid, rotting scent deep into nostrils, set the men to tightening their lips or spitting as if, in this way, they could get rid of it.

At the bend where the battlefield began the trucks turned off the road and bumped over uneven ground. There, as if meant for a signpost, lay a cow, bloated and stiff, its stomach three times normal size in a weird pregnancy.

Following the others Jim's truck bumped off the road, scraping against the low branch of a tree. It crunched over a loose arm, squishing it into the oozing mud.

Their bodies were thrown as seeds are scattered to the soil. Some had lain for a week unburied. And worse than the odor were the flies. The alive men had continually to brush them away with their gloved hands. The dead men made no protest.

He, Carter, Johnson and Richards hopped down from their truck. As he jumped, his foot placed itself on a piece of rubbery human flesh and skidded away. There was no way of telling what part of a body it had been. Jim lifted his head and stared at the far trees on sun-warmed hills. For a moment his stomach tightened and seemed about to revolt. Then he spat and was well. Look and remember. He turned his face down. Remember. At his feet lay a hand, upturned. Only a hand. Remember. He followed the other men.

The truck backed up with a grinding of gears. The first two, Johnson and Richards, picked up a dead body by head and legs, lifted it to the side, scraped the stretcher underneath, forced the body onto the stretcher, and tossed the dead soldier into the truck. It made a thumping sound as it hit inside the truck. Like a sack of potatoes. And another. And another. Like sides of bacon. But only the Americans. Let the enemy bury its dead. And another. Another. Thump! Thump! Thump! And now a loose leg. And now a single arm. The truck drivers were calloused. They had seen plenty of it. Jim had no gloves. He took a pair from the raincoat of a dead German. When he reached in, the pocket was full of blood. Not dried. Jim, with Carter, bent to his work. The face was shattered on one side with only a grinning socket and an empty jaw. The other half of the face was as if the boy were asleep. Jim pulled his eyes away. Look! He forced his glance back and looked with clear blue eyes. Remember!

*Thump!*

Another. This one had become a black, swollen, decomposing mass, alive with maggots. Remember.

*Thump!*

As they lifted this one a leg slipped halfway off in Carter's hand.

Jim looked. Carter, keeping his face sternly tough, kept his eyes fixed stiffly to the side of the thing he ported from ground to truck.

*Thump!*

The men bent to their work. The trucks began to slowly fill up.

Insignias were cut from enemy soldier's uniforms for souvenirs. And one fellow wanted a ring. And another a Luger. They picked up the dead bodies and passed them around.

Johnson, under a clump of trees, had laughed. His laughter rang out strangely, weirdly on the blue air of the day.

"Wonder how many arms and legs there is to a ton?" Johnson said. He laughed again. The laughter tinkled away into the sunlight.

"Here, you sonofabitch!" a man called out and, when Johnson turned to look, the arm came hurtling slowly through the air with sunlight on it like a poorly punted football.

They came upon a dead German. Look! Jim told himself.

This corpse had been shot while running—attacking. He had been shot in the throat. His mouth was wide open. His hands were frozen on his throat as if trying to stop the flow of blood. His legs were in a running position as if still pawing the air. His mouth was open as if he had been screaming as he died. His eyes were wide open, looking with terror at the blank blue sky. He had been bleeding through the mouth and nostrils. The blood was crusted, scaly. Remember!

The men gathered around him. One of them turned him on his side. They went through his pockets. Jim stood watching. A harmonica tumbled from his pocket and lay on a green thatch of grass in the sunlight. A little battered harmonica.

None of them could take it. A man said, "Somebody might as well take it. It won't do him any good any more."

Their trucks were filled and sagging with their loads. The trucks ground up out of the place of ended war and onto the road. The trucks moved through sunlight, under trees, to the cemetery. There had been war here too. Shells had unburied some of the dead. Here a face, half clothed in dirt, grinned mockingly on all things alive, in bitter distaste. Here an arm, out of its hiding-place, seemed to clutch the air with dead, twisted, frozen, swastika-curled fingers. Vainly, as if to pull itself erect . . .

Somewhere in Germany on the way back home, after victory, the V-E day that was to be the beginning of the new world . . . the displaced people, men and women, children, in rags, sprawling weakly, hungrily, diseased, across the roads—back to home—back to the beginning—back to the start of the New World. Sleeping like animals in the fields. Crawling to their knees, their feet, the next day and continuing the long pilgrimage home. Hungry. A few of them ganging up together and stealing the farmers' chickens. The farmers running to the American Military Police and the M.P.'s going out to quiet those awful D.P.'s and protect the German farmers . . . somewhere in Germany when the war was on . . .

The night was a dead thing. The woods through which they penetrated on the outskirts of the town hid the sky and there was no moon. The night was alive with death. It came from the sky. It came from behind the next clump of trees. In this town ahead the Jews had been hunted. They had been tortured. They had been thrown into concentration camps. Parent torn from child. Often never to see one another again, through all of life. Here on the outskirts they had been trailed. Only the animals of forest and field had been safe and at peace. The rabbits in their burrows. The spiders in their silken webs on tall grass supports. The bats in tree limbs and the worms in the ground. The field mice and the moles and infinitesimal ants in honeyed cells; the squirrels with hidden provisions. Even the mosquitoes and the flies; the fish of the river and the clumsy waddling crabs; the wood ticks in their diggings. All nature held her creatures and gave security in the night—even unto the broad day with the sun at noon. All were safe in nature and in man. All but man himself.

Now they, the Americans, came that way. In the blackness. They were the hunters and the hunted. In the night. And the night frowned menace. The night promised death. For hunter and hunted . . .

Day came and they were the searchers and the searched. Carter was saying he wished they'd get somewhere, take some town, so that he could get screwed. It was then that they came upon the fifteen German soldiers by total surprise and took them captive. He, Carter, Johnson and four others.

The Germans stood pale, frightened, their hands on their heads. Johnson was in command. Johnson had said wantonly, "We ain't going to take all the sonsabitches back to M.P. We're going to shoot half the bastards." He leered into the line of Germans.

One was hardly more than a boy. One was an aging man. The boy, in his fright, could hardly hold the tears back but was trying hard, for his elders were there, the soldiers, and one in the uniform of the SS. His lips quivered enormously and now the tears spilled down. For Hitler and the SS trooper and all of Germany he had failed.

"You—" Johnson said, motioning to the SS trooper, "step forward." The SS trooper understood and stepped forward. The blast of Johnson's gun caught him in the chest and face. He fell forward.

In the line the aging man trembled:

Next. Hitler and the world had no further use for the elderly.

"Pick one you want to save," Johnson told Carter over his shoulder. Carter shrugged. "The boy," he said.

"You," Johnson said to Jim. Jim only looked at him, levelly.

"Well, Norris?" Johnson said.

Jim turned away.

"You," Johnson said to one of the other men.

They picked them by looks. If they were intelligent-looking. Scholarly-looking. Or good-looking. Or appeared to have personality. Or slightly resembled someone from your past. If you didn't like the guy's face or looks that was his tough luck.

Jim's face was averted. He forced himself to look. And he knew that they, the aggressors, and murderers here, could have been any soldiers —from any country. And at any appointed time in history.

They had picked those who were to live.

Johnson and two others, trigger-happy, mowed the others down.

Jim was sick by the side of the road . . .

Jim stared up from his newspaper. Stared across the room. "You—" he said, half-aloud, "if I had had my choice. You, Johnson."

Louise came into the room. Jim half stumbled out of his chair. He squeezed her hand. "I'm going for a walk, Skinny," he said. He didn't look at her.

Under the starry sky he walked realizing that he could have saved a life and hadn't. Which one of the dead might have been alive now if he had but made a choice? Which bereaved family might now be happy? Walking under the starry sky his carelessness seemed to him now to be worse than Johnson's brutality.

The memories pursued him . . .

The Germans were begining to lose, beginning to bend back off the land of France toward their own frontier. The broken and bleeding Axis Army was in full retreat.

Dying machinery and dead men. The whole fluid front of the now incredible war. No one knew where he was going, in what direction, for what reason. Hundreds of Jerries giving up. So many that there was no attempt to do other than say, "Throw your guns down—go that way—" pointing toward the direction from which the Americans had come . . .

Entering a town. A soldier among the few with whom Jim marched stopped to cut a ring from a dead woman's finger. And then they moved on. Jim and the two others. Said the first soldier, rubbing the ring clean against his coat, "I'd like to find a good-lookin' one," meaning the woman.

"Yeah," the second soldier said, "one not cold yet."

It was all part of their life now. No one was shocked at anything.

# XIII

Don's job was simple but it was a white-collar job. He sat at a desk. He had few duties and they were of a mechanical nature. He was a supervisor.

Smiling, he puffed on his cigarette with deep enjoyment and glanced down at the cover of the thick instruction manual: CREDIT ADJUSTMENT DEPARTMENT and underneath, WELCOME TO THE HAINES FAMILY. He leafed through the manual—SUPERVISORS: GENERAL DUTIES—*Check time sheets and issue absentee reports. Distribute general store and executive notices. Schedule and check lunch and pass periods.*

Don, lifting his head, looked proudly out the door of his little office and over the heads of a hundred girls. The room into which he looked was large, oblong, completely encased in a paneling of frosted glass. At the hundred little desks, crowded close together with just walking space between them, the girls sat hunched over, talking swiftly into their speakers. The mumble of voices cloaked the huge room and the needles of the machines cut into the black disks. "Form Letter F3 . . . form letter A2 . . ." The typists in the next huge room would understand and with deft fingers pound out quickly the particular form letter their particular back accounts required. On droned the voices of the collection correspondents. . . .

Don smiled, looking out of his little cubicle of office over the heads of the girls and then at the far wall where, inside a private office, draped too in glass, the department head sat and had the honor of his name on the door: B. G. WILMINGTON. Inside Wilmington's office Don could see Jerry half seated on the edge of the Boss's desk: she was pounding one hand into the palm of the other, swiftly, emphatically. She was frowning. Under her arm she clamped a ledger. Don watched, a little awed. From where he sat there were five other little offices in a row, each with a supervisor behind a desk. Don ruffled the pages of the instruction manual with idle fingers. There was little for the supervisors to do. They sat there. They walked around and chewed the fat with the other supervisors. Occasionally they walked through the aisle, distributing notices or just nosing around. Whenever they walked past the correspondents, the girls became frightened, bent closer to their mouthpieces and started dictating faster. Once in a while a supervisor had to call a girl in and politely bawl her out if the collections were down or if she wasn't keeping up the rate.

Don opened the instruction manual and began to read. He had never thought he could hold a job like this. He'd study hard and go as far as he could with the company. Maybe one day he'd get to the top and be a department manager. The fantasy was pleasant on the screen of his mind. Name on the door. Big shiny-topped desk under glass. Phone. Two phones . . . It was damned nice of Sue to get the job for him. His thoughts began to stray. He looked out at the girls. He enjoyed looking at them—and he was their boss. He enjoyed looking at their legs, their breasts—for future reference . . . Rebecca was tied up in his thoughts too. Boy, a nice lay! Timid. Holding back at first. Then as frantic as he had been. He had brought her out, made a woman of her. She hadn't let him take her all the way home, nor would she tell him where she lived. She had been awfully ashamed afterwards and made him promise never to tell anyone. He felt himself growing, thinking about it, and tried to concentrate on the manual. Boy, was she pretty! And what a body! She had walked beside him with her head down, ashamed to look at him and pulling her arm away when he tried, several times, to take it.

He tried to kiss her good night but she had turned her face down into the collar of his coat. He had kissed only her cheek. She had broken away from him then and sprinted down the sidewalk.

Don lit another cigarette and stared at its red coal. He guessed that he was half in love with her. He must see her again. He knew she worked here. But where? In what department? With thousands of girls employed there he would have to be lucky to run into her. And he'd have to be careful about Sue; not let her know anything about it. Rebecca Friedman! he said to himself, liking the sound of the name in his mouth. Becky. He saw her face.

Someone walked into his office. "Oh—hi, Jerry."

"I'm sore, Lockwood, damned sore," Jerry said.

"Oh?"

Jerry was the only woman supervisor in the department. She was Miss Brooks to anyone but the other supervisors. And was the only woman allowed to smoke at her desk. She wore a tailored suit and a shirt like a man. Jerry was sophisticated, smooth-looking, the personality girl of the department; good-looking but not pretty. There was a lot of energy about her. When she talked her whole body talked, her arms, her face; her back muscles stiffened and relaxed alternately, her head poised first on one side and then the other and she took every opportunity to talk long and loud. Though most of her remarks were insignificant they were delivered like orations. There was nothing mousy about Jerry.

She sat down in the chair in front of Don's desk with her head thrust back and her jaw stuck out. "I just had an argument with Wilmington," she said, snapping her head angrily toward the department head's office. "He flunked out in every course at the University of Chicago. What kind of a letter does he want me to write anyway? You can't write decent English to these people." She gestured with the ledger. "And do you know what it's all about? A typist sent back a special letter *I* wrote with an annotated correction! I had to write the letter because the damn correspondent didn't know what to say in answer." She slapped the ledger against her knees. "What does she mean, a *typist* telling *me* how to write a letter! Maybe *she* wants my job."

Jerry talked on and on for half an hour, lighting one cigarette on the butt of the other. She crunched out a final butt and stood up, looking down at Don. "Say! Do you belong to the union?"

Don looked away and then back into her eyes: be careful. Don't want to lose this job. "Well—no—I—I—"

"There's a union meeting tonight," Jerry said bluntly and gave him the address.

Don laughed uncomfortably. "Well, I can't make it tonight. Got a date." Sure I believe in unions, he told himself.

Jerry turned toward the door. "Maybe next meeting," she said over her shoulder. "It's damned important."

"Yeah—we'll see," Don said.

Don signed in for work and then, as every morning, was ready for coffee; as every morning Krendesky, one of the other supervisors, stuck his head in the door and asked, "Coffee?" Krendesky was a tall, lean, rather sinister-looking young man in his late twenties. He seemed never able to talk until he had his coffee but only cast sidelong glances through slitted eyes at the girls as he walked through the department, and additional sidelong, half-raping looks at the typists. In the hallway going toward the elevator there was invariably some girl walking on tapping high heels who brought his hair bristling along his scalp. He'd always catch Don tightly by the arm and stand staring at her, his whole body stiffening. "Whew!"

Then the elevator and the coffee. The modulated and chuckling voices of the leisure class floated around them in the big and crowded cafeteria; the smooth, satisfied faces looked from business suits and smart dresses. The suits had three-pronged handkerchiefs standing erect from breast pockets. The dresses had costume jewelry riding the rich cloth over breasts.

Krendesky was always recovering from a hangover or the girl he was out with last night. With his finger looped in the handle of the coffee cup he spoke of the night before, now that the coffee had taken some of the slack out of his face, "At three o'clock I had her in her vestibule." Then shifting to another night, "Took a widow out. Met her at a bar. She told me I was scared of women—" He laughed. "Sure, I'm scared of getting involved."

A couple of the other supervisors joined them. Everybody had had a big time the night before. Everybody told about it. The spots they had been to along Rush Street, the amount of money they had spent. For half an hour they idled in the cafeteria, then unhurriedly wandered back to their desks chuckling, patting each other comradely across the shoulders, stopping to light cigarettes as they moved through the hundreds of back-bent typists, file clerks, shipping clerks.

In his office, with boredom settling around him and the low droning voices of the correspondents humming in over his desk, Don, for something to do, read some of the letters the company had received on back accounts. Some were angry. Others apologetic. Some were amusing: *Soon as I sell my corn I'll send what I owe you. . . . I been abed with a baby case and the town hada pay for it while my husband was asporting around. He's lazy and he's a drunkard. If you're going to sue him you'll have to sneak up on him. I been trying to sue him for a year for nonsupport and I can't get ahold of him. . . .*

In general they were pathetic letters. The letters told every detail of their plight. Their wives were in hospitals for operations and they had no money for food but they were forwarding a few dollars to pay on the bill so that the Haines Company would please keep their credit in good standing. Of course it wasn't by that time. But they had the idea that it might be.

Don was staring at the wall, thinking about the letters, when Miss Jennings stuck her head in the door and then followed it with her body. Miss Jennings was the floor manager of the girls Don supervised. Miss Jennings was a busybody. She came swiftly to Don's desk, talking even before she was leaning over it on her thin little arms while her neurotic eyes flitted to his face. "God, has Miss Phillips, that new girl, got body odor! Does she smell! Did you smell her?"

Don shook his head no and frowned slightly.

Miss Jennings' spinster forty-year-old face leaned further over the desk. "And I wish you'd speak to Miss Grover and Miss Stein. Grover's not making her rate and Stein—well, she just isn't bringing in her collections." Miss Jennings bobbed her head up and down angrily. "Humph! Just because she's studying opera and made a couple of guest appearances on radio, she don't need to think she can be any prima donna around here!"

Don sighed. "All right, Miss Jennings. I'll speak to them."

Miss Jennings went back to her desk. Don waited the discreet amount of time and then walked along the little, tight line of correspondents' desks. "Miss Stein—may I see you a minute?" The girl looked up and nodded quickly. She unclamped her speaker and went toward his office. As she went, Miss Jennings flashed her a smiling, triumphant glance.

When Don tapped Miss Grover on the shoulder the words she was speaking into the receiver choked in her throat and she trembled under his touch and looked up fearfully into his eyes. "May I see you when Miss Stein leaves my office?"

"Y-yes, sir." Her hands trembled and she put them out of sight on her lap.

Miss Stein was standing by his desk when Don entered the office. "Sit down." He waved at the chair. Then he closed the office door. Leaning over the desk and adjusting his tie he smiled at her. "Miss Jennings tells me you are studying opera."

Miss Stein nodded but said nothing.

"I was an actor before I got this job," Don said. He smiled again. "Well, you'll get married when the right guy comes along and then you can spend all your time studying music."

"He has come along."

"Oh, you're engaged?"

"Well—I'm not going to get married for about a year."

Don chuckled. "Why so long?"

"He just got out of service."

"Oh, he's got to find himself, huh?" Don asked jokingly.

Miss Stein said, very seriously, "He needs to be alone for a year. He needs to be quiet. If people will just leave him alone he'll be all right."

Don nodded as if he understood what she meant. He stood up, smiling at her. "Well, stick to the music," he said.

Miss Grover was nervous when she slipped into his office and, behind the closed door, twisted her fingers in her lap. "Your rate is down a little, Miss Grover," Don said, looking at her record sheet.

"Well, I'll tell you, Mr. Lockwood—I'll tell you—" Her eyes brimmed with tears. She looked down into her lap and went on speaking. "I've got to keep this job. I've got to keep it as long as I can.

I—well, you see—I'm pregnant. I've just got to keep it as long as I can."

Don looked and saw no wedding ring on her finger. He came around the desk and offered her a cigarette. He wanted to tell her how small and unimportant he was with the company and that she needn't fear that he could fire her. Instead he told her, "Don't be afraid—we're hard up for help around here." He told her, making his voice chuckle, "For Christ sake don't cry! They'll think your boss beats you."

They smoked in silence, he sitting at his desk, she looking down into her lap. Then she went back to her dictaphone.

Krendesky stuck his head in the door and said, "Un-huh!" and grinning, disappeared. Miss Jennings came sneaking around the corner and into his office. "Did you smell her? Did you smell that new girl?"

"No, I didn't," Don said.

The afternoon dragged. Along about three o'clock Krendesky stuck his head in the door. "Coffee?"

Don got up to go with him. They stepped onto the elevator. Mr. Wilmington, the department head, was already on the elevator and nodded at Don in a friendly manner. "How are you, Lockwood? Afternoon, Krendesky."

"Fine, thank you, sir," Don said. He was flattered. Then he glanced at the elevator operator and saw that it was O'Keefe in the company's blue uniform with the yellow-gold shield: THE HAINES COMPANY. Don turned his face away, hoping O'Keefe wouldn't see him and speak.

There were a bunch of men, executives and white-collar workers, on the elevator. One of them was telling a dirty story. At the fifth floor several women got on the elevator and the story suddenly stopped. It was only half over and amid the dead silence Mr. Wilmington said, laughing jovially, "If I were less intelligent I'd ask what was the rest of that story."

The elevator stopped at the cafeteria level and Don, keeping his face carefully turned away from O'Keefe, squeezed out with Krendesky.

Then, walking along the corridor with Krendesky and the department head, Don was ashamed of himself. Jesus, I've been a bastard again! I acted like a shitheel. He halted. "I—forgot something in the office. I'll meet you soon as I get it."

He rang the elevator buzzer and said in surprise when the door opened, "Oh, hello, O'Keefe! How are you?"

# XIV

Don's heart beat fast. There on the sidewalk approaching him as he stepped out of the restaurant was Rebecca. She was looking past the man in front of her and at Aaron who walked a third of a block ahead of her. Her eyes were sad and wistful.

Don stepped directly in front of her, blocking her path. "Hello!"

Rebecca stared up into his face. Her cheeks flushed crimson and she looked down at the sidewalk, then quickly over Don's shoulder at Aaron disappearing under the neon signs, and back at the sidewalk.

"Hello," she said.

"I've looked all over for you!" Don said.

Rebecca stole a frightened and shamed little look up into his face and glanced away.

"Want a soda?"

She shook her head.

"Want to take a walk?"

She took a long time answering. Finally she said, "All right."

"Which way?" he asked.

She glanced frightenedly in the direction Aaron had disappeared. "This way—over on Dearborn Street," she said, nodding toward a side street.

He took her arm. He could feel it tremble. "Gee, it's good to see you again," he said cheerfully. "I thought I had lost you." She glanced sideways at him and dropped her eyes.

Don started talking fast and cheerfully. He tried to be as interesting as possible. He made little jokes. She glanced at him occasionally and seemed to want to say something. But the words never came. Instead she spoke only when he asked her a direct question.

"I've got a job at the Haines Company," he told her. "I'm a supervisor. You work there, too, don't you?"

"That's a good job," she said impressed.

"What department do you work in?"

"I'm a salesgirl in the bargain basement."

"Here's the park!" Don said as if he were surprised. "Want to walk in the park?"

"I don't care."

They walked into the darkened park, back behind the Historical Society and past Lincoln's statue. The moon was yellow and the trees stood in dark leafy patterns. They walked slowly and Rebecca, once in a while, glanced at him. It was at once a glance of fear and of fascination. He took her hand. Her fingers trembled slightly under the touch of his.

Don said, "It's early yet. Would you like to go to the show?"

"I don't care."

He took her to the Surf and sat looking at her rather than the picture. When it was over he said, "You're going to have something to eat now," and his fingers, firm on her arm, guided her across the street to the Dale drugstore. Inside she said, "Just a soda." For a fleeting moment her eyes were looking directly into his and she flushed.

When the soda glasses were fringed with their drying curtains of pink froth and the paper straws were bent she said she had better go home. On the sidewalk where her streetcar would take her home he said, "I hate to see you go."

Her car came. He pressed her arm a little. "Please wait for the next one."

"All right."

He watched the car move away from the corner with relief.

"Becky," he said.

She glanced at him and flushed. "Becky, come over to my place for a minute—just for a little while."

Again she seemed about to say something but instead caught her bottom lip between her teeth. She nodded.

In his room she sat on the single upright chair. Don sat on the couch. "Want a little wine?" he asked.

She shook her head.

He poured himself a little and again sat on the couch, dramatically, one leg propped up at a right angle with the sole of his shoe against the plaid cover. In his hand he held the wineglass, holding it against the light and twirling it slowly while he squinted at it. Rebecca sat upright on her hard-backed chair, tensely. She avoided looking at him.

Don twirled the glass and squinted at it: he wouldn't try. He would be real nice to her and not try and she would admire him for it and let him see her again. A little of the wine spilled over the rim of the glass and reddened his thumb. But if he didn't the opportunity might slip away forever and he might never again be able to get her to come up to his room. "Why don't you sit over here?"

She hesitated, then got up slowly and sat next to him. She put her forehead down on his knee. "I'm ashamed," she said.

Don set his glass aside. He stroked her hair. "Don't be ashamed. It's nothing to be ashamed of. It's natural." He stroked her hair a while longer, then gently lifted her head and looked into her wide green eyes, admired her long lashes, her ivory skin. He slipped his arm around her and drew her close. Looking into her green eyes he said, "I love you." He meant it.

"I—I—" she said. She thought of Aaron.

He kissed her and she was staring into his eyes as again their lips met, staring in fascination. Her young arms encircled his neck; his mustache was rough against her young red mouth. She was breathing hard. She said, "You better give me some of that wine if—if—"

# XV

Aaron walked the night streets of the city as usual. His mind raced along ahead of him and he tried to slow it down from its strangely spinning and spiraling thoughts. He stared up from out of his slumped head at the people passing him on the sidewalk. Those people out there are only a pencil-shading. Walk. Walk. Walk. Fire hydrant. Red fire hydrant. Walk. Walk. Walk. Hock-shop. Typewriter in window. He seemed suddenly shaken by some inner terror. He was trying to express himself on the dark surface of civilization. Again he shivered in thinking of it and drew his shoulders up about his neck. Was suddenly fearful of the city itself, the people around him, the very buildings. Shivering, drawing in his shoulders, he walked as fast as he could toward his room.

He undressed and got into bed, curled himself into a ball: the embryo position.

I'm through.

I'm washed up.

I resign from the human race.

He didn't eat. He didn't sleep. He didn't drink. He didn't get out of the bed. For a week he stayed in bed.

Then . . . slowly . . . like someone recovering from an almost fatal illness he came back to the reality of the moment, the time, the place.

He got up. He drank some milk. He stayed for another week alone in the room.

He finally worked his way to the window, to the back porch, then down to the street.

He was like a child learning to walk. Like a man awakening from bad dreams and shaking himself.

What had O'Keefe said?—The nation needs every man, the world needs every man. Aaron slowly nodded his head. His sanity depended upon action. Everyone's did. The world wasn't there for a man with long pants crying like a child.

And his mind, as he walked through the sunny street, went over the statistics it had catalogued: forty million killed, wounded, captured, during the war. Ten million killed on battlefields. Ten million casualties. Two and a half billion casualties one way or another. And—his mind bringing up the figures he had searched out—51,000 American veterans of both World Wars hospitalized by the Veterans Administration with neuropsychiatric disabilities. Enough to populate a city.

Aaron ground his hands to fists. His stride was firm on the sidewalk and his jaw toughened. They say, Peace—it's wonderful. But where would they find peace? Where, for the two and a half billion, was peace? Oh, Dave, Milo, I too am a conscientious objector. I can't sit back and let it happen again. The way the world is now there is no time to be a poet. I must be a man of action. A man of action for the poets to come. I must keep my senses open to a clue from the men of good will who want a world of peace and plenty for all, and I will join them.

He saw a face. Milo's face. Another face. Dave's face. Faces. Jim, O'Keefe, his father. They all seemed to be smiling at him. Through his whole being rode a feeling of triumph. He strode along the sidewalk, swinging his arms. Life had touched him. He looked up out of a stronger face at the daylight. Where to turn? How to begin? To be a good American on his new terms was to be concerned with the good of all men. The tree has many branches. And there was something good in America.

There are good people in America working for good causes, working and fighting for those causes. Working in many ways. The new mind, the new heart, was moving in. They might cut it down in a hundred places, it would spring back in a thousand. You couldn't stop the people. They were meeting, mixing, mingling. He felt the shiver of a thrill go up his spine and tingle at the roots of his hair.

There is no time for writing. This is the time for action.

He was ready for action.

He was looking for some link with the people. Some chain of action. Some dove of peace.

And he knew that people wanted this chance to love and were taught to fear and hate. He had seen the picture that appeared in all the newspapers of the American and Russian GI hugging each other when the two armies made contact. And the picture of the white Cleveland pitcher hugging the Negro outfielder when they had combined to win a World Series game 1-0. And he knew that Negro athletes and musicians were doing more to overcome race prejudice than any other group in America. He knew, too, that the thing wrong with the Jew, the Negro, with women, with all minority groups, was that they were too sensitive. They lived in their mental ghettos. They moved through the night, the day, through the long years with their scars like the birthmark on Rebecca's face. And now the young Negroes, Jews, women, were freeing themselves from themselves. They appeared like strange new flowers, straight in the soil. For too long a time he had been too concerned about being half Jewish.

Aaron moved on down the street . . . and his thoughts were good to him . . .

Man, man, who traversed the seas and weighed the world and measured the stars. Man, man, puny man, who couldn't live alone and couldn't get along with his fellow man. Man. Man. Vain, egotistical, long-suffering man. You, the individual. You, the each of us. In some buried fiber, in some not alien tissue, all men knew they were all alike and all wanted the same things.

Aaron lifted his head. He wanted to sing it. To shout it: Arise, people! Arise from your sore spots of prejudice and hate. He could feel the hair tingle on his scalp. He could see all the people arising from hatred.

In Aaron there was an urgency. There was no time to wait.

He walked into Bughouse Square. In front of the solemn stones of the Newberry Library the ragtag army of broken and beaten men and women from flophouses and tenement rooms on North Clark Street stood listening to the soapbox speakers who had come that night with their world-saving speeches. Aaron moved from speaker to speaker.

Around this old man with a gray beard, who looked as if he had stepped from the pages of the Bible, gathered some of the old men and women of the neighborhood as he, with flashlight on the pages of his limp-covered Bible, read the words of the Lord.

Around this woman had gathered the listeners who were through with religion, through with God. She was a blond woman, her crisp hair frizzed. She was about fifty and wore glasses with thin gold stems and no rims. She looked like a grammar school teacher when her eyes were not sliding mischievously behind her glasses. And sometimes, as she spoke, she stuck her tongue out in a comical grimace. "They put Chiang Kai-shek on your back and they put Greece on your back," she bawled out at the crowd. "How strong do they think our back is? And how weak do they think our mind is?"

Aaron stood looking up at her. Someone moved close to him in the crowd, pushing forward for a better look. Aaron glanced sideways into the youthful face. The fellow grinned at him in friendliness. It was a very pleasant grin. Aaron smiled back.

The blond school-teacherish-looking woman was saying, "And what about the workers? They make silk suspenders and hold their pants up with string. They build the railroad cars and ride the rods. They butcher the meat into steaks and eat soupbones. And what are they offered!—Pie in the sky!"

Aaron and the other young fellow stood grinning at each other. "She's surely giving it to them," the boy said.

They moved together as if by mutual consent to the next speaker and stood listening. This was the Communist box. The Communists had the largest army of listeners in the park, the broken and beaten, youngish and middle-aged men and women from the flophouses and tenements down the street and for many blocks west. The speaker was finishing up. He was saying, "The danger is that the real criminals, the men who really caused the war, will walk right through our fingers—the monopolists, the bankers of Germany and the industrialists. The people who do know who caused the war won't be listened to. Of course—" his voice grew angry and derisive, "you and I and every Tom, Dick and Harry know who caused the war—it was that Hitler, that goddamn crazy paper hanger."

There was laughter and hand clapping and the hat was passed around for the collection and a woman sold copies of *The Daily Worker*.

Aaron walked out of the park. How to find his place of action and best turn his small contribution to the uses of the people? There was no pattern. No track to travel on.

The next day he went down to City College. He had heard that there were a lot of liberal and progressive young people in the school. Maybe he would enroll there—at least maybe he could make friends with some of them. But once in the large entrance of the school he was shy and didn't know just what to do. Self-conscious, he walked into the cafeteria and bought a cup of coffee. Then, carrying it toward a table, he saw the young man who had smiled at him in Bughouse Square standing by a table near the window talking to two or three other people. He stood in blue jeans and gray sweat shirt. He lifted his arm to Aaron in greeting.

"Hi! Want to join us?" His hand was already on the back of a chair, pulling it out. Aaron sat down. "Thanks."

"My name's Dick," the fellow said, holding out his hand. Dick introduced Aaron to the other young people.

"You go to school here?" Aaron asked Dick.

"No," Dick said. "I'm at the Art Institute. I was going to ask you the same thing."

And Aaron got to know Dick. Dick talked like a truck driver. He gestured like a truck driver. He cursed like one. And yet when he smiled that smile belonged to you. You were the only person in the world. He talked and cursed like a truck driver. And yet he painted. He was in his last year at the Art Institute.

Invited, Aaron went up to his barnlike studio. He was amazed at all the canvases Dick had painted, at the vigor of the brush strokes, the violent colors in his work, the huge-muscled figures, the gaunt faces—slum faces, workers' faces. All the vitality, iconoclasm and rebellion of youth were in his canvases.

And through Dick, Aaron got to know Mary Ellen. Mary Ellen painted and sculpted and made ceramics. She wore blue jeans turned up at the cuffs and T-shirts and her hair was cut almost as short as a boy's. She shared Dick's barnlike four-room studio. "Don't get the idea that Dick and I are having an affair, Levin. Not that I'm a virgin. But we aren't." Her hand waved impatiently. "A lot of people think we are but we don't give a good goddamn. You know—" standing with her feet spread wide and squinting down at the design for a ceramic bowl she was making "—the artist, if he's worth his salt, always has to rebel—against something, anyway. Sometimes it's established art." She shrugged. "Maybe his family." Again her shoulders leaped in their shrug. "Maybe society itself." She squinted at him. "Gimme a cigarette." When the smoke was curling up into the hair of her forehead, she said, "Me." And was silent; then went on, "I come from a good middle-class family from the North Side. Above average income. Good Irish stock. Old settlers." She exhaled a cloud of smoke. "Didn't want me to paint. Thought certain people were—not to be—ah—considered."

She was a thorn and a challenge to Aaron.

"You worry too much, Levin. Don't be so precious, baby, just get the words on paper."

A comradery grew up among the three of them. Aaron saw as much of them as possible. Coffee and cigarettes until three and four in the morning in cafeterias and hash-houses. The Black Belt on the South Side to listen to music or eat barbecued ribs. Mary Ellen said, walking along 35th and State Street with them, "Yeah, this is the Negro's territory. He can move around anywhere in the Black Belt. He can take a woman. He has his music. He has his people. Of course, he knows he has this big hostile world outside that will stamp on him if he gets too far out of bounds. Do you think that's right? Oh, hell, let's stop somewhere for a drink!"

And there were conversations with Dick:

"You know, Aaron, the way this country was set up by its founders there was room for a man to say 'I think the way you're doing it is wrong—everything you're doing is wrong.' His room has been rented."

Their legs pushed under a table and the plates pushed away to make room for their elbows. Dick saying, "A man isn't penalized so much these days as he was for his race, religion or color. He's penalized—" Dick tapped his forehead with his finger, "for what he thinks."

And another time Dick saying, "Take the Orient—this tidal wave of words—Communist—and all the crap they feed you in the papers. This upheaval of the people on the absolute bottom from our standard. Wait—just wait until the little nobody finds out he's as good as anybody else." Dick shook his head slowly from side to side. "I'm really afraid—I'm really afraid—to be on the other side." He smiled the smile that belonged to Aaron alone.

. . . and the night at Dick's studio when they had sat around talking until the early hours.

Dick and Mary Ellen said why didn't he stay all night?

"Yeah," Dick said, motioning to the door of the fourth room, "we use that as a library but there's a cot in there."

Aaron agreed to stay. He sat on the edge of the cot. Then he looked curiously across the room at a huge bookcase full of books. He went over and looked at the titles. His mouth fell open. The books and pamphlets of Marx, Engels, Lenin, Stalin, the whole array of Communist thought and philosophy looked out at him.

Hearing movement Aaron turned his head toward the door. Dick stood there with an extra blanket in his arms. When he saw the astonished expression on Aaron's face he threw back his head and laughed. "Yeah, I'm a Party member," he told Aaron, his eyes still twinkling. He tossed the blanket to Aaron in friendliness. "Look inside any of those books you want."

Aaron closed the door. He opened a book. He laced his long black hair behind one ear.

"Listen, Levin," Mary Ellen said, "how about coming down to the Workers' School and sitting in on a couple of classes?"

"I don't know," Aaron said.

Mary Ellen's eyes stabbed him with amusement. "What's the matter? Gutless?"

Aaron angered. "All right. I'll go."

Dick and Mary Ellen took him downtown the next evening and they rode the old-fashioned iron grillwork elevator in the 1895 Chicago building to one of the upper floors and went along the corridor to the four office rooms that had been converted into classrooms and headquarters of the Workers' School.

Aaron sat in the first class with them and an hour later sat on one of the fifteen or twenty chairs facing a desk in the second class. He was surprised to see and hear seated around him young college students, workers from factories, housewives and Negroes. Surprised at the mixture of well-educated and almost illiterate people gathered together here in a room in a Loop office building, a sincere and enthusiastic group of disparates. His deep brown eyes looked and his whole being reached out in an embrace. The instructor walked in and to the desk. Aaron looked at him in amazement.

Eric! Milo's friend. Eric who was a writer. Eric whom he had met at Thompson's restaurant.

All through the Marxian Economics class Aaron stared at Eric and heard little. Eric was slim and erect and handsome, his face thin, his hair clipped short, his jaw strong, his eyes calm but penetrating and deep-set. His mouth was clean and strong with his words. There was conviction in every sentence. And Aaron remembered leaving Thompson's after meeting him, going to the library the next day and getting the novel he had written. He had admired Eric's book. It was poetic, full of strength and idealism, crashing to a vital and important conclusion. It was much like Dick's paintings.

After class he went up to say hello to Eric. Eric remembered him but not his name.

Aaron went with Mary Ellen and Dick to the fourth room. Its outer section served as a bookstore and on long tables were Marxist books and pamphlets, *The Daily Worker,* novels approved by the party. The other part of the office room was sectioned off into two small offices. From one of these offices a man came. He was a short man, strongly built with a very large head, bald, and eyes that fastened on a person, a thing, penetratingly and seemed unwilling to let go until they had decided something for the tremendously large skull.

"That's Mr. Hamilton," Mary Ellen whispered. "He's the head of the school."

He was approachable. He made himself so. Mr. Hamilton walked over to them and called Dick and Mary Ellen by name. Smiling he shook hands with Aaron and welcomed him to the school. His eyes probed Aaron and catalogued. Then, as if thinking of something far more important, he nodded, smiled, and moved away.

Two weeks later Aaron enrolled in classes at the Workers' School. Most of every day and every night when there was no school he lay on his belly on the cot in Dick's studio reading volume after volume from Dick's bookcases. He had Dick and Mary Ellen as companions in their fight against oppression of the underdog; as companions in art. He met many other students. They were gracious and sincere and he fell into easy conversation with them. They were dogmatic and tenacious in argument and that was good too. This was the companionship of struggle: he had found something to grab hold of. Some force to devote his life to. Something that gave purpose and meaning to his life. He wanted to sacrifice himself to something. He now had this sacrifice which offered nothing to him personally and demanded everything. The people. The abstraction of the people. Everything for their good. He had found a branch of the tree. This was logic. These were rules to live by. They made sense. They gave a harmony to life and living. He was in the *avant-garde* of the future. Two centuries from now communism would have the same sanctity surrounding it that Christianity now had. He was happy to throw his lot in with the common man and it had been the common man who had gotten himself torn apart by the lions in the early days of Christianity. They had said peace, it's wonderful, and the war went on—the nice, civilized war of everyday life, of man against man, class against class and creed, color, of man against himself. And now, he was engaged in the good fight.

He had never been happier. Communism was the answer. He had found a track to travel on.

# XVI

I want to do something for the Party," Aaron confided to Dick and Mary Ellen.

They were happy about it. Dick lugged out a bottle of wine from under a bed and they drank, looking out of his skylight window at the star-studded night.

Aaron's other friends, members of the Party, said, "It won't be long now. Soon Aaron will join the Party."

Dick and Mary Ellen must have spoken to Mr. Hamilton about him. Mr. Hamilton asked him if he would like to help out on the school newspaper.

Happily Aaron accepted the duty and set out fresh paper and new pencils on his desk at home. But the first weeks on the newspaper meant nothing more than turning the crank on the mimeograph machine, doing menial jobs for the editor, addressing envelopes and taking orders from everyone on the staff. Also he was caught in a web of petty politics and small jealousies among members of the staff.

There were other things that rasped against his sensitivity. In one of his classes the instructor, a Mr. Fisher, taught Dialectical Materialism. This subject was tough going for Aaron, for the housewife who sat next to him, for the Negro woman from the South. It was even hard to grasp for the two eager freshmen from City College.

Mr. Fisher was patient at first and explained again, very carefully. And they didn't understand. Then, a little more impatiently, he explained in more detail. If they still didn't understand he put it down to stupidity and changed the subject. Words always steamroller over a student's thinking. And this was so in most classes. It was dogma. There was little room for questioning or arguing.

Confusion came to Aaron's mind. There were things he didn't understand and things he didn't agree with. But there was no arguing them. There was the school and there was the Party line.

Aaron took his difficulties to Dick. Dick slapped him across the shoulder and laughed and said, "It takes time, boy, but it's the right thing. The only thing."

He took his difficulties to Mary Ellen. "Look, baby," she said, "I think you need an affair." She took his cheeks roughly between the palms of her hands and kissed him on the lips. Then she took his hand. "Come on, let's go for a walk. Walking always cures the blues."

At last he was assigned to do an article for the newspaper. Enthusiastically he worked on it, three days running, and turned it in. The next day Mr. Hamilton called him to his office. "Levin," Mr. Hamilton said, clearing his soft-spoken throat, "there are falsities here. This—" he nicked off a sentence "—this is Positivism. Here—" he nicked off another "—bourgeois idealism." He nicked off many more phrases, giving them impressive names as he did so, until Aaron's brain was completely confused. "But—" Aaron said weakly. Mr. Hamilton was accusing him of all manner of heresies.

The smile was fatherly, all-knowing, ironical, condescending. "Do this article over and—I'd like to see it when you have rewritten it."

"Yes, sir." And as Aaron departed, Mr. Hamilton said softly after him, "You know, Aaron, a liberal is a worse enemy of the people than arrant reactionaries are. Remember that."

"Yes, sir," Aaron said.

Aaron waited alone in the classroom. Then he moved from his seat to Eric's desk. For a moment he looked down at Eric, who was bent over some papers. He didn't seem like a writer and a teacher. More like a kid his own age. Only the gray hairs coming, a few, sneaking to his temples. That must have been from the war.

Aaron didn't say what was on his mind. "I don't understand," he said, "all the things the Party stands for. I'm confused. Sometimes the Communists—we Communists," he said in amendment and hoped Eric had heard.

Eric grinned. It was a boyish grin. His eyes wrinkled down almost to a close and the wrinkles streaked out across his temples. "Well, there are a few of us," Eric said, "but we're awfully lonely."

The words were disconcerting to Aaron, "I—I—" Aaron said. Milo's friend, Aaron thought, looking at Eric. "Sometimes I wonder if there's enough room for your own private thoughts. You have to watch out for—so many things—I mean, well Mr. Hamilton—he always knows where your thinking is wrong—"

Eric seemed to know what he meant, for he smiled sympathetically. "Remember this, Aaron, Mr. Hamilton is a brilliant Party strategist. He's used to working out programs of action. He's just come to the school recently and that's why sometimes he may seem so exacting."

The next day Aaron took Eric's second book from the shelf of the public library. He took it home and lay on his stomach reading it. He had admired Eric so much because of his first book. The tremendous difference to him in the second book shocked him. It seemed only a recital of the Party line. The framework, the perfectly constructed novel, was there, and the clear, clean style. But to him it seemed as though it had lost all the poetry of the former book, all the penetrating and inspired observations. His work now was neat, like Mr. Hamilton's mind.

Aaron rewrote the article and handed it in. It came back with Mr. Hamilton's red-penciled notations. He tried writing it again. This time he started on an entirely new track, and when he was through he felt that he had an important article.

The evening he handed the article in again he said at a meeting that he would like to join the Party. No one said anything. The members of the newspaper staff glanced at one another.

Mr. Hamilton called to him from his office.

"You didn't remember what I said, Aaron."

Aaron looked down in confusion. How could it be! This was one of the best things he had ever written. He knew it! He had written out of his heart about willingly giving up the freedom of expression for the greater goal of achieving a true communist society. He had torn individualism to shreds. Or so it seemed to him.

And now Mr. Hamilton's eyes told him that his efforts were completely unsatisfactory.

Mr. Hamilton was talking in his precise, soft way: "How can you say that you will willingly give up freedom of expression? How can you imply that this is what the Party demands? Capitalistic society does not allow freedom of expression. Freedom of expression only comes when a society completely controls itself, and capitalism does not control its own economic and social life.

". . . I'm afraid, Aaron, you will have to work very hard to rid yourself of the bourgeois idea that self-control means loss of freedom. . . . I understand you wish to join the Party, but the Party does not want members who feel that they are giving up their freedom by joining. Such members always turn renegade."

"But I didn't mean that," Aaron said desperately. "I meant that one must be willing to give up something, some ideas—"

"The Party—" Mr. Hamilton interrupted, "is a *voluntary* organization of people who fundamentally hold the same viewpoint."

Aaron stood crestfallen, hurt—and worst, confused. How could Mr. Hamilton so misunderstand him? The Party didn't want him, Mr. Hamilton had said.

Mr. Hamilton put his hand on Aaron's shoulder. "We can't afford to make mistakes. Learn. Study. Think. Discipline yourself. Examine what you really think. When you do this you will know if the Party is for you. And the Party will know if you are for it."

Hurt, defeated, Aaron moved toward home. He argued with Hamilton in his mind on the way home. "I don't care what you call it, it was the truth that I wrote in my article," he said half-aloud. Then he was shocked at himself. He must remain a student. Hamilton was the master.

Again he waited in Eric's class after the others had left.

Eric laid his pencil aside. Eric smiled. "Well, Aaron?"

Again Aaron didn't say what was on his mind. Instead he said, "The newspapers—all the stuff about the Iron Curtain and slave labor—"

Eric sighed. He tensed in his chair. Then he leaned back. He looked with his gray, deep-set eyes into Aaron's brown eyes. "You don't know the facts," he said. "It's—" he spread his hands, "it's a matter of which you believe in—the people who have betrayed you before and who have every newspaper in the country through which to betray you again—or the people from whom you haven't been able to hear." Eric's eyebrows knotted. He looked at Aaron seriously, and for a long time. His gray eyes asked understanding. His lips said, "I've read Koestler. I've even read Trotsky's *History of the Russian Revolution.*" He said this jokingly, for they both knew the heresy involved. Then his face was serious again. "Those books have confused me. I don't know all the answers, Aaron. No one knows all the answers. Come on, I'll pop for a beer."

In the tavern, sitting in a booth facing each other, the rich suds high on their steins of beer, Eric said again, "Go along with Hamilton. He is really an amazing man. He's called the right shots all along the line. He predicted the turn against Russia after the war. He predicted our own imperialist moves into Greece, into the Far East. He predicted that we'd start making deals with Franco—oh, so many things. And not because he's Hamilton, but because he is an expert Marxist." Aaron's face was not responding. "Look, Aaron," Eric said, "you can know nothing with certainty. You have the feeling of being in a blind alley, a cul-de-sac. Go ahead, retreat into yourself—but that is a blind alley too. Or you can take faith from the examples of history that there is always a solution found by those who need it most." He paused. He looked deep into Aaron. He said, "Hamilton and I hold the same point of view—basically."

Aaron said, "I don't want to be just a cog in a machine—I had that in the army." Whipping the black hair off his forehead with a snap of his neck, "If the Communist Party is out to establish truth—it means everybody has to be a thinker." He gestured with his shoulders and big hands. "Mr. Hamilton is trying to force me to give up my right to think." Pitifully he pulled the red-penciled article from his pocket. "Look," he said, "I didn't say anything against the Party." His eyes were hurt.

"You don't understand—there are some basic contradictions here. You're not versed enough yet in Marxism. Many of the statements you make here are still—still tinged with individualism and a need for self-expression rather than an interest in fact."

Aaron broke in. "Does that mean that if you're a member of the Party you do like Hamilton says—you give up freedom of expression and at the same time delude yourself that you're not giving it up at all?"

Eric evaded an answer. "Be patient," he consoled.

"Your second book—" Aaron started to stay but Eric interrupted him. "I know," he said, "that my second book isn't as good as my first one. But I don't have as much time to write now. There are—" he gestured "—more important things to do." He looked across the booth at Aaron. The little shiftings of Aaron's eyes, the slight accusation there.

Slowly, sadly, Eric twisted his glass, swishing the beer around. Looking down into the sudsy white foam, he said, "When I write about capitalists I make them evil—I probably wouldn't have done that before. They become symbols, not people—although, of course, I know this isn't true. My father was a capitalist and a wonderful man. But he was an enemy of the people. If you want people to recognize their enemies you do not speak of these enemies sympathetically. You see, the intellectual is always anxious to show that he sees both sides of a question. He is a bystander. If you believe the class struggle is more important than your right to express your own subtlety, if you can wait for that luxury, perhaps even give it up altogether, then the Hamiltons won't bother you." Eric smiled in a kindly but penetrating way. "You can't recognize the truth of class differences because you don't want to belong to a class. You have avoided being a Jew, for instance. . . . Class opposition is something real, something independent of whatever you may think about it."

Eric went on, wearily, but he hoped in a way Aaron would understand: "You came here because you hate war. But that is not enough. You must hate war so much that you are willing to fight the one war that is necessary to end all wars—the class-war revolution."

"How does that differ from the last war they told us would end all wars?" Aaron said. "I want no part of any more wars."

"Then you don't belong to the Party," Eric said.

"Only the men who refuse to fight can stop war!"

"That's Milo's point of view." Eric smiled. "You see, I had this all out with Milo once. You want to take the sitting-duck position with Milo. Sitting ducks are easily knocked off."

"Then the Marxists are only interested really in the struggle between the men who have and the men who have not?"

Eric looked at him. He smiled, he shrugged, he gave up the conversation.

Aaron left for home. He walked. His walk was troubled. Eric was right. He must be right. Hadn't he himself said that this was no time for writing but a time for action? Did he want it to happen again? Didn't he want to put all of his force behind the one movement that really meant ultimate peace? Didn't peace come when all the peoples of the world met in a single family? The family of humanity? One world? Eric must be right. He had been a rich man's son. He had sacrificed everything for the ideal. He, Aaron, wanted to be a part of what Eric and Dick and Mary Ellen were part of. He had never been as close to anyone before in art, in friendship, in purpose and ideal, as he now was to them.

He was depressed.

Depressed.

He walked into Thompson's and looked around. Nobody was there that he knew. He slumped at a table with a cup of coffee at his elbow.

Steve, on his night off, came into the restaurant, got a cup of coffee and sat down at the table with Aaron. "Hi, keed."

"Hello."

Steve shook a newspaper under Aaron's nose. "Look," he said and went on in monologue, telling about plans for atomic bomb shelters. "We're second on the list. It's New York first and then Chicago. Sure, they've got the bomb and we've got it and we'll both use it. It's the end of the human race. The hell with it! What the hell. Why not? We gave it a try and just look around. Let's let the monkeys or the insects have a try at it. They won't do any worse job than we did." He went on and on.

Aaron stood up. He had to get out of there. "I've got to go, Steve—"

He hurried to the sidewalk.

Depressed.

On the street he remembered Steve months ago telling him how Russian musicians, artists, writers, had to use their art as propaganda for the good of the state.

But what's so wrong in that? Aaron asked himself. Didn't the great artists of the past propagandize for Christianity, for church and state? Yes, the artist had to use himself too for the furthering of ideals. Ideals. Hamilton didn't like the word.

Depressed.

Solace. He needed solace.

He climbed the stairs to Dick's studio. Mary Ellen was bent over a drawing board making some sketches. "Hi," she yelled when he entered, and went on working.

"Where's Dick?"

"Huh? Oh, he's out."

Aaron sat in a corner leafing through the pages of a book. The stars began to brighten in the skylight overhead and after a while he heard Mary Ellen say, "Damn!" and toss the pencil aside. He heard her get up and walk toward him. "Want a glass of wine?" she asked.

He stood up. He took her roughly by the wrist, and pulling her to him, kissed her roughly. He was surprised at himself.

"Hey!" she said, pushing him away. "Just because I said you needed an affair I didn't mean you needed it with me."

"I'm sorry."

He picked up his hat and went home.

He sat at his desk and wrote the article exactly as they wanted it —paraphrased from a Marxist book.

The article was accepted. He was given more articles to write. He didn't cross Mr. Hamilton any more. He wrote strictly along the Party line. But his writing was mechanical. He retreated from thought. He put the words down. He walked the treadmill. He wasn't satisfied with what he had to say, or dissatisfied. He just didn't think about it.

He went on writing mechanically. But he was confused and depressed. The crack had come. He read the newspapers. It couldn't all be propaganda, what the American press was writing about Russia, could it? And he couldn't talk to Eric any more. Eric had shut himself off, it seemed. Eric didn't even listen when he came with unpopular questions and probings about communism. Or had Eric shut him off? I can't tell. He looks at me. He says things in answer. . . . One thing Eric had said: "You're looking for intellectual satisfaction, Aaron. The Party distrusts, and rightly so, those who have nothing to gain except intellectual satisfaction. The mind can relinquish ideas as quickly as it accepts them—and so the intellectual is not to be trusted. But the worker—he has everything to gain, if he wins what he wants—and the capitalist has everything to lose. So the Party recognizes the hard validity of the capitalist's struggle to keep what he has even though he is an enemy."

But I don't understand, maybe I don't really know what he means. All I know is I'm against war. All I want is to try to listen to what I, Aaron, want to hear—all the truths.

Mary Ellen found him alone in Dick's studio. His head was down on the drawing board. She rubbed her fingers into his hair, started to massage his head sympathetically. "What's the matter, baby?"

He shook his head and kept his face down in his arms.

Mary Ellen leaned down and kissed him on the head. "Come on now, baby, snap out of it."

He didn't snap out of it. Then, after a long while, he turned toward her and put both arms around her, clung to her in despair.

She kissed him. And the floodgates of youth were open to them. They clung together.

They held hands. They kissed. They went to the cot.

Aaron said, "I'm a virgin. I don't know anything about it." But his nerves knew their desire. And she was teacher and lover.

# XVII

The days moved to weeks and the weeks became months. There were nights for Aaron at Dick's studio with Mary Ellen. There was relief in it. It took away some of his doubts and fears. And there was his writing for the Workers' School newspaper. His writing didn't mean anything to him. It was just words. And he filled many pages with the words. Mechanically. Each word followed Party dictum. And the time came when Mr. Hamilton called Aaron aside after a meeting and said, "The time has come, I think, Aaron, for you to join the Party."

"I—I have to go home and—and think about it."

He saw Mr. Hamilton's eyes staring unblinkingly at him. They seemed as if they would never unclutch him and let him go. He turned and left the office in confusion, took the elevator down, hurried out onto the sidewalk.

Why did I say that? Why do I have to think about it? I have to think about it, yes, I have to think about it. But I wanted to join. All the time I wanted so badly to join.

He wandered around. If his thinking wasn't clear it was at least sincere. And he saw nations, governments. Russia is a name and America is a name. But the good of all mankind is a better name. Wasn't Russia for that? I don't know. I used to think so. Self-sacrifice is important, yes. For the good of the whole. But individuality, self-expression, is important too. War. This threat of war. Must there always be wars? The two big powers were preparing in threat or for actual conflict. And this was a truth. This he knew for a truth.

They didn't care about people. They only cared about the importance of the nation as a world power. *The* world power. And bow your heads, all other nations. They only cared about the military machine poised for action.

And now he was accusing them both, Russia and America. They didn't care about lives and deaths.

He looked down at his feet. He looked up at the sky. Eternally it turned its calm, inscrutable face down over him, the city, the people, buildings, lampposts. Its suns and worlds burned in pin points of light, uncaring.

Isn't the world all one hunk of land? What part of a river, what high path of a mountain, what gigantic and perilous sea had given consent and become a chalk mark among people across which others must not move?

He halted. He leaned his head against the black upright of a lamppost. He hung on with both hands. The blood in him heated and cooled and heated. He took his lip between his teeth. I must hurry back. I must do what I have to do. School is just about out. I must hurry. . . .

Slowly, slowly he retraced his steps, went into the office building, took the elevator up, went down the corridor to the Workers' School.

He stood in front of Eric. He stood mute. He wanted to say:

Something shiny has been taken away from me. The whole world with, in it, men, all men of good will.

He did not say this. He said, "I'm leaving the school." He stood yet a moment longer looking at Eric with his wistful eyes, hoping he would understand, knowing he wouldn't. He said, "I know it's popular right now to talk against communism and Communists. I won't do that. I'll never speak against the ideal. I believe in the ideal."

Aaron stumbled up the steps to Dick's studio. "They asked me to join the Party."

Dick smiled his wide, wide grin. "Swell!" he said. "Swell!" and pounded Aaron's shoulder.

Aaron looked down at the floor. He would miss these good friends, Dick and Mary Ellen. He would miss Eric's kindness and sincerity, his devotion to a cause he felt good and true. Aaron looked up at Dick. "I'm not going to join the Party." He dragged his eyes away. He looked at the far wall. "I'm leaving the school." He looked back at Dick pleadingly.

Astonishment was in Dick's face, and argument.

Aaron shook his head slowly. "Don't try to talk me into it, Dick."

Dick looked at him, deep into him. He smiled the smile that belonged to Aaron alone. The smile said, I'm sorry for you.

"Good-by," Aaron said. He knew it was good-by. Gone the bond that had held them. . . .

Down the steps. Out into the black night. Alone on the street.

Dick! he said. Mary Ellen! he said.

But it was good-by and he knew it. The door locked. The bolt thrust across. The chain secured and the light put out to him.

Dick! Mary Ellen!

He was their enemy without wanting to be. He was the Party's enemy, the ideal's enemy, without wanting to be.

And he knew that Dick's face, Mary Ellen's face, Eric's face, were as important to the Party as Hamilton's face. But he knew that whenever he thought of the Party he would see Hamilton's face and those like him.

# XVIII

Blue and depressed, Jim headed for the tavern. If he could forget about the war. If he could run into Dave or Milo and sit around and talk about the old days. About high school and football. . . .

The window was painted with the name: NICK'S VETERAN BAR. The place was full of ex-GI's. It was their tavern, their hangout. Many of them came every night to lean against the bar or group together in the booths and talk about their experiences overseas or to gripe about civilians and civilian life. Some of them had put parts of their service uniforms to civilian use. Two or three fellows wore army shirts with their civilian pants. Here a navy coat was turned up in a circle of blue collar. Toward the end of the bar a field jacket had its elbow propped up on the mahogany.

Few men who hadn't been in service came to Nick's place. When they did, the ex-servicemen got into conversation with them over beer mugs or shots of whisky—telling their grim stories of killing and bombing, the women they had slept with, the drunks they had been on. Telling it in part as a release, partly to amaze, shock: I've lived. I've seen things. See how dull your life has been. I wouldn't trade all the days and hours of your existence. You haven't lived. I've got muscles. The ex-serviceman was the professor standing up on the lecture platform telling you a lot of things you didn't know. And among themselves: You shot down twenty planes and you were a hero. You shot down one and you were a deadbeat. You shot down a man face to face and you were a hero. You screwed all the women, raped a few of the enemy's women, gambled all your money away, drank a barrel of liquor in a single night, threw a couple taverns up for grabs. You were a man.

Gray-haired Nick, veteran of the First World War, stood behind the bar in his white apron. On one side of the cash register there was a framed salutation with a reproduction of the ex-serviceman's lapel pin above it. The salutation read: WELCOME BACK WEARER OF THIS BADGE OF HONOR. YOU HAVE SERVED YOUR COUNTRY WELL. WE THANK YOU.

The juke box blared. The ex-servicemen leaned on their elbows toward each other, laughing, talking, punctuating their conversation with frequent curses. Tomas, drunk and with an arm flung loosely over Max's shoulder, was telling dirty jokes. "Now this one," he said, "could be told in church. It can be taken either way. It all depends on your mind—whether it's at a forty-five degree angle or straight down." He gestured illustratively with his hands.

"Hey! Keep it clean! I got a picture of my mother in my pocket!" an ex-GI shouted.

Tomas told his story. Max grinned out of his tan Mexican face. "Is that all you learned in the army, bud?" he asked, his eyes crinkling.

"Did you have to go all the way to Italy for that one?" George asked in good-humored derision.

Jim walked in. He took his bottle of beer to the back booth and sat there alone.

He heard someone say, "I want to be so drunk that I don't make any sense—not even to myself." Jim heard and felt the same way.

The juke box said loudly:

*You get your kiiiiicks*
*On roooooute Sixty-Six!*
*It winds from Chi-ca-go to L. A.*
*More than two thousand mi-les away*

Down the bar a voice said:

"So this kid, he says 'Hey, Sarge! I haven't had a chance to kill a German yet!' So the Sarge says, 'Well, take your pick.' So he does and he says, 'Thanks, Sarge!' "

Bruno walked in and over to the bar, pushing between stools. "Hi, Nick!" he called; and when Nick came down along the bar, "How was the black market while I was—" He nodded his head toward the windowpane and Europe. He looked around in admiration. "From the stock of whisky it looks like it was good."

In the back booth Jim brooded over his beer and the memories flowed home.

And the juke box:

*Now you go through St. Looey*
*And Jop-lin Mi-ssour-i*
*And Ok-la-ho-ma City is migh-ty pre-tty*

At the bar Max was saying to the fellow on the stool next to him, "I was in the Pacific. Where were you?"

"Europe."

"You had buildings to look at and lights," Max said, grinning.

"You had imagination, didn't you?"

"We didn't have anywhere to go."

"If you were fighting it was tough. If you weren't it was tough," the ex-GI said.

"Yeah," Max said.

"Yeah, we had towns," the ex-GI said, "but most of the time we just thought how nice it would be to go to them. Either we were fighting to win them or when we got to town we were told to take the other side."

And the juke box:

*You'll see Am-a-ril-lo*
*Gallup New Mex-i-co*
*Flag-staff Ar-i-zo-na*
*Don't for-get Wi-no-na*
*Kingman, Barstow, San Bernadino*

A young fellow standing at the bar behind Max pushed his head forward and said, "Boy, was I glad to go into the army! It was the first time I had been away from my mother and my wife! I could be alone! I could look at women!"

Max was saying, "My ship had the most beautiful bow that ever cut a wave, boy."

His drinking partner said, "You sound as if you're talking about a woman."

"She's more than that," Max said.

And down along the bar toward the middle stood three ex-servicemen talking. The first one said, "In Hawaii you'd get in a great big line, way at the end, and wait your turn." He waved his hand, showing where the front of the line was. "The madam would be up there —'Old-fashioned, half and half, 96, around-the-world—' " He lifted his arms away from his body and, with his eyes squinted as if he were half asleep, moved his hands like a blind man feeling his way. "You'd find the proper door. I only tried it once myself. Boy, those gals made the money!" And laughing, "Sometimes I wished I was a woman."

And the second one, "They were clean over there. They were inspected regularly."

And the third, "What does it mean to a woman? You may get satisfied. She doesn't have to. All she has to do is just lay there." He shrugged.

The second ex-serviceman said, "A lot of them nurses turned plenty of tricks—a hundred dollars a crack. But the guys were glad to get it. Glad to pay. What the hell, fifty dollars was like five dollars here."

The first ex-serviceman looked down at his partner's arms. "When'd you get tattooed? In the navy?"

"Naw. When I was seventeen."

The first fellow said in answer, "I started to get tattooed but I got laid instead. After I got laid I wished I'd got tattooed."

They all laughed.

And the juke box:

*You get your kiiiiiicks*
*On roooooooute Sixty-Six!*
*It winds from Chi-ca-go to L. A.*
*More than two thousand mi-les a-way*

Max was saying, "The crazy things the navy does— lets you know the enemy is going to attack you. Let's you know they're—twenty miles away—over the P. A. system—" His voice imitated the P. A. system. *"Boogie Woogie—approaching two points off starboard bow—"* Max grabbed his drinking partner's arm and squeezed his fingers into it. He said, "It's like taking a violin string and making it tighter—tighter—I've seen men get down on their knees and scream."

Down the bar a way an ex-soldier said to an ex-sailor, "So you flogged your dummy. Is that anything to be ashamed of? We all did in service."

Max got off the bar stool and went to the head. The sign along the urinal advertising a product said: GOOD FOR HEARTBURN—BREATH ODOR—LOST VITALITY—SLEEPLESS NIGHTS—HEADACHES.

Max watched the water swirl in the urinal. He shivered. He went back to the bar, but not to his scrape-acquaintance drinking partner. He sat alone and ordered a beer.

Max shivered and stared down into the foam of his beer. The sea lifted and tilted. The sky was a bare, blue roof lifting and tilting. They were burying another one. Another sailor who had caught it. They had laid him on his canvas hammock. The mortician had sewed him into his hammock, starting at his feet and sewing to his head. The last stitch was through his nose to tell if he was still alive. And that was tradition. Between his teeth and his lips was a piece of silver, a dime, to pay his way to heaven. And that was tradition too.

Carpenter's horses were placed on deck with a couple of planks across them. The dead man was put on them, just a body sewed in canvas, draped with an American flag, the stars across his heart. At his feet were tied two five-inch shells, each approximately thirty-five pounds in weight.

The whole ship's company is called on deck. Six marines are standing at attention. The minister mumbles his prayers. The lieutenant says: "Aim! *Fiah!*" The six marines six times fire at the empty sky.

Then taps. And the body is tipped into the sea. Splash of the body. The circles of the sea spreading out and taking the body greedily. The ship is under way as the ceremony takes place. The lonely man is soon left behind in his lonely place in the sea. He stands in the sea with the two thirty-five pound weights holding him erect. He stands at attention in the sea. He looks longingly after his ship.

The bugle blows.

"Resume your regular routine."

The quartermaster records in the ship's log that so and so was buried at such and such meridian and such and such degree.

They buried the dead any time they had a chance to. Sometimes there were many carpenter's horses with the stiff, still bodies sewed in their canvases, a long loop of thread through each nostril, a piece of silver between teeth and lips. And, stooping over the sacked bodies, Catholic, Jewish, Protestant clergymen mumbling prayers. The splashes of the bodies and the circles spreading like lassos, like nooses.

In the bottom of the sea the dead men stood erect. The little fish would swim near, and the big fish. First in curiosity and then ripping through the canvas, nibbling at the dead, water-soaked flesh.

Max shivered, looking down into his beer, watching the bubbles rise to the surface of the beer.

"Hey, Mac! What's your trouble?" an unknown ex-serviceman said in gruff friendliness to Max, slapping him across the back.

Max swirled the beer in his glass and, turning his head, looked sideways at the stranger. Max shook his head nothing. Then he grinned slowly. "Have a drink, mate," he said to the stranger.

Max drained his glass and when he set it down he was grinning. He had thought of Ollie. "Hey Rebel!" "Hey Fur-ner!" they yelled at each other. "Pal, when I die, sneak a can of beer in my canvas for me. Frig the fish. Take a drink for me down there," they said to each other. . . .

In the booth ahead of Jim's sat three young fellows. One wore GI summer issues and was telling an experience. He was in his early twenties, good-looking, and as he talked he looked at his friends with deep brown eyes, clear and youthful. He was saying, "A German civilian told us there was an SS general and his staff in the woods. I had a machine gun mounted on a truck. I sprayed the woods. Our anti-aircraft guns sprayed it too. We had trucks circling this area and some of our men went into the woods searching for them. But it got dark too quick so we went back to our battery positions and that night about eight o'clock me and two of my buddies went to the village looking for something to drink—"

Don walked into the tavern. "Let each man render me his bloody hand!" He stood grinning, posing a moment on the floor, and then slapped his hand down on the shoulder of one of his friends. "Who's popping for my drink?"

"We always used searching for German soldiers as an excuse to look for something to drink," the handsome young man in the booth said. "To search the houses for liquor."

In the booth behind him Jim heard the word *drink* and began to listen.

"At one house we spotted a young German *Fräulein* that looked pretty good so we made up our minds that when everybody was bedded down for the night we'd come back and get a little of that."

And the juke box:

*You get your kiiiiicks*
*On route Sixty-Six!*

And at the bar:

"What the hell did we go over there to fight for? We come back and the country is in worse shape than when we left."

"You come back," the second ex-GI said, "and the Jews get hold of you. You try to rent a place and they got their hands in your pocket."

"In the army I got my three hots a day, my clothes and fifty dollars a month," the first ex-GI said.

The handsome fellow in the booth lifted his glass to his lips and gulped the shot. "Eventually," he said, "we found something to drink in another house and proceeded to get drunk. I crawled into my pup tent and went to sleep—thanks." He took and lit the cigarette offered him. "I got up at 1 A.M. for guard duty and when I was off, me and five other fellows took off for this house where this good-looking *Fräulein* was. We got there and knocked on the door." He rapped his knuckles hard against the table and grinned. It was a handsome but hard grin. "We got everybody up and herded them into the living room of their house—three old people and this one girl. We grabbed ahold of the girl and took her upstairs while one man stood guard over the old folks." He grinned again, in pleasurable memory. "We got the girl upstairs. She was screaming and yelling—she knew what we was after and she wouldn't let us have it." He smiled, boyishly.

Jim lifted his glass for the first time and emptied it of its beer. In the booth ahead the young fellow said, "One big guy about six feet two or three said, 'Get out of the way! I'll get in!' He does all right. So the rest of us got her too." He laughed outright now. "She said to me, 'Please! Please! My husband is in the army. How would you feel if somebody was doing this to your wife while you're in the army?' " He looked smilingly at his two friends. He said, "That didn't do her no good. Everybody knocked off a piece anyway."

At the bar one fellow yelled angrily at the noncombatant, "You're talking to an ex-GI!"

"Aw, pipe down!" a couple of the fellows near him said.

Don laughed. He said to his companions, "Sudden and quick in quarrels." He nudged one of them with his elbow. "That's from Shakespeare," he said. "That's what he said about soldiers."

At the far end of the bar a man said, "But you were in the Pacific, Les. It was different there." Les smiled. He was a big-boned man, broad-shouldered, and above his square jaw and warm gray eyes his short-cropped hair was mixed with gray. He said, "There's a rhythm in the South Pacific that takes you in. Yes." He nodded in remembered enjoyment and his eyes roved across a small area of the ceiling as he tried to find words to explain. "You know how palm trees bend and wave with the breeze. You know there's a rhythm to it. And the sea matched it." His big hands tried to move in that rhythm above the bar. "And in time you fall into that. You talk in it and you live in it. They call it some kind of mystery. But it isn't. There's something about the equatorial South Pacific that takes you in and lulls you down. Slows you down to that rhythm. The natives all move by it. They talk by it and it's a wonderful thing. It's restful. There is civilization there. . . ."

Dave had come into the tavern. A man at a table said loudly, sneering it in Dave's direction, "I thought only white men came in here." Dave heard but his face did not change expression. He walked toward the bar. Nick had heard and came from around the bar. He scowled at the man and shook his head emphatically. "Not in here," he told him. "None of that stuff in here." He pointed toward the door.

Max saw Dave and sang his name out loudly. Dave walked over to Max. Max hugged him to himself. "Dave—" grinning, "what are you doing down here?"

"I promised Milo I'd meet him here. How's things?"

Max scowled a gesture and nodded his head slowly up and down indicating that things were okay. "So Mi's coming down," he said, and grinning, "Good! We'll get him drunk. Do the writer good."

Don had seen Dave, and leaving his friends, came over. "Hi, Dave!" They shook hands. "Come over to see me sometimes," Don said. "I've got a room in a hotel near here." He scrawled the address on the back of an envelope and handed it to Dave. Dave introduced him to Max. Don insisted on buying a round and stood talking easily to the Mexican and the Negro.

*It winds from Chicago to L. A.*
*More than two thousand miles away*
*You get your kiiiiiicks*
*On Route Sixty-Six*

—the juke box said.

"So," the handsome fellow in the booth in front of Jim's said, "while we're waiting turns somebody found her jewel box and broke it open and took all her jewelry. We kept all the lights off but one so that none of them could recognize us and took turns guarding the old folks. These old folks—" he laughed "—cringed back in the corner as if somebody was getting ready to shoot them. If they made a move toward the door we'd throw a rifle in their faces." His smile was vicious across his handsome face. "They'd get back. They couldn't do a thing. They were helpless. The old woman kept rolling her eyes toward the stairs to where the girl was."

Outside the tavern a truck backfired loudly. In the crowded tavern a big hulk of a man over six foot tall jumped straight up with his arms thrust out wildly and yelled, "Look out! Look out!" He hit the floor.

For a second, part of the conversation died down. One ex-GI shrugged his shoulders. Another ex-sailor staggered over the prone figure on the floor and, leaning down, tapped the ex-GI on the shoulder. "It's okay now, Mac."

And the juke box:

*Now you go through St. Looey*
*And Jop-lin Mis-sour-i*
*And Ok-la-ho-ma City is migh-ty pre-tty.*

Les was saying, "We anchored in New Guinea in a place where white men had never been before, and these natives' youngsters—they couldn't have been more than six or seven years old—they paddled out in those dugout things near the ship and then ran them back. And each day they came a little closer to the ship. Each day a little closer." He smiled. "We finally got them on board. You know, never seen white men before. Seven years old. That much courage they had. And they came up the ladder. We took them into the mess hall and gave them something to eat. You know, jelly and bread." Les grinned slowly and completely. "Their eyes popped!" Smiling, he lit a cigarette. "Next day they came back and brought us some oranges and stuff that was growing wild—you know, to even it up. But—" he laughed "—everyone on board that ship was afraid to go ashore alone."

Milo entered the tavern, and standing between Dave and Max put an arm over a shoulder of each. "Hi, fellows." He nodded at Don. "What are you fellows drinking?"

"No, it's my turn!" Don said. He put his hand on Dave's shoulder and smiled at him. "I like your people. I want to help them. You can help them too, Dave." He looked up earnestly into Dave's brown Negro face.

Milo glanced at Don in amusement and at Dave in sympathy and embarrassment; and then in half anger. Why did so many people have to start like this? But he supposed they meant well. Yes, they meant well. Only—he shrugged to himself.

"Yeah, I want to help them," Don said again.

"I think," Milo said, "that Dave thinks people are just people." He said it with a slight edge of anger in his voice. "He's not interested in just the—" he slurred it "—the Negro problem."

Don laughed with embarrassment. "Yeah," he said, "yeah, that's the way I feel too." He laughed again, weakly; and with his hand on Dave's shoulder in sympathetic compassion, "When you were a conscientious objector did they put you in jail because you were colored?" He said it because he wanted to be friendly and understanding—and having said it, wished he had kept still.

Milo answered for Dave. "No," Milo said, squinting hard-eyed at the wall ahead. "Dave didn't hide behind God. I did, though. Dave said he was an atheist and was a C.O. only on philosophical grounds—not on religious grounds. I didn't have that much guts." He smiled, a trifle hard-lipped, and stopped. And Don felt the coolness of both of them and was hurt. They don't appreciate what I'm doing. I want to tell them I feel like them. I'm one of them too in my way and they won't let me be.

He smiled impotently at them and wished they'd understand, accept him. He genuinely liked Dave. Dave should have the same chance as a white man. Dave was different.

Bruno had seen them. He came lumbering over on his big feet, his broad, beefy shoulders and slightly puffing stomach making a path through the crowd for him. "Hey!" Bruno shouted. "Jesus Christ!" He grinned. "The whole gang's here!" His little blue eyes twinkled at them from behind his glasses. He kissed each of them on the forehead playfully, making smacking sounds: Max, Dave, Milo.

Max introduced Milo to his new drinking partner on the next stool, his arm thrown loosely over Milo's shoulder. "When he sold his first story he almost came all over himself. The magazine didn't have any money and he got merchandise—a sweater." He grinned at Milo in friendliness.

"The sweater kept me warm three whole winters down there in the slums," Milo said.

Near them stood a short, husky little man with a big voice. With much waving of his stubby little arms and many gestures he was keeping his friends amused by his war experiences. Using his palm for a piece of paper and the finger of his other hand for a pencil he said, "Roosevelt said 'Greetings—' I said 'Hello there.' —Good-by —that's all—Guadacanal." He slapped the backs of his hands against his two buddies' arms. "When I got to Guadacanal—oh, what girls!" He placed the palms of his hands together as one about to pray and then laid his cheek down on them and closed his eyes. *"Uuuuuuummm!* I didn't fight no more. I was playing pinochle with a Jap." His little brown eyes snapped wide and his short, high-pitched laugh that was half a snort went climbing up toward the ceiling. "What a canal!" he said. "What a canal!" He laughed at his own pun. Majestically he unbuttoned his suit coat and showed the roll of potbelly straining against his belt. He slapped it with a hard palm. "They say this is a sailor. This ain't no sailor—this is army." He laughed and did a half-dance away from them, spinning around on one heel and turning back to his buddies. One had been in the navy and he now razzed him. "Were you ever in the navy—taking a shower—and you try to stoop down and pick up the soap?" He laughed again and leaning forward with his little brown eyes moving in a line from buddy's face to buddy's face and lowering his voice, he said, "You know what they put on a sailor's tombstone? *This man died here. God knows who reared him!"* Again the laugh and a hard palm slapping the ex-sailor on the shoulder.

Max bought a round. He lifted Don's fresh bottle of beer from the bar and handed it to him. "Here you are, fellow," he said in friendliness. "You know," he said, talking about the navy brass, "they think they're the nuts." He scowled comically. "It took them a long time," he said, "but finally they realized that these animals talked—talked!" He struck himself in the chest, indicating that he and his fellow sailors were considered animals. He leaned forward. He grasped Don by the wrist. "Before I went into the navy I'd fight you. I'd fight you on the street. I'd fight anybody." Slowly his head shook itself no, not any more. Slowly his lips smiled. He released Don's arm. He turned toward Milo, Dave, Bruno. "Atrocities. That's all you heard about—the Nazi and Jap atrocities. Did you ever hear of the American ones?" He looked now at Don. "What are you going to do about the Americans? Put them on a pedestal and worship them?" He tilted his beer to his lips. He set it aside. He said, "The order came down that we weren't to take any prisoners. Just one or two for questioning. It came down from this admiral—" Max's eyes squinted angrily at the admiral. His lips balled out: " 'Assist them in joining their ancestors.' We hit a ship," nodding his head slowly, "yeah, we hit a ship. Every time you saw something bobbing it was a head. It was a human being. It was the Jap sailors in the water. They were licked. They were killed. But we had to shoot them."

Max drained his entire bottle, did not set it down until it was empty, banged it down on the bar, looked out of his suddenly haggard eyes at his friends. His voice came slowly, softly, and as if it were hard to speak, to go on. "I was a group captain with machine guns and men under me. I had to give the order for my men to start shooting. The order came down over the intercom to the different groups." His voice took on, but quietly, clearly, the cold tone of the official voice giving the order: "Group one, prepare to fire!—Group one prepare to fire!—Commence firing!—Commence firing! . . . tah! tah! tah! tah!"

He was living it again. His sorrowful eyes looked from one to the other of them and his hand tightened on Don's arm. He said, "Then: 'Group three commence firing! Commence firing!" Max nodded slowly, sadly, tapped himself on the chest. "That's my order. I'm supposed to tell my men to fire." He said, "I used to look at Ollie and he used to look at me. I think I knew what he wanted to say. I think he would have done the same thing." Max's voice, living it, grew louder:

*"Commence firing! Commence firing!"*

Max slowly shook his head. "I couldn't," he said. "Those heads—those *human beings*—bobbing in the water.

" 'Commence firing! Can you hear me?'

" 'Yes, I hear you,' " drearily, sadly.

It was over. Max sat slumped on the stool for a long moment more. Then he looked up at all of them. He laughed out loud. It was a sad, remembering, angry, violated-against laugh. He turned in toward the bar. "Hey, Nick! Bring us another round!"

*You get your kiiiiicks*
*On Route Sixty-Six*

"Everybody got finished knocking off a piece of tail," the handsome ex-soldier said, "and we went back to the battery and to sleep. The next morning an order came that we would round up the SS general. The colonel took half the men and led them up into the woods. We went up one side of the hill and three men from my battery went up the other side." He scratched his head over army tactics. "About three hundred men up one side of the hill and three up the other. We didn't find the general up our side of the hill. The colonel and three or four other officers stayed up on the hill and he sent the rest of us back to our units. When we got back one of the three men who had gone around the other side of the hill came running in and reported that his two buddies had got killed. One of them hadn't died yet. The top of his head had been blown off. They took him to the aid station but he died. Me and three other fellows took a jeep and went up the hill. The other fellow was deader'n a doornail."

*It winds from Chicago to L. A.*
*More than two thousand miles all the way*

At the front of the bar a loud, bawdy sailor's voice shouted to the whole tavern in sailor humor, "I liked them gash-a girls!"

In a booth one buddy was saying sympathetically to another buddy, "They really put it in you and broke it off, ain't it?"

At the bar Les still talked about the South Pacific. "We were in a hurry to build installations before the Japs could get back in there. See, they moved out to fight the battle of the Coral Sea and we moved in—and we had to get them in in short order so—ah—hurry!"

A fellow with a proud service pin riding his lapel on the thrust-out chest sidled up. "I killed one of them goddamn little monkeys," he offered. "I knocked the teeth out. Them Japs go for gold teeth, you know."

Les said, talking past the gold-teeth-owning ex-serviceman, "We were busy working twelve hours a day in that terrific heat—and every once in a while a native would stroll by."

Max was saying, "There were two types of heroes—those who were going to blow their top any day and those who were so stupid they didn't know what they were doing. I'm talking about the heroes now. The guys with the medals."

Milo said, "What type were you, Max?"

Max looked pained. He grinned sorrowfully; a smile that forgave his friend. "Now is that a nice thing to say, Mi?" he asked.

Les was saying, "And every once in a while we'd look at a native laying under a tree. And every once in a while a sailor would say, 'God! I'm glad I'm not a stupid, enslaved native. I'm glad I'm free!" Les laughed loudly and slapped his knees. "Working like—" he said, "oh hell—you know—and glad *he* was free!"

*You'll see Am-a-ril-lo*
*Gallup New Mex-i-co*

The handsome ex-serviceman was saying, "We were sitting around moping and mad because they had been killed. We were fighting mad. We wanted to go to the woods and start looking all over again. Our captain said nothin' doin' until we heard from the colonel. Pretty soon the colonel came grinding down the road in a jeep. He was sitting there smiling like a cat eating fish because he had three German prisoners on the hood of his jeep. He thought he was a hero or something. As he went by everybody started yelling, 'Kill the sonsabitches! Kill the bastards!' Then he found out what had happened. He issued an order that nobody was to go up into the woods again. It was the infantry's job to do work like that. We were artillery." He swallowed his drink, wiped his mouth. "Before the order came out an anti-aircraft unit attached to us had three or four men who took off up into the woods anyway on a search of their own. They found three krauts in the woods. Gimme a cigarette—"

He lit up, continued. "They fired a couple of shots at the krauts and they surrendered. They were so mad they decided not to take them prisoners. One fellow lined the three of them up and shot them down. He machine-gunned one of them across the legs until he shot his legs off. He machine-gunned an X across the chest of another one—"

*You get your kiiiicks*
*On Route Sixty-Six!*

Les was saying—and Bruno, Dave, Milo were listening now too as were several of the other men nearby—"There was a crew of Russian women that brought a ship up to Brisbane when Brisbane was the advance station. And they had a beautiful ship! And you know how they'd work the booms?—in rhythm. They'd be singing, their bodies bending free. From captain to cabin boy they were all women. They unloaded their ship in five and a half days. They wouldn't let you scratch a match or touch it. They were proud of it."

*Now you go through St. Looey*
*And Joplin, Mis-sour-i*

"After chow," the handsome youth said, "the captain called the battery together. The girl we had raped had squawked and was going to come around to every battery and try to identify the men. Boy! everybody got worried because there had been eighteen men out the night before. You should of seen the eighteen of us scrambling around—shaving—changing clothes—trying to make ourselves look a little different. We sweated out a two-hour worry period." He laughed. "Then finally the captain came around and was so sore because two of his men had been killed that he said he wasn't going to let no goddamn German woman come around and try to identify any of his men." The handsome youth laughed. And drank his shot. One of his companions said, "That reminds me of the time—"

*You get your kiiiiiicks*
*On Route Sixty-Six!*
*It winds from Chicago . . . to L. A. . . .*

"Jeez!" a voice said. "Some 4F must like that damn song!"

Les was saying, "In five and a half days these Russian women unloaded their ship. Our crews, the best they could do was twelve or thirteen days. Because everybody was ducking away from work, you know. So I said to our commanding officer—ah—he's from Denver. I can't remember his name—I said, 'Wouldn't it be something if we could indoctrinate the idealism into our people to work like that?' "

Jim had seen Milo's face through the crowd in the tavern. He walked over to Milo. Slid down the bar next to him, grinned. "Hi!"

Les said, "I told him, 'You know—ah—like the Russians say—we want to get so much and give so little and they want to give as much and get as little—' " Les looked at the ceiling with his warm twinkling eyes and then around at the men who stood listening. "Well he said, 'If we educated our people to do that—we—' " Les slapped his chest with a hard, open hand, "meaning his type, the officer class—'would have to work for a living.' He said proud-like, 'I'd rather match my wits against these sons of bitches for a day's work any time.' Meaning his own men." Again Les laughed. But the laughter died. "See how they are?" he said.

*And Ok-la-ho-ma Ci-ty is might-y pre-tty . . .*

Les said, "The chiefs are separated from the enlisted men and the gold braid separated from the chiefs. They have three different classifications. Rigid. Yes. So tied to the past. And that's holier than winning, than beating the enemy—the hell with that." His voice was angry now. "Believe it or not, it's more important." He frowned along the line of listeners. "Capitalism must have some kind of understanding between all nations," he said.

Jim nudged Milo and nodded toward Les.

Les said, "You have to salute a Jap officer. If you're a prisoner, you know." He frowned again. "The class distinction runs all the way through. And it's the holiest of holiest. You can't violate that—other things aren't as important—if you fail to do this and that, something that might win against the enemy. The hell with that."

"Hey, Mac!" a half-drunk ex-sailor yelled out. "How do you like the civilian attitude?"

"You mean," bawled out an ex-soldier, "like why don't they send those veterans back where they came from?"

"Yeah—and the typical attitude—" his voice, ringing down along the bar, became scornful "—them coming back and taking their wives back from the men who were sleeping with them."

Along the bar, near the middle, an ex-GI was saying in a new-found wisdom, "They want to know if you've killed a man and how many. They're curious about it. They want to hear all about it. They're the easy kind to make. You tell them all about it."

His partner said knowingly, "Like some of them go for wrestlers and fighters." He laughed.

The first ex-GI laughed too. He said, "They think we're well-hung, I guess."

"Hey, Mac," the voice rang down along the length of the bar, "civilian life ain't what it's cracked up to be, huh?"

And several voices, roaring back, "HELL NO!"

In a booth two ex-servicemen were talking to a fellow who had missed it. The one called George was saying, "It was sure okay in Japan. For eighty yen I got my laundry washed, my back scratched and my ashes hauled." He waved a big palm at his buddy. "Jimmy was a paratrooper—" and impressing the poor fellow who had missed it all: "How many men did you kill with a knife, Jimmy?"

"Oh—a couple," Jimmy said casually, conversationally, as if speaking of the weather.

"How did you feel?" the young fellow who had missed it all asked.

"I felt nothing."

"Who was the first one you killed?"

"I killed a boy—the first one I killed."

The conversation went somewhere else to the war. Then later Jimmy turned to the young fellow who had missed the war and said, "You know, I think that's the first time anyone ever asked me that. . . . I don't know how I felt. . . . " Then, after a pause, "I didn't feel anything. It was all part of a job we had to do."

His buddy said, "You saw the roughest part of it."

He said, "As far as I'm concerned I saw the best part of it."

*You get your kiiiiiicks*

Max tapped Milo on the shoulder and grinned. "I want to tell you a dirty joke," and disparagingly, "oh, it ain't so dirty."

Milo grinned. "Go ahead."

Max said, "See, there was this guy and he got out of service and wanted to surprise his wife. He didn't tell her he was coming home." Max's wink was a humorous scowl. "So he comes home and walks in the house. His wife ain't there. He sees a baby-crib in the kitchen with a baby in it and he scratches his head. The poor sonofabitch has been in Europe for three years. So—" Max said, puffing out his lips in another scowl, "he walks into the front room and glances in the bedroom. It's a hot day and there on the bed is a guy stretched out naked and sound asleep." Max stretched his arms over his head, showing. "Well—" he said, gesturing, "the guy's wife comes home. He says to her, 'Honey—' " Max gestured again, stretching one arm and scratching his head with his other hand to show the fellow's perplexity. " 'In the kitchen there's a baby—in the bedroom—' " Max gestured toward the bedroom. "So his wife says 'Dear, when you went away we owed two thousand dollars on the house.'

" 'Yes.' " Max nodded agreement.

" 'Well, the house is paid for now.' " Max waved his finger in Milo's face. " 'When you went away you didn't have a car.'

" 'No.'

" 'We got a new car now.' He looked out the window and saw a brand new Cadillac. 'When you went away you didn't have any clothes.'

" 'Yes, that's right.'

" 'Look in the closet. You got a closet full of clothes now!' "

Max grinned. "So," he said, "the guy looks in the closet and sure enough it's full of clothes. And the guy looks at his wife and nods his head toward the bedroom and says, 'Honey, cover that sonofabitch up before he catches cold!' "

Milo roared and so did Dave, Don, Jim and the others listening.

*You get your kiiicks*
*On Route Sixty-Six!*
*It winds from Chicago to L. A.*
*More than two thousand miles all the way. . . .*

The music came out the open door of the tavern, and the talking, the cursing, the laughter. Until 2 A. M. Closing time. Then all over again the next night.

They who had endured so long, and whose hope, in the end, was so small, living their memories, griping, telling their dirty stories, looking for a little pleasure, a little comradeship, releasing their tensions, night after night in the bright new world.

# XIX

He had one last vow to make. He dedicated himself to it. The liberal was the man of good will. That was where he stood. Wherever the men of good will were he would be there too.

Only the weak quit. There were things to put on paper. With his pen maybe he could let in a little light. He would put his war experiences on paper, every moment of it until his crackup—and the hospital too. He would include that. It didn't frighten him now. It would be like a malignant growth he would cut from out of himself.

He would show it all. He would speak for the millions of soldiers. His little effort.

He would speak for peace.

To this, in vow, he dedicated his life.

He closeted himself in his little room. He wrote in a frenzy as if there wasn't time enough. Ten, twelve hours a day he sat at his desk pounding on his hockshop typewriter.

One evening when he was working someone knocked. Irritated by the interruption Aaron scraped his chair back and went to the door. Milo stood in the hallway.

"Hi," Milo said, smiling and coming across the doorsill, "you haven't been around so I thought I'd look you up."

Aaron grinned shyly. "I've been writing. Sit down!" He pulled a chair out. "I'll go get us some beer."

Milo walked over to the desk where alongside the typewriter was a neat stack of manuscript. "You really have been working! Care if I take a look?"

"If you—" Aaron gestured with his big hand shyly "—if you want to."

Milo picked up the manuscript and sat in the chair. Aaron stood trembling a little, looking out of his wistful eyes as Milo began to read. "I'll—I'll get us some beer," he said.

He ran down the steps and bought a couple of quarts of beer at the corner liquor store. Then, clutching their wet, cold necks, he walked around the block several times. I hope Milo likes it! I hope he likes it!

When he got back he glanced quickly at Milo. Milo was frowning down at a page of manuscript. He doesn't like it! Maybe, maybe it's just concentration. No, he doesn't like it. Aaron poured beer into two glasses. He handed one to Milo. Milo set it absently aside. Aaron sat across from him, scared.

Milo turned a page. He looked up at Aaron. His forehead was knotted and his mouth was pushed out in a scowl but his head nodded up and down. He picked up his glass of beer, drank, went back to reading. And now Aaron was breathing hard, happily.

An hour later Milo looked up and across the room at Aaron. "It's good, Aaron. It's damn good!"

Aaron piled the page on page. Every day he wrote, all day long. Over a hundred pages had come out of the typewriter. But even in this perfect world of creation, even in his writing, he couldn't shut himself off from events and people:

A headline said:

DEFENSE AGAINST
A-BOMB POSSIBLE

A newspaper item read:

> Casualties can be greatly
> reduced by carefully planned
> civilian defense measures.

There was talk of having everybody in America tattooed with the initial of his type blood.

People said:

Colonel McCormick was building an A-bomb shelter under the Tribune Tower.

People said:

Two Chicago socialites had gone to the Arizona desert and were digging a large atom-bomb shelter for themselves and their friends in the side of a mountain.

One rich man had withdrawn the bulk of his money in bills of large denominations and hidden them in the vaults of small banks in towns and villages near his farm.

A Highland Park man was building a basement shelter. He had made out a list of things to store away. Canned food and bottled water were high on the list. Stacks of fifty-dollar bills were to be hidden. Toothpaste, soap, razor blades, warm clothing, lots of cigars, books, playing cards, records and a phonograph, a radio and a few bottles of whisky were included in his storage plans.

People were saying this. And the newspapers began to suggest that any peace group or movement to outlaw the atom bomb was Communist and Russian inspired. It was un-American, undemocratic, inhumane to suggest that humanity should not be destroyed by atom bombs. It was un-American to say that humanity had no right to destroy itself.

Aaron sat staring at his sheets of manuscript.

There were more headlines to meet his eyes:

RUSSIA HAS A-BOMB
U. S. HAS STOCK PILE OF A-BOMBS

Aaron walked on the city street with the other people. This, the peace. This, the new world. This was what we fought for.

He looked up fearfully at the sky. He looked around at the people. They were going their accustomed ways. There was no fear in their faces. No concern.

He stared at them unbelievingly. A brief case and a fedora striding down the sidewalk here. Ladies waiting for a bus on Michigan Boulevard. A smiling mustache flirting with a girl. Boy peddling a bicycle. Lady out airing her cat. Waitress slamming down cups. Radiolike male voices of insurance salesmen, promoters, business executives talking loudly about deals. Woman pushing a baby carriage. An ego striding the sidewalk here. And now the shoppers, a whole bunch of women, housewives, rushing, pushing one another into dime stores, out of department stores, milling around the counters of canned goods, vegetables, meat, cut-price dog food, dresses, silk stockings, men's ties, men's shirts, cigarettes, soda fountains.

Aaron shook his head unbelievingly. They were worrying about the goddamnedest things! Their husbands might not get home in time for dinner. They might not be able to get a baby sitter for Saturday night.

An airplane droned across the Loop sky, high above its tall towers. Aaron looked up at the sky fearfully. The atom bomb had become giant landlord of all the world.

Aaron again looked at the casual or hurrying people going their uncaring ways. Didn't they know? Or didn't they care?

Hate had sown watermelon seeds. It walked across borders, back and forth. War was at the gates. War was always at the gates.

He looked out of his wistful dark eyes at the people. No one was alone in the black sleep. The whole world had at last been lumped together, to live or die. And Mars was the evening star.

Standing there as the unthinking, the uncaring, those who thought they were helpless to do anything, swarmed past him, he could imagine a real people concerned with mankind, or only with themselves and their children. It was almost as if a signal had been given. As if Pied Piper had blown his flute. As if Gabriel had called the dead to life. They came, as the locusts come. They swarmed as the ants swarm. They flew as the birds fly to warm sunlight and open day. Every ear heard the same sound. Every head lifted to the morning. Every foot moved in the same direction. Even the beggar, the lame, the one-legged. The housewife put down her dust cloth and put on her hat. The schoolboy tossed his football aside. The sweetheart turned her lips away from kissing. The mother baked no cakes that day. The worker didn't go to his job. Nor the doctor to the hospital. Nor the professor to classes. The scientist to his laboratory. Like a swarm they came, like a horde, but quietly, purposefully, they came. Like locusts, like ants, storming the city hall. And around the city hall and in all the streets until no traffic could move. And now all the city stands ringed around the city hall. All the faces look up. And voices speak:

The housewife says: No, never again. Not my husband.

The schoolboy says: No. Not my arms, my legs, my brains.

The sweetheart says: No, not my lover.

The mother speaks, saying: Not my son. I will hide him first. I will kill him first.

The doctor says: There are enough sick and maimed without making more.

The scientist speaks: Nor my brain for destructive uses.

The professor says: We will learn. We will learn. But not through fighting.

. . . and all over the world Aaron could see in all the cities the same scene before the city halls, hear the same words . . . and soon the church bells and factory whistles are sounding across the broad daylight sky. And man had come of age. Had come into his own.

He wanted to hold out his arms and stop them, tell them. He stood, weak, on the corner, staring at the people passing by. And he could see them only as weak. As stupid. As zeros floating to their soap bubble security. He shook his head sadly. These were the people whose forebears had made America, hewn it from the mountains, chopped it from the forests, bridged it across rivers, thrown railroad tracks from coast to coast. He watched the present-day American pass him by going complacently about his business, waiting—unconcerned—the dropping of atom bombs and the ending of humanity. He watched the zeros pass him by. The zeros seemed without muscles or vitality.

Aaron stood weak and shaken on the street corner. Then he turned and walked on down the street.

He walked into the mouth of the tunnel, the lower level of the city, at Grand Avenue. He walked under the city now, below the proud boulevard. It was better here. It was like an atom-bomb shelter.

Like a grave. Like a coffin. He was shut in by warehouses and the back ends of hotels. By receiving and shipping doors and loading platforms. By the parked cars of those who in the city above had gone to jobs, or shopping or to theaters. He walked in the long tunnel.

This was old Chicago down here. This was the old city. The enterprise of old Chicago. These the aged and ancient buildings that was Chicago before the city up there had been built on top of it. This was the hidden city.

Overhead the rumble of traffic along Michigan Boulevard, the tread of many feet, were like a headache. As if the bombardment of the city had already begun. And he grew afraid. He went up to the city. But the city was ugly. The people ugly and stupid. He shuddered and went back down into the hole. Better here. He sat on a loading platform in the hidden city. Again the rumble and roar, the steady rhythm of traffic overhead, frightened him. What if an atom bomb were dropped right now? The city up there would all come tumbling down. It would be rubble. It would be worse than the Chicago Fire. There would be nothing left alive in it and nothing erect. Only a scarred hole in the face of the earth. A mute crater. A death valley. A grand canyon. And the huge mushroom rising away from it to show its work.

Again the trembling vibration of traffic frightened him. He left the hidden city and went home.

But because of his fear he went back. He knew it was neurotic to be afraid of the noises of a city and he went back to get over his fear. He wandered the bowels of the city. He was drawn back again and again. It became an obsession with him. Night and day he wandered in the tunnel. Despair and loneliness were his again. Again he couldn't sleep. Again he had no appetite. And under the city he walked . . .

Aaron wanders . . .

He sees the huge yellow automatic city garbage trucks lined row after row with their ludicrous radiator adornments attached there by the drivers—a bunch of artificial flowers, a rag doll, a lady's hat, baby shoes, a dinner bell.

And Aaron begins to tremble with an unknown fear. Was the city still there?

Aaron went up into the night. The city was still there.

He looked up at the sky that would be the enemy. The eternal stars looked back at him. The silent stars. Without life, but with dignity. Aaron looked at the tall towers, the skyscrapers of the city. They clustered together there, many, many stories high. On each of the highest buildings on a long pole in warning to airplanes was a large red light, throbbing, throbbing. On, off. Throbbing, throbbing. The bleeding, dying heart of the city awaiting death. Forming a bleeding red net to catch the atom bomb.

He sits, huddled, on a loading platform, his big head back against the wall, his black hair falling over his forehead in a scythe, his knees drawn up, his feet on a crumpled newspaper caught there by the soles and heels of his shoes. . . . Gradually his head sinks forward and down. His feet are on headlines, half obscuring them, their meaning:

GI RAPED DEMS
KI GI VOTE

His eyes look down. His eyes see one word in a headline. He moves his feet and lifts the crumpled newspaper up toward his face. His eyes take in the word he had seen. Between his shaking hands the other two headlines his shoes had half hidden read:

GIRL SEVEN RAPED,
KILLED BY EX-GI

DEMS ACCUSED OF
VOTE STEALING

Aaron's eyes focus on the word of the headline he had seen:

KILLERS

He reads the entire headline:

HERSHEY TELLS
NATION'S NEED
FOR KILLERS

He reads the article:

> Cincinnati (UP)—The armed forces need "killers" and a lot of World War II veterans are too old for the job now, Selective Service Director Lewis B. Hershey declared Thursday.
>
> Hershey, director of the draft in World War II who is again marshalling the nation's civilians for war, said in an interview that war is legalized murder and indicated the U. S. is not too well prepared for it. "In the last war," he said, "we had 7,000,000 killers and another 7,000,000 to back them up. But the killers are old now, 32 or 33. Many of them are used up, burned out, in spite of brilliant war records."
>
> "There's a peacetime classification for a killer," he continued. "Men who fall into that category are anti-social. Except in wartime, homicide is an illegal profession."
>
> Hershey is here to address a Rotary Club luncheon.

Aaron crumpled the newspaper into his balled fists in a large, impotent protest. Then, still clutching the newspaper, he put his head down on his arms.

After a long while, he rose. He started for home.

He ran the last two blocks and up the steps. With frantic fingers he pulled open the box containing the pages he had written on his novel. He tore them, slowly, methodically, into two-inch squares, and opening the window, let them fall in a slow snowstorm to the hard sidewalk below.

He put his head down upon the window sill. He had nothing to say. Nothing. He was without anchor. Again without root. The people were ugly, stupid, foolish. Better to be dead in a world like this. Again he resigned from the human race.

The slow snow of manuscript pages settled upon the concrete sidewalk.

# XX

**K**rendesky stuck his head into Don's office.

"Coffee?"

Don shoved away from the desk. "Sure thing!"

They walked through the department. Krendesky squinted at the girls' legs or nodded and smiled out of his gaunt face at any girl who happened to look up as he passed. Outside the department Krendesky pressed Don's arm and said, "Ummmm! Some of those babes!" He had no words for it. He gave a vulgar jerk with his body. "Ummmm!"

Over the coffee Krendesky said, "Say, I'm going to an American Legion dance at my post tonight! Like to go along?"

Over his coffee cup Don smiled at Krendesky. It was a superior smile: American Legion. That lousy, reactionary outfit. But he said, "Sure, I'll go."

Krendesky was saying, "There's free beer. And a lot of choice little chicks up there." He clucked his tongue. "You can take your pick. I'm taking a babe with me, though." He smiled knowingly at Don. "You got someone to go or you want me to fix up a blind date for you?"

"I've got a girl to take," Don said.

After work, when he knew she would be home, he dialed the number.

"Hello," a woman's voice said.

"Can I speak to Rebecca Friedman?" He made his voice as official as he could, slightly melodious and older.

"Excuse me—?" There was a large question in the woman's voice.

"Can I speak to Rebecca Friedman?"

"To mine Rebecca you want to speak?"

Don smiled at the Jewish accent.

"Yes, if you please."

There was a long pause. He could almost see Mrs. Friedman frowning and peering suspiciously into the phone. Then, "Why do you want to speak with mine Rebecca?"

"Ah—well, I am her supervisor at Haines, and I have an important message to give her."

"Oh—" The voice was still suspicious. "I'll see if she is at home—" She hesitated. "And you are her boss, you say?"

"That's right, madam," Don spoke, repressing a smile.

He heard the receiver click down on a hard surface and heard Mrs. Friedman calling, "Rebecca! For you it is. Some man who says he is your boss. Now why, I ask, would your boss be calling you when you just left there?" There was a pause and then Rebecca's voice saying, very frightenedly, into the phone, "Hello."

"Hi, sweetheart! It's Don." He spoke as if he were giving her a great gift.

"Yes," she said and her voice was even more frightened.

"I know I shouldn't have called," he said, "but, honey, there's a dance tonight and I'd really like to take you."

"Yes, sir," her small, frightened voice said and he could almost see her fearful eyes going to her mother.

"Can you make it? Can you make some excuse to get out of the house?"

"I'll tr—yes, sir," softly.

"Don't worry, honey," Don said, "tell her my name is Hymie Goldstein." He chuckled. "And look, I'll meet you at the corner of Clark and Division at eight-thirty. Front of the drugstore."

"Yes, sir," softly.

He hung up and strode out of the booth chuckling. He'd take his Jewish girl to the American Legion dance. It would be ironic. Trouble was they wouldn't know she was Jewish. He'd tell them she was.

Rebecca was on the corner when he got there. They took a streetcar.

Krendesky and his date were waiting in the doorway below the Legion hall. Don glanced at the girl and was surprised that she was so homely, after all the bragging Krendesky had done about the women he went out with. She was one of that whole race of girls who, in their middle twenties, have found it difficult to get a date, wear too much makeup on their plain, sharp, irregularly featured faces, and have awkward, slightly fleshed bodies that are too long and bony. She squinted a little as if she had left her glasses at home. Krendesky had his arm about her waist, high on her waist with the fingers pointed up, searching, and she stood against him with one shoulder lifted as if trying to work her breast down into the searching palm of his hand. A friendly, almost gushy smile broke across her hard features as Krendesky shouted "Hi!" and winked at Don. It was a smile seeking warmth and kindness from a person. A smile that tried desperately to make up for other deficiencies.

"Miss Franklin, Mr. Lockwood."

She smiled and held out her hand. Her teeth were large, a little crooked and with space in between them.

Krendesky looked quickly and approvingly at Rebecca. And already his eyes were sliding down to her legs.

"Miss Franklin—" Don said, and Miss Franklin's face was already smiling, big-toothed, at Rebecca, "my girl, Miss—" and he said it slowly, proudly, "Rebecca Friedman."

The smile had begun to fall away from Miss Franklin's face. She nodded curtly and with a hand already outstretched shook Rebecca's hand briefly. "How do you do?" The greeting was chilly.

They climbed the long narrow flight of steps and went up into the Legion hall, Krendesky and his date walking behind by Krendesky's own maneuver so that he could look at Rebecca's legs and hips.

The American Legion hall was on the second floor up above a hardware store. The Legion hall was one huge room. There were card tables in one section of the room and two pool tables and across the far wall a long bar and toilets marked POINTERS and SETTERS.

Entering the hall they were the only people who looked as if they had come to dance. There were a few people at the bar, men sitting at the tables playing cards and drinking beer. Two fellows in army issue trousers moved around one of the pool tables, lazily poking the balls toward the pockets.

Krendesky led his party to one of the square tables and brought beer to them from the bar. They sat drinking, waiting for the music. Don leaned toward Krendesky and said in an undertone, "Don't get any ideas about my girl. I think I'll marry her." He chuckled.

Miss Franklin tried to be sparkling in her conversation. She limited all of it to the two men. There was a woman who waited bar along with the other bartender. Elsie was her name. Everybody wanted Elsie to sing because she had the kind of voice that would almost knock the ceiling off. Elsie was plump and about forty-five. She was about one-tenth good-looking and had a big smile, big teeth, big breasts and a big voice. Elsie came out from behind the bar, stood leaning against the piano with a cigarette held in her hand and sang a couple of half-dirty songs.

Don glanced at Rebecca. Color had come to her cheeks as Elsie sang and she dropped her eyes.

"Come on, honey," Don said, "let's see what we can do with the one-arm bandit."

"I never played," Rebecca said.

"I'll show you how, Becky," he said.

He pulled back her chair for her, and taking her arm, led her to the slot machines. Miss Franklin leaned over toward Krendesky. "Does he go with a *Jewish* girl?" she asked.

The three-piece orchestra began to play its sour notes from the little bandstand as if the place were full of people. The master of ceremonies cracked his corny, off-color jokes into the microphone.

Other people began to come up the stairs and into the Legion hall. Young men with girls for the dancing. Older people. The hall became quite crowded, noisy, almost hilarious. The floor was crowded now. The legionnaires swayed, in dance, with their girls and their wives, the young legionnaires and the bald-headed or gray-haired ones clutching their girls close. Around the bar they swayed from the free beer and drank more of the free beer and talked loudly, laughed.

Don danced with Rebecca. He danced with precision if not with grace on his false leg. He put his hand on the small of Rebecca's back and pulled her a little closer to him, hummed the music in her ear. Don danced with Miss Franklin. She looked over his shoulder, her weak glass-less eyes following Krendesky and Rebecca while her face flooded with a certain fear. "Thank you so very much," she said when the dance was over, her large red mouth circling, her big-toothed smile a wide oval, and her eyes searching for Krendesky.

After a bit Krendesky appeared. His big hands held four steins of beer and he was smiling down at Rebecca, as they moved to the table, while his mouth worked swiftly over a pleasantry. They sat down. Miss Franklin said tensely with a voice edging upon hysteria, "Please excuse me a minute." And the forced, begging smile. Wanting to be excused to use more makeup, or gain control of herself in her jealous, fearful feeling of inferiority.

"If you're going to—" Rebecca motioned naïvely, "to the—the bathroom—" and the word made her blush.

Miss Franklin shivered visibly. Then the wide, wide smile. "Why, of course!" But she didn't walk close to Rebecca.

Don looked around at the crowd. He turned to Krendesky. He said philosophically, but with judgment in his tones, "This place is full of people who wear a suit once a week. Can't you tell a guy who wears a suit once a week?" His mustache wrinkled scornfully. "That's what it's full of. Those kind of people." He smiled. "They've got a hat and they've got a suit and they've got a tie and they put it on one day a week." And though he was Krendesky's guest he went on,"The American Legion is a lousy organization. It's full of reactionaries. The kind of people who would like to see fascism in this country."

Krendesky's face showed anger and disagreement. But most of all it showed hurt. Then someone smacked him on the shoulder. "Hello, Kren!" a young fellow shouted.

Krendesky's face lifted in a quick, welcoming smile. "Hi Bill! Bill, this is Don Lockwood. Don, this is Bill Sawyer—one of the members." And to Sawyer, "Sit down, you bastard!"

Sawyer straddled a chair. "Say, is there anything here worth picking up?" was his first question, followed with a sly sidelong wink.

"I'm with someone," Krendesky said.

"Does she push?"

Krendesky shrugged. "First time I've been out with her. I think so. If—" and his face became sly behind the gauntness, "I wasn't with her we could go out wolfing for something. Don here's with a nice number."

"Oh yeah?" Sawyer asked, eying Don approvingly.

Don, man of the world, said laughingly, "Yeah, she's a Jewish girl, too."

Krendesky and Sawyer, swilling their beer, began chuckling over the other night when they had been out with a woman in Sawyer's car after he had taken his wife to her bridge club, and the woman they picked up had wanted to go to bed with both of them but in a hotel, not in a car. They didn't have the price for a hotel, they remembered, and wondered what it would have been like? Don listened and glanced at them in secret disgust, though he kept his face easy and man of the world. He hid his real feelings in the going-along-with-them laugh.

When Rebecca and Miss Franklin came back to the table they were still talking about it. Sawyer said, laughing good-fellow-in-the-know at Don, "Don't worry, after you get married you'd still go to bed with Betty Grable if you had the chance."

Don laughed his self-conscious and embarrassed laugh and stood up. "Want to dance, Becky?"

When they came back from the dance floor Sawyer was gone and Krendesky just returning from the bar with refilled glasses of beer. Don seated Rebecca. Then he gestured over his shoulder toward the toilet with his chin. "Gotta go."

Don moved toward the toilet and, as he approached the bar, saw at its far end the man who had complimented him on his speech in Bughouse Square; or rather he saw the hand with the large diamond ring lifting the cigarette, and with his eyes, followed the hand to the face and immediately recognized the distinguished features, the red-flushed, blue-veined face. Don stood at a distance looking at him: The hair turning a handsome steel-gray all at once but the eyebrows still black. The well-featured, straight-nosed face with the eyes moving intelligently as he talked to another man. The lips spreading out, the eyebrows wrinkling, the large head poised at an angle. And now the diamond ring made a little flash, cold and brilliant, as he again brought the cigarette to his lips.

Don wanted to step forward and say hello to him. He hesitated. He tried to remember the name he had fleetingly read on the card the man had given him but couldn't. He turned and pushed the toilet door open. Inside he hastily pulled out his billfold and searched through it, found the card, now discolored, that the man had given him. On it he read:

THOMAS McCARREN

*Ward Committeeman*

REGULAR DEMOCRATIC ORGANIZATION

There was a Gold Coast home address, a LaSalle Street office address and telephone number. Jesus! And he told me to call him up sometime! I didn't even notice who he was. Too hot after Rebecca at the time.

At the bar Thomas McCarren stood talking with another man, a man of medium height and broad shoulders who wore a wrinkled brown suit. The pants were baggy and his shoes hadn't been shined since the day before. "Tom!" the man said, laughing loudly and without repression. "You're a damn liar!" He laughed so heartily now, after his statement, that he put his hand up on the bar to help support himself.

"It's the truth, D.S.," Tom McCarren said, humor showing in the twist of his facial muscles and the cleverness of his eyes.

Still chuckling, D.S. looked up into Tom McCarren's face. He put both of his big hands, hands that were large-knuckled and husky and looked as if they must have callouses on the other side, up on the bar and went on laughing. There was a healthy vigor in his face, a face that was square, strong, with a large forceful mouth and strong jawline. And now the laughter slowed to a chuckling. "Never thought," he said, "when I was twenty-five that anybody would ever call me by my initials." He had chocolate-brown eyes with humor close to laughter lying in them always. Winking at McCarren, he jerked his head over one shoulder in a pointing gesture. "I've got my daughter over there." McCarren glanced in the direction D.S. had gestured and both of them caught a glimpse, through the crowd, of the girl. She had her father's chocolate-brown eyes and, smiling, darted a flirtatious glance at her father and McCarren while she deftly pulled herself away from the young man who was trying to whisper something in her ear. Pulling her head far away until it was tilted to the side while her lips still smiled at the young man, she lifted a gloved hand and waved in their direction. McCarren nodded. D.S. laughed loudly in a short but bellowing sound that reached her ears at the other end of the hall. Her lips smiled wider in answer.

D. S. turned back to McCarren and nodded at their beer glasses. They drank. D. S. leaned toward McCarren and said, slyly, "I don't know if those GI's were getting into her when she was in the Red Cross overseas or not. I'm—" he winked again, "taking her to all the joints tonight. I'm going to teach her life. I'm going to make either a bitch or a nice girl out of her." He laughed again. And he said it in such a way that you knew he couldn't believe any daughter of his could be a bitch; could be anything other than a virgin.

In the toilet Don stuffed his billfold back into his pocket. He adjusted the knot in his tie, lifted the tie clasp a little higher until it rode brazenly on the crest of his shirt. Finished, he looked at himself, tilted his head a little to the side, admired his cheekbones and his deep-set green eyes into which he could bring many expressions.

Mr. McCarren, he thought, strolling out of the toilet; Mr. McCarren, memorizing the name as he tried to nonchalantly stroll toward the bar until he would be standing next to him as if quite by accident and as if he had come for beer. Then the surprising look of recognition and—Mr. McCarren!

His training in the theater gave him the mechanical poise and he strolled toward the bar.

D. S. turned on the bar stool just as Don arrived for the curtain call. And he and D. S. were looking into each other's eyes. Don felt like a fool. He had muffed it. The man was a complete barricade between him and McCarren.

D. S. looked into Don's face in straightforward friendliness. And now his eyes were twinkling in humor, looking at Don's serious and embarrassed face. "Hello!" D. S. said loudly and in good nature. Don gulped. "Hello," he said. Twisting his head toward McCarren, D. S. said over his shoulder, "Gotta join my daughter. Gotta show her life." Crowding past Don he went off toward his daughter, laughing. It was a robust laugh. The music had no chance with it. It bounded over his shoulder and left McCarren smiling in friendliness even after he was halfway across the room and shouting to his daughter, "Well, my dear, want another drink in this dump or shall we move on?"

Don stepped self-consciously to the bar and McCarren, turning his eyes away from D. S., saw him. "Why—!" McCarren stood up and held his hand out at arm's length. "Hello, young man! It's good to see you! Sit down! Sit down! Have a drink!" Don took the outstretched hand. "Hello, Mr. McCarren." McCarren pumped his hand hard and didn't immediately let go and with his other hand slapped him on the shoulder. "How've you been? Why haven't I seen you?" McCarren asked and without awaiting an answer, "Hey—bartender! Bring the young man here a drink!"

"Say, Tom," a slow, lazy voice said from the stool on McCarren's other side, "who was that fellow you were just talking to?" The face came around on the neck to look questioningly at McCarren. His eyes had the curiosity of a ward heeler.

McCarren let go of Don's hand and turned on the stool. "D. S.? Why D. S. is one of the richest men in Chicago. That was Daniel S. Matthews."

Don craned his neck trying to see through the crowd of dancers this multimillionaire who had said hello to him. The dancers were shoulder to shoulder and there was a lot of cigarette smoke and he had completely disappeared in the crowd. Don felt disappointment. Then vanity. He had never been that close to a millionaire before! And he spoke to me!

"No!" the politician said and whistled, long-drawn.

"Yes, sir!" McCarren said. "He got there in the good old American way. Worked himself up from the bottom. Didn't get no more education than I did. Just grade school. We went to grade school together, matter of fact. Only he didn't go all the way through—old pal of mine." McCarren swung back on his stool to Don. "Well," he said, "tell me what you've been doing. Where you're working." McCarren's eyes were heavy-lidded, almost sleepy-looking, but they were too carefully observing to be sleepy eyes. They were paunched a little, with thin, many-crossed red veins showing.

"I'm a supervisor at the Haines Company," Don said.

"Ummmm!" McCarren grunted as if impressed. "Good company!" he said in approval. There might have been the beginning of a second chin but his jaw line was strong and he tilted his head, looking with his observing eyes at Don. He smiled and put a hand on Don's shoulder. "Enjoyed your speech in Bughouse Square. We need more young men like you with your kind of ideas. Young vets with—" He balled his hand and punched his fist triflingly into Don's arm.

Don smiled, warmed by the praise. "Bartender!" McCarren called. "Bring us two more on the double." His command was casual, as if he were used to giving orders.

At the bar Don looked at Mr. McCarren's suit admiringly. Tailormade. Expensive tie and— "By the way," McCarren said, though he had never heard it, "your name has slipped my memory."

"Don Lockwood."

"Oh yes! Of course! That was some speech!" He shook his head and smiled. The fresh beer came. "Tell me," he said, "how everything is going—I mean—" He nodded at Don's crippled leg and frowned his sorrow. "Are they doing the right thing by you? If not—" He paused cleverly so that Don would have to speak and he wouldn't have to make any definite commitment.

"Oh yes," Don said, nodding.

McCarren slapped him on the shoulder. "I want to have a long talk with you soon. Say, are you with your girl?"

"Yes," Don said, flushing a little.

"Why don't you bring her over for a drink?"

"Well—ah—" He became slightly panicky. "We—we have to go soon." He didn't want to have to bring Krendesky and his girl over and introduce them, he told himself.

"Too bad," McCarren said. His eyebrows frowned his disappointment while his observing eyes studied Don carefully and seemed to be thinking of something he hadn't mentioned. But now he smiled again, that wide, winning smile. "Could you come to see me—say—the first of the month?" He handed Don another of his cards. "There's something I'd like to talk over with you." He nodded his head secretly. "It might mean a lot to you—" The easy gesture and the ring taking momentary fire. "After we talk it over—" He stood up to shake hands good-by. "Remember to come in. Please do. My—" again the ring flashed, "business office. I'll keep one o'clock open for you." And McCarren smiled again, comradely and in a signal of dismissal. "Don't fail me now—" in very gracious tones.

"No, sir, I won't," Don said. "I'll be there before one."

Don moved through the crowd. Gosh, he's a swell guy! He knows millionaires too. Guess he's rich too. I'm—he was smiling down at Rebecca—moving in the right circles now! "Hi!" he said to Rebecca. "Want to leave?"

Don looked at Krendesky. Krendesky shook his head no and winked at Don covertly as he put his arm around Miss Franklin's chair and his cheek close to hers.

Through the crowd toward their table came Mr. McCarren with D. S. Matthews and his daughter. McCarren walked in the middle and had his arms looped in theirs. "Brought some people over to meet you, Don," he said when they reached his table. Don stood up smiling. D. S., smiling, winked in friendliness at Don as he had done at the bar. Rebecca, Miss Franklin and Krendesky stood up too.

"Daniel S. Matthews—" McCarren said, easily, casually.

"Oh!" Miss Franklin said in a loud gasp. D. S. laughed his booming laugh.

"—Donald Lockwood."

"Howdy, Lockwood." D. S. held out his big strong hand and shook Don's hand warmly.

"And," McCarren said, "Miss Irene Matthews."

Irene Matthews looked at Don. She blinked her eyes quickly and some clouded memory stuck its foot halfway inside the door.

Don nodded and said, in stage voice, "How do you do." He introduced all of them to his friends. "Miss Rebecca Friedman," he said distinctly. D. S. shook hands with everybody. Miss Franklin, when he took her hand, looked as if she were about to faint. He had supplied her with the one big topic of the rest of her life.

Don glanced back at Irene Matthews. She was still looking at him. Her oiled red lips were slightly parted and her eyes glanced at him secretly. She seemed to be looking him up and down. Don looked at her:

She was a rich man's daughter and probably thought she was the greatest. He slipped an arm around Rebecca's waist. He was glad and proud to be standing looking across at her with an arm around a Jewish girl. He smiled at Irene Matthews almost defiantly. She smiled back, coldly, with her chocolate-brown eyes. Mr. McCarren said something and Don answered him. Then he glanced back at Irene Matthews. She was still looking at him. Her eyes were receptive, eager. Her lips slightly parted. He looked at her with amused, deriding and then bored eyes, taking them the whole gamut he had learned from his days in the theater. Irene Matthews smiled. "Let's go, D. S.!" she said. Her chocolate-brown eyes danced back, half-flirtatiously, to Don. But when they met his they became cool and she looked him up and down, coldly, dismissingly. She took her father's arm. "Good-by," she said and she didn't look at him again.

"See you on the first," McCarren called over his shoulder to Don.

"You bet!" Don yelled back and waved.

"How'd you meet them?" Miss Franklin asked incredulously.

"Oh," Don said, casually, "Mr. McCarren is an old friend of mine."

"Who was the other man?" Rebecca asked.

"Who was he!" Miss Franklin almost screeched it.

"Oh," Don said, gesturing open-palmed, "one of Chicago's millionaires."

Outside the Legion hall Don slipped his arm around Rebecca's waist and squeezed her up close to him. "Come on over to my place."

She shook her head and edged away.

"We'll have a good time," he promised her.

"Not tonight, Don. Please." She blushed. Worked the toe of her shoe against the sidewalk. Leaned against him for a moment, helpless, caught in the spider web of her emotions.

"Come on, honey," he pleaded. "It's been such a long time."

Again she shook her head. "Why do we always have to do that?" She blushed. "Why can't we just be together? I—I—next time."

Then he understood. And he didn't want to be too demanding. It would take a long time yet until she would want to be with him as often as he wanted to be with her.

He knocked loudly. "Come in," Sue said immediately.

He opened the door and saw Sue sitting in the large armchair under the floor lamp with her legs drawn up under her. A book of plays was open on the floor at her feet and she was reading from another book of plays. "Oh, hello, Don. You don't get over this way often." She tried to say it casually.

He walked over to her and, stooping, kissed her on the cheek dutifully.

"Thanks," she said ironically as he withdrew his cool lips.

He pulled his tie loose and began to unbutton his shirt.

"Just like that, eh?" Sue said and put her feet down on the floor. He could see that she was angry.

"Aw now, honey," he said.

But there was no relenting in her eyes. He laughed a little. "Me take it the lady doth protest too much."

"The quote isn't correct," she said; and she had already put her fingers up to his shirt and was buttoning it. Her eyes stood steady, looking into his. "You're in love with someone." It wasn't a question. It was a statement.

"No, I'm not." He laughed his nervous laugh and glanced over the edge of her plump shoulder.

"Look at me, Don." She put her hands to the sides of his face and, as with a child, forced his eyes back to hers, probed his face with her eyes. He grinned weakly. "No, I'm not."

She looked into him, dropped her hands from his cheeks and nodded. Turned. Walked across the room. Lit a cigarette. Returned and sat down next to him with her hand on his knee. "It's all right." She laughed. It was a throaty laugh and not very sincere.

"Let me stay here tonight," he said.

Smiling, she shook her head no. And got up and walked to the dresser. She snuffed the cigarette out in the ash tray there. With her powder puff she patted away the droop of her lips and again smiled at him. "I've got to get used to the idea first," she said. She put on her coat. "Take me out somewhere," she said. Her smile tightened on her face, taking some of the plumpness. Maybe if he got her a little bit tight, he thought.

They made the rounds. Sue drank more than he had ever seen her drink before. She got to that point of drunkenness where he wanted her to be but she seemed to know what she was doing and kept a reserve between them.

She didn't talk much but, instead, seemed to be deeply thinking.

When he caught her eyes, as he frequently tried to, she smiled at him, slowly, but smiled.

All the taverns were closing. "Let's go to your place," Don said. Sue shook her head no. "We could take a bottle up there." Sue shook her head no. In angry amusement Don thought, they're all turning me down tonight. Even Sue.

"I'm hungry," he said. Sue gathered up her coat. They went to a barbecue pit on North Clark. Don ordered a steak. Sue drank coffee but ate nothing.

"You're awfully quiet," Don said.

Sue forced a smile. "Thinking."

They were silent again, Don cutting into the steak and chewing it hungrily.

"How's the steak?"

Don wrinkled his forehead approvingly. "Great!"

She looked at him and felt like crying.

Behind them someone had put a nickel into the juke box and the words of the song came to Sue's ears:

*. . . Some day you'll want me to want you*
*When I am strong for somebody new*
*And though you don't want me now*
*I'll get along somehow*
*And then I won't want you.*

The muscles in her face twitched. She could feel Don studying her face and kept her eyes averted, afraid she would betray herself, afraid the tears would show. "Yes, you're awfully quiet," she heard him say and was sure he was smiling at her in amusement. She looked down into her coffee cup. She lifted the teaspoon and, frowning the tears away, frowning in concentration, tried to get the teaspoon under the small bit of cigarette tobacco floating in the cup.

*You expect me to be true*
*And keep on loving you*
*Though I am feeling blue*

She listened to the sentimental words. They gave expression to what she felt. She wanted Don to be aware of the words.

Stretching her arm across the table she said, to call his attention to the words, "That's one of my favorite songs."

"Yes. That's nice," Don said absently. He didn't hear the words or get the implication.

Her eyes were misted but a half-smile came to her face: there's a song for everything.

On the sidewalk she said, smiling grimly, "Well, I go south."
"Let me go with you."
"No."
"Then come up to my place."
"No," she said. She meant it. She smiled again. "When I can get used to taking leftovers," she said. Don shrugged in anger. "Okay!" He walked away angrily.

Sue stood in front of the mirror at home. There were tears in her eyes. "All right, Sue," she said, "get control of yourself. Come on! Come on, you old bitch, you." She said it jokingly and tried to smile at herself. She looked into the mirror. Inside the mirror was another mirror. It was dusty. She peered into it. . . . The girl was slim, petite. She was pretty. She was young. Seventeen, and she had left home for New York. Her parents, intellectuals, artistic, had approved: "We always wanted a child who would run away from home," smiling, anxious, wanting her to go beyond their place in life.

She was stage-struck. New York! The Bohemians! The actors! The wonderful life of New York! . . .

There was another dusty mirror behind that one too. . . . Half a year later she got her chance. She was doing bit parts in plays . . . she had talent. And got the breaks. A year later she got the ingenue lead in a Broadway play. He had the lead male role. An elderly man. Tall, distinguished-looking. She was youthful, enthusiastic, a virgin, full of life and the wonder of it. Her aunt warned her against him. It did no good and they were married quickly, on a week end. Their sex relations . . . another mirror presented its past surface . . . he would jump on and off. It got so he'd tap her on the shoulder: "Okay, come on." She was afraid to display emotion or aggressiveness and was only receptive; aroused, but not satiated. It became a drudgery. . . .

Another mirror sliding before her eyes, showing its face of the past. . . . He was *the* actor. He was the hail-fellow-well-met. The party man. He liked drinking with the boys. Drinking all night, leaving his wife at home. He wanted center stage. He didn't want her to act. When he got mad at her he didn't speak to her for days. He'd go to his room and slam the door—that was to indicate that he was mad. . . .

The mirrors moved swiftly before her eyes. . . . He hadn't lasted long on Broadway, though he was a good actor. A broken-down, drunken, out-of-work actor is a sad sight. She stuck with him. The only man she had ever known sexually. She felt protective. He had talent. She stuck with him.

They were broke. She got a job. She stuck to him, not knowing why, even hating him for his weaknesses, for his talent he was throwing down the drain. Stuck with him maybe out of a doglike loyalty. . . . Her shoulders shrugged at herself in the mirror . . . and the mirrors changed, the mirrors moved forward, more polished, clearer now. . . . The years can move swiftly. Instead of being petite she began to become a little plump, a little stout . . . he stayed less and less at home, drank more and more, seemed not to want her even for economic security . . . but New York. You can't live in New York and brush shoulders with intellectuals, Bohemians, the theater, art circles, radical movements, thought, thought on that plane, hunger, being on relief without taking much of it home with you . . . he drank more and more . . . she had her friends . . . he drank more and more . . . she left him at last, divorced him . . . Chicago . . . meeting Don, a young kid working as a messenger at the Haines Company . . . seeking, finally, the thrill of sex for the first time in her life and with a boy—just a boy . . . the roles had reversed themselves. She had been the young girl with the older man and now she was the older woman with the young man. She had worn herself out, her youth, her attractiveness, on her husband, an older man. Now, this younger man. What would become of her? What would happen to her?

Sue looked back into the top mirror at the woman. The woman, plump, no longer attractive.

"Old bitch!" she said again. The smile slowly became a little fuller but tears still ran down her cheeks. She moved her powder puff over her cheeks, over the tears.

# XXI

Jim lay under the car. The ancient Chevie had been backed out of the little frame garage and stood in the middle of the back yard in noon sunlight. Only Jim's legs protruded from under the car. Near the running board Feezer had crouched down on his front legs with his back legs held stiffly erect and his tail slowly wagging at the top of the long, lean upward slope his body made. He peered curiously under the car, sniffed, sniffed again, barked playfully. He bounded to another spot on the lawn and again sniffed, backed up slowly, tensely, wagged his tail and waited for a responding playfulness.

Louise came out on the little porch overlooking the yard. "Jim!" she called. "Oh Jim! Come on and wash up. We've got a good lunch."

After lunch, groaning pleasurably and patting his stomach with a hard hand, Jim sat on the sofa in the front room with his legs sprawled out lazily in front of him and his arms dropped loosely on the cushions at either side of him. Junior crawled over one long, fallen-tree of a leg and, standing between his father's legs, looked up at him. "Did you eat enough, Papa?"

Jim put his big palms on his son's cheeks, leveled his face and tilted it upward toward his own. Holding the boy's face steady he looked down at his son. "Look at those eyes," he said proudly to Louise. "I'll bet the girls are going to go for him."

Junior had squirmed away, and climbing past his father's big foot and knee went to the corner where his toys were piled. Picking up the boxing gloves he brought them to Jim and held them out. Jim laced them in place and then strapped on his own and pulled the strings tight with his teeth while Junior was already hitting him. "No! No!" Jim protested, hiding his chin in the hollow of his neck, "That isn't fair!" Feezer opened one eye and then the other from his curled position under a chair.

Jim shoved the cocktail table over into a corner and knelt down in the center of the floor. Laughing and squinting his eyes closed, Junior rushed at his father and set the gloves to pounding on Jim's arm in a hand over hand swimming stroke. "No, like this," Jim instructed, taking the small arm and pushing it straight forward into his face in a short jab. Louise turned the pages of the newspaper.

And now Jim and the boy were boxing again. Junior was laughing and flailing away with his short little arms puffed at their ends with the large boxing gloves. Feezer, under the chair, opened one eye and then closed it ignoringly. Sometimes Jim let Junior hit him all over the face, in the stomach. Occasionally he tapped Junior on top of the head with a soft glove or whacked him resoundingly across the behind. They both laughed and giggled and puffed. And now they were both out of breath.

"He just ate, Jim," Louise protested mildly.

But the boxing went on.

"He's winded, Jim. You'll upset him," Louise said without sternness but in wisdom.

"Like this," Jim said, leaving his stomach open and pushing it out while he nodded toward it. Junior brought the fist in. Jim scowled in pretended agony and fell over sideways to the floor. Junior squealed with laughter and danced around him, hitting him with both gloves.

"One—two—three—" Jim counted and then crawled erect. Junior came in, throwing punches. Jim covered up and backed away on his knees.

"Jim, he's all excited. He's got to take his nap," Louise said. "If you upset him you'll have to put him to sleep." Louise had brought some paper and crayons to the sofa. "Let's play something quiet. Let's draw some pictures before it's time for a nap," she told Junior, gently tousling his hair.

Jim went down to work on the car again. A girl was passing along outside the fence. He glanced at her.

Jim squinted his eyes against the dirty brown oil that dripped down from the clutch and across his cheek. He'd like to take Louise to the show tonight. He tightened the wrench against the rust-gripped nut and strained for leverage. Maybe if Mrs. Bush would watch the kids. He stuck his head and shoulders out from under the car. "Hey! Skinny!" he called. Then he lay back weakly against the grass and closed his eyes. He began to tremble. He saw the whole thing again. The thing he had been trying to hide from himself. Had hidden all these months. He bit his lip in shame, and sweat stood out on his forehead. His shoulders shook with a quick and violent shudder and the bitter birds of memory flew back home to him:

. . . he was alone and lonely. He had fought it when it first crawled to the edge of consciousness. He had fought it harder when it had reoccurred unclothed and unashamed and looked him square in the face and smiled wantonly at him. He had fought and won.

Then in Paris, alone and lonely. Walking in Montmartre. The dimly lighted street. The dimly lit string of bars and music coming out. It had smiled at him again and taken human form and looked him in the face from out of the eyes of a shabbily dressed girl who came out of the shadows of a building and stood in the half-light of the circle of a lamp, looking up at him out of a gaunt and hungry face with large sad eyes. The others on the street, and there were many, had been smiling, painted, behind-twisting whores flirting and bargaining for their stint on hotel beds. She was not like the rest, though as gaudily painted. She was very still and looked up at him with grave eyes from a bowed head. Her mouth had twitched. She opened her mouth to speak, closed her lips, looked down at the sidewalk and then up into his eyes, staring and afraid. She seemed about nineteen.

"You go with me?"

He looked at her and did not move away though he knew that he should. Again she said the words and her voice was pleading. He looked at her and felt tenderness and longing and an undefined tingling across his skin—pleasurable and alarming and of guilt. And her voice, struck with beggary, cut a knot of pity in his throat. He swallowed and stuffed his hand into his pocket. The prostitute with her luridly painted face and beggar's eyes made signs of an empty stomach and signs of eating. His hands touched money in his pocket. His fingers drew away from the touch and came out of his pocket and took her arm.

And he walked along with her as if in a dream and not understanding himself or his actions.

He saw Louise's face but it did not stop him. He seemed to walk, as a ghost, through her face.

And felt only a warmth and desire for this prostitute.

She walked with her head down and hurried him along through a dark space between buildings as if she were afraid of being caught.

In his pocket he found a candy bar. He handed it to her. She tore off the paper and ate the candy bar greedily, licking her fingers of the last chocolate sweetness.

The hotel room was small, like all rooms all over the world used for the purpose. There was a stern, bare look to the room, as if it held but one repeated secret and yet told the secret in its furnishings, its scent, its half darkness. There was a pipestem bed, the blankets mussed, the sheet not very clean, the pillow tousled as if from the heads of the hundreds of restless men who had come here and rubbed it to its weary ball and gone to seek other rooms and other girls like this through a long procession of lifetimes in search for the unfound security, identity, craving: for the road away from frustration.

There was linoleum on the floor worn patternless from many feet and a bare and dirty electric bulb that hung over the bed on a long cord. In a corner was a small washstand with a *bidet* under it.

The prostitute came with a towel. "Wash," she said. It was a command and she thrust the towel into his hand.

There was no soap. Jim washed with the cold water that for a moment took away desire. But now that he was here desire again rose.

The prostitute was undressing. She undressed mechanically.

Jim undressed quickly and approached her. She was sexily made. He approached her. He found himself hungry for her mouth.

He swayed a little in his emotion there in the center of the floor with his arms clenched tightly about her. He drew her quickly to the bed.

Over the edge of her shoulder the floor slanted downward and the bed rode the red-brown linoleum at an angle. And exhausted he lay back on the pillow on which many heads had come to rest themselves at this period of the act.

The prostitute had stirred and sat up with her breasts leaning over him. He lay on his back staring up into her face. He lifted his hand to her breast. She asked him if there was an additional favor he wanted her to do. He shook his head no and drew her to him. She kissed him fiercely. And not yet relieved, or for a higher pay, she nestled her body tight against his and made womanly movements.

And then it was over. And Jim felt guilt. He didn't get much out of it, he told himself. He should have waited for Louise. He didn't get anything out of it, he told himself. He owed this prostitute something.

He dressed hurriedly and moved back to the bed, reaching in his pocket for money. She had not stirred. Her face was turned away from him. He touched her on the arm and, leaning closer, saw that she was crying. Silently crying with the tears salting the crushed, dirty pillow.

In high school he had taken a little French. He searched for the words.

"What is it that bothers you?"

She shook her head.

Jim sat on the side of the bed. He touched her again and searched for words: "Don't cry!"

She smiled now. But it was a tight smile.

In sudden sympathy Jim lay next to her on the bed and put his arm around her gently, held her protectively.

"Don't cry."

In French she said, "I am not crying."

He patted her shoulder consolingly.

In French he said, thinking about the war outside, "Have you brothers?"

She shook her head no. And shaking it no said, "Two. In Germany. Dead."

"A father?"

She shook her head no.

"A mother?"

She nodded yes.

"Why don't you live with her?"

She laughed. "I do."

She laughed again. "We work together."

Again she laughed. "First the Germans. Then the Americans, the English." And her hand moved piteously across the dirty bedsheet as if to soothe away some secret pain. "You have to eat," she said. Her face was stony now and she sat up. She looked at him as if to dismiss him.

He touched her hand and shook his head no, trying, in this gesture for which he had no words in either French or English, to tell her not to be bitter, to forgive us, we men, German and English and American. And then he looked closely at her. Her face was smeared free of its paint. Her skin was very smooth and it was a young face. She wasn't pretty but only young.

"How old are you?" he asked in surprise and almost in fear of her answer.

"Fourteen," she said.

His whole body stiffened on the bed and he closed his eyes. My God! His body came limp with his shame. He sat up and walked across the room and looked out the window, down onto the street. He couldn't look at her. The girl sat on the side of the bed.

"How many times?" he asked her from the window, staring out.

She shrugged her shoulders. "Many," she said.

The girl dressed. He walked over to her and avoided looking into her face. From his billfold he took two ten-dollar bills and kept only three dollars for himself. He stuffed the bills into her hand. "Here." She looked up into his face in disbelief, her mouth held open and her grave, childish eyes seeking his. She shook her head no. "Too much—too much!" she said. He looked at her for a moment and felt his face grow warm as he blushed. He closed her hands roughly on the bills. He felt his fingers tremble on her hands. He remembered another young face. Other trembling young hands. "Keep it," he told her gruffly. He searched his pockets, found three full packs of cigarettes. He dropped two of them on the bed. "You can get a good price for them on the black market," he said in English. He stood an awkward moment. Then he reached down, and flushing, squeezed her hand. "Take it easy."

He walked out of the room and along the boulevard. Prostitutes walked with American soldiers. Prostitutes smiled at him and plucked at his sleeve. Prostitutes whispered invitations: *"Faire zig-zag avec moi?"*

Jim went into a bar and drank whisky for an hour. He came out again and walked down Paris' night streets smoking cigarette after cigarette. And he knew he had enjoyed it. And there were flashes of sexual activity as a kid. The first time. And Flora. He was fifteen and she was fourteen. Those few times with her had been the completest fulfillment he had ever had. Never since then that feeling—no, not even with Louise. God! the one thing he had been trying to forget all of his life.

The shame and the guilt and the disgust came—of this time and that long time ago. But the need for a woman too. And after that the drinking and the whoring around. Perhaps to forget about that fourteen-year-old kid . . . the drinking and the whoring. . . . Always wanting to be drunk or half drunk . . . looking for women too.

He was alone and lonely. He was alive and afraid and unhappy and none of it meant anything. Anything at all. This was only their lives over here. In the hidden night of war they could do as they pleased. Without censor. Without guilt. No secret feelings of guilt or shame would come creeping back home to them, stealthily, across battlefields and from out of conquered and freed towns, cities, countries. This was their lives over here. It had nothing to do with home. Or with them. They would go back to their wives and sweethearts and leave this part of their lives here. It had nothing to do with what they were at home and would be again at home.

# XXII

Jim combed his hair in front of the dresser in the bedroom. To one of the curved mahogany uprights that held the oval mirror in place was fastened the little pipe-cleaner dancing Hawaiian doll frozen in its seductive position. Dust had collected. Its whiteness was now a grayness. Jim glanced at it a moment and gave his hair a final pat.

Louise was bathing Junior for bed. Jim gave her a peck on the cheek on his way out and started down to union headquarters.

When he got to the high twin towers of the Haines Company he decided that he needed a beer before starting to nail posters to their standards. He went into Bernie's Tavern-Restaurant across from the mail order house.

"There's our boy!" Bernie bawled loudly when he saw Jim, and a couple of the men turned on their stools. "Hi, Jim!" they shouted. There was admiration and respect in the way they said it and Bernie, without being told, was bringing Jim's beer down along the bar.

"Well, how they hangin'?" Bernie asked in his everyday humor.

Jim nodded. "Straight down," he replied in the kind of answer Bernie wanted.

Jim drained his glass and walked over to the 26-table to try his luck.

Fran was on her stool behind the green felt and seeing him coming, averted her eyes a little. Jim walked up. "Hello, honey!" he said quickly, grasping her chin between his thumb and forefinger. He liked her. She was a thin, sensitive-looking girl from a small southern Illinois town, two years of college, and generally had a serious novel propped up on the green felt while she waited for customers. Jim grinned. Different from any other 26-girl he had ever run into. She was the only 26-girl in Chicago who tried to convert customers to communism. It wasn't: "How about going home with me, baby?" It was: "Have you ever read Engels' book on dialectical materialism?"

Fran snatched her chin away. "Cut it out," she said gruffly. Her eyes reached up into his face. "What number do you want?"

"Sixes," Jim said.

Jim had no luck. "See ya," he told Fran. He left and walked down the street to union headquarters and went in.

"Hi, Jim!" Kovac called.

"Hi, Kovac." Jim nodded; he frowned and moved further into the office as the nasty thought ran across his mind: Kovac visiting his wife often while he was overseas. No, Louise wouldn't do that. So many stories when you're over there. He moved over to Kovac. "Cigarette, Stan?" he asked, offering his pack.

Edna was in the basement. Jim put an arm around her shoulders affectionately for a moment and, looking down at her graying hair, asked about her kids.

In the back O'Keefe sat at a long table with eight or ten others folding and piling mimeographed handbills. He sat next to Jennie, a healthy-looking pink-cheeked woman wearing a house dress. Her arms were plump, her bosom full, her skin smooth and milky with freckles peppered across her cheeks and down her arms. Jennie was popular. She laughed often and in a warm, womanly way.

Jim nailed and lettered signs in a far part of the room and occasionally glanced toward the long table at O'Keefe and Jennie.

They worked several hours. Then Jennie and two other women made coffee, set it out for them in paper cups. Someone brought Jim a cup. He saw the plump, freckled arm and the short, flowered sleeve. He looked up. "Thanks."

He worked for a while longer and, remembering that Louise had a headache, decided to leave.

One beer first.

He entered the tavern and waved at Fran. She looked up over the cover of her book and smiled at him. He went to the bar and Bernie was already there with the beer.

"Which side did you dress on today?" Bernie asked from his stock of sex jokes.

"Left side," Jim said.

"I right-dressed," Bernie said and went off into a guffaw.

Jim drank and went out into the night. His mind felt curiously alerted and stimulated. He would walk.

It was dark along Sedgewick and it was now late at night. Ahead of him as he turned the corner off Division onto Sedgewick a woman walked. On one side of her stretched the vacant lot. On the other the empty car tracks and the high dark wall of the school building. When the woman heard his footsteps she looked over her shoulder in fright. Jim walked twenty feet behind her. She looked back again and hastened her footsteps. Jim walked faster too. Looking back again she slowed down, not sure now whether he was following her or not, hoping he would continue to walk fast and pass her. Jim slowed down too. The woman, completely alarmed, walked faster and Jim matched her stride. She crossed the street. Jim crossed the street. She walked, almost running. Jim's long legs fanned out wider. The panic-stricken woman finally got to her house and broke into a run along the little sidewalk and up the flight of steps. The door opened and banged. Jim hurried home.

At home Louise was sitting up in bed reading a magazine.

"I forgot something at the union hall," he told her. "I'll be right back."

He got into his car and drove back to the union hall. He hadn't forgotten anything. Inside he looked around and was disappointed. He went back out onto the street shouting to his fellow workers, "See you in the morning! Yeah, I'll be down early."

Outside, looking up at the tall twin towers of the Haines Company he suddenly realized that he had come all the way back to look at Jennie. And hadn't known it. And was disappointed because she wasn't there.

# XXIII

Aaron got up off his bed of pain in the cheap little Near North Side room. He fastened his sweaty palms to the top of the dresser to keep from falling. . . . I better go take a walk . . . let the night embrace me . . . there is only one way out . . . let the night embrace you . . . one way out. . . .

He wandered around the city, letting any corner take him down its way.

Into the sleeping arms of the city he walked. Along the sour streets of North Clark, West Madison, South State. To the river he found his way—

Sat on the bridge, looking down with his feet hanging over the water. All about him the great uprights of the city stood like spectators watching a scene and far at his back in the western sky the twin towers of the Haines Company yawned forty-eight stories high.

He looked down into the water. The water moved endlessly. He kicked his feet against the bridge. It would be easy here. He pushed his behind a little further out on its small perch, and a little further. Looked down into the black and wrinkled, ageless water. "Float scum—" he said, "float scum—" Kicking his heels, half-chanting it, "Float scum—float scum."

No, not here.

He waited until he knew his father would be on the picket line. Then he went to his father's house, got the key from under the scrub pail on the back porch, let himself in. At the kitchen table he wrote the note and set it up against the sugar bowl.

As he emerged from the house Rebecca came across the sidewalk toward him. "Aaron!" she called. He looked at her. He smiled at her and said, "Hello, Rebecca!"

He put his arms around her. He kissed her, and for the first time passionately.

"Can I—can I walk along with you?" Rebecca asked.

"No." He smiled at her. "I have somewhere to go."

He rented a room at a downtown hotel. It wasn't high enough. He left and rented another room. It was on the fifteenth floor.

He took the elevator. Got off. Went toward the room. He smiled wisely, indifferently.

And now the bellhop was gone. He was alone in the room.

He locked the door and moved quickly to the window, looking out and down, thinking, man owes God but one death. He who dies this year is quit for next. All Chicago spread below him.

He opened the window quickly. It was a French window and, parted in the middle, rose almost to the ceiling.

There was a wind. The curtains blew back into the room and the white clouds moved swiftly across the sky. Aaron climbed up on the window sill. The window was a wound and his way out. Standing on the sill in the open window he was fat and rather grotesque-looking with his big, rounded shoulders hunched down, his long black hair weedy in the wind, his behind large in his tight pants and his big feet planted wide. He closed his eyes. He edged with his toes to the tip of the window sill and squinted his eyes tighter. Then he got down out of the window, closed it, locked it, sat in a chair with his face in his hands.

Suddenly he sat up.

The note!

What if his father came home from the strike and found it! What if his sister came home!

He leaped to his feet and rushed out of the room. Forgetful of the elevator he ran down, down, down the flights of steps and stood weak and panting in the lobby. Even before his breath came he ran out of the hotel and down the street—tiring—slowing up—running again—panting and sweating. Saw a cab. Ran out in front of it and gestured wildly with his arms.

The cab didn't go fast enough. His father was on the stairway, was opening the door, had picked up the note.

He gave the cabbie a bill and turning away ran blindly up the steps, scrambled with nervous fingers under the scrub pail for the key.

He opened the door and the note was like a bedsheet in front of his face. He laughed, weakly, piteously. His fingers tore the note across, and again across. He flushed the toilet. The water boiled and the torn bits of paper swirled in a slow downward circle on their way down. Looking into the bowl, Aaron chanted, "Float scum—float scum—"

# XXIV

When Don arrived in front of the Haines Company the picket line was already weaving around the building in a long, slow-marching procession, placards bobbing above heads in the early morning wind, bold and defiant placards:

WE DEMAND
20% WAGE INCREASE!
IN CHAINES AT HAINES—THE LOWEST PAY IN THE CITY!
JOIN THE UNION AND
BREAK YOUR CHAINS

Don walked on the opposite side of the street, uncomfortable and ashamed. He looked for people he knew in the line of marchers: there was O'Keefe in a raveled blue knit sweater handing out mimeographed leaflets on the corner . . . a girl from his department . . . but most of all he looked for Jim Norris: and there was Jim now, smiling and broad-shouldered and as defiant as the banner he carried: BRADLEY GET OFF YOUR PILES!

Don stood across the street in the shadow of the Butler Building watching. He waited until Jim was down almost the length of the block and then, as fast as his false leg would carry him, crossed the streetcar tracks and, pulling his hat over his eyes, moved through the strikers toward the entrance. "Don't go in!" a woman shouted.

Another woman, a husky middle-aged woman, her hair graying, deliberately placed her shoulder against his and pushed him sharply. He staggered a little on his false prop and, still with his head down and his chin drawn into the hollow between his collarbones, moved quickly toward the door. A chorus of boos followed him. A girl's umbrella sliced into his hat, creasing it, and the boos and derisive laughter followed him in past the glass and chrome doors of the Haines Company. But he was safe.

He hurried nervously along the hallway, ashamed and embarrassed, and quickly got onto the elevator. Behind him bell-like chimes tinkled in a cheerful, four-noted jingle: *Bing! Bing! Bing! Biiiing!*

"Mornin', boss," the Negro elevator operator said. Don nodded and didn't answer. The Negro put his hand on the control of O'Keefe's elevator and they eased upward through the steel and concrete building.

Wilmington, the department head, idled nervously near the entrance of the department. As his supervisors entered he greeted them with instant and wide smiles. And now Effingham, the ex-minister, entered and Wilmington awaited him with a smile that came as soon as he was within speaking distance. "Good morning, Mr. Effingham! How are you?"

Effingham nodded curtly. Wilmington shouldered himself directly in front of Effingham and, still smiling, held out a cigar. "Care for a smoke, Mr. Effingham?"

Effingham looked at the cigar for a long moment. Then he took it, turned it in his fingers, frowned at it. "Thank you." He moved off to his little office, past Wilmington's smiling face, past the many girls already bent to their machines, taking note, as he went, of the very few empty chairs.

And now Don came to the entrance and Wilmington was there, smiling broadly, to greet him. "Good morning, Mr. Lockwood!"

"Good morning, sir." Don's hat was still bent over his face as a shield against recognition. He now lifted it from his head and smiled at Wilmington sheepishly. Mr. Wilmington put his hand upon Don's shoulder. "Won't you have a cigar?" And the Wilmington company smile.

"Oh! Thank you very much, sir!" Don said, pleased and proud that his boss had taken this special interest in him. He must be getting recognition in the department. Mr. Wilmington's hand on his shoulder made him warm inside.

In his office Don arranged his work on top of the desk. All over the department the girls' voices were speaking their letters onto the cylinders in a many-voiced low monotony. Don glanced out and saw Miss Grover bent to her work. He looked and imagined her stomach filling with the child she was to have, and the arms and legs growing full, the fingers, without a single ring, thickening. No, she couldn't afford to stay away from work or join the strikers. He looked across the many-voiced section counting the few empty places. Oh God, because they have little white-collar jobs they think they're better than the strikers. He didn't think of himself. Or of being on the job.

A girl walked in, late, with a tense and scared look on her face. Don leaned back in his chair and bit his lip, remembering the scene on the street below. Didn't the strikers know he was on their side? He wouldn't have come in only—well, he needed the money.

Krendesky slouched into Don's office. "Oh man!" he moaned and put his hand up across his forehead. "What a night!" Then Mr. Wilmington was standing in the doorway chuckling. "Let me take you down for coffee, men!" he said. His company smile embraced them lovingly. "Come along!" And Mr. Wilmington, like a proud father taking them to some special treat, led them toward the door.

They followed him. He picked up supervisors at the other offices. Effingham looked up with his solemn preacher eyes when they stood at his door and shook his head no.

Going past Geraldine Brooks' office Don saw that she wasn't at her desk in a smart business suit, the only woman supervisor in the department. And, looking at her desk, he could tell that Jerry hadn't been there. Was she sick? Was she with the strikers? Was she pretending to be sick so that she wouldn't have to make an issue out of it? And Don, heading toward the elevator with the others: I should have called up and said I was sick.

In the cramped little elevator, standing close together, the four of them and their department head smiled at each other in a strained and overfriendly way this morning, almost as if they now stood alone against what was happening down on the street and sought an unspoken protection in allying themselves together.

At the cafeteria table they talked shop, and incidentals—about the weather, what they did last night, their families. They chuckled often. They didn't mention the strike or the barricade of unwashed pickets on the sidewalk below. It was as if it didn't exist for them. The bell-like chime tinkled again: *Bing! Bing! Bing! Biiiing!*

"Say, what is that anyway?" Don asked.

Wilmington smiled jovially. "Why, that's Happy Worker!" He put his hand up on Don's shoulder and again Don felt the warmth of flattery. "Don't you know who Happy Worker is?" Wilmington asked, chuckling. "Well—you'll find out today." He leaned back in his chair importantly and stroked his gray hair. "The old man," he said, referring in secret familiarity to Emerson Bradley, "gave an official order that—" he nodded toward the retreated sound of the bell, "everything go on as scheduled through the entire plant despite—" He consulted his watch. "Nine-fifty," he said; and in picnic spirit, "We're all going to the theater. The whole department's going. Even Effingham." His chuckle was slightly malicious. "The whole floor's going. The bargain basement salespeople, too." He waved his upturned palm in modest knowledge. "The whole plant will eventually see it."

They filed into Emerson Bradley's gray and green marble theater on the sixteenth floor. The seats began to fill with typists, stenographers, salespeople, minor executives—cynical men forty to fifty years old who had flopped from one white-collar job to another.

The theater was full now. The lights went off and the title of the movie flashed on the screen: HAPPY WORKER.

The movie began to unfold.

Don had a hangover from the night before and felt terrible. He looked across at Krendesky and Krendesky, with his hangover, looked at him and they were both sick to their stomachs. They scowled and shook their heads. The cynical middle-aged men sat in boredom. The women watched the screen.

Don leaned back in his seat, fitting himself to a more comfortable position, and tried to go to sleep, but the saleswoman behind him kept popping her gum. Bored and sneeringly amused, he watched the screen.

The picture unfolded showing the happy worker as a typical member of the Haines Family, showing him advancing on the job and getting a raise.

Don groaned and squirmed in his seat. All around him the big fat salesladies were swallowing it up. Meanwhile the strikers walked the pavement sixteen stories below with their banners.

The movie faded. The lights came on. Don sneered. The little screen went up and there was a table with a pitcher and a glass of water on the stage.

Don watched him walk out onto the stage. He was a man in a brown suit. A big executive from upstairs where you never see him. Some big shot of the company. A clean-cut, sharp guy. Don watched him. Jesus Christ! He'd take a drink in a minute—he couldn't have been that insane, but he walked out with the same harp that had been used in the movie. And he had a big smile. He said, "Well—" He walked over and sat down at the desk, very formally, and went *"Plink!"* on the harp. Don, smiling cynically, watched him: He's got a desk with a whisky bottle in the drawer on the right-hand side and a golf bag on the left-hand side.

The man put the harp on the table. He said, "Well—" and proceeded to tell them the moral. "Now you understand what we're trying to put across here. Every time a bad situation comes up—" and he picked up the harp and plinked it. He smiled at them blandly. "I talked to the star who made this picture and he said to me, 'Al! I enjoyed making the movie and I really got something out of it!' " He smiled again, too patiently, and plucked the harp. Don looked across at Krendesky and grimaced.

They went back to their jobs. Every hour on the hour Happy Worker's *bing! bing! bing! biiiiing!* was heard throughout the plant. Everybody in the plant laughed about it. And the morning wore away. And noon came. The strikers were outside. None of the people in the plant went outside for lunch. They ate in the cafeteria. Or went without.

The afternoon came. Don, with nothing much to do, read through some of the letters that had come into their department. One he read twice.

Holding the letter in his hand Don walked into Effingham's office. "Say, Effingham, what's this all about? This stuff about National Administrators?" He held the letter out toward Effingham. "And what does this mean—'Thanks for the penny'?"

Mr. Effingham looked up over the desk at Don. His eyes held Don's for a long moment and then began to squint in a frown. Slowly he stood up and closed the door. His tall, gaunt figure came back to the desk. He was still frowning and, motioning with his hand, said, "Sit down, Lockwood." Effingham put his bony hands upon the desk and leaned forward, his fingers tightening together and showing large knuckles flecked with freckles. "That," he said deliberately, "is the Haines Company's famous spying system. Inheritance!" He laughed dryly. His eyes narrowed. "They trace people that way. And they finally send them a penny to make it legal. The system has an initial which is very secret. You aren't supposed to talk about it outside the organization at all." As his voice stirred to anger his hands trembled slightly on the desk top. "It's a scheme," he said, "for finding out certain things about people who are very unsophisticated, whether they have a job and where they are working and if they have any relatives who might be made responsible for their debts. The Haines Company," Effingham said, "doesn't print those inheritance letters. Some company up in Wisconsin does. You send these letters around to any one who might have information on the customer, saying that you are looking for the customer or for relatives under this name, that he has been left an inheritance and that it is in the care of this custodian—'National Administrators.' " Effingham laughed through his nose. "There is no way it can be connected with Haines. The girls just say on their spools that an ID is to be sent. Haines buys the ID forms from this company in Wisconsin who sends them out and Haines stands by the Wisconsin people legally."

Effingham pulled a pencil from his pocket and scrawled on the glass top of his desk. "If the information is sent in the customer is sent a penny. In order to legalize the thing." Effingham leaned back in his chair. The lower drawer of his desk was open and he kicked it closed. Don watched the elderly ex-minister in surprise as his foot kicked viciously at the desk. Effingham said, "They get a terrific amount of information, if they get any. Most customers ignore them. Once in a while a customer will send in the complete details of his job—where he works, how much he gets per hour, how long he has been there, the names of his parents, brothers, relatives. And that information is used to try to collect the money owed the company. Sometimes we finally send a telegram or special delivery letter or return-receipt-requested letter stating that the bill must be paid within twenty-four hours or legal steps will be taken immediately to collect the bill and that the consequences will be costly and unpleasant. Imagine this—" he said, smoothing his long straight hair sideways over his bald spot, "you are working on your job and a telegram comes in care of your employer. Of course your employer calls you into his office. Naturally you open the telegram right then and there and your boss says, 'Is it bad news?' Of course you could say no but you might say 'It's about a bill I owe,' and your employer puts the pressure on you to pay your bill." Nodding, he said, "It works quite frequently.

"Sometimes," he went on, searching Don out with his dull blue eyes, "we send letters to relatives—which is illegal, but they are carefully worded—in such a way that nothing can be done about them. You can write a brother and say that you would like to know the whereabouts of—of the customer because you have something important which you are holding for him and that you are unable to find his address or his whereabouts. You sign such a letter with a fictitious name of course."

His grimness, his big-knuckled hands gesturing, his bony, wrinkled face with the eyes unpleasant as he talked, held Don and drew Don close to him. Effingham said, smiling without humor, "Oh, we have all sorts of methods of tracing people. We trace them through employers, one to the other. Employers are very co-operative. 'Where did he go when he left you?' Then you write to that one. Maybe he left the state. Maybe he went to a small town where there are no large companies. Maybe he is working for a friend or someone you can't trace. Ah—!" Effingham held up a large forefinger. "We write to the post office. Say that we are holding important mail for him. In that way you can sometimes get his address. It isn't legal to give out an address through the post office. But it's done." Effingham tapped the point of his pencil hard against the desk top. It made sharp, angry sounds in the room.

He smiled sarcastically, and with the smile his eyes grew more dull. "You know, Lockwood," he said, again smoothing the hair down flat against his bald spot, "I used to be a minister in a small town. I was sincere. I was happy. I never lifted my hand to injure any man. Perhaps I was too sincere, too God-loving—the bishop—well—I left off preaching." The smile was slow and sad. He looked across the desk top at Don. "This is a dirty job we have," he said. It was a wretched old man's face that looked across at Don. Its mouth said, "I'm a little ashamed at night when I kneel down to say my prayers. I wonder what God thinks of me."

In his hand Don balled the letter he had brought to Effingham's office. It was now a tight, crumpled ball in the fist of his hand. Effingham smiled sadly across the desk. He reached with his hand as if to touch Don or only ask understanding. "I'm an old man," he said. "I have to make a living—for the declining years of my life. You're a young man." He stopped. Seemed to gather control of himself. He smiled. "You know, sometimes," he said, nodding toward the window, "I think those people down on the street have the right idea."

Don stood up. "Thanks," he said. He turned and limped toward the door. "Thanks," he said over his shoulder.

Sue would be down there too.

He got into his coat. He wedged his hat tightly onto his head. Mr. Wilmington hurried from his office and approached him with a bewildered, half-frowning, half-smiling look. "Hello, Mr. Lockwood!"

Don didn't answer or look at him.

"Going out for a cup of coffee?" Mr. Wilmington asked.

Don didn't answer or look at him. He took the elevator to the ground floor. He walked to the chrome and glass door of the main entrance and watched the strikers march by. When Jim came in sight Don stepped quickly outside and fell in step with him.

"Hello, Jim."

"Hi, Lockwood!"

"Let me carry the banner for a while," Don said.

Grinning, Jim handed it to him. Behind Don a girl's voice shouted, "Hello, Don! Took you a long time to make up your mind!" Her voice was laughing in excitement and pleasure and he looked back toward the voice, knowing who it was. "Hello, Jerry," he said before he saw her. She moved up to their line of strikers and linked arms with him.

The marching line swung back around. Don saw O'Keefe and yelled but O'Keefe did not see him. Don laughed aloud. He felt freer than he had ever been. And with his laughter a bit of moisture stung the corner of his eyes, thinking of Wayne. Wayne would be proud of him. He was carrying on for Wayne. He turned his face toward Jim. "I want to join the union."

"Swell!" Jim said. His big hand folded comradely on Don's arm.

Don threw his head back. The wind whipped the banners. It stung his cheeks. Laughing and singing the strikers marched.

Don threw his head back farther and laughed. He belonged to something. He belonged to the people. To something big. The people.

# XXV

D. S. Matthews sat in *his* Chicago. It was as much his Chicago as it was Emerson Bradley's. He sat chuckling over the headline in the newspaper:

STRIKE TIES UP
HAINES COMPANY

D. S. Matthews leaned his head back against the sofa and roared with laughter. His broad chest and shoulders shook with his laughter and his big hands, wrapped into fists, beat the sofa cushions pleasurably. When the laughter became only a chuckling he sat up, reached for the silver decanter on the cocktail table and filled his highball glass half full of Scotch. His big hand wrapped around the glass and he swirled the liquor gently while his chocolate-brown eyes smiled at it. He gulped a large mouthful and lit a cigar. Then leaning back he closed his eyes and the strong line of his jaw tightened into round knots of muscles at each end where they fit into the upper part of his strong, square face. . . .

So . . . old Bradley was in trouble again. He liked to see the silver-spoon boys in trouble. The millionaires who hadn't turned a hand to get their money. He took another large swallow of Scotch. He flicked his cigar, careless of the ashes that spotted the thick Persian rug.

Again he leaned back against the sofa cushions, the glass held in front of him, his eyes staring at the richly carved ceiling. D. S. was reliving a triumph. His eyes kindled with it and his strong, purposeful mouth smiled with it. When he had suddenly become a millionaire his chief ambition, apart from drinking as much as possible, had been to become a member of the Country Club. But, in a city like Chicago, with its packing-house, railroad and department-store aristocracy, that was almost impossible, because established society had decided it couldn't handle one of the plumbing aristocracy among its number.

But D. S. wangled around until he found a big real estate man, a member of the club, who was willing to propose him for membership. The real estate man had said, "Well, I'll do my best but I have my doubts. You know they're very prejudiced."

He succeeded in getting someone to second D. S., but when his name came up before the membership committee, he was blackballed.

On the sofa at each side of him D. S.'s hands tightened into fists.

When Daniels, the real estate man, brought back the news, D. S. had flown into a terrible rage. . . . He had told Daniels, "I'll make that place my garage if it takes the rest of my life!"

D. S. chuckled now in remembrance.

Daniels discovered that the land next to the Country Club on the shore of Lake Michigan was for sale. Claiming to represent a client who wished to remain anonymous for the moment, Daniels, after a lot of maneuvering, secured the piece of ground.

And, of course, the millionaires in the community wanted to know what it was for.

The real estate man completely satisfied them by saying that the owner was a New York banker who wanted to build a summer home there.

The millionaires thought, Well, that's all right. New York bankers are, you know, pretty good members of society.

D. S.'s mirth bubbled over again and he poured himself another Scotch.

After a while barges came up the lake and started unloading material—massive stuff. There was pink marble from Sicily and building materials from all over the world.

He was regarded, in those days, as a bad nickel. He was always drunk and raising hell. Always the broad-shouldered competitor who beat the other fellow at his own game.

D. S. began laughing aloud and stretched his short, muscular legs out across the cocktail table.

A million dollars worth of building materials alone were used on the construction and the work went on apace. After the building was almost completed, one of the members who was in the club looked out through a window and saw a strange man, magnificently dressed, strolling about the new building.

"Who is that man?"

None of the members who were around the club at the time knew who he was. And, of course, at that time he wasn't a celebrity but just a grimy kind of a character who was known in the saloons and hotels. But Sarah, one of the maids, knew.

"Why, that's D. S. Matthews, the famous plumbing manufacturer, sir!"

"What is he—what is *he*—nosing around here for?" one club member asked suspiciously.

Another member answered: "I don't know. He's that kind of a fellow anyway. He pokes in everywhere."

One of the stewards was sent out to talk to the contractor, who said, "Why, that's the man I'm building the house for."

D. S. smiled at the memory and drank his Scotch.

The fat was in the fire. Inquiries became serious. Club members elicited the information that the whole place was the property of D. S. Matthews. . . .

With the result that the Country Club gradually faded out and closed its doors, the members drifted away and picked out a piece of ground miles away on another part of Lake Michigan's shores and put up a new building there.

"So I was left, *mmmmm* (chuckling) with an empty club next door to my palatial house which I could have bought for a song and made into a garage if I'd wanted to," D. S. said aloud.

He stood up, draining the glass, and chuckled good-naturedly. Now, over twenty years later, he had been offered membership in all of the most exclusive clubs, all of which he had turned down time and again. He now tilted the decanter, emptying it of its last drops. I'll go nose around over at Bradley's place. He slapped his hands together in amusement.

He went into the bathroom and got under the shower. The bathroom was unique. He had designed it himself. The huge sunken tub was octagon-shaped. A mirror completely covered one wall. Another wall was of glass out of which he could look but into which no one could see from outside. Flowers bloomed inside the bathroom against this window and continued on the penthouse roof outside.

D. S. stood before the mirror, bunching the muscles of his hairy arms and chest and could find no fault or flabbiness in them for a man of his age. He was well built, hefty. He turned, staring out the window, over the penthouse roof down the Lake Shore Drive at his Chicago and the starry night, the walls of lights from hotel and sky-scraper. He put a big bare foot up on the chromium bath fixtures. One little mechanical invention had catapulted him into the millionaire class. Time had made him one of Chicago's wealthiest men. Drainage, that was it. An invention used all over the world. No damn bathtub you could get into without it.

In his early days when he owned just a little plumbing shop on West Harrison Street, when he was just a poor man who lived on credit like most of the small plumbing shop owners, he had struck upon his drainage idea. From then on—

He smiled.

He looked at his big-knuckled, bare hands. With these he had done it. And this—tapping his forehead with his knuckles. Best damn plumbing in the world. With a hairy big toe he twisted the water on. It hissed down over him.

He did everything in a big way. Drank in a big way. Lathered himself, now, until he looked like a polar bear, let the water blast down, finally turned it to its coldest spot and endured it enjoyably.

With a big Turkish towel he rubbed himself red and began dressing. He put on his gold cuff links that always ended by being rolled up into the sleeves of his shirt. He put on his trousers in which there was no crease, his big handmade shoes that were always scuffed, and his coat.

He still looked and acted like a poor man. He walked so fast that others could hardly keep up with him and he always walked a little ahead on his short, hefty legs, and got a sort of delight out of this. He stood straddle-legged when a woman came around, tightening his thigh muscles, arching his chest in a gesture almost like hitching up his pants.

Just now he stood in the paneled library with his hands behind him, arching his back, feeling his muscles roll over his back and and along his shoulders and arms. He again smiled over Old Bradley's troubles, and going to the phone, had his limousine brought around.

He pulled on his fedora with the long rakish sweep of the creased brim over his right ear and eye. His hats were always a little too big and rested on one ear at an angle.

He left his penthouse in the exclusive Lake Shore Drive apartment house where only mayors and millionaires lived and walked to his limousine. When the chauffeur reached back to open the door D. S. punched him playfully in the arm. "Hello, Chuck, you old bastard, you!" he said. He shouted it. There was never anything modulated about his voice.

Getting inside he said, "Drive me around to old Bradley's Company." He began to laugh.

Just as they moved away from the curb a car, with a loud screeching of brakes, cut them off and came to a dead stop, the fenders of the two automobiles only a fraction of an inch apart. From the driver's seat of the cream-colored Cadillac convertible with the top down, Irene Matthews waved gayly at her father. "Hi'ya, darling!" she yelled.

"Hello, sweetheart!" He smiled in proud and fatherly affection. "Staying here tonight or going to the other place?" he asked.

"Staying here," she said. "Having a few friends in for drinks."

With a screeching of brakes she backed out of the way until she was at a level with her father's face. "Coming back for a few?" she asked.

He shrugged and chuckled.

She backed behind his car. "Have a good time," he shouted. He waved the chauffeur on and shortly the long black limousine was bumping over the cobblestones under the elevated structure on Lake Street. It turned off on Canal Street and stopped in front of the main entrance of the Haines Company where the strikers in hundreds marched with their defiant banners.

When the marchers saw the chauffeur-driven limousine they began to boo. Then someone shouted, "That's D. S. Matthews!" and he felt a thrill of pride at being recognized by the workers. He laughed and rolled the window down and shouted with his head sticking out, "Keep up the good work! Give old Bradley hell!" They began to cheer him. He lifted his arm out the window with the fist held up in salute and laughed. The car slowly trod the block at the pace the workers set.

The marchers wheeled around and at the head of the procession D. S. saw the tall and handsome Jim Norris and, next to him, Don Lockwood.

The huge Cadillac drove up alongside Don and the man in the back seat shouted, "Hey, Donald! Hey, Donald!"

D. S. stopped the car and got out. He waved his arms at Don. Don saw him and came out of the line and onto the street. D. S. slapped him across the back heartily. "Good going, boy! Give old Bradley hell!" And in a spirit of fun, "When are you through?"

Don looked at D. S., the millionaire, with admiration, respect and awe. A thrill went through all of him when he realized that D. S. Matthews himself had remembered him. He lowered his eyes. "I was just going to quit now, sir. I've been marching since early afternoon."

"Climb in!" D. S. said, holding the door of the car open.

Don was astonished, almost competely overcome, at finding himself in the limousine with D. S. Matthews.

"How about having a little drink with me?" D. S. asked.

"Well, sir, I—I—well, look at me," he ended desperately. His face was grimed and sooted, streaked with dirt and sweat from having marched with the pickets for hours, his suit was baggy and soiled, damp ovals of perspiration stood under the cloth of each armpit and he was convinced he needed a fresh shave, talcum and cologne, to go anywhere with D. S. Matthews.

"Aw *Hell!"* D. S. said, "that doesn't matter. See those callouses—" He held his palms out proudly, showing the hard lumps of flesh. "I don't just sit on my can giving orders. I worked my way up the hard way and I don't give a damn how anyone's dressed! Came up the hard way, yes sir. That's why I hate bastards like old Emerson Bradley. Never had a day's work to do in their lives—Hey, Chuck, you old monkey-face!" he called to the chauffeur. "The Ambassador East."

Don sat in embarrassment on the rich cushions of the limousine. D. S. bit the tip off a cigar and stuck it in his mouth. He offered a second cigar to Don. Don took it and stared sideways at D. S. as the millionaire cupped the match and held it for him. "They're especially made for me—handmade," D. S. said. "They're not especially good—not as good as some of the standard brands. But it gives you a feeling of power—especially if you rose from nothing." He laughed. He chewed on the cigar, blew a cloud of smoke and kneaded the palms of his calloused hands into his knees.

The huge Cadillac drove up in front of the Ambassador. The doorman opened the door for them.

"I can't go in there!" Don said in desperation, in a panic of embarrassment. It was *the* spot in Chicago, the real spot where the silk stocking people hung out. Who was he? How could he go in there? Look how he was dressed!

"The hell you can't. You're with D. S. Matthews!" D. S. said with his hand on Don's elbow pulling him out of the car.

Frantically Don tried to reknot the pulled-loose tie as he found himself being led toward the entrance. "Noooo, I'm not going in there dressed like this. Do you want me to be thrown out?"

D. S. laughed loudly, in a crashing bellow. "Anyone with me is never thrown out," he shouted; and to the chauffeur, "Leave the car, Chuck, and go back to the apartment. If I need you, I'll call you."

D. S. led Don up the steps of the Ambassador and into the Pump Room. The waiter in his smart knee breeches and hunting pink uniform came to attention when he saw D. S. Matthews but looked slightly askance at his dirty and wrinkled companion as he escorted them to a choice table. "What will it be, Mr. Matthews?"

Don slumped down in his chair and wished he could crawl under the table.

All about him was the beauty and the glamour of one of America's most famous eating and drinking places. Don glanced at the luxurious white leather settees. At the white plumes of the blackamoor coffee boys who wound their way through the tables. He swallowed and pulled his embarrassed knees tightly together under the table.

D. S. said, "Give us a bottle of Haig and Haig Pinch."

The waiter put a bottle on the table and two glasses. D. S. and Don started drinking. Don glanced at D. S. in shy embarrassment.

Nobody he told would believe it. Here he was in the Pump Room with D. S. Matthews! *He,* D. S. Matthews' guest!

They drank the bottle, Don in deep embarrassment feeling sure that everyone was staring at him, and D. S. in enjoyment, laughing raucously while heads turned around and stared at the table where the noise came from, but smiling in that well-bred tolerance when they saw who was making the noise.

D. S. ordered another bottle. Don didn't know how to get to the toilet. He was afraid to get up amid all this elegance and walk between the tables of richly dressed men and women. He clamped his knees together.

Meanwhile D. S. proceeded to get drunk, laughing loudly, telling Don stories about the times when he was poor and working in his little shop on West Harrison Street, slapping Don on the shoulder, going into peals of laughter, putting his hand on Don's knee in friendship and saying he envied Don, a young man capable of working his way to the top, standing right now where he had once stood, that all the fun was in the struggle to the top of the heap. Again he drank, banging his glass noisily against Don's. "Drink up, son," he said in a big voice. "There's plenty where this came from!"

D. S. leaned over toward Don. He said, "Did you ever think—if everybody thought the same thing we'd all be in love with the same girl?" He leaned his head back and laughed. He filled their glasses.

"Mr. Matthews, I think I'd—"

D. S. stopped him with a hand on his arm. D. S. was very drunk. "My friends call me D. S. You're my friend. From this—from this moment on you're my friend." He lifted his glass to click it with Don's. Don lifted his glass.

Don was getting drunk now too. He didn't give a damn any more how he looked. What did he care about these people here? They were just people. No they weren't. They were the rich bastards that caused wars. No, not D. S. here. D. S. was his friend. Good old D. S. He'd drink all night with his pal D. S. What if he couldn't hold his liquor any longer and lost it right here in the Pump Room —what would they say? Nothing. His pal D. S. was with him. What if he did do that? He laughed. He threw an elbow up on D. S.' shoulder.

"Say, D. S., old pal—"

"What, buddy?" This was a lark. He was showing the kid a good time.

"Say D. S., buddy, you'd pick me up, wouldn't you?"

"How're you doing?"

"Fine. Fine. Les' have a little drink—say, when do they close this joint up?"

D. S. bellowed his laugh. "We'll close it up for them."

They did. They staggered, arm in arm, between the tables and D. S. had a hard time getting into his car.

# XXVI

Aaron came to with a start. He was lying on his stomach. His eyes were blurred and he tried to focus them . . . legs . . . bars . . . were those the legs of soldiers . . . or tree trunks . . . or bars . . . ?

He blinked his eyes.

"Oh. Hello, Denny."

He was back with his outfit.

"Hi, Aaron!"

He was the only Jew in the outfit. They were all older than he was. Some of them were even married men with children. They were always talking about women. About going to bed with them. He always walked away when they talked about women. They'd say they did this and did that and tell what the women did and he'd get up and walk away.

They'd laugh at him. "Look at the kid blush!" they'd say. "Didn't you ever get your ashes hauled, kid?" they'd say. "We got to take the kid out and get him fixed up."

The wise looks, the grinning faces, the passed winks. "You'll like it!" they said. "Once you taste blood—*uuuhhhhh!*" It was wise, fatherly, worldly, the way the words fit their mouths and the way the hands fit compassionately about his shoulder.

Embarrassed, blushing, he'd walk away. And the grinning faces watching him . . .

. . . trees . . . legs . . . bars . . .

Then today. They got him cornered. They hemmed him in with their khaki arms and legs. Their broad shoulders and grinning faces. The grinning faces looked at one another and then at him. The dirty talk about women began. It was dirtier than it had ever been. He stood, backed against the wall. He looked from one grinning face to the other. He stood trapped. He couldn't get past the khakied legs and arms and the broad shoulders. He lowered his head in shame and embarrassment. He burst into tears. The tears rolled down his cheeks and his wistful, pleading brown eyes looked from one face to the other.

"Okay, cut it out," gruffly. "Let the kid alone." That was Denny speaking.

Blinking his eyes . . . is it soldiers' legs or . . .

And after that the fellows were sort of embarrassed in front of him. And they were friendly to him. They were very nice to him. They called him kid most of the time. It was an affectionate nickname.

"Hey Kid, want to see this letter I got from my wife?"

"Hey Kid! Hey Levin—can't you hear good?"

"Aaron!—catch!—that's a book you might like to read."

Ties of great strength grew among him and all the other thirty-nine men of his platoon. There was a sense of fidelity among all of them, one for the other, all for the group. He was accepted. They genuinely liked him. For the first time in his life he wasn't conscious of his Jewishness. He was one of the group. One of the platoon. One of the forty. Accepted.

. . . yes, they're trees. I'm lying in Lincoln Park with my head in Rebecca's lap . . .

"The kid turned out to be a depressive."

"The kid was about nineteen—a good-looking kid."

"Don't you remember him? A big kid."

"No, I don't remember him—not from where I am."

He raised his rifle . . .

He couldn't distinguish between actual combat conditions and a safe environment . . . between reality and his world of fantasy.

"The kid saw five Germans approaching at some distance."

"I raised my rifle."

"Now go over your story. Go over it, word for word . . . word for word . . . WORD!—FOR!—WORD!"

"I want to go back. *Please* let me go back!"

His platoon was Intelligence and Reconnaisance. They got all the dirty work, the miserable missions, the scouting. Did it happen this way? Yes . . . I think so . . . or did it happen this way?

His platoon was trapped. They were practically surrounded. They were cut off and the only way he could join them was to infiltrate the enemy lines. He lay on the ground with his forehead against the earth. I've got to join them. I must! I must! They're doomed. But I've got to join them. I must! I must! He scraped his forehead back and forth against the earth. I can't! I can't! I must!

He lay on the ground at safe distance. I belong with them. I want to join them. I can't! I must!

He lay in a calm grove surrounded by white birch trees . . . He lay on an open battlefield . . . He lay in jail, penned in by bars . . .

All he knew, positively, was that his whole platoon had been wiped out and that he had deserted them, abandoned them. He could have joined them and he hadn't. They were all dead. He was alive and safe . . . The sky accused him. The earth beneath. All nature. He was alive and alone. Not a man. Not a soldier. Not a man. Tree trunks . . . soldiers' legs . . . bars.

*"Hey Kid! . . . want to see this book?"*

*"Come on into town with us, Aaron, to the show."*

*"Aaron! . . . . . . . . Aaron! . . . . . . . . "*

He was alive . . . and . . .

He saw five Germans approaching at some distance. He raised his rifle and couldn't shoot. He threw his gun away. He ran.

He was ringed around by soldier legs . . . he looked up . . .

Almost immediately court-martial proceedings began. Throughout all the treatment for psychoneurosis the army court-martial board kept making him go over his story against the wishes of the psychiatrists.

He counted the bars . . . no . . . trees . . . soldiers' legs . . . thirty-nine pairs of legs . . . his were missing . . . BARS!

He lay twisting from side to side in the hospital bed of the psychiatric ward.

Not a man.

Not a soldier.

Not a man.

He told the psychiatrist that he thought he should be court-martialed and shot. He wanted to be shot. He never wrote home. He received a letter from Rebecca with her photograph in it. He wouldn't answer it.

"I'm not fit to look at her," he told the psychiatrist.

He improved slightly.

He wanted to know when he could go back to his outfit.

"I want to go back. I want to go back and get killed."

Aaron twisted from his stomach to his back. His eyes began to focus—

He shivered and sat up straight in the bed. He put his hands over his face—

They were bars.

Then he remembered. He had hitch-hiked all the way back to the coast and had voluntarily re-committed himself to the neuropsychiatric Veteran's Administration Hospital.

# XXVII

On the first of the month Don dressed carefully and went downtown to McCarren's office, high in a building on LaSalle Street. Painted on the frosted pane of the outer office door were the words:

McCarren, Connors & Rosenberg
*Law Offices*

Don read the black-lettered words. Mr. McCarren was a lawyer as well as a ward committeeman! He gave his hair a final careful pat and, swaggering just a little, pushed the door open.

More cautiously now, and without swagger, Don approached the receptionist.

"I—I—want to see Mr. McCarren."

"What is your name, sir?"

"Mr. Lockwood. Mr. Donald Lockwood."

The receptionist switched her voice into McCarren's office and said through the speaker, "Mr. Donald Lockwood to see Mr. McCarren."

"Send him in in ten minutes," McCarren said back.

The receptionist glanced secretly at her wrist watch. "Mr. McCarren is busy just now. Have a seat, won't you?"

Don sat on the edge of the chair and nervously tapped his fingers against the brim of his hat.

In his office McCarren called Connors' office down the hall one door. "The boy is here—the Lockwood boy I talked to you about. Remember, I told you I had some friends in from out of town and I was taking them around to show them the sights and I ran into the kid in Bughouse Square making a speech. I think he's just what we need. I want you to look him over—give us twenty minutes and then come on in." McCarren hung up and began studying the racing form again.

The receptionist glanced at her watch. "Mr. McCarren will see you now, sir—through that door and to your right."

Don knocked timidly on the door. McCarren slipped the racing form into a drawer. "Come in!"

McCarren rose, smiling in pleasure, and came from around the desk to meet him. "Well! Hello, Donald! Nice of you to drop in on me!" He shook hands warmly. "How have you been?" He pulled a red leather chair up to his desk, near his own in almost a love-seat arrangement. "Sit down! Sit down!" He pulled the leather case across his desk. "Cigarette?"

"Thank you, sir."

McCarren snapped the lighter to flame and held it to Don's cigarette, lit one himself and leaned back in his chair, smiling warmly. "You know, Donald, I still remember a lot of that speech you made in the Square!" Smiling he shook his head in admiration. Don flushed red with pleasure. "But—" McCarren said, gesturing with his hand; and the large diamond struck its many colors in the air, "tell me something about yourself—your war experiences."

Don dampened his lips. He saw Wayne lying dead. He moved his eyes away from the scene. He dampened his lips again. McCarren studied his face. Don squinted and blew smoke. "Well—" He began telling about the trip across and the invasion. McCarren asked many questions and all the while studied him carefully. He asked about Don's background. Don told the same lie he had once told Sue. He was an orphan. His parents had died in Oregon. He had come to Chicago when he was old enough to be on his own. The door opened and Connors pushed his head and shoulders into the room.

"Come on in, Frank," McCarren called. "I want you to meet this young man. Mr. Lockwood, Mr. Connors."

Connors lifted his eyebrows. "Oh—Lockwood!" Shaking hands with Don he said, "Mac has told me a lot about you."

Don laughed his self-conscious, nervous laugh. Connors took a cigarette from his case in a deliberate manner. He seemed to concentrate all his attention on secretly sizing Don up.

McCarren said, "Donald was telling me about his war experiences—he lost his leg in the war, you know." Connors looked pained.

"Go ahead," McCarren said, gesturing to Don, and the sparkle of the ring blinded Don for a moment. "This is something you should hear, Frank," McCarren told Connors.

Don looked at the dead body of Wayne, and away. He began again telling of his war experiences. They listened, frowning. And Connors clucked his tongue and shook his head sadly.

"They must have gone through hell," McCarren said to Connors.

"We did," Don said, looking again at Wayne, "and I'm against war. I want to do all I can to stop another one."

McCarren and Connors exchanged meaningful glances.

"You were the first wounded serviceman in the African invasion, weren't you?" McCarren asked, and his eyes slid over to Connors.

"No, I wasn't."

"Oh, you must have been."

"What did you think of the segregation of Negroes in the army?" Connors asked.

"I don't think it was right," Don said honestly. "If they were good enough to put their lives on the line just like us they were good enough to fight alongside of us." And rather defiantly—"I don't go for that stuff."

McCarren and Connors exchanged glances again.

They drew him out on various subjects, on politics in particular. McCarren listened in a calculating way. His eyes were almost dead things in his otherwise friendly and handsome face.

At last Connors stood up. "Well, I'm a busy lawyer," he said chidingly to McCarren, "I've got to get back," and to Don, "It was pleasant meeting you and talking to you, Lockwood." And jerking his head sympathetically, "Awfully sorry about your leg." Then he maneuvered to get his back turned to Don and, looking McCarren in the face, poked out his lips and lifted his eyebrows in a grimace of approval.

When Connors was gone and the door closed, McCarren drew his chair even closer to Don's. He began to discuss politics in earnest. He talked about saving good government and about Republican inroads. "What we want," he said, "is good sound government built on the principles of F.D.R."

Suddenly he turned his friendly, red-flushed, blue-veined face full toward Don and lifted his eyebrows while, for a moment, the diamond sparkled against his steel-gray hair. His lips spread out in a smile and he said, "You, no doubt, wondered why I wanted to talk to you. We—the Democratic party—want to put you up for office in the November elections—want to run you for State Representative."

He smiled with his well-featured face tilted at an angle as his eyes stared into Don's.

Don gulped. "You—want—to—" he stared incredulously, "put—*me*—up for office?"

McCarren laughed, nodded, held out the cigarette case.

"I don't know anything about it—about politics."

McCarren laughed again and patted him on his false knee. "Don't worry about that. We'll coach you. Well—what do you say?"

Don stared in disbelief, breathing, all the time, through his mouth.

McCarren chuckled and patted his shoulder. "You with your *fine* army record. One of the first wounded of the African campaign."

"But I wasn't one of the first."

Chidingly, "Oh yes you were."

Don sat ill-at-ease, puffing on his cigarette to hide his confusion and his embarrassment.

"Well, what do you say?" McCarren asked again.

"If you think—" Don said, "if you think I should—that I could—"

"Of course I do!" Whack! a hard hand slap across the back. "This calls for a celebration!" McCarren took the whisky bottle from his desk and two glasses. Don's hand trembled violently bringing the glass to his lips and his heart pounded in fearful triumph.

"Look—" McCarren said, lifting a political chart of the area from his desk drawer. "Here—pull your chair around here."

They sat side by side in front of the big desk and McCarren picked up a pencil, pointing out, circling. "Look—this is what we have to do. See—right here—from here to here—" The diamond ring broke color over the chart. "This is a large Negro section—and this here is Eye-talian. We've got to get that vote. The Republicans are getting stronger in these areas. A lot of Negroes still vote Republican despite what Roosevelt— This—" the pencil slid to the right, guided by the headlight of the diamond ring, "this is Polish. A large number of our voters work at the Haines Company." He swung his head up from the map. "By the way—you better join the Polish National Alliance."

Don flushed. "But I'm not Polish."

"You don't have to be. Show yourself around their meetings. It'll help." McCarren's face fell back to the map. "Too bad you're not Polish. A lot of these Polacks won't listen to anybody but one of their own—and we've got to get that vote too." With his pencil he pointed out the boundaries of their district. "By the way—" and again he looked up, "we'll get you a job."

"I have a job," Don said.

McCarren laughed. "Yes, I know. But we'll get you one down at the city hall."

City hall!

"One you—" he smiled slyly, "you—won't have to work at too hard. You know, now that you're a candidate you'll have to do a lot of campaigning." The diamond fluttered on the gesturing hand. "You'll have to let people see you. Have an ear for everybody's troubles."

He looked laughingly into Don's scared face and patted him on the back encouragingly. "But don't worry about anything. We'll take care of everything. We'll call the signals and give you the ball. All you have to do is run with it." His diamonded hand was around the bottle. "Well, let's drink to it!"

They drank. As McCarren set the glass down and pressed his lips together, taking the last of the liquor, he said, inserting it very tactfully, "There's one suggestion I have—I, eh—" clearing his throat, "suggest that you get your hair cut a little shorter—"

Don's hand came up automatically, protectively, to his long, theatrical haircut.

"You know, so you'll look like the typical ex-GI." He laughed. "One of those army haircuts."

"Y-y-yes, sir," Don said.

"Well, Mr. State's Representative," McCarren said, "let's drink to it!"

They drank. McCarren explained some of the technicalities of getting Don's name on the ballot. "In a couple of days," he said, "we'll go around and meet some of the people." The diamond ring caressed the steel-gray hair above the black eyebrows. McCarren said, "Your girl—the girl you were with at the Legion hall—she—" he put it gently, "she's Jewish, isn't she?"

Don's blond face flushed up color and he looked away. Then he looked back into McCarren's eyes. "Yes, sir."

"Well, that's fine!" McCarren said. "Now I know we have the man we want." He poured liquor while Don looked down at his lap and flushed with pride.

McCarren, having finished his shot glass said, "But—ah—during the campaign I wouldn't—if I were you—be seen too much with her—too openly with her—not that she looks Jewish but when you introduced her and I knew—" He laughed. "No, I wouldn't be seen with her too openly—" He laughed again. "Discretion is the better part of valor." He laughed in jovial friendliness, in paternal kindliness. "You know how that sort of thing can go bad for you, create the wrong kind of publicity." He held up his hand and the diamond was a stop light. "Not that I care, understand." His lips spread out in his fatherly smile. "I'm for that kind of thing. After all—America—you know—" He laughed and didn't say what he meant about America.

They talked a while longer. McCarren wrote down Don's address and telephone number. "I'll call you day after tomorrow and take you around a bit. See you then."

It was a dismissing gesture of the diamond.

Don pulled himself up erectly and squared his shoulders. "Thank you, Mr. McCarren. Thanks a lot!"

They shook hands warmly. McCarren walked him out into the anteroom past the receptionist and to the door with his arm thrown comradely around Don's shoulder.

The elevator took him down and Don stood on the Loop sidewalk with the people swarming around him. He stood as if planted into the sidewalk in front of the building housing Mr. McCarren's office. It was like being in a dream. He watched the unimportant crowd with its unimportant faces swarm past him. If they only knew who he was! His heart beat elatedly and his eyes glistened. He tilted his hat to one side. Mr. State's Representative! He walked along jauntily, sprightly, on his one good, his one bad leg, swaggering, whistling to himself.

He went to the barbershop and sat uneasily in the chair. "Don't take too much off." He flinched with every snip of the scissors. "Now, now, now! Not too short! Not a crew cut!"

Every five minutes he asked for the mirror. But like all helpless mankind in the barber's chair, the barber had his way with him. On the floor he saw his long strands of hair that had fit in a sweep over his temples, back along his ears and rested together at the back of his head in folded, glistening wings.

At last it was over and talcum dusted his neck, tickling it, giving a pleasant odor of sweetness to his nose. He stood up and looked into the long horizontal mirror. It didn't look bad at all. Not bad at all! He began to strut in front of the mirror, turning his head this way and that way. I look good. It's just like a part in a play. I look the part. Well *I am!* I'm a politician now. I'll give the greatest performance of my career!

He bought a gray Homburg for his haircut and tilted it over one ear. He bought a cigar and fitted it into the side of his mouth.

His leg ached. He was sure of it. He went to his mother's house. She was astonished to see him. It had been several months since he had been near them. "Hi," he said and went toward what had been his but was now Helen's room.

The cheap perfume-powder-deodorant smells were heavy. Several slips and dirty pairs of stockings were thrown on the bed where he had memorized the lines of great plays and thought of Edwin Booth and John Barrymore.

He went to the closet. Helen's clothes were there. But back in the dark depths of the closet was the cardboard box, gathering dust, that was all that was left of Grandpa except a blurred memory. He felt in the dark corner of the closet and his hand closed on it. He drew out the gnarled walking stick with its gnarl-carved handle. Holding the cane by the handle something of grandfather passed into grandson and his eyes filled with tears. "You're going to be proud of me, old man," he said aloud.

He went back into the kitchen. "My poor son," his mother said, "is your leg heavy under you? Is it bad with you?"

"Yeah," Don said, "it's been giving me trouble the last couple of days."

He looked at his mother. Gee! Could he surprise her! Walking over to her with the aid of the cane he kissed her on the cheek and that was surprise enough. She started to cry.

"Whatcha cryin' for, Ma?"

He hugged her a little and rocked her a little.

"I gotta go. Tell Helen and the kids hello."

He looked around the house. When he was State Representative he'd take care of Ma and the kids; he'd help Helen too. That was for sure.

Unconsciously posing at the door he lifted the cane and winked at Ma. "See 'ya."

The next day, drawing his meager savings from the bank he bought a diamond ring at a hockshop. Not as big or shiny as Mr. McCarren's —but a diamond ring.

In his room with his cane leaning against his false leg, he polished the ring. Out on the street he kept polishing it against the sleeve of his suit coat, and with his Homburg tilted over one eye, the cigar clenched in his teeth, kept lifting it to lamplight, to store-front light, to starlight to see it glisten and sparkle. He was, unconsciously, still the small-time actor. This was another role.

In the dark, on the empty street, whistling, he twirled his cane, even if his leg did bother him. Whistling in the dark he even did a couple of fancy dance turns, twirling the cane.

His head was as big as all Chicago.

# Book Five

## EVENING DARKENS

### I

In his little theater days he had learned to tie a Windsor knot and wear a yellow scarf. Now he was learning to wear a Homburg hat and smoke a cigar. His cane was his constant companion. With the Homburg tilted to one side and the cigar clenched in his jaw he walked along the street. Lifting the cigar from his mouth and snapping the ash from it, he could see the diamond ring flash. And the job. What a job! All he did was collect his $425 a month through checks in the mail every two weeks. He was a pay-roller in the county treasurer's office: an assistant chief clerk. It sounded good too—assistant chief clerk.

Meanwhile THE POWER, Ward Committeeman McCarren, went to work. He told his secretary to have telegrams sent to all his precinct captains instructing them to be at the clubhouse Thursday night. Then McCarren called Don and said into the phone, "Hello, my boy! We're going to spring it Thursday night. Be down at organization headquarters around eight o'clock."

Thursday evening Don entered organization headquarters uneasily and looked around. The clubroom was a large hall with a stage and five hundred dusty folding chairs, many of which were stacked against the wall. Others were lined up in front of the stage, stiffly awaiting their occupants. On the stage was hung an American flag and framed photographs of Roosevelt and Truman behind dirty glass. There were several chairs on the stage and a small table with a pitcher of water. Off to one side was a cardroom. On the other side was the ward committeeman's office and, next to it, the alderman's office.

McCarren waved to Don in generous salute from the doorway of his office. Don came on his cane to the office, holding his Homburg in his other hand. THE POWER saw the cane and smiled to himself: The kid's doing all right! "Hello, my boy!" he called. THE POWER shook hands with Don and then, circling his shoulders with his arm, drew him into the office. "Fellows—" THE POWER said; and it was then that Don saw there were two other men in the office, "this is my new man. This is our next State Representative. Donald Lockwood—Alderman Flynn," and Don found his hand being tightly squeezed in the big paw of a tall, portly, florid-faced man.

"Donald Lockwood—Judge Rizak," THE POWER said. The wizened little man with bushy gray hair looked at Don through his gold-rimmed glasses in a quizzical, judging, pouting way. But he smiled, too broadly, and turning to THE POWER nodded his head in a falsely approving manner.

"Have a cigar, Mr. Lockwood," the alderman said.

"It's a pleasure to meet you," the judge said; and wincing in bland sympathy: "Heard about your leg."

"Glad to have you in the organization," the alderman said.

They hovered near him, overly attentive; but their eyes occasionally moved to McCarren as if to take their cues from him.

McCarren rubbed the palms of his hands together, and smiling at both of them in a friendly, superior, amused way, THE POWER said, "Well, what say we go with him." It wasn't a question. It was a decision. His amused eyes held theirs and they nodded solemnly. From his picture frame the President of the City Council's face looked down at them. THE POWER gestured toward the door with his head. Judge and alderman, after again shaking hands with Don, left the office.

"Well—" THE POWER said laughing, "sit down."

Don sat, pulling the cane in between his legs and tightening them against it. THE POWER's cold and amused eyes traveled slowly across Don's face. It was a possessive, speculative look. "Well—" THE POWER said, "how do you feel?"

Don laughed nervously. "I guess I'm kind of scared, Mr. McCarren," he said honestly.

Outside the office there was the mumble of voices and chairs scraping as the precinct captains began sitting down facing the stage.

"Nervous?" THE POWER asked. THE POWER laughed, and getting up from his chair came over to where Don sat. He put his hand on Don's shoulder. "Never," THE POWER said, "say too much—just sit and listen." He laughed again, good-naturedly, mechanically. "Let's go," THE POWER said; and on the way out of the office: "The precinct captains are our foot soldiers. They're the real vote getters. They—" THE POWER's face took on a look of grimness and pride, "do as I tell them."

As they walked onto the stage, Don following McCarren, the alderman and judge, who were already seated there, stood up and remained standing until they had taken their chairs, THE POWER seating Don between himself and the alderman.

The mumble of voices in the audience died down and out front the over a hundred precinct captains sat on their folding chairs looking up at the stage. Above their heads hung the blue cloud of smoke from many cigars and cigarettes. At their feet were the squeezed-out butts from the long period of waiting. The faces looked up.

THE POWER rose and went to the front of the stage. He held up his hand and the diamond ring flashed back at Don. "Well—" THE POWER said. "The meeting is going to come to order. Let's get on with our business. We're going to run a new man. I want to introduce Don Lockwood—"

Don flushed, smiled, bowed in theatrical fashion, standing with his cane knob encircled by the moist, frightened palm of his hand.

THE POWER said, "I'm going to nominate him to run for State Representative at the north end of the ward."

The words had barely left McCarren's mouth when up, out of the audience of precinct captains, popped some suckhole lap-sitter and seconded the motion.

"All those in favor say Aye," THE POWER said.

Everybody yelled *Aye*. But they were all startled. Where did *he* come from? Who was *he*? They stared at Don in jealousy, envy, hatred.

"All those opposed say No," THE POWER said.

Not a sound.

"Well then, it's unanimous," THE POWER said.

Everyone applauded.

THE POWER turned toward Don.

Immediately the buzzing went on between the precinct captains. They leaned toward each other, whispering, speaking out of the corners of their mouths.

"Who's that guy?"

"What's that guy?—Is he related to the ward committeeman?"

"What is he—a syndicate man and we have to put him up?"

THE POWER called on Mr. Lockwood to make a little speech.

Don, nervous, walked on his cane to the center of the stage. "I don't know you well," he began, "but I want to get acquainted with you and give you a good administration." He said a few more words and sat down.

Don got plenty of applause. They had to eat him whether they wanted to or not.

After Don sat down McCarren said, "Well, let's hear from the alderman."

In ringing tones and political phrases the alderman told them what a swell guy Don was, what a sterling war record he had, how—his voice caught falsely with tears—he had lost his leg in defense of his country against the fascist beasts of the torrid African shoreline after having made a gigantically valiant but vain attempt to save the lives of three buddies and his lieutenant.

THE POWER sat with his chair tilted back, his eyes half-closed, his mouth lifted in a thin-lipped, tight smile.

"I know him well," the alderman said, though he had never seen Don before. But he had to swallow him like everybody else. "I want all of you precinct captains to get acquainted with him and know him personally. Then you will know, as I do, that this young veteran will be one of the greatest State Representatives our party has ever had down in Springfield. And—before we close this meeting—I want you fellows to be sure and come up and get your petitions for Mr. Lockwood."

Immediately a couple of the precinct captains in the front rows who resented Don's being State Representative but knew that they couldn't do anything about it clambered to the stage to shake his hand and congratulate him. They were followed by the others: all the precinct captains wanted to get acquainted with him because he was going to be a little power. They became very friendly and started to suckhole up to him.

And now the alderman had a sheet of paper and was calling off the names of the captains.

"Evans!"

Evans came forward. "Eighty-first," Evans said, indicating his precinct.

"Hi, Lou!" the alderman said.

"Hello, Alderman."

Don, with a big smile on his face, handed the precinct captain two petitions.

"Riley!"

"Ninety-third."

"Hello, Tim."

"Hello, Alderman."

"Now I want you to get twenty-five names—and positively legitimate names. Street written out. Chicago written out."

"O'Brien!"

"Ninety-seventh."

Don handed out the petitions with his big, friendly smile. Each of the precinct captains, playing up to him, shook hands.

"I'll really get out for you," they said.

"Come and visit me election day. Everything's going to be wholesale at my place," they said.

"I'll have them all lined up for you," they said.

About every fifth precinct captain the alderman told Don, "He's a good man." Automatically, every fifth man.

At last the meeting began to break up. Some of the precinct captains, after assuring Don that they were solid behind him, went into the cardroom to start a game of Polish rummy and talk about THE POWER's new right-hand man, wonder who the hell he was, what his connection was and how come. A couple of precinct captains had wives waiting outside in their automobiles for them and drove home complaining to their wives about the new guy, how it should have been them instead, after all they had done for THE POWER all these years.

Meanwhile THE POWER stood in the center of the hall with a hand-licking precinct captain saying to him, "I see the little czar of the North Side is going to do it again—with a vet this time."

THE POWER smiled and gestured as if offended by the name. But he loved it. They all loved it—all the ward committeemen who had been given public-enemy nicknames by the newspapers in campaigns against them.

And now a couple of the precinct captains who had hung around to ask THE POWER for favors in their precincts sidled up to him.

"See the alderman," THE POWER said. "He'll take care of you."

The usual brigade hung around and didn't leave until McCarren did. "Are you going home? I'll take you. I've got my car outside," they said, just to get their apple in.

And the precinct captains were trying to get close to Don now, too. He's THE POWER's new right-hand man. He's the Little Power. They stood, the usual brigade, around the two of them, smiling, their eyes climbing up to THE POWER's face. "Where are you going from here? Are you going downtown? I can drive you downtown."

They actually helped McCarren into his coat. When THE POWER had a pain in his stomach, they felt pain. When THE POWER broke wind, they smelled.

# II

THE POWER went to work. He had a list compiled of all the other prospective candidates for State Representative. Then he called Don and told him he would pick him up in fifteen minutes.

Don, waiting in front of the apartment building, posed on his cane. McCarren drove up in his car, a big black Cadillac. Don looked at it admiringly. He glanced at the license plate—only two numbers. His eyes took in the long, sleek lines of the limousine. Some day!

"Hop in!" McCarren said.

McCarren took him down to the city hall and filed his petitions. Even before they got out of the building and with people wandering all through the long, wide corridor that connected County and City buildings McCarren slapped him on the shoulder and said loudly, "You're the next State Representative!"

Don laughed nervously but with pleasure. "You mean—I'm going to win? Is it as easy as that?" he asked.

McCarren's cold eyes narrowed above his blue-veined nose. "I'm the boss of the organization," he said. "So you're in the organization. So nobody likes you. But do you think anybody's going to oppose me? NO!" His mouth tightened. "They'd find their ass on the street—so they all applaud."

They came out onto Clark Street where McCarren's car was parked beside the No Parking sign. A cop lounged there. He tipped his hat and said, "Hello, Mr. McCarren." He held the door of the car open for them.

McCarren wheeled the car across the street from the city hall to Randolph and LaSalle and parked in front of another No Parking sign. They went into the Metropolitan Building where there were many law and insurance offices. On one of the upper floors they went to a glass door upon which was painted SAFETY INSURANCE COMPANY, THOMAS MCCARREN, President. Don looked at the name and at McCarren with growing admiration and respect. Jesus! How many businesses was he in?

They entered. The secretary smiled and said good afternoon and they went into an inner office. "You'll be working out of here a lot," McCarren said. "You'll accept telephone calls here from the precinct captains—" He swung around in the chair to the interoffice com. "Miss Brooks, call Buckley—tell him to get hold of that Bill Kelly character and have him up here in an hour." McCarren clicked the interoffice com off. He pulled out a sheet of paper on which were written the names:

WILLIAM KELLY
EDWARD DAVIS
JAMES SCHMIDT
JOSEPH POLANEK
ANTHONY MARTINELLI
GEORGE REED

"These are the men who think they're going to run against you." McCarren's pencil checked them—WILLIAM KELLY √ EDWARD DAVIS √ "He's a Negro," McCarren said. "He'll draw so many votes in the Negro section and pull them away from you." McCarren swung around to his private phone and dialed. THE POWER said into the phone, "Hello, Bob—this is Tom. Say, you have a fellow in your precinct by the name of Edward Davis—yeah," nodding, " a Negro. He's got a crazy idea about running for State Representative. Tell him the ward committeeman would like to see him. Bring him downtown—make it—" McCarren glanced at his watch, "down here at about 2:30. That gives you something like an hour and a half."

THE POWER hung up. THE POWER checked the next name, JAMES SCHMIDT √. THE POWER said to Don, "Schmidt's a legitimate businessman. We can't knock him off the ballot." He smiled tightly. "We'll leave him there for the election." THE POWER laughed. His cold eyes looked at the wall on the other side of the desk. He smiled slowly, almost sneeringly. Then the pencil against the paper. JOSEPH POLANEK. The pencil made an angry check. "This one—" McCarren said, "is a half-ass hoodlum without a record—never served time." THE POWER swung back to the phone and dialed a well-known hoodlum. "Tom McCarren," THE POWER said to the front-page public enemy. "I want you to go see Joe Polanek. He wants to be in politics." THE POWER chuckled into the phone and hung up on the chuckling sound without saying good-by. THE POWER glanced at Don, getting amused pleasure out of the stare of admiration he saw in the boy's eyes; getting a kick out of showing off his power to the kid. He lifted a box of expensive cigars from a drawer, "Have a cigar—stick some in your pocket. They're always in here," pointing, "when you start taking over at my office here."

"Thanks, Mr. McCarren," Don said.

THE POWER put his hand on Don's shoulder. "Call me Tom, kid."

McCarren picked up the pencil and checked the name, ANTHONY MARTINELLI.

Miss Brooks said into the interoffice com, "Mr. Buckley is here with Mr. Kelly."

"Send them in."

The two men came in. THE POWER stood up and Don, watching him, did so too. THE POWER turned on the personality. "Hello, John!" he said to his precinct captain. "John, this is my man. This is Don Lockwood, our next State Representative." THE POWER let his eyes slip to William Kelly meaningly. "Ohhh, hello," THE POWER said, holding out his hand generously, "You're William Kelly. Glad to know you."

"Glad to know you, sir," Kelly said.

"William Kelly—this is Don Lockwood, my man for State Representative." Smiling, but in his mind thinking, You bastard, do you think you have a chance?

Kelly and Don shook hands and Kelly in turn put on the personality, knowing that Don was started for big things with THE POWER behind him. Lockwood was a good man to know. Might have to ask him for a favor someday.

"Sit down, Kelly," McCarren said genially. From a wall cabinet McCarren brought a bottle of Scotch and four glasses. "Well—" lifting his, "first today." They all drank. When THE POWER laughs everybody laughs, when THE POWER drinks everybody drinks. Kelly, lowering his glass, looked quickly at McCarren, knowing this was the pay-off, the kiss-off. He had known that he couldn't win but thought he'd try it anyway. What would the kiss-off be? A job? Money?

THE POWER leaned over the desk with his hand to his chin and smiled. "I hear you're running against us, Kelly."

Kelly hedged. "Well, I—I thought I'd try it." He shrugged, smiled foolishly and let his eyes drop away from McCarren's. Looking at the edge of the desk he again wondered what he'd get out of it, what the take would be.

"Well, now, look," THE POWER said, "I'm not one to hurt my own people. Tell you what I'm going to do for you. There's a job at the city hall—"

Kelly's hands tightened on his knees in greedy acceptance.

"And—" THE POWER, his cold eyes sliding back and forth and his lips half sneering as he thought how he could buy and sell them, "there's a chance I might need a precinct captain—now mind you—that's not a promise—but—" He shrugged dismissingly and started to fill the glasses again.

Kelly stood up, smiling broadly. "No, thank you, Mr. McCarren. It's a little early in the day for me to have another. Thank you, sir." He held out his hand. He said, "If there is anything I can do at all—any time—"

"I'll remember that, Kelly. Glad to have had this talk with you." THE POWER bowed Kelly out of the room.

At the door, Kelly turned back. "Glad to have met you, Mr. Lockwood!" He almost ran back to the desk and held out his hand to Don. "Best of luck." He dropped his eyes and shrugged self-deprecatingly. In patronizing friendliness, his hand sawed the air, "Ah, ah—I hope you'll like it in Springfield."

"Thanks." Don barreled out his chest.

Buckley, the precinct captain, was as friendly to Don as Kelly had been. "I'll get the vote out for you. I'll push as hard as I can," he said from the door.

Buckley and Kelly left together. The precinct captain took Kelly over to the city hall and put him on the payroll in a county clerk job, knowing that THE POWER could wipe this job out any time he wanted to. Then the precinct captain walked Kelly over to the election commission office and withdrew his name from the election.

At the same moment over in one of the river precincts the big-time, front-page hood stopped his car in front of the small-time hood's joint. The hoodlum had a big Cadillac too. He went inside. "Say—" he said to Polanek, slurring out of the corner of his mouth, "since when do you want to be a politician! I'll hit ya in the mibb! Do you want your ass put in the garbage can fer ya. Get off the friggin' ticket or I'll send ya over to the undertaker's."

The big-time hood turned grandiosely on his heels and swaggered out of the joint in his three-hundred-dollar tailor-made suit, got into his brand new Cadillac and drove out of the river precinct. He lit an expensive cigar and smiled grimly, looking out the window at *his* city, knowing that the petty-ass hood would run right downtown and withdraw his name. He smiled grimly: and the petty hood would get word to him that he was going to take a vacation until after the election, to assure them that he didn't want no trouble.

When they were alone again THE POWER checked the name ANTHONY MARTINELLI. "This one," he said, "we're a little worried about. He may cut up our vote a little. We'll contest his petition. I think he has a lot of forged names and we'll get him thrown off the ballot."

Miss Brooks' voice said into the room, "Mr. Burns is here with Mr. Davis."

"Send him in," THE POWER said, and checking the last name on the list—GEORGE REED—"He's an organization man. It's him and you for office."

Burns entered the room with Davis, the Negro. Davis was a tall thin dark man who looked as if he had never had enough to eat. There was a nervousness to his speech and his movements. His big hand reached out as THE POWER stood holding his hand out graciously. The Negro's smile was hesitant and lifted up off a couple of gold teeth. "Glad to know you, Mr. McCarren."

"Sit down, Davis," McCarren said casually. "Burns," McCarren said, "this is my man for State Representative—Don Lockwood."

The handshakes went the rounds while McCarren rinsed the glasses and poured new Scotch into them. Already Precinct Captain Burns was warming up to Don, the boss's new right-hand man.

McCarren sat down and handed Davis a glass first and then passed the other glasses around. They drank silently. Burns eyed Don and smiled at him. Don had his head tilted majestically and held the glass in the hand that wore the diamond ring. There was pride in him and wonder in him too. This isn't me sitting here. This isn't real. This is like a play. Wish Sue could see me in this role. And Don was acting all the hero roles he had lived and played and dreamed about, ever since he was a boy of seven on an empty lot playing the hero with his wooden sword. And it was he here at this desk with these important people. And all the time it was in me. And I *am* like Wayne. And I'm not a Polish slob from the slums of Grand Avenue. And I'm going to do a lot of things—a lot. Don, this is your chance to give the greatest performance of your life.

He set the glass down because his hand was trembling. He looked around at the people, at McCarren first. And this man—this man—his throat filled. He drew his hand down onto his lap, no longer conscious of the diamond. And if he hadn't heard me in Bughouse Square . . . He drew his grandfather's cane against his leg and held it tightly in his hand until the warmth of his hand went into the old polished wood. Old man, you're going to be proud of me—and Bronislawa with all your suffering . . . and great-grandmother who never saw her son again . . . and great-grandparents who I never saw, whoever you are, whoever you were . . . in centuries of centuries. . . . He had to blink now because his eyes were filling.

Davis the Negro stared down at his feet. THE POWER glanced around the desk at all of them paternally.

THE POWER rubbed the palms of his hands together and smiled patiently over the desk at Davis. Lifting the box of expensive cigars, he offered Davis one.

"No, thanks—I don't think I want one," the Negro said nervously.

"Want to have a little lunch?" THE POWER asked. "We want to talk things over."

"I—I ain't hungry," Davis said.

THE POWER said, "You know what we are up here for. You knew that before you came down here." THE POWER looked out of his handsome face with his cold, dead eyes. "Now, look, Ed, you've got no possible chance in the world to beat my man—but if I thought you were going to hurt my candidate, I'd spend an extra fifty thousand dollars to beat you, but I don't have to—because I have an organization with plenty of patronage. You're a nice fel-low. Some day we could do you a favor. We could hurt you if we wanted to, but we're not that kind of people." THE POWER glanced at him meaningfully: in other words, we're liable to give you a frigging when this thing is over.

THE POWER leaned way back in his swivel chair with his fingers in a little church steeple over his stomach. "What's your reason for getting on the ticket?"

"Well," Davis said, "I like politics, and—and," he stuttered nervously, knowing it was a lot of bull but trying to think of something to say.

THE POWER leaned way forward on his swivel chair. "You're sen-si-ble, but what the hell," THE POWER said, filling the glasses with Scotch, "you can't get anywhere." THE POWER tilted the glass and tilted his head. The Scotch poured in. THE POWER said, "How much was your expenses to have your petition filed and things like that?"

"A hundred and twenty-two dollars," Davis said, and nervously dropped his eyes to his untouched glass of Scotch, knowing that they had actually cost him only forty dollars.

"Well-l-l-l, I'll tell you what I'm going to do," THE POWER said. "Let's go get some lunch. I'll give you five hundred dollars—you get off the ticket."

Davis agreed. They took him out to eat. They made a big fuss over him.

After lunch they stayed with him all the time. They didn't let him out of their sight. They took him to the election commissioner's office. He filled out a little form withdrawing from the election.

THE POWER gave him five C notes, patted him on the back and told him what a swell kid he was.

Walking down the street away from them, with the five hundred bucks in his back pocket, Davis smiled and his gold teeth shone almost as much as Don's diamond ring.

Walking with Don, his candidate, his new right-hand man, THE POWER philosophized. "It happens every election. They file as candidates just to get a little loot. That's their main purpose in getting on the ballot."

Back in his office THE POWER showed Don the new list of candidates. There were only four names now.

"Martinelli we'll give the bounce to when we contest his petition. Schmidt—an Independent—" THE POWER sneered, "won't get anything." THE POWER slapped Don on the back. "Just you and your stablemate, Reed."

THE POWER had a drink of Scotch. THE POWER smiled.

# III

How do you get your name changed? How do you become a good American? How do you get Kosinski changed to an American name?

It was simpler than he had imagined. He paid a lawyer forty dollars and the lawyer filled out the necessary papers for him. Reasons for name change: It's hard to pronounce. There's resentment against foreign names. It's hard to spell.

He had to appear in court before a judge with the others, about forty in all, who had come that day to become American in name too, saying:

"It's hard to pronounce."

"People don't like people with foreign names."

"Nobody can spell it—nobody can say it."

In his turn Don stood before the judge and the American flag.

The judge intoned monotonously, "An appeal to change name from Kosinski to Lockwood."

Don recited his reasons.

The judge didn't even listen. "Granted," the judge said.

His name was now legally Donald Lockwood.

# IV

It was Don's day of triumph. The campaign cards had come. And the sample ballot with his name on it. He looked at the little political card like a calling card with his picture on it and underneath:

VOTE FOR
DONALD LOCKWOOD

STATE REPRESENTATIVE
303RD SENATORIAL DISTRICT

FIRST WOUNDED VETERAN
OF WORLD WAR II

He turned the card over and read:

HE STANDS FOR
PEACE—NOT WAR

*Equal opportunity regardless of race, color or creed*

*Public housing*

*Full benefits for veterans and their families*

*Higher wages*

Don turned the card over and over in his hand. He looked at his photograph again and then up into McCarren's face. He smiled slowly. "Thanks—thanks for everything, Mr. McCarren. I'll—" he dropped his eyes and ran a forefinger along the edge of the desk, "I'll try to do my best. I'll—" his hand tightened on the cane, "fight for those things it says on the card."

THE POWER looked at Don's bowed head and his lips smiled in amusement. His fingers curled in his steel-gray hair and the diamond sparkled, then was hidden. "Good!" he said in a political tone of voice, "I knew I had just the man I needed for the job." THE POWER, perfectly attired in his midnight-blue suit with the three-pronged handkerchief neat in its breast pocket, bit off the end of a cigar and lit it. He handed Don one and held the match for him.

Don looked over the flare of the match at him. "Are there going to be campaign posters too?" Don asked, imagining the big placards with his picture on them displayed from the sides of empty buildings and attached to lampposts.

"No," McCarren said.

Don was disappointed.

THE POWER said, "We're not going to make a big splash with billboards. We'd sooner buy the votes than advertise. We'll spend the money with the people. They don't forget favors." THE POWER tapped his cigar against the ash tray in meditation. "The Poles," he said, "have me a little worried. They can be so goddamned stubborn and," nodding, "we have plenty of them in our senatorial district."

Don took a deep breath. "I can speak Polish," he said.

"You *what!*" McCarren said.

"I—" Don looked away from McCarren's eyes. "I learned it in

Catholic school. I—" he thought fast. "I went to a Polish Catholic school. We—lived in a Polish neighborhood."

"Good!" McCarren said. He began to laugh. He said, "We'll give some parties for the Polacks. You talk to them in Polish."

Don glanced away. "Yes, sir."

THE POWER put his big arms up on the desk and poured a shot for each of them. Scattered across the desk were several hundred of the newly printed little cards with Don's picture on them and half a dozen book matches with his picture on one side and campaign promises on the other. On the edge of the desk and on a table were stacked cases containing thousands more of them. THE POWER pushed away from the desk. "Come on, we'll take a little ride—through some of the precincts."

Don stuffed his pockets with the literature about himself. In his arm he carried a carton of the book matches and one filled with cards.

They got into the Cadillac. They drove over into one of the precincts. From the car window, with his arm around Don's shoulder and his finger pointing, he showed Don a store-front sign. It read:

THE WILDCAT SOCIAL-ATHLETIC CLUB
MEMBERS ONLY

"Kids have a club there. They have beer and screw their girls there. Sundays they have crap games among themselves but the police come in and bother them." THE POWER leaned back against the cushions of the car and looked out the windshield with squinted eyes. THE POWER said, very softly, as if speaking of a beautiful girl, "You figure twenty-five members . . . their families and their friends are all voters in the ward. Figure all the votes that amounts to . . . there are four more boys' clubs like that in the neighborhood." He handed Don some money and told him what to do with it.

THE POWER climbed out of the car and Don followed him. THE POWER went into the boys' club. He stood at the entrance in his magnificent clothes.

Inside there was, set at an angle on the bare, warped floor, a pool table, two battered card tables, a coke machine, and a charter on the wall. Two boys, in T-shirts and sloppy pants, were shooting pool and in a corner four others were playing poker for money. They wore their hats. The brims were turned up and the hats were worn on the napes of their necks. At the pool table the two boys passed their last cigarette from mouth to mouth, spat on the floor, poked at the balls and cursed their bad luck.

The banging of the door brought the heads of the six boys to attention.

A quick hand scooped the money from the gamblers' table. All six of the boys came forward, slowly, suspiciously, moving close together as a gang moves when it suspects attack. Their eyes were fearful. But they were narrowed too.

"Hi, fellows!" McCarren shouted jovially.

One boy nodded his head sharply, hostilely. And they all moved forward together, forming a half circle around McCarren and Don.

"Yeah?" the boy who appeared to be the leader asked. He spat sideways. His eyes stared into McCarren's coldly.

"I hear," McCarren said, "that you've been having a little trouble with the police."

"Naw, we ain't been having no trouble with anybody—yet," the leader said. He was ready for a fight.

"Do you gamble in here?" McCarren asked.

The boy poked out his lips in ugly grimace, shook his head and tilted his hat back even farther on his neck.

"Nothing wrong with gambling," McCarren said, laughing. "Oh," he said, as if just thinking of it, "this is Don Lockwood. He's running for State Representative."

The six boys held out fish hands and didn't say what their names were.

"I think he can help you," McCarren said, putting his forefinger against the chest of the leader and chuckling. "Keep you out of trouble with the police. Don will be around to see you fellows in a couple of days."

McCarren laughed again, good-naturedly, turned and walked out.

Don, before leaving, threw a twenty-dollar bill on the pool table for the fellows. "Get yourself some beer."

Outside McCarren said to Don, "I'll give you the addresses of the four other boys' clubs. I want you to go there and treat it just like I did. I'll tell you what the pitch is later." He looked down the street and laughed. He pointed out a woman climbing the stairs to an apartment building three doors away. She was an attractive woman in her late twenties. "There go the Communists," he said.

"What do you mean?" Don asked.

"Ho—" chuckling, "that's Jane Morris. She's running against you on the Progressive Party ticket. War widow. Has three kids. She's got herself set up in a store front over in the Eye-talian and Negro district." He was much amused.

At the curb a slight, not very well-dressed man with a pockmarked face, his Adam's apple loose in the creased skin of his neck, stepped forward. In a stage whisper filled with surprise he said, "Well, *no*—if it ain't the little czar of the North Side!"

McCarren laughed. "Hello, Bernie!" he said and slapped the man on the shoulder. "I thought all you Republican precinct captains had hibernated until after election. Bernie—" turning toward Don, "this is your next State Representative."

The pockmarked man with the Adam's apple that moved up and down like a miniature elevator when he talked looked at Don with a sneering smile. He unbuttoned his coat and tapped the pocket of his vest. He said jeeringly while his fingers tapped in rhythm with his words, "I got the nigger vote right here in my vest pocket. You might as well stay home."

Don smiled a thin-lipped smile. He didn't like the word and he didn't like the man. "We'll see," Don said, still smiling.

McCarren and Don got back into the car. Don pulled out the sample ballot and admired it:

☐ DONALD LOCKWOOD
☐ GEORGE REED
☐ JAMES SCHMIDT

When Don left McCarren he went over to his mother's house. He went up the steps quickly without the aid of the cane, rapped it against the door and then flung the door open. "Hi, Ma!"

She was cooking as usual. She was drinking as usual. The place was as dirty as ever. A strange man, big, dirty in his overalls and with tattoos on his arms, sat at the table with a plate in front of him and a bottle of whisky in his hands. He was filling two shot glasses.

Don went in happily and pinched his mother on the arm. She turned her squinted eyes toward him. "Huh! So the bad penny rolls back home. The whole of my life is sown with thorns. This thorn must always catch in my skirt." She turned from him and walked to the table, snatched the shot glass from the overalled man and drank the whisky quickly while all the time her eyes angrily regarded her son. "So—you have forgotten that you have here a mother and brothers and sisters. Perhaps you have forgotten them so I shall remind you who they are. The name of one is Helcia—" she tolled them off on her fingers, "of the other Ewa, of the third Alina, of another Julka, and another Kazio."

"Aw, Ma! Ma!" Don said, laughing, trying to hug her to good-nature.

"So—" his mother said, "I will tell you this—as you make your bed, so you will sleep."

Don stood grinning at her. He pulled the ballot out of his pocket. "I've got good news for you. Look, Ma! I'm your next State Representative!"

She came over curiously, pushing the hair back off her forehead. "But I do not understand." She peered down at the ballot. Don's fingers scrambled in his pocket and drew out one of the cards with his picture on it. "Donald Lockwood!" his mother said contemptuously. "I spit on it. Is not the name you were born with fitting to you?" She took the card to tear it in half but instead looked at it, read it and began to understand. "So!" She stared at him in astonishment. But resentment returned. "You forget us. You reproach us. But we are not angry. It is you who are angry with us, for you don't remember us." Her eyes began to fill. With one hand she drew Don toward the table and with the other she pushed the hair from her face. "Mr. Markiewicz," she said formally, "this is my son, my boy who remembers his mother and comes home to see her. This is my dear wounded son who lost his leg in the war and who is now to be a politician." The tears were running down her cheeks.

Don laughed, and hugging his mother with one arm shook Markiewicz's hand, not even angry because his mother had a man in the house.

Don pulled out a card and handed it to Markiewicz. "This is my card and my platform. Vote for me," he said.

"Come," his mother said, "come and eat with us. I will spread a board here next to Mr. Markiewicz for you and you can talk your politics."

Don grinned and shook his head. "No. I have somewhere to go."

Mr. Markiewicz had poured him a shot. Don drank it, shook hands again, pinched his mother's cheek, glanced at his picture over the sink where his mother had pinned it, put on his Homburg, picked up his cane and left.

But outside the door he suddenly thought of something and grew fearful. He opened the door. "Ma, can I see you?"

He gave her a ten-dollar bill. He said, "Nobody knows that my real name is Kosinski. Don't tell anybody who I—don't talk it all over the neighborhood. Don't—tell—anybody."

Ma Kosinski put her hands on her hips. She laughed at him. She went on laughing. "I'll tell them all. I will tell them that you are a Polack who does not honor his mother."

He smiled at her. He knew she wouldn't. All he had to do was to tell her to keep quiet. It was like when he lived there and every day she threatened to kick him out, but kept him on.

He hopped into a cab and went to Sue's room.

"Hi, stranger," Sue said in cool casualness.

Don grinned at her and tried to slip his arm around her. She wasn't there. "Let me take you out to dinner," Don said.

"You must be hard up to be asking me," Sue said.

"Aw, honey, don't be like that!"

Sue came over to him. She blinked her eyes, but they remained moist. She put the palms of her hands up to his cheeks and took his face between her hands. She looked into his eyes, deeply into his eyes.

"You don't seem to be as much in love as you used to be with this girl, whoever she is."

Don laughed foolishly. He glanced away. He felt guilty about Rebecca. After what Mr. McCarren had said he had been afraid to go out with Rebecca. He had made excuses for not seeing her. She had been to his room. That was all.

He kissed Sue's hair. "Let me take you out to dinner." He patted her shoulder. And into her hair, close to her ear, he whispered, "I'll come back." He felt himself grow.

They went to Riccardo's near the foot of Rush Street.

He saved it until after dinner. He waited until she went to the ladies' room. Then he slipped the sample ballot and the card with his picture on it in front of her place.

When Sue came back she picked the card up, read it, turned it over, read that side—very slowly—as if she would never look up. When, finally, she looked across the table at him she was smiling at him gently, but with something else in the smile too.

"What's the matter?" he asked.

She smiled. It was a brittle smile.

"What are you smiling about?"

"I'm against you," she said. "I'm working for Jane Morris and the Progressive Party."

"Against me?" He couldn't believe her.

She looked up. "Oh, you fool," she said, "don't you know they're using you? Don't you know what that crowd stands for? Don't you know what a bunch of crooks they are?"

"You're crazy!"

"Don't you read the papers? Don't you know anything about the little czar of the North Side?" She bit her lip. She shook her head. "I'm sorry, Don."

"Look," he said, "you're going to tell me what you mean."

The bartender was standing alongside them. "Two more," Don said, frowning.

She didn't speak until the drinks were set on the table. There was bitterness in the tone of her voice. "They'd like to have you on the appropriations committee. There are labor bills they want nullified and twisted—" She pulled her lower lip in between her teeth, slowly let it go. "Oh, God, don't you know what McCarren stands for?"

"He liked my speech in Bughouse Square."

"What speech?" Sue asked wearily.

"He's a liberal."

Sue laughed.

"He's for public housing and racial equality. He thinks like you—honest he does, Sue. Like you and Wayne."

Sue laughed at him.

"Look," he said, "the Progressive Party is cutting up the liberal vote. You're helping the reactionaries. The Progressive Party is Communist-inspired."

"Did the little czar tell you that?"

"You'll take part of our vote and let the reactionaries in."

"Tax bills especially—" Sue said. "He'll want you working for him on that down in Springfield. Sales tax—the handling of that mass of money—"

"I'm going," Don said angrily. "Are you ready?"

"All right, Don."

Outside he said, "I suppose you don't want me to go home with you then." He said it in wounded pride and in anger.

"I didn't say that."

He went with her. They undressed. They got into bed. "You're a Communist, honey. When a Communist and a Capitalist lie down in bed together—" he said, making a joke of it.

"No, I'm not a Communist," Sue said.

To himself, straining close to her, Don said: Tonight I give the greatest performance of my life. But underneath he knew his need for her.

It wasn't a good performance. She wanted him to stay. He wouldn't.

He was home only a short while when the telephone rang. It was Rebecca. "I haven't heard from you. Oh, Don, I want to see you so badly. Can I come over?"

"Sure, come on over, honey."

When she was there and leaning against the sofa he showed her the cards and the sample ballot.

"Oh, Don, Don! I'm so glad for you!"

She held him close with his head down against her breast. He wanted to tell her he was in love with her. But he was weak. He had almost been afraid to see her, even here, after what Mr. McCarren had said. He was weak. He lifted his lips to be kissed. He saw the faint outline of the birthmark under the makeup.

She was happy for him. "Let's go for a walk."

"I don't feel like it," he said fearfully.

"Let's go celebrate," she said. "Let's go to the show."

He looked again at the faint outline of birthmark . . . "I just want to be here with you."

It wasn't a good performance either. Afterwards he called a cab for her and stood fearfully in the doorway while she ran out, hopped in and yelled back, "Goodnight, Don!"

Don went to Thompson's restaurant carrying a pocketful of the campaign cards and the match books. He walked in, leaning heavily on his cane but with the Homburg at a jaunty angle.

Don saw O'Keefe and Jim Norris sitting at a table. He went over to them. He told them that he was running for State Representative. "Vote for me," he said, handing them his cards and match books. "I'll give you good government." He left extra match books and cards for them to give to their friends.

He went to the other tables where acquaintances sat. He told them about his candidacy and left literature with them.

On his way out of the cafeteria he left cards and match books at all the empty tables, walking on his cane with an exaggerated limp.

He went through the clear glass doors and onto Chicago Avenue.

He left laughter behind him.

Don walked proudly in the night. Jesus Christ, it was something to brag about! Running for office! Having a big man, a powerful man like Mr. McCarren backing him. And yes . . . he could live Wayne's life for him. He could do the things Wayne would have done. He could carry on for Wayne. Wayne's parents would be proud of him if they knew . . . the Democrats . . . the merits of their cause were good. The principles of F.D.R. Those principles that Truman would follow. Sue would be proud of him, even after what she had said tonight. Wayne hadn't died in vain. . . .

These, the days of his triumph. . . .

# V

Aaron stood in the center of the long, wide room. The concrete moved away from under his feet to the barred windows. In past the bars filtered the warm coastal sun. Somewhere on the road below a car tortuously climbed a hill. Severe depressive reaction, they called it. Schizophrenia. They had given him electric shock because of his depression. He shivered violently, remembering being strapped down. They had borrowed lightning and shot it through his brain.

He lifted his head and his dark eyes looked from behind the black strands of hair that fell across his face. All about him were the others. They sat or stood, the forty or fifty, assuming all sorts of weird and horrible postures. They were childish positions, grotesque positions. Some of them were completely indifferent. Some highly excited. Some utterly sad. Their eyes stared at nothing, and their loose, flabby mouths drooped open. They were like rag dolls in their loose postures or like robots fastened in their frozen positions. All along the walls they sat, each day, staring at each other or at nothing . . . all day long . . . day into day. . . .

One patient squatted in a corner in his loose gown with his hands touching the floor and his forehead pressed against the wall. Another sat on a chair talking to himself and wildly gesturing to the invisible companion with whom he was conversing. Then he stopped, twisted his head so that his ear would catch the answer. Then he began talking again angrily: listened, laughed, jabbered on to the unseen companion. Next to him sat a patient with his legs propped upon the chair and widespread in the position of a woman. His arms were wrapped around his legs, his hands at his ankles, trying to spread them even further apart. He stared down at himself and played continually with the long strand of his shoelace, which was a symbol to him and which he had been caressing between long, lean fingers for hours, sometimes lifting it erectly as if to inject it into himself.

Aaron stared at him. Should I have spread my legs to be a woman? And across the floor came a veteran cradling an invisible baby in his arms, rocking the baby back and forth, softly lullabying to the baby. Suddenly he looked up from his cradled arms and said aloud, "How could they take a mother?"

It was as if some deeper part of themselves had made them like women so they wouldn't have to fight.

All along the walls the patients, the ex-servicemen, sat slumped. Many of them had their legs crossed and continually jiggled their legs in what the psychiatrists called masturbation. Others patted their feet against the concrete floor, swiftly, swiftly, continuously. Now from a bench one patient slowly arose and lifted his arms out in front of him, the fingers of one hand tensing wide apart, the other hand drooping down from a stiff wrist, the hand so loose that it seemed about to fall from the arm. He froze into his position.

On the floor next to him with his trousers pulled down sat a tall handsome ex-pilot. His eyes had a weird, faraway look and his lips were sculptured into a foolish smile.

Near Aaron hobbled a blue-eyed, innocent-eyed boy of nineteen or twenty in restrainers, his arms and hands fastened across his stomach in the semi-straitjacket, his ankles shackled so that he could take only half a step at a time. Not far away a skinny dark-faced youth stood with his back against the post. He looked up at the top of it. His pupils had gone up into his head somewhere. Only the whites of his eyes showed. He rose to his toes, rubbing his back against the post and stayed, like a trapeze artist, on his toes for a moment. The glazed glare of the whites of his eyes. The open mouth. The glint of the white teeth. . . . Then he walked to another post, again only the whites of his eyes showing. And another post. Another post. The doorjamb. Another post. All day long.

. . . And now Aaron wasn't sure if this was the same day or some other day. . . . He was moved from ward to ward—or so he thought—he wasn't sure. . . .

Across the floor scooted an ex-lieutenant on his bare rump. He was wearing only the top of his hospital pajamas, open in the back and caught by a single lacing at the back of his neck. In front of him were his two grotesque stumps, he like a gargoyle, following them, grimacing with a perpetual tic. At his sides were his arms in restrainers. The ex-lieutenant who had been a hero before he cracked up and who had, since being in the hospital, killed two patients by holding them down with his hands while he beat them to death with his stumps, hunched along the concrete floor.

On a bench sat a youth who looked as if he might have been a college graduate were it not for some horrible experience that had wiped his face of intelligence as a sponge across a blackboard. He kept trying to pull his leg off. He had one that shouldn't be there. He was a garden-variety catatonic. "Go there." He went there. "Eat your rice." He ate his rice. It had to be somebody in white giving the orders.

Near the barred door an old man from the First World War supplied almost comic relief or would have were he not so fantastically sad-looking and lost-looking. His pinched face bobbed from his thin neck. His body was like a slender dried weedstalk leaning awry, its only support in the ground of the concrete floor. His head was like the dried and dead, the drooped circle of a sunflower. Slobber dribbled in long spider trails from his mouth. His lips were loose and flabby as if the muscles beneath had no control any longer. He carried a tin cup in which to spit. And a push broom. He moved the broom round and round in one place, one small oval on the concrete floor. His hair bushed stiffly, like the dried, fibery petals of a dead sunflower. His eyes were glossed and nowhere, looking at nothing, not even the empty space two inches in front of him. He worked on and on in his tight circle. Then spread the little dirt out again, to again sweep it up. Then halfway through a stroke he'd stop in a frozen position, the broom his only support, he in a dizzy angle from the floor but immobile there. There he would stay, the tin cup hanging lopsided from his hand, spit drooling down his lip in long strands to the floor until the attendant saw him and came over, saying, "I'm going to take the broom away from you." Immediately the old man would begin his tremendously important job of scraping the small amount of dirt around and around in his small area of the big room.

Standing on a bench and making a speech stood a husky, handsome man of twenty-six or -seven who looked as if he were perfectly sane. He had his jaw set and his arm raised in Hitler's gesture. Though there had been many Napoleons in asylums, he was their first Hitler. "The Reich will last a thousand years," he proclaimed loudly. He could have been expected to laugh and jump down from the bench at any moment. But he was Hitler. He never lost the role.

. . . and on the benches all day long, the eyes staring, the sudden insane bursts of laughter or of cursing, the jiggling legs, the drooped slobbering mouths, the vacant eyes, the foolish fixed smiles.

Aaron gazed around as in a horrible dream. His palms were sweating and he rubbed them against his thighs as if to rub the flesh off. He wandered, weakly, over to the window with his big shoulders slumped and his head sunken in between them. At the window he looked out.

He looked at the hills that rolled away in the distance under the taffy-yellow sun and the blue sky dotted with the froth of a few small clouds that lazed above the brown-and-greenness of the hills. At the foot of the hills were houses, the homes of people, the houses of the coastal sun, varicolored stucco with flat roofs and picture windows.

Just across the road from the hospital was the soldiers' cemetery. Underneath the mourning trees and evenly arrayed in the crew-cut grass were, row on row, a mile across it seemed, and row on row in length as far as the eye could stretch in either direction from the hospital window, the granite tombstones, all alike in size and height. They bruised the greenness of the grass in mute testimonial. To his eyes they all wore the appearance of bullets sitting upright in cruel rows. And the generous earth, the covering grass, tucked away the dead of two world wars.

Aaron put his forehead against the cold pane of the window inside the black, standing bars. He shut his eyes and lay there with his head pressing . . . and rubbed his forehead back and forth across the cold pane with the tears trying to come past his clenched eyelids. . . . One tear spilled down behind the bars to the windowsill, and another. He ground his feet against the concrete. He forced his eyes open and looked around the ward. All about him were the young men who had gone out to fight the war. These were the young and healthy in body and mind who had cracked up.

Soldiers into rag dolls. Come home with your shield or on it . . . Mother America, we have come home on our shields. We, the living dead.

Many of them were paralyzed. Others were blind though they, according to all sane standards, all medical standards, should be able to see. Others who were unable to talk. Others whose bodies shook and twitched continually.

He glanced around at the rag dolls and the mechanical robots. He stood motionless on the hard concrete and looked down into the cemetery.

The bitter granite gravestones marched along in silent, immobile close file. He was like a dead, insane general reviewing the dead. Some of those who marched before his eyes bore the dates of 1917 and 1918. Others those of the 1940's. He could see through his tears the bright yellows, reds, blues, of flowers.

Some of the graves had fresh flowers on them. Some had flowers that were dying. Many had no flowers. The gravestones of the war dead marched away into eternity before his eyes to the hills, over the houses, over the hills, to the sky itself.

He looked down again into the graveyard. And he laughed. At last they lay in peace. At last there was no hate. Dead people get along well together. The cemeteries just wait there and laugh.

Aaron laughed aloud, a choking, sobbing laugh. "Control yourself," he told himself. "Don't become disturbed."

His thoughts meant nothing to the world. He was crazy.

# VI

He was big time. You could see that he took himself seriously by the way he leaned on his cane, twisted his mouth and frowned importantly with his eyes squinted. His diamond ring was a part of every gesture he made.

He stood in front of what had been the Wildcat Social-Athletic Club, polishing his ring against the lapel of his coat, and smiled proudly at the row of houses across the street and the blank blue sky. Behind him the new lettering on the window said 98TH PRECINCT DEMOCRATIC CLUB, DONALD LOCKWOOD HONORARY MEMBER.

The boys had played softball this Sunday morning and Don, at McCarren's suggestion, had umpired the game for them and would, at THE POWER's suggestion, do so every Sunday morning. Don had also had a barrel of beer and sandwiches sent to the club after the game for all the boys. In a moment he would go in and have a couple beers with the fellows. Again he polished his ring.

The squad car, looking for loot, drove slowly past. The cops on their big behinds inside saw the new lettering on the dirty window. And the figure posing in front. The cops drove on, knowing that the new sign was for their benefit: it meant stay out of there. If they went in Don would defend the club members. What's the sense of getting involved with the politicians?

The Democratic precinct captain walked along the sidewalk toward Don. He was a dapper little man who could be found at almost any time of the day in one of the neighborhood taverns. Seeing Don, he put on his best Sunday smile and came with his hand held out.

"Hello! Hello, Senator!"

"Hello, Hogan," Don said.

"How are you, Mr. Lockwood?"

Don pursed out his lips and nodded okay.

"Not me!" Hogan said, looking at his wrist watch. "Taverns don't open until noon on Sundays." In his Sunday suit and with his thirst for a drink he walked on down the street, saying over his shoulder, "Anything you want done in my precinct, Mr. Lockwood, just let me know."

Don walked east in the Sunday sunlight, crossing Clark Street, crossing over to Dearborn.

"Don!" a girl's voice called.

Don turned and saw Rebecca coming toward him. He colored. But waited for her. Waited in a panic. Jesus!

"Oh, Don!" Rebecca said, catching up with him. "I'm so glad to see you!" She stood beside him and slipped her hand under his arm. "My mother is away and I sneaked down."

Don laughed nervously. "Oh, swell!" His eyes searched the concrete sidewalk. What shall I do? Where can I take her? He looked up. A man was coming along the sidewalk toward them and, on his arm, a woman. Don bit his lip. Precinct Captain McGuire.

And now McGuire stood smiling at him, waiting to be recognized.

Don glanced up over Rebecca's shoulder. "Hello, McGuire."

"Why—*why*—hello, Mr. Lockwood!" He beamed. "I want to introduce you to the Mrs. Just—" he laughed in nervous, boot-licking pleasure, "just came from Mass at the cathedral—dear—" turning to his wife, "this is Mr. Lockwood, our next State Representative."

The woman held out her gloved hand and bowed, smiled at Don. Don stood awkward. "Oh—ah—" Don said, "Mr. and Mrs. McGuire —this is—ah—" he gestured awkwardly, "Miss Beth Freeman."

Rebecca's eyes were like a startled child's, then she flushed and hung her head. Her hand came up, in the old gesture, to the cheek with the birthmark on it. They were speaking to her. She looked up, squinting to keep the tears from showing. "H-h-hello."

Mrs. McGuire smiled at her, patted her arm. "Hello, dear." Mr. McGuire grinned at her in a flirting way. "Pretty girl, Mr. Lockwood," he said. "You've got good taste, Senator."

They were down the street now. Rebecca walked swiftly and Don followed on his false leg, trying to keep up with her, and when he had caught up, glancing sideways at her wretchedly. He tried to touch her arm.

"Don't!"

"Rebecca," he said. "Becky—"

"Don't!" Her voice trembled close to tears.

"I'm sorry, honey—don't you see—" He glanced down at his shoes. "Aw—look, please—it's just that—that—well, I'm running for office and Mr. McCarren—well, people—you know how people are—it's—aw—please, honey!"

She was almost running.

He hurried to catch up with her, his cane held above the surface of the sidewalk. He restrained her with his hand. "Please, honey."

She twisted away from him, her head down.

"Becky," he said, "I love you."

She turned then and was crying on his shoulder. "Don't," he said, patting her shoulder, "people are looking."

"Oh, Don!" she said, and started all over again.

His head twisted one way and then the other, fearfully. "Let's go."

He got her to his room as soon as he could.

She pulled off her hat and tossed it on the couch and stood looking out the window with one knee on the couch and her back to him. Ashamed of having come back here. It was all over between them. He had made her feel a Jew instead of just a person. Tears brimmed in her eyes. She would never have believed that he felt that way. And she loved him. Aaron was gone. Gone forever. Like one dead.

Don came to her and put his hands on her shoulders. "I'm sorry, honey." He turned her around. "Oh, honey, don't look like that!" He took her face between his hands.

She looked at him with unhappy eyes. "I never thought you—" She shook her head no. "I never thought you would do a thing like that."

Again ashamed, and genuinely sorry, Don told her why he had had to do it.

Don stood in front of the grimed church that had once been a synagogue before the Jews had moved to new streets, new neighborhoods. He tilted his head back and read the crudely lettered crayon sign in rainbow colors:

THE GOD IN CHRIST HOLY
APOSTOLIC CHURCH OF ZION

*Sister Emmie Smith and Her Gospel Singers*

Don touched his breast pocket where he carried the big contribution for the church and went in.

The reverend, a black, baldheaded man with a roll of fat at the back of his neck and a heavy gold chain around his neck from which hung a heavy crucifix that bounced against the protruding ball of his stomach, came forward eagerly to meet Don. He held out his pale fat palm.

"Mr. Lockwood, Ah'm sure. Mr. Donald Lockwood." He grasped Don's hand and held on to it like a man drowning. "Mr. McCarren, that good friend of my people, said you would be with us tonight, sir, and our humble flock welcomes you. Ah'm Reverend Johnson, Reverend Paul Z. Johnson." There was the lazy, rounded blur of the South in his voice mingled with the accent of the North. He stood there grinning, waiting.

"Glad to be here, Reverend," Don said.

The reverend grinned broader and rubbed his pale palms together.

Don took out the hundred-dollar bill McCarren had promised the reverend and handed it to Preacher Johnson.

The reverend took the money.

Don was ready with a speech: "It is a great honor, Reverend Johnson, to—" But the reverend took him by the arm and, grinning servilely, walked him briskly down the aisle to the front of the church, seated him in the front pew.

The flock gathered. The reverend with the heavy, nooselike chain around his neck over the black frock suit he wore and the huge crucifix hanging like a weight from it, put on a purple peaked cap and a red cape. He held up his black hands, and his pale palms signaled to the flock that the services were about to begin.

It was a revival meeting: Reverend Johnson worked himself into a sweat, rubbed it off with a towel-sized handkerchief, worked himself into another sweat. There were loud *A-MENS!* and *HALLELUJAHS!* that were sighs and sobs and pleas for forgiveness, and frenzied shouts. There were testimonials. One woman had consorted with the devil and sold her soul to the devil's black subdevils until she got religion and now—*praise the Lord!* A man had drunk that old devil juice and gone evil ways until one day right smack in the middle of Wells and Oak Street on the car track God had spoke to him out of the window of an old tenement house in a voice like thunder and from that day on—*ohhhhhhhh—hallelujah!*

"AAAAAAAA-MEN!" the flock chorused. "Praise the Lord!"

The preacher called on God over the heads of the repentants who, giving their testimonials, knelt in groveling positions at his feet. The flock from the tenements and alleys and broken stairways, lamplit, musty rooms of the nearby neighborhood prayed for them and shouted their amens. The sad Jewish windows of the church looked down, the flickering candles in variegated colors from black to pink and bought from the Greek's candle shop on Polk and Halsted Streets sputtered in their metal stems.

When the revival meeting was over the reverend stood outside on the top step of the church with Don, introducing him to the congregation.

"This is Mr. Donald Lockwood, the gentleman who gave our church a hundred dollar donation! The gentleman who is going to be our next State Representative!"

The people came forward gently, eagerly, shyly, in humble thanksgiving and took Don's hand.

But one Negro woman, an old woman, asked, "And what party are you-all with?"

"The Democratic Party."

"Not," the old woman said, "for a basket of fruit would I vote Democratic, because Abraham Lincoln freed us slaves." She went with proud dignity from the steps of the church, her unyielding head held high.

"Thank you, sah! God bless you, white man, for what you done for our church. You's a good man and I'll 'member you in my prayers," the others said.

THE POWER had bought their votes. He had put Don up to it and made Don feel that he should help this church. He had promised the preacher that he was going to help this church as much as possible. And the preacher believed every word of it because nobody but their own people had ever offered to help them before.

# VII

The automobile sped out away from the city toward the veterans' hospital. The last snow of winter was blackened and rain splattered against the curbstones and spring's first blueness was in the sky. Trees stood ready to leaf their buds. Don glanced sideways at Sue. Sue had said, "If you can leave your cane at home and forget you're a wounded vet and—a politician—you'll find out that they're much worse off." He frowned in shame and moved away from her a little. He looked down at the knee of his false leg and out the car window.

"Know your part?" Sue asked.

"Yeah." He could drop it around a bit that he was up for office. Everything helped. Had to keep it before the public's eyes.

The hospital was something on the edge of town hidden from the eyes and sensitivity of the people. The buildings were gray; a grayness that spoke of prisons, hospitals, sanitariums, old folks' homes. Inside were the men, the old men of World War I, the young men of World War II.

In the corridor, smiling and approaching them, was a small handsome woman. White circles of earrings shone out from the curling cluster of her auburn hair and her eyes were a warm brown. Down the corridor in a wheel chair came a boy peddling fast with his hands. He scooted his wheel chair into the woman. "Hi, Mrs. Q!" he shouted.

And now Sue and Don were standing in front of the woman. "Hello, Sue!" the woman said cheerfully. "Glad you're here early."

"Hello, Mrs. Quitman. This is Don Lockwood," Sue said. "Don, Mrs. Quitman."

The woman held out her hand. "Are you going to help entertain the boys?"

"Yes," Don said. "I'm a vet, too. I lost my leg in the war." He tapped it with his fingers and the hollow sound echoed in the corridor.

"So?" Mrs. Quitman said. "So you think you got it bad?" She nodded toward the boy in the wheel chair who had run into her. "See that boy? He'll never walk again. He's a paraplegic. He's paralyzed from the waist down."

"Oh?" Don said and looked away from Mrs. Quitman, ashamed.

Mrs. Quitman took Don and Sue each by an arm, leading them toward the auditorium. "They're the swellest bunch of kids you ever saw," she said. "They don't miss out on anything. They play basketball from wheel chairs, and golf and bowl. The boys go swimming. You should see how they swim! I asked them once, 'What's with the legs?' and they said, 'Oh, we can do it all right.' Someone just puts them in the water and they take care of themselves."

Mrs. Quitman, Don and Sue walked down the corridor and into the auditorium. Everything was wide—wide halls, wide doors. They were built that way for fellows on stretchers, on crutches, in iron lungs, in wheel chairs, and the floor was of linoleum to give crutch-hold.

The stretchers were borne in. The iron lungs were wheeled in and faced away from the stage so that their occupants could look through their mirrors at the stage. And the paraplegics came in their wheel chairs and pushed with their hands to places around the stage.

"Hello, Mrs. Q! Hello, Mrs. Q!" they shouted as they wheeled themselves in. And a boy came pushing himself in a stroller, like a child uses to learn to walk in. Over his pants were braces up to his knees. His tall legs took their pitiful, unsure, rubbery steps.

"Some of them are very thin and very sick yet." Mrs. Q. said in answer to a question from Don. "There are thirty to a ward in this one veteran hospital. There are twelve wards. They are sick and thin, or bitter and resentful, or living for whatever kicks they can get out of life—while life lasts. They have no control over their bladders and wear bottles strapped to their right ankles with a tube attached. The bottles are concealed under their trouser cuffs. Hello, Jerry. What's with you?" Mrs. Quitman called out to a boy with broad, husky shoulders, a deep square chest, muscular arms and withered legs.

"Hello, Mrs. Q!"

She leaned over and put her hand on Don's hollow knee. "That boy," she said, "didn't want to make up to anybody. I had the hardest time with him to get him to be friends with me. Even to this day he's bitter and conscious of himself. He was an athlete before. He drinks a lot. While he's living he's going to live. That's all. It bothers him to see a football game because that's what he used to do."

Don glanced at the ex-football player pedaling his wheel chair close to the stage with calloused hands.

"They have no sex life. This is an important factor in their mental attitude. And yet they all have girl friends. Many of them get married, and generally to the young cadet nurses. These marriages are a mystery even to the doctors," Mrs. Q. said.

"Hello, Bobby!" Mrs. Quitman called to one of the boys.

Sue, leaning toward Don, said, "He lives in Chicago and sometimes drives his car to his folks' home. His folks live on the third floor. It's even an inconvenience for him to go home. He can't even go up to his house. He toots the horn, they come down to see him and then he comes back to the hospital."

"Hello, Mrs. Q! Hello, Sue!" another of the boys shouted.

"He raises stud horses," Sue told Don.

"How do you know so much about them?" Don asked.

"I come out to help Mrs. Quitman once a week," Sue said.

Don glanced back at her: Jesus! Like McCarren she has her fingers in a lot of pies! Little Theater. Job at the Haines Company. Union. Progressive Party. Paraplegics. . . . It was like Sue to do things without talking about them. Again he felt a surge of shame. He always had to talk about what he was doing.

"Some of them work. A group of ten works at the post office, four hours a day. Some don't move from the hospital. They could go out but don't. They are sitting in the same position every Tuesday when I come to visit them," Mrs. Q. said. "I beg them, coax them, kid them. Nothing does any good. They sit around playing cards all day. Bed is their domain, their home, their life. They're like stray dogs. They have that unwanted feeling."

And now the auditorium was filling with veterans in wheel chairs, on crutches, on stretchers, in iron lungs. Was filling with the war's devastation.

They came into the auditorium, hobbling, being carried, pedaling themselves. The vets of the first war didn't care any more and came in bathrobes. The vets of the second war fixed themselves up. Some even wore ties.

Sue, Don, the Junior League girls and the other entertainers went to the dressing rooms to prepare for the entertainment. Don dressed in his black tuxedo and stuck his long, pointed black mustache to his upper lip, donned his top hat in the role of the barker. Someone thrust a cane into his hands. Sue had told him to leave his cane home. So they stick a cane in my hand. Huh!

The lights were dimmed in the auditorium. The piano player took his place. And the accordionist, the Junior Leaguer with a guitar.

Don stepped out from the theater wings as the show barker, and lifting his hat, twirling his cane, did a prancing step with pointing knees and pointing toes across the stage to its center. "Hur-ry! Hur-ry to the show!" he bawled, looking out at the audience.

He took center stage and made his top hat do a little spiraling dance on the end of his arm. "Hur-ry! Hur-ry! Hur-ry! It's fantastic! It's mad! It's sensational! It's *new! New! New!* The only show of its kind in the world!"

He twirled his cane and hat. "—introducing Molly O'Dea, tap-toe dancer who has entertained kings and gamblers! Blackguards and saints—!"

With a flourish Don held the flap of the tent back and the girl tumbled out onto the stage in a fast tap dance in pink toe shoes, sequin dust in her hair.

*Oh you beautiful doll, you great big beautiful doll!* the music said. The girl danced, twirling, posturing, snapping her tiny skirting out at the audience.

Don threw in a couple of gags. The veterans whistled and shouted and some from different parts of the hall went:

"*B-ooooong!*"

With a last snapping of the little behind, skirt and girl disappeared into the tent.

A clown tumbled out from behind the tent flap as the accordion played "Over the Waves," and a magician came out pulling panties and brassieres from his hat. . . .

More tap dancers. Two girls this time, very small, one dressed like a man, very Junior Leaguish, very sentimental about the boys, very anxious to do their number.

Madame Adeline was an older woman trying to be young again. She had large, healthy breasts that seemed about to burst out of their red satin and disks of rouge that stood out on her cheeks like stop lights.

Madame Adeline sang, shaking her hips, posing with her chubby, pinkish, dimpled arms:

*"Do I need you*
*Do I?*
*Oh my, darlin'*
*'Deed I do."*

Madame Adeline lifted her bountiful skirt and did a dance—with bumps and grinds. Her long string of choker pearls bounced against her breasts, rebounded and bounced far away.

The veterans loved her. The hand clapping was loud and long, punctuated with shrill whistles of approval. . . .

Don was enjoying himself. "And now—fellows—that lovely bit of pulchritude—star of radio, screen and television—"

Don pointed his cane at the flap of the tent, the piano played its attention chords.

The girl strode out onto the stage. She was a society girl who thought she had a voice. In her plunging neckline gown she strode to the center of the stage and clasped her hands together down around her knees, thrust out her not very ample breasts. She began to sing.

The fellows didn't like her. Catcalls went up from the vets. "Boo! Boo!" they shouted. "Get the hook! Bring back Madame Adeline! I want my money back! Booooo! Boooooo!" the jeering voices yelled.

The girl had to leave and two ballet students came out doing a comic. One of them danced seriously and the other burlesqued her.

The vets liked it. . . .

"And—*now*—our grand fi-na-le! The only living Fatima girl—direct from India—right out of the harem of the Maharajah of Bengal!—smuggled over here by the GI's for her first performance—this performance for you—*this!*—the first time she has been seen by male eyes!"

Don pulled back the tent flap and bowed low. The girl stepped out. The points of her gold Turkish shoes were turned up in front. Her voluminous chiffon pantalettes of pale green were gathered tight at the ankles. Between her red satin sash and the tiny jeweled bandeau that cupped her breasts her midriff gleamed white in the spotlight that sought out the entrance from the tent. A half-mask, black chiffon, lacy, concealed the upper part of her face. On her arm, twined around it, she carried an artificial snake.

As she stepped out from behind the tent flap her eyes for a moment met Don's and they smiled at him in an amused, flirting, coquettish way. For a moment she caught her heavily rouged lip between her teeth in a mischievous and half-concealed smile. Then she moved out across the stage in her sensual dance.

The accordion music weaved and throbbed. The drum beat its rhythm. The girl danced, twisting her hips, falling away in sensual glides, twisting her shoulders, looking down through her black mask at their soft bareness. She did the shakes, slowly, in rhythm to the whine and slide of the accordion, and her hips moved like tongues of flame licking the logs of a fire. She twirled her hands above her head, snake held aloft. She did bumps and grinds. And all the while the artificial snake crawled up her arms, around her shoulders, around her waist, rose, slithered to her lips for a kiss.

The music was sexy. Words to it formed in Don's mind: *Oh the dance they do, is enough to kill a—*. He was ashamed of the remembered schoolboy words.

She brought the house down. If the veterans could have gotten out of their wheel chairs, they would have mobbed her.

The entertainers mingled with the veterans in the canteen. Madame Adeline was patting a boy's cheek. The magician was showing one of the paraplegics how he did his tricks. The two Junior League girls were beating time with their hands and doing an unscheduled tap dance before a cluster of wheel chairs.

Don, accepting the congratulations of the veterans, smiling, shaking hands, moved from the canteen. He went into the cloakroom. Someone followed him. He turned around. Fatima, the dancing girl, was standing in the door in her colorful costume, her eyes and the upper half of her face hidden by her black lace mask.

"Hello," she said. Her creamed lips smiled at him.

Don nodded seriously, questioningly, and stared at her.

The girl came to him quickly and put one bare arm around his neck. She pulled his face to hers. She kissed him.

Don lifted his hands to the side of her face to take the mask away. She shook her head no and laughed, and from the little slits in the mask she looked into his eyes. With her bare arm still around his neck she reached with the other arm and put out the light. Her hand touched his zipper.

When the light was on again the girl took off her mask.

Don's mouth opened in astonishment. He stared at her with wide-stretched eyes.

Irene Matthews! D. S. Matthews the millionaire's daughter.

She laughed. Her eyes were amused and contemptuous.

"I'm Donald Lockwood."

"Hello, Don." They both spoke at once. Then laughed.

"Oh, I know your name," Irene said.

"You mean—you remember me?"

She nodded devilishly. "You got a haircut."

"I'm running for State Representative."

"My! What a big chest you have!" She laid her hand against his chest. She eyed him with amusement.

"Can I take you home?"

"I'm here with someone else," she said coolly.

"When can I see you again?"

"Oh, I'll see you sometime."

He tried to kiss her but she moved her face away. She laughed and twisted past him and out of the cloakroom. He followed her.

"Can I get you a drink?"

"I don't care."

He hurried on his false leg to the canteen and brought her an iced coke. She didn't like it and sent it back. Obediently he went for a soda.

From a far corner of the canteen Sue, talking to Mrs. Quitman, occasionally and secretly glanced across the room at Don and the pretty girl he was smiling at, talking to, in a way that Sue knew for its meaning. Was it good that he was attracted by the Junior Leaguer? What about the girl he was in love with? Was he tiring of her? Could she, Sue, again gain him back now that that love had died a little? The way he was smiling at that girl! Had she, Sue, lost him less or more?

. . . the months of loneliness, of waiting for him, thinking he might come over tonight, and sitting home alone, waiting, waiting.

"Yes, that's very true, Mrs. Quitman," Sue said, still looking across the room at Don.

Across the room Don said pleadingly, "Can I see you again?"

Irene shrugged. She made him hold her drink while she powdered her face—and smiled secretly as over the corner of the little square of mirror she could see him staring at her intently—in that way she knew so well.

And Irene, finishing her drink, left with her escort.

"Well, are you through flirting? Are you ready to go?" Sue asked Don. *Why do I say things like that? Why can't I keep quiet? I'll just drive him further away from me.* But moved by her hurt and anger: "Or would you rather stay? You might make out."

Don lowered his eyes. He felt guilty, thrilled, wondered if what had happened in the cloakroom was obvious to anyone, especially to Sue.

He looked up. "Oh now, Sue." He touched her arm. "Don't be like that."

"No, you can stay if you want," Sue said. "Someone will drive you home." *Why can't I shut up!*

"Well," he said, half posing, half angry, "there are a couple of cute little gals over there I haven't talked to yet. D. S. Matthew's daughter took up all my time, you know. She's—" he grinned at Sue, "a pretty girl and—" his grin grew more contemptuous, "money in the family."

Mrs. Quitman walked over to them. "I'll see you Tuesday, Sue?"

"Yes."

"Thanks for being so nice and coming out to help us," Mrs. Quitman said to Don and held her hand out to him.

Sue and Don walked to the car in silence, got in, drove back toward the city without words for ten minutes.

Sue broke the silence. "You just met a wonderful woman," she said.

Don heard but went on thinking about Irene Matthews and the cloakroom.

"Mrs. Quitman has been working with the paraplegics for four and a half years," Sue said. "It took her about two years to get them worked away from their bitterness."

*. . . in the cloakroom, in the dark, with her lips fastened tightly, hungrily to his.*

"Later she got them started going out to restaurants and other places." Sue slowed the car and lit a cigarette.

*. . . the mask taken away from the brown eyes. "Oh, I know who you are!" She knew who he was!*

"Un-huh," Don said in answer to Sue . . . *she had put her arm around his neck and kissed him. She had put the light out. . . .*

The car moved through the night back toward the city and the familiar. Sue, remembering the year she had been out at the hospital helping Mrs. Quitman, was silent with her eyes on the road ahead and her mind remembering the faces of the boys, the words they had spoken. Ronnie, who had read all that was printed on his condition: "I know everything about paraplegics that anyone can know." He didn't want to take therapy because "this is as far as I can go." . . . She and Mrs. Quitman with a group of the boys at the theater. One of the boys, pointing at his bottled leg, "Gee, Mrs. Q., does that show? Pull my trousers down." Mrs. Quitman stooping, high light on her soft auburn hair, and pulling the trouser down over the bottle.

*. . . she had smiled and shook her head no when he had tried to take her mask off. Oh boy! What a lay! . . .*

At the theater they were complaining because they had to sit in the seats instead of in their wheel chairs on their pillows.

Mrs. Quitman saying, "So, what's with it? You're at the show, aren't you?"

"Well, gee, Mrs. Q., you know, you're uncomfortable and you might have an accident."

"What do you mean, an accident?"

"Oh gee, can't you read between the lines?"

*. . . I laid a millionaire's daughter! ME!*

Sue stopped for a light to change. She glanced at Don. Don was staring dreamily ahead with a slight and tender smile on his lips. Sue felt the tightness of desire and the automobile behind her was honking because the light had changed.

And Don and Sue drove on toward the city . . .

Mr. Crowe of the Erlanger Theater had been good to them, had started it with *Mr. Roberts*. They had taken four boys every Saturday to see *Mr. Roberts,* their wheel chairs in the loge of the theater. Every boy who could get out of bed had seen it. Mrs. Quitman saying to the boys, "Look, no changing of the minds. Unless you're sick you're going to be there. That's all."

Sue, smiling out of the windshield at the night . . . this little boy was from Tennessee. A cute little southern boy only twenty years old. He had never been in anything but a small town before. Mrs. Quitman had said to him, "We're going to have a wonderful dinner, wonderful entertainment. How could you miss that? What is it I hear, you're not going to see *Mr. Roberts?* Look, you go get a ticket."

They had driven up in front of the Erlanger and the boy said, "I'm not going in. I couldn't get out if somebody paid me a thousand dollars."

"What did you say?" Mrs. Quitman asked.

"Second of all," the boy said, "there are too many people in the lobby. I'd never make it."

"Third reason?"

"The curb is too high."

"All the other boys got out."

"My legs don't move that way." He was scared. He was almost crying.

"Well, Harold," Mrs. Quitman said, "you're going in if I have to carry you in."

"Look at all the traffic! I—I—just can't make it!"

And Mrs. Quitman, with her hands on her hips, "You're going in, Harold."

"I think—" the boy said, pointing, "I could get out on this side."

"Okay, Harold, you're getting out on this side then."

The boy got out. And was more frightened. "Oh, look at all the people! I'd *never* make it!"

And how nice everybody was. Men started yelling "Heads up! Heads up!" They moved him into the lobby immediately through the throng of people.

Sue's eyes misted.

There was an America you loved.

Inside, Mrs. Quitman said, "Well, was that so bad?"

"No, but I *never* saw a downtown like this before."

The boy had never seen a legitimate play. After the performance he wanted to meet the star of the show.

"But how'd I get to him, Mrs. Q?"

"He'll get to you."

He got to him. . . .

Sue rubbed her fingers through her short-cropped hair, remembering.

And the man at the race track who knew what horse was going to win a certain race coming over and giving each of the boys a two-dollar ticket and then disappearing into the crowd.

There was an America you loved.

Dreamily, in the seat next to her, Don went over every detail, every spoken word in the cloakroom. Would he see her again? How could he get to see her again?

Sue smiled out of the windshield but there was a hard hurting place in her throat.

Christmas. Mrs. Quitman had invited her over. And she had brought two of the boys to her home for dinner. Turkey and all the trimmings. It was the first time either of the boys had been in a private home since before the war. It was the first time they had sat at a dining-room table with a family since they had been injured. This Jewish woman giving the boys this Christian meal on their most religious holiday.

There's an America you love. That America is people.

Through the windshield Sue could see the faces of the boys, and their immobile legs. She was hurt by their hurt. Her eyes teared. She took one hand from the steering wheel and placed it in Don's. To touch some human, in one's sorrow, to feel a hand, to express love, understanding, sympathy, through a look, through the touch of a human hand.

*Don was looking into the cloakroom and into Irene Matthews' chocolate-brown eyes. The light had just clicked off. Her damp, hungry lips against his. Their bodies meeting and straining.*

He hadn't even been conscious of Sue's hand in his.

And Sue, staring out the windshield with tears in her eyes, love and humility in all of her:

There's an America you love. That America is people.

# VIII

Jim awakened and groggily reached a hand out from under the cover, limply pressed the button down on the alarm clock to stop its jarring command. For a moment he lay there rubbing his big-palmed hands across his eyes and forehead.

Then he sat up in bed and switched on the table lamp. It cast its dim circle of light and in the other twin bed Louise moaned in her sleep and turned over on her back.

Jim lit a cigarette and sat on the side of the bed. He looked across at his wife. There had been love the night before and in his loins there was a quiet satisfaction. With the smoke curling up slowly from his cigarette he sat staring at his wife.

She lay flat on her back with one leg drawn up in a triangle under the covers. The blankets were pulled down off her shoulders and the thin cloth of her pajamas showed the imprint of her breasts, the nipples no longer firm with youth. He saw the sunken wells of her collarbones and the bones themselves standing pronounced beneath the thin skin. His eyes moved up to her mouth, thin, colorless without lipstick, open a little as she breathed. Her eyes were puffed with sleep. Long lines from the edges of her eyes had begun to scratch themselves minutely across her temples. Jim, lifting his cigarette to his mouth, continued to stare at her. Inhaled. Well, nobody looks good when they're asleep. But he felt a depression as he looked again at her face.

The baby began to cry in its crib in the next room. Jim got up and went to the crib. He lifted the baby up into his arms. As he held the child against one shoulder he thought of his wife and how he could have done better. Momentarily hated her.

"There, there—don't cry," he told the baby. He patted the child gently on the back and felt the baby's damp bottom. Jim changed the diaper. Leaning over the child he felt guilty and frowned. Well, every man wishes he hadn't gotten married at one time or another.

He left the baby standing, holding to the bars of the crib while he went back to the bedroom to dress.

Louise was awake and sitting up.

"Hi, Skinny," he said and looked away guiltily.

"Baby crying?"

"He's all right. I changed him."

"Come sit down a minute." She stroked her uncurled hair off her cheek and made room for him on the bed.

He sat next to her. She began to rub the palm of her hand across his forearm and watched the little gold hairs curl back and forth with her caress. "Oh!" she said suddenly. "You'll be late!" And gave him a little push.

Jim leaned his mouth to hers impulsively. When their lips met he felt only as if he were kissing his mother or a sister. She put her arms around him and clung there. Dutifully he put his arms around her.

The baby began to cry again and Jim released himself.

He went about his work at the union mechanically. Occasionally the remembrance of drinking and whoring around all over Europe came back to him. But that was their lives over there, they had told themselves. Once they were back home—

After work he stood on the corner for a long time watching all the young women and girls going home from work. Then suddenly fearful, with his guilt rising to the surface of his mind, he turned away afraid that some one he knew would see him—know—or that the women themselves would see him—know.

After supper he told Louise that he was going out for a while.

He parked his old Chevie and went into Thompson's restaurant. Seeing Milo and O'Keefe sitting at one of the tables in the back he walked over to them; slid into a chair between them and smiled. "Hello, Jim!" O'Keefe said, his face lighting with pleasure, and went on talking with now one more listener to hear: "And they talk about war. They talk about walking into blood tomorrow just as if it were a picnic. But history writes with a bloody finger. When people begin counting the casualties of their families and when a crepe is hanging on the door of every house in the United States it won't seem like a picnic then."

Steve, now working at Thompson's and on his fifteen-minute break, carried his cup of black coffee to the table and sat down. O'Keefe broke off in the middle of what he was saying and immediately unrolled his newspaper and held it up close in front of his face with his hands tightened into the margins. Steve looked in his direction in amusement and his sneering smile bristled his mustache. Then he looked at Milo. "Hi'ya, keed. It looks like Aaron has really—" he put emphasis on the really—"blown his top. I hear he's back in the nuthouse for keeps."

O'Keefe's hands pulled the paper down until just his eyes, fierce, the purple irises pin-pointed to black, stared over the top of the paper, looking directly into Steve. "You'd like that, wouldn't you?" he said and lifted the paper back over his face.

Steve smiled debonairly, and in a little shrug of the shoulders to Jim and Milo, said, "Well, statistics show that one out of every ten of us goes nuts at one time or another." His lifted smile showed discolored teeth. "That gives us a better chance."

O'Keefe's fingers rattled his newspaper angrily. Jim put out his cigarette and said nothing. Milo, glancing occasionally in O'Keefe's direction, tried to make polite conversation with Steve. And while he did, Jim began to drift away. Again he saw his wife's aging face twisting, in sleep, on the pillow. How old was she? Two years older than he. That made her almost thirty-five. For a brief moment Jennie's face superimposed itself on his wife's and he saw her full breasts, her generously freckled plumpishness. There was the inevitable comparison in his mind. He turned his mind from it. He stared vacantly at the smoke that rose from his cigarette . . .

Wonder what it would be like with Jennie?

O'Keefe was saying to Milo and Jim, "The rabble that fought with cobblestones and pitchforks in Paris now have airplanes and flame throwers. The rabble now can stand even with them."

Jim's attention began to float away from what O'Keefe was saying. His eyes reached to the young woman coming into the restaurant. His eyes glanced at the fullness of her coat in front. Edged down to her legs. Then a familiar limp caught his eye.

"Here comes the politician!" Jim warned out of the corner of his mouth and got up to go.

"We're in for it now!" Milo said softly to O'Keefe. O'Keefe nodded grimly and edged his newspaper over to his shirtfront, ready to prop it up in front of his face.

Don intercepted Jim halfway to the door. With his cane held under one arm, Don extended his hand to Jim and smiled, smiled a huge, friendly, backslapping smile. "Hi, Jimmy! How are you! Good to see you! How are things over at the union?"

Jim got away as quickly as he could. Walking out the door and onto the street he saw, in memory, the young French girl. Remembering her young body, her firm young breasts, he shivered in shame.

Don, walking proudly on his cane, exaggerating his limp a little, moved toward the table where Milo and O'Keefe sat.

Walking down the street with the French girl striding alongside of him, Jim remembered something else:

Suddenly he was standing in the alley. He was the boy aged fifteen. The alley was a slum alley behind Halsted Street near Maxwell, near where his mother, his sister and he lived when they had first come North from the South. He was with his friends, the gang of young boys he played baseball with, ran around with and went to the shows with. The fellows had the girl back behind a stairway. She was willing. It was another gang-screw. "Come on, Jim! Come on!" the fellows kept encouraging. He never went with them. But he was fascinated just the same. And ashamed of his fascination.

# IX

Life was good to Don. He was running for office. They told him he was in. THE POWER was behind him. He couldn't lose.

"Hello, Tom," Don said to THE POWER.

"Hello, m'boy!" THE POWER said, punching Don in the arm playfully. "Now, look," drawing a chair up close to Don, "this is what I want you to do." THE POWER told him about John Caspitolli down at the Toronto Avenue police station and handed him the schedule of precinct parties he had doped out.

THE POWER said, "Caspitolli was in a drunken brawl and is booked on disorderly conduct. He'd ordinarily get a twenty-five-dollar fine and be released *but*—there are twelve votes in that family. *Now* —"and THE POWER'S eyes glinted with the same hard light that reflected from his diamond ring, "this is how you handle it," and laughing, "those votes mean something to you on Election Day." It was the hard laugh of the streets and came from this handsome man in his magnificent clothes.

Don went down to see Caspitolli and introduced himself. Caspitolli looked out through the basement cell fearfully from his dissipated face. *"Jesus,"* Don said, throwing a scare into him, "they're liable to throw the book at you! Jesus Christ! You might cop thirty days. Even six months. I—" drawing himself up in a posture he had copied from McCarren, "I've got to go in and talk to the judge."

Caspitolli was scared and began to plead with Don. "My God! Anything you can do for me—anything—I'll never forget it."

Don went in and talked to the judge. "Hi, Graham, how are you? I'm Don Lockwood, Tom McCarren's candidate for State Representative."

"Oh!" Judge Graham said, coming from behind his desk in his private chamber. "Come sit down! Have a cigar! A drink?" He chortled pleasantly. "Well—" leaning back on the swivel chair, "how is my old friend Tom? That's fine! Fine! And what can I do for you?"

"There's a fellow named Caspitolli locked up downstairs." Don tapped ashes from his cigar. "Nice chap, really. From the thirty-ninth precinct. From a big family. Family of twelve."

The judge nodded pleasantly.

"Got in a little scrap," Don said. "Nothing much. Had one drink too many. Tom thinks—" Don shrugged. He handed the judge a card with Caspitolli's name written on it.

The judge stood up. He shook Don's hand warmly. "Say hello to Tom for me, won't you? And—Mr. Lockwood—" halting Don with his hand, "if there is ever anything I can do for you—well—" He smiled most affably and again shook hands warmly with THE POWER's candidate.

Don gathered up his cane and went to the courtroom.

The judge put on a good show. He bawled Caspitolli out pontifically. "Don't do this again!" An angry finger snapped at him from over the bench. "Don't ever let me see you in this courtroom again!"

He discharged Caspitolli.

Don's time was tied up at THE POWER's Safety Insurance office doing favors for the precinct captains, getting the people—the voters—in the district out of jams, going to bat for them, doing favors for them. Don was making himself a big guy. A swell guy. The people were thankful: Jesus, he's a good guy! How can you help voting for a guy like that?

Meanwhile THE POWER had an American Legion program started within the organization and paid for by the politicians. Each precinct captain was told to get the names of all the veterans in his precinct and a mailing list was made. The program was run by precinct captains who had been in the war. Literature, signed by Don Lockwood, Mr. Veteran of World War II, the first wounded of World War II, was sent out to all the veterans in the district. Baseball teams were promoted. Parties were given for them. Free beer and cigarettes. And at each party at the height of the festivities some precinct captain or ward heeler, or judge, sometimes the alderman, sometimes even THE POWER himself, got up and said, "Now this affair is being given through the good graces of our candidate for State Representative, Mr. Donald Lockwood."

There were many other parties given in the district. Bunco and Bingo parties for the women. Dances. Saturday afternoon ice-cream parties for the kids.

And THE POWER had even better schemes. He arranged parties at the organization headquarters for all the people of the district, three precincts at a time. The people mingled, grateful to the organization and Mr. McCarren and Mr. Lockwood for the free drinks, the good time.

Always Don was called on to make a speech for them, and gesturing with his diamond-ringed hand, he thanked the people for turning out. Always he ended, "But who wants speeches on a night like this —the beer is over there—"

THE POWER had strategic plans. He called in some of his precinct captains. "Now," THE POWER said, "I want to explain this as a good political angle. Let's get some of the colored and some of the white voters to a party. We don't separate them—see? We invite the colored precincts and I want you precinct captains all to come. I don't want the colored people to feel funny. I don't want any white voters there who would resent the colored people. I want more colored people than white but—" THE POWER held up his hand and smiled handsomely, commandingly. *"But*—I want the white people spotted all around—not hanging around together, but spotted all over the hall to give the colored people a glad hand. Get it?" THE POWER'S strong mouth flattened out grimly, his forefinger waggled out over the heads of the precinct captains. "And I want all of my precinct captains out to the party to show the colored people a good time—show them we don't have any prejudice. Show them we're one hundred per cent behind Mr. Truman and his Civil Rights program." THE POWER smiled boldly, aggressively, and sat down.

The mixed party was a great success. The white people, especially the precinct captains, gave the Negroes a glad hand. Don got up and gave a speech showing that there was no prejudice among his people—the people of the Democratic Party.

Don was very happy and very proud. He was extending the frontier. He was fighting for equality and, if Wayne had consciousness wherever Wayne was, he was proud of him. If Wayne had no consciousness wherever he was, he Don was bringing a last wreath, a last tribute to Wayne who had not, for his beliefs, died in vain.

THE POWER knew his way around. There was no hole in his armor.

Don. Don was cast in the hero's role. He had what he had always wanted. He had prestige. His humble slum beginnings were known by no one. Nor the fact that he was Polish.

Life had cast him in the hero's role.

# X

The automobile horn was honking so loudly and so continuously that Don, like several other people along the block, put his head out the window. A cream-colored convertible Cadillac with the top down was parked in front of his building. Irene Matthews sat in the front seat. She waved a small, gloved hand and shouted, "Hi, Don!" It was as if she had seen him yesterday. Not weeks and weeks ago at the veterans' hospital.

He came down the elevator as fast as he could, forgetting his cane, and stood alongside her car. He looked at the automobile and then at her.

Another Cadillac.

"Hello!" he said eagerly, smiling his best smile with his eyebrows wrinkled into it. And he looked at her deeply. In fascination. She was Michigan Boulevard beautiful.

"Get in. I'll take you for a ride," she said.

He didn't have to be asked twice.

She spun the steering wheel, and turning the car in a half-circle, pointed its yellow nose toward the outer drive, gunned the accelerator.

As soon as they hit the outer drive her small slippered foot pressed down on the gas pedal. Don said nothing but pulled out a cigarette and looked at her covertly from the corners of his eyes. Without looking at him she gestured to the cigarette lighter in the dash panel. He lit up.

"Where are we going?"

She smiled.

The motor hummed. She seemed interested in passing all the cars on the drive. They were already past Belmont Avenue. She came up close to the rear ends of cars, cut around them, zoomed out in front of others and fastened her foot down more firmly on the gas.

"How are your girl friends?"

"What girls?"

"Your Jewish girl—Miss Rebecca Friedman."

"Huh?"

"And Miss Franklin?"

"You've got a good memory."

"Like my dad."

"They aren't my girls."

She laughed at him.

It made him mad. "You can let me out, you know."

She slowed and pulled the car over to the edge of the drive.

"Okay, Mr. State's Representative." She stopped the car. Then gunned it, her fender narrowly missing another fender. Her hair blew straight out in the wind, rich, brown, curly hair blowing away from her temples. "I wouldn't have gotten out anyway," he teased.

"Light me a cigarette."

He lit one. She took it without looking, keeping her foot far down on the pedal.

"You'll get us killed," Don said with a shaky little laugh.

Steering with one hand, she held the cigarette between the fingers of the other, wiping it dry with her thumb. "You soup your cigarettes." She was teasing him.

They took the sharp curve near the lake and drove past the Edgewater Beach Hotel.

Her foot was impatient with the string of stop lights. The car moved along the lake, through Evanston, past Northwestern University, through the suburbs: Glencoe, Highland Park, Lake Forest. The sun was warm on them. Lofty estates and country homes of the rich towered like bank accounts to left and right, screened by trees or proud on trim lawns.

There were curves on the ever-winding upward path of Lake Bluff. Every time they came to a sharp curve Don, as if by accident, let his body slide on the leather upholstery until his shoulder was touching hers. She moved away from him and slung her arm out over the window. Smiling, laughing at him, catching her lower lip between her teeth.

The trees were above them, the smooth road below them. "Well, Mr. State Representative," Irene said, "how do you like it?"

He nodded approval without answering. He held two cigarettes in his mouth and lit them, passed one to her. He put his arm up around her on the upholstery. She cut her eyes at him. Embarrassed, he took his arm away.

She turned the car around and circled back through Lake Bluff, driving very slowly. "I bet," Irene said, "Miss Friedman wouldn't like this if she could see you now."

"Aw, she doesn't mean anything to me," Don said.

In Highland Park they drove down in front of a huge and impressive gate. Irene nosed the car speedily down the drive and with the screeching of brakes came to a spring-jarring halt on the half-circle driveway in front of the huge Georgian manor house.

"Who lives here?"

"I do."

They got out. She said, "Let's go find Dad. He's probably out in the orchard."

The grounds were enormous. The house itself looked like a small and expensive hotel. There were two guest houses, and far at the back of the estate near the orchard were the servants' quarters.

As they approached the orchard Don saw two men. One of them, his white flannel trousers rolled up over his ankles and bare to the waist, was chopping down a tree with an ax. In between lusty hacks at the tree which sent the chips flying in hard-rocked sprays, Don heard him saying, "Now, Bill, you stay out of the way. You don't know how to do things like this."

"Which one is your father?" Don asked in a joke.

Irene laughed over her shoulder and broke into a run toward the orchard. Don followed, hopping and hobbling as well as he could.

"Hi, D. S.!" Irene called; and when they stood beside him, "You remember Donald from the Legion hall, don't you?"

With one arm D. S. thrust the ax powerfully into the tree and made it stick there. With his hairy forearm he wiped the sweat from his brow. "Oh yes, I remember Donald." His eyes were laughing. "How are you, son? We had quite a night of it, eh?" He winked. Irene mussed her father's hair and kissed him. D. S. heaved his sweaty shoulders and said to Don, "It's great to be out in the sun—to get out and do a little work. Keeps you sharp. Keeps your mind sharp. Been doing it since I was a boy."

"Come along," Irene said to Don; and to her father, "We'll see you later, D. S."

She walked swiftly, and a little ahead of Don. He hobbled along, trying to keep up with her. Turning her head over her shoulder, Irene said, "What's the matter with you?"

Don looked down at the ground. Cripple. He was ashamed to look up. "I've got an artificial leg." Then slowly meeting her eyes in a little boy look; then squaring his shoulders back in the gesture of a man who can take things: "I lost it in the war."

She fell back in step with him. "Oh, I'm sorry." Her fingers slipped down into his in a little gesture of sympathy. She walked along with him, swinging his arm. She could be natural and unaffected when she wanted to be.

She took him into the house. Jesus! he thought. It's like a palace!

She rang for the servant and, sinking down on a low divan, patted the cushion next to her. "Sit down." He sat down and made an accident of letting his fingers barely touch hers.

The maid came. "Two martinis, please, Clara," Irene said, "with onions." Tucking her feet up under her, Irene settled back into a corner of the sofa and turned toward him. "During the war," she said "I was in Cairo—with the Red Cross."

Don stared at her. She was in service. Her with all her money. Don continued to stare in admiration.

"How was it over there?" he asked. It was the only thing he could think to say.

She combed her hair back from her temples with her fingers. "Terrific. There were a hundred and seventy-five of us." She laughed. "We had a greater impact on the troops than the Afrika Corps. A lot of the men hadn't seen any white women for a long time." She looked down, seeing the memories, smiling over them. "It was fun." She raised her eyes. He was staring at her and she knew what that stare meant. She had seen it so many times. It amused her. Then she glanced down. Her eyes brushed his knees and, the mood gone, she glanced away from his legs, her eyes more serious. "I might have been over about the same time you were," she said.

D. S. had come in and gone to the shower, one more elaborate than the one in Chicago. When he hopped out from under the needles of cold water, impatient to show Don his collection, he knotted a bath towel around his waist without drying himself and tramped barefooted, wet-footed, through the house.

He found them in the drawing room.

"Hi, honey!" he shouted at Irene.

"D. S!" Irene said in a tone of mock reproval.

D. S. put back his head and bellowed a laugh. He flopped down on the divan next to them and propped his dripping legs up on the cocktail table. "Hey, Clara!" he bawled out to the maid who appeared in the doorway with the martinis. "Bring me a bottle of Scotch!" He looked down at the palms of his hands, enjoying the raw-rubbed callouses there. "Feels good," he said, "to swing an ax. Used to work in a lumber camp up in the State of Washington, up in Oregon too, as a boy." He lifted the silver cigar box and took one. "Here, boy—" to Don, "have one of the handmade ones." He set the silver box down. "Don't wear glasses either. Strong eyes," he said, biting off the end of the cigar and spitting it at the air. "Comes from looking at the sun in a lumber camp. I worked my way up, boy!"

The Scotch came.

"Come along," he said to Don when he had poured himself a tumblerful of neat Scotch, "I want to show you something."

"Better fortify yourself with this," Irene said, passing him her half-emptied martini glass.

D. S. took him into his den. He moved Don to a whole wall of glass-enclosed showcases. They were all filled with miniature boats: full-rigged sailboats, pirate galleys, ancient war vessels of Greece and Rome, Spanish galleons.

Glancing across the room, angry words suddenly crashed across D. S.'s mind in memory. "Goddamn it, Miss Society! Why couldn't she marry who she wanted to?" And the words, the memory left.

D. S. stood in front of one of the cases, gazing in with a lonely pride. He put his hand up to slide back one of the doors and, seeing a few specks of dust on the glass, took them away with his thumb.

"Everybody has a weakness," D. S. said to Don. "This is mine." He drew ship after ship out of the cases and told Don all about them. "And some of these models, boy, are worth thousands of dollars—take this—" He lifted it off its rack: "This is a galley from the year 1571—notice it is propelled by the oar, or sweep as it is called. Now this one here, five hundred dollars for this little sailboat but—" Holding it in his hands the light of enjoyment softened his eyes. He put the boat back, and closing the case, put his hand up on Don's shoulder. He said, "Every man wants something he can't have." He shrugged at the room, the house, his wealth, and moved toward the door. "Let's go find Irene—or you find her—I'm going to dress."

And going out the door, squinting at the open sky, "Yes, every man wants something he can't have. His goodies of life."

They made him stay for dinner. It was not as in Omaha when Hilda sat at the table with the family. Here a butler and second man stood in the deep shadows beyond the light cast by the candelabra at the long refectory table, emerging ghostlike only to remove the plates, to refill the glasses, to serve the next course. Irene had changed into another dress and was beautiful to him in the candlelight. D. S. talked loudly from the head of the table, gesturing with his knife.

Don had never been more ill-at-ease. He didn't know which fork, which knife to use, and waited with his eyes cast down, sure that they noticed this waiting, until D. S. or Irene picked up the proper piece of silver. When a servant came near him to offer a dish he started, glanced up in embarrassment: now what do I do? Looked to Irene, D. S.—awkwardly stumbled through getting served.

Dessert.

Coffee in demitasse cups. And later a splashing of brandy in the bottom of huge, tulip-shaped glasses, sipped in the drawing room.

Irene went out of the room for a while and returned. "Don't let D. S. bore you—come on—" She held out her hands to help him up from the divan. "I want to show you the whole ranch."

She took him into several of the rooms in the huge, luxurious house. They came to a final door. "And here is where I sleep."

It was like a Hollywood set.

In the bedroom he tried to kiss her, trying to be manful about it, pulling her close to him with his arms laced tightly about her. It was a silent, competitive wrestling. She forced his face away with the palm of her hand against his forehead while, silently, her red-oiled lips laughed at him.

She drove him home. He was silent in the car and sat turned toward her, his eyes looking at her profile on the long trip back to Chicago. He was uncomfortable in the car. Felt inferior to her and everything she was and had. And thought he was in love.

At last they drove up in front of his apartment building on Dearborn Street.

"Well I got you back, safe and sound," she said. "No bones broken."

He looked at her longingly, forgetting even to be theatrical. "When will I see you again?" It was a soft, pleading voice.

"Oh, I'll call you sometime," she said carelessly.

Smiling, she watched him move toward his apartment building.

"Oh!" She called him back to the car. "I'm giving a small cocktail party Sunday afternoon. At our Chicago apartment. How'd you like to come?"

"Gee! I'd love to!"

She gave him the Lake Shore address.

He got back into the car. "Can I kiss you good night?"

"No, you mayn't!"

"Please."

"No."

Crestfallen, not knowing how to handle the situation, feeling awkward and foolish, he got out of the car.

She smiled over the edge of the door. "And do say hello to Miss Friedman for me."

"I will," he said, angry for the instant. Then he tried to put his hand on top of hers on the door. It wasn't there.

"Good night, Donald." She smiled at him. The car jumped away from the curb.

Don stood looking after it. The little red light in back winked as she slowed at a street crossing.

Jesus! She's beautiful! Jesus! Jesus! was all he could think. What a home! What a life! Jesus!

# XI

Don, dressed in his best and a little nervous, pushed the bell on the top floor of the Lake Shore apartment building. He touched his tie and looked down at the tops of his toes.

The door was suddenly flung open by a maid, and Don, in complete confusion, stepped into the richly appointed apartment.

He knew no one in the crowded room but everyone was friendly to him. Women smiled at him, men nodded and the butler offered a tray filled with cocktail glasses. Don took one and, out of place, wishing he hadn't come, glanced self-consciously around looking for Irene, afraid to find her here in this beautiful apartment with her friends. He wouldn't know what to say to her.

He edged into a corner against the wall, and lowering his eyes in embarrassment, lifted the cocktail glass to his lips.

Then he saw her.

She was seated on the soft, low-cushioned sofa. She was beautiful. Her ankle-length taffeta dress, with its wide black and white horizontal stripes, swirled out into a full skirt from the tight dirndl waist. She was sipping her martini and talking animatedly with one of the young men standing around her, when she saw Don.

"Don!" she called. "Come on over!" She held her hand out to him.

Don walked self-consciously across the room.

She took his hand and rose, handing her glass to one of her admirers to hold or to dispose of for her. She introduced Don to the young men around her. Their eyes cut down across his face curiously, with cool courtesy and detachment, even as their polite voices acknowledged the introductions and their hands gripped his.

"And don't forget, Irene," one of them said, looking at Don, "we're going riding tomorrow."

Irene shrugged her shoulders in a petulant little gesture.

"Ever been riding with Irene, Bob?" he asked.

"She rides much too hard and fast for me," Bob said.

Irene patted Bob's cheek with her hand. "Come along, Don," she said, "there are some other people I want you to meet."

Sweeping her skirt up out of the path of milling people, she wove through the crowd. Taking Don's arm, pressing it warmly, she led him across the wide and crowded room, introduced him to names he would forget as soon as they moved to the next group.

Leading him across the crowded room Irene leaned over and whispered, "Missed you!" She tightened her fingers on his arm again. "Why don't you stay after the others leave?" she asked. She moved across the room, nodding at the smiling faces that bowed to her. "There are a lot of barbarians here," she said, smiling up into Don's eyes.

"What do you mean, barbarians?"

"Society people."

Don grew more frightened.

She hurried him over toward where D. S. stood talking to another man. Immediately Don recognized the man from the many pictures of him he had seen in the paper. D. S. had a water glass of Scotch in his hand and, frowning good-naturedly, said to the man, "Oh now, Oscar! That's a lot of bunk!"

Irene, her arm linked in Don's, pulled the man called Oscar by his ear until his face was even with her lips and kissed him on the cheek. "Hello, dear," she said, and taking his arm, drew him around until he and Don were facing each other. "Mr. O'Brien—Mr. Lockwood."

Don gulped and said something incoherent and shook the outstretched hand. D. S. swished the Scotch in his glass, and grinning, winked at Don.

"Don is running for State Representative," Irene told the President of the City Council. "I want you to help him," she commanded.

The president smiled at Don and wished him luck.

"Come on, Donald," Irene said, drawing him away, "there are other people I want you to meet."

Another man was saying to D. S., laughing in good humor as he said it and they moved away, "Harvard, that's my alma mater. What's yours, you sonofabitch, Senn High School?"

In a corner, withdrawn from everyone else, watching Irene's progress from group to group, was a tall slim handsome young man with curly black hair and a curiously smooth face.

"Hi, darling!" Irene called, and followed by Don, walked over to the young man. She kissed him on the cheek. "Donald, this is Christopher." Don nodded curtly. Christopher responded with a smile. He smelled of eau de cologne, good breeding and wealth.

Leading Don to meet other people, she said, "I'm very fond of Christopher."

"Oh?" Don said jealously.

Suddenly Irene, seeing someone she knew who had just arrived, left him standing in the center of the floor. He glanced around nervously at the guests. He didn't belong here. He didn't dare join any of the groups that were talking so animatedly all around him.

His glass was empty and he went toward the butler for another, to help him over his nervousness. There were many people there. Society people, business people. A couple of professors from the university. Political figures. But most of all they were rich and careless and graceful people. There were also two Negroes present. One was an up-and-coming young artist. The other had begun discussing the Negro problem before the artist, Don and several of the other guests. The young artist tactfully moved away and isolated himself at the other end of the room from his fellow Negro. For the rest of the afternoon they studiously avoided each other.

Carrying two glasses and avoiding all the young men who tried to corner her, Irene sought Don out.

"Look what I brought you!" she said, holding one of the glasses out to him.

"Thanks." His eyes were solemn on her.

He stayed after all the other guests had gone as she had asked him to.

Irene took Don's hand. "I want to show you our roof."

She led him out onto a large flower-decked roof high above the city. Sunset was coming in its many colors of orange, red, lavender.

"Come, sit over here," Irene told Don, indicating the hammock with its gaudily-striped awning. She held it so that he could easily sit down. "Put your feet up," she said. He did so and lay full length on the hammock, looking over its edge into her eyes. She wrinkled her nose at him and drawing a hassock up close, sat near him.

"Like it up here?"

He nodded yes.

"You remind me of someone," she said. Her eyes saddened. "Someday I'll tell you."

She put her hand on the edge of the hammock and swung him back and forth, slowly, smiling in at him. "Comfortable?" "Uh-huh," he nodded. He lay there looking, looking at her. She glanced up over the edge of his shoulder and her mouth opened in small surprise. "Oh look—!" Her finger pointed at the far sky. Don turned on his shoulder and looked too. The whole western sky was ablaze with the sunset. Red and orange in huge extravagances were bold and unbelievably beautiful strokes across Chicago's western wall. In front of the backdrop of sunset the water towers and smokestacks of the city's slums strode in giantlike structure.

Don looked out across the city. He saw the slums down there. He saw the water towers, crude-legged on the tops of factory buildings, the smoke-smeared stacks of factories, the mile on mile of tenement houses down below this lush apartment building. He saw his own mother's crumbling tenement building. The rusted front. The dirty rooms.

He compared Irene's life to his own. He saw his mother. He saw her dragging in, dead-tired from work at night. He saw his sisters. He felt the pain of sympathy. He felt love for them.

For a moment Don put the palm of his hand over his eyes. He was ashamed, in that moment, of being here in this hammock with this rich girl and felt guilt.

"Isn't it beautiful!" she said.

"Yeah," he said.

# XII

The feeling of guilt did not easily leave him. From the cocktail party he went to his mother's house.

His kid brother Kazio sat on the steps in front. Kazio was telling a young girl, "Hold your tongue and say, 'I found gold in my back yard.' "

Don grinned. "Hey! Cut that out!" he yelled at his brother. And went up the steps into his mother's house.

"Hi, Ma."

"You do not forget us. You do come to see us," his mother said. She came and stood beside him and he let her kiss him on the cheek.

Don drew ten dollars from his billfold. He put the money on the table embarrassedly because it was something he had seldom done before. "There's something for you, Ma."

His mother picked the money up in her thin, hard-worked hands and looked at her son. "I knew you would help your mother once you made your way. Like Grandpa, I always believed in my son."

Helen came from the bedroom. "Well," she said, "I thought I heard you out here! How are you, Don? Long time no see." She moved to him and put her hands on his shoulders. "Let me look at you." Don grinned. Helen looked him up and down, at his new suit, his polished shoes. She nodded approval. She took his hand to look at his diamond ring and whistled her approval.

"How are you, Helen?" Don asked.

Helen shrugged. "All I know," she said, "is *smiało,* be of good cheer."

But once home, once in the familiarity of the house, his sense of guilt left him. Home with his family he was full of himself. "I just came from a cocktail party," he said. "The President of the City Council was there. He shook hands with me. All the people there were rich. You should have seen how the women were dressed!"

Helen poked out her lips and nodded. Ma Kosinski smiled proudly and said, "Grandpa always said you would be a great man some day."

Don laughed with pleasure. "When I'm elected," he said, "I'm going to take care of you, Ma."

"Grandpa and I always said you would make good," Ma said.

Julka, the baby, toddled over to Don and held on to the columns of his legs. Laughing, Don lifted her up and tossed her above his head, held her there. "And Julka, you're going to have all the candy you want." He set the baby down. "And Helen, I'm going to put you in business or get you a job at the city hall."

"Save your money, kid," Helen said. She took her dried slip from the line and went back into the bedroom.

"And Ma," Don said, "I'm going to see that you and the kids get a good place to live. And you, Eva," he said, "I'm going to buy you a black silk dress. How would you like that?"

"She runs out late at night," Ma said.

"I'll take a dollar now," Eva said.

Don laughed and gave her the dollar.

"She stays out late with boys," Ma said. "You must talk to her. You should be the head of the house now. You should move back home."

"Aw, Ma!" Irritated.

"Where's Alina?" Don asked.

"At church," Eva said, laughing contemptuously.

Ma fingered the ten-dollar bill. "I am going down to get my son some beer," she said. She slipped into her coat. "Is my boy hungry? Would you like to eat?" Don shook his head no.

He went to the bedroom door and knocked. "Come in," Helen said. He opened and closed the door. Helen stood before the mirror in her slip and was arching the black eyebrows high on her forehead.

"Gee! There was a lot of rich people there! I was invited by a rich girl. It was at her house. I go around with her."

Helen laughed and poked him in the side with her elbow. "I always say nobody's going to hold against you what you can get for free," she said.

"That's for sure," Don said.

Don frowned a little. "Is Ma sore because I don't come over often?"

Helen turned from the mirror. She put the hand holding the eyebrow pencil up on Don's shoulder and looked her brother squarely in the eye. "We don't mean you no good. We can't do nothing for you. You live your own life," she said.

# XIII

This was big business. This was the party machine. This was a smooth-running corporation.

The Power called in all the bookmakers of his district. It wasn't done in the open. They met at his downtown insurance office and sat around nervously. Frowning, chain-smoking, looking at their watches in McCarren's inner office.

"Wonder what the little czar's up to?" one voice said.

Shoulders shrugged in answer and the waiting to find out went on.

They had the look of gamblers and were flashily dressed, wore diamonds, had loud ties and loud, matching handkerchiefs that sprouted out of their breast pockets. Their nails were polished, their cigars clenched in the corners of their mouths. The short ones had built-up heels, the fat ones had had facials. There was the mingling scent of talcum, cologne and tobacco smoke. No shirt was cheaper than twenty dollars. They all looked like real sharp characters. They were bookmakers but they all had homes in the suburbs. They all had big cars. They were always complaining that business is bad, the reason being that somebody might ask them for something.

McCarren came in smiling. "Hi, fellows!" He waved a big hand. He spoke to them all by their first names. Don followed McCarren into the room.

McCarren brought glasses and a good bottle of Scotch from the wall cabinet. Looking around from man to man he filled the correct number of glasses.

"What's the dope, Tom?" one of the bookies asked impatiently.

The Power glanced up and smiled but said nothing. He handed the glasses around. Holding his as in a salute he nodded to the men to drink; he drank and they all drank. The diamond rings and the other-stoned rings lifted glasses, lifted cigarettes and cigars to mouths. The bookies gathered around the desk in a half-circle. The Power smiled at them again in grim amusement. The Power gestured to Don with an open palm. "Now, here's my new man—here's my collector."

The eyes glanced across at Don. The heads nodded.

They had barely left the office when The Power had another caller whom both Don and McCarren could hear greeting the bookies in the outer office:

"Hello, Jerry!"

"What do you say, Tony?"

The caller knocked and entered at The Power's loud "Come in!"

THE POWER had his back turned to the man and was getting still another glass from the cabinet. "Hello, Jim," THE POWER said with his back turned.

"You wanted to see me," the man said.

"That's right, Jim," THE POWER said; and turning around, "Jim, this is Don Lockwood—Don, this is Police Captain Jim Gowan."

They shook hands.

"In case anything comes up," THE POWER said, indicating Don, "this is my man."

They had their drink. And another.

"He'll drop in to see you—day or so," THE POWER said. He swung around to the police captain. "By the way, some very nice fellows are running the Blinking Owl. Good friends of mine." He paused. "So—" he shrugged, "they prostitute out of the joint. So—" THE POWER shrugged again, "a few fairies cruise in there. So—" another shrug, "there's a little marijuana around the place. Welllll—after all—" Another shrug. "It's North Clark Street." THE POWER smiled. And THE POWER added, "The place will go along with you and the organization one hundred per cent."

"Okay, Tom," the police captain said.

As instructed, Don dropped around to the police station to see Captain Gowan. The police captain had his right-hand man too so that he also could keep his nose clean. The police captain's right-hand man took THE POWER's right-hand man around to the bookie joint.

It was a huge room behind a stage-setting cigar store. There was a double door entrance with a watchman at each door so that, in case of a raid from downtown, the first guard would be arrested while the second watchman rang the buzzer and the place was cleared of equipment and bettors.

The bookie joint was huge, with boards attached to the wall showing the tracks, races, horses and odds. To the wall was also attached a loud-speaker that, in a rasping frenzied voice, kept everyone posted on the outcome of the races. The room was so full of smoke that Don couldn't see very well but, with the captain's man, edged his way through the crowd. At the far end of the room was a long counter with three men sitting on stools writing tickets for the races. One man wore a shirt with the sleeves rolled up. Another wore a polo shirt and had a pencil sticking behind his ear and one in his hand. There was a cigarette with a long ash stuck in his mouth. The third man was schemingly friendly. He laughed and joked with all his customers and got very chummy with everybody, thinking that if they win they'll come back and give him a five-spot or a sawbuck. Next to this bench was the pay-off cashier where the winners collected. It was to this window that the captain's man led Don.

The captain's man said to the cashier, "This is the ward committeeman's man."

An envelope containing money was shoved across the counter to Don. One was shoved out to the police captain's man too.

On the first and second day of the month the bookmakers hung around their spots to pay off. They were too important and busy to hang around at other times.

Don did the collecting. And in case he saw that a joint was doing good business, he picked up a little payroll job for one of his precinct captains—especially Buckley and Ryan, who had sucked in good with him. Don got the petty cash payroll jobs for his men. The bookmakers couldn't say no to him. He was THE POWER's right-hand man.

And Don learned that insurance was a big thing too. All the big firms and corporations turned their insurance over to the County Central Committee. The committee turned it over to whomever it wished.

From the downtown license bureau, when tavern licenses were due for renewal, a list was sent to the police captains to see if they should okay the license or not. In turn the police captains sent it to the ward committeeman for approval.

"Show it to Don," THE POWER told the police captain. "I don't handle that." THE POWER smiled and fingered the bridge of his nose.

The list was sent to Don. Don checked off those who didn't have McCarren's Safety Insurance. Then he called in the precinct captains and, seated at McCarren's desk, leaning back in McCarren's chair, Don said, "O'Brien, you've got three taverns in your precinct." Don bit off the tip of a cigar and lit it. "This fellow hasn't got our insurance." He tapped the name with a red pencil. "Go see him and tell him we've got very good insurance and unless he gets it I don't think his license is going to be okay.

"Schuman, in your precinct there's two taverns without our insurance—"

THE POWER said, "Every year the organization puts on some half-assed fights. But there's big revenue in it, boy! The precinct captains go out soliciting ads for the ad book. Those program books bring in thirty-five and forty thousand dollars and those ads don't bring them ten cents' worth of business in return." THE POWER laughed tonelessly. "But," THE POWER said, "main thing is I want the precinct captains to report to you—and the ward superintendent and his five foremen. This is where they get part of the money used for Election Day to buy votes. Those five—" he smiled, "are the main go-getters. They put a little pressure on the tavern owners and they're glad to give them an ad. Well—" THE POWER stood up. "I'm going to run along. Going out to the track. Just wanted to tell you they'll report to you."

"Say, Tom—" Don said, "a guy came in—name's Williams—wants to start a policy wheel."

"Work him over," THE POWER said, laughing as he went out the door. "We aren't going to let him operate for peanuts."

The precinct captains and the ward superintendent and his five foremen went out to collect for the ad book. They collected from the same taverns that had their insurance. And they also collected from grocery stores, butcher shops, restaurants, poolrooms. Those proprietors didn't know when they'd need a favor, had to stay in good with the party. The small taverns were charged ten to twenty dollars for an ad. The strip-tease joints and the B-girl taverns—the shady places—had to take a hundred-dollar ad. The ad book was a must.

"Can't I take a ten-dollar ad instead of fifty dollars this time?"

"Well, after all, if you get in trouble we'll take care of it."

"Well, I've been here five years and I've given you my insurance business. I'm in a legitimate business. I've never asked for anything. I've never had any trouble."

The shakedown came:

"Yeah, but the organization has pretty nice people at the head of it. They don't want you to get hurt"—meaning, come across or you might get hurt.

A legitimate businessman wasn't worth much to the police or the political setup. The police and the politicians were there to sell the privilege of violating. Law had deteriorated to nothing more than fix. It had almost become an American tradition.

Don made the collections for McCarren. McCarren left him up in his office and Don accepted all the phone calls from the precinct captains and the people of the district. McCarren used him as a runner. Used him as a flunky too. And in his running, in his collecting for THE POWER, Don picked up twenty-five dollars, fifty dollars, here and there for himself.

McCarren invited a couple of the other powers down to go to lunch with Don at Henrici's on Randolph Street. He was schooling Don. Schooling him to be a right-hand man. And Don was grasping it all, all the machinery behind the politics.

Don was learning more, much more than McCarren realized.

Don mingled with the people of the district at the parties that were still being given. He now had the professional capacity to appear to be everybody's friend and seemed to serve the voters while serving himself.

The Poles wanted to know what he would do when he got in office: The Jews won't get more than we do, will they?

He spoke then fluently in Polish, saying he had a great fondness for the great Polish people, and assured them that they would be taken care of first and most.

The Negroes wanted to know what he was going to do for their people; the more intelligent ones, what his stand was on covenants, on equal rights and the FEPC.

Labor had its questions. The vets had theirs and he gave his answer as one of them.

He gave all the right answers.

All the time Don was becoming a bigger and bigger man.

But there were moments when he was alone with himself, with his conscience . . . well, he'd go along . . . when he got in office things would be different. He'd see that a lot of this graft was done away with, that the poor people got good government. He had to play along with them—until he was in office. . . . I got a terrific break—one in a million. This *great* man, this *great* man McCarren, had picked him up. I've been cheated all my life. I'm not going to be cheated again. It's kind of an easy and a swell game I got into. It's easy to do when you believe in something. When I'm in office . . .

He had had a little taste of the money, the power. He liked that money. He liked the power.

# XIV

He went looking for Sue. He hadn't seen her in over a month and wondered how she would receive him. Climbing up the steps to her room he could hear the phonograph playing a worker's song, but he couldn't remember the name of it though they had often listened to it together along with other records the turntable had offered. Walking to the door he heard a man's voice saying, "Well, that's about it."

Don stiffened. Who did she have in there? With jealousy he moved quietly to the door and put his hand on the knob. He threw the door open. He stopped in the doorway, startled. Inside the room he recognized a lot of old acquaintances.

Jim Norris was there. Sean O'Keefe. Milo. Aaron Levin's father. Dave. And another Negro, a slim, elderly, dark-skinned man. A couple of college-looking young people, one a Japanese; and a good-looking woman in her late twenties or early thirties. They were in various positions on the floor, bed, and at a card table. They were all folding some sort of literature. It was Jim Norris who had said, "Well, that's about it." Then everybody looked toward the opened door.

Don stood there, embarrassed and feeling foolish. "The old crowd from Haines," he said, for something to say. He laughed. It was an embarrassed, nervous laugh. "Oh, I guess I'm not wanted here," he said. He laughed again.

Jim looked at Don strangely. "We were just getting ready to go."

Sue was at the stove, reaching above it for coffee cups. She too had turned at the sound of the door opening. "You're not going," she said, "not until we all have coffee. Hello, Don. Come on in."

He came across the doorsill. Dave was looking at him. "Hello, Dave," he said to the Negro in true friendliness.

"Sit down, Don," Sue said, "I'll introduce you in a minute."

Don sat on the edge of the bed. Sue brought the cups and set them, piled together, on the cocktail table. She introduced Don to the people he didn't know. "And this is Jane Morris."

Don stood up and bowed. Jane Morris held out her hand. "Hello, Don." She smiled and her cheeks dimpled.

"I guess we're running against each other," Don said.

"I guess we are." She smiled again. "Here, let me take your hat and cane." Don handed her the hat and cane and continued to stare at her. Then he sat again, stupidly, on the side of the bed. He picked up one of the leaflets. "Care if I look?"

"Of course not."

He unfolded it. Her picture peered smilingly out at him:

VOTE FOR JANE

*War Widow and Mother of Three Children*

JANE MORRIS STANDS FOR—

Moratorium on Evictions
Schools Free From Machine Politics
End of Discrimination in Housing
Fair Employment Practices
Safeguarding the Peace
Keeping Rent Ceilings
Checking Runaway Prices
Building Low-Cost Homes

Don looked across at Jane Morris. "I'm for the same things," he said.

"Well, that's good," she said.

Sue brought the sugar and creamer and began pouring the coffee. Don balanced his on his knee and looked around the room uncomfortably. "I feel like a spy." He laughed self-consciously.

Sue looked at Don and at the others. She was rather amused and enjoyed his discomfort. Milo looked from one to the other with a writer's curiosity.

When her coffee was finished Jane set her cup on the floor beside the sofa. She smiled at Don as she twisted her shoes off. "My feet are killing me—I've walked up and down so many steps in the last couple of months. Got a headache tonight, too." She stretched out on the sofa, putting her head in the gray-haired Negro's lap. "How are your feet holding out?" she asked Don. The Negro began stroking the headache away with the palm of a gentle hand. Don glanced at her and away, then back with his lie: "Not so good. I know what you mean about going to see voters."

"Well," Dave said, having stacked the dishes despite Sue's protests, "I guess we better go."

"Yeah," Jim said. "I have my car and can drop some of you off."

They all began getting into their coats and hats and piling their Jane Morris literature under their arms.

Don stood self-consciously. He smiled and shook hands with all of them. "So long, Dave; Good-by, Milo; See'ya, O'Keefe" and, "Good-by, Mr. Levin," thinking of Rebecca.

Jane Morris was charming, saying good-by, holding his hand in friendliness. "Well, best of luck," he told her cockily.

"You the same," she said, her face dimpling.

And the door closing. And their steps going in a little parade to the sidewalk below.

Don turned to Sue. He was upset. "Those people are my friends," he said. And, looking at her desperately, "Do they know about you and me?"

"I don't know," Sue said wearily, and went to the phonograph to turn off the record that had been playing over and over.

"I hope not," Don said.

"Well, you did walk in without knocking."

"I'm sorry," he said, coming over and sitting next to her.

"Oh, it doesn't matter," she said. She put her head down on his shoulder. "I love you, Don. Whatever you are—"

"What do you mean—whatever I am?"

"Whatever happens to you, whatever you do with your life—"

And the guilt speaking silently to him: Sue, I'm taking graft. I'm getting corrupt.

"Whatever, I'll always care for you as I care for you now," Sue said.

# XV

After Jim had left Sue's house and dropped some of the others off he drove around a while and parked in front of a tavern. He walked into the bar. He couldn't have said why. But when he was sitting at the bar he knew that it was because he wanted to look at women.

"Bottle of beer," he said, and while the bartender got it he glanced secretly down the length of the tavern. He had made a bad choice. There was only one other customer there at the near-closing hour, a broad-shouldered fellow in his late twenties who sat at the far end of the bar.

Jim sat twisting his glass and, looking down into it, thought of the women he had known in Europe. The large hand of the clock over his head began dropping away from two-fifteen. The bartender, with but two lone customers, sat lazily picking his teeth with his fingers. Jim, his head down, continued to twist his glass. The other young man automatically lifted his shot glass and tossed the liquor into his mouth.

When the two girls, wearing sports suits and hats set jauntily on the sides of their heads, came in the young man at the other end of the bar immediately gave them the eye, then let his glance drop again to the shot glass in front of him and the rings encircling rings on the glossed mahogany that told of repeated hoistings of the glass to the thick, pale lips behind which his buckteeth met irregularly.

Jim lowered his eyes and, without turning his head, glanced at the girls' legs.

The girls, chattering, sat at the middle of the bar. They ordered drinks. While the bartender mixed them Jim slowly twisted on his stool so that he could, without being obvious, look in their direction. Then, while the bartender set the drinks in front of the girls, Jim's eyes went searching them out, followed their legs up the stool along the line of their hips and up to their breasts.

The young man at the other end of the bar lifted his khaki sleeve from which a stripe had been removed, leaving a faded and inverted V, and signaled to the bartender with his finger. He pushed the glass forward for refilling. His eyes glanced sideways at the girls and then moved in a line to the eyes of the bartender. "Ask the young lady and her sister if they'll have a drink."

The girls looked first at him, then at each other and shrugged. They looked again at the young man. One of them smiled. "Thank you," she said.

Sliding along the bar with his glass in his hand, the young man came and sat on the stool next to the girls. "Ain't you girls starting awful late?" There was a slight foreign sound to his words, as if he were second-generation American.

"We're just getting in," one of them said.

"Same here," he said, twisting on the stool till he faced them. "Only I'm not getting in till after midnight tomorrow. I'm a auto racer. Midget autos." From his billfold in the back pocket of the wrinkled olive drabs he produced a photograph of himself smiling at the steering wheel of a racing car that looked too small for him. He shoved it under their chins. "I'm racing tomorrow. At Soldier's Field."

"We believe you, honey," one of the girls said.

With a finger he brought the bartender. With a finger and silently, he pointed from the bottle to his glass. And as an afterthought, turning again to the girls, "My name's Bill."

"Our names are Hilda and Rose," they said.

"Ever see a race?"

"No."

The finger signaled the barkeeper. "The girls too," he said.

"If you've got to race today—it's today now," said the girl named Hilda, nodding toward the glass beading at the top with a silver chain as the bartender poured, "why don't you take it easy?"

"Don't give me a rough time, sister," the young man said gruffly.

"You were in service, weren't you?" the girl named Rose asked, noticing the faded and inverted V where the stripe had been, as he raised the shot to his mouth, his lips spreading out flat to receive it.

"Yeah." He grinned boyishly, his broad shoulders slightly hunched. "How'd you like to go to the races with me tonight?"

"Oh sure! First I'll have to ask my mother."

"What outfit were you with, soldier?" Hilda asked.

His lips flattened out for speaking. "I was with Patton," he said. He looked at both of them, straight in the face, and pulled his shoulders back. Spoke with a hard tone of conviction. "You know what kept me awake? Patton, that's what. You know what kept me alive? Patton, that's what. You goddamn right!" He wiped his lips with the back of his sleeve and screwed around, in his enthusiasm, on the seat of the stool. His arms waved in gestures. "You know what Patton said when we crossed the Rhine? You know what Patton said?—'There's only one thing coming back—ambulances, that's all.' You goddamn right!" He smacked the huge palm of his hand against his knee. "And that's all that did come back." His finger pointed at the bartender, the whisky bottle, his glass.

Jim listened. And he could look all he wanted to now. The girls were turned toward the young man. The bartender was bent over the comics. Jim let his eyes rove over the girls' figures, let his eyes concentrate on their legs and on the top of the stool. The little one wasn't bad. Nice legs . . . the way she sat on her stool. Uhhhhh!

"Hey, barkeep! The girls' glasses are empty!" Bill called, waving down something Hilda had said with an irritated motion of his hand. He turned back to the girls, putting the soles of his big feet down squarely on the floor and dashing the hair off his forehead with a rough hand. "I want to go back. There are too many Germans left."

"Oh look, honey," Hilda said, coloring a little, "all the German people aren't bad. It wasn't the fault of all the German people."

The young man made a disgusted sound, an imaginary spitting at the far wall. Then, leaning toward them, he became very confidential. "You know what? I'd like to be there right now. I don't want to be here." Lighting a cigarette he let it hang loosely from his mouth, the smoke curling up past his dull gray eyes as he talked. "You know why I want to be over there? Because this war isn't over yet. Because there are Germans living. You goddamn right!"

Jim's secret glance traveled to the girls' faces. They were both attractive to him. He would like to be with either of them. How can I get in the conversation?

But he didn't know what to say. Instead he ordered another beer. Bill was saying, "Patton had the right idea. If it had been up to Patton there wouldn't be a stick, a stone or a blade of grass or even an ant crawling around and that's why I'd like to be over there."

Hilda placed her hand on his forearm. "Now, honey, you can't be cynical like that."

"Cynical! Who's cynical?" He shook her hand off his arm. "I'm not cynical. You goddamn right!"

"Well now, look," Rose said. "You've done half of the war and the other half is up to you too—unions, petitions and things like—"

"Ahk!" the young man said in a spitting shout. "Unions!"

"The unions help people," Rose said.

"I got a friend," the young man said, "and his father was killed by those union racketeers. My friend's bucking the union right now."

Jim heard the anti-union words but his mind was dulled and he continued to stare at the girls' legs and hips with his hand hiding the roving of his eyes from the bartender.

Bill was saying, "He's going to kill them fellows that killed his father and I'm going to help him. He's looking for them right now. You goddamn right!"

His voice brought the bartender from his stool at the front windowpane.

"Well now look, now look," Hilda said in good humor, "let's calm down. Let's get this straight. I know you're a good guy and you've got a fine heart. I know you're a good person." She reached over and patted his knee. "But, honey," she said, moving her finger back and forth close under his eyes, "you can't go on feeling like that." She smiled. "Now let me ask you a question. How does it feel to be sitting right here at this bar? Doesn't that make you feel good?"

The young man made a spitting sound. "Aw, nuts!" he said. "Stop giving me a rough time. Sharpen up, girl, sharpen up!" And as a stamp of approval on his own thoughts: "You goddamn right!"

"Three o'clock," the bartender said. "Time to close up." He began turning the lights down.

Jim got off the stool and went out of the tavern.

Going out the door he said to himself: Damn it! Why didn't I think fast enough? When he started talking about unions. I could have got in the conversation then.

He started the motor of his car, then turned it off and sat waiting. The girls came out. Bill was with them and they appeared to be having a hard time getting rid of him, but finally they turned away and went off down the street while he went the other way.

Jim started the motor and drove slowly, watching the girls as they walked. Then, driving fast, he turned four corners in a square so as to be approaching them. There they were! He drove slower, looking out at them. Damn it, why did there have to be two of them? If there was only one maybe he could have picked her up. And now, already, his car was down the street past them and they, their legs and bodies, were only pleasant memories. He squinted into the backview mirror but they were lost in the darkness of the street behind him.

He drove on toward home through the 3 A.M. streets. He turned onto Clark and at Lake Street was stopped by the traffic light. On the curb, alone, stood a girl waiting for a streetcar. He glanced out the open window at her. She smiled back at him. He held her eyes.

"Hello," she said. It was a throaty, sexy hello.

"Want a lift?" he asked.

She was already off the curb and walking toward his car. He opened the door and she looked in at his handsome face.

In the car she deliberately leaned against his shoulder. "You're out late," she said. She smelled of cheap perfume. It oozed from under the armpits of her dress, the lobes of her ears, the bosom of her dress. She wore a gardenia in her hair.

"You're out late too," he said, and heard his voice tremble, felt his knee shake a little. He almost missed the stop light for his eyes were glancing down at her knees.

"Cigarette?" she asked.

He nodded.

She lit one and lifted it to his lips, held her fingers against his lips as he secured the cigarette and inhaled.

She nestled a little closer to him. "Wouldn't you like to have a drink somewhere?"

"Do you know a place that's open?" Again his voice quivered a little.

She directed him to an after-hours spot. They drank there for an hour. Then Jim said, "Let's go."

It was as if it had been arranged by words. He drove her to a neighborhood where Negro and white districts met at a streetcar line and frowned across the car tracks at each other. Facing the car track was a dingy little hotel with a face-lifted front and a neon HOTEL sign.

He helped her out of the car. They signed as Mr. and Mrs. and went to the room. It was like Europe and the war.

When she was dressing she asked, "Do you want to see me again?"

"I'm married."

She shrugged. "Want to see me again?"

Jim nodded.

She wrote her first name and a telephone number.

They left the hotel. She told him to drop her over on North Clark. He did. Then he tore up the slip of paper with her phone number on it.

Driving home he felt no guilt. He felt free instead. He began to whistle. But the whistling stopped. Louise would want to know where he was so long. He began to think of something to tell her.

. . . and the days following.

Jim looked out the window of the union office and chewed on the end of his pencil. He wished that he again went into the plant to repair machines. He had known so many of the girls there. They had kidded with him and flirted with him. A lot of the flirting had been serious. At the time he had known that he could have had many of them. And didn't want any of them. He had been able to talk union to and gain the confidence of most of the women and girls simply because he was good-looking. Conscious of this, he had been ashamed of his looks. Now—

Jim dropped his pencil down on the desk top and stared out the window.

He sat watching the passing women. In Jim the fever grew.

He made an excuse, that night, to get out of the house. He went into a tavern. Sat watching a girl who had picked up a fellow at the bar. It was strictly a commercial deal. The girl was getting as many drinks out of the man as she could. But it excited him, watching them. He hoped they wouldn't leave.

Jim sat in the tavern booth drinking too much. The women and their bodies floated across the back of the other booth in erotic fantasy. He fastened the soles of his shoes against the floor and cramped his toes down tight. There was an overpowering fascination in the thoughts of women. His strict and religious mother. Southern Baptist. The moral background. The religious upbringing. His mother making a sin of sex. The first experiments with his own body, the days of masturbation. The feeling of guilt and the washing of himself afterwards. But once the dam had been broken . . .

The first girl. The other girls. Those that he wanted. For he had always been handsome. And a high school football hero. Marriage. Love and loyalty for his wife. Through those years before the war. Then—the war and the final letting down of all moral standards. The war that left to each man only his basic instincts. The war that made self-survival and sex the only animal desires of the moment. So tonight let's drink and have sex for tomorrow you may die. There wasn't much more to our lives over there. It was all of pleasure we had. And now it was almost as if the moral, the allowed, the licensed, was the less attractive . . .

He knew where he could go. He had heard about it for years. The girls were attractive and you had your pick.

He picked one. He paid for her.

When the desire had been loosened there was no joy in him. It had been like buying something at the grocery store.

# XVI

Another day and another and another . . .

On the bench in a corner a patient picking at his scalp, picking, tearing away tiny bits of flesh, pulling away a hair, two hairs, three. His head a mass of scabbed or half-healed and bloody little spots. . . . Here a young boy sitting with his face in his hands, muttering over and over, "Planes and bombs, bombs and planes . . ." Here a trembling young man saying, "I can't stop shaking."

With the others Aaron sat. Have they forgotten me? How will I ever get out?

Ned came up to the attendant, Stan, and stroked his arm. Stroking his arm and looking up into his face Ned sang, as always, his favorite number "My Silent Love." He didn't know all the words and made up words as he went along, any that would fit. He sang with all the gestures of the movie hero who was making love to his lady fair. His eyes were half-closed and his arms were spread out from his body: "Darling, I love you" or anything to make the song.

"Yeah, yeah, Ned," Stan said and walked away.

Aaron pressed his hot forehead against the cold pane of glass behind the bars. All I want to do is forget everything.

The attendant, the little tough one, was saying, "Sweep the floor, Ned, and stop making so damn much noise."

"Aw shut up, you sonofabitch," Ned said. "You can't tell me what to do. I'm tough."

Rolling his eyes away from the scene Aaron looked down into the graveyard.

"I'm tough. I'm rugged," Ned said.

And the attendant, looking at him: "What did you say?"

And Aaron, looking down into the graveyard.

And Ned, to the attendant, raising his arms protectively around his face, "Don't hit me! Don't hit me!" Ned, lying in the corner, "Don't pick on me. Don't hit me again!"

And Aaron to the graveyard, "All I want to do is to forget everything."

Major Goodman, psychiatrist, entered the ward.

Major Goodman walked to Ned and touched him on the arm. "It's all right, Ned. Get up. Nobody's going to hurt you."

Ned rose. "Doctor," he said, "when are you going to let me go home? I'm all right. There's nothing wrong with me."

Laughing Boy came up to the doctor and said loudly, "You should get a program so that you can tell the patients from the attendants." He nudged Dr. Goodman in the side with his elbow and chuckled.

"Hello, Gus," Doctor Goodman said, smiling. Aaron looked at the doctor gravely from the other end of the room. Mother Malloy cradling the invisible baby in his arms, cradling it back and forth, walked up to Dr. Goodman and looking up into his face with sad eyes asked, "How could they have taken a mother?" Then he walked away, softly singing a lullaby to the invisible child in his arms.

An elderly man said, "Come here, Doctor. I have something to show you." He dropped his pants.

"Well, what is it?" the doctor asked.

"See that there?"
The doctor saw nothing but the human body. "I don't see anything."
"That's what's wrong with me."
"Oh," Doctor Goodman said. He walked away with no other comment.
They grouped around him. Each with a few pitiful words to say. It was as if they were all children playing games or adults playing charades. He was part of the game even while he tried to help them. He, too, was drawn into the web of reality and fancy.
Dr. Goodman looked along the rows of immobile patients in their postures against the wall. He glanced at the man who, with his fingers, had torn one of his eyes from its socket in the act of castration that was not at all uncommon among the insane.
A patient came up to Doctor Goodman. "I signed myself in," he said, "because I was beginning to feel bad, Doctor. I was getting headaches. And now they won't let me out. There's nothing wrong with me any more. Will you speak to them, Doctor?"
From the table came a man with a sheet of paper. He offered it to the doctor. There was a music staff and some notes on it. "This is for you, Doctor. I was a musician before I came here. I'm not going to be here long." He had soft white hands and slick black hair. Major Goodman took the sheet of paper. And knew the patient would be there forever. He was a sex maniac and had raped three little girls before he had been caught.
Aaron glanced at the doctor and then came forward and stood in front of him with his head down. Slowly he lifted his head and his sad, wistful eyes looked into Dr. Goodman's eyes with the look of a small, completely defeated, completely lost child. "Doctor—" he said; and his eyes dropped, his limp black hair fell over his forehead. "I—I—" he said, "maybe they forgot about me but I don't have a doctor."
Major Goodman looked at him sharply.
"You haven't a doctor?" He still looked at Aaron, trying to sift reality from fancy.
Aaron looked up. "No, sir."
"What is your name?"
"Aaron Levin."
The doctor wrote the name on an envelope.
The door unlocked, and locked again.
Major Goodman walked down the long corridor.

# XVII

Just before the primaries, the newspapers—the Republican *Chicago Tribune* and the *Herald-American*—began blasting Don. Articles appeared stating that Don was just the front for a corrupt organization. That he was a Charlie McCarthy for "smooth, sophisticated, tyrannical Tom McCarren, the little czar of the North Side." A cartoon was run showing Don and George Reed, the other organization candidate, sitting dwarfed on the knee of a leering and diabolical-looking McCarren.

James Schmidt, the Independent Democrat, was spoken of with faint praise. Was written up as a reputable businessman having no connection with the organization. Schmidt was an upright citizen, a capable man: the Republican papers were supporting him. Supporting Schmidt as well as the Republican candidate for State Representative—in the interest of good, honest organization—free government, the paper stated sanctimoniously.

Meanwhile the Republican precinct captains and the Democratic precinct captains of the district had their own little deal cooking. Three votes were allowed for State Representatives—three men would go to Springfield. The Republican candidate was alone on the ticket and had no opposition; the Republicans couldn't swing three State Representatives from the district and so were running only one strong man. One vote elected him. The Republicans could swing over to the Democrats. The Republican precinct captains made a deal to swing twenty-five of their votes from each precinct over to Don and his running mate George Reed, and in this way insured defeat of the Independent Democrat. THE POWER suggested it and financed it. The Republican precinct captains were not averse to a little extra loot.

The people went to the polls. The newspapers had done their damage to McCarren. The vote was so small between THE POWER's two candidates and Schmidt that they would all have to go again in the big election in the fall.

But Don had won the primary. He and Reed, THE POWER's men. Even if they did have to run against Schmidt and Jane Morris again in November.

Don swaggered more than he ever had before in his life.

Come November—

"Senator," he called himself secretly.

"Mr. State Representative," he said to himself in the privacy of his room.

# XVIII

Rebecca had tried to stay away from him. He hadn't seen her for three weeks. He felt relieved. It took the pressure off him, the fear of people finding out she was Jewish and he was going with her. He frowned a little as guilt came to the surface of his mind. Not that he cared that she was Jewish. Hell, everybody was just the same. And she was a nice kid, only . . . And guilt flooded in again, around his thoughts. . . . You're being a bastard again. You know you're a heel. But I can't take a chance like that, being seen with her and spoiling my chances of getting elected. You bastard you! No. No, I'm not.

He walked under the marquee of the Allerton Hotel and went up to the Tip-Top-Tap, walking importantly on his cane.

"Don!" a girl called. He looked across the room at Irene. She beckoned to him. "Don!" She held out both hands to him as he reached the table. "Sit down, Don. Do sit down!"

He sat down.

"You remember Christopher, don't you?"

Christopher said, "Hi," and nodded coolly; asked, "What'll you have?"

"Nothing for me, thanks. I can't stay long," Don said. "I'm on—ah—business."

"Well, run along when you have to," Irene said with sudden indifference. She turned back to Christopher, who was complimenting her on her horseback riding. "Oh," she said, laughing, "Daddy set me on a horse when I was three years old. He used to take me on long hikes. He taught me how to hit a baseball and kick a football." She laughed again. "I guess D. S. thought he almost had a boy. We did everything together."

The next time Don saw her was on Michigan Boulevard. A horn honked and her voice was shouting "Don!" and he saw her in a gray Lincoln Continental convertible. She had stopped the car and was waiting for him. He got down off the curb and went to her.

Traffic was tied up behind her and horns began to honk. It didn't bother her. "I'm going shopping at Field's," she said. "Why don't you take the car and meet me with it?" She hopped out and looked at her wrist watch. "Meet me in two hours at—well, let's say five-thirty. I'll be on the library steps by the I.C."

The horns continued to honk. Don got in behind the wheel. "I'll walk across to Field's," Irene said, and waving her gloved hand, strode away from him.

Outside the Loop, Don stopped the car. Even though it was a chilly day he put the top down so people could see him; he lifted the collar of his coat on one side and tilted his Homburg over one ear. He drove back through the Loop, slowly, down State Street, down Michigan Boulevard. Then he drove slowly all around the Near North Side, out along the drive. Then he wheeled the car over to his mother's house.

Kazio, whistling astonishment, came running boyishly from the steps, all his bored and rough hoodlum swagger gone. "Whew! Is it yours?"

"Naw. It belongs to my girl."

"Whew!—Hey!" Kazio tilted his man's hat further back on his head. "Take me for a ride!"

Don laughed. Kids from along the street and Don's younger brothers and sisters came straggling up to look at the swell car.

"Take us for a ride! Take us for a ride!" One of them had slipped in behind the wheel and was honking the horn. They were climbing all over the car.

"Hey! Cut that out!"

Don piled them all in and, grinning, took them for a short ride.

Parking in front of his house he saw his mother coming from work. "Hey, Ma! Want to go for a ride?"

He took her shopping and waited proudly outside. He could see his mother gesturing toward him and the car, and the grocer nodding his head up and down looking out the window at him.

When they got back home Alina had a little box camera in her hand and wanted to take pictures. He posed smiling alongside the car with his arm around his mother, and with his kid brothers and sisters standing by the fender.

Alina took a whole roll of film. Kazio said, "Hey, let we wash the car!"

"No, I've got to go."

Don drove off. And suddenly he became fearful. He shouldn't have let them take pictures! He shouldn't have posed with them! Nobody knew who his family was.

He drove back. "Hey, where's that film?"

Alina gave it to him. "I'll get it developed," he said, and felt relief when it was in his pocket. "Hey, Ma," he told her, "I want to talk to you alone."

In Helen's room with the door closed he said, as he had before when he took the campaign advertisements home, "Look! Don't tell anybody I'm up for office—I mean that I'm your son—understand?"

"I'll tell them all—and what a bad son you are, what your real name is, how you hate your people and forget your family." She smiled in conquest, in revenge.

He smiled back at her. All he had to do was tell her to keep quiet, despite what she said, and she would.

And she was smiling at him, saying, in Helen's philosophy, "Get all you can for nothing," and in Grandpa's words, "That way success lies," and craftily, "And then you can help your mother who has bred you."

He saw more and more of Irene. She did a lot of drinking. She seemed to know all the headwaiters and every bartender in Chicago. She never went to a table. She looked good on a bar stool and knew it. "Hi, Norm!" she called to the bartender at the Cuban Village. "Make it strong, whatever it is. Scotch!" . . . "Hello, Ric!" at Riccardo's, slipping her arm around the proprietor's shoulders. "And when does the house buy a drink?" . . . at Hoffman's East Inn, "Hello, hello, hello—how are you, Frank? This is Don Lockwood. He wants something strong. He's going to be our next State Representative." . . . at the Rancho Grande, "Hello, Hi!" . . .

She ran Don around. She moved him from one night spot to another. Chez Paree. Club Alabam. The Spa. The Blue Note. The Singers' Rendezvous. The Steak House bar. The Croydon bar. She took him to little intimate bars. To hotel bars. To roadhouse bars.

After their first date she had said, "If you bring that old cane again I won't go with you." Days he used the cane. Evenings with her he left it at home.

Up and down Rush Street she took him. It was the same everywhere. Always to the bar. Never to a table. And always Don hated the toilets where the porters stood servilely smiling, wiping shoes, brushing backs, offering soap, towels, doing everything but flushing the toilets. He was ashamed of having someone kneel and dust his shoes. He felt self-conscious about it.

In his collecting for THE POWER Don continued to pick up twenty-five dollars here, fifty there for himself. The twenty-five, the fifty, helped him finance his evenings with Irene. The money became easier and easier to take. He became less and less averse to a little graft, a few easy bucks here and there. It helped with cover charges, bar checks. Irene knew the best places and knew how to throw money away.

She ran him around. She took him to Tito's on Halsted and Polk. "Hi, Koko!" she called to the bartender. She took him to places along North Clark Street. But now he wanted to go only to the better places. Don wanted to go up and down Rush Street. Not Irene. She wanted to go slumming. She took him to the Peek-A-Boo, The Victory Club, The Shanty, to places on West Madison Street where Don was always afraid he'd run into his sister.

But he was happy being with her. Being around her. And Irene, driving her car with Don in it, had a feeling of possession, a feeling of power and aggressiveness. And liked that feeling. . . .

She arched herself upon a bar stool and Don helped her out of her mink, took it to the cloakroom. When he was seated next to her he looked at the lines of her body, her clothes. He had never seen her in the same dress twice. She was always the best-dressed woman in the place.

And he was seeing more and more of her. But she held him off. As far as she was concerned, it seemed, he was only a drinking partner. Leaning over he kissed her on the ear. She appeared not to notice, and started talking about her father. Very often in conversation she mentioned her father, little incidents about him. Always with affection. With admiration.

"And do you know, Don," she said when the new drinks were before them, "D. S. would take me down to his office when I was a little girl. I'd climb up on his lap and braid his hair or play with his ears or pull his nose. He'd never even look up." She sipped her drink, smiling. "I'd move my hand across his desk in imitation, pretending I was writing too. I wouldn't have known what to do if he had told me to get down. I would have been completely lost."

"Hey!" Don said. "You're always talking about your father. You never talk about your mother. What happened to her?"

"Oh, she—" Irene said. Her lips curled a little. "Miss Society is traveling somewhere in Europe."

Don signaled the bartender. Irene said, "We can't stay long. We have to meet Christopher at the Pump Room."

"Do we have to meet him?"

"Of course we do. I couldn't do a thing like that to Christopher."

When they had had only three drinks Irene said, "Let's go," and got down from her stool. "Bring my purse, Don."

Obediently he picked it up, and her gloves, and followed her.

Christopher saw them come in. He was already standing when they reached him. He nodded at Don curtly. "Sorry, Irene," he said, "but I've got to go," and in an undertone to her, " I thought you were coming alone." He walked away.

Don's eyes showed satisfaction. Irene smiled a little. "Well, sit down, Don. I guess he doesn't like you."

Who did she think she was? Did she think it didn't smell? Don, angry, walked along the sidewalk deciding he'd stand her up. Show her. After all, all she means to me is a lay. I've been wasting too much time on her anyway. Rebecca is worth two of her any day.

He turned into a bar and ordered a shot. Miss Rich Bitch! They were born on a bed of roses. They'd die on a bed of roses. Screw you if you can't climb up on this bed of roses. Well, he'd climb up there. And once there—He rubbed his fist into the palm of his hand.

He ordered a drink. He'd show her.

She had said over the phone, "You say I stood you up last night? That you waited there for me two hours—well, that's character building, Don. . . . I wouldn't stand Christopher up? . . . Oh now, Don, don't be like that! Yes, I'll meet you there tonight if you want me to."

Well, he wouldn't show up tonight.

He ordered another shot. I won't see her again. He didn't want her. Just to go to bed with, maybe. Nothing else. She was rich. He was against that class of people. Yeah, she'd just be a good lay. And he'd sure like to make her again.

He ordered another shot.

He met her. She was already at the bar in the Cuban Village. He sat down next to her. "Hello," gruffly.

"Oh, hello, Don!"

He got drunk. He was silent and moody. He got drunker. She occupied her time laughing and talking to Norm, the good-looking bartender, half flirting with him. "Hey," Don said to her when he was good and drunk and when Norm was down the bar a way, "I'm not in love with you. You couldn't have me if you wanted me."

"No?" Irene asked and tish-tished with her tongue. "Then I'm wasting my time."

Irene paid no more attention to him but talked to Norm when he wasn't busy. She drank a lot. Don got drunker. He put his head down on the bar and, drunk, looked up at her, smiling sheepishly. "I'm sorry, honey."

In her car, later, he tried to neck with her. "Don't," she said. "I don't want someone always trying to make me. Let's leave it like it is."

Tears began to form in her eyes. . . . Once is enough to be hurt. Once is enough to love any one person. She'd never get serious about any man. Damn it! Why did he remind her of him?

"Let's go to a tavern," she said.

She had one drink.

"I want to go," she told him.

She got up from the stool. Don picked up her purse, and putting the strap over his shoulder in the fashion in which she wore it, he followed her. On her long-striding legs she was several feet ahead of him. Carrying her purse he followed her through the crowded night club like a happy puppy.

# XIX

In desperation, in sexual hunger, he went to see Sue.

"Hello," he said, trying to be casual.

"I haven't eaten, Don," Sue said. "Want to come out with me somewhere?"

"Oh, all right!" He was angry in his tension.

"You're coming back to the place?" she asked over coffee and pie.

"Yeah," he said eagerly.

She wanted to stop for a drink. "Aw, let's not!" But she insisted. And then, at the bar, she didn't seem very happy over her liquor.

Don sipped his beer. He glanced at her. Sue stared broodingly into space. Don snapped his match book against the tip of her nose. "Hey, wake up!" he said, grinning.

She smiled at him, a sad smile, and gathered up her purse. "Want to go?"

He was more than ready to go.

They went back to her room. She was restive.

"What's the matter?" he asked.

"I'm worried about you."

"Worried about me? Hey, look—!" He grinned at her. "I'm on the way up!"

She nodded. "Yes, I know."

He was both pleased and angry that she was worried about him. The anger took form in words. "Oh, you can always get someone else!" He gave a little grunt of a laugh. A laugh of scorn.

"Cut it out, Don, or go home."

"I'm sorry, Sue." Only placating her, keeping her in a good mood for bed.

He picked up a book and turned the pages, not wanting to approach her, make it obvious. "Well—why are you worried about me?"

"The people you're tied up with."

Here it came. But he knew what he was doing. Sometimes he had even thought Wayne wouldn't like what he was doing but Wayne's life had been sheltered. You have to be realistic. Yeah, it would be nice if most people could be good people but there were crooks and you have to realize it. You have to work within the group. You have to be realistic. Sure, it would be good to be like Jane Morris if you could—but that was why they always lost—you have to be realistic.

He closed the book, slamming it a little in his anger. "Jesus! Can't you lay off? I know what I'm doing. What do you think I am—a kid?" He walked to the window and looked out. With his back to her: "I know what you're thinking. And you might be half right about—" He gestured with his hand, his back still turned to her. "But once I get the power, do you think I'm going back on what I believe? And McCarren, whatever you might think of him, is all right. He gave me a break. Gave me a real start." His voice took on earnestness. He turned in toward the room, in toward her. "I'm campaigning for labor and housing and racial equality. I'm campaigning against the evils of society. I'm—" he smiled a little grimly, "campaigning for the same things your Jane Morris is." And his eyes frowned. "You ought to know that." He moved a step toward her. "I'm a liberal. You ought to know that."

"In my book," Sue said, and her frown became a tight-lipped smile, "*liberal* is the most hated word in the language—liberal!" She laughed. She took off her glasses and ran their stem through her short-cropped hair. "Liberal! There are all kinds of liberals. Jews who are liberals only because they are Jewish and pro-Semitic—and think only of the suffering of their people. Negroes who are liberals only because they are race-conscious and their liberalism bleeds for their poor suffering people. White people, businessmen, rich people who are liberals simply because they are suffering from feelings of guilt. Liberal!" She snapped her glasses back over her eyes. "Do you know what the word means?" —almost derisively and in direct attack on his lack of education—"The dictionary definition is 'independent in opinion, not conservative, having tendency toward democratic or republican as distinguished from monarchical or aristocratic forms, one who is liberal in thoughts or opinions.' " The laugh was bitter. "There are liberals who are liberals only because it serves their personal or racial or political purpose." She smiled at him almost contemptuously. "You're not even a liberal."

Don laughed. He walked to her and put his arms around her. Tightly around her. She turned her mouth away from his kiss. He continued to tighten his arms. And then she was only a woman who cares for someone else, weak though he may be, stupid though he may be, or selfish, or vain, or insensitive, or even vicious or sadistic. She moved her mouth back and pressed her lips hard against his, then opened her mouth for his entry. He laughed. "You're in love with me," he said. "You want me. My body."

It was his turn to be contemptuous. He lit a cigarette and let her light her own.

He finished his cigarette in silence. Snuffed it out. And was then penitent. He came toward her where she sat on the side of the bed. "You're right, Sue." He gestured with a humble hand. "I wish I was different." His deep-set eyes asked forgiveness. "I guess I'm not much. But—"

He came all the way across the room and sat at her feet with his head against her knees. "I guess I need you. I guess I love you. I guess I was trying to run after something I couldn't have or don't even really want. We're—we're both kind of unhappy people."

She stroked his forehead. There was no contempt left in her. She leaned down toward him. He kissed her glasses, both lenses, behind which tears ran.

She stroked his forehead and, leaning over, kissed his hair, his mouth. "Take care of yourself, Don. Don't get hurt. They're going to hurt you—don't let them hurt you." She was talking as if to a child and she stroked his hair.

# XX

The doctor sighed and shook the pages of Aaron Levin's case history. The doctor frowned, rubbed the butt of his pen across his forehead and began studying the case history.

Father: ABRAHAM LEVIN (living)
Mother: MILDRED LARSON (living)

*gentile mother:*

The doctor read more concentratedly.

To the case history was attached a little sheaf of poems. These the doctor loosened and read.

Aaron was brought into the doctor's room and stood there, now that the attendant was gone, alone in front of the desk.

Dr. Goodman smiled from behind his glasses. "Sit down, won't you?"

Aaron flushed. He slid apprehensively into the chair and tightened his feet against the floor.

The doctor smiled at him. "I'm Major Goodman. Maybe you could tell me a bit about yourself."

Aaron couldn't hold the doctor's glance. His eyes slid upward to the short-clipped black hair, upward to the ceiling, then fell to the top of the desk. He began to sweat. He could feel his hands under the desk and his knees shaking.

"I—I feel nervous. I can't sleep."

And suddenly he put his forehead down on the desk and was unable to lift it up although he kept telling himself no, no. Sit up straight. Don't do this. They will never let you out.

"I—I—" he stammered, "guess I'm just crazy." The big shoulders shrugged above the pressed-down forehead. "I vomit and I can't keep my food down. Sometimes I'm hungry. Soon as I see the food I can't eat a mouthful. I can't stay in this hospital any longer. I can't stand it here. I'll die here. I can't sleep and I'm scared all the time. I'm scared of everything. I'm scared of people. I'm just scared. I guess I'm a coward, I don't know. I don't want to be this way. I don't like the army. I object to soldiers everywhere. I just can't take anything GI any more. I hate everything GI. I don't like soldiers. Somehow I'm different. Not a soldier. Even when I went to town there were soldiers everywhere. You can't get away from it. And the killing. Everybody killing everybody else. I used to write poetry. Isn't that silly? A soldier writing poetry. They stole my poems."

He wept unashamedly, the tears falling on the floor between his trembling legs and feet.

"I tell myself, 'You have to grow up. The pubic hairs don't mean anything.' "

His voice was so choked with his sobbing that he had to stop talking. That only made his legs tremble more violently. He lifted his tear-stained face with his long black hair spilling over it in a series of bars, closing him in. He spread his hands out for the doctor to see and laughed a little. "Coarse tremor of both hands, they call it."

He put his forehead back on the desk and the tears spattered to the concrete floor. "Someday I'll write about something. Someday I'll show them. I wanted a mother to talk to when I was young. I didn't have one. I had an obligation to my father and I failed him. You should see my father's back. I feel a great sense of failure. And of guilt too, I guess. I even failed when I tried to kill myself. I'm the greatest failure life ever spawned."

And then he was quieter. He was sitting up, rubbing the backs of his hands across his cheeks, taking the tears. "I guess you think I'm a big cry-baby. I'm sorry. I shouldn't have done that. And I shouldn't have said all those things."

Then he was silent and sat across from the doctor, kneading the damp moisture of the palms of his hands into his knees. Major Goodman said, "Well, you should say and feel what you think and feel. You just talk and don't worry." He smiled gently at Aaron. "What you—what we all—think about ourselves isn't necessarily true. That's true of you and that's what we have to find out. Now—just talk—about anything you want to." He gestured with his hand.

Aaron glanced at him, and away, as if he carried an inner wound and wanted nobody to see it. He bit his lip, and when words came, said, with a lump in his throat, "I—I guess I don't have anything to say." And to himself: I better be careful what I say. He'll think I'm crazy and keep me here. He wants me to talk. I won't let him make me talk.

"You seem more relaxed today."

"Yes. I guess I am."

"Is there anything you would like to tell me?"

"No. I don't think so." He's a nice man. He's so kind.

"You told me the other day that you wrote poetry in civilian life. Have you written any since you were here?"

Aaron began to tremble. "No," he said.

"Do you think you would like to?"

Aaron looked down and shook his head no.

Dr. Goodman looked at the bowed head. "What was your mother like?" he asked gently.

Aaron bit his lip. "I don't remember," he said. "She died when I was a baby."

"What is your father like?"

"He's a—" Aaron shrugged his shoulders. Aaron gestured ineffectually with his hands. "I don't know." Again the gesture. "He's a good father, I guess."

"Your mother was a gentile, wasn't she?"

Aaron nodded. "And my father is half-gentile," he lied.

. . . And the next time.

"Are you a virgin, Aaron?"

Aaron glanced at the doctor with guarded eyes. Then, looking away, he laughed. "No," he said, "I've whored around a lot just like any other guy. I've had lots of girls." He glanced at the doctor but couldn't hold the gentle but inscrutable look of the eyes. Staring down at his hands, he said, "My mother can bawl me out whenever she wants but not these damn GI nurses. If you don't let me go home and get away from everything GI, I'll go completely nuts. I know I will."

Aaron walked in and smiled. "What shall we talk about?"

"That's up to you," Doctor Goodman said, smiling with friendliness.

Aaron looked at him with liking and admiration: there is nothing about him of the major except his uniform with its sharp lapels, its insignia, its decorations, the knife-edge of the trousers. "I'd like to talk about home," he said with a smile. And began to talk:

"Chicago, it's dirty and ugly and has a lot of slums. But it's beautiful too and it's home. It's my place where I know myself. My friends all live there—on the Near North Side. There's—" counting them on his fingers, "Milo and O'Keefe and Don. Yes, and Steve. There's Saul—only Saul's in the army. Dave's a Negro. I like Milo and O'Keefe best of all. You'd like them too, Doctor. Only I can't follow O'Keefe where he goes. He gets irritated with me sometimes. I guess he's a Communist even if he doesn't belong to the Party. He's a radical anyway. And Milo's always trying to talk me into writing realistic stuff like he does. I don't like realistic writing. Steve's a cynic. He says people stink. He says people are pigs. Steve gives expression to all his hatreds. He writes poetry too. He's about thirty-six and all his poetry is sensual. I'll be sitting around in Thompson's restaurant with Milo and O'Keefe, feeling comfortable with them. Steve will sneer at them, at what they say, and I'm glad Steve does because then I feel aloof from them and at the same time I hate myself because I don't tell Steve he's wrong. I guess I see O'Keefe as a man sitting at a roulette table putting hope on people and I don't know. And Steve says they stink and I don't know. And Milo is silly and sentimental about them. I guess I've lived a question-mark life, searching for answers to so many things." He shrugged his shoulders despairingly. His eyes saddened. "We're so young, so young yet. All of us boys in this war. We became friends with pain so young. We've never had a chance to place our coin in the slot and wait for the three lemons to appear . . . I wonder if there is such a thing as a jack-pot? . . ."

Aaron talked on. He was very co-operative and anxious to help himself and the doctor.

Doctor Goodman leaned forward and looked Aaron full in the eyes. He smiled at Aaron. His smile touched only the corners of his lips but stayed there, truant to his depth of concentration, and his objective scientific approach. And his quiet voice asked, "Would you like to talk a little about your mother?"

Aaron tensed. "I don't remember anything about her, Doctor. Please don't ask me." He rubbed his sweaty palms together. "Death whispers in my ear every night. And why am I so scared of windows—I guess I may jump out of one some day."

It had been hard to wait until the next time when he could talk to Doctor Goodman. And now it was time. He hurried along the corridor. He was envious of and hostile to the patients in the ward who shared Doctor Goodman's attentions. Doctor Goodman liked him best of all.

Doctor Goodman would help him and he would be completely well again.

Aaron dropped his eyes in embarrassment as Doctor Goodman glanced up at him.

"I have something for you," the doctor said. He pulled open a desk drawer and drew out Aaron's sheaf of poems. He set them on the desk in front of Aaron. Aaron looked down at them and then up into Doctor Goodman's face. He began to tremble. His eyes grew misty and he hung his head. With a hesitant hand he reached out and touched the paper, the words he had put on paper.

"I read them. I read all of them," Doctor Goodman said. Aaron's head drooped lower. "I like them," the doctor said. Aaron's eyes came up unbelievingly and his mouth stretched open in surprise.

Aaron sat staring at the doctor. He read it as poetry. And went on reading it. And finished.

The doctor was talking about Ezra Pound and Gerard Manley Hopkins. Now he had said something about Baudelaire. Aaron's hands were trembling and there were tears in his eyes. Did he mean—did he mean that his poetry—! There was ecstasy in Aaron.

The minutes went and it was time for him to go back to the ward.

"I'm having you transferred to an open ward," Doctor Goodman said and this was something hard for Aaron to believe too.

He said thank you with a lump in his throat and stepped timidly toward the door.

"Your poetry—" Doctor Goodman said, pointing to it.

"You mean—" Aaron asked, "that I can have it?"

Aaron picked up the little sheaf of poems. With one finger of the other hand he stopped the tear that was halfway down his cheek. He smiled at Doctor Goodman. Then he laughed and the doctor was laughing too.

With gentle hands Aaron carried the poetry. His heart was beating fast.

Doctor Goodman slowly injected a 5.0 per-cent solution of the drug intravenously. From the couch Aaron looked up into his eyes trustingly and followed his instructions. And now Aaron's counting aloud ceased. He began to take deep, sleeping breaths. Doctor Goodman injected still a little more of the drug. He held the needle in the vein until he was sure that Aaron had reached and maintained the proper responsiveness.

And Aaron, speaking ". . . I feel guilty about something. I have a deep sense of failure. I don't know what it is. My mother? You asked about my mother, Doctor. I didn't have a mother. She died when I was a baby . . . Babes? Lots of 'em. All over. Place is filthy, crawling with 'em. Some pretty nice, I mean they go to bed with a smile. And that always helps (haha). They love poets—some of 'em. Love amorous poets. Love young poets. Love long-haired, sensitive-faced, oversexed poets. We-e-elll . . . I wrote a poem once. Honest, I did. And that other stuff—well, maybe yes . . . maybe no. What the hell's the diff anyway when you find yourself between the warm thick covers and some pig pressed-glued-stuck to you tight and hot and the lights out and the radio playing soft tinny music all the time and—jesuschrist! what's the diff anyway when you're halfway around the . . . world and you're feeling good and snappy inside? They bite. Sure they bite. Don't pigs all bite? Sure they do. Bite like hell. Tell 'em anything—I'm a hero, babe. I'm a lover. I'm a warrior. A poet. Your one-and-only loving . . . VAMPIRE! Anything at all. They bite. They wanna bite. They love it. Sure, they do. Okay then. So I'm a long-haired, sensitive-faced, oversexed poet. Okay, okay. Milo believes that crap I feed the babes. He thinks I spend my evenings writing poetry. Can you imagine? Well, that's something too. Why not? If he's happy why not, huh? Let 'im believe I'm sincere. Levin the poet. Levin the writer. Levin the . . . fake, really. Hell, why not? Huh? Why run through all evenings feeling lousy and mixed-up because all these people believe you and you keep telling them it doesn't matter—writing, I mean—and your friends getting blue and sullen all over the place thinking he's bad off Aaron is and if they could only help—do something—anything—anything at all. No, it's nuts. Nuts to sit around and feel that way all night. Sometimes it takes me a week to get over those hangovers. Uh-uh. It's nuts. To Milo I'm still the writer, still the warrior with a sword-sharp pen. I'm going to keep it that way . . . but Babes—lots of 'em. All over. They sit around Thompson's restaurant all night. Nothing to do. Waiting. Waiting. Hoping that some guy—you, yes, you—might give them a tumble. And if you write poetry and if you're sorta sensitive and feeling things (that's a joke)—well, that's even better in a way. That's how they like 'em. Souls—medium done . . . I don't deserve to live . . ."

Aaron began to twist and turn on the couch. Tears streaked down his cheeks. "Don't lose me, Milo—don't let me lose myself, O'Keefe . . ."

And "No, I'm just a virgin. I've never had a girl. Isn't that something, now? A great big guy like me. I'm old enough too. That's why I put all that stuff in my poetry—that sensual stuff. The sexual things that shock everybody. Aaron! And you look like a little boy and you've had all these experiences! You know all these things (haha)."

And suddenly becoming extremely nervous, turning from side to side, covering his face, crying into his hands: "My father loves my sister. He doesn't love me. When we were little—when my mother went away—he would rock her, he would hold her in his arms, he would sing to her. Never me. I was alone. I've always been alone. Only once my mother held me in her arms and kissed me that I can remember. My father hates me. That's why he sent me to fight. He wants me to get killed. I know it. He does."

Aaron clenching his fists. The knuckles stood out white and hard: "Jews! Jews! Jews! The goddamn dirty kikes! They caused the war. They've caused everything bad in the world. They with their crooked noses and their religion and everything that makes them different from other people." He said many violent and obscene things about the Jews. Then his fists collapsed to his sides and became big, awkward, weak hands clutching at the couch for support from their trembling; his head rolled from side to side, the tears tumbled down. "No. That isn't so. The Jews have suffered for over two thousand years. My poor suffering people. I have failed my whole race. I don't want to be a Jew. What chance has a Jew in the world? What chance has a Negro? Why doesn't Dave feel his Negro-ness? Why does he think he's just a human being like everybody else? Who's he kidding?" He began to sob again, his whole body shaking with his sobs.

"What happened to your mother?" Doctor Goodman asked quietly.

"I want to write because then, if I could become famous, I won't feel so bad about my mother."

"What happened to your mother?"

Aaron began to cry even louder and could hardly talk. He rolled from side to side. "She's—she's—" and when he could talk again, "a whore, Doctor. Just a common whore. She left my father and us kids. She lived with a gangster first, and now anyone. That's my good gentile mother, Doctor. I'm no good. I don't deserve to live . . .

"If I'm a 4F or a soldier I'll—I'll be a failure. I want to be a good soldier. I want to go home. My sister is home alone. If she's up she'll be crying too. She's been through hell. I don't want to put her through any more. My mother had every chance. She didn't have a bad environment or anything. She came from a good Swedish-Irish background. She just wasn't any good. We had the pleasure of having everybody in the neighborhood know about her . . . I went to Clark Street before I came here tonight. Standing there looking down the street—I'm too young. I don't understand anything.

"I see all those boys killing each other with the points of different flags." He stared weepily. "What's wrong with them. I'm too young. I don't know anything—I can't understand anything. I'm just no good, I guess . . .

"I could have gone to them. Yes, I could have if I had really wanted to. I . . . I . . ."

Fear and pain were in his face.

"I—I—No!—No!—" He rolled face down. He went on talking . . . pain and fear were in his face. "Like I said, I'm going to enlist. I'll try to do the best I can wherever they put me. I'm soft—not only physically—and it may make a man out of me—maybe it will put a backbone where there is no backbone. And it will help me with my writing." He rolled on his back. He made no noise crying. The tears ran down his cheeks and off his face. He shook his head, trying to rid himself of them. But more came.

"Like I said, I'm too young. I just don't understand. It isn't just me. It's all the boys in the world and what they're doing to them." He wiped his eyes with the back of his hand. "I'll probably write precious stuff. I'll probably end up like Steve feeling sorry for myself and saying people are no good, people are pigs. You're right, Milo—people are good—all people are good. You write about them, Milo. Make them stop hating each other. Make them stop killing each other. You can do it. You can help to do it."

He sat up straight, the black scythes of hair falling over his temples. "I want to tell you something, Doctor. I lied when I said I didn't have a mother. I want to tell you something I haven't told anybody. My mother is a prostitute. She deserted my sister and me when we were little kids and ran away with a gangster—one of Al Capone's gang. My sister doesn't know anything about it. We thought my mother was dead. That's what my father told us—then one day—then one day—" His shoulders shook with his dry, silent sobs. "One day my father told me all about it. I think he hates me. He must hate me or he wouldn't have told me. And he told me that I had to become something and he told me why—about my mother. He told me that she had become a—a—prostitute—and she was down on North Clark Street and my sister must never know. I went down there. I went into every tavern looking for her—I don't know why. I saw a lot of women who could have been my mother." He put the big palms of his hand up over his face and talked through them. "They were drunk. They were picking up men. Some of them had black eyes. Once I saw her. When I was little. Just the top of her head. She cursed at my father and told him that unless he gave her some money she'd tell us kids who she was. My father shook her and kept shaking her. He said he'd give her the money if she'd promise never to come to the house again. She laughed. She cursed him some more. She said she didn't want to ever see us kids . . . we moved right after that."

Aaron rolled again and lay face down. "All I want to do is to forget," he muttered, "just forget."

"For a long time," the doctor said, "you have tried to forget and you have not succeeded. First you must remember and then you will know what problem you have to solve."

For a moment he seemed to be listening.

The doctor said intently, "You are working in the hospital where you tried to commit suicide. It is evening. You have just taken a bedpan away. You go out into the ward corridor and swallow poison—"

Aaron sat up, wringing his hands together, the tears flooding down his cheeks. He said:

"I look around the ward at all the patients. I think of all the hospitals all over the world filled with sick and maimed young fellows of every country and all the dead ones too—I tried to tell the governments and the military leaders that—looking out of the window and down into the cemetery. I look around. I take the bedpan out. I have no friends in the army. Nobody likes me. I'm a poet. Who wants a poet around? I didn't want to be a hero. I couldn't kill anyone. I could never even fight with anyone. Even in grammar school when the kids pushed me around. I wanted to be a conscientious objector but I didn't have the courage. I guess it takes courage. I was afraid of what people would say. I guess I'm a coward. And then my father shows me his back. He was beaten in a pogrom. He asks me to do the right thing—what is the right thing? I enlisted. I hoped they wouldn't take me but they did. I have no friends in the army. I hate everything GI. Everything that suggests killing. The soldiers sit around writing home, getting letters and packages from their mothers and wives. I used to pretend I got packages from my mother—cookies, cigarettes. I used to write letters to her and then tear them up."

Aaron lay back sobbing loudly. "I take the bedpan out. I'm a Jew. Who wants a Jew around? All the time I heard that anti-Jewish talk even among the soldiers. I set the bedpan down and I think what's the use of it all? Nothing solves anything. The war wouldn't. It would just take the lives away from millions of young fellows, lives that were owed to them. I couldn't kill a German or a Japanese. Whenever I want to I can stop this pain and unhappiness. I can't kill anybody else but I can kill myself whenever I want. I set the bedpan down. I am faced with my failure for the rest of my life. I am suddenly depressed. I can't make another effort to write another poem. What does it matter? What does anything matter? Back into the womb or wherever you came from. That's all! Good-by. That's what all the countries were saying to their soldiers. I set the bedpan down. I swallow poison.

". . . everybody around me is a chalk doll. I live on a shelf at the carnival. I live with my chalk lovers, my chalk mother, my chalk friends. I live with my chalk thoughts—the thoughts that go home with cheap little girls undressing in the penny arcade night.

". . . I swallow the poison . . .

"I have been rejected by everyone. Now I reject all of them. There is no place in the world for me so I won't live in the world. And it's Steve, I'm always afraid of becoming Steve. So I swallow the poison. My hand is shaking but I swallow the poison."

The doctor leaned back and sighed. He looked at Aaron. Aaron lay as if in a stupor. "Aaron—" he called, "want to read this book? Aaron, you're one of us! Aaron! Aaron! We're under fire!"

Aaron sat upright, groaning. And the tears came again. In a new violence. His mouth slobbered with his crying. His nose ran.

"No! No! No!" he shouted.

He fell back against the bed and lay there. His mouth said words, torturingly, miserably: "I ran out on my buddies. I let them die. I don't deserve to live."

He cried long and hard.

Then he seemed asleep. Then the pentothal wore off.

The doctor sighed. He smiled slowly, reassuringly. "Now," he said, "we will go over what you have just told me while you were under the drug and in that way you will bring these things to your consciousness and you will know—" he made a little gesture with his hands, "what problem you have to solve—and that you alone can solve." Again the gesture with his hands. "I can only help you."

# XXI

They sat at the bar in Riccardo's. She lifted the shot glass to her lips, and smiling at him, said, "How you doing?"

Don nodded seriously. As she turned back to her drink he watched her hair slide off her shoulder, leaving it bare. He wanted, intensely, to lean over, kiss her shoulder, bite it. And he sensed she would enjoy it. His eyes, staring at her bare shoulder, became fevered with the thought.

"What are you thinking?" Irene asked.

He laughed self-consciously, guiltily. "How pretty you are."

"Oh?" Her lips parted in the smallest of smiles. Then suddenly bored, Irene said, "Let's go." She slid off the bar stool.

Don gathered up her purse and gloves and followed her out to the car.

It was a chilly June night with a threat of rain in the obscuring sky and they had to put the top up.

"Want to drive out to my place?"

Don nodded yes.

Irene turned onto the Outer Drive. The rain came. Came in a torrent. It tattooed the canvas roof and the tires squished through it and Irene drove faster than was safe. But Don didn't notice. He sat with his hat on his lap, his head back against the red leather upholstery and his eyes closed. Irene! Irene! his mind called out.

"Asleep?"

He shook his head.

They drove through the rain. In the windshield she saw a vision.

And out on the lonely road. She caught her lip between her teeth and pressed down hard.

Don opened his lips to speak but closed them again, afraid of being laughed at or of drawing irritation. But at length he said, "I love you, Irene."

Irene's teeth released her lip. "Oh, do you?" She chuckled as if she didn't believe him. Her shoulders twisted in slight irritation.

And on through the rain. Both silent again. The lonely vision riding the windshield.

When they reached the house, Irene unlocked the door. "Go on into the drawing room," she said. "I'll get us something to drink."

Don sat down on the sofa in front of the fireplace. The huge hearth was piled with white birch logs ready to have a match touched to them. On the grand piano, flowers bloomed from a vase. Don laced his fingers together and stared into the fireplace.

Irene came in bringing highballs, which she set on the low cocktail table in front of Don. He looked up. "Where's your father?"

"He's in New York for a few days."

Don glanced at her. And away. He could never tell about her. Why the hell had he let her talk him into driving all the way out here just so she could tease him?

She circled the cocktail table and, sitting next to him for a moment, patted the back of his hand.

He glanced at her and tried to take her hand. "Don't," she said. The irritation in her voice was softened by a tremor of pathos.

She stood up. "Mix us some drinks, Don."

She went to the fireplace and touched a match to the logs. Then she came back and sat alongside him and took the drink he offered. The flames rose high, yellow and ambitious and crackling. The rain sounded against the windows. Irene stared into the fire and swished the drink around in her glass. Slowly she turned her face to his. The fire cast its dark flickering shadows across her face. Never before had he seen this mixture of tenderness and sadness in her eyes. "You remind me of a boy I used to know," she said. She said it very simply and stared back into the fireplace. "You know, I told you once that you reminded me of someone." Her eyes traveled up the flames and down to the logs where the white birch was beginning to curl away.

"Who was he?" Don asked.

She shook her head no. Slowly she swirled her drink.

The fire began to lose a bit of its yellowness. Irene lifted her glass and drank quickly. She laughed. But the laugh caught, for a moment, in her throat. Without speaking she held her glass for another drink.

In silence they drank two, three more. The fire was low tongues of purple.

Irene set her glass down and went to the fireplace. Kneeling there, sitting back on her heels, she poked the fire to renewed flame. Her black and gold quilted ballerina skirt belled out around her and onto the edge of the carpet. The narrow band of ruby and gold sequins that edged the deep rounded neck of her blouse caught the light of the re-kindled fire in a thousand tiny points of light that reflected a ruddiness across her smooth bare shoulders. Gilded and molded them with its light. Etched her profile with its orange, red, yellow, purple flames. Left a feather of darkness under her cheekbone. Don tightened his fingers together. Irene! Irene!

And now she was frowning a little and moving back away from the heat. And now she stood up. Don watched her skirt take the molding of her hips and legs. Half of the room was lit by the fire and she moved to the lamp, switched it off. "It's cozier this way."

She came back and sat next to him but with an expanse of sofa between them. She drank again and was very cheerful now. Clicking her glass with his, she laughed and her laughter was deep in her throat.

"Again," she said and held her glass.

When it was half finished she set it down and, restive, got up, walked to the piano. From the bowl of flowers she took a red rose and put it behind her ear. She moved in front of the fire. "Want me to entertain you, Don?" she asked laughing. Bending she took off her shoes and stockings and there, in the space in front of the fire, she pirouetted several times like a ballet dancer, her skirt flaring out in a swirling bell. The fire threw its stage of light, and summer thunder crackled against the roof.

Laughing she glanced at him and winked. Then deliberately, slowly, churning to a faster and faster rhythm, she went through the sensual steps of the Fatima dance she had done at the hospital. She twisted her hips, and under the ballerina skirt they fell away in long glides. They moved like the flames licking the logs in the fireplace. And now the dance centered around her navel. And all the while the imaginary snake crawled up her arms, around her shoulders, around her waist, rose, slithered to her lips for a kiss.

Exhausted, panting a little, Irene walked to the sofa to pick up her glass. Don grabbed her bare arm and pulled her down alongside him. He kissed her roughly, passionately, on the lips and she let him. Then she twisted her face away from his kiss. "Let me go, Don." She tried to sit up straight. His mouth was against her neck. "Your lips tell me no, no, but there's yes, yes in your eyes," he said in the words of the popular song.

"Let me go."

His arms fell away obediently. His eyes searched hers pleadingly.

She was composed now and smiling in that aloof and brittle way that always kept him at arm's length.

"You thought I was a little bitch, didn't you?" she said, still smiling.

"In the cloakroom. Out at the veterans' hospital." She lifted her glass and sipped from it. "I wanted to get even with you." She sipped again and set the glass down. "I didn't like the way you put your arms around those two girls and looked at me that night at the Legion dance." She tossed her head a little. "You acted as if I were dirt. As if I were a little bitch." She smiled again, a tight, poised, inscrutable smile. "Well, maybe I am."

Don moved close to her on the couch. He put his arms around her. He kissed her on the neck. Her body stiffened and she sat erect with her head up and her face turned away from him. But she was letting him kiss her. She wasn't pushing him away. He began brushing her throat with his lips and wondered how it made her feel.

He pulled her closer, but she was stiff and icy cold in his arms. His arms tightened and he pressed his lips against her neck. She was cold and withdrawn. Then suddenly she turned to him, and putting her arms around his neck fiercely, kissed him on the lips hard, hard.

He pulled her down onto the sofa with him. His excited fingers loosened the fastening of her blouse. Her skirt was like the petals of a flower that have been spread open. The fire crackled in its low flames on the charred logs. Her arms were about him. Don moved closer, and more aggressively. Rain stung the windows in needles. Flames in the logs moved in straight-standing, unsheathed spears. Irene's arms came from their clutched hold around him. The butts of her hands were against his chin. She pushed him off. "It's no use. It's no good."

She got up off the sofa. One side of her blouse was almost completely pulled down. She pulled it up and tightened the little black drawstring. She whipped her hair up off her forehead with a snap of her neck and looked at him. "It's no use."

Don pulled himself up clumsily, awkwardly, embarrassedly, from the couch. His blond face pumped up red anger. "You little bitch! You cheap little teaser!" The hard palm of his hand moved in a quick, angry arc and smacked across her cheek. "You cheap little bitch, you!"

Irene moved back a step. Her mouth opened in a circle of astonishment. Her cheek was red where his hand had slapped. She looked at him. Her lips began to stretch out into the beginnings of a smile. It fell away almost immediately. A contemptuous anger snapped up into her eyes. But it too went, swiftly, and she was crying with her hands up over her face.

"Irene—Irene—" Miserably. He touched her gently on the shoulder. "Irene—" She swayed there.

"Nobody ever slapped me before." It was in unbelieving tones. "Nobody ever slapped me before." The tears ran beyond the butts of her small hands and fell on the floor.

"Irene—" Gently, tenderly, he guided her to the sofa and his palm, with kindness in it, forced her to sit down.

She was still crying. She went on crying. He sat, miserable, with a soothing hand on her shoulder. "Don't—don't—"

At last she drew in deeply and wiped her nose on the back of her hand like a little girl—"Oh, I'm sorry—" and searched around blindly for a handkerchief. He gave her his.

Silently she pointed to her glass. He filled it, and ashamed of himself, looked away when he handed it to her.

She drank slowly, sipping and staring into the fireplace where the last logs were dimly glimmering in charred red ash.

"I told you," she said, not looking at him, "that you reminded me of a boy I knew. His name was Ken—Ken Bailey. He was poor." Her sad lips smiled at the fireplace. "He was working his way through the university—" She grew quiet. She began remembering:

. . . she had gone to Northwestern University. Daddy had said to Sybil, "Well, Miss Society, she's not going to any finishing school. She's going right here in this state. I want my little girl close to me where I can see her."

She had dated at Northwestern, along with the other girls. For two years she was bored with the smooth, groomed, slick-talking young men from frat houses who had turned up at all the social affairs and dances. Christopher was fun—sometimes—but nobody she could ever get serious over. Then she had met Ken. He was quiet, serious, from Chicago's West Side. There was an idealism in him—an idealism about everything. He was awkward. His clothes were baggy. His hair needed cutting most of the time . . .

On the sofa beside Don her lips smiled below the sadness of her eyes.

. . . he had a warm and generous smile but always, in his deep-set eyes, was the seriousness, the idealism. Something about Don reminded her of him . . .

She glanced at Don and lowered her eyes. Again glanced at Don . . . then . . . the memories plaguing her:

She fell in love with him. At first they had dated in a carefree way and he had counted his money carefully to make sure that he could afford a show, a dinner, an occasional few beers at the run-down tavern outside the dry town of Evanston.

Then he found out who she was.

He had avoided her. She had had to call him. He was polite but aloof and made excuses about the next date.

She had pursued him. But he kept their relationship on only the friendliest of bases; had never allowed himself to become really serious about her. And yet in the workings of the muscles of his face when they were together, in the look of his eyes, in the sternness of his mouth tightening over unsaid things, she knew that he cared for her.

Recklessly she had driven to his dorm in her car. "You're going out to my house with me. I want my parents to see you."

"But, Irene—"

"I want them to see the kind of man I date."

"Now, look—Irene—"

His awkward hands were on the top of the car door but he hadn't opened it. He snapped his head and the uncombed and uncut hair flew back in place. Her eyes had filled, looking at him, and her face had become tense. "Oh, Ken—" she had said, "don't be a snob. We can't help it if we have money. Please get in."

"All right, Irene—only I don't think—"

"Please get in—" Her voice cracking.

He got in in his baggy pants and sweater, shirt open at the neck. "Do you really think it's a good i—"

Her palm had caressingly pressed his lips and pushed back the rest of the words.

She took him to the house—once. D. S., in a pair of pants as baggy as Ken's, had been nice to him. Sybil treated him in a cool, hospitable way, and watching her mother, Irene knew. When she had driven him back to Chicago and returned home, Sybil asked immediately, "Who was that young man?"

"Why," Irene said, "a boy from the university."

"Who are his parents?" Her mother's nostrils began to quiver. They always quivered in her thin blond face when she was angry.

"I don't know. Does it matter?"

"You know perfectly well that it matters! I won't have my daughter—"

D. S. slapped his paper down on the arm of the chair and smacked his fist down on top of the paper. "Well, Miss Society," he said, "what have you got to say about it? She's *my* daughter. *My* daughter, Miss Society!"

Sybil's eyes glanced in scorn from her husband to Irene. Always she had been opposed to the two of them. To the mother, Irene was completely lost. She hadn't fitted into any of the places her mother had selected for her. "I hope you're not serious about that boy." Her nostrils contracted and expanded. "I won't have it."

"Look—Miss Society—" D. S. said, "she's *my* daughter. The Matthews don't give a damn about money and titles and social position. I want my little girl happy. That's all."

The nostrils expanded. "Then why did you marry me?" The head was high and the nostrils contracted and she was looking at Irene again.

The scene dissolved.

Irene leaned toward Don and wide-eyed, tears in her lashes, searched his face. "Did you ever," she asked, "hate your mother?"

Don straightened up uncomfortably. He laughed nervously. "No," he said.

Irene leaned back against the cushions with her glass held against the tip of her lips but forgotten.

. . . the Germans had overrun Poland. The campus ran with political talk, war talk. "Will you marry me?" she asked him.

He put his hands on her shoulders. "Now, now," he said, grinning.

"No, I mean it."

"I couldn't—look who you are."

"Who am I?" Piteously. Begging. Dried up inside.

"Now, now."

"Tell me—please tell me—do you love me or not?"

"I couldn't marry you—I don't have anything—"

"You're not serious. You don't think—"

"Your parents would never—"

"Do you think—"

"Irene, look—I'm poor. My people are poor. Let's be practical. It would be years, if then, before I could ever give you the kind of life—well, no, I could never give you that."

"I don't want that kind of life," she said, seeing her mother. "I hate it!"

She swayed under his touch and put her head down against his chest. He held her close to him and kissed her, slowly, gently. Then kidding, pushing her away—"Let me go!" Taking her hand, "Come on, I'll pop for coffee." Across the campus, their fingers laced, their arms swinging.

The war came. He enlisted. He didn't tell her good-by or write. She thought he was breaking it off . . . and the other memory, bruising her consciousness . . . she and D. S. horseback riding. Suddenly she had spurred her horse and started off at a wild gallop across the dangerous terrain. "Irene!" Her father's voice calling to her in alarm. She lashed the horse with her whip. Her father's mount came galloping after them. He caught her in the forest, under low trees, and grabbed the rein.

"You gave me a scare, Irene."

She sat her mount with her head down.

"You're in love with him, aren't you?" D. S. asked, lifting her chin.

She nodded.

He tapped her cheek gently. "When he comes back—if you want him—you can have him."

Irene, tossing her head, her hair flying back over her shoulder: "Sybil?"

"The hell with her!" . . .

"Donald," Irene said humbly.

Don looked up at her.

"Would you please fix me a drink?"

He did. She watched him with her unhappy eyes.

He lit a cigarette and handed it to her. She nodded her thanks without speaking. She looked at his deep-set eyes, so like Ken's. Or was it something in his posture? Something in his seriousness? You can never, of certainty, lay a finger on what in one person reminds you of another. She drew the glass up close to her lips and, vacant-eyed, watched the purple smoke of the cigarette trail upward.

. . . he didn't write. He was trying to break it off. She had quit school and joined the Red Cross. She sat in the Red Cross office. A list was given her of those who had been killed in the area. She and other workers were to go visit the families. Her eyes ran down the list. And then she knew why he hadn't written. He had been dead all this long while.

She put on her coat and left the office, carrying the list in her hand. She went into the cocktail lounge. She sat at the bar with the typed list in her hand. She ordered a drink. She sat with the list in her hand, staring straight ahead. She folded the list neatly, once, twice, opened her purse and put it inside, closed her purse. She drank her drink. Drank another. And another. They were all straight shots of whisky. Her eyes, as she calmly sipped her drinks, were very bright.

Into the cocktail lounge walked Christopher. Neat. Smelling of cologne. Funny she should notice that. Remember it.

She smiled at him with her red-creamed lips. "Oh, hello, Christopher!" she called brightly. "Come and have a drink with me!"

When he stood next to her she turned on her stool, put her arms around him tightly and kissed him warmly on the lips, kissed him with abandon.

"Well!" he said, chuckling. "That's a surprise! What's got into you?"

She smiled, and unable to speak for fear of hearing her voice crack pointed to her shot glass.

"Let's have another," he said.

She nodded.

The drink came. She could remember clicking her glass with his . . . and all of her flooded back and around the memory of the dead Kenny. Why had she not gone off with him? Or slept with him when she could? Now she never could. Her teeth took her lip. She forced them to release it. She smiled up at Christopher.

His eyes were the inscrutable male's. He asked politely, casually, if she would have another.

"Why, of course!"

They had one and another. Several others. Glancing at her, Christopher said with sudden casualness, "Why don't you drop up to my place for a while? I've some imported stuff." His eyes dropped away, concealing their real intent, but she knew what he meant.

"All right," she said, smiling, and he helped her down from the stool.

It was her first time. It hurt horribly. But it was good to have physical pain. In the numbness of her it was good to have physical pain. "I've got to get up." She got up and stood by the tall French windows overlooking the lake, steeling herself. She went back to him.

She was sober when she got home. She parked the car on the driveway and walked into the house on quick, angry legs, taking the long strides her father took.

D. S. and Sybil were at the table. Irene took the list from her purse. She unfolded it. She smiled, narrow-eyed, at her mother, and turning her head to D. S., smiled in a frightened, tortured way at her father. She dropped the list on the table between them. "Well—" looking at each of them again, slowly, "Kenny is dead."

She turned and walked in long strides from the room. They could hear her heels hammering on the stairs as she ran up to the second floor to her bedroom.

She went to bed and stayed there for a week. She wouldn't even talk to her father. Then, late one night, she had heard them quarreling loudly.

"Goddamn you!" D. S. shouted. "Why couldn't she marry who she wanted to? Goddamn you! Goddamn you! That kid's heart is broken."

Irene turned face down on the bed, trying to stop the tears with her pillow. Her mother's voice came up the steps to her. She could see her mother's nostrils quivering. Her mother was saying, "I never loved you. I hate you. I've hated you for years." Her voice had dignity and outrage in it. "I've only stayed with you for—for convenience's sake." She heard her mother's chair scrape back from the table and heard her mother's controlled laughter tinkling in a contemptuous and revengeful key.

"Goddamn it! Get out!" D. S. shouted. And Irene heard her father's chair bang back away from the table and her father's footsteps, wide on the floor, and the slamming of the front door. Then after a bit, the hopeless, helpless sobbing of her mother.

Irene lay there listening. And she was glad that her mother was crying.

Hours later she heard her father come back into the house and heard his voice, drunken now. "I want you out of this house tonight!"

"I'll get out when I please."

But she began to pack. And in the room next to hers, Irene heard her mother's desperate, angry words, her father's drunken cursing.

She put on a robe and went out into the hall. D. S. stood in the doorway watching Sybil pack. He held his Scotch bottle in one hand. He was very drunk and very angry. He lifted the bottle to his lips and drank and some of the Scotch ran down his chin and neck. "I've been waiting twenty-five years for this minute," he said.

Irene came for him. She took his hand. "Come on, D. S. Come on, Daddy."

Sybil glanced up and threw Irene a contemptuous look. D. S. let Irene take his hand and followed her like a child.

Irene took him to his bedroom and gently twisting the bottle out of his hand set it on the floor. Kneeling down alongside the bed she unlaced his shoes. He patted her head and ran his fingers through her hair. "I'm sorry, honey, about your boy." And big childish tears, driven out by the Scotch, fell from his eyes. "It's all my fault, honey."

"Now, now," Irene said, finding strength in his weakness.

But he went on crying. He nodded his head toward Sybil's room. "She's not a bad woman. Vain, yes. Snobbish . . . it's all my fault. I shouldn't have married her. I guess I'm vain too. Look—I had a lot of money—" He was rubbing his eyes with his fists. "I'm drunk," he said. "I had a lot of money. I wanted to get in society." He laughed at his own youth and snobbery. "They wouldn't have me. She—" he again nodded his head toward Sybil's room, "had a good social name but she was poor." He laughed again. "She couldn't be choosy. I married her because—" Again he rubbed his fists into his eyes. "I'm drunk—"

"Lie down, Daddy."

He did as he was told but clutched her hand. Irene began to cry too. She lay on the bed beside her father with her arms around him. . . .

Irene again looked up into the room and at Don. So like Kenny, somehow.

The crock was broken and she was trying to pour the liquid into another crock.

"This boy Kenny," she said to Don, "was killed in the war."

Don mixed drinks and handed her a glass. She looked down into the glass. "I could have slept with him," she said, "I know that. And I wanted to. It wasn't that I felt any way about it. It was just that I knew I'd love him even more and—and—maybe he—well, I didn't." She looked up straight into Don's eyes. "After that I slept around. I slept around a lot. At first I imagined every fellow was Kenny. Then —well," she shrugged, "call me a nymphomaniac if you like." She put one lonely finger on his shoulder and ran it down along his arm. "I would have slept with you a long time ago—only—and you are like him. You—well I didn't want to give you that kind of a deal." She leaned against him and laced her fingers with his. She put her head down against his shoulder. "I'm sorry I gave you a bad time."

"That's all right," Don said.

They sat perhaps an hour. The room was almost completely dark. At length Irene said, "Let's try again."

It was what Don had wanted all these weeks of waiting. It was good and over too soon and he was in love.

# XXII

Electric Shock.

The days seeped in through the bars to the eyes reaching for the ceiling, the patting feet, the torso, Hitler making his violent speeches, the boy coddling the invisible baby—seeped into the rag dolls and the mechanical robots. The days slid back out through the bars.

Electric shock again.

Again.

Again.

And finally Aaron was discharged from the hospital as cured.

He went back to Chicago. But not to his father's house. Not to see Rebecca. They didn't even know he was out of the hospital.

Aaron's days were of despair, his nights of grief. Even though he was out of the hospital. Even though he was supposed to be cured. He spent the long evenings in darkness. He could not write. The desire was gone.

Home from the hospital now . . . he lived secretly, away from everyone he had known.

If only he could write—explain himself on paper. Once . . . years ago in the Marquis restaurant the evangelist had told him to go home and pray and that then he would be able to write. He had laughed and gone home. He believed in no god. But almost as a game, in the superstitious aid-by-charms ritual, he had knelt down and prayed to the Christian God, the God of his mother.

Tonight out of the travail of his mind and its accusing confusion he undressed and went to bed . . . slept . . . dreamed that bad dream . . . the fever came to his forehead . . . a woman's fingers were stroking his forehead—his mother's fingers! From the sky a huge rock was falling on him. A rock bigger than a mountain. But he opened his fingers a fraction of an inch and, in this small space, was trying to catch the rock . . . his fear grew great . . .

He awakened in sweat, his head tossing from side to side on the pillow.

"Jesus God Almighty!" he cried aloud. "I had that dream again!" And sat upright in the bed.

Amazement came. Why had he, a Jew, called out aloud the name of Jesus?

He arose, trembling, and sat on the side of the bed.

For some reason beyond his reasoning he thought of the Virgin Mary. He knelt beside the rumpled bed and prayed to her with his face in his palms, prayed her to lift the burden from his shoulders.

And calmness came. He began to think of communism. And to think of Christ. Christ had said *all men are brothers,* had said, *do unto others* . . . communism was based on Christianity and communism had failed him. All men are brothers was a very radical thing when Christ had uttered it. It was still a radical thing today. Man professed it, mouthed it, but didn't believe it. Nor could he, Aaron, believe any longer that men, through reason, wanted the same things. Somewhere he had sensed the spark in mankind that was good, and the church taught that man, without grace, was an animal. And hadn't he seen that men, even though they had reason, were without grace? Could be interested only in power. If there was a heaven where this good part of man could find itself, he wanted that heaven. He had made his mistake in thinking that the earth mattered, when it was all eternity that was more important.

Almost as a somnambulist Aaron stood naked beside the bed and drew on his clothes.

As a somnambulist he went to the door and let himself out. He pushed open the huge arched door and stepped inside. He stood in the great aisle of the Catholic church. Twilight color stood in the church, deepening at its high-arched ceiling and scenting the air with its sweet-dusty smell of incense. Over the altar on its long thin golden chain a golden lamp burned like a red star through its crimson glass. All about him the angels and saints stood in their frozen plaster. But the many tiny sparks of holy candles moved their shadows on the walls. Gave breath and life and eternity to the angels and saints.

Aaron trod the holy aisle looking with his deep brown eyes for the Virgin Mary and the saintly, tortured, all-men-are-brothers face of Christ. He came like a thief up the aisle and like a thief moved to where Christ stood with his hands outstretched and his bleeding heart showing. He looked up into the saintly, tortured face. Moved by a compelling force, he knelt before the statue, and though he had no money to pay for it, he lit one of the candles in the little red cups at Christ's feet, adding its humble, worshiping tongue to the rest of the praying tongues of light. He sighed. An intense feeling of goodness, of purity, of sinlessness passed through him. The dark night lifted its curtain a bit. He said aloud, "You were a Jew. I was born a Jew and circumcised a Jew as you were, and like you I am not really a Jew. Is this what you too felt?" And in the flickering of the candles the plaster statue became human. The face softened. Here was a man, a human being, looking down on him with compassion and love.

He put his forehead down against the rail that shielded the red-cupped candles and they cast their fluttering light into his black hair . . . *blessed are they that mourn, for they shall be comforted* . . . and with the candlelight flickering in his hair he wondered from where inside of him came the words.

He had lit a candle. He had prayed. After going through all the motions he wondered at himself and wondered if he really believed? Were the motions without meaning? Others had joined, made the motions, come to believe, had felt peace inside themselves.

He tried making the motions. If mind and body were one, as the good doctors, the good psychiatrists said, perhaps here he could be mended and made whole again.

Once more he made the motions, the faltering sign of the cross.

The next morning he went to mass and knelt, imitating the rising and kneeling of the devout, and through the entire mass he felt humble and dirty and unworthy; had the feeling that he must identify with this.

After the mass he went to the priest's house.

"Father, I want to become a Catholic."

The priest smiled. Sat down. "Tell me about yourself."

Aaron put his hand upon the edge of the table and looked at it. "Father, I'm Jewish—well, half-Jewish, anyway." He looked up at the priest and rolled his eyes away, wet his lips, "I have no hold on life. I'm just living to die. I'm grasping for—" Again he looked at his hand on the edge of the table.

The priest cleared his throat and smiled kindly. "From the way you're talking," he said, "I don't think you're ready for it yet." The priest's hand touched his shoulder. "Go into the church and just meditate."

He went back into the church. He prostrated himself there. He went back to the priest. "Father, I want to be a Catholic."

"Well, you will have to undergo instructions."

He bought a blessed medal for his neck. He learned the *Our Father* and *Hail Mary*. He went every day to mass and every night into the church to kneel before the Virgin Mary and the high altar and the crypt . . . some day he would join an order.

And there was the Sunday at mass when the others went to the altar rail for communion. He found himself standing, moving to the altar rail, kneeling there. The priest coming in his white and gold robes and the chalice held on high, the host lifted in his hand and then placed on the tongues of the devout. Christ in the wafer to take home with them. And the priest coming nearer . . . you haven't been baptized! You're not a Catholic! . . . But his tongue went out and accepted the holy communion.

He was baptized. He was confirmed. The motions were only motions. It seemed to him that he was doing the same thing he had done in the Communist Party. Was going through the same sort of ritual. There was no surcease from the pain inside him, the agony of him. He was still alone and lonely. He was again cast on the sea of his despair and separateness.

# XXIII

The campaign was growing hot. At first the Democrats who ruled the district had considered Jane Morris as of no importance other than nuisance value. Early in the campaign she and her committee had gone to see McCarren and asked his support against Patterson, the Republican incumbent who had voted reactionary on every issue in Springfield.

"Yes . . . Yes." THE POWER was agreeable about little things.

"Now—" THE POWER had said, "why don't you people get out a little leaflet against Patterson—bring out these points—" THE POWER enumerated them. Then THE POWER looked across the desk at Jane. "And I'll pay for the printing of the leaflet."

"Why," Jane said, "we can't prove those things!" She tapped a cigarette against the desk and put it in her mouth. THE POWER held his lighter across the desk for her. Over its flare Jane looked into McCarren's eyes. "Why don't *you* print the leaflet?"

THE POWER leaned back in his chair and laughed and laughed.

Later THE POWER admitted to those close to him that he'd rather have Patterson down in Springfield than this woman, but that he didn't mind knifing him a little.

The Progressive Party had no money. They set up headquarters in a store front in the slum center of the district.

They had the borrowed cars of friends to use in street parades. Placards attached to the cars read: A WAR WIDOW FIGHTS FOR YOU—

JANE MORRIS, MOTHER OF THREE CHILDREN, FIGHTS FOR YOU.

Jane Morris's workers were all volunteer workers. They were project-housing people, veterans, housewives, college students, neighborhood people. They went out every night ringing doorbells, distributing literature, talking to people about the campaign. They arranged house parties to raise money. They worked hard for Jane Morris, the candidate of the slum dweller, the worker, the poor. The candidate of the many races of people who lived in the district.

The confident Democratic precinct captains and workers stood on street corners watching the parades and smiled and waved in good-humored raillery.

Jane Morris and her group began to gain real influence. Many of the families in the Sparrow Flats housing project were listening intently. Workers at the Haines Company had taken her seriously.

THE POWER called Jane in for an audience. He was overfriendly and sat her down across the desk from him in gallant style. THE POWER smiled his handsome smile at her. "I hear you're thinking of going to Northwestern Law School."

Jane smiled at him and said nothing. THE POWER smiled back. "Don't you think you should stop all this nonsense?" he asked pleasantly.

Jane smiled and again said nothing; smiled back into the teeth of THE POWER.

"I'll tell you, Jane," McCarren said pleasantly, "you're a nice girl. You don't belong in a game like politics. I'll tell you what. You've got a family to take care of." McCarren got down to brass tacks. "I'll tell you what—I'll give you a lump sum of five hundred dollars and two hundred dollars a month plus a good job until the end of the year—" THE POWER chuckled and wagged his finger across the table at her in a jovial manner, "if you just keep your mouth shut. You know—soft pedal it."

Jane smiled back pleasantly. "I'm more interested in a political career."

The Progressive Party began to give McCarren a little trouble, began to chip off a few promised votes here, a few there. A whisper campaign of REDS! COMMUNISTS! was started against Jane and her group. A little businessman, Olson, owner of a restaurant, who was one of Jane's precinct captains and a hard worker for the party, was approached and offered a job as a Democratic precinct captain —a paying job. When he refused, all the weight of the Democratic machine in the district was thrown against him. Though a previous restaurant owner had operated the place for years and had not been molested, the squeeze was put on Olson. He had to have special plumbing. The fire department paid him visits. His place was unsafe. He had to have special wiring put in. The health department arrived. He had to do several things to meet their specifications.

In her Sparrow Flats housing project apartment Sue held the pages of the speech and Jane recited it aloud in practice for the evening's meeting. They heard the uncertain rattling and banging of a car outside and then its tinny horn and Jim Norris was bursting in the front door with a big grin. "You gals ready?"

"Right away, Jim!" They got their coats.

When they drove up in front of the store the big windowpanes had all been broken out. House bricks and glass were sprayed across the floor inside. Chairs had been overturned.

Jim ground his teeth and rubbed his fist in the palm of his hand and cursed.

"We'll hold our meeting anyway," Jane said, getting a broom.

They swept up the mess. They set the chairs upright before the little platform. Then they took up posts outside to greet people and assure them that the meeting was on.

By eight-thirty the store-front hall was almost filled.

Don walked past and peered in through the broken windows. He walked past again and then, gaining nerve, stepped quickly inside and sat in the last seat of the last row. On the platform he saw Jane, Jim, Sue, and two people he didn't know. Slumped in his seat and half hidden by the woman in front of him, he felt the thrill of the spy.

Jim was introduced by the chairman. Jim said, "I'll make it short. I am here as a representative of the union at the Haines Company to endorse Jane Morris's candidacy. We of the union have come to know her as the friend of the working class. We have . . . "

Don listened with something of a smirk and with something of respect. Then he wasn't listening but looking at the tall, handsome, squarely built Jim Norris with envy. And then Jim's words snagged into his hearing:

"We know that Emerson Bradley is the archenemy of labor. We know further that millionaire D. S. Matthews has always given at least lip service to the workers, that his whole vast fortune was amassed through the efforts of the worker. We know that these two men have been bitter enemies—supposedly on moral and political grounds—and that they have often clashed openly. Their battles have always been front-page news. We know of Emerson Bradley as a Republican. The Republicans are—or so they feel—fairly sure of electing their man for State Representative. Well, here's something you may not know—both Emerson Bradley and D. S. Matthews have made large contributions to Boss McCarren of the Democratic Party to insure the election of his candidates."

Don didn't hear any more of Jim's speech. His mind was reeling: Emerson Bradley and D. S. Matthews! He couldn't believe it! He didn't believe it! Jim was lying just to get votes for Jane Morris.

Don's attention was recaptured by a burst of applause.

Then Jane rose smiling, and moved to the center of the stage, looking down at the faces of the housing-project people, the housewives, the workers. Looking down into the faces of whites, northern whites and a sprinkling from the South who had come North during the war to make money and had stayed. Looking down into the faces of Italians and Poles. The faces of Negroes, Japanese, Filipinos. These were her neighbors. She smiled out at them and began quietly to talk to them.

Don listened to her words and agreed with them. He even tried to memorize some of her statements so that he could use them himself. He felt a thrill of kinship with her and what she said.

And Jane Morris, moving closer to the edge of the platform, speaking as she would to a small group of friends in her own front room:

". . . as you know, I live in a public housing project—I am proud to say a biracial public housing project. My program also includes a state FEPC—a man should be hired and paid according to his ability to do work, not on his race, color or creed. We must have equal opportunity and equal pay. We must make discrimination in employment illegal . . ."

Don nodded his head. He looked up into Jane Morris's face.

". . . we need emergency housing for vets and non-vets in order to relieve the present crisis. Once we have done that we can make plans for long-term, city-wide housing. Slums and overcrowded housing conditions are at the bottom of most of the city's social problems. Improve housing and we'll be fighting disease, juvenile delinquency and crime. . . . This," and Jane pulled herself erect and looked out across the hall, "is my program. I dedicate myself to the winning of deep and lasting gains toward a better way of life."

She sat down. The hand clapping lasted a long time. The chairman put records on the phonograph and the people milled round to shake hands with Jane and to get the coffee and cookies various housewives were handing out. Don sneaked out of the hall.

# XXIV

It was now a month before the election.

The precinct captains went out across the district like an army of ants. They canvassed every house. They began lining up the vote.

They did favors for their voters. Fixed tickets for them. Got their delinquent children out of trouble. Ran small errands for their voters. Supplied a bit of the rent money to large families in the poorer neighborhoods. Fixed a leaky faucet or took care of a burned-out fuse. Offered a job at the polls to the heads of large families. Brought inexpensive toys to the kiddies. If something came up in court—robbery, fight, drunken driving, assault—they fixed that too. It was a remember-I-helped-you method.

They praised Bishop Sheil to Catholic families, commented on the greatness of Rabbi Wise to a Jew, condemned Russia to the Poles, told the Negroes that after this election things were going to be different for them.

They worked hard for the boss.

The newspapers began again to bum-rap Don. The little czar had put him on the ticket as a good front for himself. Now, sincere Democrats would vote for Schmidt as the lesser of two evils. They came out against Don because he was THE POWER's right-hand man. Reed, running for re-election, had been a representative for twelve years. Don was a new man and it would be harder to put him over. They left Reed alone. They knew that when it came time to deal with the Republicans, Reed would deal. He had before. They accused THE POWER of running Don so that it would appear that he didn't want to forget the vets—that he was doing something for them and that Don, in office, would fight for them. All a political scheme—the newspapers said.

For the entire month before the election the newspapers kept blasting THE POWER and his candidate.

THE POWER smiled blandly. THE POWER clipped the news stories, underlined *the little czar of the North Side* in red pencil, and pasted the articles in his scrapbook.

Don, worried about the newspaper articles, visited in the precincts himself.

The Polish man said, "Blood of a dog—they are all bad—all the politicians. Into my pocket all of them put their hands. Why should I vote? When they come buy I take the Republican money and I take the Democrat money. Then I stay home."

Don said, *"Mów pan ze mna po polsku*—speak Polish with me."

"You are one of us!" the Pole asked in astonished English.

"I am as one of you," Don said in Polish. He gave the man a cigar—and one of his political cards.

The Pole slapped him on the back and grinned underneath his bushed blond hair. "For you I will vote!" He shook his head incredulously. "You speak Polish! You speak Polish!"

Don knocked.

*"Kto tam?"* the Polish voice asked.

"I am here," Don said in Polish. "Don Lockwood."

The door came open.

THE POWER found out that Don had been canvassing in the precincts. He called Don in and, frowning paternally while he waggled his finger across the desk at him, said, "You keep yourself away from those precincts. You hold yourself aloof from the voters. You're not easy to contact or to see—" And THE POWER smiled. "You're not running on the Progressive Party ticket. Jane Morris and their candidates have to do their own leg work. They don't have any money or any workers. And you're not visionary Schmidt, the Independent. We've got the power and patronage. We don't go begging for votes. We let our precinct captains get the vote out."

Don flushed. "Yes, sir—yes, Tom."

Don, still worried about the newspaper stories, went back to see McCarren. THE POWER laughed.

"The newspapers!" THE POWER put his head back and bellowed. When he stopped laughing and wiped the tears from his cheeks he said, "Look at me. I go along, year after year, year in, year out. You think they can touch me? Or you? With me behind you!"

THE POWER waited until the election got close. Then he got pictures of Don in the papers. Pictures of Mr. Donald Lockwood, wounded veteran posing with other wounded veterans out at the hospital. Mr. Donald Lockwood, an orphan running for office, photographed with children at the orphans' home. Mr. Donald Lockwood, an orphan and a veteran.

THE POWER smiled and felt his power and knew he would win.

The precinct captains covered the district like a horde of locusts. They knocked on doors and rang doorbells day and night. They wore their political smiles and bland, friendly political voices. They made promises. They sent their assistant precinct captains out with literature about the candidates and with still more promises, more bribes, more small favors. They were cynical about their work and about politics. They knew they were flunkies. They knew that as long as they got the vote out, as long as they were good precinct captains, their jobs were safe. Even if the other party came into power.

But they had no self-respect.

Their loyalty was built on easy living.

They had their jobs at good money. Five days a week. Two hours work a day. And actually they did nothing. Where can I make that kind of money anywhere else? I'd have to work.

They had no ambition. A *hope* for a break—politically. That was all.

The job made bums out of them.

McCarren was right. He should stay aloof from the voters. The newspapers couldn't hurt him. McCarren was backing him. The Party was backing him. Nothing could beat the Party machine.

Getting cocky and conceited, and sure now of his election, Don swaggered more than ever. And there were women—three women in his life—to make him even more proud of himself.

There was Irene whom he loved.

There was Rebecca. She hadn't been able to stay away from him. She cried in his room and told him she loved him.

Smirking: "You mean you can get what you want from me." He said it cruelly because even if she had stayed away and he had felt relieved, he had also felt hurt.

"Oh, Don, you know I love you."

More tears.

"Well, look, Becky, I've been sort of a real bastard. If you get rid of me it's best for you." And now it was like a part in a play and he was enjoying the role—when you want to get them in real deep all you have to do is play the martyr. It fed his ego.

She cried some more and clung to him and said she just wanted to be with him, that she wouldn't even let on that she was Jewish.

It fed his ego.

"Love overcomes race and religion every time, huh?" he said.

And then angry at himself, at the part he was playing, recognizing himself as a bastard, he said, "I'm sorry. That was lousy of me. Honest I'm sorry." He got his hat and coat. "Goddamn them," he said. "Come on, we're going to walk through the park, we're going to go out to eat somewhere."

"You can call me Beth. It's all right," she said.

They walked through Lincoln Park. They went to eat. He faced up with himself. But he had his shaky moments on the street, afraid someone—McCarren—a precinct captain—

And for Don there was Sue. As a boy in his early teens, obsessed by sex, he had imagined how romantic and worldly it would be to have a mistress. It proved you were a real man. He supposed that Sue was sort of his mistress. And there was more than that to it. He found himself drawn back time and time again to Sue. When he doubted himself. When he was really lonely inside himself. When he needed someone to whom he could really talk and who really knew him. He even suspected that he wasn't really himself when he was with Rebecca, with Irene. He had to act the part they and he together had created for him. He saw all three of them. He was with Irene much of the time. He saw Rebecca through a sense of duty. He went to see Sue through a sense of need.

He was proud of himself. Very proud of himself, even when he said, You're a rat the way you treat Rebecca and Sue. A no good bastard. A rat.

But he was still proud of himself.

Irene, Rebecca, Sue.

What other guy could brag about having three women crazy about him?

He supposed it was because he was well hung. Thank God for that!

# XXV

Election was less than two weeks away. The precinct captains went all out for THE POWER. The newspapers kept blasting away every day or so.

LITTLE CZAR'S CANDIDATE LOCKWOOD
CABARETS WITH MILLIONAIRE'S DAUGHTER

> Don Lockwood, the little czar's candidate for State Representative, who is being built up as the first wounded vet of World War II and running on a platform as the protector and champion of the wretched and the poor is evidently feathering his own nest well. He is seen almost every night squiring the daughter of millionaire D. S. Matthews, the plumbing magnate, around town to the most swank and expensive bars and after-hour spots Chicago affords.
>
> D. S. Matthews is the schoolboy chum of McCarren, the North Side's little czar, and has contributed large sums to the czar's organization for years. Lockwood has also been seen with a woman worker of the Progressive Party and it is evi-

> dent that he is trying to entice her to get the Progressives to swing some of their votes his way since their candidate for State Representative has small chance of winning.
>
> Lockwood, an ex-actor and quite the Don Juan around town, is also, it is rumored, dating a Jewish girl in an attempt to swing Jewish votes his way.

Don walked into Sue's room and took off his coat.

"I've been reading about you in the paper."

"About me?" He came over. Sue pointed the column out to him with her finger. Don's eyes took in the headline.

LITTLE CZAR'S CANDIDATE LOCKWOOD
CABARETS WITH MILLIONAIRE'S DAUGHTER

"Oh," Don said, laughing weakly.

"Christ," Sue said, "what are you trying to do? Sleep with everybody in Chicago and the visitors too?"

Don looked at the article as if he had never seen it before.

"So it looks like taking you out to the veterans' hospital led to big things for you," Sue said.

"Huh?" He was reading.

Sue glanced across the room. There was hurt in her eyes. And then she was angry. "First it was the Jewish girl and now this rich girl." She smiled at him. "You're quite the man! Congratulations!"

"Thanks!" Don was pleased with himself. He liked the write-up. "You're mentioned too," he said, laughing.

He tossed the newspaper aside and began wrestling boyishly with her, trying to kiss her. She held him off stiffly. "Oh, I'm not young, Don, I'm not pretty."

That made him angry and he stopped. "Got anything to eat?"

She fixed him something.

Putting the plates of food on the table she looked across at him and smiled. "Don, do you know what I think? I think you'll always come back to me. It's nice to sit and wait." She smiled bitterly and sat down.

He narrowed his eyes at her. "Yes, I suppose I'll always come back." He tightened his lips; and opened them. "Goddamn it, I don't know why!" He looked at her angrily. "I suppose it's because you remind me of my mother." That hurt and he knew it. "I suppose I've got a mother complex." He pushed his chair away from the table. "I'm not hungry." He went to the cabinet and poured himself a glass of Sue's wine, then sat on the sofa sullenly drinking it.

Sue acted as if nothing were wrong. She picked up the paper and began reading it. She tried to eat but wasn't hungry and only toyed with the food. The newsprint blurred together.

The clock ticked fifteen minutes of their hurt and anger away. Don walked over to the table. He was repentant. "I'm sorry, Sue."

She looked up at him. "Oh, it's all right." Looking at him she recognized his weakness and the good in him too; and she supposed that the weak would always prey upon the strong—if she were strong. And she loved him. Maybe the strong always loved the weak and the weak the strong. And maybe each always carried a small parcel of contempt for the other. "Come on and eat now," she said, "I'll warm the coffee."

"All right," Don said humbly.

Going to the stove to warm the coffee she touched his hair: knew that the men women loved would hurt them. Coming back from the stove she touched his shoulder: that was why, too, a woman's love was more full of abandon than a man's. Woman's love is not passive. It abandons self. It takes on another self.

She sat down at the table and smiled at Don. Don looked back at her. "You'll always have me," he said, "I'll always have you." It was a confession of truth beyond right or wrong, good or bad, misunderstandings and small angers, envies, contempts. And they both knew it. Knew that they would always have each other.

# XXVI

The precinct captains with their glad hands and their small favors and their two dollars went all out for THE POWER.

Big John Buckley had a private meeting in the neutral corner of a tavern booth with the Republican precinct captain of their area. "Look, Charlie," Big Buckley said, "I been in here five years. I spend plenty of money and I see you hustling and you don't get any more than forty votes anyway regardless of how hard you work. I spend money—you don't get but them forty votes." He spread his hands. "Now, look—I'll tell you what I'll do. I'll give you fifty dollars. I know you get about fifteen dollars from the Republican organization—" Buckley winked, all-knowing. He waved his hand to the bartender and signaled two of the same while what he had said sank in. "So—" Buckley said, tapping a finger against the table. "I give you fifty—and the fifteen that the Republican organization gives you—stick that in your kick. You don't have to canvass or do anything. And—" he impressed the Republican with his eyes, "I'm going to give you forty-five votes—five of my Democratic votes—that's five more than you ordinarily get—and you're still a good guy with your organization."

"It's a deal, Buck," the Republican precinct captain said, picking up the fifty dollars.

That was all Buckley wanted. When he went out to canvass the people who were Republican, who weren't regular Democratic voters or who hadn't made up their minds, he gave a valid argument: "You never see the Republican precinct captain. They can't do you any favors. You vote for me. I'll do you a little favor whenever you need it."

He kept his opposition out of the limelight. And when the floaters came in to vote, when at night, after the election, all the stealing of votes went on, he could give the Republican precinct captain the extra five votes and lose nothing himself.

All for fifty bucks.

Bob Ryan worked hard in his precinct. He had a couple of jobs to give his voters. He won his precinct because he worked hard and got money from the organization to buy votes whereas the opposition didn't have money.

Then there was Precinct Captain Mucci, a fat, fleshy, oily man. He had a big potbelly and a vocabulary of nine words. But he knew his business; he knew politics. The song "Mr. Five-By-Five" might have been written for him. A little over five feet tall he was almost as wide as he was high and had popped frog-eyes in a greasy, puffy, swarthy face. He was in the corner tavern as much as at home and, with his sleeves rolled up, played poker week ends with his neighbors and voters. A self-effacing winner, he was a good loser. In solid with the ward committeeman, he had been given seven jobs by THE POWER to dole out in his one precinct alone where they would do the most good—get the most votes in return. All the voters in his precinct had his telephone number and could call him day or night. Anybody could come to him for a favor—Democrat or Republican—and they were all greeted the same—as old and fond friends. He could clasp a hand and talk loud and long while he smiled and, giving nothing, make people who had come for favors think that he had given them a lot. In the neighborhood, in the precinct, it was Mucci this and Mucci that.

He didn't go around canvassing. He had his assistant precinct captains do that for him and they always put in a good word for him, built him up: "Don't forget Mucci! He's a great guy!" It was a page out of the assistant precinct captains' rule book: *Always build up the precinct captain.*

Sometimes before election Mucci made a canvass with his assistant precinct captains.

"Here's Mr. Mucci," the worker said, "here's your precinct captain."

"Oh yes! We feel that we know you. He—" pointing to the worker, "always talks about you."

Mucci, like most of the precinct captains, always had lots of money around election time.

"You know, Mr. Mucci—times are tough—"

And Mucci, paying for the vote, "Well, how much did Joe here give you?"

"Well—I got three dollars."

"How much do you think you're worth?"

"Well—five dollars."

"Here's two dollars more."

On the street Jane Morris accosted and accused him.

"Sure," he said, "I got the money." He showed her a wad fat enough to choke a cow. "Sure, I buy votes." And, "I'm only working for McCarren because he bought me my first pair of pants. When we was poor he found a place for my family to live." And laughing, slapping a hand on Jane Morris's shoulder, "If you get on top, I'll work for you."

Jane laughed. "You're what I call an honest crook," she said.

And there were Democratic precinct captains, flush with money, who went to see people on relief and people in the housing project who they knew were having a hard time. The precinct captains gave them ten and fifteen dollars to put Democratic posters in their windows. Made them outright gifts of twenty-five and thirty dollars.

The precinct captains went all out for Don. "Here's a nice fellow—a veteran," they said. "Don Lockwood is his name."

"What a great guy he is!" they said. "He lost his leg in the war."

But there were Kostner and McGuire. Precinct captains in Don's district, they had been there for years. Both resented Don as a candidate for Representative and felt they should have had it. They weren't going to work their cans off for the punk bastard. They gave Reed a big play instead and didn't mention Don.

There were other elements working against Don. His running mate, Reed, began to worry about himself. THE POWER wasn't behind him the way he was behind Don. He got his four key men—

precinct captains—together and told them to get a bigger vote out for him: "Push me. Don't worry about Lockwood too much."

There was plenty of scheming going on in the district. Anyone would buy or sell anyone else if it was to his advantage.

Schmidt, the Independent Democrat, put German precinct captains in the German part of the district. They said to the voters, "We've got a businessman on the ticket—a German. We've got to stick with our own people. He's a fine businessman and people are saying there's a Nazi on our ticket. We Germans have to stick together."

The church hurt Don a bit. Knowing he was running around with all the women from what they had read in the papers, ministers got up in their pulpits and denounced him.

Don, in a countermove, closed a couple of the policy joints to make a showing with the people, showing them that he was going to knock out gambling.

The gamblers, the three or four who ran the policy wheel, in their own move against Don, in a secret hate for him but one that they couldn't afford to let get back to him or THE POWER, spent money secretly. They handed out five hundred dollars to the precinct captains of the opposition to buy up votes.

THE POWER, without knowing who to name, knew that there was a lot of conniving going on in the district. THE POWER shrugged and laughed. He was THE POWER in the district and had been for years. They couldn't beat him. The day after election they'd all be there licking his boots. THE POWER poured out liquid, drank and felt his power.

# XXVII

It was a week before the election. The newspapers went to the University of Chicago and Roosevelt College and got students to sign up to volunteer their services election day as poll watchers. They were schooled to watch for the stealing of ballots that belonged to Don's opponents.

A reporter, with the influence of his newspaper behind him, went to the election commissioners' office and convinced the officials that THE POWER was going to steal the election for Don. The election commissioners' office, in deference to the reporter's newspaper, promised to send a couple of watchers into each of the tough river precincts where most of the stealing was expected. Meanwhile the Women's Council of Voters also planned to send watchers.

Election day drew nearer. THE POWER planned a big mass meeting for his candidates. THE POWER handed Don a copy of the speech he was to make. "Can you remember it?"

"Can I memorize it? Are you kidding?" Don said. "I was on the stage." His legs began to tremble. This was his final speech to the people. Maybe this one speech stood between winning and losing.

He took the speech home and memorized it. It sounded good in his mind and tasted good in his mouth.

As the election grew even nearer the spider web was spun tighter. Don was sent around in a limousine to see some of the important ladies of the district. Don was sent with a little something for the ladies—a pair of stockings, a box of candy.

A precinct captain said to a man who had a couple of roomers in his house, "Send the boys around and I'll fix them up—see that they get enough for a bottle."

Precinct captains said, "Don't forget Lockwood, the veteran. He's our man."

And two days before the election the alderman took a little walk along West Madison's Skid Row and strolled into three of the largest flophouse hotels on the street, each housing two or three hundred men. With him he took forty or fifty dollars in quarters.

"Here's the alderman!" the proprietor shouted loudly, doing a little bootlicking himself.

The alderman gave a quarter to the first bum. He's a big shot. They all line up. He gives a quarter to each man. "You're all right!" the alderman says, doling out a quarter. And another George Washington profile into another grimed palm. "You're all right!"

The bedraggled, forlorn bums line up. Four hundred quarters are given out in one hotel alone. The alderman is a big shot.

After election a bum could no more get near him than an office clerk to an atomic research laboratory.

THE POWER, on the same night, was ready for his before-election mass meeting.

An hour before the mass meeting he called his precinct captains together. THE POWER sat looking out across the hall at his precinct captains, seeing all of them as one lumped-together man, a little underling, a little flunky carrying out the boss's wishes and orders: *I let him make an easy living but I keep him broke. Keep a precinct captain broke and you've got a good precinct captain.*

THE POWER signaled for attention. THE POWER, standing wide-legged on the platform, let them have it: You and I know what a political machine is—it's jobs and more jobs and if you want to keep yours you'd better deliver a good precinct. The county central committee expects me to carry the ward and I expect you to land every voter in your precinct. Don't fool yourself—we know what work you are doing. You'll hear from us the day after Lockwood and Reed get in. I don't want any alibis when this is over. If you need more money or have any grievances, now is the time to speak up."

THE POWER left the stage and went to his office. He sat down with his bottle and put his feet up on the desk, smoothed a weary hand over his brow, setting the handsome steel-gray hair in place above the strong, handsomely featured face with the hard eyes, and awaited the alderman.

The precinct captains sat around, lying to each other, awaiting their voters, clasping them by the hand and slapping them across the back as they arrived, escorting them to good seats, telling them how glad they were to see them out to the meeting and how much they depended on them two days from now. A few dollars passed hands from precinct captains to voters.

The hall began to fill. A three-piece band, sent from one of the taverns in the ward without pay so that the proprietor would stay in THE POWER's good graces, played monotonously. A couple of photographers set their cameras on window sills and, with their hats perched on the backs of their heads, chain smoked and talked football scores, argued the merits of Notre Dame and Army.

Reed, middle-aged and bald and bored and twelve years in Springfield as a representative, arrived and dutifully took his place on the stage, yawned into a cupped palm, frequently glanced at his watch in boredom. A judge, two congressmen and other minor dignitaries paced their way to the stage in great and aloof dignity.

The alderman arrived and went to McCarren's office. THE POWER poured drinks for himself and the alderman.

THE POWER lifted his glass, and so did the alderman. When THE POWER drinks the alderman drinks.

THE POWER turned toward the alderman. "I wish you'd take over for me tonight, Neil." THE POWER touched his stomach. "Stomach's a little upset."

The alderman winced. When THE POWER felt pain the alderman felt pain.

"Want me to get you something—something to settle your stomach?" the flunky asked.

"No." THE POWER frowned.

The alderman strode to the platform.

Don came late on purpose and stood, by previous arrangement, at the back of the hall accepting the praise of suckholes and well-wishers. The alderman caught his eye and lifted his hand in salute, then gestured comradely for him to stay at the back of the hall with his friends. Don smiled and nodded with equal comradery.

In the toilet two precinct captains who couldn't take it stood with their feet up on a toilet bowl and shared a pint of whisky.

The alderman's smooth, syrupy tones flowed in political sweetness over the heads of the audience. He nodded and smiled at Reed and Reed walked wearily to center stage, spoke in a low mumbling voice, in much-used and bored phrases for as short a time as he felt he could get away with, and sat down. He was glad it was over. No matter what he did he knew he couldn't lose. He looked out over the audience and thought what fools the voters were. He looked out at them in half-sneering contempt.

Reed was followed by the one judge, the two congressmen and the minor dignitaries. They all gave glowing plugs to Don.

The alderman again spoke sweetly to the audience and, his voice rising, ringing, said:

"And now we will hear from our next State Representative who, wounded in the war—the first wounded of World War II—left his leg in Africa but brought his heart and spirit back to campaign for the ideals—the democracy—he so recently defended on the battle-field of Africa. Our next State Representative—Mr. Don Lock-wood!"

The alderman himself, facing out toward Don, began the applause, his palms slapping together loudly.

Don, smiling, gesturing with his upraised cane, moved down the center aisle from the back of the hall. Everybody applauded, some of the people standing and clapping, patting him on the back as he moved through the throng toward the stage.

On the stage Don faced the audience, and with uplifted arms and smiling face, tried to silence the loud applause. Loudly the three-piece band played "Hail, Hail, the Gang's All Here!" Don turned his profile left and right, looking out, smiling out over his audience.

The applause gradually diminished.

One of the lap-sitters ran up with a fresh glass of water.

Now, on the support of his grandfather's cane, he came forward. His jaw tightened. He lifted his head at an angle. He spoke the words that had been on the paper. The words burned in him. They were part of him, what he stood for. They were Wayne and the soldiers who had suffered and died. They were the poor people of the slums. They were all nationalities. They were democracy and America. His face flushed with his sincerity and a small trickling of perspiration rolled down his forehead from beneath the short-cropped blond hair. He smacked the balled fist, grasping the cane into the palm of his other hand. The two photographers with bored faces pointed their bored cameras. Don stuck out his hand and spoke before the flash bulbs, gesturing with his cane, grimacing into the cameras.

" . . . that they have not died in vain—we—they, the young—who gave so much to the last drop of good American blood that this country and its democratic way of life might survive. They who have suffered that this democracy go on reaching even further toward the people—toward all our population—embracing them in their great need—I, standing here, speak to you as one who has come back from the war and pledge my everlasting support to the veterans and their families—to what they fought and died for—to better wages for all our people—to equality and democracy for all under this—the good and bountiful land of—"

THE POWER, in his office, filled his glass and a glass for his flunky. THE POWER, with his ear tilted toward the sound of Don's voice and his eyes and lips amused, swallowed his drink. With a twinkle in his hard eyes he looked across the desk at his flunky. "Our boy is doing okay," he said. And THE POWER threw back his head and laughed heartily. "From the sound of that speech you would think he was running for the governor's job."

In the toilet the two little precinct captains with their feet propped up on the toilet bowl again uncorked the bottle and passed it from hand to hand. "Let's drink to the tin god again or should we say THE POWER's chief gimp."

"They're sure using him," the first precinct captain said. He laughed. "Gimp—peg-leg—that's good! Say, he probably wore patches on his ass all his life. Now he has the gall to tell of all the good he is going to do!"

". . . that good and adequate housing, that decent jobs and wages be had by all, regardless of race, color, or creed," Don said.

In the toilet the second little precinct captain said, "Politics is the filthiest, friggiest business in the world. They use you as a whore. You have to have six faces in this game. Promise a lot and give nothing."

# XXVIII

Aaron stood in front of the synagogue. He felt his Jewishness. In the early morning light he looked at the frame building wearily leaning to the side, its once-bright color faded by many seasons of rains and snows and harsh sunlights.

He moved forward toward the door. . . .

Yesterday he had been sitting on the beach watching the white sails of boats against the blueness of the sky. The beach had been crowded but in the whole mob he had seen the old man. The old Jew had a long beard and wore the little flat yameka on his head. He also wore a bathing suit, an old-fashioned loose one with baggy legs. He walked along the beach holding a little boy by the hand.

Looking at him Aaron had felt his own Jewishness. He tried to avoid it, to turn his face from the Jew so often despised by the society in which he lived . . .

. . . But he felt his Jewishness . . . one old man on a beach in a yameka . . . he thought of his father. . . .

As he approached his father's house the first three stars of the Friday evening were in the sky and the Sabbath had begun. He went up the steps and pushed the door open. His father sat at the table alone in his work clothes and wore his hat as was the custom, partaking of the meal. The cup of wine near the fluttering candle on its golden holder, his father's old and only valuable possession. On the table was the food he remembered: the two loaves of bread covered by a napkin—the double portion of manna that fell on the Sabbath in the wilderness. Gefüllte fish brought over by Rebecca's mother. The other foods. This, the kiddush.

His father's aging and lined face looked at him. His father seemed not surprised to see him. Aaron looked back. "Hello, Papa."

His father motioned him to the table and Aaron sat down.

The old man blessed the cup of wine, drank and passed it to Aaron. He gave Aaron a portion of the Sabbath loaves.

Then followed the habdalah and Papa Levin chanted the prayer of separation, dividing the holy day from the days of work. And, after a bit, Aaron, like his father, held up his hands and they both gazed at their fingers in the promise to work hard during the coming week.

Eating, Aaron glanced quickly at his father: this was a good father. He had had a pushcart, had a horse and wagon, had a wife and two children. Papa was a Jew on the Sabbath, on Passover and other holidays. If a light was on on the Sabbath it must stay on; if it was off it must stay off. I used to say he was buying his way into heaven. And Papa is a hard worker—just a laborer at the Haines Company—always will be. Aaron glanced at the stump of a finger long ago mutilated by a machine. I'll never help him, never be any use to him. Aaron bit his lip. Then secretly looked at the lined face. A good father. Saw that I received the rite of circumcision on the prescribed day, eight days after I was born and with a godfather present, a pious Jew. The chair was in readiness for the prophet Elijah in the synagogue on that day.

"I wish you had remained a Communist." They were the first words to his son.

Aaron shrugged. "I have taught my tongue to say I do not know," Aaron said, quoting back the words from that ancient day when his father had given him the *Communist Manifesto.*

The father looked at him and then shrugged in turn. It was a weary but patient movement of the shoulders.

"Where is Muriel?" Aaron asked.

Papa's eyes came to his and, saddening, moved away. "The young grow increasingly away from the old."

And the meal was finished. The wine remaining in the cup was poured upon a plate, the burning candle was extinguished in the wine.

Leaving his father's house Aaron devoutly touched his fingers to the mezuzah and then kissed them.

. . . And now he stood in front of the synagogue.

He went forward toward the door.

He stood in the synagogue, in the home of his grandparents, his great-grandparents, his race. He looked again at the old men sitting there with their hats on, as is the custom, with their feet close together, as is the custom, and with their heads bowed a little. And Aaron could see a tremendous history stretching back for thousands of years from the synagogue. With solemn eyes he looked up at the ark containing the Torah inscribed with the ten commandments. Above the ark was the holy light that never went out. He was home. He had come home to his people. Elation struck him. He moved forward to his place among his people.

He was home.

But the next day his Jewishness was gone. We Jews. We cry. We lament. We know we're going to be hurt. We're even disappointed when we're not hurt.

As communism, as Christianity had failed him, now too, Judaism failed him.

He tightened his mind in a hard fist against religion. Religion hadn't saved the world. It had only helped divide it.

# XXIX

The day before the election The Power called his precinct captains together at the Democratic headquarters of the district.

It was the same old routine that had been used election after election by whatever party had been in power at the time. Money won elections. And money alone.

The spending of money is no object on Election Day.

The precinct captains waited in the hall outside McCarren's office for the money that would buy the election. Three o'clock afternoon sun filtered through the dirty windows. The precinct captains stood around in the hall asking one another how many votes they were going to get. There was jealousy and a feeling of competition among them. They stood around lying to each other.

"How many you going to get?" Hurst asked Mucci.

Mucci threw up his little fat hands in his fishes' fins gesture. "Three hundred," Mucci said, knowing he was going to get four hundred.

Inside The Power's office, card tables had been pushed together to form a long table. Behind this table sat Ward Committeeman McCarren like a czar with a long box full of envelopes, each containing money and each with the number of a precinct on it and the precinct captain's name. On the floor at The Power's feet was a large black bag with money in it in case he needed more. Money is no object on Election Day.

Next to The Power sat Don and next to Don the alderman. At each end of the table sat a secretary. They were not really secretaries though they went by that title. Instead they were two little flunkies, lap-sitters who suckholed around The Power and stooled for him.

The precinct captains came into the room one at a time to pick up their money. They were each given about three hundred dollars so that they could buy votes tomorrow. The votes would cost the captains anywhere from a dollar apiece to two for five dollars. They all had their complaints, each trying to get a little more money so that he could really pay off to everybody, pay off well and make a good showing in his precinct. Bring in the vote.

Money was no object, and McCarren, if he knew a man was a good vote-getter, a good flunky, kicked in with more money. He knew his precinct captains inside-out. He knew their strengths and their weaknesses—at the polls and in their personal lives. He knew just what the vote in the district would be, to within a few hundred votes. He was the little czar of the North Side.

And he'd kick in with a little more money. These were the boys, his boys, who kept him where he was.

THE POWER let Don hand out the money. Don, each time, handed the money out with a big smile. It was a begging smile, begging the precinct captains to give him their best.

They all shook hands with Don when they took their envelopes, and called him Senator.

Come tomorrow evening—well, they'd better butter him up and get as close to him as they could. "Thank you, Senator—we'll have you in there tomorrow evening!" A gracious smile, a bow, a conniving suckholing eye.

THE POWER looked up at Precinct Captain Miller. "Well—" THE POWER said, "What are you going to get—how many votes?"

It was a stock question to each of his men.

Miller's forefinger circled the brim of his hat on top of the table. "I'm going to get three hundred Democrat. I'm going to get a hundred and twenty-five Republican this trip."

THE POWER let his feet fall off the rung of the chair noisily and leaned forward with his hard eyes holding Miller. "You're going to get a hundred and twenty-five Republican! What's the matter with you? Why, you sonofabitch!—you've got four jobs in there. Why are these Republican votes going to get out?"

Miller hedged. Miller knew he was going to get more money. It was a game. A clever, strategical game. He knew he stood pretty high with THE POWER. His precinct, after the vote, was always up there near the top in the district. He had his job in the city hall. He had four ward heelers under him in the precinct. THE POWER had turned over four jobs—patronage—to him for distribution among his voters. One was a garbage bureau sanitation job. The others were a job as a janitor in the neighborhood public school, a window washer at the county hospital and a truck driver for the sign division. He had put up a hundred dollars for the organization election expenses himself and had collected fifty apiece from his two workers. He'd kicked his in for the buying of votes.

Miller shrugged at McCarren—and kept the smile inside himself.

"Well—" THE POWER said, "you're going to get three hundred

and fifty dollars and you're going to get three hundred votes and the Republicans are going to get a hundred and twenty-five votes. They're weak. They haven't any jobs to give out. They aren't working in the schools or city hall or bureau of sanitation. And—" THE POWER frowned, "they're going to pull a hundred and twenty-five. How do you explain that? They never got a hundred and twenty-five before."

Miller shrugged hopelessly. "Well, there are a hundred and twenty-five Republicans I can't stop."

"Listen—" McCarren said, "we got to get this election. It's an important election. I'll be around tomorrow afternoon to give you a little more money." His forefinger snapped back and forth in Miller's face. "You go pay those Republican voters to stay away from the polls."

Don, with his big pleading, friendly smile, handed Miller his envelope and the VOTE DEMOCRATIC badges, tally sheet, red and blue pencil, a precinct list of the names of the eligible voters and their addresses pasted to a cardboard, the candidate pins and poll watchers' credentials.

The next precinct captain came in.

"How many you going to get over there, Jimmy?" McCarren asked.

"I'll get two hundred votes," the precinct captain said.

McCarren pulled over a sheaf of records that lay on the table at his side. He glanced down at it. "The record shows last election you got three hundred and ten."

"Well—I got a fellow in my precinct," the captain said. "He has a policy station and a tavern and he wants to go into politics and he's out there canvassing against me."

"You ever collect anything from him?" McCarren asked.

"No, I never trouble him."

"What's his name?"

"John Marsack."

THE POWER pulled one of the telephones over under his mouth. THE POWER called the police station and spoke to the captain. "Hello—this is McCarren. A man by the name of John Marsack has a tavern over in the ninety-third precinct. They're getting kind of rowdy in his place. I'd like to have him picked up now and don't let him out until 5 P.M. tomorrow."

THE POWER hung up. THE POWER lit a cigar. From behind the smoke THE POWER said to the precinct captain, "Now don't come in with this two hundred vote. Otherwise I might put someone else in your place who can bring in more votes than that."

The last envelope was given out and THE POWER and his candidates were ready for the election. Were ready to go to the people for an honest, Democratic vote.

Precinct Captain Casey had early that morning gone down to the courtroom of his local police station where the bums were arrested and up for trial.

Casey knew all the bums on West Madison. Casey stood before the bench with his legs spread wide. Casey talked up to the judge for the bums. "He's a good Democrat," Casey said to the judge. "He's from Tom McCarren's district. . . . This one too, judge."

"Okay, Bill! Okay, Bill!" the judge said. And to the bums Casey knew and vouched for, "Get out of here!"

It's a joke.

"He's a Democrat," Casey says to the judge about the arrested bums. "He's from the third precinct . . . now this one, judge, votes out of my precinct . . . this is old Bobo Wolfe. Drinks too much. Hello, Bobo, you old tramp! Here's for coffee an' (*giving a dime*) . . . Say, judge! This man is from the twenty-second precinct. Hello, Gus. So they got you again! Better stop drinking that two-bit wine and passing out on them curbstones. . . . He's from the ninety-sixth, judge, never voted anything but Democratic."

And the judge to the bums:

"Get out of here!"

It's a joke.

Casey is a smart precinct captain. That night, the eve of the election, he had his whole election board of five women pinched so they would be sober election day.

Casey knows his way around. Casey's a good precinct captain. Casey never lost an election, never lost his precinct.

And that night in the precincts, the assistants and the little helpers went, late at night, with their armloads of literature so that the voters would be greeted with it first thing in the morning, and slipped the reading matter under doorways, rolled it securely against door-knobs, placed it under the windshield wipers of cars, covered the districts all over the city, with Democratic, Republican, Progressive Party literature.

The Democrats destroyed Republican literature and put their own in its place, the Progressive Party destroyed Democratic literature and put their own in its place. Whoever got there second and third left only his own candidates' pictures and promises. It was like a card game. You play your card and I'll play mine.

All through the city . . . and daylight was beginning to filter in, over the city.

It was Election Day. The city was to go to the polls to elect the best man, the finest candidates.

# XXX

November thrust a cold palm over the city.

In the early morning quiet, lights were turned on in the many polling places. Already on the sidewalks on street corners and outside of polling places the paid workers stood with their badges and ribbons—VOTE DEMOCRATIC. VOTE REPUBLICAN—and their armloads of literature about the various candidates.

Everything was all right with Mucci on election morning. He owned his election board. He had bought them. In Mucci's precinct, the 97th, an odd-number precinct, there were supposed to be two Republican judges, a Democratic judge, a Republican clerk and a Democratic clerk on the election board at the polling place. In the even precincts it was just the opposite.

Mucci owned his board. He had his two Democrats on the board and he had said to one of his week-end poker-playing friends, "Look, Bill, I know you're a Democrat. You're my pal. You go down to the election commissioners and register as a Republican."

Bill did so and was appointed a judge.

Mucci had the other two "Republican" members of the election board go down and register as Republicans. On the election board of his polling place, sitting behind the table where the ballots were given out to see that the elections were run honestly, were two Democrats and three "Republicans." They were all Mucci's people. Mucci knew he couldn't lose. He would even have to keep the Republican vote up a little so that there would be no investigation as to the legality of the vote he'd pull.

Mucci, at the polling place before it opened, made certain that the poll books and ballots were there and that his watchers and challengers with their check lists of the registered voters were ready to guard his party's interests.

Everything went well for Mucci. Mucci went over and handed the policeman on duty twenty dollars. Mucci owned and ran his polling place.

Walters, the Republican precinct captain, came in, sleepy-eyed, handsome in a square-cut, brown-haired, strong-faced way. "Hi, Mucci!"

"Hello, Walters, you old bastard!"

In the back of the polling place the bookie ran wide-open. We don't care. Let them run.

Into the polling place came the Progressive Party poll watchers. A young Negro from Roosevelt College, a middle-aged Swedish-looking woman with her hair piled on top and a pencil sticking in it, and a slim taut-faced Jewish girl in her late twenties. In a pleasant but thoroughly assured manner they presented their credentials as poll watchers to the judge of the election.

In one of the river precincts everything was okay with Precinct Captain Casey. He owned his board too. He had his fifty bums lined up outside the barbershop window early in the morning, ready to come in and vote the way he wanted them to. The bums leaned together in their old clothes in a breadline, leaning together for warmth against the November morning cold.

Casey went into the barbershop polling place, past the red and white candy-stripe barber pole.

"You dirty bastard!" one of the women judges of his board said to him, remembering the night before in jail. The woman laughed and Casey laughed. The other four women on the board laughed too. Outside, the first bum was ready to come in with his marked ballot and vote; was anxious to get his fifty cents and go back to West Madison Street for his bottle of wine. In the tavern he could walk in through the back door, Election Day or not.

In past the candy-stripe barber pole came Miss Thorndyke Peterson, head of the Women's Council of Voters. Dressed in black and like a militant present-day Jane Addams or Harriet Vittum, Miss Peterson entered the polling place and sat stiff and stern with her unyielding eyes watching the ballot box, watching every move made by the judges, the clerks, the voters.

Casey saw her there and began to sweat. His fifty bums waited on the sidewalk outside. Casey stroked his unshaven chin and ground his teeth.

Casey had to think his way out of it. He walked around the block puffing on three cigarettes, one after the other, and thought his way out.

Coming back to the barbershop polling place, he leaned his face toward the portly Miss Thorndyke Peterson's face. "What," Casey asked loudly, for all to hear, "in the goddamn are you doing here, you old hatchet-faced bitch? Why don't you go home and do your dishes? You ain't got business around here, you fat-assed slut, you!"

It worked. Miss Peterson, flushing and breathing through a shocked, wide-open mouth, gathered up her two hundred pounds, her purse and her umbrella, and with head held high marched out of the polling place.

Casey had won. Quickly he had his fifty bums go down into the barbershop. The steal was on. Casey stood with the first bum on the sidewalk outside and handed him the ballot he wanted the bum to put in the box. It had been stolen by someone on the election board. It was marked by Casey the way he wanted it marked.

"Now you," Casey said to the bum on the sidewalk outside in the meager sunlight of early morning, "go in and put this one in the box. I'll—" Casey patted the bum's crummy shoulder "—pay you when you come out with the ballot."

The bum went in. It was the old business. The old chain vote. The tramp brought out the fresh ballot. Casey, on the sidewalk, in front of anybody who wanted to look, marked this ballot and sent the next bum in to push it into the ballot box and bring out still another new ballot. To the floater who had just voted he handed a fifty-cent piece.

In went the fifty. And the last bum put not only the marked ballot in the box but the extra one as well.

Everything was all right with Casey. Casey knew his way around. Casey had fifty sure votes there in the ballot box for himself.

And Miss Peterson came back with officers from the election commissioners' office:

"This man cursed at me!"

"Who *me,* lady?" Casey said in hurt and shocked surprise, lifting his hands in astonishment, moving his eyes to the men with her. "She must be mistaken!" Anger in his face. Then a big-hearted, generous shrug. "She must be wrong. Not me, lady. You must be confusing me with somebody else. Me, I'd never curse at a lady." And to the officers, "You can ask the board. *Me!* Swear at a lady!"

And the board of judges and clerks, the board Casey owned: "No, we didn't hear nothing. Mr. Casey's a gentleman. No, he never talks bad to a woman."

And Casey had his votes in. Let her sit there all day. Let her sit and snoop till the polls closed.

In the other twenty-five river precincts they weren't doing so well. They were having a shaky time. There was little or no stealing with the college kid poll watchers meddling, challenging voters, taking notes. And the threat of men from the commissioners' office coming in at any moment. They had to keep it clean. The board couldn't do any stealing for THE POWER's precinct captains. The precinct captains could do little stealing for themselves.

And over in a precinct bordering on the Gold Coast, big Buckley early in the morning slapped a hand on the shoulder of his Republican precinct captain opponent. John Majewsky looked at Buckley and smiled. Majewsky was a big Pole who worked in the steel mills, had no patronage to offer the voters and no money to give them.

Buckley massaged the palm of his hand in Majewsky's shoulder. "Let's get a bottle of whisky, John."

Majewsky grinned. He didn't even have to answer and Buckley smiled in cunning triumph: big Polish slob.

Buckley had his man.

Majewsky was a heavy-drinking Pole. By ten in the morning he was drunk. Buckley was free to do all the stealing he wanted to.

The precinct captains were polishing off their work across the district, across the city. They had their paid workers stationed outside the polls to greet the voters, to canvass for their candidates, to remind, to threaten, to pay off.

In Hurst's precinct the Republican election judge found a hundred nonresident and disqualified names on the books. He pointed it out to the Democratic judge.

"Yeah," the Democratic judge said, chewing on the end of a pencil, "that's true. There ain't no voters in this precinct by them names." He chewed on the other end of the pencil as the Republican judge started to clear the names from the book. Then he lifted his pencil from his mouth and put it across the Republican judge's hand as a restraint. "Tell you what—" His eyes, with a bargaining and amused light, came up to the face of the other man. "We'll give you half of them if you leave them there."

The names remained on the registry.

The morning wore on and the ballot boxes across the district, across the city, were beginning to stuff full with the wishes of the people.

The Progressive Party candidates were out canvassing for themselves, appealing to people to get to the polls. Schmidt, the Independent, was appealing to the voters, seeing them in a last desperate effort to get their votes for himself. He had no organization behind him. He didn't have enough precinct captains to cover the whole ward. He only had his friends. And his precinct captains began to realize that he didn't stand a chance because there was too much money against him. They began to sell out for a hundred dollars each to the Democrats. They didn't even hang around in the precinct. They too gave the Democrats every opportunity to do their stealing.

THE POWER laughed at Schmidt. THE POWER and Don appeared together early in the morning in Don's precinct for Don to cast his vote for himself and smile with THE POWER for the cameras. THE POWER sent Don to make the rounds of the precincts in McCarren's limousine with two big detectives for escorts. The precinct captains introduced him to members of their election boards. "Our next State Representative, Mr. Don Lockwood."

Don left boxes of candy for the boards. It was his own money he was coming up with. But it was worth it. Tomorrow—

Don shook hands with the policemen on duty at the polling places and handed out cigars to them.

The police smiled and gave him a big hand: I don't know. This guy may be the winner.

The November morning filtered its meager sunlight and coldness to noon. The Democrats had all the money. The Democratic precinct captains saw to it that the whole board got plenty to eat. They had bought breakfast and sent in coffee and pop at regular intervals. They now sent in big lunches—anything the board wanted. And boxes of candy for the women board members to munch on during the long hours of the afternoon. They even treated the poll watchers.

In Mucci's precinct the Progressive Party poll watchers refused the food. The Jewish girl was even insulting in refusing.

In the river precincts the board of judges and clerks was afraid to steal votes for THE POWER. There was so much heat on that they didn't make one move for the precinct captains. There were so many poll watchers in the polling places that they were even afraid to accept the precinct captain's food. And in the river precincts the captains couldn't pay the voters right on the outside or in the voting places as usual. Too much heat.

The bums resented this. They were used to getting their money right out in the open. They thought they were going to be screwed. Many of them refused to vote and wandered away angrily.

Jane Morris made the rounds of the precincts too. The Democratic captains said to her, "You're making too much trouble. We'll have to do away with you. Take you out to the country." They were laughing on top, but there was a meaningful ring underneath. She went from precinct to precinct. They were men and she was a woman. In the polling places they grabbed her by the arms in pretended friendliness. "Well, *hello* Janie! How are you?" and left a month's black and blue marks. Or, greeting her warmly, slapped her across the hips vulgarly and made wise, insulting remarks. She went, later in the day, escorted by veterans, big fellows wearing part of their uniforms, and the Democrats tried to provoke fights, tried to get them to hit someone so they could be thrown in jail. And in one polling place a youth claimed he wanted to vote but didn't know how to write. "Did you go to high school?" Jane asked. "Yeah, I graduated."

"Well," Jane said, "I'll admit the Chicago high schools are bad—

but they're not that bad." They threw her out of the polling place for "politicalizing on Election Day."

Visiting her voters' homes, Jane found that many of them were afraid to go to the polls and refused to unless they were escorted: they had been warned not to show up.

And the prices of votes had gone up to five and ten dollars. There was the open buying of votes on the street. One Progressive Party member had tried to take a photograph of it and was beaten up.

Over in Buckley's polling place where Buckley owns his election board and is the typical precinct captain, the judge has a pencil in her hand. Generally the voters hand the judge the ballot to put in the box. When the judge knows it's a Republican ballot she marks the ballot with the pencil or sticks a hole in it with the pencil while pretending to stuff it down into the filled ballot box. Automatically it is a spoiled ballot. There must be no mark on it but the X's in the proper places.

If the Republican precinct captain beefs, the woman judge says, "Listen, we're running it in here! If you have any beefs call the election commissioners and have them send their investigators."

Over in Mucci's polling place Mucci isn't sure how this man is going to vote and he has promised to pay him. Mucci gives the cop on duty a side glance. The voter goes into the voting booth. The cop pretends he's fixing the curtain that slides across so that no one can see how the man is voting. And if the vote is okay the cop lifts his hat off his head. If he doesn't the voter has double-crossed Mucci.

If the vote is okay Mucci nods to one of his ward heelers outside and the ward heeler pays the voter when he comes outside.

And this, too, is happening all over the city.

The police are always on the side of THE POWER, whether he is Democratic or Republican. The policeman may want to be promoted to sergeant or want plain clothes and then he has to go to THE POWER.

And always, in all the precincts, there are at least twenty-five people who are old people who don't understand or who are blind, or foreigners with a language difficulty, or illiterates. They need instructions. One Republican and one Democratic judge is supposed to go into the booth with them. In Mucci's precinct, or Casey's, or Buckley's, Hurst's, in the precincts where the boards are owned by the precinct captains:

"You want to vote Republican, lady? Oh, sure, that's fine!"

And bang, they hit the Democratic column.

This too, all over the city.

The day was wearing toward evening. In Mucci's polling place there had been the flaring of tempers. The Negro and the Swedish woman from the Progressive Party had challenged votes in loud suspicious voices. Walters, the Republican precinct captain, and Mucci, his rival, had ganged up on the Progressive Party representatives, arguing, cajoling, dismissing. They had, time after time, worked it together like a well-executed double-play. The Jewish girl had been openly hostile and argumentative. They had called her a Red. She had spoken to them superiorly and quoted from the voting procedure rule book, the Constitution, the Bill of Rights. She had even used Lenin and Lincoln and Thomas Jefferson and Tom Paine and the Communist Manifesto. Both Walters and Mucci had been angry with her. And the board had yelled at her. And Mucci had told her to go to Russia if she liked it better there, even before she had quoted the Communist Manifesto. But Walters, square-cut, brown-haired, a card shark and a gambler and a lady's man, was gallant. And now, half flirting, half sneering, seated near her he showed her card tricks. "Now you see it, now you don't—pick a card—any card—put it anywhere in the deck."

His deft hands shuffled the cards. His slim fingers pulled a card out of the deck. "That's your card, ain't it?"

The Prohibition candidates' poll watcher, a tall, slim girl, bony-faced, in plain dress and without makeup, watched disapprovingly.

And Schmidt was wearing out his shoe leather and his temper climbing stairways, seeing people, getting them to the polling place in his own car. The Progressive Party candidates were doing the same and had had trouble with a crowd in the Gold Coast polling place because the woman candidate had entered with a Negro worker. And over in the intelligent part of the ward the voters knew that Don was strictly a "go-for." They were voting for Schmidt, for the Republican candidate, for Reed, and occasionally, very occasionally, for the Progressive Party.

And Kostner and McGuire were campaigning for Reed, went out to get Don. And THE POWER was laughing. Knowing all the time that he was the organization, they couldn't beat him.

"Looks like the little czar is doing it again," a backslapping suck-hole said. THE POWER smiled. They all like those names.

Mucci stood outside his polling place. Across the cobblestones of the street was a school yard and beyond its open space of playground the tall steeple of a church pierced the gray November sky. Mucci stood with two priests. The priests wore their black street clothes, their holy collars and their black hats. Both smoked cigarettes. One was a short man, soft-looking and piously smiling. The other was a tall young man with fingers yellowed from nicotine. They stood, amused at Mucci; but stood, also, to impress the voters with their now unspoken opinions. With them too stood Walters, the half-handsome forty-year-old Republican precinct captain. Mucci had a hand on Walters' shoulder.

Mucci turned his round, pockmarked dark face toward a sidewalk doorway from which a redheaded boy in his middle teens came. "Hey, Red!" Mucci shouted.

The kid came over across the cracked sidewalk and Mucci yelled, "Hey, Red, I'll give you three dollars to go vote."

The kid grinned. Mucci laughed. The priests laughed too. The kid went on about his business.

"How much did you spend?" Mucci asked Walters.

Walters showed his money with a rubber band around it and grinned as if to say, Well this is my take, this is what's left and it's mine.

A woman with a shawl drawn over her head came along the sidewalk toward the polling place.

"Hey, Walters," Mucci said, "loan me five bucks to pay her off."

"We canvassed her house," Walters said.

The Negro poll watcher for the Progressive Party was eavesdropping. He moved a little closer to the group.

"How much did you spend?" Walters asked Mucci.

"Oh—just the food," Mucci said. He put out his little arms, half embracing Walters and singing, "I'm a big fat papa—a big fat papa—" Singing and laughing with his arms holding Walters in the embrace of a dance he made several little fat-legged, rotund-bodied dance steps on the sidewalk in his humor and satisfaction at the way the vote had gone for him.

The Negro sidled up to the priests and started a conversation. "Well," the Negro said to the priests, "the Progressive Party didn't pay anybody to vote."

"Aw—" the Republican Walters said, big-handed, "they didn't have any money to spend."

"It's too bad," said the pious and elderly priest, "that any party has to pay for votes."

"I'm a big fat papa—big fat papa—" Mucci sang, laughing, snapping his little fat fingers, rolling his frog-eyes in the round pudgy face.

"Do you think it's right?" the Negro asked the priests.

The young one lit a cigarette. The older one said, "With either one in we'll go to war. Three weeks and we go to war with Russia."

"I like it over there," Mucci said happily. "I'll see all my relatives again."

Walters moved down the sidewalk to accost and try to influence a late-arriving voter.

"I'm a big fat papa—big fat papa," Mucci sang happily, snapping his fingers, taking his dumpy, grotesque little figure through twirling dance steps on the sidewalk outside the polling place.

The precinct captains gave their final try. They sent private cars after voters who hadn't yet arrived at the polls. They sent relatives and friends and voters who had received favors in the past to squeeze-play the people into the polling places. They went themselves and counted off five-dollar bills from their rolls.

And the big clocks in the city buildings boomed five. The polls closed. The taverns opened. The vote was in. It was now only to tabulate the count and record whether or not the best man had won.

All over the district, all over the city, votes were being stolen. Watchers had to have eyes that were everywhere at once.

In Mucci's now they were counting the vote. Mucci showed a roll of money in a fistful wad. "Well, I can put this in *my* pocket now."

"You bought a lot of votes," the Jewish Progressive Party girl said grimly.

"A few," Mucci said, nodding.

"You're a lousy bastard," the girl said.

"I know it. It pays off," Mucci said.

Walters, the Republican captain, said, grinning, "We only paid twenty-two dollars—the food we bought." He winked at Mucci.

Mucci winked back and they chuckled together and it was a good joke.

And up came a vote that was questioned. "You can have this one," Mucci said to Walters, meaning the next questionable one is mine.

And the count went on.

"No fooling," Mucci said to Walters, "how much did you spend today?"

Walters said, showing the roll of bills, "Twenty-two dollars. Just the money for the food."

The Jewish girl jumped up for the twentieth time to challenge a ballot. "Aw, quiet down!" the cop said.

"Let me show you some more card tricks," Walters said, and gave her body the eye.

"Look—" Mucci told her. "Don't give us a hard way to go."

"You wanta get home sometime tonight, don't you?" the Democratic judge said. The Republican judge just gave her a dirty look.

And up she popped again to challenge the next ballot, waving her instruction book, arguing, pointing out the rule.

"Come on, girlie," Mucci said, "don't be like that. You ain't bad-looking. Get over that nasty temper of yours."

And over in Buckley's precinct Majewsky, the heavy-drinking Pole, is just coming out of it, just sobering up. Majewsky has just twenty votes. He has to go back to his organization headquarters to report.

"Well, John," Buckley says, "I'll give you twenty-five votes to protect yourself."

He gives them to Majewsky and says, "Do what you want with them."

Majewsky is greedy. He starts erasing the Democratic X's and starts writing in Republican X's.

Buckley's brow creases down and his lips crease down. And it was a smile.

If he erases only one ballot he's as dirty as me. He can't beef on me. I might have stolen two hundred votes but his one makes him as dirty as me.

And this was the democratic process. This was the foundations of government. This decided city, state, federal rule. Decided the fate of the poor, the slum dweller, the laborer, the great masses of the middle-class, housing, health, the young and the old. This, the democratic process that led from city and town government to the White House itself. This was what decided national policy. And international policy. War or peace.

This was the free, democratic process. This was what Don had lost his leg for, Aaron had lost his mind for, Jim had lost his balance for.

# XXXI

THE POWER sat in organization headquarters with his feet on the desk. THE POWER was not in a good mood. The returns had begun to come in and the vote was not the landslide for his candidates that it had always been. Lockwood and Reed were only a few votes, less than a hundred, ahead of Schmidt, and the Republican candidate was running out in front. The river precincts hadn't, with all the bad newspaper publicity and with all the poll watchers from the colleges, been able to come in solid for THE POWER.

THE POWER chewed on his cigar, pulled the latest returns over to him and tabulated.

And now the ninety-ninth and the hundred-and-first precincts were in and the vote was even closer. THE POWER frowned. When THE POWER frowns everybody frowns.

THE POWER yelled for the returns from the thirty-ninth, one of the biggest precincts. All of his flunkies hopped toward the telephone to call the thirty-ninth.

"They're not finished counting there yet, Mr. McCarren," a flunky said.

Don sat with his cane drawn up close to him and his shoulders hunched up. He too kept a tab sheet and as new returns came in looked over next to him at McCarren's master sheet.

Mucci came into headquarters chuckling, snapping his puffy little fingers, rolling his frog-eyes in conquest at the other precinct captains who had come to headquarters with their count.

Mucci flopped down in a chair across from THE POWER, and throwing back his head, laughed.

"Six hundred and twenty-nine Democratic, seventy-five Republican," Mucci said. "Five—" he laughed, he drawled it "—five Progressive."

"Good!" McCarren said. "Good! Have a drink." He drew the decanter over and poured for Mucci and himself.

Buckley reported in and things were looking better.

THE POWER laughed grimly and polished his diamond ring against the sleeve of his coat, looked at it glisten under the electric light. "What are we worrying about? I run this district. Only a third of the precincts are in. *I* run this district."

One o'clock.

McGuire came in. He had fallen back about a hundred and fifty votes. Those he did pull in were in Reed's column.

"You dirty sonofabitch!" THE POWER said. "How come you get only two-hundred and fifty-six? You've got a job there. How come Hurst in the next block pulls all of his and over last time? He didn't have a job to give out over there—but *goddamn* you, he's going to get patronage from now on!"

Two o'clock.

Kostner came in. He had lost his precinct and came in with the excuse that Schmidt lives in his district and he couldn't swing it Don's way. "Schmidt spent a lot of money," Kostner alibied.

Two-thirty.

Most of the precincts were in. Don was running only even.

It was now after three o'clock.

The east of Michigan Avenue vote, the hospital vote, came in. These votes went Republican and for Schmidt, the Independent, the man not tied up with THE POWER's machine.

The newspapers had done a good job against Don and McCarren.

The last precincts reported in. Pencils at headquarters went down sheets of paper, tabulating. The votes were totaled—

Schmidt was in!
The Republican was in.
And Reed.
Don, THE POWER's man, his right-hand man, was defeated.

Don went down from organization headquarters and out onto the street. He tightened his hand on his cane and walked along under the street lamps. He had forgotten his hat and his blond, crew-cut hair took light from the street lamps. There were tears in his eyes and he had to keep blinking to keep from crying. He looked up at the night sky and ground his teeth. He was hurt and bitter and hugely disappointed. Again he blinked his eyes. And anger came. He thought of the people in the slums, the people he had made speeches for and had wanted to help. He could see their faces again. The Polish and Italian and Negro faces. He saw their dingy and ugly slum houses. He saw the Negro faces crowded in the church that night when he had given the minister a hundred-dollar bill. More anger came. He had been repulsed by the very elements he had tried to help. "You can't help these people," he muttered half aloud.

And now his head was down. He had lost and they had told him he would win. And now his eyes were filling.

He rubbed his hand across his ear in the gesture of a child. He had to close his eyes to keep the tears back. His hand rubbing his ear touched his hair. Well, at least he could let his hair grow again.

# XXXII

When Don got home, Rebecca was there. She stood up, the magazine sliding off her lap onto the floor. "Don," she said, and came toward him, her green eyes searching his face.

"What are you doing here?" Don asked, staring at her blindly.

"I told my mother I was staying with my girl friend. I had to be with you."

Don threw his cane into a corner and sank down into a chair.

"What happened, Don? Did you win?"

Don put his fingers over his eyes.

"No, I lost."

Rebecca came to him. "Oh, I'm sorry, honey. I'm—I'm sorry." She put her fingers into his hair at his temples. Leaning over she kissed his forehead. "I'm sorry. It doesn't matter. Please don't feel bad." She slid to the floor at his feet and, sitting there, put her arm on his knees and her head down against her arm.

"Don't," Don said. He drew away from her. "Get up!"

Rebecca went and sat on the edge of the couch with her misty green eyes looking at him sympathetically. Don sat with the tips of his fingers against his eyes. They sat like this for a long time. At length Don lifted his fingers away from his eyes.

"They told me I would win," he said.

"Don't feel bad," Rebecca said, wanting to come to him.

"I wanted to win," Don said, rubbing the palm of his hand against his knee. His jaw tightened and his eyes frowned. "If the nigger vote hadn't gone the other way I would have won. They sold me out. They promised me their vote."

"Don't say that," Rebecca said.

"Say what?"

"Nigger." She hung her head.

"Well, it was the nigger vote that beat me." He was angry. "And I'll say nigger if I want to."

"Please, Don, don't say that."

Don looked at her sneeringly. "Efen you don't like the zoot poot it beck on the reck," he said in Jewish dialect.

Rebecca's face flooded red. She stood up and her mouth was held open loosely. She walked to him. "Please, Don." She held out her hand for his but he didn't take it. He stared at her birthmark, covered with theatrical makeup. "What are you so high-hat about? You're nothing but a bitch," he said. "The first time you came up here I laid you."

Rebecca lowered her head. "But, Don, we're in love," she said. Her eyes came to his face pleadingly.

"Oh nuts!" Don said. He kept staring at her birthmark covered with theatrical makeup. He opened his lips a little in the sneering, cynical smile. He was hurting her, hurting her horribly. And he knew it. "Efen you don't like the zoot poot it beck on the reck," he said again.

Tears.

Rebecca walked to the couch and sat there drawn into herself and staring at the floor. Across the room Don, with the tips of his fingers over his eyes.

For half an hour they sat in the silent room. Then Rebecca stood up. She glanced at Don and her eyes flooded with tears. "I'm going, Don."

He sat motionless without looking at her.

She stood there a moment, her eyes staring at him pleadingly, asking return, asking love, sympathy, asking to be allowed to love him, to give him comfort and warmth, her arms to shield him in his great disappointment. And again she half whispered, "I'm going, Don." Her voice broke on his name.

"Yeah," Don said. With his elbows on his knees he ran his hands up across his forehead and his fingers into his hair. "Yeah."

Rebecca left.

# XXXIII

He lay across the bed. He lay there an hour. Then he got up. He couldn't stay here, in this room. Forgetting his no-longer-useful cane, Don went down to the sidewalk and wandered around the streets. It was cold and he turned up his suit collar. He walked, miserable, through the city's endless and uncaring ways. Soon—he shivered—the newspapers would be out and acclaim his defeat. It was to have been his proud day. He lowered his head and shoved his hands deep into his pockets. And he had lost Irene too. She wouldn't want him now. He was just a nobody.

His feet took him where they would. He had lost. But he'd stay in politics if he could. No, he guessed McCarren was through with him now. Overhead the rumble of an early morning El. And McCarren had done so much for him too.

Down the endless ways of slum streets leading to slum houses he walked . . . city dawn came . . . the city gave back its hard, impersonal stare. Don looked up, wondering where he was. Recognition came. A block from his mother's house.

On slow legs he climbed the stairs and opened the door. The little kids were sleeping in a pile in the bed behind the stove. He looked at them there under the frayed and dirty blankets, wearing the clothes they had worn all day. He guessed he belonged there. He was just another Polack. His eyes looked across the doorsill at his mother. She, breaking wood by the sink to give morning warmth to the room, looked back into her son's eyes.

"Ma, I lost."

He walked across the doorsill. His mother met him on the warped boards. "It is all right, my son." Her thin arms went around him. "Come," she said, "Helcia did not come home last night." She led him to his old bedroom and he sank on the side of the bed. Yes, he was home. He had never left home. Just a Polack. A dumb Polack.

And his mother's arm enfolding him, his mother's words, in Polish: "There, there, child. Do not grieve. All will be well."

Don rubbed his cheek against the rough weave of his mother's ragged sweater. He heard the Polish words. In his mind, Polish words spoke to him in an old proverb: *natura ciàgnie wilka do lasu:* what's bred in the bone, can never be out of the flesh . . . just a Polack.

"Speak Polish to me," he said to his mother without any reason.

Some Polish words passed between them. Then the mother arose. "A little warm milk will do you more good than words."

She went to fix it.

Don lay back across the bed . . . just a . . .

When his mother returned he was asleep. Gently her hard-worked hands pulled a blanket over him, her calloused palm stroked his forehead. Tears stood for a moment in her eyes. Then she raised up proudly. Her son had come home to her. She would not go to work this day. She would lose five dollars and twenty-three cents. But she would take care of her son. He had come home to her.

Quietly she closed the bedroom door and went into the kitchen so that the little kids would not make noise and disturb her son's rest.

# XXXIV

A big upset like this had hurt THE POWER's pride. The newspapers had beaten him and he knew it. The defeat was his, more so than the puppet he had put on the ballot to run. THE POWER's pride was hurt.

THE POWER started yelling that his white-haired boy, Lockwood, had been robbed of the election. Lockwood's opponent had won by the small margin of nine hundred and some votes. "They stole the election from us!" McCarren howled. To make a good stink THE POWER said that he was going to demand a recount.

But this was all ballyhoo to save his own face after his defeat, for he had nothing to back his statement. Knowing that this recount would take a year and a half and cost him a tremendous amount of money, he was only blowing hard just to have something to say after the election; have an alibi.

THE POWER raised hell. And just for the show.

Meanwhile, in their homes, in the privacy of their minds, a number of the precinct captains were glad. They had hoped that THE POWER would be pushed out but they would never dare say anything aloud because of their jobs. These precinct captains had a hidden hate for THE POWER. Many of them felt that they should have been given better jobs, more money, or should have been put up for office. But always it was the suckholes who came first.

They chuckled to themselves and listened to THE POWER's ballyhoo.

The third day after the election McCarren phoned Don and asked him to come down to the office. Sheepishly, and with his eyes averted, Don entered. "I—I'm sorry—" He gestured ineffectually with his hand. "I didn't think you'd want to see me any more."

McCarren snorted and slapped Don on the shoulder. Don had been a good boy. He had done McCarren's bidding all along the line. McCarren had an affection for him. He could still use him.

"I've got a job for you, Don," he said.

He made Don a ward superintendent, a civil service job.

Don was supposed to have his name on the lists for the job after passing a test. He didn't even have to take the test. The connection passed him. He was installed in his new position with five foremen under him. His duty, in his official capacity, was to take care of all the garbage disposal in McCarren's ward, the Ninety-ninth.

And Irene called him. Her voice was cool and casual. "You haven't called me," she said. She didn't mention the elections. Instead she asked him it he'd like to go have a few drinks.

He went. Everything was okay there. Was as it had been. And he felt shame, too, about the way he had treated Rebecca. But wouldn't let his mind stay too long thinking about it. He shrugged. After all he had to break it off sometime.

City trucks were not supposed to collect garbage from restaurants, taverns and other places of business. This was all supposed to be done by private scavengers.

Don, feeling his way around, liking the money, got acquainted with all the businessmen in the ward and had their garbage picked up by the city trucks at half price. This gave him a little extra loot.

And Don as usual made all the collections for THE POWER.

If trouble came Don would be left holding the bag. He knew that.

And he was strictly a yes-man now. But one false move and THE POWER would say *out* and he'd be *out*.

He knew this too. And he didn't want to go back to the slums. He didn't want to be miserable again. At any price he wanted escape.

Don was a good boy. There was nothing more important than being a money-maker. Don made good money for THE POWER.

# Book Six

## WATCHMAN, WHAT OF THE NIGHT?

*The dirty jokes in the men's toilets were beginning to be signed* KILROY WAS HERE. *The OPA was off. The war was over. A sigh of relief went up. It was a world sigh. The war was over. People were taking the small and pleasant things of peace. They laughed and cried at the movies.* The Best Years of Our Lives *and* The Jolson Story *put lumps in their throats. But there were Bob Hope and Jack Carson to laugh at. Bing Crosby, Ingrid Bergman and Van Johnson were the leading box office attractions. "The Gypsy" was the most popular song in the country and you had to have a drag to get a new car. Winchell and Jack Benny were Sunday rituals.*

*It was the day of high prices, of markets flooded with meat, with wheat, and prices going up higher and higher. But the people were told there's no hoarding of meat, no hoarding of wheat. It's all going to starving Europe. Prices were going higher. They were soaring to new records. You couldn't rent a house to live in. It was the day of the black market and then the day of the gray market.*

*But these were the best years of our lives. These peaceful years here and now.*

*Emperor Hirohito had, in this time, in these years after the war, told the Japanese people over the air that his divinity was really only a matter of legends and myths. On the trains the Japanese had been segregated by their conquerors. FOR JAPANESE—FOR OCCUPATION FORCES and in America, in its Southern states, the population was soon to learn that Negroes and whites standing out under the open air were to be segregated one from the other. Jackie Robinson was playing ball in the major leagues and that was a selling point for democracy. American diplomats from Southern states where Ne-*

*groes couldn't vote traveled to Europe in Gilbert and Sullivan satire to shout that Europe must have the freedom and democracy of America. America was building a stock pile of atom bombs. America was maintaining an army larger than ever before in its history and a navy larger than all the other navies in the world combined.*

*And the body of little six-year-old Suzanne Degnan was found, the head there, the torso here, an arm somewhere else. And the Pope created thirty-two new cardinals in all the pomp and glory that is Vatican City. And some of the most exciting news to hit the front page was the marriage of an English girl, called Elizabeth, while a girl from Chicago, near the Stockyards, sent her a gift of a green taffeta dress and was invited to the wedding.*

*There were strikes and more strikes. And a man came all the way from England to the small town of Fulton, Missouri, to denounce a man in Russia to an American audience as a warmonger and to advocate a fraternal Anglo-American association against Russia, as if he were custodian for all the English-speaking people.*

*In the days of our peace. In the days after the war.*

*And General McNarney ordered a more rigid discipline among the armed troops of the United States Army, saying that black market activities and drunkenness had caused loss of respect for United States soldiers throughout Europe and Asia.*

*These the days of our lives. The days of our peace.*

*And Joe Louis knocked out Billy Conn in the eighth round and Frances Xavier Cabrini of Chicago was canonized by Pope Pius XII.*

*Meanwhile Russia was filling American skies with flying discs. The UN was having a hard time finding a place to call home in the United States and the American government had distributed a billion dollars worth of war materials overseas and Mr. Truman told Mr. Wallace, here is your Secretary of Commerce hat, and the Hindus and Moslems were rioting, the Jews and Arabs were fighting, and it took the St. Louis Cardinals seven games to win the World Series with Harry, the Cat, Breechen winning three games after St. Louis got into the series through a league playoff with Brooklyn and America was allowing her army and navy officers to talk openly of attacking Russia before she had time to recover from her war effort and before she had the atom bomb. And Hermann Goering fooled everybody by committing suicide under the noses of his guards by swallowing poison less than two hours before he was to be hanged while his ten buddies were strung up for crimes against humanity by the International War Crime tribunal.*

*And the Un-American activities committee was having a field day, the Taft-Hartley labor bill was law, few days went by without some boy or girl under fifteen killing someone, generally another boy or girl.*

*And the most popular songs, according to the Hit Parade, were*

*"Near You," "Now Is the Hour" and "Nature Boy." Then, suddenly, "Some Enchanted Evening" was the most popular song across the length and breadth of the land.*

*The headlines were full of spy stories. The newspapers had declared war on Russia. Almost everybody agreed that atomic warfare would mean an end to man: almost everybody said, We've got to fight Russia! The dirty jokes in toilets were being signed* KINSEY WAS HERE.

# I

The first snowflakes came to the city as the first stars come to the evening sky. They swirled far overhead and then began gradually to drift down. They etched window frames and laced the sidewalks with a delicate powdering and were swirled about the heels of the people by gusts of wind. The high towers of the Haines Company stood tall on the western fringe of the Chicago Loop. Stood as a mighty potentate and gave work, food, shelter, to the people.

Jim, the new vice-president of the union, doubled his work and his energy but the small stone of shame was frigid inside of him. Max brought his truckloads to and from the Haines Company. O'Keefe, sitting at a Thompson table over coffee, talked about the boss.

And at home alone in his house Papa Levin put his hands up to his temples and mourned his boy.

And Rebecca had thoughts about Don. There were nights when she cried. But she did not go to see him. And there were nights when she cried over Aaron.

And Don, though defeated, was successful. He was still THE POWER'S right-hand man. In him was a great gratitude toward McCarren. And loyalty. There was nothing he wouldn't do for THE POWER. He did all the dirty jobs, collected all the graft, was ruthless with those who failed to kick in. In a short time he had doubled McCarren's take. And THE POWER just sat back and raked in the gold. Left more and more authority to Don. And Don was helping himself to money. Was doing better than he ever had done before. Had five new suits. Had money in his pockets all the time. And if he stopped to think about the rightness or wrongness of what he was doing, if Wayne's image appeared, he quickly substituted thoughts of McCarren and what he owed him, substituted the faces of his mother and the kids and how he wanted to help them.

He smiled at his mother importantly and set his Homburg down carefully on the kitchen table. From his pocket he took the keys and the address written on a piece of paper. "I rented a new place for you, Ma. It's nice and clean. Seven rooms, too. Plenty of room for the kids." He tilted his head a little, looking at her, and smiled and saw the first tears gathering. "The rent's paid for six months and I'll keep it up for you. Here's some money as a start, for new furniture." He put a couple of hundred-dollar bills on the table. "Leave all this junk here. Oh—there'll be a fellow around in the morning to take your clothes and whatever other stuff you want to take." His face lost its confident, cocky self-assuredness. But only for a moment. Only as he said, "Will you take Grandpa's stuff too?"

The new apartment was far away from where Don lived. It was on West Division in the Polish neighborhood. But still in the district so his mother and Helen could vote for him. And the kids, too, when they got older. Politics was all right and he wasn't getting out. Someday he'd be able to do a lot for the poor people. Some day I'll be a Power and then I'll change things. Then I'll help the poor . . . don't worry, Wayne. I haven't forgotten.

Aaron—walking along the sidewalk. There were a million beetles on the sidewalk at his feet. Look. Levin, it's only snow. It's only footprints in the snow. You can't go on like this, Aaron, you can't. You've got to grab hold of yourself.

He walked into Thompson's. Like everybody else he needed people and had begun to come back there.

Immediately Rebecca said, "I'll get you a cup of coffee, Aaron." She had found out now where he spent part of his time. She came often to the Thompson tables just to be near him. She brought the coffee and a slice of pie. His deep brown eyes looked at her and he said thanks and laced his black hair behind his ear. He was hungry. He hadn't eaten since morning. He didn't have any money.

O'Keefe was talking to Rebecca about the Haines Company, but Rebecca was watching Aaron in a sad pleading way. O'Keefe was saying, "You should hear the girls over there. 'Oh we were over to the Bit of Sweden last night! Was it crowded!' The fact that someone's elbow was in your teeth was unimportant. The important thing was that they were part of the mob and the mob was lovely. The mob was enjoying itself." He went rambling on in the way a man does who lives alone in a room and has a chance to be with people and talk to them.

Aaron opened his pocket notebook. He tore out a page. With his lower lip pouted out he wrote words in his precise handwriting.

Aaron pushed the slip of paper across the table to Rebecca. She read:

Twin sleek breasts
tense
in the shrubbery of your shirtwaist.

Her eyes looked over the paper at Aaron. "It's nice," she said softly.

It didn't mean anything to Aaron. Just the poetic expression. Or maybe paying for the pie.

O'Keefe looked up toward the front of the restaurant. "Here comes the politician!" he said.

When Don saw Rebecca his blond face flushed red. Her cheeks reddened in turn. Don quickly pulled his eyes away. "Hello," he said to everyone at the table, gruffly, and sat down.

"You remember Rebecca?" Aaron asked.

Don nodded into Aaron's face and his eyes moved to Rebecca. They glanced at each other and their eyes fell away. Don looked down at the table top, remembering the words he had used. Ashamed now.

O'Keefe said with some relish, "Well, the election didn't come off too well for you."

Jesus, if Wayne had heard what I said to her: Then he heard what O'Keefe had said. He looked up and squared his shoulders and frowned with his eyes. "They robbed me of the election. You know that, don't you? Why I only lost by nine hundred votes and they stole a good three thousand." He went on talking, blowing himself up big and glancing at Rebecca. "McCarren's going to demand a recount. Didn't you read that in the papers?"

Rebecca's eyes fluttered to Don's face and away. There was a secret between them and this other thing, now, this racial thing. And she was on guard, too, against anything Aaron might think or guess. But she couldn't help looking at him. She felt again his fingers against her cheek applying the theatrical makeup to her birthmark.

"I'm not through with politics. McCarren's going to run me again." He looked at Aaron. "And when I get in I'm going to do things for your people and for colored people." As he said it he knew it was in bad taste but it was an apology in words to Rebecca. He stole a glance at her. She was staring at her hands. He laughed nervously. "I mean I'm going to help all the people."

He went into one of his political speeches while O'Keefe read his newspaper or pretended to.

But nobody was listening and he stood up and carefully molded his hat to his head. Stood there self-consciously a moment. Then he smiled at everybody and said good-by and glanced at Rebecca. She didn't look at him.

But when he had gone, because she had to talk about him, she said to O'Keefe, "You don't like him, do you, Sean?"

O'Keefe answered slowly, wanting to be kind, "He's useless as a friend and harmless as an enemy. That's how I'd sum him up."

Again Rebecca's face flushed. She stayed just a little longer and then said she had to go. As Don had glanced at her she now glanced at Aaron before leaving.

As she moved toward the door Steve, on his half-hour break, carried a cup of coffee to the table where Aaron sat and O'Keefe again lifted his newspaper in front of his face.

Steve flopped down opposite Aaron and looked at him out of his muddy, red-rimmed eyes. He knew his influence on Aaron, he knew his destructiveness and the vicious poison pills of conversation he had been doling out to Aaron. He knew his half-poetic language had a fascination for Aaron. His eyes were as cold and scheming as McCarren's. He said, "I want to be a gazelle. I want to run through the wild woods and piss against the trees as they present themselves to me. Do you think I can? Here I am, a poet, dishing up hash." His smile was cynical and bitter. "I've had a marvelous life—a marvelous life—so people tell me. I've decided that I'm a very lucky fellow—after talking to everybody else. How can you end such a life? How do you start such a life?"

O'Keefe stood up, folded his paper, stuffed it angrily into his pocket, gave Steve a fierce, black-eyebrowed Irish frown and walked out of the restaurant.

Steve reached across the table and took hold of the wrist of Aaron's coat and held on as if it were a lifesaver. "We know how rotten life is," he said. "People are pigs. Any way you look at it people are pigs. People stink."

Aaron began to tremble. But his fascination was strong. Oh, save yourself, save yourself! He tried by thinking of Steve's eyes: small gray buttons hanging loosely from black cords. But the words poured in from Steve's monologue:

"People stink. People are lousy. They're petty. They're little. At the top or at the bottom you'll find them all the same. And the middle is worst. They've got petty larceny in their hearts. They go for pennies. Look—take doctors—they're cruel in their way. They use you for copy. They use you for study. This fellow I go to, he's trying to break me from living in the past. He told me, 'You say your mother needs you and your son needs you. They don't need you—you need yourself. I know the world's a lousy, stinking place. But other people get along.' "

Steve's mind took a sharp curve. "Take women. All they're good for is screwing—and most of them aren't any good at that. People!" He laughed bitterly. "Let me get what you have otherwise I can't sleep tonight."

Aaron began to sweat. He had to get out of there. He had to get out right away. "I've got to go, Steve." He half stumbled on his big feet as he hurried to the door.

Steve watched him. His lips lifted in a sneer. He wanted him to be as unhappy as he was. He wanted him for a son. A disciple to influence.

Outside, in the winter night, fear chased Aaron through his mind and down the streets. It was after him, the black shadow of it, wherever he went. He began to run. If anyone had stopped him and asked him why he ran or what it was that frightened him he would have said, "I don't know." But he ran on down the street through the night trying to get away from it.

Christmas came closer. Trees were bought at vacant lots and carried home. Would there be snow? Everybody wished for a white Christmas except the people who lived in the slums. Snow meant colder weather and that meant more money for coal.

The Christmas spirit hit the city. Father and Mother spent too much. Everybody spent too much. Everybody went into debt a little. But the kids have to have a good time. It's their holiday. . . . And made it more than a children's holiday. The big companies made their greatest profits of the year. The Haines Company would break all records for profit. They were standing six and seven deep around counters. The river brought cargo to the jaws of the building. The building shipped to all parts of the country in stamping-machine regularity and at the tempo of the beating of a giant heart.

People spent their money. They even remembered, as they did every year at this season, that there were poor people in the world. Newspaper charts showed how much was donated to give the poor this one big meal of the year with turkey and trimmings.

Fellowship was a warm, ruddy lamp in every person's heart across the city. Hatreds were packed away somewhere. Prejudices were not, in this season, hard icy snowballs of intolerance. Peace on earth, good will . . .

On Christmas Eve the spirit had reached its peak. At the Haines Company a family really existed. Once a year. On this day. A family. The bosses were proud parents and the workers their children. But a family.

On Christmas Eve, law and order were out. In the afternoon, after lunch until quitting time, there were parties all throughout the building. Liquor flowed in the various departments. Executives got drunk in their offices and had to be carried to cabs. Little gifts were exchanged. Boxes of candy and cigars. Ties and pairs of nylons.

O'Keefe ran his elevator up and down the spine of the building and in the late afternoon began unloading the high in spirit, the happy, the half-drunk and the drunk. Gifts were brought to him and were a little gayly colored pile in the corner of his elevator. Drinks from whisky bottles were forced on him by drunken executives and shouting half-drunk office boys.

In Don's old department Wilmington, the department head, was throwing a party for the typists and correspondents and supervisors. Wilmington wanted to take them all into his arms at the Christmas party and make up for the things he had done during the year. He now set down his water glass of whisky and walked over to Krendesky with his hand stuck out. "I wish you a very happy—merry Christmas."

Krendesky stood with a group of the girl correspondents and a couple of the other supervisors. Krendesky was a little drunk. "Well, I don't know if I'll accept," he said. "You didn't treat me so good this last year. I'm not going to wish you a Merry Christmas." He wove back and forth on his legs. "I'll tell you what. I'll put you on probation until next year and we'll see."

Wilmington laughed ha-ha-ha good-naturedly and looked around at all of them—ha-ha-ha. He had long legs. He moved quickly to another part of the room.

Jerry in her smartly tailored suit with a corsage on the lapel put her arms around Krendesky. "Good for you," she said and part of her drink spilled down his back. "Good for you." She kissed him wetly on the lips.

Jerry was filled with love and the Christmas spirit. Walking not very evenly, she searched Wilmington out. She had a wet kiss for him, too. "Now I'll tell you what, Wilmy," she said. "I'm going to sign you up for the union." And she kissed him again.

O'Keefe brought his elevator up to one of the middle floors. Edna, with her arms piled full of presents for her children and a little high on liquor herself, stepped inside. Down the hall ran others toward the elevator, dignified men and women laughing and shouting like children. O'Keefe, grinning at Edna and rubbing the soles of his shoes against the floor of the elevator like a boy, said, "Here I've been taking you down in the elevator all year and I think you ought to give me a Christmas kiss."

"*Awwww,* you don't want to kiss me!"

"Yes I do too!"

"Well, hurry up before someone catches us," she said.

And on his next load he took Sue and a bunch down from their office party. O'Keefe leaned close to Sue and said softly, "I stayed late just to take a friend of mine down on the elevator." Sue was a little drunk but didn't want him to know it so she didn't answer him, just smiled a little hazily. Her arms, too, were full of colorfully wrapped bundles.

Over at the Stevens Hotel in one of the private ballrooms there was an entirely different kind of party. This was for the top executives of the company. This was the party that Emerson Bradley threw for his group, his big men in the company, although he himself never appeared.

It was a terrifying kind of party. The executives sat around getting drunk sullenly and practically without speaking. Pouring the liquor in mechanically, dourly. Pouring it in in clocklike regularity. Then, as the liquor settled in them and they were half-drunk, they each and every one began to denounce Bradley. Each with his story about him. Each denouncing him in turn.

They ripped him apart. They used scalpel and broadax on him. Nothing was too petty or too gossipy or too scandalous for them to say about him. It was their yearly hate-Bradley party.

Then they began denouncing the Haines Company and ripped it and its practices apart. And one gray-haired man in his fine dress suit and bow tie and solid-gold cuff links sat down on the edge of a French period chair and actually wept because he hadn't left the company years ago.

The next day, Christmas, Aaron went to his father's house to spend the day and eat dinner. Not because he was broke but because the link that is a family drew him back. Muriel was there, cooking for her father. There was a small artificial Christmas tree on the table, memory to his lost gentile wife, and a sadness rimming his father's eyes that lifted a little when Aaron entered.

Secretly Muriel let Rebecca know that Aaron was there and Rebecca came over.

But none of them had a good time. There was a shadow over the house. And to Papa Levin the shadow was his wife and his son on this day when there should be a warmth and laughter in a house. To Aaron it was his life and what was happening to him over which he had no power. Like being tunneled through the night in a pilotless subterranean plane. To Rebecca it was Aaron and Don.

Don, too, went to his mother's house for Christmas dinner. He went in a cab, piling all the presents for everybody in his family on the seat next to him. Expensive presents. Boy, life had been good to him! Gee, they'd all like the presents! Two dresses for Ma. A sixty-dollar coat for Helen. He felt proud of himself, and smiling in quiet happiness, he looked out the cab window at his city, Chicago. He had bought a Christmas card for Rebecca and a gift but had torn the card up at the last minute and left the gift in his drawer. After all it was a Christian holiday and she might be insulted. Jesus, he had screwed things up there!

The cab stopped in front of the new Kosinski apartment. He looked at his watch. Fifteen to three. At seven he had to leave to meet Irene.

He'd see Sue after Irene. He'd make some excuse so he could go to see her. Couldn't let Christmas pass without seeing her. And he had something nice for her.

All of his brothers and sisters were glad to see him and eagerly tore the wrappings from the presents he had brought and there was a Christmas tree, a big one, and the smell of turkey coming from the kitchen and Ma put her arms around him and held him a long time and he was happy and comfortable in her embrace.

The tree, the kids, the happy smiles and the shouts. It was the kind of Christmas he should have had when he was a kid and had never had. Now he could at least give that to his family. And McCarren had made it all possible. Good old McCarren! A wonderful man! Jesus, I'd do anything for him!

Happily Don uncorked the gallon jug of wine he had brought and poured for Ma and Helen, who had the coat on and was modeling it heavy-hipped for Don and the rest of them.

Ma looked proudly at her son. Her eyes clouded a little. "Grandpa ought to be here today."

Don nodded. Yes. Grandpa. To see his success. Grandpa who had predicted it. The thought of Grandpa not being there spoiled his day a little.

In the front room Eva had turned the radio on. One program had just ended and another was beginning. The identifying theme song filled the room and then subsided and Gregory Martin, the announcer, was saying:

"Ladies and gentlemen, The Haines Family Hour . . . we greet you and wish you all a very Merry Christmas. Today, as every week we bring you another dramatic radio play featuring that beautiful star of screen, radio and television, Loretta Lawson. But before we announce today's drama we are pleased and honored to again bring you another of Mr. Emerson Bradley's ten-minute speeches on Americanism . . ."

Eva had changed the station. "Leave that on a minute," Don said and Eva's fingers brought Bradley's voice back into focus in the room.

Bradley's garbled, monotonous monotone spoke into the room: "On this great day, this great Christian holiday when God gave his own Son to man it should also be the occasion for all Americans everywhere to give worshipful thanksgiving . . ."

"I don't know why you want to hear that!" Eva said petulantly.

". . . for the liberties and freedoms all of us are blessed with here in this country, and, I might add, we have here in this country men of ill-will who are spying and endeavoring in every way they know how to destroy our way of life, are trying, indeed, to take from us, everything that has made us, as a nation, a family of happy people, feared and respected all over the world. Let us then be, on this Christmas holiday . . . "

"You can turn it off now," Don told Eva.

At the radio station the *Haines Family Hour* was over. Emerson Bradley's chauffeured limousine waited for him at a side entrance with the door open. He and Loretta Lawson came out of the side entrance and as she got into the car he pinched her affectionately in an unorthodox place. Laughing, he got in beside her. They knew where her husband would be for the next two hours. Announcer Gregory Martin would be at the station. Settling back on the cushions and taking Loretta Lawson's hand he felt more than the Christmas spirit. He felt the heady intoxication of power over people and events.

In the Norris home this Christmas day Louise and Jim were entertaining. Edna sat smiling happily at them. Her daughters were with her. Marion, the oldest, was a strikingly beautiful girl with long, shoulder-length blond hair, wide blue eyes and a good figure. Her every gesture, smile, word, indicated that she was well aware of her beauty.

Jim was painfully conscious of her. Occasionally he glanced at her but tried to keep his eyes cool and impersonal.

And Jim acted the part of the typical happy family man. No one saw his scars. He sat in his chair while his older boy went whooping through the house with his toys or came to ask a hundred different questions, all of which Jim patiently answered. When Louise went to prepare drinks for them in the kitchen, Jim stood up on his long legs and gave a shout toward the kitchen, "Want me to help you, Louise?" He never called her Skinny any more because of the guilt that was in him from the morning when he had sat on the side of the bed looking at her.

"No, honey. I can do it," Louise called back cheerfully.

And the younger boy, the baby, stumbling against a toy truck, grasped the tall trunk of Jim's leg for support. Jim, leaning down, steadied him and said, "Safe at second." Then he lifted him up into his arms and sat again in his chair holding the little boy. Quickly, secretly, his eyes darted to Marion. Jesus, is she good-looking! Sixteen or seventeen years old.

"I've never had a nicer Christmas," Edna said. Louise brought the drinks. Jim went to her and put his arms around her. "Don't work so hard." He drew her gently to the couch and sat with his arm around her as they talked to Edna.

And the last days leafed themselves away from the tree of the year. The days were brittle and cracked away like ice melting from a storefront window. The days were but a few more left to the year.

And New Year's came and the city went a little bit insane and drunk celebrating—a division of time

And Emerson Bradley carried on in the feudal lord way on New Year's Day. It was a tradition with him. A tradition he had created. Each New Year's Day he greeted his employees, all of them, in the windy corridor of the Haines Company. No matter if you're a truck driver, no matter what the hell, you have to show up. You're all checked off. He is in formal clothes, he and his wife. Department heads are all checked too, and woe unto you if you don't show up. They with their kids and their hangovers from the night before. Emerson Bradley bows and smiles in that windy corridor. His flunkies hand out presents. A quarter-pound box of candy for each woman. A cigar for each man. A trinket for the children.

He bows and smiles in that windy corridor.

And the days come on swiftly into a new year, the days take stride. The new year is a baby howling in a world of fear and anxiety and threats of war and the atomic destruction of mankind.

And Aaron had lost touch with life.

And Jim was torn a hundred ways in his mind.

And Don got a telephone call.

# II

Mucci said into the phone, "I'd like to see you, Lockwood."

"Sure. Come on up to the insurance office."

There was a long pause. Then Mucci said, "I'd like to make it private."

"Okay. Come up to my place . . . huh? Yeah, eight o'clock will be all right." Don hung up. Now I wonder what he wants?

At eight sharp Mucci wedged his fat little body in past the door and held out one of his fat arms to shake hands with Don. "Howya doing?" The political, overfriendly smile cut across the roundness of Mucci's face and his little frog-eyes popped wide and looked into Don.

Mucci sat down. Don got a bottle of whisky and glasses, poured, offered a cigarette. And all the time Mucci laughed good-naturedly and talked in a cheerful, buddylike way. And all the time his popped eyes behind their sleepy lids minutely studied Don.

"What's on your mind?" Don asked.

Mucci set his glass down and smacked his lips. "Good liquor." He smacked his lips again. He moved out to the edge of the chair and leaned toward Don. He leaned so far forward that his little round belly almost rested on his knees. "I've got a proposition for you. I'll make it fast," he said. One little fat arm gestured in a fish's fin. And then his eyes rolled left and right as if to ascertain that they were alone, telling Don in their flitting that this was very important and very secret. And then his voice dropped to a hoarse whisper, confidential, to keep the words here in this room between them and away from any ear that might be pressed against the door. His eyes sidled to Don's face. They were half closed as he whispered but they scrutinized Don like twin tigers hidden in tall reeds, crouched, ready to leap out in attack. "It's foolproof, see. It'll mean three-four thousand dollars apiece for each of us. Only thing, we got to keep it on the q.t. We can't afford to let McCarren know nothing about it. That way we won't have to cut him in."

What's he trying to do, frame me? Be careful what you say. And McCarren's my friend.

"That way we won't have to cut him in. You can cover the whole thing up and without taking no chance whatever." The whispering went on and the half-closed popeyes watching, watching, had the glaze of greed, the concentration of the hypnotist.

Don listened.

It *was* foolproof. There *was* good money in it for them. Don listened in grudging admiration. That was a lot of money. McCarren would never find out.

"And you want me to do this behind McCarren's back?"

The frog-eyes popped wide open in anticipation. "That's the idea."

Don nodded slowly and kept his own opinion to himself.

And Mucci's mouth, twisted to a distorted oval, leaned its misshapen funnel closer to Don's ear, went on in its hoarse whisper. The fish-fin arms reached out, gesturing, almost encircling Don in the secrecy of the spoken words and the anticipated act.

Don lit a cigarette and watched Mucci's face as the purple-gray smoke curled upward past his eyes and into his blond hair. It was a good deal. Though it was graft, he had grafted before. That was enough money to buy a new car. McCarren would be cut out. McCarren would never find out. But McCarren had always played it square with him.

Don pressed his lips down over the cigarette and closed his eyes and inhaled.

The twin tigers lay low in the swarth of Mucci's face, watching.

Don exhaled and looked at Mucci. Mucci sat with his open mouth already beginning to form the clever, scheming smile. Don lowered his eyes.

Yeah, he had grafted before. But this. This was against all his principles. It had to do with housing and it knifed labor and the veteran and the poor people in the back at the same time. Against all his principles—and against McCarren's principles. Against all his speeches while he was campaigning.

He looked up at Mucci. "I can't do it, Mucci."

The concealing frog-eyes blinked in astonishment. "You can't do it?" Mucci swallowed hard. Refusing three-four thousand dollars. He stared incredulously and leaned back in his chair, still staring as if he had suddenly seen some strange new type of human. "Why not?"

Don looked at him. Dirty, fat little politician. And then the expression of disgust on Don's face gave way to one of earnest sincerity. "I can't double-cross McCarren." He spoke swiftly, with conviction, wanting Mucci to really understand why he couldn't do it. "McCarren and I believe the same way about housing and labor. McCarren wanted me to win because he wanted me down in Springfield fighting for the things I set up as my platform when I was campaigning. McCarren—"

And he halted, not knowing what else to say, how to explain to this greasy little precinct captain that he and McCarren were honest when it came to the election campaign, that they both wanted to change things for the people.

Mucci's dark, oily face was without expression for a moment. Then he lay back against the chair and laughed. His laughter rose and rose and went on in its loud, howling vulgar tones. His belly shook. His little fat legs wriggled out and his heels kicked against the floor in his paroxysm. When he had finally finished laughing and sat up, the tears of laughter were streaming down his pockmarked face. He wiped them away with the backs of his hands.

He sat upright. There was amused contempt in his face now. Everybody in politics is everybody else's enemy in the machine. That's why politicians smiled at each other and shook hands with each other so often. To cover up. That was all. And they'd cut each other's throats at the drop of a hat if it benefited them. Sure he'd graft on McCarren. Why not! Didn't he bring in the best precinct in the district to McCarren year after year? Had McCarren done anything for *him?* Ever put *him* up for office? Hadn't he run this young punk? And this kid thought the little czar was serious. That was funny. Funny as hell. No, he didn't like this punk and had had to run his legs off getting out the vote for him. Here was his chance to get even with McCarren and twist Lockwood's balls at the same time. Punch his idealism to a pulp—if he really had any.

There was amused contempt in his face. "Look, kid," he said, "you're green. You ain't dry behind the ears yet. Your pants are still a little wet. Do you—" He began to laugh again. But caught himself up quickly in his anger, said bitterly, "Did you really eat that stuff?

Did you really believe all that bull you were giving the people? Even if you was honest about it do you think McCarren would have let you carry such a program down to Springfield? Are you *kidding?* Say, the little czar controls the representatives he puts in office. They vote the way he dictates it. Reed's working against housing for McCarren down in Springfield right now. He's been voting McCarren's antilabor way down there for twelve years—and you—" the contempt was strident across his voice "—are too *idealistic*—" he slurred the idealistic "—to take a big hunk of money because it will hurt the chances of things that won't ever happen anyway. Say, do you know why McCarren picked you up anyway? Because you're a cripple."

*Cripple*. The word was like a torch applied to the end of his stub.

Mucci's voice cooled and grew singsong and pleasant. "Because you had a leg off. Because you were a vet. Jesus, are you that dumb? Why, the little czar was just playing on the emotions of the crowd. He was trying to sweet-talk the vets and the niggers and the dagoes and Polacks into voting for him."

Funny. Even in that moment of hurt and resentment his mind, as if it stood apart somewhere, observing, said, Don't say *dago* even if you are Italian. And that was Wayne. He felt his eyes filling with tears. He got up quickly and went into the toilet. He tensed himself there. He looked into the mirror at himself: you fool! you fool!

When he came out Mucci was standing up getting ready to leave. Mucci said, "From here on in, you're on your way out. McCarren will ease you out. Now's the time to be one step ahead of him. I know these people twenty-five years before you met them. I know how they operate. You may think you do, but—" Mucci shook his head; and went on. "How do you think McCarren got there? By being honest? He had to double-cross a lot of people to get to the top. This game's strictly business—there's very little honesty." Mucci laughed through his nose in contempt. "So you go back to McCarren with my little plan." Mucci lifted his shoulders in a shrug and his fish-fin arms stood out away from his dumpy, grotesquely fat body. "Do you think that makes any difference? McCarren will laugh and tell me, you sonofabitch you, you tried to pull a fast one on me. It'll be a great big joke. I'm solid behind him with the vote come Election Day. That's all he's interested in."

Mucci lifted his arm in a farewell gesture and went out of the room.

I don't believe it. He was behind everything I said. Mucci is a goddamn liar.

But there was doubt in him. He picked up the telephone book and looked for Reed's number. Just on the chance that he was in Chicago and not in Springfield Don dialed the number.

"Reed, this is Don Lockwood. Can I see you tonight for a few minutes?"

When Don arrived it was after ten o'clock. Reed lived, when he was in Chicago, in a lavish apartment on the Gold Coast. Reed answered the door wearing a dark-blue lounge robe and slippers. "Hello, Lockwood." They shook hands, politically, and Reed led him into the front room which was perfectly appointed with antique furniture. On a low table an electric coffeepot was bubbling. "Sit down, Lockwood." Reed gestured in his bored way. "Anywhere at all." And Reed, middle-aged and bald and bored and twelve years in Springfield, sat down himself and crossed his legs, poured coffee into a cup. "Care for a cup of coffee?"

"I need a drink," Don said.

"Never touch the stuff myself," Reed said and yawned slowly. "I was just brewing a cup of coffee before I went to bed. Have to get back to Springfield in the morning. Never keeps me awake. Wife's in Florida for the season."

Reed went on to sugar and cream his coffee and was now tasting it. Don looked at him. Didn't drink. He was a pious-looking man with his bald head and his long doleful face. Looked like a minister in that dark-blue robe. His lean face. His slow movements, sipping the coffee and setting the cup down in the saucer, his long bony fingers. The eyes behind glasses gave him a kindly, generous, even suffering-for-mankind look. My answer. I must get my answer from Reed.

Reed looked up at him over the brim of the coffee cup and smiled slowly with his thin, colorless lips. "It must be something important that brings you here," he said. It was quietly insulting. And from behind his glasses he looked at Don quizzically. This was McCarren's right-hand man. This was the young upstart McCarren had put up for office. Reed licked at the coffee on his lips but licked, too, the pleasure of having seen Don's defeat in the last election. What does he want with me? Or has the little czar sent him on an errand?

"Say, Reed, tell me," Don said, "how did you vote on that housing bill down in Springfield?"

Reed smiled. His smile turned his lips down at the end and gave his face the philosophical look of a priest, sadly, gently smiling over the shortcomings of humanity.

"Against it."

"Against it?"

Reed nodded slowly. Two infinitesimal sparks of amusement stood in his eyes like far lights you are not sure you see.

"Why?"

Reed set his cup in the saucer and it made a little singing sound that seemed to echo and re-echo among the pieces of dark antique furniture and against the heavy draperies.

"McCarren."

"What do you mean?"

Patiently Reed said, "I voted the way McCarren wanted me to vote. I always do. McCarren made me a State Representative. I do as the boss says. If I didn't—just as he made me a State Representative he can kick me out any time he wants." His face was calm, his eyes pious, his voice gently bored. But he was getting his revenge on Don. He was the professor instructing the pupil in political science. "Sure, I vote the way McCarren tells me to. I've been doing so for twelve years. I intend to as long as I'm in office and as long as he's in power. How do you suppose I stay in office? How do you suppose I maintain this apartment? And one in Springfield? Look—" He enumerated on his fingers, gently touching them, quietly speaking. "I have my car, servants, leisure. I go to Florida or Hot Springs when I please." He smiled blandly. "Sure, I work for McCarren. I do. You do. We all do. The people? . . . Their good?" He shrugged lazily. He smiled slowly. He chuckled as over a joke and slowly shook his head no, slowly. His glasses, catching high light from the lamp, gave his eyes a blind look. "You're doing all right under the boss. He took you off the street." It was advice. "Why don't you let it drop or you'll be wearing shiny pants again."

So it was true. All those speeches. All those speeches McCarren had written for him were just lies. McCarren had only been using him. Don laughed nervously. What if Reed talked. Protect yourself! Don said, "Well I just blew my top. That's all. I guess I felt like an honest John."

Reed sighed slowly and stroked his bald head. "Yeah. I understand. There were things I wanted to do and I had to shut up about them." Reed was parrying too. Reed was saying he wasn't going to go back to THE POWER with their conversation. He might be able to use the kid one of these days.

Don looked around. He smiled broadly. "Quite a setup you've got here. Well, I don't want to keep you up." He smiled brightly and stood up. He shook hands. "Thanks, Reed!"

Outside he began to tremble with hurt and rage.

He walked without being aware of it. Only his false leg. It was a heavier weight than it had ever been before. Need a drink. Need one bad. He wished he could unbuckle it and leave it standing on a street corner. There, America, that's what I did for you. Hop along down the street on one leg.

He saw the sign: CLOVERLEAF LOUNGE. He went down the seven steps, counting them without knowing why and into the basement tavern. Blindly he moved through the crowd to the bar, bought a shot and a beer and carried them to an empty booth near the bar. He drank them and when the waitress came another set, and another, another. "Hey, Joe!" people were yelling and that must be the bartender's name. Another, another, and another. They were talking about good and evil, right and wrong. Now that's a funny thing to be talking about at a bar. He looked around. Textbooks were heaped on the bar and on the floor in a corner. Students. What did they know? About anything? Oh—Loyola University. That's where they're from. Good and evil. Right and wrong. What did they know about it with their schoolbook answers? Their Jesuit priest answers? I don't want to hear about right and wrong, good and evil. It doesn't mean anything. I should be in a sewer somewhere. Where is the Sewer? That's the name of a bar. Yeah, that's a bar. It's down on North State Street. Which way? I ought to go there. I belong there. Another and another and another.

So they used me. So they exploited me. They exploited my false leg. "Hey, Joe!" That's what everybody else yelled.

"I'm not Joe. My name's Madeline."

"Oh," and he laughed, "well, bring me a bottle of whisky. Sit it right here. Here—" fumbling through his bills, "take what it costs."

And the full bottle of whisky at his elbow.

So I really got a screwing. McCarren was just using me for his own ends. Don laid his forehead down against the top of the whisky bottle. They exploited my leg. I was too dumb to know that the shell hit me instead of somebody else. That I lived on a particular street. That he heard me because I happened to go into Bughouse Square that night. That they picked me up instead of somebody else. The Democrats, they are the liberals, and they selected me simply because I could be manipulated. He half sobbed and caught his lip between his teeth. The phony bastards! The crooked sonsabitches!

The bottle lopsided its way to his lips. He got up, and staggering to the telephone, called Irene.

"Yeah, yeah, it's me. Where am I? I'm in a basement. I've been in a basement all my life. Yes, I'm drunk. What basement? The Cloverleaf—" and staggering away from the phone, shouting, "Where is this place?"

Somebody told him. "Fifty East Chicago," he said into the phone. "Meet me . . .

*"I said meet me!*

"Listen, bitch, I'm going to wait here and you better show up."

He hung up and staggered back to the booth on the heavy weight of his false leg.

He flopped down. He drank from the bottle. They just used me. He drank again. Sue was right. He drank again. Jesus! the way I treated Rebecca! Right and wrong, good and evil, ha-ha-ha. His bleary eyes came up from the booth and looked across the bar. The Carstairs white seal was balancing the slowly whirling ball on the tip of its nose. Around and around the ball spun. The juke box played loudly and the Dixieland music sweated its tones against the walls. The blues singer's voice crept along the floor at the ankles of the people . . . and the bottle lifting to his lips again. So that was the way they played their damn dirty game? Everybody out for himself. Well he'd be out for himself too . . . like a teacher once told me, "Well, can you do it?"

"No, ma'am."

"Well, are you going to sit there and cry or are you going to make an effort!"

I knew how to make an effort then. I'll make an effort now.

His fist crashing against the table startled him. He looked down at it and tightened it harder. It's a stinking game. But I'm not getting out. I'm going to frig some people. I'll give McCarren a screwing! The biggest screwing he ever got. I'll work for that. Live for that.

Someone was tugging at his arm. He looked up sideways and it was all he could do to lift his head on his shoulders.

"Sit down," he said.

"When did you become so domineering?" Irene asked.

"Sit down, honey."

"I don't want to sit down."

"Okay! Okay! Go away then."

She sat down.

"Do you know what they did to me?" Don asked. "The bastards framed me." He dissolved into tears. "Take me home, Irene."

In Irene's car with his head against her shoulder the tears ran down his cheeks. This was the man I was loyal to. But—and a little bit of himself crept up to the surface, asking, Are these real tears? Or are they phony tears? He shook his head against her shoulder. Always the actor. No, no, I'm not acting . . . this was the man I was loyal to.

Against her shoulder, incoherently, drunkenly, he told her what had happened.

Irene stayed the night with him. Daylight somehow found its way down the narrow shaft between the two tall buildings and smeared the room with grayness and Don blinked his eyes open. The whole thing came back to him. He tensed his body, feeling the hard knot of anger grow in his head.

Life played a dirty trick on me. Life made me a Pole and put me in the slums and gave me a prostitute for a mother. And I know what I want.

He lay in bed with Irene. He thought about what he wanted.

I want just the opposite. And I'm going to prove it. I'm going to get it. I'm going to profit and get everything I ever wanted. I've got to prove it or I'll hate life.

I want a nice home. I want to be able to wear ten-dollar ties. I want a feeling of extravagance. I want to be able to tear a twenty-dollar bill into tiny little pieces and throw it down a grate. And if I did I guess I'd hate myself. But that's what I want to be able to do.

He wanted a feeling of security. He wanted it so badly that he didn't know what it meant. To him security meant having more than enough. This would give him a sense of power. As with Emerson Bradley. As with D. S. Matthews. Everybody must have been laughing at me, all the precinct captains, knowing what McCarren was doing. I'm going to make them swallow those laughs.

What had bothered him all his life was running through alleys with relief sacks showing and the feeling of shame it gave.

He had never had enough. Enough love. Enough of anything.

He even needed three women instead of one.

Maybe he had been looking for an excuse to be a power. Maybe his loyalty to McCarren had been superficial. Yeah, why not admit it. He had envied McCarren and had wanted to be McCarren—to be in McCarren's shoes. And deep inside him where he hardly recognized it himself and through his sense of the dramatic he was glad he had lost his leg. It set him apart. It gave him more demands on life. And he had never had enough of anything.

He got up out of bed. Irene arose too. Smiling, little-boy, but cynically too, he said, "How'd you like to be married to me and wake up in a rathole like this every morning?"

"It wouldn't be the worst thing in the world." She looked into his eyes. "I think I'm in love with you." Her hands were cool on his cheeks. "Don," she said, looking into him and remembering the one she had lost, "you don't have to stay in politics."

He pulled his face away roughly. "I'm going to stay."

He turned his back and looked out the window at the tall wall of windows he could have reached and touched with his hand. "I don't want to take anything from your father." Stop being dramatic, he told himself. And even while he said it a part of his mind told him he might be able to use D. S. Matthews one of these days.

Irene drew him back to bed. And while he went through the familiar motions he felt good about what he was going to do. He felt a great relief. Now nothing stood in his way.

I'll show them.

The scheme began to grow large in his mind.

# III

"Mucci—this is Lockwood—let's go with that deal," Don said into the telephone. His voice over the phone was as tight as his smile. He hung up and sat back for a moment while his eyes narrowed. Then he got up and went about THE POWER's business for him.

At the bookie joints and at the big night clubs where there was gambling, at all the other places that paid off, Don said, "We're going to have to ask for a little more from here on in. We got a buzz that some of our precincts are going to be in trouble with the election commissioners' office and we have to have dough to squash it before they start pouring on the heat."

They all came through with more.

"Hello, Tom," Don said. There was a smile deep in his eyes. The same sort of wise, cynical, hard look that was always at the back of McCarren's eyes. He tossed the envelope across the desk to McCarren.

"Sit down, Don," McCarren said.

Don sat across the desk from McCarren, watching him. THE POWER opened the envelope and thumbed through the thick wad of bills. He looked up at Don and whistled softly as his eyebrows lifted in satisfied surprise. He tossed Don's cut across the table to him. He laughed. "Let's have a drink."

Don laughed too. "Yeah, I could use one, Tom."

Twisting on his swivel chair, McCarren got the bottle and glasses from his cabinet. Don watched. His lips twisted cynically.

THE POWER filled the glasses. THE POWER winked and held his glass up in salute. Don smiled and winked back.

"Here's best," McCarren said.

"Best," Don said.

They clicked glasses.

# IV

He had a longing to see Rebecca He called her on the phone. There was a long pause at the other end of the wire.

"It's Don."

"Yes. I know."

She saw his face and it was dear to her. The blond-brown short-cropped hair. She had liked it better, though, when it was long, her fingers curling through it. His deep-set eyes staring out at her. For a moment Aaron's face clouded the picture. But Don's face came back to her. His long mouth, the top lip thin, the lower one pouted out a little, petulantly. The lips reddish and the cleft in his chin. In imagination she put her finger in the cleft of his chin and leaned toward him. Her desire for him was great.

"Can I see you?"

There was another long pause.

"All right."

"Could you meet me in front of Isbell's on Rush Street at seven-thirty and we could eat there?"

"Isbell's—" Her voice trembled on the name. "All right." And she knew she was close to tears.

He hung up. Poor kid. I'll make it up to her.

She was nervous when he met her and dropped her eyes and they went inside to a table. She only picked at her food and they both lowered their eyes when they glanced at each other. Don laughed nervously and ordered more wine.

The glasses of the dark wine. The fleeting catching-together of their eyes.

There was this thing between them. The dark angry words that he had spoken. The scabs of words that must heal and the scars of long-ago-spoken-things that would forever leave their mark though the scars dimmed away to only thinly etched lines.

And dinner was over. Don touching her arm. The taxicab to his room.

Inside they were all the more conscious of the last time they had been together. Things could never be as they had once been. There were few words. And the embarrassment flooding their faces. And Don pouring wine for them. And Rebecca drinking, as if for strength —or weakness—to go back into his arms, but sitting far away from him. And blackness at the square of window. And the two lamps casting their circles of light out on the carpet and slightly touching, making a segment of one lighter circle in the shadow-lightness of the other.

Rebecca lifted her eyes. "Aren't you drinking too much, Don?" Rebecca lowered her eyes.

"No." He laughed quickly, nervously. And hurt and resentment came. She had stayed away from him. She had hurt him too. When he needed her sympathy she had forced ugly, angry words on him. The night he lost the election she forced the words from his lips and walked out on him. When he needed her. Yes, maybe he was drinking too much. The red wine blotched his lips. "I should never have lost the election," he said. "You know that." More red wine stained his mouth. "The niggers sold me out. They promised me their vote."

The red wine of a flush came into Rebecca's cheeks. With her head lowered she said, "Don't talk like that. I don't like to hear you say that. You know I don't."

Don walked over to her. "All right—Negroes." He pronounced it nastily.

Leave. Don't stay. But love forced her there, pressed her down immobile on the sofa.

And again he was sorry. He sat down next to her. "I'm sorry."

"It's all right."

She didn't look at him. She lifted her wineglass and wanted to go and couldn't.

Bit by bit, red inch by red inch, the wine went down in the bottle. There were no words now. The embarrassment of silence was better than the embarrassment of words. And bit by bit.

Don touched her hands. "Let's go to bed. We've been sitting here a *thousand* years."

And there was the desire to see Sue, to tell her all about McCarren's dirty trick. It was a confessional sitting in Sue's room, telling her all about McCarren and how he had been used. It started with, "You were right, Sue" and it ended with every detail of the political setup and the corruption. In confidence, in trust he told Sue.

"What are you going to do now?" Sue asked.

Hard light glinted on Don's weak chin. His eyes narrowed in a frown and his jaws tightened as he clenched his teeth. "I'm going to stay in politics."

Sue sighed in resignation.

Don's jaw clenched even tighter and his eyes were ugly in their squint. His fist tightened too. "All I know is that I want power. From here on in I want power." He tapped his pocket where he carried his money. "As long as I have this I have my entrance anywhere. I like a buck just like anybody else. As long as you have money you can buy just about anything you want."

There was Rebecca and Sue and Irene again. There was a tenderness in his relations with all three of them. He needed them. Each of them. And each of them for different reasons.

But he was really unhappy. He wished that Sue could be Rebecca and Irene and Sue all at the same time. Why didn't the world give you everything at once instead of eking it out? It wasn't his fault that all of these girls were lacking. Most people were unhappy most of the time and then happy for a while. Sue had adjusted. She didn't want wealth or power. She had faced obscurity. She can live with it. Maybe I can adopt Sue's attitude and be at peace about it all. No, it's no good. I never had enough of anything. I need all three of them. And for different reasons.

# V

This is the library: REFERENCE NON-FICTION FICTION May I help you? RETURN BOOKS HERE So little of it, life I mean. The hand, ladeez and gen'lemen, is quicker than the eye. We've lost a boy.

Aaron gathered the books up in his arms. He spent the entire morning reading the poetry of Ezra Pound, Kenneth Fearing, T. S. Eliot. In the downtown library. Until early afternoon. And then home. His room.

His was a twilight state. His the pleasure of being sad. His mind was in a certain atmosphere. "When," he said aloud, his forehead down upon the typewriter, "your motives are friendly with pain, then you can write, not before." You see some pretty damn good paintings coming out of insane asylums, he told himself. He lifted his head and his big, awkward hands. Placed his fingers on the keyboard. His mind was clogged now with erect rabbit ears listening for sounds, the sounds of poetry.

Seated in the quiet house of his hoarse typing machine he put the few words slowly on paper. The words came and were torn from the machine and the crumpled paper tossed on the floor.

He pressed his forehead against the window, looking down into the street. And felt behind him the presence in the room of his record, *Clair de Lune:* music on discs, smooth black raven wings . . .

Black raven wings. He thought of war, shivering, and those who died . . . Mother earth had taken them home to her heart, back to her black womb, long before their time. Yet each had wanted only to crawl home from out the hell. Home to a house, a family, someone waiting. Home to their stake in the future. Home to a familiar old age, a familiar death in keeping with the living and dying of peoples, and nations, of all things.

He went from the room and down into the ravine of the street . . .

Time, 3:35 in the late afternoon of a sun.

He walked through the crowds. The wittling knife of frustration was at his throat again. To laugh—to cry. He walked, instead, pulling his shoulder in tight.

And suddenly, in the Loop of the city Chicago, he sat on a curb and pulled his notebook from his pocket, sat while the downtown people stared, passing in a flood of humanity—and he wrote:

The breast is a bubble and it is blown
From the clitorus of a dark pomegranate

Got up off the curb. Stuffed the notebook into his pocket. Wandered through the city. Looked up at the houses: there was not a house where there was not one dead. That's from the Bible. Christianity. Judaism. He had tried them both and found them wanting. He had tried everything. Each time he had been on the floor for the count of nine. But he had gotten up. And each time he had assumed another attitude. There were no attitudes left to him. He was too weak. He was stuck with himself. He was ending as he had started, without anchor. It wasn't, after all, father, father, why hast thou forsaken me? It was mother, mother why—? But it snarled in his mind. Why fool himself? He had met perpetual motion life with his ego and had failed.

Into the empty arms of night he walked. Inside him was a jungle of wild animals. He had, inside him, no quiet pool, no meadow in which to walk, no tree under which to sit.

He looked up and saw the Thompson restaurant sign. Aaron, the ex-Jew, and then ex-Communist, and then the ex-Christian, and then once again the ex-Jew, walked into Thompson's. They were over there at a table, O'Keefe, Milo, Dave and Jim. Aaron's large, awkward shadow fell across the table. "Are the Communists having a meeting?" he asked. He smiled bitterly and sat down.

O'Keefe's bushy eyebrows arched together into a single continuous frowning brow but he tried to joke, saying gently in Aaron's direction, "Just for a ribbon to wear in his coat, just for a handful of silver he left us."

And more talk of politics. But every time the door opened and a woman entered, Jim, with his sentences dangling into silence, looked up at her and then dropped his eyes.

Secretly Aaron glanced at all of them. Everybody seemed to be in a little prison and everybody seemed to be rattling the bars. Oh, the prisons we make for ourselves. His eyes rested for a moment on Jim. There was something wrong with Jim. He sensed it.

They grew uncomfortable with Aaron there among them. His silence had an unnatural quality. His silences had become almost frightening.

O'Keefe was saying, with the black Irish eyebrows scowled together, "And now we want another. The common man is afraid he'll have to go to war with Russia just as he is afraid it might rain tomorrow. No more than that."

Aaron pulled over a clean napkin and wrote on it . . .

> This is the time that cats get fat with young.
> They slink-slank down deep passages at night
> Who knows the limitations of a cat's libido
> Through the night . . .

His attention strayed from his writing and their conversation. While they were talking he got up, walked over into the corner of his mind and went to sleep without moving from the table.

Outside, the night loomed large. And O'Keefe, who had nurtured, fathered, mothered the young brood that had come to him in his loneliness, in his refuge here in American soil; O'Keefe who placed his loss and his faith in the hands of the young; O'Keefe who had believed in Milo, Dave, Jim, Eric, even Max, even the prideful and vain Don, even the sensitive and (he now told himself) precious Aaron, felt build in himself a dislike—and saw the worn Jewish face of Aaron's father in the Haines Company picket lines, the struggle and sacrifice Aaron's father had made for his son. To O'Keefe came a contempt for Aaron who had had America as a child, its chances of education and knowledge, its weapons of an anvil against those ills old O'Keefe (and in that moment he felt old) saw in the American society that spawned in slums and prejudices, in hatred and vice, in group against group. He had lost Aaron. He had lost a son. He had contempt for Aaron and his early and unmuscled death.

And O'Keefe pulled at the edge of his newspaper and frowned. The tight lines of his mouth were drawn downward. He unrolled his newspaper and buried his face in the editorial page. His feet were angry and impatient with youth, scratching across the floor. He had lost a son.

On a loose piece of paper, pouting, poising his pencil, lacing his slack strings of fine black hair behind his ear, Aaron wrote:

> spring-slime-crap-so, die.

# VI

Don began to scheme. He made himself indispensable to McCarren. He had doubled McCarren's take. Handling a hot potato he knew he might get burned any minute and be left holding the bag—but—he was doing all right for himself. He was working with the vigor and enthusiasm and angry revenge of youth. He handed McCarren more and more money. And made more and more for himself. Touching his pocket, "This is my entrance anywhere."

He took a room in the Tennyson Hotel but continued to maintain his room on Dearborn Street. The politicians all hung out at the Tennyson, made many deals there. And Don started dropping in at the Stone and O'Brien's tavern on Clark and Randolph where the politicians also hung out. He knew them all in a short time and they all knew him as McCarren's right-hand man.

Mucci and Don, with their deal made and the money in their pockets, became the best of buddies. They sat around talking at Stone and O'Brien's or up in Don's room at the Tennyson. Their friendship grew. Mucci became Don's mentor. All of his years of learning as a precinct captain he translated into information in two weeks time and Don's active mind absorbed it like a sponge; the things Don hadn't learned from McCarren, and they were few, he now took from Mucci. Mucci gave him all the pitches and all the angles. Mucci, sleepy-eyed, watchful under lowered lashes, sat evening after evening puffing on his ragged cigar, flailing at the air with his short, pudgy arms. Mucci was dealing from the top of the deck to Don; and he was dealing from the bottom of the deck for himself. He had cards up his sleeve for both Don and himself. Was giving Don all the bricks to throw.

"You know," he said lazily, "Kostner and McGuire clammed up on you during the campaign." Sleepy eyes watching.

"Yeah?—what do you mean?"

The dark lips curled. The short neck fell away to ridges of fat flesh. "Sold you out. Gave Reed a big play. Played you down." The popped eyes watching; the clever words coming. "Wanted their revenge on McCarren. Thought they should of got the nomination. So you were the fall guy for McCarren."

Don went down into the precincts. He found Kostner at the bar of a small neighborhood tavern. Slouched at the bar. Talking to the owner, one of his voters. Drinking his lunch.

"Hi Kostner," and they shook hands. "Let me buy you a drink."
Kostner was agreeable and smiled, lap-sitter-like, at Don.
With the drinks on the hard mahogany in front of them, Don said, "Here's a ten-dollar job—why don't you pick it up? You need it."
Kostner looked up at Don: the guy's all right.
"It's a sheet writer in a book," Don said. He gave Kostner the address of the bookie joint. "Tell them I sent you around."
"Thanks, Lockwood! Thanks a lot!" Ten dollars a day as a sheet writer—that's good money!
McGuire was sitting at home cutting his toenails with a razor blade when Don dropped by. "How'd you like to pick up a little extra money as dealer in a blackjack game?"

"Say, Tom," Don said, walking over and placing some last election return tabulations and other data on the desk in front of McCarren, "Look at this. There are two or three precincts here that could have been better if we had had a couple of jobs in there. Why, we could have had another fifty votes in each of them if we had had another job apiece for the precinct captains to hand out."
McCarren gave the charts a casual glance. "Well, go down to the city hall and get two more jobs for each of those precincts," he told Don. He looked at him in crafty admiration: the kid's on the ball.
McCarren felt Don was doing it for his good. Greater grew his trust in him, and greater still until eventually he left all the political dealings to Don.

Don got the jobs—janitor in the public schools, window washer at the city hall, bridge tender, clerk in the County Recorder's office and watchman at the sanitary district. He gave them to Kostner and McGuire to hand out to the men in their precincts who had the largest families of voters.

To McCarren's desk came a letter from the Haines Company. It was from one of Emerson Bradley's secretaries.
"You handle it, Don," McCarren said.
When McCarren put on his coat and left, Don sat in THE POWER's swivel chair, leaned back and laughed. Then he read the letter again.
This was good! This was rich! He got a big kick out of it. Here was one of the richest men in the country, one of the biggest shots and most powerful men in Chicago, asking him for a favor. His old boss asking a favor of him! And one he could do.
Emerson Bradley wanted NO PARKING signs put up in front of his plant on Orleans Street. Don put them all around his buildings where there were not already NO PARKING signs. He had McCarren's

secretary write a letter to Emerson Bradley: "I am delighted to be able to be of assistance to you in this small matter. If there is ever again any request I can . . . "

Don signed his own name with a flourish.

Favors never ended it seemed. Another request by the Haines Company came through the mail. This time there was not enough light in front of the plant along Canal Street.

Don had a couple of extra lampposts put up and had a night-shift policeman posted in front of the building. Emerson Bradley himself answered with a letter of gratitude.

And Don began to strengthen himself in the district. He began making the intimate acquaintance of all the precinct captains. Nor did he forget Casey. Casey who never lost an election. Never lost his precinct. He gave Casey a piece of the west end of his district in gambling—gave him two book joints down there.

If you act the part and dress the part, then get with it, Don told himself bitterly.

# VII

He had a car—not a Cadillac yet—only a Buick. Not a new one—but the top went down and the people could see him when the weather got good and he put it down. And he was making a big shot of himself.

He went out and became friends with the people. He became a great guy with all the precinct captains. He went against McCarren's theory that if you keep a precinct captain broke you have a good precinct captain. If he—lifting his shoulders in a shrug and frowning under the Homburg hat—wrecked McCarren's little empire—well that was all a part of his plan.

He handed out jobs to the precinct captains. "Say Bob, how'd you like to pick up a little extra change as doorman at a book?" . . . "Oh, by the way, Jim, want to deal dice at night?"

Buckley, a good vote-getter, was working in the State Treasurer's office drawing down three hundred dollars a month and knew he could get more money if McCarren had yelped about a raise for him. He went to see Don about it. Don got him a seven-hundred-dollar-a-year raise. And a little money on the side in a deal.

Don became known in the district as Mr. Veteran. He took good care of the precinct captains, all of them. They became very fond of Mr. Veteran. They were doing much better with him than they ever had with the ward committeeman.

Emerson Bradley wrote for another favor. He wanted new driveways on three sides of the street for the parking lot he was building for his customers.

Don knew the pitch on this too. The city would get only ten dollars for each permit after the city council okayed them. The council wouldn't pass on the permits without the alderman's okay and the alderman, in turn, wouldn't allow the permits until after he got his graft.

The alderman wanted seven hundred dollars for each driveway. Don, in McCarren's office where he had told the alderman to meet him, leaned back in the swivel chair and after biting off the end of a cigar and lighting it said quietly to the alderman, "Now, now, Jerry, we might as well be friendly with a man like this." He polished his diamond ring against his coat sleeve.

Don got the new driveways at a reasonable price for Bradley and wrote a letter which he again signed with his name.

Shortly after this he learned that the city wanted Bradley to build his smokestacks higher. Don squashed this too and wrote Emerson Bradley a letter about it. It was like making love by mail.

Mrs. W. L. J. Gardener, one of the chairmen of the Urban League, sat in McCarren's office with Don by appointment. A nervous, high-strung woman, she tapped a cigarette vigorously against the desk before fitting it to her mouth. Don came around the desk and held the match for her.

"Thank you—" looking up into his face with that strained look of Negroes who are tense about the problem and who always expect to be rebuffed by white people. Not a beggar but one who made demands with the strength of pressure groups behind her, she rushed immediately into her subject: "I'll speak quickly and not take your time and tell you exactly why I made this appointment with you. You know the Negro settlement in your district—know it as well as I do. You know the population. Now I'm sure that you don't think that asking for fifteen jobs in a private industry for them is asking too much. And I wondered what we could work out—where we could place some of my people—in some industry where they haven't had a chance to work before." Her voice, without southern dialect, like her coloring and her intelligence seemed to be the balance between the old and the new and the bridge that would sweep the Negro into the full flood of American life. "Now I have a list—" searching in her purse and putting it on the desk—"of factories not too far removed from their homes but where they have never been employed and I thought that perhaps you—"

Don listened politely. And there was a part of his mind that didn't hear her words but had its private discussion with him: This might be the way to get the colored vote.

"I'll see what I can do, Mrs. Gardener," he said when she was finished. "Can't really promise anything but I'll do all I can. I have always had a deep admiration for your people and fully understand their problems. One of my best friends—" he smiled broadly, unprejudicedly, "perhaps you know him—Dave Wilson—is a colored fellow."

No, she didn't know him.

Too bad. He was a fine fellow.

He held the door open for her. "I'll do all I can."

At the desk he stared abstractedly at his hands and didn't even look at the list she had left. He knew the problem. He knew that he'd get nowhere with the men who ran those places. No use going, saying, they're the same as we are; meaning, this is political and will help me. . . . He had been in that Negro settlement during his campaign for office. He knew those people. Sue would argue with him about what he was thinking. But he knew better. That's why people were anti-Negro and anti-Semitic. Wayne had never had to work with them but he had. They had a chance to help themselves but they never did. Dave was different.

That evening Don got into his car and drove out to the Matthews estate.

"Come on in and have a drink!" D. S. shouted. "Irene isn't home."

Don sat with D. S. and drank Scotch, had several before he gained courage enough to say what he wanted to. Then—

"D. S.," Don said.

"Yeah, Donnie m'boy."

"What do you think of colored people?"

The chocolate-brown eyes twinkled in the red-flushed face. "Why, they're Irish turned inside out. As a kid we used to say that." He chuckled and his lids began to lower.

"D. S.," Don said, "would you give fifteen colored people jobs in one of your plants?"

"Fifteen," D. S. said, with his eyes closed. "Why fifteen? Tell you what. You can have fifty jobs to hand out to them." His eyes looked into Don's mischievously, knowingly. "It's political, isn't it?"

Don's eyes drifted away from D. S. "Yes," he said, "it is."

Don felt his hands tighten together in triumph. He finished his drink and started to stand up to leave. Then he heard a car drive up in front of the house and the motor go off. He accepted another drink and sipped it slowly. There was silence outside for five or ten minutes while he waited and listened. Then the motor was started again and the car drove away, the front door came open. High heels through the front of the room and toward the den.

Irene stood in the doorway. She arched her eyebrows. "Hello, Don."

When D. S. had left the room saying, "Well, I'll leave you two kids alone," Don asked Irene jealously, "Who were you with?"

"Christopher." She tossed her head.

"Well, I'm going."

"Sit down a minute."

Grudgingly he sat on the sofa. She sat next to him immediately and, turning toward him, put her hands on his forearms. She searched his face and his eyes and the lines of his body for the other boy, the lost boy, Kenny.

Donahue, another precinct captain, was in trouble. Donahue had been a sales investigator for three years. For three years he had been going into business establishments and shaking people down. He had two methods when he went in to check up on the proprietors:

"I have to look at your books. Everybody's books are a little shady."

"I won't have to look at your books. I know they're messed up."

Both methods worked equally well. The proprietors generally paid off.

Until a few days ago it had been a lucrative racket for Donahue. Then he had been caught taking a bribe. It looked like a jail sentence.

Donahue went to see Don. Don fixed it for him.

Each day Don became better liked in the district by the voters and the precinct captains alike. Mr. Veteran was running free shows for the kids. Mr. Veteran sponsored bunco parties for the ladies and threw free beer parties for the men. He had given fifty Negroes jobs in a factory where, until then, only whites had been employed. He was already planning summer picnics and vacation camps for the underprivileged.

And all in his own name.

Mr. Veteran had become the idol of the district.

# VIII

Spring was a promise. The little shoots came in buds to the branches of the trees and looked timidly out of their windows. New grass was tiny yellow-green needles in the moss of last year's carpets. The remembrance of winter was in the snow that lay in blackened patches along the gutters. Spring was coming early this year; or so people said.

McCarren told Don that he'd like to get out of the city, rest up somewhere for a while and come back when the weather was good.

"Yes, why don't you, Tom?"

"Well, I'll give it some thought (yawning). It would sure be good to get away from town for a while."

Don didn't even bother to say good-by when McCarren, bored, left the office to go down to the city hall.

The money and the power were going to Don's head. When a man comes into money and gets power he begins to talk different, walk different and even smell different. Don laid in several new suits for the spring season—and they were tailor-made. He had his weekly massage and an occasional Turkish bath. He had his nails manicured at the hotel barbershop. He had additional appointments with his tailor for fittings for a couple of topcoats and had worked himself up into the ten-dollar-tie class. He bought Sue expensive gifts of things she didn't want, and was trying to break it off with Rebecca. He gave his mother money every week. He did the precinct captains more and more favors. Mr. Veteran was known all over the district by the people and loved by them. Mr. Veteran was their hero, their father-confessor, social worker, defense attorney in trouble and kind benefactor at play. Mr. Veteran was prideful and swaggering and forever confidently smiling, even cockily smiling, and always willing to help anyone. He joined a couple of the city's best clubs. And, Mr. Veteran had himself elected Commander of his American Legion post. After all, the most popular man is generally picked as Commander and who was more popular than he? The vets elected him by an overwhelming vote. Immediately he had slot machines put in the clubroom and this was profitable for the post.

The first time he officiated as Commander he made a speech and proposed a bill for the building of a housing project for veterans only. The applause was like warm sunlight after a long winter.

He was going down to Springfield, he told them, to see if he could put it through. And while he spoke he knew that it would never go through. But it sounded good to the veterans.

The newspapers picked up the story. McCarren came into the insurance office waving the paper. His square, handsome face was angry and his hard, cold, expressionless eyes brushed Don's. "You're getting a little too big for your pants, aren't you?"

Don smiled and held it as if looking into a camera. "No. I don't think so." He tapped ashes from his cigar. "Look, Tom—it's good for you, it's good for the organization." Don chuckled and his eyes brushed McCarren's face in a secret and disdainful way. "Everybody knows I'm your mouthpiece. That little piece sounded good to the veterans but—" he lifted his shoulders and dropped them in a McCarren gesture "—do you think it has a chance? Just talk." He chuckled again. "Keeps the organization up there—we Democrats are the liberals and—" he smiled secretly, sneeringly at McCarren, "we have to talk that way. Anyway—" His voice imitated the dissenters to the proposed bill. " 'What the hell! Just because I'm not a vet—just because I didn't go—what are they trying to pull? I probably did more right here than half of them.' " Don's voice and face fell back to its naturalness. "It doesn't mean a thing, Tom."

McCarren smiled in grudging admiration with just the edge of his mouth. But, disgruntled, he said, "Well, I didn't tell you to start anything like that."

"I'm sorry, Tom." Smooth, polished tones.

"Oh—it's all right."

McCarren stooped down behind the desk and fished around in the metal cabinet for the bottle of Scotch and glasses. He was half-laughing. "You're on your toes," he said, still half-laughing.

Don cut his glance down across McCarren's back. His eyes were hard and amused.

But it was Mr. Veteran's bill and became known as Don's proposal and there was more and more talk about Don Lockwood.

He had won the confidence of the Urban League when he had handed out the fifty jobs to Negroes in his district—and that was five or six votes picked up in each of those families. He now called Mrs. Gardener up and had lunch with her in one of the large downtown hotel dining rooms. Over cocktails he asked her to have the Urban League sketch out a program in the very poor Negro area. They also discussed a campaign to condemn all of that property for public housing—and this was just between him and her, for the time being, and would be carried on through the Urban League.

Don leaned back, after lunch, inhaling on his cigarette and squinting his eyes in a self-pleased manner. He was building up an organization right under THE POWER's nose without McCarren seeing it. He had many of the precinct captains on his side. He had buttered their bread for them. He had the people with him. And he had old Deacon Johnson, the Negro preacher he had given the hundred dollars to during his campaign for State Representative, on his side. Reverend Johnson, who was well known in the Negro district, handled all the trouble there among his people and Don took care of it for him, did all the political favors for the deacon.

Mrs. Gardener tapped her gloves energetically and said she had to get back. Don helped her into her coat as courteously as a lover would have and, holding her arm, walked her to the door. He hailed a cab for her. He handed the cabbie the money for the fare as soon as she stepped in. He knew his way around.

Now Emerson Bradley wanted something else. He had a long, friendly letter written to Don thanking him for past favors and asking what the sale price of the alley adjacent to his property, his west bank of the river building, was at this time.

Don investigated. When his investigation was over he discovered that Bradley had been trying to buy the alley from the city for several years so that he could add to his main building. Knowing that Bradley needed the alley, the city was in no hurry to sell. The city council knew that it would get its price. That price was an outrageous sum.

Don made a deal with the alderman, put out money in the right spots and got the alley for Emerson Bradley for a decent price.

As soon as the Haines Company had been informed, Don got a telephone call. Emerson Bradley's private secretary was on the other end of the wire saying that Mr. Bradley would like very much to take Mr. Lockwood to dinner and personally thank him for the consummation of the sale of the alley.

Don dressed carefully in his most expensive tailor-made suit. The nervousness of a year ago was gone. That nervousness and fear and feeling of inferiority when he came into the presence of such men as McCarren and D. S. Matthews, men of importance or wealth.

He hailed a cab and soon found himself seated across a table from Emerson Bradley in a small private dining room in one of the better places. He had been escorted into the presence of Mr. Bradley and introduced by a private secretary who immediately disappeared. After the handshake and even before he had sat down, Emerson Bradley had said, "I'll have to ask you to refrain from smoking. Smoke annoys me." Don now sat looking across the table at his host.

Here was a man worth millions and millions of dollars. A powerful man used to having his own way.

"I am very glad to have this opportunity to thank you, Mr. Lockwood," Emerson Bradley said. There was neither warmth nor friendliness in the voice. The voice and the face never changed expression.

Even laughter never changed the face muscles. Laughter was only a low-keyed, growling eruption.

"If you ever tire of politics I think I could find a place for you in my organization. You get things done. Most people have forgotten how these days." It was the monotonous voice Don had heard on the radio over *The Haines Family Hour* on Sundays and always turned off.

The dinner was a dull and boring affair. A uniformed waiter served it on whispering feet. Emerson Bradley's false teeth made a clicking sound as he ate and he sighed and breathed hard while he chewed and swallowed. At the end of the dinner Emerson Bradley took an envelope from his pocket and placed it before Don. "This is for the favor you did for me," the monotonous voice said. It was like handing the lowliest of servants his pay.

Don smiled the smile he had used over the footlights. Don played his ace card. He handed the moneyed envelope back across the table. "I like to do favors," he said; and he knew that he would get more in the long run: they like money more than anybody else. Like getting the driveways for less.

Emerson Bradley was a bit confused and settled back in his chair. Very unusual! Very unusual for a politician to refuse money for his services.

Emerson Bradley said a few polite things and then summarily dismissed Don.

In the insurance office McCarren said, "I'd like to get out of town but with the April elections coming up—" he yawned and stretched his arms out wide, "and the election of ward committeemen—"

"Why don't you?" Don said. "I can take care of things for you."

"Jeez, no one is running against me—I'm the people's choice," McCarren said. He laughed.

McCarren went to Hot Springs for the baths, knowing he had no opposition.

# IX

He'd have to move fast now.

McCarren was hardly on the train before Don began collecting campaign funds for the April primaries. He went the rounds of the big night clubs where there was gambling—cards, dice, roulette wheels. Where there were women. He went to the bookie joints, the numbers wheels.

"We're collecting for the April primaries."

McCarren, THE POWER, had said, "This is my man." There was, as usual, no questioning it.

All the spots came up with money. A thousand to five thousand dollars wasn't an unusual sum for the biggest book joints in town to pay.

When checks were written, Don said, "Instead of making it out to the Democratic Party, make it out in my name," or, "No, I'll take it in cash."

There was no questioning THE POWER's man.

Don got in touch with the precinct captains. "Pass the word around that we're collecting for the campaign. Have them come up to headquarters Tuesday night."

The precinct captains knew what that meant. They passed the word around in the taverns, poolrooms, restaurants; in all of the places of business in their precincts. Up and down North Clark, North State, West Madison they went, in and out of door after door of taverns, hash houses, flophouses.

Tuesday night the proprietors lined up outside of McCarren's office at headquarters. Don sat at McCarren's desk. The green-shaded drop light made his face ugly. The proprietors shuffled in with their envelopes containing offerings. And they were all there, every proprietor in the neighborhood. And the tavern owners sweetened their envelopes a little more, knowing that if they didn't show up or didn't give enough they'd have the police in their places every half an hour bothering their customers. Don pulled the money out of each envelope and counted it before nodding dismissal to the proprietors.

At Don's side sat Mucci with a list of every place in the district. As each proprietor paid off, Mucci ran a pencil line through his name. And just now a North Clark Street tavern owner stood in front of the desk. He laid down his envelope. Don counted the money. Then, pushing it back into the envelope, he tossed the envelope back across the desk. He looked up and the hard, bright light cut harshness across his face, left his eyes in deep black shadow. "I can get that much from the newsboy on the corner," Don said.

The tavern owner shuffled away. He pulled more money out of his pocket, stuffed it in the envelope and got back in line.

The scavengers contributed. If they wanted to stay in the district they had to. They got together and gave Don a hundred dollars apiece which came to another two thousand dollars.

Don deposited all of the campaign money in the bank in his name.

In Don's Tennyson Hotel room, where he had been summoned by Don, Mucci sat in a soft chair with his hands on the arm rests and his belt loosened a little to give his stomach freer play. Don offered the bottle again and Mucci lazily made a no more gesture with his hand. Don poured for himself and squinted at the glass as he held it up to the light. Then he drank. Set the glass down.

"I've got something cooking, Mucci."

Mucci dummied-up. His frog-eyes were passive and patient.

Don pulled out the bankbook and tossed it on the cocktail table. "I've got sixty thousand dollars here in my name."

Mucci's patient frog-eyes drooped sleepily but his hands tightened on the knobs of the chair.

Don said, "I want to run against McCarren. Will you run the campaign for me?"

He had put it in words. It was out. He sat staring at Mucci in the semidarkness of the room while his arms and legs trembled. It was like signing to fight the champion. A vein pounded in his forehead and his throat was so tense it hurt. He went on staring at Mucci.

Mucci stirred lazily in the chair and sat half-upright. Behind him his shadow stirred on the wall like an ape. His popeyes were wide open now and looked back into Don's as if measuring him. "I'll have that drink now," he said.

With trembling hands Don filled Mucci's glass. Mucci drank silently while Don's heart pounded and his hands shook.

Mucci drained the glass and set it down on the floor. He leaned forward, halfway out of the chair, and held his hand out to Don.

Don grasped the pudgy hand on the end of the finlike arm. Don smiled. It was a McCarren smile. Perspiration of nervousness that had popped out when he had told Mucci began to trickle down his armpits.

Mucci picked up the bankbook and, with his round, pockmarked face close to it, read the figures.

"It's all in my name," Don said.

Mucci began to chuckle. But the chuckling shut off. His frog-eyes looked over the bankbook at Don. "I want to be alderman."

Don nodded.

# X

Mucci rolled the big cannons into place for Don.

"You go down to the city hall," Mucci told Don. "You get an audience with the county central committee. But first—you call a meeting of all the precinct captains."

Mucci held a long, all-night session with Don and planned it with him, step by step. Mucci got in touch with Casey and Buckley and Ryan, the big boys, the big vote-getters of McCarren's organization.

Don walked out onto the stage at Democratic headquarters and faced the precinct captains. He started speaking immediately:

"You probably wonder why I asked you to show up here tonight. I'll get right down to brass tacks. Now I've done right by you precinct captains. I've always taken care of you. I've seen that you made extra money. I think you'll agree that I've treated you better than McCarren did. Well—here it is—I'm going to run against McCarren for ward committeeman and—" he pointed out to Mucci as they had arranged it, "Mucci is going to run my campaign for me."

Mucci got up immediately, and as prearranged came smiling to the stage, shook hands with Don, pumping his hand up and down and voicing phrases of congratulations, as prearranged. Then Mucci, in the stunned silence of the hall, turned to the precinct captains and held his little fat fins up for a silence that already existed. Grinning with his fat, flabby lips he spoke into that silence:

"I guess this comes as a surprise, men. But it's true. And Don Lockwood is going to be our next ward committeeman so you'd better go along with him. Lockwood has sixty thousand dollars in campaign funds and we all know that money buys the vote. McCarren hasn't got a red cent! McCarren's a dead duck. Now what we're asking you is to come along with us. We have a petition here on the table that you can sign pledging yourself to Lockwood's election. Now—" fat little fin stuck up in the air, "you don't have to sign tonight. You've got a day or two to think it over but we want to get as many signers tonight as possible." Mucci picked up the petition and waved it out at the audience after first signing it himself. "Now, who's going to be next to sign and swing over to the precinct captain's friend—Don Lockwood—our next ward committeeman!"

Casey, Buckley, Ryan, the big boys of McCarren's organization got up and went to the stage to sign it as had been prearranged. Other precinct captains followed. Kostner and McGuire got up and went to the stage. The precinct captains began signing the conspiracy.

Mucci waited up in Don's hotel room while Don went over to the city hall. Pleasant were Don's steps through the early spring sunlight and the jostling crowds of people, the traffic that halted at stop lights to let him pass as if from a command of his own. Pleasant the look of the city hall and its wide corridors. Day of triumph. I am Don Lockwood. Hero. They have to go along. I am Don Lockwood. His foot was sprightly and his eye clear with the spring of victory.

Around a huge glass-topped desk in comfortable leather-bound chairs the President of the City Council, the gentlemen of the County Central Committee, and Mr. Louis Martin, the County Organizer, awaited him. They had only been names to him before and now emerged as men in dark blue and pin-striped suits who arose and shook his hand and acknowledged his greetings. And he was seated in the circle with them, their polite but slightly aloof eyes regarding him. A tray of cigars was presented to him and a light held for him. Polite and frosty was the air. And the President of the City Council was making some casual joke.

The head of the central committee leaned forward and looked at his watch, leaned back in his chair and stroked his wavy gray hair. He cleared his throat. "Mr. Lockwood, you—ah—" he paused, "asked to see us on some very important business pertaining to the political picture in Tom McCarren's district. Mr. McCarren—ah—" he paused again, "Tom—my old and good friend—ah—has done a particularly brilliant job in his district—ah—over the years."

Don glanced from the organizer of the committee to the President of the City Council. The president was looking out the window. Don looked again at the committee organizer, the other gentlemen. Unconsciously he touched his breast pocket where the bankbook was: his entrance anywhere, and he must give the greatest performance of his career.

Don dampened his lips. "Mr. President, Mr. Martin, gentlemen—" picking them each up with his eyes and nodding pleasantly, "I'll make it short, gentlemen. I don't want to take up your valuable time. I've—" he strengthened himself in his chair like a diver gaining courage for the leap from the high board "—decided to run against McCarren." And he spoke quickly then, drawing the bankbook from his pocket, pulling out the other papers he had brought. "I've got sixty thousand dollars here. I've got fifty-five precinct captains." He laid bankbook and documents on the table.

The president picked up the bankbook, started to look at it, instead handed it to Mr. Martin, the County Central Committee Organizer.

"No, you first, Mr. President," the organizer said generously.

The president looked at the bankbook and then handed it to Mr. Martin without speaking. The committee organizer looked at the figures in the book and nodded his head up and down slowly. He handed the book to the others of the group. Each fingered through and looked at the total: $60,000.

The committee organizer took the sheet of paper Don offered. "That's a list of the precinct captains, signed by them, who have pledged themselves to support me," Don said. "That's two-thirds of the precinct captains in the district." His voice came a little more naturally now and with independence behind it. "Next to their names you will find the number of votes each of them pulled in the last election. At the bottom you will find the total number of votes they were responsible for. That's their petition in support of my candidacy."

The committee organizer's eyes came over in a staring appraisal of Don. The president's lips were now silently tabulating the vote. The president leaned sideways and handed the list to the gentleman next to him. Don looked down as if unconcerned and applied a new match to his cigar that had gone out. He saw his diamond ring and the sparkle of it. The tally was over. The eyes of president, organizer and the other gentlemen were on him. They, the big shots of the party, had known of Don only through hearing THE POWER boast about him. Now they realized that he was certainly smart and cagy. A little of the official sternness was gone from the faces confronting him. Winter was lifting a little from the room.

The president and the county organizer cleared their throats at the same time and looked at each other and smiled. Mr. Martin nodded deference to the president.

The president said, "Well, young man—" gesturing with his hand for forgiveness at the loose usage of the words, "Mr.—ah—Lockwood—do you realize what handling a huge district like that entails? The experience necessary—the years of—"

Don broke in. "I've worked for McCarren. I've done his work for him. He's in Hot Springs right now. I've done all of his dir—all of his work for him since before the last election. I am now the best-known man in the district. I can beat him easily and I'm quite capable of handling the district. I have $60,000. I'll spend all of it and more, if necessary."

The president, the county organizer, the other gentlemen, smiled and nodded pleasantly. They each had something to say. And during the course of the discussion the president suggested that if Don would go along with McCarren, they would get McCarren to dump the alderman and make Don alderman.

Don was purposely dramatic and purposely impolite. He stood up, almost as if to go. He laughed. He put his palms on the table and leaned over toward the president, the organizer, the other gentlemen. He knew that he would still be a tool for McCarren and that by the time the aldermanic elections came up McCarren would get him out of the picture and make a pauper of him again.

Don laughed again. "I won't go for that kind of deal."

Fat bellies shook and elderly faces relaxed into smiles. Caught in their own trap they all chuckled patronizingly. They now knew more than ever that he was a good politician.

Organizer Martin's eyes came over to Don's face in a sort of salute.

Don sat down. He began to talk.

But threatening still was the air. There was an interruption. It was a polite interruption and the polite voice of the county organizer said, "You know, Mr. Lockwood, that we could take all the jobs—all the patronage—away from your precinct captains and let McCarren keep it."

Don smiled. "I don't think you will though." His shoulders lifted in the smallest of shrugs. "After all—election is only a few weeks off and—after I win—you'd give me all the patronage back because you know I'm an organization man and your policies will be mine."

Their eyes were now attentive.

"I know—" and he stood up again "—even if I did win you could break me. You could send a top man in there to collect, saying, 'This is my acting ward committeeman.' " Don sat down. His eyes went earnestly from face to face. "I'm an organization man. I'll be strictly an organization man."

The eyes looked deep into him. The eyes liked what they saw.

Polite and warming was the air.

Knowing how he got the money they were amused. The kid was alert. He was on his toes—any time a kid can stick it into an old timer like that he deserves the spot.

They went on talking. Cigar smoke blued the conference table over their heads in a low-hanging cloud. But was summer far away?

The political, the knowing, the crafty eyes began to exchange glances.

They talked.

McCarren is getting old. They needed some new, young, clever blood in there. Organizer Martin looked up at the president. "Mr. President, McCarren has been making too many demands on us the past couple of years."

Don's heart thumped hard.

Organizer Martin continued, "This is a good time to dump him."

Don's heart stopped.

"Yes, this is a good time to dump him."

The president looked at Don. The president was amused and astonished that McCarren had let the grass grow under his feet and this kid was stealing the play away from him. The president was not in love with any ward committeeman. All he was concerned with was who can bring in the biggest vote for the party.

The president looked at Don again and agreed that he was going to make him. Under one condition. If he gets out of line after we make him we'll break him.

The president and the county central committee organizer exchanged glances and nods. The president assured Don that his precinct captains would not lose their patronage or their jobs. There was much shaking of hands.

Summer sunlight was the air.

When Don left, the men exchanged amused, significant glances. Laughter ran in a chain around the table. It was like the hard, linked chain of a political organization. It subsided to a smile. A political, cynical, clever smile. But a group smile.

Organizer Martin walked to the window.

"Poor old McCarren," the president said, chuckling.

Looking out the window with his back to the group, Organizer Martin began to howl with laughter.

Don didn't wait for the elevator. He almost ran down the steps, almost got hit by a car. In a drugstore he called his room. "Get a bottle of champagne!" he told Mucci excitedly and hung up on Mucci's shout of triumph.

In the hotel room they clapped each other across the back and hugged each other and did a little dance with their arms around each other. Into the glasses the champagne fizzed like laughter and anger and excitement and competition and war.

Over the blue rug of the room Mucci danced in a weird little fatman shuffle, holding his glass above his head.

Don went to the window and looked out at his city, Chicago. He hugged himself and grinned out of the window at Chicago.

Mucci, in the steps of his dance, with champagne spilling out of his glass, shouted, "We got McCarren by his whisky nose!"

Don threw back his head and burst into laughter. "We'll give him ulcers!" he shouted back.

# XI

Spring was more than a promise. Spring gurgled in the gutters. Sunlight warmed the streets and green were the boughs of the trees and blue the skies above. The city smiled with spring.

Jim's blue eyes widened and sun made his blond hair golden. Spring moved into his body, his mind. On the boulevards and side streets women walked. Jim's blue eyes met and followed them. Their heavy fur coats of winter had been laid away and their bodies blossomed like flowers in the clothing of spring. Jim walked, aware of every pretty woman on the street, his eyes concentrating on them, their hair, their legs, their hips. Often he followed them just to watch the movements of their bodies. Many times he hurried in the crowds to fall in step with and then to get a step ahead of a woman who looked attractive from the back so that, in that instant of passing her, he could glance quickly into her face. There were those times when they were not good-looking and he was disappointed. And there were those times when their beauty left him short of breath and he carried a picture of their faces in his memory as long as he could. The sounds of women's heels against the sidewalks, their perfume, the high music of their voices, the tinkling cords of their laughter sent a thrill of excitement through him.

There were times when, like the flash of a fever or the sudden pain of a headache, to his mind came the French girl. And he would shudder with shame. My God! She was only fourteen!

Forget it! Forget it! he told himself; and her face, her age, would vanish from the mirror of his memory. Almost vanish.

He was good-looking and got women. He found out it was easy to get laid. But even this was not enough.

His was a sex hunger. A restlessness. The city with its well-dressed women, its music and taverns, its night clubs and bright lights, its painted prostitutes, plunging necklines and neat round bottoms on the stools of cocktail lounges were a constant stimulation to him.

. . . the French girl came back . . . the French girl haunted him. And with her she brought a friend . . . a broken battlefield and the man whose life he could have saved and didn't when Johnson said "Pick one." This haunted him too. And he had killed an old woman. This too haunted him.

He stopped his car with a jolt and climbed out. He had to see it better! He crossed the sidewalk and cinders crunched under his feet. He stood wide-legged looking up.

The huge billboard was set at an angle on the vacant lot. Three spotlights curved over it like curious eyes. One figure half reclined across all the billboard like an *Esquire* drawing. She was smiling. She wore a bra that was as tight and as firm as chrome discs. Her long, shapely legs, almost half the length of the billboard, wore the sheerest of silk stockings.

Jim stood a long time, wide-legged before the billboard.

. . . Often now he thought of the French girl. The clouds of shame came over his mind and over his eyes.

Across the room Louise, darning his socks. In the bedroom the children slept.

He lowered his eyes. He stood up. "I'm going for a walk."

He kept his eyes lowered and moved out of the room. His wife watched him go, her sad eyes following him.

Outside he breathed the warm air of night. Outside he walked, to walk his shame away. But there were women on the street. His eyes followed them.

There were times when instead of driving his car home he rode on the crowded streetcars, jostling with the home-hurrying people, managing to crowd close to a woman, his thigh touching hers. Or the sway of the streetcar touching her womanness against him and withdrawing it. And the time he often thought of later when, crowded so tight in the car, his hand had touched the young woman's breast and could not be removed: her breast secretly cupped in his careful hand.

Nights that he took the streetcar home he told Louise: "There's something wrong with that damn car again! As soon as we can afford it we'll have to get a new one."

He watched the women . . . if I could have any woman I wanted . . . and he watched them, started looking for the one he would select . . . no, not that one . . . *uhhh!* He selected one in this block and discarded her only when he found one he liked better . . . if he could have all the women he wanted, any woman, changing when he wanted . . . women of all nationalities . . . lots of women . . . and walking on the boulevard in the city streets he had sexual intercourse with those of his choosing . . . like a king, like a maharajah . . . having them brought to him as they walked down the street toward him.

He brought union work home from the office. He put it off after supper. He kept putting it off. He snapped at Louise. It became an argument. She apologized. He didn't say he was sorry and that was the first time since their marriage when, after a quarrel, he hadn't put his arms around her, and tilting her face up to his, said, "I'm sorry, Skinny."

But not tonight.

Louise looked at him and was worried. It must be what she had always feared—it must be another woman.

In the bathroom she cried a little and washed her face with cold water to take the telltale red from under her eyes. In the bedroom she undressed. From the bedroom she made her voice gentle and enticing. "Are you coming to bed, Jim?"

"I'm not sleepy yet."

Restless, he wandered through the house. He made himself some coffee. Pouring it, he looked across the table and saw the French girl sitting there. Shame, disgust and guilt were his.

He wandered around the house. Tiptoed in to see if the children were asleep. Got out his union work. Lay on the sofa with the papers he had to go over tonight.

He looked at the sheets of paper. Fantasies of women appeared to him. He tried to concentrate on his work. It was no use. He conjured up a girl. And on the sofa in the dim light he drew up more and more enjoyable fantasies. And went to the bathroom for a long, excited time before crawling into bed with Louise.

# XII

From his Tennyson Hotel room Don drove out to Highland Park. D. S. was out of town for a few days. He met her in front of the fireplace. He embraced her and, when their lips had parted, while their arms were still tightly about each other, he looked over her shoulder and into the huge mirror, capturing his face with his eyes, smiling at himself, proudly, even vainly.

Don was full of himself. He told her about the meeting in the city hall, about how he was sure of winning, about how the way was up for him politically.

While she got the liquor from the cabinet. While she mixed the drinks and handed him one. While she drank and took the empty glasses and filled them again. While she sat toying with her cigarette, making lazy little circles of smoke.

After a while she said petulantly, "I don't want to hear any more about your old politics. Make love to me."

Don laughed and slid next to her on the sofa, making love to her. For hours on the sofa; and later in her room, in the lace and brocade and perfume of the rich girl's boudoir. All night long they clung together in the silk of her bed, sleeping, awakening. And in the morning, in the gray morning light when drowsiness is to the body what music is to the ear, turned lazily toward each other, playing in the little fondlings of lovers.

In the early afternoon they arose and Irene went to bathe. In the tub with the warm water lacing its soothing fingers over her body Irene came to what was a resolution. Over the smooth concrete roads of life to this point of her existence she had come. Rich girl. Happy rich girl. Or so it should have been. In books and movies it was that way.

She sat before the mirror powdering; and now looking deep into her own eyes. When had she sucked the sweetness from the persimmon? Too often her lips had come away bitter. She wondered, stroking the powder puff over her cheek, when she had been happy. That brief time with Kenny. And even then there had been more hurt than happiness. As a little girl with her father, riding, going to the circus, astride his lap at the office twisting his hair down over his forehead in curls. Her mother she had despised and formed allegiance against with her father. And had had her own way. There hadn't been much happiness. Anything she had seen or wanted she had been able to buy or to get. It was true that good-looking people and wealthy people had, really, the hardest, the most unhappy lives. Life spoiled them young. Temptation was always sitting on the doorstep or beckoning through the windowpane. All things came too easily and most things came to be nothing in the hands of the handsome and the wealthy. Loneliness was an infirmity, a senile old age, an empty bag propped up with air. And now in the welter of that loneliness, that brittle gaiety of parties and dances and the all-alike faces and forms and polite ways, saying the right thing, the clever thing, the all-alike smell of the cologne from the expensive clothing of all the smart young men of her set with never the invigorating, exciting smell of the body, the armpits: sterile, the all-alike men, the same conversations, over and over. Don had come, crude, vain, as unpolished as her father was; had come with something of the slums sticking to him, a something that attracted her as the truck drivers always had, the cabbies, the delivery boy at the back door with a parcel from Marshall Field's. In Don she saw what she wanted: for now, at least. And was it only for now or for a longer time? Would he, too, become but a bauble in her rich girl's hands? She wanted him because he was like Kenny and like her father. He was the memory of Kenny. The shadow thrown from the grave across the face of life. And more than that. She faced herself squarely in the mirror. She told herself the truth. That truth was that sex with him had been more satisfactory than with anyone else. His body brought a violence. His words of love were coarse. From his body exuded not the smell of cologne but the armpit smell of a man. There was satisfaction in the tearing away at her that he brought. Not the polite or flattering or concerned or mechanical or stale-sterile or diverse of the bored young men of her crowd that she had known, the rich and casual and bored, as she was bored.

At the doorway Don was knocking and saying, "Hey! I'm going to make some coffee!"

A smile lifted Irene's mouth and tears came to her eyes: I'm a fool—the biggest fool—it won't work.

"Okay!" she said.

In the kitchen with the cups of coffee set before them Irene suddenly looked across at Don. "I think I'll marry you."

"Oh yeah?" Don said. His heart beat fast. Irene Matthews! D. S. Matthews' son-in-law! "Oh yeah?" he said again as if he were hard to get.

That evening he called Irene. "I've *got* to see you."

He drove out to the estate and they sat alone in the huge front room. I've got to ask her. I'm scared.

No words came to him. But at length he lifted her hands out of her lap, stretched out on the low couch and put his head in her lap. Idly she played with his hair. He put his hand up over his eyes, feeling his inferiority. When he spoke, and the way he acted, he was little boy about it and didn't even know it. In the same way he had been years ago, when Sue had wanted to reach out her hand and help him.

"Look," he said, "I'm nuts about you." And silent a moment, then, "I know you were kidding today." Silent again a while, then, "I want to marry you. But I know you wouldn't marry me, would you?"

Irene leaned her face to his. She kissed him on the lips tenderly, slowly, touching his lips with hers, slowly lifting them away. "I love you, Don. I'll marry you."

And going home an exhilaration hit him. Happy, happier than he had ever been before. The husband of Irene Matthews!

Marrying Irene was like acquiring the diamond ring and the Homburg hat.

And he didn't even know it.

# XIII

McCarren flew into town, having found out through a stool pigeon that Don was running against him. And that suited Don fine. He wanted McCarren to know. This, the moment when his revenge was sweetest.

McCarren tried to get in touch with Don. Don let it be known that, "I'm too busy. I've got no time to see him."

Frantically McCarren tried to contact Don.

"I only see my friends."

McCarren tried to collect campaign money from the bookie joints and the other places. The money was gone. The books and the others couldn't beef. And they couldn't get their money back. After all, McCarren had said of Don, "This is my man. This is my collector."

And now that word had gone around that Lockwood had the okay from the city hall, they were all with him for their own good.

A thief doesn't like to be robbed of anything. McCarren let up a howl. He went down to see the County Central Committee and found out that he was washed up.

Storming in front of the big glass-topped conference desk, walking back and forth with his handsome face flushed, McCarren smashed his fist into the palm of his hand. "This kid don't stand a chance. When it's all over you'll beg me to come back into the organization."

Organizer Martin said quietly, "On the contrary, *you* don't stand a chance."

McCarren, pounding his fist now into the glass of the conference desk, shouted, "I'll be elected because the people want me because of all the good I've done for the people. I don't need any precinct captains. The people want me."

Central Organizer Martin said in his quiet voice, "If you feel you want to run—go ahead—we like competition anyway."

McCarren ran. His pride made him. He came up with his own money for the campaign. He went down deep into his own pockets. He began organizing what was left of his outfit. Don hadn't taken all of McCarren's precinct captains. But those who hadn't originally been on Don's side found out that he had the go-light and, knowing he was going to win, started to sway over to his side. The only ones who stayed with McCarren were fifteen men who had been with him twenty years, making money all the time. And a lot of the assistant precinct captains stayed because they knew that if McCarren won they'd be precinct captains.

Meanwhile Don, with his sense of the dramatic, rented a vacant lot in the district and had a huge army tent put up on it. A sign in foot-tall letters was erected above the entrance flap:

CAMPAIGN HEADQUARTERS OF DON LOCKWOOD
FIRST WOUNDED VETERAN OF WORLD WAR II

Good things were happening inside the tent. Other ward committeemen who had known McCarren and hated his guts but could never say so openly because he had always been a big power in the organization, contacted Don and gave him a little money to help beat McCarren. It was their only way of getting even with him.

State Representative Reed found out through the Council President that Lockwood was going to win. He sent telegrams from Springfield to all of his key men instructing them to support Don to the fullest.

The alderman wanted to come over to Don. Don refused him. He was going to make Mucci alderman—that was their deal.

Don girded his precinct captains. Standing wide-legged under the tent top he spoke to them forcefully:

"I'm going to make a pledge to you men. When this thing is over with I'm not going to accept any of McCarren's men. The fellows from McCarren's organization will never be accepted in my organization after I win. There are no favors in this organization. Those of you who bring in the best precincts will get the best jobs . . . "

Even while he spoke he knew that any one of McCarren's men who carried a precinct against him would be welcomed back and given a job. What he was interested in was a powerful organization. He might as well have them on his side—they were good vote-getters.

" . . . that's my solemn pledge to all of you. . . . "

Clever things were hapening inside the tent. Don brought two colored precinct captains into the organization to work in the Negro district. They could talk to their own people. They could show how their own people were making a buck now. The Urban League was for him. And the fifty jobs he had given out in the area—that had gone the rounds. He was the friend of the colored people. They had been sneaking with a policy station without paying off. Don let them go wide open with the policy station.

Don talked to the Republican ward committeeman and made a deal with him. Don promised him a couple of books on the south end of the district, five state, five county and five city jobs for his men. The Republicans had no patronage so Don made the deal this way: the Democrats always give the Republicans jobs when it's time to deal with them.

Don and the Republican ward committeeman shook hands warmly. The Republican ward committeeman instructed his precinct captains to get the vote out for Don.

All the tricks—all the dirt Don had learned from McCarren he now used—against him.

Old walls and lampposts all over the district began to flower with red, white and blue signs. Each bore a large, smiling portrait of Don. The signs said:

VOTE FOR
DON LOCKWOOD
FIRST WOUNDED VETERAN
OF WORLD WAR II

Late at night Don walked the streets of the district admiring his portrait that smiled back at him all over the district.

# XIV

D. S. Matthews stood in his den. The sleeves of his shirt were rolled up with the gold cuff links hidden in their folds. He ran the palm of his hand over his hairy forearm and stared abstractedly out of the window . . . the good old days. Well now, were they, really? Yes, they were. His invention.

The big deal was brewing. The big deal was on. He was on his way to being a millionaire. The good old days . . . of struggle . . . of success. But if he lost all of his money and this home and his car, wouldn't he think back on these as the good old days? They had been days of pleasure and of competition. Days of great wealth and of helping those he loved, crushing those who were his enemies. They had been days of marriage. He thought of Miss Society and smiled tenderly. They had had some real brawls—argue! The little unpleasant things of life always sifted through the sieve of time leaving in solid lumps only—the good old days—and the days had all, so to speak, been good to him.

He walked over and looked into one of the cabinets containing his collection of ships. But he looked in with out-of-focus eyes and saw only their vague shapes. And still he had never been very happy, really. What were his goodies of life? He liked calling them that, the things that each man wanted most or prized most in life.

Everything had been a contest to him. The grain pit. The stock market. A game entered into lustily. For the game. For the feeling of power. He had wrestled with men for power and money. Wrestled and won. There were people, many people, who envied him. But how many goodies had he had? The model ships loomed up largely before his eyes. Most of the goodies were always somewhere else. The ships loomed even larger.

"D. S."

Startled, he turned and saw his daughter standing in the doorway.

"Yes, honey?"

Irene strode into the room in slacks. She walked up to her father and looked up into his face. Her eyes were tense and her voice strained and she spoke quickly. "What do you think of Don, D. S.?"

"Well—" D. S. said, putting all the things he had been thinking about back into the chest and shutting the lid on them in the attic of his mind, "I like the boy. He—generally knows what he wants and goes out and gets it."

"I want to marry him."

"What!"

"Now you don't need to argue with me. I've made up my mind. He isn't educated—neither are you. If it doesn't work I'll divorce him. If you don't let me marry him I'll sleep with him anyway. I might even become a high-class whore."

"Now is that a nice way for my little girl to talk?"

"I'm not a little girl. I'm twenty-four and well able to do anything I please."

D. S. smiled proudly, seeing his own willfulness in his daughter.

"So he's one of your goodies—no—" waving his hand, "never mind." He put his arm around her. "Let's have a drink."

D. S. got the decanter and poured. Father and daughter drank together.

Irene laughed. She said, "I generally get what I want."

D. S. chuckled. "Miss Society should hear about this!" he said.

Irene's chocolate-brown eyes looked into her father's chocolate-brown eyes and they laughed together.

When D. S. was alone again and pouring more liquor into his glass he said to himself: so it takes away the hurt of the other boy. And the kid is going to go places. A little conceited. A little cocky. But—

And D. S. had his own little joke on his daughter. Only yesterday he had mailed a large check toward helping Don's campaign after talking to the President of the City Council.

The boy was going to be ward committeeman. He could be pushed far. I can see to it that he's pushed as far as he can go. If he treats my little girl right.

Don parked his Buick on Skid Row and walked to the 26-table. "Hello, Helen."

"Oh, hello, honey!" Her eyes leaped with pleasure.

He grinned at her and said, "I'm getting married," and told her who it was. "Don't tell Ma," he said.

"Oh, I won't, Don!" And again she warned, "We don't mean you no good." Her eyes were proud on him, and tender with love: "I'm so glad for you, Don, and that's for sure."

She had a favor to ask him. She asked it fearfully, afraid that he might refuse. She opened her mouth twice with it and closed her mouth before asking. Then she blurted it out. "Bring her down and let me look at her. I'd be proud to have you come down sometimes—and I won't let on that I'm your sister."

And he spoke the words of love between brother and sister in farewell, "*Smiało*—be of good cheer."

The next night he brought Irene down, swaggering over to the 26-table.

"What number, sir?" Helen asked, her voice trembling a little.

"What number should I take, Irene?"

"Aces," she said, holding his arm, looking up smilingly into his face.

And as the dice rolled out, Helen held the image of her in her eyes, traced every feature, looked in humble admiration at the girl who was to be her sister-in-law.

There was a great difference between the two girls. Irene, petite, sophisticated, pretty, polished and lacquered at the beauty shop to give that prettiness every advantage, her features small, her eyes knowing how to sparkle and smile, her mouth how to exclaim in delight as Don's numbers rolled up. Helen, large, almost plump, her full lips and her cheeks too heavily made-up, her eyebrows plucked and painted on her forehead, her bushy brown hair like two large earmuffs at the sides of her head. All about them in the tavern was spit on the floor and drunks at the tables.

He was going to marry Irene. He could hardly believe it himself. He had had to tell Irene and D. S. the same lie he had told Sue. . . .

"My parents are dead. I'm an orphan. I came from Oregon when I was old enough to be on my own."

He was going to marry Irene. Guilt was upon him. He thought of going to see Sue and telling her about it. He couldn't face telling her. He stayed away from her.

Rebecca saw it in the society section of the Sunday paper: Don and Irene standing smiling at each other before a Highland Park home. The caption reading, . . . *to be married in a simple ceremony* . . . and knew it was all over between them. Sue also saw it in the paper. And Don's mother, fancifully reading the society column as she did every Sunday, transporting herself to her weekly make-believe world, turned the picture up.

Don went, a few days after the wedding, to tell his mother. Answering the door, her stern Polish eyes looked at him angrily as she asked what he wanted there. She opened the door so that he could step inside and she could have her way in words with him. "You are no son of mine. It is not you who are ashamed of us but we who bow our heads in shame of you."

"But now I can help you," Don said guiltily. "Now I am in a position to help you."

His mother came across the room with her hands on her hips. "How help us? Move us somewhere where we don't want to live? Give us your fine wife's charity? Move us again somewhere out of sight so that you need sneak to see us only once or twice a year? So that we can never see them or they us?" She dragged up one of the dead grandfather's expressions. "I spit on all this!"

Don, angry and also guilty, slammed out of the house and went back to the apartment on the Gold Coast that his father-in-law had given him as a wedding present.

# XV

Spring was the fulfillment. Lilacs gave their colors and their scents to the city. People were sleeping with their windows open again.

Jim sat at a bar with a bottle of beer in front of him. The French girl sat with him at the bar. There was no beauty to him like the beauty of a young girl. Often, now, in the early spring afternoons when school was getting out he would drive to one of the nearby high schools and, parking, sit watching the high school girls on their way home. He had, for a long time, when he thought of the French girl, shuddered and thought, But she was only fourteen. Now he was fascinated by the thought of her. And he knew a truth that all older men knew in less or larger degree—the younger girl and the older man's attraction for her.

In Jim's mind was the thought of younger women, younger woman. And a fear for himself. Where would it lead him? His attraction was not innocent. Nor was it an attraction alone that would want nothing else. Where would it lead him? And now he began to look back upon the time of war with nostalgia, wanted to live over again the time with the French girl.

He drove his car and parked it in front of the school where, slumped behind the wheel, he could watch the girls go home from school. The grammar and high schools were on the same large plot of ground and he now saw that these were the little girls from grammar school. For a moment he thought of his sister. He started the motor and drove to the other end of the school grounds.

Now the high school girls came from under the archway and towards avenues and streetcar lines on the way home.

Jim sat hunched over the steering wheel, staring out of the windshield. His legs trembled a little watching the girls. There was a beauty to them, a charm to them, you couldn't find in older women. First of all it was the freshness of them, of their young bodies and their young skin. Their fresh, unspoiled faces. Unspoiled even by makeup. Generally only a little lipstick. Their small, tight young breasts, their youthful dresses, books under their arms. Their hair was worn differently from a woman's. Most often it was worn in a page boy style. He liked, too, their high school sweaters, their skirts—skirts and sweaters—it gave them a youthful beauty—their firm-looking young legs going down to saddle shoes, gym shoes, shoes with low heels. They poured from the school, sometimes shrilling, sometimes chasing each other down the sidewalk, walking backwards talking to each other.

And there was a fear in Jim, watching, a large fear. If he didn't contain himself—if he ever let himself go. He was tall, handsome, very handsome, and he knew it. It would be easy to get acquainted with any of them he wanted: the young girl's attraction for the older man and, in his case, the tall, handsome older man. He must just look at them and never speak to them. Oh God, give me the strength!

He watched the high school girls. This one—she was young yet. She hadn't learned to walk like a woman with the dainty, calculated twisting of a woman. None of them had. Oh God, only a little strength!

At home in the newspaper after dinner he read a headline:

MOLESTER GETS
TWENTY YEAR
JAIL TERM

Sex offense against
children ended today in . . .

There was business for the union that had to be done quickly. He went over to Mr. Baker's house and he and the union secretary worked almost until midnight. But while they were on their charts and records, Jim's candid blue eyes came up secretly from their bookkeeping to look at Mr. Baker's granddaughter curled on a couch under a lamp where she was doing her high school homework.

Mr. Baker waved Jim good night from the doorway and the French girl walked from under a lamppost, fell in step with him, got into his car with him. And the pleasures of war. The sensual and sexual pleasures of the soldier moving from country to country, conquering or liberating the countries he went through.

Jim walked the streets at night when, with plausible excuse, he could get out of the house. He walked unhappy, in despair, afraid of himself and his appetites, miserable because he knew of the unnamed fear he had brought to Louise, miserable because of his children whom he loved. He walked until he was weary and his mind eased a little because of the exercise, his body relaxed. Then he was conscious of the fact that he was following a woman. But he continued to follow her because he was going that way too, headed, now, for home.

The woman went up the steps of a building, opened a door, stood in the bold bright light for a moment, closed the door.

Jim turned a corner. Ahead of him a young girl carried a loaf of bread toward home. Jim looked at her. My God! He began to tremble. He stopped and sat on a doorstep with his face in his hands. He could hear the police saying into his home, into the four rooms, into his wife's ear before his two sons playing in the living room, "We have your husband in jail on a morals charge."

Jim sat on the unfamiliar doorstep almost sobbing, his hands over his face. The French girl, in shadow, a small smile on her lips, sat next to him. An old woman, dead, killed by a soldier's bullet, lay at his feet. Across the banister, doubled over the banister, lay the dead body of a human being—a German soldier, but a human being—a man Jim had refused to save by not selecting one to live when Johnson with the girl's name, Evelyn Johnson, had mowed down the enemy prisoners. It had begun to rain but Jim didn't notice. It rained hard and he didn't notice. He was drenched now and he didn't care. He sat immobile, his hands over his face. Three people waited for him. Silently, motionlessly waited. Until he got up and moved down the street they would wait and then they would move down the street with him. The French girl. The old woman killed by his gun. The dead German soldier.

And the rain made a river in the gutter. The gutter gurgled its little spring song of rain and spring and greenness and hope.

# XVI

He waited under his father's window, watching the apartment across the areaway until she came home from work. Then he came from out of the shadows.

"Rebecca!"

Her startled eyes looked up out of the darkness into his towering face. "Oh! Hello, Aaron."

"Come to my room with me."

She glanced up quickly at her mother's window, and then, quickly, into his face before her eyes dropped away. "All right."

He took her arm. He lead her to the streetcar line. She was trembling.

They got on the streetcar. Sitting in the double seat Aaron put his big arm up around her, clumsily. He could feel her shoulders trembling.

She turned her face toward him and looked up into his face with tender eyes. The clanging streetcar moved through the night.

"We get off here."

She was surprised to see that the corner was Clark and Chicago.

He led her to a door on North Clark Street and up a long, narrow flight of rickety, poorly lighted stairs to a room over a Skid Row tavern.

He inserted the key and opened the door.

It was a musty room, sour with the smells of street and building. Laughing voices rose from the tavern below. And curses. The vulgar sounds of obscene songs.

"You live here?"

He nodded and closed the door, moved across the telephone-booth-wide room furnished with a narrow bed, a small table, a chair, nothing else, the upper portion of the rotted, whitewashed board walls finished from six feet high to the ceiling with chicken wire.

Aaron turned off the light and sat on the bed. He took her hand and pulled her down next to him on the bed. They sat, looking down at the bums and drunks and prostitutes on North Clark Street. Neon lights—BAR—DRINKS—GIRLS—LIQUOR STORE—gave the room its only light.

After the long dark silence Aaron's awkward body turned toward her, his clumsy hands groped her shoulders and his pouted lips looked for hers. He kissed her. He dropped his hands away. "This is why I wanted you to come here," he said. She leaned toward him and put her head on his shoulder. His mind made a hairpin turn. "You better go home."

"No."

"If you don't—"

"No."

They sat like this a long time, the coarse songs, the vulgar laughter, the curses, the juke box, a vibrating carpet at their feet, the neon signs a wall that held them, the drunks and bums a grim tableau on the broken pavement below. Then his fumbling hands on her . . .

And for a while she was Mary Ellen to him. And for a while he was Don to her. It was the only other knowledge either of them had. Then he was Aaron to Rebecca. What he had been in the green, sunlit park, long ago, before he was eighteen. It was the two windows facing each other and she looking across the areaway at him. It was young love. To her it was much. To him it was nothing—a satisfaction of short duration.

"I'll never leave you," she told him.

She stayed all night, hugged close to him. And in the morning: "I'm not going to work."

That night she brought her clothes from her mother's house to Aaron's room over the tavern on North Clark Street.

# XVII

Mr. Veteran did not hold himself aloof from the people and let the precinct captains make the personal contacts as McCarren had. Don, the people's friend, was always available at the army tent to give everybody the glad hand.

Mucci took him into the slum basement apartment where the southern family lived. They went in knowing they were going to buy those votes up. There were eight or ten towheaded kids, beautiful kids. They were running around the house barefooted but still there was a half gallon bottle of beer on the table.

Don patted towheads and handed out shiny quarters. He shook hands with Mr. and Mrs.

"We'll put you on as a worker—come down and vote." He'd give each of them three dollars. "After all, the organization gives us the money to spread around."

"Here's enough for a pair of stockings."

"Enough for cab fare so you won't be late to work after you vote."

Don, the Negroes' friend, went to a NAACP meeting with Mucci at the invitation of Mrs. Sawyer, a Republican from the district. The NAACP had called together all the colored charity organizations in a fund-raising drive to send their key men to Washington to help pass the F.E.P.C. Don and Mucci were the only white people there. Don made a brief speech about the equality of people and the brotherhood of man. Don contributed five hundred dollars at the end of his speech, knowing that he would get front-page publicity in the *Chicago Defender,* the city's Negro newspaper.

Afterwards, when they had let Mrs. Sawyer out of the car in front of her house, Mucci said from the corner of his mouth, his frog-eyes rolling sleepily in his skull, "Let's pick up that vote! There are seven votes in that house!"

"No," Don said. "She'll tell all of her friends about us going to the meeting and help us more."

It hit the front page of the *Chicago Defender,* along with a picture of Don, and told of his donation, extolled him as a friend of the colored people.

Don bought up several hundred of the newspapers and had them distributed free among the Negroes of his district.

Everybody was happy. Don was happy, the newspaper circulation management was happy, and so were the Negroes who read about this new champion for their people.

And Don, his own best friend, made an appointment with Emerson Bradley.

Sitting across the desk from Bradley and looking into his ugly pink face Don explained that he was running for ward committeeman. "Can you possibly do me a favor?" he concluded.

"Glad to do it," Bradley said in his monotone and then caught himself up swiftly. "If I can."

"Well I—ah—wondered if it would be asking too much if—I wondered if I could have some of my campaign literature put up on a couple of your bulletin boards."

"I'll see what I can do for you," Emerson Bradley said. He smiled his frosty, noncommittal smile and shook hands in dismissal.

The people of the Haines Company, the little office girls, the superintendents, the order packers and the greasy workers from the bowels of the plant were all surprised when they opened their pay envelopes to find a little card included telling them to vote for Lockwood, first wounded veteran of World War II.

A favor had been paid off and oddly enough D. S. Matthews and Emerson Bradley, hated rivals over a good period of Chicago history, were both on the same side, both backing Don.

Election Day came nearer and they began lining up the vote. Don called Deacon Johnson in to have a little talk with him. He told the reverend how much he liked his people. He enumerated to him all the things he had done for his people and told him that he expected them to turn out for him. "Last election—" Don said, "last election I donated a hundred dollars to your church. This year—" He went magnanimously into his pocket. "I want to donate two hundred dollars."

Deacon Johnson rubbed the pale palm of his hand over his bald head. He found a spot that itched there and scratched it. "Well, church business is a little different," he said; and holding out his pale palm and grinning, "A little money for myself!"

Don smiled in his greater knowledge of people since being in politics and felt less guilty himself. He began to chuckle. He went into his pocket and put a hundred-dollar bill in the deacon's hand. "That's for you," he said. They both laughed. It was a hearty laugh. They put back their heads and laughed.

When the deacon left, Don slapped him across the back affectionately. There was an understanding bond of friendship between them.

A few days before the election Mucci had yet another plan. He told Don about it. After midnight he got his crew of three together. They were trusted assistant precinct captains. With knives they ripped the sides and front of the canvas army tent.

They blamed it on McCarren and his crowd. It made a good newspaper story.

And the clock of time swung its slow pendulum to Election Day. Don's precinct captains went across the district, getting the vote out. They stood outside of the polling places, indicating to people how to vote, paying them off. Everything was ready for victory; all the machinery was set and the gears revolved together smoothly.

Don was prepared. He knew how they stole and how they didn't steal. Who worked chain ballots and who didn't. He knew what to watch. And he had the money. You can't beat money. He knew he could buy the votes. And if he couldn't buy them he could steal them.

He went out into the district.

"Got enough money, Hurst?"

"No, I need more."

"Well how much do you need?"

"Three hundred dollars."

"Well I'm going to give you five hundred—get me fifty of those Republican votes. Pay ten dollars a vote if you have to. Get them at any price."

On Clark Street and on West Madison they had filled the flophouses with floaters. Kostner was short of votes. He called Casey. "Listen, you got any guys over there?"

"Yeah. I got ten."

"Bring them over."

Casey brought the bums over and they told them how to vote.

The precinct where they have doctors and students has a tendency to go Republican. You can't pay them. And McCarren might hurt Don over there on the Democratic ticket. Olson knows he might drop it three to one. He's trying to figure a way to beat them. Olson's been walking around the block all day long trying to figure a way. His right-hand man has been bringing in voters all day long but hasn't voted himself. Olson finally figures it out. At four-thirty when the rush is on he sends his right-hand man in to vote and gives him the pitch.

His right-hand man takes a ballot and goes into the booth. In the booth he lights two cigarettes. He wraps them up in the ballot, puts it in the ballot box and walks out. In ten minutes the ballots all start to burn. The ballots are all spoiled. None of them count. This is a victory for Olson. He's a smart precinct captain.

In the army-tent headquarters Don waited for the returns. Irene waited with him, beautifully gowned and furred. His precinct captains began bringing them in. From the gun they were way ahead of McCarren.

By ten it was a landslide.

Photographers took pictures for the morning newspapers of Don and his beautiful wife. After they had gone Irene, bored, said, "Let's go home, Don. Let's get out of here."

He didn't want to go yet. "You go home, honey. I'll be there later." He called a cab for her.

By eleven o'clock the army tent was the scene of a wild victory celebration. Beer bottles and whisky bottles were open and sitting on the desk and benches. Paper cups were filled and refilled. All the precinct captains were there. Don had shaken hands with them all a dozen times. Everybody was shouting and drunk and happy. Telegrams of congratulations had been received from the President of the City Council, the committee organizer, the other ward committeemen.

By twelve o'clock a few of the captains had gone.

By two o'clock Don's big boys were still clustered about him—getting drunker, shouting, laughing, drinking more. His big boys—Mucci, Ryan, Buckley, Casey, Donahue, Kostner and McGuire. The hierarchy.

Mucci slapped Don across the back drunkenly, affectionately. "Mr. Veteran, The World-Beater," Mucci shouted affectionately, drunkenly.

Don had his name.

He finally sent them all home. He had trouble getting them to leave but he was THE POWER now and had his way. For some sentimental reason he wanted to be alone in the tent. When at last he was alone in the tent with its knife-cut sides flapping in the wind Don leaned back in the swivel chair, put his feet up on the desk and grinned. He squeezed his fists together in satisfaction.

He had screwed McCarren and beaten him. He had thrown the guy out who had made him. He, Don, was the guy from the slums who had succeeded. He had control of the whole district. The gambling, the vice, the patronage. The jobs, all 550 of them, automatically came to him. Every precinct captain would owe his job to him. In a dog-eat-dog world he was right up near the top. He dreamed bigger and bigger things and more important positions for himself. He had been dreaming these things five minutes after he won the election. He knew he wasn't the President but his dreams were that big. They were bigger than a reefer smoker's dreams. He never thought—two, three years ago—never thought those times when he was a dirty, hungry kid with lice in his hair and hamburger for Christmas dinner—that today he—

Don squeezed his fists together and grinned to himself in the empty tent: Success story. Slum boy makes good.

# XVIII

Rebecca tried, pitifully, to clean the room. She went to work at the Haines Company and came home. She brought cartons of coffee and hamburgers to him, pencils and notebooks. She picked up his clothes and bought him socks and shirts.

Sometimes he was there and sometimes he wasn't. She went looking for him—found him at Thompson's sitting alone against the wall away from his friends, O'Keefe, Milo, the others he knew—found him wandering the streets or in dingy little cafeterias, bars. When she found him he was either writing on sheets of paper and stuffing them into his pockets or just sitting, staring.

Sometimes she didn't know what he was talking about. And sometimes he'd say, dully, "I'm just a Jew-boy. Just a kike."

"Please, Aaron," she would say, putting her fingers over his lips as she had with Don when he had said nigger.

"No, I know," Aaron would say, "and I'm a coward. I left them. I didn't join them. They knew I could have joined them and I didn't. I bet they said you can never trust a Jew. They were my buddies and I let them down."

Sometimes he needed her in bed, but not often. Many times he fell asleep across the bed with his clothes on. She would pull his shoes off and the covers over him. Then she would crawl in next to him. "Move over . . . leave me alone . . . stay on your side of the bed." And she would roll to the other edge of the bed.

She loved him and she took care of him. It became a burden, but a burden she gladly, at first, accepted. She neglected herself to care for him. Her clothes gathered lint and were never dusted and became shabby. But she did keep her birthmark covered with theatrical makeup. It was her one vanity left.

She lost her job. They lived on what the government gave him for his war disability.

She had begun to drink and was sometimes drunk.

A baby was coming.

# XIX

Don Lockwood, THE POWER, got into his Cadillac. He drove through his city, Chicago, toward the Tennyson Hotel. A pleased with himself smile rode his face beneath his gray Homburg. It was a good life now. A cushy life. He had climbed up with the best of them. Everything was under control. He'd never make the mistakes McCarren had made. First off he had changed the police captains right away after his victory at the polls through connections downtown. He was strictly boss of the police stations. He had sent his man, and that was Casey, into the police captains with a list of his precinct captains so that when they went down there they could be shown a little courtesy, done a few favors. McCarren's good friends had come back into the organization. He had beaten McCarren and they needed him from here on in. Meekly they had come back into the fold of the regular organization.

He had his own insurance company now that took care of the spots in the district. He had gained control of a furniture company and was going to put new furniture in the city hall. He had control of the parking concession at the race track. And a liquor business which he was going to turn over to his boys—his boys Mucci, Casey, Buckley, Kostner and McGuire. He was buying a home for his mother and the kids.

Irene was forever throwing lavish parties where he—*he*—mixed with society people as well as topnotch figures in the theater, sports, movies, art. Next year he'd have to get a two-number license plate for the Cadillac.

The way was up. There was no other way. After a few years he might even be organizer of the County Central Committee, dictate to all the ward committeemen and distribute the patronage to them. His rear end was comfortable on the soft cushions of the Cadillac and his smile was wide. Through the summer sunlight he drove with the top down toward the Tennyson Hotel; the big new diamond glistened on his hand that clutched the steering wheel.

"Yes, sir! Mr. Lockwood!" the doorman said when he arrived and held the door open for him, got in to park his car for him. Don slipped him a silver dollar.

"Thank you, sir!"

He needed the taste of good liquor in his mouth and went in to the bar.

"Good afternoon, Mr. Lockwood."

"Hello, George."

He had a martini, sipping it enjoyably. When he was finished he paid for the drink and then waited until the bartender had walked down toward him again. With his Homburg tilted to the side of his head he flipped the silver dollar on the bar toward the bartender with a gentle but resounding metallic clicking. With his mouth half open in a little puckered smile and his eyebrows lifted. Until the bartender looking up from the silver dollar met his eyes with the astonished, servile look and said most respectfully, "Thank you, sir!"

Don went to the toilet. The porter held the towel for his hands. The porter brushed his coat and trousers. There was a feeling of well-being, of power, of importance when the porter half knelt and wiped his shoes off.

A silver dollar into the black hand.

He carried this roll of silver dollars for tips.

# XX

Summer heated Jim's blood, sweated his brow and his armpits, over all of his body under his clothes. Jim's urge came often to him and his was a struggle to keep it in leash.

The weather turned even hotter and women wore thin summer dresses tight across their stomachs and tight over their breasts, their hips.

And the hot summer evening came when Jim worked until late at night at union headquarters. He was almost finished when Edna's young daughter Marion, now old enough to work at the Haines Company and working the evening shift, slowly passed the window, peered inside and saw him at the front office desk. Broadly smiling, she tapped her knuckles against the plate glass.

Jim looked up. His blue eyes stared through the plate glass at her and his pencil rested against the paper. He smiled at her.

Marion pushed the door open and entered. "Hello, Jim!—Mr. Norris, I mean. Are you still here?" She smiled flirtingly, and her chewing gum smacked in her mouth.

Jim looked at her wide, strikingly beautiful face, the long, shoulder-length blond hair, loose and luxuriant, her wide blue eyes, smiling, flirting with him. He nodded yes, slowly.

"Ma wants you to come over to dinner sometime soon. So do I," she said.

Again Jim nodded slowly. His eyes did not leave her face. She was beautiful. And she knew it. She was sixteen, maybe seventeen. Jim flushed and lowered his eyes from hers. But slowly, unable to do otherwise, his eyes took complete inventory of her figure.

She smacked her gum. Red, red lips smiled at him. "How soon before you go home?" the red, red lips asked.

"I'm all finished." His fingers tightened under the desk and his insides tightened. "I—ah—are you finished work?" he asked.

She nodded. Her hair bounced in shoulder-length blondness at her oval of dress collar. "Un-huh."

"Well—ah—" He stood up. "I'll give you a lift." He made his voice gruff. "First I have to lock up."

"I'll wait," she said. "Can I help you?"

"No."

She sat on the edge of the desk. He secured the windows. He took the key from his pocket. He looked at her legs and her hips as he turned off the light. "Let's go."

She made a pretense of catching onto his arm for support in hopping down off the desk. "Thanks," she said and tightened her fingers on the muscle of his arm.

They went outside and got into his car. He knew the way to Edna's house but took a longer route. She nestled close to him in the front seat. She talked about work and about the union and how proud he must be to be such a big, important man in the union. While she talked she now and then rubbed her head, her loose luxuriant blond hair, against his shoulder. He could hardly breathe without parting his lips. His heart pounded hard and summer was an itching and an urge all over his skin. He knew where, along the way, was the quiet neighborhood, the dark street and the two vacant lots facing each other. He wouldn't have to say anything. He would stop the car and put his arms around her. He stopped the car. He clicked off the motor.

"What's the matter?" she asked. "Are we out of gas?" She giggled. She looked flirtingly up into his face with her lips parted. His long arms hung loosely at his side. For a moment he sat like this. Then he said, "I think we have a flat tire." And there was still another moment when he sat. Just sat there. Then he said, "I better look."

He got out of the car and walked around it. "No," he said when he came back. He got in, started the motor and drove almost too swiftly for safety to Edna's house where he let Edna's daughter out of his car.

Summer. He wandered the beach looking at the seminude bodies. And the French girl came to him. Was in his memory all the time. Was constant companion. Sweet companion now. The touch of her remembered body now, over all the silence, across the battlefields . . . and the city . . . and her sisters in the city, in this city Chicago. War had given him a craving.

He sat at home with his wife.

The urge was on him.

He gathered his children around him. He played with them and tried to amuse himself with them, find surcease here, at home.

The urge was on him.

He took a cold shower, standing tall, athletic, broad-shouldered and handsome under the icy needles of the water.

The urge was on him.

He told Louise he was going to take a walk. In the early night through Lincoln Park he walked. He saw the girl walking ahead of him and alone in the park. There were no people near and silently, fearfully at first, he followed her. Grew closer to her. Then, like an animal stalking its prey he followed, silently, grew closer, closer, followed, her shadow almost touching him now and she unaware that he was behind her, following, stealthily, drawing closer, closer—

Here—

He moved quickly toward her and up behind her in the shielding grove of trees and bushes. On firm athletic legs he stepped and stood behind her. His large, big-fingered, square-fingered hand clasped itself over her mouth and his free arm secured her as surely as deft fingers stay the flight of a butterfly. And his clear, wide blue eyes looked down at the captured prey. The curly blond hair was tousled on the handsome square forehead.

And for a moment, only a moment, they stood silent and stiff in the secret night, more quiet than the trees, more lifeless than the far statue of Abraham Lincoln. Stiffer. More immobile.

Then . . . suddenly . . . Jim let go. Jim turned and broke and ran away from the girl and through the park as fast as he could. Her scream followed him.

He ran out of the park. He kept running. He ran until he had little breath left. Then he walked as fast as he could, rested only a short while, walked fast again. His face was tortured. Haggard. His mind was sick with what he had almost attempted. The street lamps were large, watchful eyes as he trudged his way toward home, his wife, his two small children.

The weeks were weeks of fear for him, fear that this urge, this thing inside of him might return, might break loose at any moment. But he curbed it as best he could, in the only way he knew how. He worked hard at the union office. As soon as he was finished with his union business he went home. He stayed home. Until I am sure of myself. Until I know that it will never happen again. And if Louise was worried, if he was silent or snapped at her, or tried sporadically to be affectionate; if she cried secretly and felt that she had somehow lost her husband, lost the Jim who had loved her—she did not know why. Could never have guessed why.

Headlines assailed him and he read them avidly, read the articles like a man taking a drug. Slumped in a chair secretly, he read all such headlines:

WIFE FAINTS AS HUSBAND
IS ACCUSED IN RAPE CASE

...held to the Grand Jury on a charge of assault with intent to commit rape on a 16-year-old girl...

EX-GI RAPES GIRL

But you can stay home only so long. What will your wife think? She wants to go to the show. Let's take the kids out. "It's so hot, so hot! Let's take the children to the beach."

Tall, handsome, he lay on the beach with his eyes shielded by the crook of his arm. Well, at least he had kept himself in control. He hadn't even looked at anyone. Only casually. The sun felt good. He was glad he could be with Louise like this. She seemed happy—well, pleased anyway. The sun was good for the kids too.

"What's your name, mister?"

He sat up and opened his eyes. He grinned at the little girl. "Jim," he said.

"Oh, I like you," she said.

"Oh, do you, honey?" He laughed.

"Catch," she said and threw her beach ball. He caught it and threw it back to her.

"Come here, Dorothy!" her mother called. "You stop annoying that man!"

Dorothy went obediently to her mother. Jim watched her innocently. Funny little girl. Suddenly he began to sweat. "Let's go," he said to Louise, "let's go home." He put on his clothes and they went home.

But that night...

He got out of the house. He went looking for a woman. A young woman.

He went to a low-down bar. Sat there. Saw in his room, attached to the mirror post, the little pipe-cleaner dancing doll frozen in her hula step. He drank. He kept drinking. The French girl, now that he was drunk, came and sat alongside of him at the bar. She touched his sleeve. He got drunk. And drunker. She touched his sleeve again. He turned and looked at her and her face was vaguely familiar.

Where had he seen her before? Where out of the past? He kept drinking.

A girl of about nineteen came and sat next to him on the other stool. She was blond, much as he was, and had blue eyes like his. He sat between her and the French girl. He drank. There was something familiar in this. Too familiar. "Hey! Bartender! Another shot!"

He tossed it down. "Honey, what about buying me a drink?" the blond girl said, nestling up close to him, her head on his shoulder. "We could go to my place later," she said.

He ordered another shot. Tossed it down. And then he knew. He dared not look at the French girl. He ordered and drank another shot. The French girl touched his sleeve. He turned and looked her in the face. And then he recognized her. It wasn't the French girl. It was his sister.

He looked down, miserably, at the bar. He looked from a long way off. But it all came into perfect focus.

It was almost as if he were looking down into a toy street, into a nightmare. The street lamps leaned awry. The crooked, warped floor to the hall toilet in the slum house, West Side, Chicago. The boy was himself. The girl was his sister. They were eight and nine years old. Their mother had caught them in their innocent explorations of each other's bodies. Their mother's hard hand across their faces and heads. His sister had screamed and dropped her skirt down. In fear he had urinated down the front of his pants. It was bad, bad, bad! For a week it was bad. For a month. Forever. He had never gotten over his mother's face and eyes and mouth saying it was bad, bad, bad!

# XXI

Now, I must get on a streetcar. I must have thirteen cents in change. I must get on a Clark-Wentworth streetcar. I am going to Chicago Avenue.

Aaron got on the car.

O'Keefe came into Thompson's restaurant waving his paper hello. Jim and Milo looked up and smiled.

Shortly afterwards Aaron walked in. He saw Milo and O'Keefe and went toward their table. He said hello and sat down. "What about some coffee, Aaron?" O'Keefe asked, already rising from his chair.

"Okay," Aaron said, "I didn't eat today."

As O'Keefe went toward the counter Aaron turned to Milo. "Will you loan me fifty cents, Milo? I'm broke."

"Sure." Milo gave him the fifty cents and O'Keefe returned with a bowl of chili, salad, pie, coffee. Aaron accepted the food. He wasn't gracious about it. He just accepted it. He was living off people now. He was lost to everything but his writing. The world was his mother. Rebecca was his mother.

He ate greedily and paid no attention to Milo, O'Keefe, Jim. He licked his fingers when he was done and, silently, O'Keefe went for another cup of coffee for him, set it before him.

The others talked and Aaron sat there staring. Then from one pocket he pulled a tiny slip of paper and wrote something on it, stuffed it into his other pocket. He took another piece of paper, the napkin in front of him. He wrote slowly, laboriously. The words attached themselves in pencil to the paper:

SERPENT

beat, Beat, BEAT!<br>
heart-hard<br>
pound, Pound, POUND!<br>
Spear-eye<br>
Drip-nude<br>
Two: I<br>
Pant-love<br>
Sobsigh<br>
Pishpoo

Aaron stuffed the napkin into the treasury of his pocket.

Steve, on his half-hour break from behind the counter serving up coffee and hamburgers, came over to their table in his white apron and flopped down.

Aaron stared at nothing. Aaron blinked his eyes. He looked around . . .

I have coffee. The table is red. I'm in Thompson's.

"Oh, at that time," O'Keefe was saying, "everything was going magnificently there. Every man was called into Hoffman's office and his record was laid out before him and you had to qualify in fourteen different points before you could be judged a raise. Punctuality and reliability and—anda—oh Jesus, I couldn't tell you half the qualifications you had to have and there was no raise for me." O'Keefe ended it grimly, his mouth tightening down on the words and his eyes scowling. He continued, "And I said—" he spoke the next words quietly, " 'just a minute.' " He paused and gestured with his hand. "Hoffman was there and Anderson was sitting back like one of those English bulldogs, you know, sitting there and watching his master's face, and Hoffman said to me, 'You see you've got to be qualified on all these things before you're entitled to a raise. Maybe next time you'll do better.'

"I said, 'Just a minute.' I said," and O'Keefe's next words came quietly, quickly, in one rush of a sentence, " 'Listen, since I came into this place I have never been an hour late in the morning, I have never left a job unfinished at night if it took until nine o'clock at night, I have put in more overtime than any man in this building. How's that?' "

At the table Milo and Jim were laughing.

O'Keefe's contemptuous voice imitated Hoffman's: " 'Oh, you don't understand. Don't you see—?'

" 'I do understand. It looks to me like downright discrimination. You can call that anything you like.'

" 'Ohhhhhh—' " O'Keefe said, imitating Hoffman and explaining to Jim and Milo. "You know, that patronizing smile. 'Well, it's because you don't understand our system. Mr. er—Mr. Anderson, will you explain to this man how our system works?' "

Jim and Milo chuckled and went on laughing as O'Keefe continued. "And I turned around to Anderson. He said, 'Didn't you stand over in the lobby one—'

"I said, 'Is that the only time you saw me? Did you see me when I was working?'

" 'Well, but you're paid to work all the time.'

"I said, 'Yeah? Even if I don't find any work I'm supposed to run and start tearing down the wall?' I said, 'To me the whole thing looks like discrimination and I know who's responsible for it.'

"Gee, he got red! He said, 'No such thing!' and he yelled and yelled—yelled at me, you know—and we started yelling back and forth and I said, 'Nothing I can do about it. But somebody will!' And I got up to go.

" 'Hold on!' Mr. Hoffman said. And he said—oh, in that bland way of his—'You can improve yourself. Oh, every man can improve himself!' "

Jim and Milo burst out laughing. O'Keefe went on in the imitated voice of the boss, " 'You see these little points here—?' " And O'Keefe used his newspaper as the boss's chart on the employees and ran his forefinger along the imagined line. " 'You just bear down. Pay a little more attention to these points and next time you might have a wonderful record. We want people with wonderful records. We try to—to build up a staff that will be way above par.' "

O'Keefe's eyes came up to Jim and Milo and their purple depths stared out angrily past his shaggy eyebrows. "That was two weeks before the big strike. I said, 'I'm afraid I'm not interested right now but we're going to talk about it another time.' And I walked out of

Hoffman's office. Well, it was two weeks before the big strike burst on them.

"I told the union. I said, 'This is my statement' and I signed it and gave it to the steward and he took it up and read it out to Hoffman and the grievance committee. The union steward was supposed to argue it out.

" 'NO. NO. NO. NO. NO. NO. NO. CAN'T DO IT. NO. WE CAN'T!' "

O'Keefe leaned back in his chair and his angry purple eyes stared into Jim and Milo almost as if they were enemies. "In other words when we say no we can't ever again say yes. Because why? Because we're the bosses. Because we'd be ruined. Our position would be gone. We could give it to you a week from now but we CAN'T GIVE IT TO YOU NOW. Because when we say no we have to mean no. Don't you see how I can't be wrong? Jesus Christ! If I was wrong well then the whole system would fall to pieces. The boss can't be wrong. You know that. Why that's impossible! That's a physical and moral impossibility! Why the whole American system would fold up if the boss was wrong."

O'Keefe smiled a slow, revenged smile. "But two weeks later when the strike came they found that they were up against a thing that didn't reason on logic or in psychology at all. There were men standing on the street by the thousands, insulting them to their faces and calling them sonsabitches and everything they liked and they couldn't do anything about it either and they had to like it."

Rebecca walked in and looked around for Aaron. She saw him and moved toward the table, the hem of her skirt uneven, her stockings wrinkled, the heels of her shoes worn and turning over. O'Keefe's back was to her and standing behind him she looked over his head at Aaron. The look was tender, worried, relieved that she had found him. No one had seen her yet and she put her hand on O'Keefe's shoulder. The fingernails were dirty and broken. "Hello, Sean," she said. O'Keefe swung halfway around in his chair and smiled weakly. "Hello—er—uh—Rebecca."

She sat down. O'Keefe opened his paper to the editorial page. Aaron had not seen her or preferred not to. Milo and Jim looked at each other. "Hello," Rebecca said. They said hello and Steve's sneering mouth and eyes took in her face, her hands, her stomach. Aaron had finished writing on a slip of paper and it followed the others into his bulging pocket. Rebecca glanced tenderly at him. He was staring at a new slip of paper with his lips held half open. "How's everybody tonight?" Rebecca asked. She spoke a little too loudly and there was a faint smell of liquor on her breath. She was very pregnant. Her stomach was a large hard ball on the chair in front of her. It was covered by a drab gray coat, soiled, the restraining button about to pop away. Her hair was uncombed and straggly, her clothing dirty, she didn't bother to cover her birthmark. It was an uneven purple-red blotch on her cheek. She seemed not to care any longer about herself or anything but Aaron. She was going to love him. She was going to love his child. At the Clark Street bars, when he was wandering around the city by himself, she drank wine. She got tipsy. She got drunk. Late at night she staggered alone to their room under the dead neon signs that had long before blinked to sleep.

Rebecca turned the pages of the paper. Quite pregnant, she didn't care who knew it: and they all knew—that it was Aaron's and that they were not married.

Rebecca turned the newspaper pages. For a moment her eyes fell on a picture of Don in one of the columns. For a moment only. She glanced at it casually and turned the page as if she had never known him.

She was going to love Aaron and Aaron's child.

Into Aaron's pocket now slipped another piece of paper. He had no more paper and was now using the margin of a newspaper, writing a few words, tearing the margin from the paper, stuffing it in his pocket, writing on a new edge of newspaper margin.

"Sure there's going to be another war," Steve said.

Aaron's pencil shook violently on the newspaper margin. He had heard. The word war came through to him. The fingers of his mind counted swiftly:

My platoon!
My buddies!
The millions of kids all over the world!
No! No! No!
The hospitals!
The insane asylums!
The millions dead!

His huge hand crumpled the newspaper margin. He was looking across the table at all of them, at none of them.

Steve was saying, casually, "Sure, they've got the atom bomb too. We're second on the list. First New York and then us." He smiled indulgently. "We won't feel any pain. We might be sitting here." He shrugged his shoulders carelessly and gestured with a graceful palm, "We might be sitting in a tavern."

Aaron, slowly rising from the table, stared at all of them, at none of them:

One dead boy is argument enough against their wars. But—shaking his head no—he couldn't tell them. He was crazy. They wouldn't believe him.

Steve was saying, "Let's hope that we're all drunk when they drop the atom bomb on us."

# XXII

Reed sat stiffly on his chair across the desk from Don Lockwood and Alderman Mucci in the downtown organization headquarters. The alderman puffed lazily on his cigar with his sleepy-lidded eyes half-closed and his little legs stretched out in front of him with one ankle over the other. Don's big diamond brought his cigar to his mouth and he leaned his head way back as he inhaled. Leisurely taking the cigar from his mouth and blowing the cloud of smoke at the ceiling, he said, "Now you get it, Reed? You get how I want you to vote?" The syndicate had told Don and Don now told Reed, his State Representative, that he wanted him to vote against the crime commission bills.

Reed's long, doleful face came to stiff attention and he nodded in a slightly servile manner. "Yes, Mr. Lockwood."

Don laughed. He was pleased. It was like a gift he was giving him. "Just call me Don," he said.

A couple of precinct captains came over. One of them put his hand on Don's shoulder for a moment in political caress. "Well, how's the world-beater tonight?"

Don laughed: the world-beater. He loved his title. They all love those names.

The other precinct captain, sucking up to Don, asked, "Anything you want me to do?"

"Take it easy, George," Don said magnanimously. "Draw up a chair and relax."

Reed, looking like a sad-faced minister, stood up. "I've got to push off," he said apologetically. "Got to get to Springfield tomorrow." His long, bony fingers took Don's hand in a farewell handshake. He bowed, leaving: the kid was on top. The kid was his boss now.

Don and Mucci had a few more drinks together. Then Don stood up to go, carefully remolding his hat before putting it on. "I'll give you a lift, Mucci."

It was a command.

In the Cadillac he gave Mucci his orders on how to vote on public housing in the city council meeting the next day. Those orders were to vote against it.

Don, on the soft cushions of his Cadillac, stared moodily out the windshield. When he laughed hardest, sitting around the Tennyson Hotel or in the city hall with the other politicians, he felt worse.

And didn't know why.

# XXIII

The big Cadillac, the top up, hugged the curb close to the Haines building. The workers began to pour out of the building. As she was about to pass the car the Cadillac horn honked.

"Sue!"

She turned and looked and stood still on the sidewalk as her face took many changes. The next to the last was a frown. The last was a brittle, high-rising laugh. "Oh! The ward committeeman waits for me!"

"Get in."

"Oh! The married man wants me to get in!"

"Get in or I'll get out and get you."

She got in. She sat on her side of the seat and stared straight ahead. It was the first time she had seen him since he had been married. She had told herself, it's over, I'm through. She wanted it that way.

"Aren't you glad to see me?"

"You better drive off before someone sees you," she said sarcastically.

That was good sense. He started the motor. He drove slowly through the heavy traffic, down Michigan Boulevard, over toward Twelfth and Wabash where she lived.

"I had to see you, Sue."

She didn't answer.

"I've missed you. I want to come over." There was pleading in his voice.

She didn't answer.

They drove in silence until they reached her building. He parked the car.

"I'm going to go up with you."

"No, you're not."

"Yes, I am."

"You're not. Not if I have to sit here forever."

Her voice edged up toward a pitch he had never heard before and one that he feared. "All right. All right, Sue."

He let her out.

He watched her go up the stairs. She climbed them, holding onto the rail almost like an old woman.

Two weeks later she called him. "You may come to see me if you want to."

He was surprised at how painstakingly he dressed. He put on the suit he liked best. He looked at himself in the mirror and retied his tie twice. He looked in the mirror at himself with his coat on; then with his hat on.

He tapped quietly on the door. "Hello, Sue." He dropped his eyes in shame, guilt, embarrassment, looked past her and into the same room he had known so well.

She looked at him without answering and stepped aside so that he could enter; and closed the door.

It was like coming home. The old couch. The low bookcase with volumes of plays and Sue's radical books and pamphlets, the Chianti wine bottles stuck with candles. He looked at the wall and was surprised to see the sketch Sue had made of him still there in its usual and familiar place. Stepping into the room, he looked at his face framed and under glass. It was a young face, a boy's face. Had he ever been so young? So naïve? Or was it only Sue's interpretation?

He went to the old couch and sat down. Like coming home. But this strange woman. In her eyes there was a stranger: this unknown person looked out at him.

He sat on the edge of the couch and looked up at her. "I've missed you, Sue."

She smiled at him. It was a withdrawn smile. It held disbelief. And she looked at him, this stranger, the eyes probing while the mind found its own answers: it is like when he returned from the army. He hadn't thought of me then though he sat there saying he had. He hasn't now, either. He came just to torture me. To throw a crumb. I'm so tired of crumbs . . . it's just his ego that brings him here.

She smiled at him and did not answer. It was the smile of the disbeliever.

"There's something wrong, Sue," he said. "I'm not really happy." And was the little boy who has been bad and has come home to his mother, knowing she will understand.

"You've got everything you want," Sue said.

Yes, he guessed that was right.

Quickly her eyes took in the outline of his face as she had remembered it. The familiar features. The lines of his figure. She looked away.

She spoke with forced gayety. "Well, you're looking fine! . . . You've put on a little weight. But it looks good on you. . . . It was quite a surprise, your election . . . over at Haines they had your political cards in all the pay envelopes, pictures of you. . . . Would you like some wine?"

He could see her making herself smile.

She filled the glasses and sat in a chair opposite him. Saw his look of pleading for understanding, forgiveness. And that was what she loved about him, what always touched her, touched off the dynamite of her heart.

And in the silence as lip met wineglass she felt shame. Shame that she had let him come here. Shame for her attachment to him. He stood for everything she despised in life, in society; and fought against in her small way.

As lip met glass he felt guilt. These things he had done to get from the bottom of the pile were wrong. Everything he had done in his life was done only for himself. In his eyes his own mother, in that moment, took heroic and decent stature. She had sacrificed herself for others. For him and the kids. What was his sacrifice? What had it ever been? Sue's eyes were accusing him as lip met glass, even with her lips smiling a little at him, as lip met glass. And he had no answer to her accusation. He had sold out. He had sold her out. He had sold Wayne out. He had cheapened Rebecca and tossed her aside. He had even sold his buddies out.

The glass emptied and set aside. And he strengthened in his own being, even as her eyes still held his: what does she know about it? About politics. About things? Hers was just a woman's soft sympathetic attitude about things. And he knew he was one of the strong people of the twentieth century. He could break rules, laws, though he upheld them for others. There were many like him. They were a whole race of supermen. Laws were made for strong men to break.

These things, in a jumble, quickly through their minds.

Sue said, "It wasn't right for me to let you come up here. It wasn't right for you to come."

"Why isn't it? Because I'm married? We've—" he put it baldly, "been together before."

"It isn't right."

"That's silly," he said. "We can always be friends."

But she knew and he knew that they could never be friends. Love could only wear the mask. Love never changed to hate. Love could only change to indifference. Indifference could never be, between them.

And Sue filled the glasses again. And Sue suddenly set her full glass upon the floor and with her hands on her knees, her head down, the tears began to fall on the floor, one after the other in a silent flood.

Don went over to her. He slid onto her lap. There was no resistance in her. He put his arm around her. "Come on, come on." He comforted with his arm around her, his hand patting her shoulder.

Sue went on crying.

He tried to lift her face with his other hand. She turned it away from him. He put both of his arms around her. His tender and pleading lips murmured to her and kissed her forehead, her cheek, tasted the salt of her tears. He laughed a little, gently into her ear, in pity. And to turn her away from her sorrow, he began, softly, and in a half-jesting way to sing, *"My man, he don't love me. He treats me, oh, so mean . . ."*

stroking her hair back off her forehead. *"Love is just like a faucet. It turns off and on. Just when you think it's here it's done gone off and gone."*

And, after a bit, her breath was catching in her throat, like a child's after crying. And the tears were still running hot down her cheeks but she looked up into his face, and across the redness of her face and the dimness of her eyes a smile came fleetingly.

He held one of her hands and pressed it. She felt desire tug. She said, in confession, in admission of the lonely nights alone, "I've played 'Stormy Weather' and 'Someday.' "

"Play them. Please," he said.

She put them on the record player. And they sat side by side, as that night when, leg lost, he had come back to her. The record said, . . . *I know that someday you'll want me to want you* . . . And there was tenderness in their caress. Tears on her eyelashes. Water in his heart. The record said, *Stormy weather* . . .

They had come up against it. Against themselves. He was what he was. She was what she was. And that was years ago. The growing, the disillusion, didn't change yesterday. The picture once captured in the frame of the heart, the eye once turned to a certain landscape, star, sunrise, the rock once smitten with the sword. Once the spring has been tapped. Once the juice poured. The loyal eye and the footsteps to but the one door. . . .

By unspoken compromise, by the whisper of mutual desire, yesterday had come back to them; there was no parting.

"Mother," he said, "give me the sun."

She laughed as he said it but his words tore her apart. How many years ago? The same words. The same mood.

Sue had come home to his heart. To her heart. Love is never a freedom. They were slave to slave.

And she having, from this night on, to forever after plug the ears of her mind to what he now was and stood for. He would have to be for her the shy, sensitive, awkward delivery boy at Haines whom she had loved all these years, loved in vain, for he had never been and would never be the things she had dreamed for him.

And both of them knew and didn't know, sensed, that their love was the focal point of their lives. Tawdry, perhaps. Not romantic. Even vulgar, the world might say, if the world knew.

But love has so many faces. The heart gives so quickly, so completely. That was the hurt of some loves. There was no growing past or beyond them. Once they had said, "We will always have each other."

And had stated a truth.

That they would have each other—and most when they were apart.

# XXIV

The weeks came. The Sunday-Monday to Saturday weeks. The day-by-day existence. But the peaks of interest, excitement, climax happened not this week or last week but back in the past or in the future yet to come.

The arguments came. The little, petty frustrations in the relationship of any two people. The days had further disagreement.

"I'm sorry we argued," he said.

She pulled his head down against her bosom and kissed his ear.

"They say the first year is the hardest," Don said.

"Yes, so they say," stroking him.

The nights, the blackness of the nights, lying close in the bed, drew them back together, made the differences of the day as nothing.

The weeks passed. There was the incident of never picking up his clothes. Where he got out of a shirt—where he took off his pants, his pajamas.

"Don, I *do* wish you'd learn to pick up your clothing."

"What have we got servants for?"

"That isn't the point, Don."

He spent much of his time with his buddies, the other big-time politicians, at the city hall and at the Tennyson Hotel, impressing them with his big talk. And he had developed the voice of the politician, the supervisor of the Haines Company, the man in power. A bass tone with the reverberating growl of confidence and self-assurance underneath.

He still went into the old haunts occasionally, Thompson's restaurant and the other places where he had hung out. Went in to give them a chance to stare at him and make over him. And one evening when he went into Thompson's he saw Rebecca sitting alone at a back table. He left without speaking to her. And, going out the door: well I at least showed her how to cover her birthmark.

He and Irene had more arguments, petty disagreements. She saw his vanity. Saw him use his leg at certain times, and in a cheap way. She began to be contemptuous of his snobbery. The way he treated servants, waiters, doormen, and remembered a thing her father had said: "Don't judge a man by the way he treats his equals but by the way he treats his inferiors—servants, waiters—people who are at his mercy for a short while." He was, she had to admit, more of a snob than the wealthy young men of her circle. And he was a show-off. She had a certain guilty contempt for him.

And there was the night when the doorbell rang and this contempt grew. Ma Kosinski stood in the doorway. She was drunk and had come from West Madison Street, from the bar where her daughter Helen worked as a 26-girl.

Earlier, at the tavern . . .

Ma came into the bar with one of her men friends. He was big-knuckled, bushy-headed, and wore greasy overalls. Ma Kosinski was drunk already but she did not stagger, never staggered. There was a dignity in her. She took her boy friend to the 26-table and introduced him to Helen, her daughter.

"This is my daughter. This is the only one who loves me."

"Hello, Ma." Helen patted the rough hand. And there was dignity, a love in her relationship to her mother. There was no shame in it. Only the recognition of the strength and weakness in this woman, her mother. A recognition of who and what this human being was.

And when Ma, on the arm of the overalled man, went to the bar and straddled a stool with him Helen sent drinks over to them:

"I'm sending this over to my mother and her friend."

At the bar two hours later Ma Kosinski, angry at her slow-thinking, vulgar-mouthed friend, rose from the stool to her feet. "You're just a dumb, no-good Polack!" And thought of her son: she had behaved well. When he had bought her a home and given her money and hid her and his past she hadn't bothered him. When he had dropped in to see her once every three or four months like giving her a present she had been nice to him. Maybe she had cried when he left. But she hadn't bothered him. That dirty little Polack bastard! Out of her womb, but still a no-good bastard.

She turned, leaving her gentleman friend at the bar, and walked quickly to the street and out onto the car tracks, forcing the cabbie to stop. She went toward the cab door and put her hand on the handle.

"I can't take nobody nowhere. I'm checkin' in," the cabbie said, looking at her disheveled clothes and hair, the slip an inch below her dress, her heels turned over.

Magnificently Ma Kosinski went under her dress and into the top of her stocking. Magnificently she withdrew the ten-dollar bill and waved it before his eyes. "How far is it from West Madison Street to the Gold Coast? Not very far, is it? This covers the cost and what is left over is yours."

"Get in, lady!"

She gave the impressive address.

. . . And now she stood in her son's doorway. The servant hadn't let her come in and had closed the door. She had leaned there with her arm against the bell. Five minutes, ten. Then Irene had come to the door herself and, looking at her, had thought, One of Don's voters, come to ask a favor or complain about something.

"Are you Mrs. Donald Lockwood?" Ma Kosinski asked, her voice laughing a sneer on the name.

"Yes. I am."

Roughly Ma pushed Irene out of her path and strode into the apartment.

Irene followed her and Ma, when inside, turned with her hands on her hips. She faced Don's wife down with it: "You know what my name is? Kosinski. You know what your fine husband's name is? Kosinski. You know who I am? His mother."

Unimpressed by the wealth and splendor of the apartment, Ma Kosinski flopped down on the sofa. Irene sat next to her, staring at her. Ma Kosinski said, "I come from the slums. I'm just slums. I have none of your fine manners but I speak out. I will tell you plainly with no ifs and ands. Your fine husband," she said, "is a no-good Polack." She told her all of it. Her own life, her sacrifices for "this son who now leaves me and takes on fine manners."

Irene sat listening, thinking, Nothing like that, like his background, matters to Dad and me. Why did he have to lie?

Ma Kosinski now stood up, drunk, unkempt, her eyes and the sag of her face alone telling of her drunkenness and her misery. Irene stood too. "You are pretty," Ma Kosinski said. "I can see why he wanted you." Ma shrugged. "I have told you. I have freed myself of it." She stood there a moment longer.

"Would you like some coffee?" Irene asked.

Ma Kosinski's face became miserable and she slowly shook her head no, afraid to try to speak. Fleetingly Irene put her arms around her. "You go home then. Do you want me to have the chauffeur—to get a cab for you?"

Ma pushed her solicitous hand away. "I will go as I came." She smiled disdainfully in the rich girl's face. "You can have him. I spit on all this." She turned, slapped her behind at Irene and walked to the door and out.

Irene sat on the edge of the couch, looking through the open door at Ma Kosinski walking down the long hallway. Irene sat there, smoking cigarette after cigarette, crushing them out in the ash tray at her feet.

At first she wanted to tell him that she knew about his family, that it didn't matter. But then it did. It showed her so much about him. To him she was just another possession like his diamond ring and his car.

The disdain and contempt grew. It was a cold, unforgiving thing that set in. It showed in the glint of her eye, looking at him; in the curl of her lip, smiling at him; in the look of scorn over cocktail glasses.

She had no more respect left for him.

# XXV

Don embraced Irene in front of the mirror and, actorlike, looked over her shoulder and into the mirror to capture the picture of the embrace, see how he was doing, how he looked.

She drew away from him, and frowning, rearranged the flounces of her black lace evening gown. Later Christopher appeared at the door.

"Why don't you invite him in?" Don asked.

"I'm going to—come in, Christopher." She was like her father. She was used to having her way.

Christopher with his curly black hair and his good looks and his chiseled features stepped inside. "Hello, Don."

"Hello, Christopher."

Don shook hands with him. The politician always shakes hands.

"I'm borrowing your wife tonight."

"Fine. Hope she has a good time."

They looked at each other. Casually. Coolly. The uncouth man and the polished man. They smiled stiffly at each other and had their own thoughts about each other.

"I've got a big meeting down at headquarters myself," Don said.

After the meeting he would go to see Sue.

He wasn't too happy, nor was Irene. They were bored, having to admit it to themselves, bored with each other most of the time when they weren't in bed, spending much of their time together drinking at night clubs and exclusive bars.

Sex drew them together, time after time, in a sort of bitter way. He knew his uses to her and was almost contemptuous about it. They had an unspoken scorn for each other. In little things. Always in little things.

And he was losing what she had wanted in him. He was trying to get rid of it. He was no longer the symbol. He strutted vainly. His body exuded eau de cologne. His nails had a glisten to them. He shaved twice a day and there were no bristles of beard under the palm of her hand. He was becoming a crude and egotistical gentleman.

And for Don there was no longer pleasure in going downtown to buy a dozen thirty-dollar shirts at a time. No pleasure in the silver comb and brush set on his dresser. Nor in the knowledge that he could tear up a twenty-dollar bill if he wanted to.

The weeks went by. There is more to life than sex. More than money. Than power. More than just being a big shot.

# XXVI

There's one world. Just one world. The one world lies inside yourself. one. one. one. one. one. one. one. one.

He squeezed the palms of his hands against his ears. one. one. one . . . he tried to stop thinking it. Recently he had been repeating things over and over to himself. over. over. over. over. His platoon! His buddies! Often he saw their faces. He wanted to. He tried to. He wanted to see what expressions they would have when they looked at him. Like when you see blood you have to get close to see it good. Like when you get into trouble and have to get deeper and deeper into your trouble. . . . But when he saw his buddies' faces they were immobile and ashy-gray and looking straight ahead, past him or beyond him or at something else. . . . He felt as if he would explode. As if he would swell out over the street and ooze into the gutter with the raindrops . . . better get inside, better get off the street.

Table. Paper.

He began to write.

Door. Sidewalk.

The pockets of his coat were bulging saddlebags filled with slips of paper, bits of brown paper bags, newspaper margins filled with his writings. He walked down along the darkened street.

Door.

Bar.

"Bottle of beer."

He sat with the beer in front of him and his head propped up between his hands and the beer not touched.

Humpty-Dumpty sat on a wall, one, two, button your shoe, three four, open the door, five, six, pick up sticks, seven, eight . . . open the door, the door!

He got up. He rushed out. He saw the star of David and the Christians' cross. He ran and walked and ran. He was out of breath and half sobbing. He saw his father's face. The leather of it. His hand with the finger missing and his Haines Company work jacket. He shivered. Beneath the jacket he could see the stripes on his father's back from the pogrom. His father was eating his breakfast, his ritual breakfast never changed through all the years: half a grapefruit, a herring, a shot glass of whisky, the hard-crusted black bread and cheese, a glass of coffee. His father was lifting the glass of coffee to his mouth with the hand that had one finger missing . . . and his platoon, in even step, marched between his father's face and him. Only lampposts, Aaron, only lampposts. He stood on the sidewalk with his eyes closed and his forehead against one of the lampposts . . . he saw his mother's face. He heard her drunken voice . . . when he was a little boy. She came to the house. He stood in the dark hallway and looked down between the banister posts. She cursed and asked his father for money. She laughed and said she didn't want ever to see us kids . . . the soldier-feet of his platoon marching over the vision of his mother's face.

He walked on down the street. He had had the dream again. The nightmare. His thumb and his forefinger were pressed together and he opened them—opened them only an inch. Inside the space was a huge tree. And the tree shot up into the sky. From the sky a huge rock was falling onto him. A rock as big as a mountain. No soft, cooling hand came to his forehead. He did not catch the rock between his thumb and forefinger. The rock fell on him, crushing him . . .

Aaron walked on through the night city. He avoided stepping on the sidewalk cracks.

He walked for an hour or more. There's one world. Just one world. one. one. one. one. one. one. one. one.

He sat on a curbstone under a street lamp. He drew out a sheet of paper and spread it on his knee and wrote.

He stuffed what he had written into his already overburdened pocket and got up slowly from the curbstone. He wandered around the sad and sour city. Night looked over his shoulder.

# XXVII

Sue took a cab from the wide alabaster doors of the Haines Company, but didn't want to go home. She had the cabbie stop on Michigan Boulevard, paid him, walked with the crowd along the boulevard, stopped for a drink, two drinks, turned off Michigan down Superior Street, saw a neon sign HOFFMAN'S EAST INN and entered the bar. Inside the door, with the door closing noisily, she wished that she had gone home or had at least not come this way. Heads had turned toward the door and she stood looking into Don's eyes. A girl sat with him at the bar. A chic, sophisticated girl with dark eyes. And Sue knew.

Don had seen her. He called to her. "Sue! Hey Sue!" She smiled and, knowing, moved to where Don sat. Don grinned at her and stood up. "Hello, Sue! It's good to see you. Sue, this is my wife Irene. This is Sue, an old friend of mine." Don pulled out a bar stool for her. Sue sat down looking into Irene's eyes. Irene's chocolate-brown eyes looked back at her, frankly, with indifferent charm. Sue, looking at her, had to admit that she was pretty. "Hey, Frank!" Don called. "Give the lady here a drink—a whisky sour—that's right, isn't it, Sue?"

Sue nodded. Irene's eyes smiled at Sue. Under her breath Sue said, with some malice, "Slumming, Don?" Irene's eyes were still smiling at her. Irene said, "Do come over and see us sometime. So few of Don's friends—his old friends—come to the house. Nor does his family ever come calling. Oh, that's right, Don has no family. Don is an orphan." She smiled.

Don flushed with annoyance. His eyes caught Sue's. See what a bitch she is, his eyes said to Sue.

She was only beautiful to Sue.

Sue had a drink with them. Two drinks. She smiled and pulled her gloves over her fattish hands. "I'm so glad I met you." She had dignity. "I'll see you, Don," she said; and placed her hand in a friendly caress on his shoulder in a piece of womanly malice.

But outside. The smile fell away. Her face showed its age and its sorrow.

On the way home she bought a bottle of whisky. She skipped dinner. At home she uncorked the bottle and began to drink.

Oddly Don showed up in an hour. She let him in. Don said, "I bet you're surprised that I came over." His voice was a little cocky. "I came over," he said, "but not for sex."

Sue's hurt showed in her eyes: the bluntness, the insult of his statement. He filled a glass and lay stretched out on the sofa. In her hurt she didn't understand that he had come over because he wanted to be with her. He wanted companionship. Understanding. Conversation. He wanted to be with her and she spoiled it. "Six months from now," she said, "you'll wonder what you ever saw in a woman of my age. 'Sue, that old bag,' you'll say."

He lay stretched out on the sofa with his eyes squinted. He angered. He talked of going to see a whore. He said it to hurt her now that she had spoiled things, and sat up.

"I'm going," he said.

"Please stay," she said.

"No."

He left in anger. She followed him along the street. She begged him to come back, just to sit.

"No," he said. "Go away! Beat it, bitch!"

"I'm tired of being pushed around," she said in desperation.

"Well how much time did you spend on me? How many years? How much do I owe you?"

"I didn't mean that," she said.

"Stop following me," he said.

He walked out into the middle of the street, hailed a cab and left her standing in the street.

And the next day at work and afterwards she understood how generous and kind he was trying to be to her by coming over after she had seen him with his wife.

And that next day, that evening, he came back to her, sorry, as she was sorry. And looking at him, she thought, I love you because you are you and nobody else. I love your ears. And your silly weak chin. Don't ever do anything to your chin or you wouldn't be you. I love you because I know you better and more deeply than anyone else. Know you more frankly and more brutally. Don't ever change. I love you and thank you for being you and nobody else. I love your thin arms moving down to long, sensitive fingers, artistic fingers. I love you, too, for your imperfections, for without them you would not be you. And it isn't just a sexual thing. You may think it is but it isn't. It's when I look across a room and see you or see you walking through a door, into the atmosphere of me. And it's always, always. This is how and how much and for how long I love you.

Don stayed in the atmosphere of her love all night and part of the next day.

But when he left there was the street outside and his thoughts, even going down from her steps to the street. He felt bad inside. What's the matter with me? There was a thin layer of scum all over him. But if you scratch me, he felt, I'll be just like everybody else.

He thought of himself, walking down the city street, and his thoughts were sad ones. He thought of his political career and it was sour to his mind. Often I wish they would say—yes, I wish they would say, "You're full of shit"—and I would like them for it. What's the matter with me inside?

# XXVIII

They saw each other through a need to see each other. It drew them back together. Many times. They were both aware of this need. When they didn't see each other the thoughts were of each other. And sooner or later they would have to meet. It was like a fever upon them.

"Don."

"Sue."

Just the sound of a name.

There was sorrow and some contempt in their love for each other. Even in their little tendernesses toward each other. She was unattractive. And yet he knew she loved him as no other person ever had. Loved him in an unselfish way. Wanted good for him. He couldn't hurt her. You cannot hurt when someone loves. Love calls only for love. And he was ashamed of his own shortcomings. His inability to measure to her ideals.

"Many is the time we lay here together talking about social and political things—about—" she said, "a better world for—" her fattish hand gestured impotently "—for people."

"I'm a liberal, Sue. You know that."

She smiled, tight-faced.

Their guilt, in equal measure, was upon them. Her guilt was great. He was married. But—well (shrugging)—how important was that? They loved and needed each other—even more important was their opposite attitudes about things—all things. She could never respect him. Only love him. Need him.

Often she thought, How foolish this is, how hopeless this is. But the thorn of him was in her flesh. She found her whole mind curving back to thoughts of him, her imagination picturing out his face, his smile, her memory bringing back, sweetly, the words he had said to her.

She wanted to break it off. But she needed him. As he needed her.

The drinking alone at night at bars before she came home. To sleep. To get him out of her mind. The few extra drinks that would make her a little drunk before coming home.

And at the bars, over drinks, remembering, like a beautiful and sad motion picture seen again: her first meeting with him. How he looked. What he wore. What he said. And, in sequence, as much as she could remember of their whole relationship—the scenes coming back, one by one. Memory is a sword and a kiss.

She was the evidence of his sex. She was his mother, wife, sweetheart, mistress, instructress. She was his truth. And she knew their love for each other.

He was her son, brother, lover, husband.

By all the laws unwritten, they, two little unimportant people on the face of life, belonged to each other in shame and virtue, in strength and weakness. The ship had come home to harbor.

"We belong to each other. We need each other." Both of them said this.

Sue lay in bed. "Come to bed, Don," she said.

He did so.

"I don't know why," Sue said for the hundredth time, when he lay next to her, "I have anything to do with you. You're cheap. You're shallow. You're superficial."

"If I knew those big words," Don said, "I'd argue with you." And his tenderness, his childish boyishness toward her, increased and there was only that.

"Oh, Don!" In love, defeat, desire.

And Don, very serious, stroking her hair and speaking his truth, "I come here because it is only with you—only with you that I find any release—only with you that I feel free—that I know I am cared for—whatever I am—whatever I become."

There was Irene. Irene, his wife. And there were their quarrels. What the hell! I'm going to catch hell anyway. He didn't give a damn. He started to drink a lot. Rather than go home and have trouble with her I'd rather satisfy myself somewhere else. I'll try to get in touch with Sue. And while he thought it, he knew that all Irene wanted was some attention. The attention of the guy he was trying not to be. The guy from the slums. The guy who was sort of honest and animal and naïvely unsophisticated. But this he had only for Sue.

After a while it got so he didn't even want to go home. He'd get a room in a hotel by himself.

. . . if he ever went away and got quiet and listened to the way he felt . . . he could get in an automobile and drive away but he couldn't run away from the slums. Despite his fine clothes and his swagger and his colognes, the slums were in his blood, his walk, his language, his feelings and actions. He couldn't get away from himself. He was stuck with himself.

# XXIX

Night changed slowly to day. The night had been cold and bleak and ugly. But the night was past. Dawn had come. An ugly dawn. And it was daylight. A gray, rainy daylight. A day of night.

A million alarm clocks, thousands of factory whistles and some church bells had awakened the people from rest. Streetcars, Els, buses and suburban trains had been alerted. But something was wrong with the city. And in the gray of morning, like a stage curtain pulled aside to reveal the stage, the eye of day concentrated on the Haines Company. Morning blinked its sleepy eye at the Haines Company. There at the base of its forty-eight stories morning saw, through its sleepy eye, the little groups of workers who stood, not entering the plant but loitering defiantly outside the entrance door. Down the street the clump, clump, clump of a horse was heard and the traffic policeman rode toward his position in front of the main entrance of the administration building at Lake and Canal.

As he rode toward his post he saw O'Keefe trudging across the street. He leaned down over one side of his horse and, laughing out of his red Irish face, shouted, "Hello, you goddamn Red you! What are you doing out so early?"

O'Keefe, seeing his friend, laughed and shouted back, "Hello, you goddamn flatfoot! We're on strike!"

O'Keefe took his position at the streetcar stop. Other strikers took their posts at strategic places around the Haines buildings on either side of the river and at street corners.

In the basement of union headquarters more and more placards were being nailed to poles. In the basement, too, Edna and Sue worked steadily with the women and teen-aged girls who made coffee, sandwiches, stoked the boiler, wrapped up in warm clothing in preparation for going out on the street to walk in the picket line.

And Papa Levin picked up his pamphlets, trudged from headquarters, talked to O'Keefe on the street corner for a while before going to his post. Then he stood on the corner with his pamphlets under his arm, thinking, sorrowfully, about his son, his boy lost to him, and the places in the world he had planned for him since he was an infant. Aaron, his hope, bearer of his name, who would go far beyond him, who would put the name Levin up high somewhere for people to see—perhaps in a profession: Doctor Aaron Levin, Attorney Aaron Levin.

The night shift came out of the bowels of the basement where they had been making nuts and bolts all night long, took offered pamphlets and—weary, grease and oil from head to foot—moved like robots to streetcars on their way home to bed. The union hadn't been able to reach them. They were the ignorant and afraid. They were the Negroes, the Poles, the Mexicans. The city's poorest. And the southern whites who were too poor and too liberated by their poverty to resent working with Negroes. They, whose lot was the hardest and whose hope was the smallest, trudged down into the bowels of the basement, obedient to the unspoken voice of the boss.

And now daylight was active and no longer sleepy. Workers were getting off streetcars. Many refused to go into the building and took streetcars back home or waited outside with the strikers, indecisively. And now several hundred who should be punching time clocks were idling on the sidewalk outside of the Haines Company.

Jim strode the entrance steps and stood at the top. Jim told the crowd, "We aren't fooling. This is a real strike. We aren't going to tolerate any strikebreakers or scabs. Anybody who goes in goes in at his own risk!" And Jim was the Jim of old. The fight! The people! The strike, the working for the people, the battle. This was his. His at his peak. The winning of a strike had always been a let-down for him. He liked the competition, the battle. He had been an athlete and the game, the struggle, was the thing. He was rugged. He was ready. If he, somehow, somewhere in his makeup doubted his masculinity this, the strike, the battle, was a way of proving to himself that he was a man.

And now the Negro porter came out of the building and began with his rag to polish the huge bronze plaque anchored into the side of the building:

THE HAINES COMPANY

A NATION WITHIN A NATION

"Come on out! Come on out!" the strikers called to him.

And now more and more streetcars began to grind to stops in front of the building. An engineer started to switch cars onto the Haines Company track. Jim flagged him down. "Hey, buddy!" Jim shouted. "We're on strike. Don't cross the picket line! Don't be a strikebreaker!" The engine snorted and breathed smoke, sparks. The engineer backed his train out of the yard. Grass would grow on the tracks before he became a strikebreaker.

And now Max pulled his truck up in front of the Haines Company, abandoned it and joined the strikers.

And now the strikers ringed the two buildings of the Haines Company and started their slow-marching picket line. Each group on either side of the river was led by a man carrying an American flag and another man carrying a huge brass drum, pounding it with every *left*—right—*left* step the pickets took.

They marched. Others came to go to work but joined them instead. Few went in. Shoppers came, mostly women, doing their Christmas shopping early. Some refused to cross the picket line and went downtown to shop because their husbands belonged to unions. Some didn't go in because of fear of violence. But there were others who pushed through the picket line.

And the strikers had a new weapon. The union had a truck on either side of the river equipped with sound devices and toured in a circle around the Haines buildings explaining the strike, asking workers to co-operate and not enter the plant.

By nine o'clock the company had been alerted. The company informed the police. The police came. Over two hundred and fifty of them.

The police were Don's men. When the examinations for the police department came up they got their jobs through the ward organization. Each ward committeeman got so many police jobs. Don had okayed every new cop in his district and moved every old cop out of the district who wouldn't go along with him. He okayed only those policemen who were part of his machine. The police examination really meant nothing when a man tried to get on the force. It was just routine. They had to be Don's men and be used for all the things he would use them for. That had all been started the day they got on the force; started long before Don was even a little-theater actor. And politics alone determined who got on the force and who didn't. Politics was the supreme disciplinarian. To get on the police force was next to impossible unless you were "okayed."

It was Don's police force.

And it was Emerson Bradley's police force. The cop was always in favor of the company. The companies paid them when they were on duty during a strike. During strikes at Haines they got fifteen dollars a week extra from the company and their meals and cigarettes. The cops brought their friends for the free meals and cigarettes. And every week they got their money. The sergeant or lieutenant went to the public relations counsel who gave him the money for his men. During the present strike they were told that their pay would be twenty dollars a week. It was a company bribe sanctioned by Bradley.

They stood in a complete ring around the Haines plant, their eyes stern, mean, squinted under the hard blue bills of their caps, their chins thrust out above the blue-uniformed coats. Their guns protruded from their big hips. Their billies were ready and sometimes they touched them, caressed them lovingly. Their big feet supported them in plant protection array and their big bellies stuck out. They had no idea of what strikers' rights were. The rights of property were more important to them than the rights of men. This only they knew. It was what they were getting paid to know. Individually they were thinking all the time of telling the strikers to go on, break it up, get the hell out of here, we don't like your looks. One word had led to another before. They had used that as an excuse to beat the strikers up before. They had often beaten them up pretty bad. They were ready now. They were *the law*.

And over Lake Street, over Canal Street, around the entire Haines plant the Strike Squad prowled in a lazy, menacing circle. Looking for an incident. Looking for an excuse. Looking for trouble.

"But all police aren't bastards," O'Keefe said, walking now in the strike and talking to Jim. Sergeant Reynolds had a detail of twenty-four men, three groups of eight, on and off. He was instructed by McMahon, head of the strike detail, to take them over to the Haines Company.

"What will we do?" the police detail wanted to know.

McMahon wanted the strikers stopped immediately but didn't want to say, "Stop the pickets by force!"

He ducked what the administration wanted as far as an attitude toward the worker was concerned. He didn't want to be pinned down. "Your sergeant will instruct you," he said.

Sergeant Reynolds favored his men. They were workingmen the same as himself in his mind. In front of the head of the strike detail he told his men, "Do nothing."

McMahon called him into his office. "I'm going to report you to the commissioner," he told Sergeant Reynolds.

The sergeant took his detail to the strike and they were stationed before the plant. The company was bringing the officials and executives, the boss class, in by a private gate. Where the officials came in there were a lot of police but few pickets. Where the workers entered there were a lot of pickets but fewer police. The workers, those just now arriving, were impressed by the power of the union. But this was company strategy. They had it all worked out. They *wanted* an incident. The publicity, the press, was right there where there were few police and where the pickets were the strongest. Reporters waited for the news with trigger-happy fingers on their flash-bulb cameras. It was a dead setup. The big shots were there with their hands on their hips, waiting. Company officials. Deputy commissioners and commissioners. Waiting. Sort of grinning to themselves. A dead setup.

And Sergeant Reynolds and his men were stationed there. And there was a colored guy stopping trucks under the noses of all the big officials and cops—"Come on! Don't cross the picket line! There's a strike here!"

The officials and cops waited with their hands on their hips, waited for the incident they wanted.

Sergeant Reynolds stepped away from his detail, stepped into the street and in front of the colored fellow. "Now listen," Sergeant Reynolds said quietly to the Negro, "I don't want to humiliate you, but if that happens again I'm going to run you in the shithouse."

"Okay, okay," the colored fellow said.

Ten minutes later McMahon had Sergeant Reynolds transferred to another gate. Half an hour later he had him sent to 47th and Racine. But the sergeant had figured a way to get out from under the big guns and save a company-cop-inspired incident and that night his detail brought him a box of cigars.

And the strike went on. Peacefully. All day long. A cold rain turning to snow did not stop them. Night did not stop them.

# XXX

And into the second day the strike went. Ward Committeeman Don Lockwood read all about it in the paper. At the Tennyson Hotel, Ward Committeeman Lockwood and Alderman Mucci discussed the strike.

"You know what I'd do?" Alderman Mucci said. "I'd declare martial law. I'd say 'Get there—and get back.' "

Don nodded. He had stopped thinking about things. Thinking raised doubts and doubts stood in the way of success.

"I'd keep them on the job," Alderman Mucci said. "I'd train them. No man would be allowed to go to another state without the government knowing it. I'd crack a few heads. These people have had too much freedom."

Don started to disagree. Instead he said, "These strikes are a terrible economic loss to the country."

Alderman Mucci changed the subject to robbers, tying robbery in with strikers. Alderman Mucci said, "I always said they should kill them. I always said if I caught somebody robbin' I'd kill him. You don't know about that time when I caught that guy robbin' my store." Mucci waved his little finlike arms excitedly. "I shot him—hit him—when he ran out and he rolled over and over on the sidewalk. All he got was two years. I wish I had killed him."

And Don, speaking of the strike again, "You know a man breaking a window—"

"Yeah," Mucci said, "he'd shoot you in the back if you were coming out of your store."

That hadn't been what Don was going to say. But he shrugged and let it go.

The king was unperturbed by any plots. He ran this place! He gave his executives fifty thousand dollars a year and then began to crack down on them, making them do his will. They were ruled by fear. They were his evil men, but not in a forthright way. In a fearful way. If once they deviated from his razor-blade line of command he had their heads. And brought in other little men to rule by fear. He had the police. He had his scabs. He ran this place! He'd break this strike!

Unperturbed by any plot, Emerson Bradley stood now in his three-story-high penthouse office atop the Haines building with one of the windows open and the crackers in his wrinkled pink and white hands. He chuckled humorlessly and broke the crackers. He tossed them out to the beady-eyed pigeons that swooped and dove, catching the crackers between their beaks in mid-air. "'Morning, H.S.T.!" he called to the gray pigeon that opened its beak and took a cracker bit—and to the pigeon following, "My! my, there's that little songbird! That little opera singer!"

Tired of his play Emerson Bradley closed the window and, at his desk, swallowed one of his pills. He poured some Scotch into a glass and added water and gargled his mouth with this, swishing it from side to side and up and down before swallowing. He glanced across the room at his Rembrandt. Then he went to the wall of windows, laced his fingers behind his back, looked out and down at his Chicago spread at his feet. He stood with his feet wide on the thick rug and the $700,000,000 Haines Company under them. He lifted his little body up on his toes and lowered himself. Again. Again. Pleasurably. Looking out at his Chicago. He looked at his watch. In a few minutes he would speak over the microphone and his voice would be heard throughout the whole plant, top to bottom, wall to wall.

Again that early afternoon Emerson Bradley spoke on his plant-wide system to an almost empty plant, to his executives and to his few scabs who had come to work, to the slums of the basement where nuts and bolts were being turned out. He promised all the workers free meals and promised that any who wanted to sleep in the buildings could do so.

Later that afternoon he brought several hundred private guards into the plant. They were escorted in by the police.

Still later that afternoon he made a telephone call.

Don Lockwood the World-Beater, Ward Committeeman Lockwood, sat in his office. The phone rang and his secretary informed Ward Committeeman Lockwood that he was being called directly by Emerson Bradley.

Don Lockwood, THE POWER, picked up the phone. "Why hello there, Mr. Bradley! How are you? Anything I can do for you?" Mr. Veteran asked.

"See here, Lockwood!" Emerson Bradley said. "What are you going to do for me? I've done plenty for you." They owned each other now and could make demands on each other. They were husband and wife in the golden palace of Power. Emerson Bradley said, "I don't want this strike! I want it broken. They've got thousands down there. They're using loud-speakers on the street! I want this strike broken—do you hear!" He hung up.

Don got into his new Cadillac. He shut himself up alone with the judge in the judge's chambers.

The next day Don dug up the ordinance against loud-speakers being used on the city streets without permit. It was an old ruling that had been employed against the radicals and Communists in Bughouse Square. Don now used it against the strikers at the Haines Company.

The same day Judge Raven with whom Don had had conference

issued an injunction limiting the union to seven pickets. Judge Raven mouthed the words piously: "We are starting here, in our own country, to stop the spread of communism—and it has been demonstrated that the strike at the Haines Company is enemy inspired—"

The same day Emerson Bradley began to spend tens of thousands of dollars denouncing the union in full-page ads in the daily newspapers.

And thumbing through the newspaper to the want ads, people looking for jobs could find column-long inducements. High salaries were quoted, congenial surroundings stressed . . . anyone and everyone, housewives, laborers, students, were invited to apply for part-time or full-time employment. They could be anything from a stock clerk to an executive!

Meanwhile the newspapers buttered-up their big advertiser by suggesting that the strike was Red-inspired, that the strikers were at fault, that a strike at this time was one of the worst things that could happen to the city.

The workers defied Judge Raven's injunction. Hundreds of them were on the picket line the day after he had restrained their pickets to seven.

The police were there. The police made arrests. The police picked their people to shove into the paddy patrols and carry off to jail. The high officials of the union whom they could identify in the crowd they grabbed first.

Two union officials and several other pickets were sentenced to ninety days in jail for contempt of court by Judge Lester Raven. Judge Raven, the newspaper said, found them guilty of violating an injunction he had issued previously forbidding violence and limiting the union to seven pickets.

Jim went to see Don at his office. Jim sat on the edge of his chair after Don had shaken hands politically with him, greeted him as an old friend and smiled across the expanse of desk at him.

Jim looked back at Don. Don would help. Don had power. "I have a favor to ask of you," Jim said. "Some of our union officials have been picked up—Mr. Baker, our secretary, and Kovac, the president of the union." Jim smoothed his hair back. "And O'Keefe—you know O'Keefe—from Thompson's. If you could exert any—any influence to get them out why—"

Don smiled with his head cocked on one side. It was a hard smile. "I'm sorry, Norris," he said, "but there's nothing I can do. . . . Nothing at all."

Jim looked across the desk at Don. For a long time they stared at each other. Don lifted his shoulders in a shrug of helplessness. Jim stared back at Don. "Sue is being held, too."

Don leveled his eyes at Jim. "Well, what does that mean to me?"

Jim laughed. He shrugged. He held Don's eyes. He stood up, tall in his plaid shirt and black leather jacket. "I'll see you." He turned and walked out.

Don put his elbows up on the desk and his finger tips over his eyes. He sat like that for a long time. Then he pulled the telephone over toward his mouth.

The next day Sue, O'Keefe and the union officials were released.

The pickets defied the contempt ruling. Seven hundred strong they marched around the Haines Company. Wholesale arrests were made. Two hundred and forty-three were carted away to jail. They were charged with contempt. They were arrested for conspiracy, for disturbing the peace, for every charge Judge Raven and the police could bring against them.

All of the strikers couldn't be put in jail. The next day there were a thousand or more in a wild, angry demonstration in front of the sacred alabaster stones of the Haines Company. And the day brought disaster. Emerson Bradley had his two lines of defense. He had his company guards. He had his police with bared clubs. Emerson Bradley and the company wanted blood.

A scab, unescorted but passing through a covey of police, attempted to enter the plant. A picket stepped directly in front of him to challenge him. The circle looped in close. Tight. Cops. Company guards. A few pickets. Blood ran down the striker's head, into his eyes and his mouth. He fell. His head was split open. When he fell he was kicked. By many feet.

The scene was blocked out by a wall of blue uniforms. The squad cars, five of them, helped block the scene. The striker was taken to the hospital, his head split open, his eyes rolled back in his head.

The striker died an hour later at the hospital.

He was dead, as a soldier dead, and would no longer breathe the good air, see morning, sunlight, stars. He, the symbol of the little individual of society, the overalled man, the khakied man, was dead. Was as a rock on the earth.

# XXXI

It was war. The lines were drawn. The battle was set. The police had barricaded the streets around the Haines Company and forced the strikers back a block from the plant on all sides. The pickets, now over two thousand strong, stood in knots, in crowds, in angry mobs in their limited area.

Emerson Bradley fumed in his office atop the forty-eight-story building. Angry. Vengeful. Unrelenting. D. S. Matthews poured money into the coffers of the union and appeared himself at union headquarters in blue jeans and a sweat shirt, a Mackinaw pulled over it. Don, on the side of the company, found himself aligned against his father-in-law in this strange but objective battle for power.

They were two armies of people, the strikers and their opponents. And many of the strikers wore black arm bands for their companion who had been killed by company or police.

And Don had an idea. It was political.

A platform was erected in front of the main entrance to the Haines Company. Spotlights were fastened above it.

And Jim went again to see Don.

"I want to ask you if you will pull the police away from the strike," Jim said.

"Afraid I can't do that, Norris. I don't have anything to do with the way the police department is run."

They stood smiling tight-lipped at each other. And all the time Jim knew that Don did run the police force.

Don, his Homburg hat pushed back on his head, puffed his cigar and looked across the desk in amusement at Jim. "Can't do it," he said. He bit the words off and blew smoke at the ceiling. "Nope. Can't do it."

"Why can't you? You've got the power to if you want to."

Don shrugged and didn't answer.

"Look, Lockwood," Jim said, "once and for all I want to know where you stand."

Don squinted his eyes and tightened his lips. "Say," he said, "what have you got a hard on about anyway?"

Jim pulled a folded newspaper clipping from his pocket. "Here's a speech you made when you were running for State Representative. Here's what you said: 'I am for unions. Only through the unions does the worker better his status.' " Jim looked up, then again glanced at the newspaper clipping. "And you said, 'I pledge my everlasting support to the veterans and their families—to what they fought and died for—to better wages for all of our people—to equality and democracy.' "

Don said, "Well then—you should know I'm a liberal."

Jim stood up. "Then prove it. You've said a lot of pretty words. Now's your chance to prove you meant what you said."

Don reddened. "Maybe my ideas of the word *liberal* aren't the same as yours. Maybe I don't happen to be a Communist." He was equivocating and he knew it and the knowledge made him angry at Jim.

Jim quoted again: " 'I am for unions. Only through the unions does the worker better his status.' "

Don said, "I can't help you." His voice was very hard. THE POWER'S voice. "I don't want to see the legitimate businessman get pushed around."

"You've forgotten all the people who voted for you—you've sold out. You've sold out the Negroes, the Italians. You've sold out the Polish people. There are thousands of them at Haines. Seems to me you were a special friend of the Poles." Jim said it derisively.

Don turned fiery. What did the bastard know, what did he mean by that! "Damn your dagoes and niggers and your Polacks! I owe them nothing. They're too dumb to help themselves. I believed in them once. I tried to help them. Where did it get me! But I know better now. They're all the same. They want what I got—what I got for myself. The rest is a lot of crap. Damn the dagoes, the niggers, the Polacks!" He sneered. He was the power now. "You came here and bribed me before. I let your people out. It won't happen again. Now get out!"

"You goddamn miserable little cripple you!" Jim said. He picked Don up and threw him across the room. Don's Homburg rolled off on the floor. His cigar was knocked out of his mouth. His false leg was lopsided under him. Jim picked him up and knocked him down with his fist. Jim picked him up again. He shook him as a dog shakes a rat. He kept shaking him, knocking his head against the wall. "You dirty little no-good sonofabitch! If you weren't a cripple I'd—"

He went on shaking him.

And finally he let him go.

Both out of breath, they stared at each other. Don's hair was a mess across his forehead and his lip was beginning to swell. Jim stood two feet away from him, his tall shadow falling over him. They stared at each other. Don smiled through his painful lip. Cripple! He called me a cripple! Don went on staring smilingly at him and dusted off his clothes with his hands as he stared at Jim. Don shined his diamond against the lapel of his coat and went on staring at Jim. "I'm going to break you for this, Norris," he said.

Jim turned and walked out.

Don picked up his hat, dusted it, set it on his desk. Don pulled the phone over and dialed. He called the police captain he owned. "Pick Jim Norris up," he said. "He's vice-president of the union. Pick him up on any charge. Frame him if you have to."

When Jim left Don's office he stopped at a tavern for beer. Shamed and guilty he sat drinking bottle after bottle. Ashamed of himself for hitting Don and for calling him a cripple.

He kept drinking. His old troubles began to trouble him. Girls. Even the thought of the strike and his part in it, his duty to the union, didn't keep his mind from plunging down and down into his thoughts of women and girls.

He got drunk. He staggered out of the tavern. In a haze he set his feet upon the sidewalk.

He woke up in jail. He was held for two days. Then they brought the young girl down to identify him. She was only eleven years old. She had been raped.

She stared at him with large, grave eyes. She stared at him for a long time. Her mother looked at him with a shocked face and angry eyes from which many tears had flowed and her father stared like some animal ready to attack. They waited. And finally the girl shook her head no, no I don't think this is the man.

Jim was released. Unshaven, dirty, his body sore where the police had beaten him, Jim left the cell and looked up at the gray sky, down at the cold gray sidewalk. He didn't do it. He couldn't have done it. But he wasn't sure. He had been drunk. He didn't do it. The girl hadn't identified him. She would have been old enough to know. But the irony of it was that if he hadn't done it Don had picked his weakness. I didn't do it. But he wasn't sure. He had been drunk.

# XXXII

It was war.

Night cupped its hand over the city. Starless night. The wind was a guillotine blade. The strikers had been forced back by the police and stood two blocks away from the alabaster towers of the Haines Company. They stood in angry groups. Hundreds of them. Thousands of them. Milling around on the city sidewalks and streets.

They were a mob on the city streets.

They were an army.

At the doors of the plant and in all the first-floor windows company guards stood. Theirs was an arsenal inside the plant. And inside the plant the scabs who were escorted to and from their work by the police did Emerson Bradley's work for him. At a third of its capacity the great heart of the plant beat, slowly, slowly . . .

A clock on a high tower pointed the hour. 10:15. Nervously jerked a finger forward—one minute, another minute, another . . .

Aaron sat in the sad places of the city, the empty places of the night. His pockets, filled with scraps of paper, were like saddlebags. On the scraps of paper—bits of brown paper bags, newspaper margins, cafeteria napkins—were the words he had written. Some of the bits of paper stuffed thick in his pockets bore only single words. Others words he had made up. Others held strange lines of poetry he had written.

He stood a moment, hunch-shouldered in front of Thompson's, and then entered, fingered out five pennies and took the cup of coffee to the small back table. He sucked in on his lip. He took a nub of pencil from his pocket and, first looking furtively around, wrote the two words on a bit of paper picked up from the floor. With nervous fingers, like a squirrel storing nuts, he stuck the bit of written-upon paper into his already overburdened pocket. Then he sat staring at the far wall. Somebody touched him on the arm and he almost jumped up out of the chair.

"Hi, keed!" Steve said and sat down on the remaining chair; but the face that looked into Steve's was like an old man's face, the eyes large, deep-brown, wistfully sad.

The head nodded slowly at Steve. The black hair fell in bars over the face and the fingers did not lace it back over his ear and out of the way.

Steve was saying, "War. They forget so soon. As soon as the armistice is signed they forget all about the hell it was." He tapped his sleeve. "The guys with one arm and one leg standing on the street corners with a tin cup are the fellows who don't forget. I worked in a vet's hospital for a while," he said. "It's a terror to be around them —the basket cases. They can't see, can't hear—some of them. They're like an alimentary canal. If you can imagine a man twenty-eight years of age who has no more function than a two-year-old baby you've got a picture of what I mean. Take fellows like you," he said, "fellows who cracked up." His half-handsome, sneering, dissipated face lifted itself toward Aaron and he tapped ashes from his cigarette. "They say—'Don't you worry because you're like that. You're lucky to be alive.' " He grasped Aaron by the sleeve, fiercely, and would not let go. "Atomic energy is the good stuff," he said, sneering, "but do you think the atom bomb is something? Why that's nothing. That's only scratching the surface. Another war and there won't be anything left. We've blown it all up but the United States and there's only a fourth of it left." He sneered sardonically. "Well let them die. Let everybody die. It doesn't matter. A couple more like the last one and we're all through anyway. Every bastard living today has murder in his heart anyway. There isn't a thing worth saving anyway. We're doomed."

The nervous finger of the clock, over the heads of strikers, police, company guards and scabs, jerked forward a notch.

Jim buttoned his Mackinaw up around his neck and got ready to go to the strike. It was a worn woman's face that looked up at him. "But I want to be with you, Jim!" Louise protested.

He shook his head no. "No," he said, "there may be trouble." He put his hands on her shoulders and, bending down, kissed her on the lips. "I'll be back late."

She watched him from the window until he was out of sight, the long street and the dark night taking him. Then, pulling on her overcoat, she ran downstairs to ask Mrs. Bush to take care of the children.

She took a streetcar toward the Haines Company and the strike.

Jim walked in the dark toward the strike. He walked across a prairie, lumpy with rocks, tin cans, and under the tall legs of the elevated structure, and on into the mouth of a viaduct, through its black tunnel and out the opposite end. Then, in front of him, he saw her. She was a young girl eleven or twelve. She wore a green wool stocking cap and from underneath it two braids hung down her back, caught by little red ribbons. The childish legs were in green wool stockings and she wore high shoes against the weather. Jim followed her. Followed her down the quiet and dark neighborhood street. His elongated shadow touched her. He knew what was on his mind. He knew what he was going to do. And the night was a witness. A silent witness. The night was a panderer. Its long, black shadows fell from everywhere. The street was empty and dark. The sky black. Shadow fell across shadow. Shadow covered Jim's face. Was grasping arms across the little girl's shoulders and clutched at her feet. Far away the broken bulb of a lamppost was like a grinning, toothless skull. And the alley. The mouth of the alley yawned open as Jim and the girl approached it.

The clock in its high tower itched its long, lean finger a notch forward. And another.

Don sat in the drawing room of the apartment his father-in-law had given him for a wedding present. He was going over the notes he had made for his speech at the strike tonight. He stood up and looked at himself in the mirror, grinning at himself. This speech! He knew what it would do for him politically. He peered into the mirror at himself slyly. Yeah! And the thoughts were good. The dreams. Tonight would make him just about the most powerful man in Chicago, politically. The strategy had been worked out. The police would fall back. The strikers would advance. He glanced at his watch, checking the time. The strikers would all be there below him in the crowd when he made his speech over the loud-speaking system. The platform was there with its battery of floodlights, waiting for him . . . he needed his pretty wife there on the platform with him.

He walked into Irene's bedroom. She was looking in the mirror and powdering her shoulders. He made his eyes pleading and his voice little-boy. He tilted his head to the side as in little-theater days. "Why don't you go with me, Irene?" he asked.

She frowned at him through the mirror. "For the hundredth time, no!"

He looked at her small mouth forming and holding the no. And her chocolate-brown eyes, angry at him.

He moved over to the dresser and behind her. "Aw, come on and go with me, honey."

"No."

He wrestled with her a little.

"Look out. You're mussing my hair." There was only disdain for him in her face and her eyes.

He let go of her. "Are you going out with Christopher?" he asked, jealously. Accusingly.

"No, I'm not going out with Christopher."

"Well, why don't you go out with Christopher?"

"Well, maybe I will."

She pulled the ivory phone over and called him in front of Don. "Hello, darling, want to take me out somewhere tonight?"

Angry, jealous, Don walked through the door and into his adjoining bedroom.

He dressed. "Hey," he yelled at her when he was dressed, "will you pin this for me?"

She came into his bedroom.

Don's false leg stood in the corner. It looked grotesque with its leather straps sprawled out and its stiff metallic pose holding it rigid in the corner. A pair of crutches lay across the bed. Don had neatly folded the cloth of his one trouser leg up over the nub of his leg. "Will you pin this for me?" he asked again.

Irene flashed her eyes at him. "All right," she said contemptuously.

She had to stoop, half-kneeling to pin the trousers up over the stub of a leg. Don looked down at her. She was beautiful. He had to admit that. Don looked down at her. You bitch! he thought. You dirty little bitch!

When he was dressed he sat on the side of the bed, again going over the notes of his speech. This speech which meant so much to him, politically. Then he was ready to go to the strike as ward committeeman. Donald Lockwood, the first wounded veteran of World War II. He would wear no overcoat. The crowd must see the stub of his leg.

He fitted his Homburg hat to his head and edged the crutches under his armpits. He swung forward on them and went through the apartment.

Irene and Christopher were in the front room having a drink. Christopher, tall, slim, with his curly black hair and his chiseled features, wore the cocktail glass like a ring.

"Hello, Christopher," Don said.

"Hi, Lockwood."

"See you," Don said to his wife.

Don got into his Cadillac and drove to within a few blocks of the strike. Then he parked the car and slid the crutches out. He eased them under his armpits and, through the dark night, hobbled down the sidewalk toward the strike, one trouser leg empty.

*the ants are a people not strong*

Aaron wandered in the sad places of the city, the empty places of the night. All about him life, people moved swiftly, vibrantly. He dragged one foot after the other not even avoiding walking on the cracks in the sidewalk. His was only an inner life. A jungle with every path grown over and no way out, with the thorns of that jungle and the beasts of that jungle pressing him closer, closer.

He saw his father's hand. The nub of what was once a whole finger welled up large before his eyes. He shivered. He thought of his mother and heard her curses again and again. Saw her that night in the hallway while, in the dark, he leaned over the banister. He shivered.

He crossed a bridge over the river. My platoon! My platoon! I don't deserve to live. He walked with his eyes closed. He opened them and crossed Wacker Drive but, walking like a blind man, was unconscious of the traffic. And was lucky not to be run down.

He was now under the El structure on Lake Street a few blocks from the Haines Company. He heard, then, the noises of the city. It's like sleeping, he said, and the refrigerator motor goes off and you wake up. The noise. Many people passing by him. Crowds of people. Talking. Shouting. Some of them running. But it meant nothing to him.

Tired. Sit down. Maybe think of something to write.

He started to sit on the curbstone but there were two bums sitting on the curb under the elevated already.

The two hobos sat on the curbstone, their ragged shadows stretching out across the cobblestones from the broken soles of their battered shoes. They sat hunched in their ragged overcoats and they shared a cheap bottle of wine. One of the hobos said to the other, "Sunday night. Tomorrow we got to see if we can make it. If we can't make it we can't make it. I don't know."

*the locusts have no king yet go they forth all of them in bands*

Jim's shadow crowded closer and closer to the little girl. His big-fingered hands started to reach. They were almost even with the little red ribbons tied in bows to the girl's pigtails. Then he heard the long-drawn, shrill wail of the police siren screaming, screaming into and across the night. His eyes rolled toward the sound. He lowered his hands. The little girl was a third of a block down the street. Jim stood looking in the direction of the police siren and the Haines Company. He lifted his hands and looked at them. He looked again toward the Haines Company. And again lifted his hands, staring at their wide, square, flat palms. His hands had been calloused from using a gun . . . they had fought and they had been told that they had won.

Jim turned and walked toward the Haines Company. As he walked, his long legs eating the distance quickly, thoughts of the war came back to him, snatches of scenes . . .

He saw again the French girl and shuddered in the memory. The soldier who had been killed because he didn't choose . . . He could have saved a life and hadn't. Which one of the dead might now be alive if he had made a choice? Which bereaved family might now be happy? . . . The floodgates opened and he saw all the war, all the horror of it as if he were again in khaki and again poised with his gun against the enemy. And this was another battle, another war. A good battle. A clean battle for high principles. He hurried to the strike like a man awakening from a bad dream.

He came onto the fringe of the crowd of strikers. In the distance the shining white towers of the Haines Company rose majestically.

The strikers saw Jim. Heads began to turn toward him. Voices began greeting him. People had been to union meetings. Jim was a hero. Hands slapped him across the back in comradeship. The calloused hands of men. The lacquered hands of women. He was one of their heroes. And they were made mad all over again in their struggle against the company because Jim was their hero. It was a mood of anger and of ecstasy. It swept them up. They were the worthy. The mood flooded into them and over them. An El on its high trestle went by indifferently. The water of the Chicago River went by indifferently.

As Jim arrived the police fell back. The strikers hesitated, looked suspiciously at the police. Was this a trap? Some sort of a scheme? The strikers paused. Then they moved forward. The police fell further back as Don had planned it. They retreated further. They moved back until they ringed the Haines Company at its very doors. The strikers moved forward toward the palace walls.

Jim moved with the strikers, looking for his friends. Then he heard a voice in the crowd shouting to someone, "Hey—Red! Hello, you goddamn Red you!" and heard O'Keefe yell back, "Go on, you flatfoot you!" to his policeman friend while all the other cops stared, not knowing what it was all about. Jim grinned and fell in step with O'Keefe.

"Hi, Sean!"

"Oh, hello there, Jimmy!"

With O'Keefe were Edna, Papa Levin and Jerry. O'Keefe's face looked tired and colorless. There were deep lines like cat scratches in his face but he was cheerful in this battle against the company. He kept wisecracking. And after a bit someone else shouted, "Hello!" and Sue fell in line with them, linking arms with O'Keefe and Edna. With Sue was Jane Morris, who had run for State Representative against Don on the Progressive ticket. And in the crowd were Dave and Milo looking for Jim. And moving through the crowd looking into faces for a face was Louise. And in the crowd was Max looking for Dave and Milo, for O'Keefe. The little group of friends kept close together, Edna, O'Keefe, Papa Levin, Jerry, Sue, Jane Morris and Jim.

Jim lit a cigarette and stood quietly, silently with his friends. In the army they had stripped him of his last vestige of humanity. His hands had been calloused from using guns. They had taught him to kill. They had told him he could shoot children in the name of a cause. Women in the name of a cause. He took a long inhalation on his cigarette. He had a willingness now to walk where it was hard to walk. If trouble comes? When you have killed people for two or three years the killing of others doesn't mean much. If trouble comes—if the police use clubs or guns—cause as much damage as you can, make your cause as safe as possible.

He stood with his people, the workers from the Haines Company. He stood tall and erect and sternly handsome, his blue eyes steady with purpose. He could kill now for a cause, if necessary. They had taught him that.

The strikers were a mob on the street. Were an army on the street.

And now Louise, pressed tight in the crowd, had caught a glimpse of Jim's face.

"Jim! Jim!" Louise called, pushing through the crowd, squeezing through to get near him.

*the way of an eagle in the air*

Don now stood on the edge of the crowd of strikers. His Homburg was slanted over his head, over his deep-green eyes and his weak chin. A policeman recognized him and, tipping his hat, said, "Hello, Mr. Lockwood. How are you, sir?"

Don lifted his head in a nod of acknowledgment. Then he began moving through the crowd with his eyes dull and narrowed. The cop and another policeman began clearing an aisle through the strikers for him. "Make way there! Stand back!" Their clubs nudged the crowd back, forming a little space for the ward committeeman. Don walked the aisle with his crutches under his arms, with one trouser leg empty and a nub bandaged in midnight-blue cloth. Faces turned, looking at him. The faces of strikers. Frowning faces. Tight chins. Eyes narrowed under hats and catching hard light from lampposts. In the distance the high platform from which Don would speak bloomed like a flower under the many spotlights. Behind it, directly behind it, the forty-eight-story-tall Haines Company rose in shining alabaster white; muscled itself in this night, was swollen out and up in might and power. Don, on his crutches, moving slowly, dramatically, edged his crippled way toward this platform at the foot of this huge building: And, moving through the crowd, Don had many thoughts . . .

He was a good American. He wasn't selling out to foreign isms, to labor, to the ignorance of people who didn't know what they really wanted and didn't know what was best for them. Wayne would be proud of him. Sue should be proud of him. He was a good American.

He moved through the mob on the street, the army of workers on the street. And a little hunchbacked on his crutches, his Homburg slanted to one side, his eyes looking out at the night and the people, his path following that of the blue-uniformed policeman who was clearing the way for him, Don had certain guilt feelings. Sue would be in the crowd. Jerry from his old department would be in the crowd. And O'Keefe. But—they were wrong. Yes . . . they were wrong. He had the good of the city, the good of the country in mind. What he was doing was right. In these troubled times he was a leader with his goal set—a good goal.

But certain guilt feelings followed him. Shame sat on one shoulder. Determination on the other. And he moved through the strikers.

There in that mob of faces, hats, legs, bodies, overcoats, faces, he saw Dave. He saw Dave's brown Negro face looking into his face. He halted on his crutches. "Hello, Dave."

"Hello, Don."

Don started to hold out his hand but the dignity in the other man, the stern, unblinking, even judging face stopped him. And the fear that his hand might not be accepted. Negroes were Negroes. His personal friends were different. He liked Dave. He nodded again at Dave and tried to smile and prepared to move on. Around him the frowning faces of the strikers. Feet in heavy shoes. Angry faces under turned-down hat brims. Elevated trains moving noisily overhead. The river sucking blackly at the shore.

Swinging his body between his crutches Don moved forward toward the platform through over two thousand strikers, and little pictures of the past came back to him. They sidled up next to him in the night: "Look," and "you haven't forgotten."

He was a kid with lice in his hair. That would never happen again. He had climbed up on this bed of roses and he was going to stay there. There was a night in a tent with the sides ripped by knives and flapping in the breeze when the guy from the slums had made good. He was successful in a dog-eat-dog world. They had called him Mr. Veteran. They had given him his name—The World-Beater. He *was* Mr. Veteran. He *was* a world-beater. He *was* THE POWER now. It would stay like that. Before that he had been beaten. He had lost as the candidate for State Representative and had wandered the streets, tears in his eyes, tears rolling down his cheeks. That night he had again been the kid with lice in his hair, the kid running down alleys toward home with relief bags of food. NOT FOR SALE . . .

The little pictures of the past assailed him. Moving through the crowd of strikers the pictures of the past came back to him, came home to roost. His mother. It was Christmas. Her raw-worked hands. His mother setting the hamburger roast on the table with a turkey feather stuck in it and saying, "There, my kids got turkey too." His mother saying, crying and saying it, "My kids will never go hungry again." His mother's first man there in the house. The others. The many men. Money. A little. Just a little. The dirty house. The stinking walls. Men.

Wayne's mother.

Their house.

And a rich girl in bed with him. A rich girl married to him. He would have to save their marriage. It was important to him. He would do anything to save it. She was, yes—well, she was what he needed for—for success, prestige . . .

Guilt flooded the thoughts he had.

He turned his face away from guilt as his body swung between the props of his crutches moving toward platform and speech.

Rebecca. Sue.

He turned his face further away and closed his ears, his eyes.

. . . And D. S. Matthews, his father-in-law, smiling out of his red flushed face that was always like a smile and saying, "These are handmade cigars. They're not especially good—not as good as some of the standard brands. But it gives you a feeling of power—especially if you rose from nothing."

And now Don, hunchbacked over his crutches, was at the foot of the platform. A policeman reached out a hand to assist him in getting to the platform. Don frowned the help away. Alone he began to mount the platform. On his face was a big smile. The leftover smile from little-theater days. The political smile. His diamond ring on the hand clutching the crutch caught light and caught fire.

I'm like Wayne, Don told himself. Like Wayne, he told himself, I'm acting—no—not heroically—but like a good American.

Don mounted his platform.

*lost, and by the wind grieved*

Aaron did not even hear the hollow wind-carried shouts and yells that came from the direction of the Haines Company. Nor did he see the many people who went hurrying past him toward the Haines Company. He walked along the sidewalk under the structure of the Lake Street El. His head hung down. His weedy black hair was over his face and his shoulders were slumped. A sheet of frayed newspaper came hurling down the gritty sidewalk blown by the wind. It swirled against Aaron's ankles and clung there like a fetter, like a snake, chaining him, holding him. He pulled it off with listless fingers. And then the idea came. He sat down on the curb under a street lamp with his feet dangling on the street. He smoothed the newspaper out on his knee and drew his stub of pencil from his pocket.

The headline on the newspaper said:

NEW A-BOMB CHIEF NAMED

Aaron didn't notice the headline. He licked the stub of pencil between his pouted lips and on the newspaper margin wrote in his slow, precise handwriting: *the city was of night, perchance of death, but certainly of night.*

He stared at the words and read them again. That was the best thing he had ever written! It left him trembling with pleasure. He tore the margin from the newspaper and carefully placed his written words in his pocket.

*the spider taketh hold with her hands and is in kings' palaces*

The clock face scrawled the hour of eleven. They stood close together, Jim and the little group of friends. The people outside of the building were several thousand packed close together. It seemed as if all the city had converged upon the scene of the strike. They stood shoulder to shoulder in the black, starless night. They had their secret, protective weapons hidden beneath their overcoats. The police wore their weapons openly. The company guards did likewise.

In the crowd, squeezing through, almost fighting her way through, Louise calls out to her husband, "Jim!—Jim!" and tries to get near him.

Jim stands with his eyes half-closed, squinting at the night . . . When he first knew Louise. His eyes looking at her, his mouth fitted over the harmonica. Out at the midway, lying full-length on the grass playing his harmonica . . . The war. The grave detail. The harmonica falling out of the dead German's pocket. An American voice saying, "Well somebody better take it. He won't need it any more." . . . Jim closed his eyes against the scene. Another El went by indifferently. More water went by indifferently. Almost laughingly.

The strikers, shoulder to shoulder under street lamps and El structure and Dave moving with them, looking for friends. Dave is a short guy and most people are taller . . .

A mob upon the street.

An army upon the street.

Hats. Fists. Twisted mouths. Angry eyes. Stern eyes. Clubs under coats. Billies on big rumps. But smiles too. The smiles of strikers in their united cause. I know you and you know me. We see each other in the daytime. If at night you see someone you work with in the daytime you smile and go on. But tonight with the smile the fist is a little tighter, the heart beats a little stronger. Here is what happens. Edna isn't Edna any more. Jim isn't Jim. O'Keefe is not O'Keefe. They have left themselves for a bigger Edna, a bigger Jim, a bigger O'Keefe that belongs to all men.

At the very base of the buildings and all around them the strikers stand, muscled, now, in their cause.

The building is muscled too. It is steeling itself. Its height is swollen in the weird light of the starless night. Its top floors are lost in the darkness. It is a gem. A jewel. It would outlast them all. Rub your hand across it. It is as cold as ice. The people are just the pulp to be used by the building.

And the mob, the army, waits for any action. The faces are grim. Even looking at one another the faces are grim. And an El rumbles by. And an airplane goes overhead toward the airport. And the brown billy clubs with the blue twisted cord. And the occasional gold braid on a hat. And the steel bullets with brown noses . . .

And the strikers. The housewife, office boy, secretary, shipping clerk, order filler, saleslady, maintenance strikers . . . in the night. The starless night.

And the lights of the city burn. The lights of the city burn the same as usual. They don't even blink for this. They will burn through this night.

And suddenly unsheathed billy clubs with street lamps glossing them.

And suddenly the riot . . .

At one end of the building and spreading.

How did it start? Who knows exactly how a riot, a war starts?

Police sirens. Police clubs. Strikers' clubs, pieces of pipe. And the riot is spreading around the building. The police have knocked the flag bearer down. The flag is on the cobblestones. It is being trampled underfoot.

The police and the company guards are engaged in war with the workers. The ants, the locusts are storming the palace.

Like wildfire the rioting moves in a chain from group to group. And now it has reached the little crowd of friends: Edna, Jim, O'Keefe, Papa Levin, Sue, Jane Morris, Milo. They were caught in it, trapped in it. And as the clubs came with blue uniform sleeves above them, Edna, mother of two daughters whom she alone had reared by working at the Haines Company, saw a police club lifted over the head of a man she did not know while other police arms held him. Muscles rose in Edna's throat that had never been there before. A strange sort of screaming, shouting came out: "Leave him alone! Leave him alone!" And Edna with no thought of personal safety rushed forward, offering her forty-odd-year-old woman body in defense of the man, striving vainly to grasp the policeman's club.

And Jim, seeing the man go down on the pavement under the impact of the club and the club turning in the night in search of Edna, leaped forward to defend her.

The club caught Jim across the head. Other clubs beat his shoulders and head as Papa Levin, O'Keefe, Sue, Jane and Milo leaped forward toward Jim and the police with nothing to defend him with but their empty hands.

Jim went down. And as he went down the French girl, the old woman he had killed, the German soldier he hadn't saved, disappeared forever from his pangs of conscience and absolved him from any blame in this effort of his in the name of the people, the little people who seeded the entire world, who grew like grass across the world, who withered and died or who were cut down in youth.

Jim's curly blond head and broad shoulders lay on the cobblestones. The strikers and police fought above him. The feet surged forward and over him and moved somewhere else.

*the way of a serpent upon a rock*

Don stood on his high platform on his crutches making his speech under broad spotlight. His face was stern. His deep eyes were handsome and his weak chin was thrust forward. His lips leaned to the microphone as to a lover's mouth. His fist pounded into the palm of his hand and the riot had not yet kindled its flame to this part of the plant.

The moving through the crowd to the platform had pulled the pins loose from the blue cloth of his nub. The empty trouser leg hung down loosely between the crutches and was waved back and forth by the wind.

Don, propped up between crutches, spoke into the microphone. The empty pant leg waved listlessly back and forth. The wind sucked at it. The night nursed at it like maggots.

*In the bright sunlight of a late October day across the black asphalt of Fifth Avenue they are bringing the dead soldier bodies back to the native land. There is a police escort and their horses' hooves beat mournfully on the asphalt. Newsreel cameras are mounted on sedan tops. Generals are there. The clergy is there. Statesmen are there. And wives. Mothers.*

*They have picked up this little bit of fertilizer from off foreign battlefields. Of the fifteen million dead and missing of the war they have raked up this infinitesimal bit and brought it back to be cried over and applauded. There had been the clasping of the hands, and the breaking loose. The kissing. The tears.*

*Now the dead bodies are home. The deaf ears. The cold hands. The unseeing eyes.*

*The solemn flag of the nation drapes the coffins of the broken and defiled bodies. The solemn faces of the politicians speak platitudes.*

*The dead bodies are home. In bed. The nation's black blankets cover them over and they are marked with tufts of grass, with occasional flowers. They are watered by occasional tears as long as those live who had cared. . . .*

*The wind blows, the dust blows, the sand blows . . .*

*Rain can weep upon them.*

*Nature can mourn them.*
*Perhaps Time itself may one day ask—Why?*

*Man will forget.*
*The wind blows, the dust blows, the sand blows . . .*
*The young grass is cut down. The new grass grows up. To be cut down. Night, night, night, and the wind.*
*Why does God waste so many seeds?*

([1])